MUSHROOMS

John Hopkinson

Edition September 2021

For Lisa, Frazer and Jodie

CONTENTS

PROLOGUE

In May, 1917, newspapers in Great Britain carried a remarkable story.

Their articles told of a man serving in the British army who had been awarded two war service medals for valour on the field of combat.

For the time, at the height of the Great War, that in itself might not have been considered exceptional, but for one significant difference.

The first medal, the Distinguished Conduct Medal, was awarded to this man by the British military. The second medal, the Iron Cross, First Class, was awarded by the Imperial German Army.

A survivor of the *Titanic* disaster, the man's history and the associations of courage and cowardice surrounding these events have never been fully documented.

ONE

"You know my nose, Maurice."

The words of his editor irritated him as he sniffed the air with a particular disdain. It had rained in the early morning, and as the sun dried out the stones of the church walk, the faintest of pallid vapours rose in shafts of light between sparse canopies of trees. It could almost have been the ether of dead souls ascending from their resting places.

"This conk, Maurice, has not let me down in forty-five years. Now sod off and bring me a good one - I want a hero! - We've had enough shit from this ruddy war, I want a belter, and I'm bloody sure it's up in Yorkshire. Go get it! " Yes, yes, he knew his editor's gift for a story. Proper bloodhound, Horace was. Just perhaps the man could trip up now and again.

A hero.... Yes, couldn't everyone wish for one of those to brighten things up! It had been a rotten first half of the year which, if anything, mirrored the tone of the Western Front and the battlefields, and the man from Fleet Street was grateful for momentary relief from the gloom of his assignment. He did not like Yorkshire.

Looking around the graves, he felt an atmosphere of incongruity, the light and the warmth conspiring against the mood of the little band of mourners dwelling in their sorrows. It had not gone well. For once perhaps Horace's nose had let him down.

"I say!"

A little hatless man with wire spectacles hanging on a cord around his neck hustled along the pathway to catch up with the tall man in the black bowler and black frock coat, a white carnation squeezed clumsily into his lapel as a last-minute - mismanaged - gesture of respect. The tall man was striding casually toward the gate, one hand ruminatively tapping a pencil against his notebook as he did so.

"I say!" the little hatless man called again. The black bowler halted and turned. "Sorry," said the hatless man and grinned awkwardly.

"Atkinson. Yorkshire Observer." So much for introductions. "You're the gent from the Evening Standard, aren't yer?" It was more statement than question and the black bowler nodded.

"Ah," continued Atkinson, still smiling broadly and a little short of breath, "You've come up from London for today's memorial service, then?"

Nodding an acknowledgement that virtually ignored the inquisitive statement, the other man said, "Maurice Welch. Bloody awful journey. It's high time these blasted companies got themselves organised so we don't have to stop off every-blasted-where changing trains. Lord, don't they know this is 1917? All I had to read was the papers with damned suffragettes in action again and Hun planes bombing London. I should've brought a darn good book but forgot how tedious these journeys can be."

Welch seemed to be smelling the air, as if he could not wait to clear his nostrils. He went on, in a detached fashion, "You know, I was in this area a few years ago. Didn't enjoy it then either. Is there always this perpetual gloom about the place? Heavens, you'd never imagine it was July. And the food you people eat! – You know, I was staying at some lowly hostal at the time and they offered me what they called 'kicker' to eat."

Atkinson dropped his head and smiled to himself.

"Horse!" Welch almost cried out. "Lord in heaven - actual horse! Can you imagine?..... Oh, well, I dare say you can."

Atkinson continued to smile wordlessly. Welch was not addressing him personally: like the inclination of his gaze, his words seemed to target an imaginary higher authority that would ignore him anyway.

"Yes," Welch carried on, "Carriages filled with soldiers on leave. Rowdy lot, no peace at all, stank to high heaven and the language was all body parts. Good job the paper doesn't send me up here every week. That hotel last night was ghastly! Twenty three shillings, no less. Daylight robbery!"

"Well," Atkinson apologised with a broad gesture of the hands, "The lads on leave, it's to be expected really, in't it? Must be rotten for 'em over in France. Glad I'm not over there writin' t' Wipers

Times, that's all I shall say...... So - what d'you make of this one, then, Mr. Welch? Your paper must think summat about this to send you up 'ere. Sidney said you was from t'Evenin' Standard, like."

Welch turned to face the smaller man, regarding him not so much with his eyes but with a general inquiring mein that wanted to mask any direct intrigue. "Did you speak to any of the family?" His tone was tired and lacked the least vestige of enthusiasm.

Atkinson took his spectacles and put them into place on his face, appearing to need them fully engaged before attempting anything but spurious conversation.

"Um... Usual interviews. Difficult, in't it? – You know, like this. Young lad getting killed, you don't want to push 'em too hard, do you? We've had enough lads gettin' killed – especially this last year, ah mean, what with Arras and the Somme. But he weren't one o' the Bradford Pals any road. Ah should think they've had enough of all the publicity, wouldn't you? – Ah mean, *that* sort o' publicity."

"I spoke to his sister," Welch volunteered, appearing aloof to the smaller man's remarks. He pressed a hand into his inside pocket and pulled out a bright silver case, offered a cigarette to Atkinson without a word.

"Well, there's a gent!" said Atkinson, "Ta very much and God save the King!" Welch returned his notebook into a waistcoat pocket, took a box of matches from another pocket and offered the light to the Yorkshireman first. Atkinson took the cigarette eagerly and looked at the name printed on it. "Mm," he nodded approval, "We don't see these much. 'I'd walk a mile for a Camel', isn't that what they say?" And he laughed nervously.

"She seemed an intelligent woman, I have to admit," continued Welch, "but said the family wanted nothing more of newspapers and refused to say any more to me. It's as you say. But I really wanted a few words with his mother, poor wretch. Flatly refused."

"Mrs. Thornton? - Oh, she's bitter. Oh yes! Very upset, that poor lady. I got a few words with her last month at the Town Hall, when they finally got around to presenting the medal."

Welch's whole posture stiffened, his eyes focused on Atkinson for the first time, his reserve set aside. "Really? You were at the

3

presentation? I should perhaps have been there instead of this memorial service. Now that's interesting - what did she have to say?" Atkinson was about to reply but the pursed lips momentarily froze, he paused and looked up at Welch with a curious grin. "Is this off the record or shall it go in your paper?"

Welch loosened up and returned the wry smile. "If it suits, yes. Why? – Are you after a stipend?"

"Payment? Oh, now there's a queer idea. In a dodgy business like this. Ah mean to say, there's been enough muck flyin' about already, that thing about his lordship an' all.... An' brass passin' between newsmen like us makes it.... well, it doesn't sit right easy, let me put it that way. Not for just a few bob anyway. D'you follow me, Mr. Welch?"

He peered up coolly into the tall man's eyes and softly blew smoke out to the side. "Atkinson, Yorkshire Observer - if you're printing a story about this 'ere medal business. But if you're printing the tale of a man dressed as a female to get off that certain sinking ship that we all know about, ah've not said a word to yer. Ah want nowt to do wi' that."

"I'll remember," agreed Welch. "But, speaking of ships, you know what they say - a rising tide raises all boats." Welch's hint of avarice was not lost on the Yorkshireman.

"Alright." Atkinson gently touched the other man's elbow and led him to one side, away from where a little parade of black linen was beginning to pass down the footpath.

"Aye, she were right bitter, Mrs. Thornton. Said she wanted nothing more of the newspapers, like you said when you spoke to Grace. So then ah said to her – kindly, like – 'Mrs. Thornton, there might be a bob or two in it for yer', but she gave me a filthy look and turned away. Then she said a very queer thing, and I didn't quite understand at first. She said the newspapers and vile tongues – ah think that was the expression - 'vile tongues' had killed her boy. She said he was never the coward in that there *Titanic* sinking, it was all lies. And she said it was them up top that put blame on her lad to take some o't'muck off their own boots. Meanin' – an' you see if you agree with me, Mr. Welch – meanin' them at White Star Lines and their mates in high places. Like that Lord Wotsisname that you and I might know about. And then – here's the funny thing – then she said, 'Ned died on the *Titanic*'."

"Died on the *Titanic*?" queried Welch, astonished.

"Aye. Surprised me an' all. And I thought, 'That's a bit queer', and I said to her, 'Come again, lady - what did you say?' And she repeated it: 'My boy died on the *Titanic*'....... which I thought was a very queer thing to say about a hero of the Somme four years after."

* * * * *

TWO

"Where're you from, lad?" shouted the fireman.

In the bowels of any steamship, firemen would invariably raise their voices to make themselves understood whilst the ship's engines punctuated every second. RMS *Carpathia* was no different.

A weary smile curled up the corner of Ned Thornton's mouth. Many responses flashed through his tired mind and, in a necessarily forced voice, he chose the simplest. "Yorkshire."

"Oh, aye. Which part?" As he spoke, the large senior fireman crouched and passed Ned a cigarette he had rolled and lit for him. This man had been using the break in his routine to check those few survivors who had sought out the boiler room for its extra warmth, to satisfy himself none needed medical assistance that might disrupt his work. Ned took the cigarette, placed it gratefully between his lips and drew on it gently, as if afraid it might choke him. The fireman grinned and said, "Turkish it's not."

Ned coughed to clear his lungs and answered the question: "Ah'm from Bradford".

"Oh, aye? Ah'm from Halifax, me-sen," barked the fireman. "Ah saw that Marie Lloyd at Theatre Royal in Bradford once. D'yer know Park Parade? – Ah've an aunt that lives at Park Parade. Too bloody grand for me!"

They conversed very loudly, shouting over the din of the ship's engines and boilers. "Bit posh then, eh?" He nodded as if Ned were deaf. "You're from the posh bit, then......."

"Not me," Ned called, but the big fireman didn't hear him; he had already straightened up on his shovel. Crossing back to the boiler face, he returned to scooping up shovel-loads of coal and heaving them through the furnace hatch into the inferno. Then a gate to the rear would pull upward and a cascade of coal would shutter forth across the floor, which the firemen leapt on with their clattery shovels with a worn yet uncanny, mechanical energy. From time to time, the man from Halifax would draw a forearm across his head, then wipe it on his dirty vest, and occasionally would cast a glance around the boiler room whilst his fellow stokers largely ignored these incidental outcasts from *Titanic* as if they were not there.

Ned viewed the slumped bodies of three other men, two of them propped up on each other. Here in *Carpathia's* tight boiler space, oblivious to the dirt and coal chunks all about, this handful of survivors found minimal room in which to curl up and relieve their exhaustion in the warmth and the overpowering din of machinery that blotted out immediate memories like an opiate and lent them grateful anonymity. They found respite where they could, squeezing themselves out of the way of gauges, pumps, compressors, and pipework shooting up and around and through. *Carpathia's* crewmen had created a little space out of anarchy, and they would nudge a man carefully out of the way, knowing they had to tolerate this situation for a time. They spoke - or shouted - little, and then in some German dialect, which is perhaps why the big Yorkshireman had spoken to Ned, because he had no-one else to converse with! Ned smiled to himself at the coincidence of finding a "townie" in this unfamiliar ship half way across the world.

Something hit his boot. "Seven hundred!" It was the Halifax fireman shouting again, making a form of sign language with his wide mouth and his fingers. "Seven – seven hundred."

"What?"

"What we took aboard, lad. So they tell me. You was lucky, lad. God 'elp the rest!"

Yes. God help them. Ned dwelt on that thought. Seven hundred. And how many on other ships? The same? He could only hope that was the case. Walter and Frank, they could have made it. They could.

The Halifax fireman had turned away, happily singing 'Boiled Beef and Carrots' at the top of his voice as he went about his work. Ships sank. So a huge liner had hit an iceberg and sunk.... you have to sing, it's all you can do.

In his weakened state, it was too easy for Ned's mind to wander along several tempting avenues. If other ships had managed to rescue similar numbers, perhaps.... But 'perhaps' failed to convince.

If he had not been directed to attend those "important" first class charges, instead of checking the after cabins and steerage accommodation as Frank had been instructed, they might have stayed together.   Then later on A deck, their paths had been parted again by the order from Mr. Flynn to clear the ropes holding a lifeboat so that it was not capsized by the other boat coming down on top of it – "You two! Take a spike each and shin down those fall lines. Get the falls free, for God's sake, or they shall all be in the water. Lively!" Walter had run to the other end but before either could act, the lines had come free and more commotion had broken out to get to the next boat. Ned had lost contact with Walter in the general melee and had found himself back on the Boat deck.

He had been struggling to free one of those Englehardt rafts from abaft of the officers' quarters when another explosion below panicked a brigade of young men newly arrived on the Boat deck. Knocked off his feet, Ned had been pitched outward beyond a davit with a fall line that he desperately tried to grab. The line was icy, he burned his hands, lost his hold and dropped into the water perhaps sixty feet below. A perilous fall in itself but - Oh, the shattering, heart-stopping cold shock!

The memory of that sea pressed into all his thoughts. His mind wandered and found only nightmares. It had to somehow find reason in all this, find some hope and comfort.

Where earlier all had been calm on *Titanic*, most passengers reluctant to trade the warm solidity of a ship they believed unsinkable for an icy cold night on a dark ocean and a frightening drop to arrive there, his brain now gave him the memory of the constant wails of women and men shouting and fighting in the water.

All too vivid, the biting, scything cold that squeezed out of him his seeming last gasp, and the taste of beckoning death in that sea. At first fearing his heart would burst, he lashed out at the water in a furious panic, unaware of any good lifesaving sense. It was Ned or the sea, and the wild certainty of death in that awful fashion kept his arms and legs flailing until he was some way off the hull and grasping for oars bobbing in the water ahead of him. Swim, man, swim! Keep thrashing that water, keep those arms and legs going and the blood coursing through! Keep fighting the cold – that hellish, bloody freezing cold! Fight the water, fight the water, don't let it pull you down - fight! Still those horrible sounds went on and on..........

Turning his face into the boiler room bulkhead, Ned let an involuntary tear escape his tension and pass through the grime of his cheek as all of his torn emotions came to the surface at once. The noise of *Carpathia*'s engines put a screen of meditation around him. There was no thought of impossible conversation, it was enough just to lie there as did these men, and reflect on those events. To wonder, and for some to be thankful. Nobody prayed: God, they must have felt, had been angry with *Titanic* that night. By and by, Ned's eyes closed again and he was aware of nothing.

* * * * *

It was the sound of raised voices that woke him. In the near darkness of their attic bedroom, illuminated solely by the pallid glow of a fading moon through the cold skylight, young Ned felt his brother already sitting upright in the bed they shared, highly conscious of the quarrelling taking place downstairs in the small terrace house on Middleton Street. Cautiously, as if their footsteps would be heard above the din, James and Ned ventured down the creaking bare wood of the attic steps to the landing, where they paused, fearful of the situation and peering into the glimmers of light flickering up from below. Both boys were frightened. Yet this was not a new scenario, the boys and their sister knew it well enough.

The sudden raising of their father's voice jolted them momentarily. It was that other voice, the cruel voice, the voice he wore more and more often these winter nights. And now their mother, protesting, crying in alarm, spitting back the words in little frightened jabs of emotion. The slow, slurred, deep tones meant father had been drinking again. In the weak, dirty gaslight filtering up to them, a pallid death-glow on the starkly bare plaster of the walls, Ned's wide eyes turned to James who returned his younger brother a grimace of resolve. Grace was with them now, rubbing her eyes and pulling some wayward curling paper from her hair. "What are you doing?" she whispered loudly. James didn't answer, he was thinking: after a few seconds he began descending the jute-carpeted staircase with faltering steps and clinging to the bannister rail, and a few moments later stood trembling in the open doorway to the parlour, his fear vibrating his grey flannel nightshirt. Ned clung tightly to his engine – the green wooden engine with the wheels picked out in black, that Uncle Jack had made for his Christmas present, to run on the rusty metal tracks their mother had bought from the rag and bone man.

"Whadda *you* want?" Ned heard his father bellow at James. "Get yerself back up them stairs!" Ned and Grace were poised half-way down the flight of stairs, with an upward flow of warmer air from the living room and Grace grabbing Ned's shirt with one fist, the other clenched in her mouth.

"Go on, see thee, yer little bugger or yer'll feel the back o' my hand, lad!"

It must have been an age before James got the words out: "Ah want yer to stop shoutin' at mother, please, father." Such a fragile, tremulous voice that almost broke apart.

"Oh, yer do, do yer? Well, come 'ere!" Grace was at the doorway in time to see her brother cuffed across the neck. James cried out, then their mother yelped and jumped between them: "Stop it! Stop it, Jubal, don't hit 'im! Stop it, fer God's sake."

"Oh, Godssake now, is it? Why the ruddy 'ell not, then, eh? – Tell the little bugger to mind 'is own ruddy business!"

"Ah'll not tell 'im ought o' the sort. Bless me life, Jubal Thornton, he's yer son. Eight years old and yer've struck yer own son too often by far!"

"Aye, that he is, an' a right useless day's work an' all!" Jubal Thornton raised a foot and, off balance, tapped his pipe out on his boot, dropped the pipe on the stone floor and barked at his wife to pick it up again. Alice for a moment stood upright, glaring defiantly at him. Her husband saw the insolence in her eyes, and it was not a new sign – damn it, he *would not* have his wife talking back to him, either with words or looks or haughty gestures. "Woman - high bloody time you knew your place!"

Raising his arm high above his shoulder, he brought it crashing down on Alice's head. The children shrieked. Ned's brain suddenly slowed as he watched his mother tumble across the room and fall onto the stone flags, narrowly missing the fireplace but hitting the bronze coal scuttle with her upper body, sending lumps of coal clattering in all directions across the floor.

For several seconds there was a brittle silence, Alice trying to obey a reflexive spasm to rise whilst muffling her pain and the children riveted to the spot with trembling legs. Jubal straightened himself up, tugged at his waistcoat.

"Naah, then," he slurred, as if it said everything. "Naah, then. I - will - not," he declared, almost to his own surprise, "have a wife o' mine speak to 'er 'usband in that manner......" As his words seemed not to satisfy his air of authority, he added very loudly, "An' is that clear enough for yer? Missus? Eh?"

Ned had dropped his little green engine and stood crying in the doorway, holding onto his older sister.

* * * * *

THREE

Whilst it was widely believed the best fighter in the West Riding of Yorkshire had been Albert 'Bagsy' Baker, an Elland carpenter and French polisher, Baker himself had always rated Jubal Thornton the better man, and the only man to best him by a knockdown – twice. Thornton had injured a couple of knuckles in his time, and learned an early lesson that punches to the jaw were more likely to break a fighter's own hand. A fighter who knew how to use his body might show little outward sign of his occupation, and Jubal was considered a handsome man when Alice had first met him on that hayride. Of Jubal Thornton it was said that he had the fastest right cross of any fighter in the county. That is, until a cut eye in the ring at Piece Hall Yard in 1896 put an end to a lucrative sideline. Head punching was not considered sporting in a time when nobody died from punches to the head. Jubal, then 32 and facing his own demise as a fighter, had always laid the blame squarely on the drunken referee for not punishing his opponent's late blow after Time was called. Assertions were rife that the referee commonly succumbed to the *green fairy*. But.... People shrugged. It was over. Bets were lost. Thornton was later warned that continued activity in the ring probably would lose him the eye altogether. Jubal kept his eye but lost the purse, and many more in the future.

Alice Thornton counted that day amongst the blackest of her years with her husband, for Jubal lost – quite literally – the glint in his eye and his humour to boot; he became a taciturn, unfriendly creature who by degrees preferred the company of mates at the Spotted Cow whilst demanding more of his wife, who counted her 'relief' time in minutes per week. As a further consequence of the later reduction in the family's circumstances, it was decided that Ned's older brother James should begin work at the mill when his eleventh birthday came round. Not unaware of the recent legislature, nonetheless Jubal had decreed that family necessity came before letting children stay on at school until they were thirteen. *Wasted years*, was his opinion.

"Aye......" Through his thick dark moustache, Jubal Thornton's lips pulled thoughtfully on his treasured briarwood pipe. "He'll do alright at t'big looms, yon lad. Percy Bradshaw's lookin' for a piecer right now, yon lad'll be champion in there, it'll bring us in a bob or two, any road. And," he stressed, jabbing his pipe, "It'll be t'makin' o' the lad, just you mark my words."

For as Jubal pointed out, "That were where ah started out as a lad, cleanin' floors an' balin' out cardin' machines at no'but a tanner a week. An' if it were reet for me, it's bloody reet for 'im an' all. Ruddy books and school's all fine when yer've not got brass ter find." His father also decided that James' first couple of wage packets should go on a pair of decent boots – "Young man, there's nowt more important in all that shit on 't factory floor than the tannin' on yer feet."

In this, there was no denying their father's good sense: Jubal had spent his youth and young manhood in the dour factories of Cleckheaton and Liversedge, rising to foreman at the shoddy factory in Batley before he was twenty. '.....And was Jerusalem builded here,' went the verse extracted with pride from some obscure and distant tome by Jubal's omnipotent father a long time before. For in that time and place, in those massive stone edifices blessed with all the love that money could invest, the mythology of Jerusalem truly was reborn to fill the breast with passion. Men were proud of these dark, rigid temples to industry, and justly so by the standards of the day. No empire had ever had so firm a backbone as the Pennine country, England was the envy of the world and the mill lands of Yorkshire and Lancashire and the industrial Midlands were the engine that drove it all forward whilst the bankers and merchants of London looked on and checked their accounts with relish. With its origins in the Industrial Revolution in the Derbyshire of the 18th century, the wool and cotton textile industries quickly came to dominate not only the North but the entire economy of England for two hundred years, blossoming as England's other great industry, slavery, declined. With a wealth of cheap, replaceable labour and the damp air of the North making cloth fibre easier to craft, these lands of soft water and ample coal

13

shone out like beacons of light to the entrepreneurs of the day. Britain ruled the world, there could be no doubt of it. No matter that there was crippling poverty amidst the fortunes, this England was a place where a man with dirty hands knew he had earned his birthright.

Jubal Thornton's birthright lay in those hills alright. His family had spent several generations in and around the Heavy Woollen district and amongst the dark stones of Huddersfield, Bradford and Halifax - like so many others, 'boom towns' of their day, they attracted migrant, foreign and native workers like magnets: those workers squeezed into towns whose buildings were already bursting at the seams with dirt and squalor and quietly disgusting smells born of disease and lack of sanitation. Jubal's father had impressed on his sons with indomitable force the legacy of the Luddites and how their grandfather, a cropper, had died for the cause - hung by Englishmen from a gibbet in 1813 for destroying looms, the property of one of the town's prominent factory owners. Progress, went the absolute decree, was not to be hindered, for progress by altruistic entrepreneurial gentlemen spread the wealth down from the richest families and provided for the poorest. It was the natural law according to those who write the laws. So it was declared. So it was written. So it had to be. And yet, for all the noble rhetoric, the poor stayed sickly and very poor indeed whilst the comforts and importance of their patrons and benefactors shaped minor empires and established dynasties. Few things change, only the times and objects of desire. Lies remain the truths that rich men dictate in order to motivate the masses.

All the same, whilst mill work had been good to them in times past, by 1902 when the family moved into Southfield Place in Bradford, Jubal's nightly wheezing had been worrying Alice for a considerable time and his only remedy was increasingly through a bottle.

"Look, lass, who earns t'ruddy money in this 'ouse, eh? Ah've got a right to go out for a pint now an' again, haven't ah? Well, then..... Ah work all day wi' them ruddy 'orses. A feller needs a drink. You

14

try draggin' ruddy 'orses up an' down tracks all day, see if you'd like it!"

Alice said nothing and poked her husband's shirt through the rolls of the mangle to squeeze out the dirty water into the tub. "Well?" called Jubal at length. "Well what?" answered Alice.

"Well, am ah right or am ah not bloody right?"

"Oh, of course you are," Alice assured him diplomatically, the frailty of her voice barely audible above the clanking of the mangle and offering not a murmur of conviction.

"Well then," concluded her husband, fighting a pair of boots with a stiff brush. "An' watch what yer doin' at that mangle, woman – ah'm not made o' brass, yer broke a stud last week because yer forgot it. That's two this year! And.... And yer broke a gas mantle t'other day an' all - yer gettin' right careless, woman!"

"You do it, then!" she retaliated, a most unusual reaction for Alice. Then, in a little more considered tone, she added, "Bless me life, ah've only got one pair of 'ands."

Alice said nothing more to him and pounded one of her shifts in the tub with the dolly.

"D'yer want this jar of Condys, mum, or shall I put it back?"

"Aye, lass, pass it 'ere." And under her breath added, "Though I might just drink the bloody stuff and get shut o' meself for all that some folk care!"

Jabbing the pipe always helped. Jubal could see Alice responded better to a good pipe-jabbing.

"An' it'll not be long," Jubal continued, "till we've got young Ned workin', an' all. That right, Ned? Yer'll want to join yer brother an' bring in a man's pay, eh? Be buggered to Balfour and 'is bloody education ideas! Learnin's all well an' good fer them as can use it in big speeches. Who bloody cares if a lad drops his 'h's now and then, ey? A man needs t'earn brass, not a ha'penny every few days like these lads get." Alice paused and looked out of the parlour window at the edge of the flagstones level with her eyes. *Aye*, she pondered, *a ha'penny if they're lucky – if you've not already spent it at the pub, Mr. Thornton.*

As an afterthought, almost to himself, Jubal added, "Pity we've not more bairns as can earn some brass..... A man might put 'is feet up at forty an' watch 'em all workin'."

He had not raised his eyes from the copy of the Argus he had picked up in the station waiting room, yet Alice felt them boring into her neck. Imagined or otherwise, there would always be that edge of bitterness that she had not been as fruitful as many of her contemporaries: large families put more bread on the table for those that survived. Muriel Illingworth had been delivered of ten so far, and so easy that the girls called her 'peapod'. To his credit, Jubal had never laid blame on Alice for losing that child, he had never reproached her for becoming incapable of further children after that dangerous miscarriage when Ned was barely eighteen months old. A girl. Stillborn. There we are...... Jubal had done what was required of him to help Alice's sister tend to the household whilst Alice lay ill. All the same, it was a sense of shame which a woman felt, that she could no longer provide her husband with livestock, and the pains she felt from time to time in her abdomen were God's reminder of it. But no, Jubal had not been reproachful. He had accepted what the vicar had called the Lord's merciful bounty, clasping Alice's hand in a way that told her he was glad she had survived what many women did not. And all those bedsheets – well, they would replace them somehow. Even a new dress - "Na' then, lass! Yer've earned a new frock - hold yer head up when we go out..... Eh?.... Alice?"

Alice had said nothing. *Yes, Mr. Thornton..... Wouldn't do to go out with a woman on yer arm in a frock smeared with my disgrace, would it?*

Grace had been quiet. Observing that the fire was getting low, Jubal tapped a hand on the table to direct her attention to last week's newspaper, indicating that she should pull it out of the coal scuttle. "Fire needs drawin', lass. Can't yer see that?" Grace gestured that she could indeed see that, drew the newspaper open on the floor then placed it over the fireplace, carefully spread to provide the necessary draught without burning the paper whilst at the same time watching that her apron was well clear. Jubal followed her doing it until the fire had burst into suitable life, then glared at her again when she had folded the newspaper and returned it to the scuttle.

"Well....?"

She turned back to the accusing tone.

"Coal..... Coal!..... Fathead!" Grace responded to the shaking finger, pulled two lumps from the scuttle and placed them neatly in the centre of the conflagration.

"Look at our Jim now," Jubal carried on as if there had been no interruption. "Nigh on fifteen shillings a week at 'is age, if you please. Champion, ey? You could be doin' that in another year, our Ned, ey? That'll make a man o' yer."

Ten-year-old Ned turned a cheek toward his father as the only outward sign of acknowledgement. Without a word, he dropped the newly peeled potato into the pot and reached into the colander for another.

"Then," announced Jubal with some satisfaction, "With any luck we'll have our Grace at Bradford Tramways office – all three on 'em bringin' in some brass. In a bit we'll be so throng wi' brass, we might even tek a holiday to Scarborough! 'Ow about that, then? Champion, eh?" Alice paused at the sink, sighed a little as if reassuring herself her husband had the right plan, wiped her face with her apron and carried on pressing the clothes.

"Well, did y'hear me? - Scarborough!... Ow about that? Eh? Your fancy Mr. and Mrs. Holroyd not been to Scarborough yet, have they?.... Eh?" Alice merely looked across at her husband without a trace of a smile.

"An' don't you tell me," Jubal warned, getting to his feet, "that we can't thoil a holiday once all these wains are workin' - it's been long enough comin'. Naah then."

Again, Jubal clamped his fists on his hips and waited for a rebuttal. None came.

"Ey, Ned?" Jubal insisted on a response, his 'bad' eye twitching.

"Yes, father."

Restless, Jubal began stoking the fire: he adjusted the fender and then propped the poker up against the range. Straightening to his full height and turning to his wife, he barked with a finality, "Well 'ow about that, then? Am ah right or what?"

There was not a flicker of reaction.

"Of course you are, Mr. Thornton," he mocked, then coughed, spat on the floor, jabbed his pipe into his mouth and walked out into the evening.

* * * * *

FOUR

Carpathia's crew had passed out many blankets: passengers and crew alike had given clothing to help the less fortunate whilst their wet rags hung up in any haphazard spot. Ned pulled his blanket around him and curled up tightly against the bulkhead; he had found a little nook under a metal table where he was hardly disturbed and here he had already slept fitfully for however long he knew not, since the sea water had had its way with his pocket watch, the chain still attached to his steward's soiled jacket - wherever that was at present. Neither was there daylight down here to judge the time, but reality was coming back to him.

He remembered obtaining a broth in a metal mug from the men who were feverishly coping in the galley here. It had been a hot brew which chased away the acrid taste of the sea, he had consumed it like manna from heaven after the struggle to clamber aboard. That effort of negotiating the rope ladder from the lifeboat had wrenched out of him the last tiny ounce of fight he could ask of his chilled body. He would have fallen back without the help of others. Moving at all had felt to have all the pain he might imagine of an amputee learning to walk all over again. The sea had almost had him - Lord, how he hated the sea now!

In those early hours of Monday, there had been coffee for those that came aboard: bread and potatoes and some vegetables and hard biscuits, no meat at that hour but enough of a bounty to satisfy all. Spirits and a little hot brandy – oh, heavenly hot brandy! - strove to overcome the chills of stiff, frozen bodies as, one way or another, they had climbed aboard and were passed along to the saloons, hastily prepared to receive them, and some to one of three doctors. Smokerooms and lounges had been turned into temporary dormitories, blankets were piled there and even in gangways.

Everywhere were crewmen acting as stewards to assist whilst the ship's own passengers were asked for the moment to remain as patiently as they could in their own cabins. *Carpathia*, having not long since left New York bound for Gibraltar and Italy, was well stocked for her cruise passengers, she was certainly used to carrying two thousand emigrants from Europe to America, but the ship's resources in those early hours were strained to the utmost by the influx of seven hundred survivors. A number of *Titanic*'s first class passengers were still commanding the comforts they had paid their tickets for and demanding – most with moderation - steward service. One gentleman confronted an officer in abrasive voice with the fact he had chartered a rail carriage to meet *Titanic* at New York. The officer had smiled politely and turned away to permit the man to arrive at his own conclusion. White Star's obligations were hardly a Cunard concern at that juncture and Cunard's problems had just multiplied seven-hundred fold. Complaints that no first class accommodation existed for persons of privilege were put down with polite candour to those insensitive enough to raise them.

And whilst many survivors were left to cluster together on deck, *Carpathia* did her best to provide accommodations to the hundreds she had recovered: stewards and scullions hustled about to attend as best they could the comfort of everyone, providing nourishment and any convenient ways of helping people rest, though there were bunks at this stage only for the sick, and many survivors had to find such comfort as they might in gangways, on tops of lockers or tables, or underneath them.

Ned was coming round. No uniforms were in evidence: the male survivors here - third class passengers - had taken off their clothes to dry out. Few of the ladies amongst the survivors had any such concern. His brain regaining acuity now, Ned wondered how many were here still not knowing whether their loved ones and friends were aboard *Carpathia* or another ship – surely there had been other rescue ships. Pushing his blankets aside, he rubbed his shoulder again and peered at it as best he could: he could feel torn skin but no fresh bleeding and from moving his arm he concluded that nothing was broken. His ear and his temple would merit further attention where the oar had struck him, he had a dressing across it now though he could not yet recall who had put it there. His hearing appeared intact from what he could judge, that was something to be thankful for, and the ringing in his ear had almost gone. If he could find those responsible for slapping their oars at people in the water desperately trying to reach a lifeboat, he would personally put a rope around their necks and watch them writhe on the end of it. Yet now was no time for recriminations. He drew on the second cigarette given to him: the big Halifax fireman was right, the tobacco was rough and pungent, probably shredded from old stogies left too long on a bar rather than any decent roll of baccy. He drew twice more then flicked it aside.

Premature to be gloomy, yes. Other ships would have picked up survivors, of course they would - his shipmates among them. Yet it nagged at him - the fear he might no longer hear their shrill laughter, their quarrelling, their silly games in the messdeck, their talk of women and football and nights at the Platform or the Juniper Berry tempting the ghost to appear as they became ever more inebriated. The long sigh that left Ned's body was not an effect of the cold, not now.

* * * * *

FIVE

Senator Burgess: 'Mr. Thornton, let's continue. The board has your statement that you joined the ship on the 4th of April as a steward at Southampton following her sea trials, having been in the employ of the White Star Line for roughly a year. Correct so far?'

Mr. Thornton: 'Yes, sir. First with *Olympic* while she was going through all her troubles. That scrap with the *Hawke* and all.'

Senator Burgess: 'You had previously been a steward with Cunard.'

Mr. Thornton: 'Yes, sir. Two years. We saw White Star as a step up, like, Walter and me.'

Senator Burgess: 'Can we turn to the night in question? So your duties confined you largely to one of the bars on... B deck. Were you on duty at the time *Titanic* struck the iceberg?'

Mr. Thornton: 'Officially, no, but there had been an unplanned party that went on longer than expected and the senior steward detailed myself and another to help clear up. I had already turned in, I wasn't best pleased.'

Senator Burgess: 'So, where were you when the ship struck?'

Mr. Thornton: 'I don't know. Ken and I were carrying crates of bottles from the stores, we were aft on E deck headed for Scotland Road – '

Senator Burgess: ' – Which is, if my geography is correct, the main thoroughfare on E deck. Would that be forward of the after staircase? And what about the electric elevators - wouldn't you have taken the elevator?'

Mr. Thornton: 'No, sir, staff weren't allowed to use the lift if passengers were using it, so we let it alone. But Ken wanted to go back to our messdeck for his cigarettes, and we went that way so we could have a smoke when we'd finished.'

Senator Burgess: 'Go on. Did you feel the impact of the collision?'

Mr. Thornton: 'The engine casing down there makes a right racket, we didn't hear anything that sounded like anything – if you know what I mean. Thinking about it later, there was a bit of a judder. Somebody said they thought she'd thrown a blade, but I wouldn't know what that felt like.'

Senator Burgess: 'When did you first become aware of anything amiss?'

Mr. Thornton: 'We got up to D deck and somebody rushed past, he was headed aft through the dining room and as he nearly knocked us over he said, "Get your lifejackets, quick".'

Senator Burgess: 'At what time was that?'

Mr. Thornton: 'About a quarter to midnight. Ten to, maybe.'

Senator Burgess: 'What did you do?'

Mr. Thornton: 'We carried on up. On C deck we saw Dick Albright banging on cabin doors and calling out to people to get lifejackets on and go up on deck. I asked him what was going on and he said we'd hit a berg and an officer had told him to get everybody up and no panicking.'

Senator Burgess: 'Did he appear to be panicking?'

Mr. Thornton: 'No, not in the least. In fact he winked at me and said, "If you ask me it's a bloomin' picnic!", so I didn't think it was serious. Anyway, one of the purser's men came past us and told us to get all the passengers out of their cabins quickly and muster them on deck.'

Senator Burgess: 'Did he say the ship was sinking?'

Mr. Thornton: 'No, sir. Just to get the passengers on deck.'

Senator Burgess: 'This was...... you were on B deck now – B deck or C deck?'

Mr. Thornton: 'B deck. Ken and I split up. I saw my mates Frank and Walter and we swopped opinions. Had a bit of a laugh actually. Walter said there were big lumps of ice on the well deck and he'd heard the ship might have been holed. We still thought it wasn't serious because *Titanic* was unsinkable. Frank joked about going back down for his cigarette card book because it was the only thing of value he had! Then the matron broke us up and we carried on knocking everyone up and told them to put on life preservers. A bit later, I was told to go through the cabins on E deck and close the scuttles – but I know some were left open, and as I was about that, a

23

lady grabbed hold of me and asked me to help get her to her employer who was one of the important passengers.'

Senator Burgess: 'Who?'

Mr. Thornton: 'Mr. Ranulph Knight, sir.'

Senator Burgess: 'Ranulph Knight. Yes. Tell us about this. That would in fact be Mr. Anthony Scott-Chapelle, travelling under that name, would it not? The soap manufacturer. But you did know who he was?'

Mr. Thornton: 'Yes, sir, we all did. And Mrs. Knight. And this lady was her companion, Miss Devonshire. Well, I got her up to their stateroom, and their private steward told me to see they got to the boats whilst he went below to get her ladyship's dog, and he left. She was creating something terrible about that dog. You want me to carry on, sir?"

Senator Burgess: 'Yes, please.'

Mr. Thornton: 'Then they were joined by Mr. Caldecot, Mr. Knight's private secretary. He was outside in the corridor talking to one of the officers – I didn't see who and you could hardly hear anything for the noise of the boilers letting off steam. When he came back in the cabin he said I must see they boarded a boat, the officer had agreed. Well, I wasn't going to argue with him.'

Senator Burgess: 'And you carried out this duty, did you?'

Mr. Thornton: 'I did, sir.'

Senator Burgess: 'And I gather from your attitude, Mr. Thornton, that it was not a pleasant duty.'

Mr. Thornton: 'Mr. Knight was complaining about everything, took his time to dress and find his stuff, they didn't seem to appreciate any urgency and complained about the inconvenience. Mr. Caldecot came back in the cabin and I think he and Mr. Knight had had a row – anyway, there was a bad mood all round. I stood by waiting until they were ready, I was afraid of a reprimand from one of the officers if I didn't treat them respectfully. Mrs. Knight said she would complain to my boss – she meant Mr. Ismay, since she referred to the head of the line, and she fussed about what she was putting on. Her ladyship – oh, beg pardon, sir, the stewards had been calling her that – she insisted on wearing some of her jewellery, she said someone would ransack the cabin while they were away and steal stuff that hadn't been lodged with the purser. I promised to lock the cabin but that didn't satisfy them. Miss Devonshire wanted to take a stuffed cat, of all things, and she had a jar of toothpaste! At the time I thought it was funny. Anyway, Mr. Knight had this attaché case and they were fratching over it – '

Senator Burgess: '*Fratching*, Mr. Thornton?'

Mr. Thornton: 'Aye - squabbling as to who took it. I told him our orders were, no luggage of any kind but they ignored me and I accepted it for the sake of peace and quiet. They argued, some papers fell out of the case and Mr. Knight got really annoyed. I picked some of them up, Mr. Caldecot grabbed them off me, he seemed angry but it wasn't my fault.'

Senator Burgess: 'Did you escort them to the boat deck?'

Mr. Thornton: 'To A deck, on the starboard side.'

Senator Burgess: 'What time was this?'

Mr. Thornton: 'I think, around 12.35. Oh no, it must have been later – they'd started firing the rockets if that helps pinpoint the time. But several of the boats on that side were already swung out from the davits and lowered. In fact, I think they were all out because at first there was none for my party to board.'

Senator Burgess: 'But you did see them installed in a lifeboat?'

Mr. Thornton: 'Stayed with them, sir, as instructed. I had to look after the two ladies because Mr. Knight and Mr. Caldecot went below again, they were still arguing.'

Senator Burgess: 'They went *back*? Did you hear what they were arguing about?'

Mr. Thornton: 'No, sir, not my business. I was just annoyed they left the ladies in my charge, it made it difficult to find them a boat. Anyhow, after – oh, must have been ten minutes, Mr. Knight came back and he was waving his arms about and demanding a boat to take them off.'

Senator Burgess: 'And Caldecot?'

Mr. Thornton: 'I didn't see Mr. Caldecot. There was one of the cutters – you know. Straight away Mr. Knight started giving out orders and telling the seamen he wanted the boat swung out. I think also there was a worry that if they tried to lower a boat fully loaded they might lose the falls and capsize. By that time anyhow it was clear there was a real emergency and people were saying the old girl was going down. The officer said just to get them boarded and lower away with what people were there.'

Senator Burgess: 'Which officer?'

Mr. Thornton: 'Mr. Murdoch, sir – I knew him from the *Olympic*. He was getting the boats away, one of them snagged part way down. That boat left with about - I don't know, only twenty people in it. They had to get it clear, because they couldn't launch the other collapsibles otherwise - they used the same falls, you see. And then at that point I was told to help with the stern boats.'

Senator Burgess: 'Alright, Mr. Thornton. In fact this board is acquainted with the predicament of Mr. Knight and his party, he has made certain representations. You did know, did you, that Mr. Caldecot is amongst the missing?'

Mr. Thornton: 'No, sir, I did not know that.'

Senator Burgess: 'Very well, we will leave that matter there for the present. In your opinion, was the evacuation of passengers handled as well as it could have been?'

Mr. Thornton: 'Given the circumstances, yes: I mean, the jobs of the officers were impossible.'

Senator Burgess: 'In what way? Some boats came away far below capacity. Do you think your officers could have used better judgement filling the boats?'

Mr. Thornton: 'A lot of people didn't want to get into the boats, they thought being on an unsinkable ship waiting for rescue was better than risking a little boat on an open sea. Being so cold. Later it was pure bedlam and they were all trying to get on a boat. A lot of orders could only be given by signals, the steam blowing off from the boilers made it impossible to hear at times. And a lot of women were still aboard. To give the men their due, most hung back to let the women through, but many women wouldn't go, so you can imagine how chaotic it was. I've thought a lot about it since, I reckon our officers and crewmen were wonderful in the circumstances. It's not my place to say, but I would not want

26

anyone criticised for their conduct. Mr. Murdoch in particular, I think you should give that man's family a medal, senator, if you don't mind my saying so. I don't want to hear ought bad of those men - some of them were my friends, they were brave men. Excuse me, senator, sir, that's how I feel about it.'

Senator Burgess: 'Take your time, Mr. Thornton. Your emotions are perfectly understandable. Are you alright now? By what means, Mr. Thornton, did *you* leave the ship? Did you have your own lifejacket?'

Mr. Thornton: 'No, sir, Ken and I and the others, we just got caught up in it, we didn't have time. At one point we were told to get the windows on A deck open so boats could load from there, but they wouldn't open and it would have been dangerous to smash them, so we were ordered back up top. Mr. Lowe told us to free the Englehardt rafts but I'd just got crouched down trying to work on the lines when a bunch of chaps came running up the deck and knocked everything flying, me included. I lost my balance and grabbed for a line from the davit but missed my hold and dropped clean over the side. Luckily the boats had pulled away so I didn't hit anything, I just went in feet first and I kicked back up and thrashed my way out of there, I suppose. That water - oh! - I'll never forget it. So cold. The shock of it took your breath, you couldn't last in there for long. But you panic: it gets hold of you, you panic, so you just kick and kick. Long as I live I'll never forget how cold it was and the feeling it was going to squeeze the life out of me.'

Senator Burgess: 'Is that how you got the head wound? The report says you took a head wound: is it plain? - I can't really see.'

Mr. Thornton: 'Not then, no. It was when I reached the first boat, somebody brought an oar down on me, they were afraid people in the water would capsize the boat. There was another person in the water that they hit with an oar, I saw her - '

Senator Burgess: 'Are you alright, Thornton? Take your time.'

Mr. Thornton: 'I saw her go under and I never saw her again. I can't believe that people would do that. I took an oar on the shoulder and it grazed my head – here, and nearly took my ear off. I got patched up by the Italian doctor and it's healed pretty well.'

Senator Burgess: 'You were then taken into that lifeboat?'

Mr. Thornton: 'No, they left us. I just kicked and kicked, you had to keep swimming, if you stopped for a second the water was just too cold. After a few minutes - well, I don't know how long - another boat pulled me aboard. Maybe a bit longer and I'd have gone under, you can't stay alive in water like that.'

Senator Burgess: 'Mr. Thornton, do you have any reflections on where blame lay for *Titanic*'s loss? Do you think for instance Captain Smith was entirely responsible?'

Mr. Thornton: 'Captain Smith? Oh, I shouldn't think so. He had a fine record.   There was that thing with *Olympic* when she collided with the *Hawke*, but Captain Smith took no blame for that. One of the best skippers in the world. I saw him on deck as we were trying to get the boats away, and he was – well, he looked in command to me. With all due respect, sir, I'm not in a position to make a judgement. They were brave men.'

Senator Burgess: 'Very well. Now, you mentioned earlier that you were down on E deck, by the engine casing, and that the noise masked any sound of the ship running into the iceberg. Do we gather from this that the engines were so loud or that the noise of the collision was much less loud?'

Mr. Thornton: 'No louder than normal, so far as I could tell. I imagine the noise of the collision was not loud anyway in that part of the ship.'

Senator Burgess: 'The point I'm trying to establish, Mr. Thornton, is whether the engine noise suggested to you that the ship was at full steam and had reached a speed which may be considered excessive for the sea conditions in the area at the time.'

Mr. Thornton: 'Excessive? It's difficult to gauge on a big ship like *Titanic*, but I don't suppose I would suggest the ship was at full speed, no. Ships I've been on doing full power, they would shake to – well, they would shake violently.   And anyway, in my experience ships generally carry on at cruising speed unless visibility's really bad. To be honest, I'd hardly been out on deck since Fastnet Light or the Cow and Calf, so it's difficult for me to say that she was making excessive speed.'

Senator Burgess: 'You had not been out on deck? Were there no drills? Lifeboat drill?'

Mr. Thornton: 'In Southampton dock while we were victualling up, yes. At sea, and with the passengers, no, we'd only taken on the last passengers a couple of days before at Queenstown. The whole crew was new, though a lot had come over from *Olympic*, like Walter and me, but everybody was new. We had boat stations, but in the event everybody was all over the place. With all the noise and confusion, I imagine only the seamen knew what boat they were taking.'

Senator Burgess: 'I see. Very well. One more question, Mr. Thornton. A number of accusations – no, cancel that: a number of *suggestions* have been made regarding men escaping in lifeboats by adopting female apparel, do you know of any such occurrence? - Actually, I shall rephrase that again, excuse me: "escaping" is an inappropriate term in the circumstances, but shall we say, masquerading to get a place in a boat which may have deprived other female passengers.'

Mr. Thornton: 'I've heard that story, sir, that's all I know. There was comment in the newspapers, and a couple of people remarked on it.'

Senator Burgess: 'And you yourself?'

Mr. Thornton: 'Sir?'

Senator Burgess: 'There was a suggestion, Mr. Thornton, that one of the male passengers in boat 11 had assumed female attire as a means of getting a place. Does this mean anything to you?'

Mr. Thornton: 'Sir?.... No.... But, I don't – '

Senator Smith: 'Thank you, senator. This is a board of inquiry, Mr. Thornton; Senator Burgess is endeavouring to inquire into all aspects concerned with the loss of the vessel. That includes any culpable or inappropriate conduct by passengers or crew that might be considered prejudicial to the lives of others. Now, these enquiries will be ongoing for some time, it is going to be quite a long time before we arrive at conclusions. Some of these facts may turn out to be unpleasant. In the meantime, thank you for your information, Mr. Thornton, we may have recourse at a later date to recall you for further testimony. Please ensure that the clerk is kept informed of your whereabouts in the interim. Do you have employment?'

Mr. Thornton: 'No, sir, I am.... No, not at this precise moment. I am hoping to return to England.'

Senator Smith: 'You are not restrained from obtaining further employment but there is a legal obligation on you to make yourself available for recall within a period of three months from this date. You understand this?'

Mr. Thornton: 'Yes, sir. But – '

Senator Smith: 'No further questions, Thornton, you are excused.'

* * * * *

SIX

On *Carpathia*'s deck it was curiously quiet, save for the intermittent ship's horn and the swishing of the water against the gaining strength of the wind through departing fog. Seamen went about their duties as they would any other day but with a subdued, self-conscious air, not wanting to disrupt the mourning of passengers whilst still eager to present a brave face. People from *Titanic* stood about and watched others moving almost as if they had no right to. Notwithstanding earlier requests for the ship's outbound passengers to keep largely to their quarters, many were giving space to the survivors and treating their needs. Spare clothes: a pair of gloves here, a pullover there, a coat; whatever made them feel they were being supportive. Many went further, offering up their cabins for survivors to rest. Charity that repaid the donor.

With eyes different from those he had used before, Ned Thornton stood by a bulkhead door, looking about him, trying to take in the nature of how many lives had been wrecked or lost and wondering if he would see any familiar faces. Yes, one or two, the faces of ladies he had served - at dinner perhaps, or in the bar with their diffident menfolk. They would not recognise him - a steward was no more than an organic automaton. Yet he had overheard the conversations amongst passengers and crew alike of the huge numbers of souls lost that night and he was embarrassed at his own attitude toward these passengers here. His guilt at remaining alive pressed him back into the shadows of the ship where he rubbed at his shoulder and patted the head dressing by way of telling himself how very lucky he was.

Squinting upward at an overcast sky, so bright now after many hours in the dim light below deck, Ned pulled the blanket tightly about him. It had smelled of mothballs but out here any aroma was blasted away in a warming sooty backflow from the funnel as he sought refuge from the wind. No solace hung in that sky: a glance at the frothy, evil sea with its whitecaps brought a shudder and repulsion. The sea was his enemy now, relentlessly pluming and darkly flowing on, coldly eager for another victim. His stomach had been fed but remained irritable. He was restless, with nowhere to go.

Women sobbed quietly, most stared with a desperation of emptiness and incredulity, and most of all for many of them – as with himself - there was an intrusive guilt that they lived.

Disconsolate, Ned took to counting off the heads in turn. One face was turned toward him, it held neither a frown nor a smile but a question, asking him if he knew her, for she would not otherwise intrude on him. He raised his head in a signal of recognition to the young lady seated alone on a fan casing beside the stairway to the upper deck. Was it she? There was a faint sign of approval on her face. Slackening his blanket about his shoulders, he decided he must approach her and did so stiffly.

"It's you, isn't it?" he said to her with a faint breath of embarrassment, then shook his head in annoyance at the nonsense of his remark. She only smiled.

"Are you alright, miss?"

"More to the point," she replied, "are *you* alright? Your head.....?"

He put a hand to the dressing across his ear. "Yes, thank you, miss. The doctor here - Italian chap - he fixed me up."

Ned was feeling his way. He was a steward, she was a passenger. Should he thank her for helping him in the lifeboat, just leave it at that and move along? Then she surprised him by standing up and taking an interest in his head wound. "Ooh!" She made a noise as if feeling the blow that he took. "It's already looking a bit black there. See the doctor again before you leave the ship." Her accent was Irish: not strong - soft and pleasant with a particular sibilance. When she asked his name, he told her, "Ned Thornton, miss. Steward."

"Not a steward now, are you, Mr. Thornton?"

The remark disarmed him. "Um...."

"I mean, not on this ship. You're just another shipwrecked person, aren't you?"

"Ah.... Well, yer see, my employer is the White Star Line, miss, an' there are White Star passengers on this ship. So to look at it from that point o' view – "

"Mr. Thornton, you're an injured man. You were in an awful state on Monday morning in the boat. Rest, Mr. Thornton, for goodness sake. I'm sure you need it. Who's going to miss you?"

She had a point. And aside of Americans, none of the gentry who travelled first class on White Star and Cunard would take a second glance at who was there to serve them; he would hardly be missed.

"Suppose you're right, " he agreed. "My first chief steward gave me some advice: he said, *Remember, a good ship's steward is a ghost!* As people, we do tend to be invisible." She met his indiscretion with a sideways look and Ned shuffled on his heels. "Sorry, miss, that's unprofessional."

".... But true, I fancy!" He allowed himself a breath of relief at her response, and still he had no idea who this girl was.

"Thank you for the coat, miss."

She shook her head lightly to dismiss the need for thanks. "Well, it really didn't suit you, Mr. Thornton. I had my lifejacket, a cardigan, and under that a dress and a couple of petticoats, so I managed well enough. Even now some of the ladies here have almost nothing to wear so I'm the lucky one. You had nothing to keep you from freezing to death except your wet jacket and bow tie....."

Humour had not been her intention, but for a moment they shared an amused exchange.

"You held onto that oar like you were drunk! .... When we pulled you aboard, you looked as if you'd had it and in the poor light we couldn't see how bad your head was. The crewmen weren't happy at all that we pulled you in, they were afraid you'd upset the boat. But you were only half-aware what was going on, I had to keep shaking you – did I hurt you?"

"Ah can't remember."

"The boat was so full, wasn't it? We propped you against that oar and after a lot of coughing you seemed like you were going to live.... another chap died in the boat –" There she faltered, the only sign

33

thus far of how the experience had affected her. "But we were determined to keep you alive, we took turns to rub you up and down. Another lady had a flask of brandy." He remembered the brandy, not the lady.

Now there was a sudden tear in her eye and both stopped talking, just glanced from one to the other and then out to sea, as if somehow *Titanic* would suddenly sail into view and all would be well again. As the tear slid down her cheek, she dipped her head, letting out the tiniest of frightened sobs.

"Oh," she shuddered, raising her head, "I wish I were home!" He felt helpless. She was after all just another piece of the flotsam that *Titanic* had left behind, another person whose life had been fractured by the events of a night too horrible to want to recall.

"... If only the lookouts might have seen that dreadful iceberg sooner.... Why could they not? – It was their job to do that."

"Ah wish ah knew, miss." Ned searched in the debris of his mind for an answer. "Ah'm not good at knowin' stuff. Like that comet that they said came from out in space, what's that all about? Did it destroy all that land in Russia? See, ah don't know much about anythin'. With the ship and that iceberg, well - who knows? It were a strange night, y'know. So still and so cold, and no moon, it were almost as if we were already under a shroud. D'you know what ah mean?"

"Not really."

"Ah'm a steward, miss, not a seaman. Ah've been doin' the Atlantic runs a couple o' years now and ah know this much: when there's dark cloud over the sea, that means open water, an' that's alright; but when that cloud is sort of pale and still-looking, then there's probably ice. Seamen say they can smell ice. An' yer can feel it too, in the air. But so far as ah can tell from what folk 've said, there weren't no cloud at all, it were just black as pitch as far as the eye could see."

It meant nothing to her. He realised it was irrelevant now.

"What's your name, miss?"

Collecting herself, she drew a quaking breath. "Zena McAusland."

He nodded. "Where from? ... What d'you do?"

"I worked in a stocking factory. I made silk mittens. It's a little place called Balbriggan, north of Dublin. I have two brothers there, and two brothers in Pittsburgh. My uncle is meeting - well... going to meet the ship at New York."

"You were travelling with someone?"

"No. I was sharing a second class cabin with two other ladies. It cost my father a fortune but he insisted I shouldn't go steerage..... I didn't know those ladies, and actually I didn't want to...." Under her breath, she let slip, "... They weren't very nice."

"You got your coat back anyway."

"Two of the seamen got you aboard because the crane was busy. You were a handful – *they* thought you were drunk too! They gave the coat to an officer. A woman's coat, obviously.... not yours." That brought a little laugh out of her. "Anyhow, they got it dried out for me. See?"

Ned looked her up and down, as if judging how her coat looked on her. She had it undone at the top, and like many women of her age – which he guessed at about 20 – wore a blouse that did not cover up to her neck as an older woman might, the blanched lace ran in a curve from shoulder to shoulder with a rose motif at the centre. Aware the look of her was drawing his eye, Ned consciously glanced away. Whether she clutched from time to time at the top of her coat out of modesty or because she was cold, he had no need to guess. She had neither headscarf nor shawl, and many female survivors had lost their hats. Zena's long auburn hair was curled up in a braided coronet and evidently secured with a pin. A servant's role does not include the acknowledgement of beauty, that at least is the wisdom of it, but he took her to be a pretty girl with a freshness and a smouldering vitality that, truly, did not belong in a stocking factory by any estimation.

"I didn't see you at the service."

"Service?"

"It was yesterday, Mr. Thornton. Today is Tuesday. That actually was quite a bang on the head, wasn't it?"

"Ah would've been asleep. And actually......." His eyes turned down, he took a few moments to continue. ".... Excuse me, miss, but God didn't seem to be anywhere in all this somehow. That's a bad thing to say..... Ah have mates.... ah think they may still be back there. Seems to me, God had 'is eyes closed. Sorry, miss."

"No, Mr. Thornton, I understand. Truly. But you should remember we came safely to this ship, and that is something to be thankful for. The sea was – well, it was as calm as a millpond at the time, we could not have wished for better, apart from the horrible cold. It was almost as if...... all the sea wanted was to swallow that ship, and nothing more, and then it was satisfied and calm.... I'm rambling now."

"No. No. You're right, ah think. Perhaps we were just lucky, miss."

"Zena. Call me Zena."

"Ned," he reciprocated. He swallowed, as if to throttle back his words, but she smiled another little smile at him and patted his arm. "Don't put the bowtie back on, Ned, that's my advice."

Later in the day, she was across the saloon, sitting between two other ladies and looking forlorn. On an adjacent table, two young girls were playing draughts quite noisily.

In a moment, she said, "It's the boy... His parents are missing." She sighed a weary sigh.

"Which boy?"

"He's with the purser... Ned," she quickly changed the subject, "Have you been to the Marconi room?"

"Aye. That man looks exhausted. Ah just filled out a message form, they said it'd be for free. Ah suppose he'll get around to them all eventually."

"I sent a message to Uncle Shane in Pittsburgh... You're right, it will take him ages to get through them all." Her face turned away again and took on a worried look. "The boy was at the service on Monday..... We committed some bodies to the sea. It was just the saddest thing." He knelt at the hem of her skirt and placed a friendly hand onto her wrist.

"This lady and I searched the ship together," she continued. "Do you suppose his parents could have been picked up by another ship?"

"Of course. Never give up hope." It was clear the young boy represented to her all those who had lost someone dear in *Titanic*'s wake. How were any of them coping with the trauma and the memories?

Now he wanted to reach out and embrace her, embrace another soul ripped from the security of an ordered life. In the event, he awkwardly knelt there until she looked directly at him again and smiled to ease his discomfort.

"Come on," she said, "Let's walk around the deck. It's too smoky in here." More than that, the girls playing draughts had become too noisy for comfort.

"Ah'm a Yorkshireman. There's so much smoke at 'ome, we plait it an' bake it an' have it for supper."

Outside the saloon, the morning fog had lifted and given leave to a fresh wind to soar through the ship's upper structure and whistle across the ventilation funnels, so strong now that spray from a choppy sea was lashing the lower decks. Ned shuddered and tugged at the jumper and jacket he had borrowed from a crewman. It was cold but invigorating, they were alive and could continue to feel the thrill of an icy blast and the redeeming warmth of hot coffee in the saloon after whilst their ears thawed out. He led her to a stairway and they descended to the deck below for the shelter of the boats, Zena holding Ned's hand as her other held tightly to her billowing skirt.

"I am so relieved," she called, raising her voice into the wind, "that we're headed for New York."

"Oh?"

"Well, we didn't know, did we? This ship was headed for Gibraltar. But now.... I suppose, with all these people......"

"It would've been down to victualling and quartering arrangements. Is yer uncle meeting yer, then, in New York?"

"I suppose."

"Then what?"

"So far as I know, we stay in New York another night, then a train to Pittsburgh."

"Ah."

"Uncle Shane is a steel worker, he got the lads jobs there. He's going to find work for me too. I have no prejudice against any kind of work. As long as there's money at the end of it."

"Ah see." He nodded slowly and Zena gave him a doubtful look.

"Work," she continued, ".....it's more like a religion to us. For Irish folk, Ned, it's everything."

"Same for us. When yer've worked in the mills – "

"I've seen your mills. I spent some time with a family in Lancashire.... Ned, my dad and Uncle Shane, they hardly knew their family. My grandfather and grandmother were split up in the workhouses. The boys were split from the girls. D'you know about the workhouses? The workhouses were like penal colonies... Prisons. The famines. Do you know of the famines, Ned?" He knew little.

"Thousands died in the workhouses. If they didn't die trying to get blood out of stones in the fields, they died in the workhouses. If you or your family were in the workhouse, you died anyway – socially, if you know what I mean. You might survive physically, but nobody would want to know you. And your English lords – " There she pulled up short, fearful that to go on would be to embarrass an innocent young man who knew nothing of the crimes she held in her consciousness from many years of English rule.

"It was just awful, Ned, that's all." Her face signalled a kind of apology for coming close to an outburst. He caught the intent of it and nodded again, now convinced this box of Pandora was best left alone.

"Anyway, that was Uncle Shane. He came through it. My father...... well..... No thanks to the English. There - I said it. I'm sorry, Ned."

"No," was the most he felt he could say in his ignorance.

"And so you see......" With a huge breath, she drew a conclusion for him in the air. "America!"

The thought she was not to stay long in his acquaintance caused a twinge of anxiety in him. Zena in effect a piece of the wreckage he was clinging to now - but quite aside from that, he already realised he was attracted to her. And within a day or two, he would have to let that go.

So far, he had but lightly turned over in his mind his own situation but would try not to worry about it until he had visited White Star's Broadway offices in New York. His service on both *Olympic* and *Titanic*, that ought to be a key to further service under the Red Pennant. And, he reminded himself, Andrew Gaskell was aboard the *Adriatic*, it would be good to get together with Andy again if he could not get back aboard *Olympic*. Yes, if he could be reassigned on the Liverpool or Genoa routes, he would be feeling much happier in a few weeks.

Ned's wistful mood was interrupted right there as a figure, battered by the wind, stumbled along the deck in the lea of the boats and stopped a dozen paces opposite. Ned at once made out the tightly sculpted face of Ranulph Knight. He was trying to puff at a pipe, cupping it in his hands, and obviously recognised Ned not at all, if indeed he had even noticed anyone else. Under his arm he held that same briefcase he had been so anxious to retain as he left the ship, and he had somehow acquired a white waistcoat and bow tie visible beneath his overcoat.

Sensing that Ned was suddenly distracted, Zena pressed his arm lightly.

Then with a loud clang a bulkhead door closed and Ranulph Knight was joined by another man, his manner immediately paying respect to Knight's seniority. Ned was surprised – it was John Cade!

So...... Cade had escaped the sinking ship too. In that instant of recognition, Ned's mind reflected back on all that had happened that night, it flickered through his brain in a moment, snatches of this and that, the late-evening festivities, the assignment to Knight and his party, the eerie quiet on *Titanic*'s deck giving way to the commotion when he had been knocked over the side, and the water..... the water.....

"Thornton?"

"Cade! ... Yer made it." He was shouting lest his words should fly away on the wind.

"Bloody did! Ruddy miracle, ey? Blimey! I didn't expect to see anyone I knew now. I thought they'd all gone down with 'er. Weren't you with Tollivant?"

"Ah was. Ah haven't seen 'im, have you?"

"I ain't seen no-one, my old oppo. Until you."

"Lucky us, then."

"Yair - damn right."

Cade forced a kind of half-smile into his face, but between the two of them conversation seemed a great imposition. Cade appeared at that time beholden to Ranulph Knight, judging by their juxtaposition, and as Knight now moved away, having said not a word and only casting a perfunctory glance in Ned's direction, Cade was drawn to follow, in the manner of a dung-catcher following behind the horse. At the bulkhead door, however, Knight momentarily paused and again peered back for two seconds, as if wondering where he had seen this young man before.

They noisily threw open the door and Ned watched them disappear into the ship, whilst Zena waited until Ned was accessible again before she spoke.

"You don't like him. Do you?"

"No," he corrected, " – *he* doesn't like *me*."

* * * * *

For all the resolve of Zena McAusland that Ned should take no part in servicing passengers, nevertheless he felt a need to offer what he could, if only to combat his own emptiness, and went about with one or two of *Carpathia*'s stewards, doing what little he might to help make the life of survivors bearable. Being without livery, Ned would attend the less fortunate, who mostly had lost everything and were deeply worried that they had no means of support, a situation in which he knew he was to find himself once they arrived in America.

Time passed nervously as *Carpathia* returned to New York to deliver redemption to seven hundred souls. Boredom was a condition easily come by. There were, on the other hand, no outbursts, no hysterics of men or women giving vent to their sufferings: wives who had lost husbands silently mourned, and mothers who had lost children wept as if in quiet consideration of the feelings of others, all knowing they bore pain.

Zena met him late on the Thursday afternoon, almost at once venting her annoyance that a certain lady had no thought for anything but the notion that her jewelled pendant had been stolen.

Exasperated, she told Ned, "I don't imagine she had one in the first place. But she'll go on pretending she did, so she can put in a claim." Her low voice, mindful of the ears of others, said it all.

"Still no word on that little Italian lad, then?"

"Giulio?" Zena shook her head and simply looked directly at him with an air that might have said, 'So many lost souls, so many broken families'.

"You alright?" Ned wanted to know.

"Sure. We..... we....."

The tears came slowly. Her frame shook and her voice pulsed with tiny sobs as she spoke. "It's just the noise."

"Ah know, Zena."

"No... No, you don't. You weren't well, after all ...... The cries of those people. I never want to hear that again!....... I *shall* hear it...... I know... Almost..... almost as if they had megaphones.... We couldn't see, we could only hear..... And I don't know......I don't know what we did then. We had no lights. Such a black night. Only a couple of boats had lanterns at the helm. The voices..... one by one..... they went quiet..... And in the boat, we were all quiet..... Ghostly... One or two of the women were crying as if they were afraid to cry. It felt like a funeral. It *was* – it was a funeral. Just bobbing around in a sea of.... As long as I live ..... Those poor, poor people."

She had tailed off in the telling of it, her head slowly lowering toward him. She placed an arm on his shoulder and let her head roll forward onto his chest, so he held her there as she let the tears come, shortly putting his arm around her back and holding her more closely as she sobbed.

"Ned, what is it between you and that man Cade?"

"'E doesn't like me."

"Did you do something to him?"

"Not summat that yer'd call anything. Does it matter?"

"Of course it matters! It's not nice when somebody doesn't like you, is it? You always feel uncomfortable, like you did on Tuesday when he passed us, and again this morning when he ignored you while we were eating."

Ned smiled and gave a little snort down his nostrils. "Alright, I'll tell yer. He were Royal Navy, that chap. He was a killick in the Navy, and 'e did something and they discharged him – I don't know what, none of us found out."

"You mean, a dishonourable discharge?"

Ned affirmed. "So then 'e came into t' merchant ships as a steward. Walter and I came up against him on the *Olympic*, we didn't know 'e had a sharp temper."

"Why? What happened?"

"He'd been drinking ashore. Came back aboard an' shoved a bottle o' claret under his pillow. Next morning we looked and shook him awake – his pillow was all red, we thought he'd been bleeding to death!"

Ned stopped for a moment and grinned, the bitter-sweet memory passing before his eyes, prompting a laugh. "Silly bastard! - Oops, sorry, miss." He excused himself by touching her arm.

"And so Cade sat up right quick, an' banged his head on the bunk above, and then 'e really *was* bleeding! Walter an' I thought it were funny, but Cade didn't see t' funny side of it. Next thing ah knew, there was a knife in front of me face."

"Oh god!" cried Zena, stopping her mouth with her hand.

"No, no, it were alright. He just hovered there for a moment or two, and ah'm there staring at this ruddy great knife two inches in front o' me nose, and then 'e blinked as if 'e were seeing stars and flopped back down again......"

"Thank heaven!"

" – An' hit 'is bloomin' head again on the rail as 'e flopped backwards!" Ned laughed out loud.

"Oh my!" said Zena, herself now trying to put her hand over a chuckle, "Was he hurt?"

"Oh aye!.... Damn near knocked 'imself out. And..... well, since that time, Cade's had it in for me. Strange, eh? Not my fault but – there we are. And the thing is, ah had no idea he were aboard *Titanic* until that second day out of Southampton, and 'e walked into the bar where I was working and just called out 'Bloody Marys for two, steward!' – meanin' yours truly here - without any sign of recognition at all. Just came straight up to me and ordered a couple of drinks for a customer. That were it. Not another word."

"Heavens! Well, didn't you say something to him?"

"Why should ah? If he wants to be like that, let 'im. Ah've got other mates." In mid-thought, he looked her straight in the face. "Ah *had* other mates," he reflected in a lower tone, then placed his cigarette back between his lips and drew deeply on it.

The pain was visible now. The pain he had been concealing. He had not spoken of it these past days.

And the other man, Zena wanted to know.

"His lordship, yer mean?.... Mr. Knight. That's the soap king. Did yer know?"

Why would she know? "So he's the grand feller that makes Vim and stuff? - Doesn't look like he has much vim in him, if you ask me."

"No!" laughed Ned. "He hasn't. Ah think his firm makes summat else. Mebbe soap, ah dunno really. Rich as Croesus, he is - somebody once said that to me, I haven't got the faintest ruddy idea who Croesus was! ... But you're right. Butter wouldn't melt in 'is mouth. Tell yer what, though, Zena - ah wouldn't want to get on 'is wrong side."

* * * * *

SEVEN

Days after the news of its star attraction foundering in the ocean depths and the arrival of the survivors, entry to the White Star Line's large offices at the ornamental terra-cotta-faced building on Broadway was thwarted by a regular queue of claimants and hopefuls mounting the steps up to the revolving door. Despite this, many important gentlemen sporting bowlers or top hats, tight waistcoats, fierce moustaches and voluminous egos processed up and down the stairs, brushing their way ceremoniously past the waiting humanity and pushing through those revolving doors with diverse badges of authority.

And in the background, littering Bowling Green with an almost sinister presence, ever the patient pressmen watched and waited for whatever scraps of infamy it might be their fortune to scrape off the sidewalk. A forlorn hope, perhaps, that a Captain Smith or a John Jacob Astor might yet break cover and confound the world by their existence. Instead, all they might note was a gentle stream of very undistinguished visitors and a number of representatives of companies wishing to take advantage of the situation by having 'sandwich-board men' parade along the boulevard brandishing advertisements for Cuticura or The Crow Truss Company or McGuyver's Hats or even a singularly sallow individual offering the comforts of Mrs. Winslow's Soothing Gastric Syrup.

Having waited almost an hour in a cool breeze, Ned finally wrestled with the revolving door and was admitted into the antechamber of the White Star enquiry desk. It was his second time here in two days. He waited a further twenty minutes before being allowed to be referred to a small balding man occupying a rear table and evidently doing his best to disappear behind a stack of white and buff papers that smothered two-thirds of his desk. His chest was held together with an enormous chain across his waistcoat, and he held two pens captive, one in his hand and one behind an ear, both of them well-tinted with ink. Consequently his collar was as almost as blue as his right hand.

"Thornton, sir."

"Thornton?"

"Thornton."

"I don't have you here," blustered the blue-collar man. "You sure you given me the right roll number?"

"Yes, sir. 73503."

"Don't have to call me 'sir', son. What's yer name again?" Ned repeated it.

"Okay. Okay......... Thornton. Fireman."

"No - Steward, sir."

Blue Collar looked up at him for the first time, agitated.. "Don't call me 'sir', son."

"No, sir."

Blue Collar heaved in a breath that pulled him up tall in his seat, then let it out again slowly as though he were being worked by a pump. The weight of all of New York was heaving itself toward him in the shape of all those people pressing into the White Star offices. A pressure he faced daily. And it showed.

"Thornton........ Nope. Aw, wait a minute. Too many goddam pursers around here, that's the trouble: too many pursers, too many goddam lists!   Thornton.....Thornton.... Did we pay you, Thornton?"

"No. That's partly what ah've come to see about. Ah've been taking handouts at Woolworths and – "

"Well, you've been signed off. Didn't you know, everyone working aboard *Titanic* was signed off? It's standard practice when a ship goes.... when a ship is decommissioned due to circumstances beyond the company's control."

"I understand that. That's not the problem. What ah'm wanting is another ship. So how do I - ?"

"Wait a minute! Pull in those horses! Hold it there, boy......" Blue Collar had his head down in another jumble of papers.

"Mmmm, just wait a minute. Let me read this...... Aha!... *Baltic*...... No, no, en route. *Olympic?*...... Oh, no, she's long gone. Which surprises me after all the trouble that ship's had..... " Blue collar was running his finger down one laborious listing after another, it seemed surprising that on the face of it he did not have a knowledge at his fingertips of each White Star vessel and its status, but evidently not.

Ned attempted to continue but Blue Collar held up a hand. "Wait, wait.... *Cedric*.... *Cedric* is outbound for Liverpool. I thought..... hmm, I guess not...... Held over..... Well, look here, the *Cedric* is going to England, I guess a lot of you Limey guys are gonna be going with her. So what about you? You could take *Cedric* back to Liverpool and let the company re-assign you from there." And Blue Collar for the first time took his eyes off his desk and looked up almost imploringly into Ned's face. Perhaps this idea was going to be the only means of getting this young man out of his way!

"Oh," Ned explained, "Ah want a ship, but ah didn't want to leave yet. We've been mandated to stay for the board of enquiry – ah think that was what they said – 'mandated'..... and I had to agree to that."

"Oh.... So you can't go on the *Cedric*... "

"No.... and there's another thing - "

"Oh, okay, okay, don't tell me, I got it. Okay. Well, then......."

"But –" Ned jumped in. "– the *Adriatic* is here. She'll be alongside 54 a while yet. And I've an oppo on *Adriatic*. Would there be any chance...... I mean, after.....?"

Blue Collar held up a hand to silence his man again. Wearily he lifted his head, smiled superciliously to indicate that this was his job, and to let him do it. And then he turned his face to his papers again but, moments later, Blue Collar stopped, as if his motor had suddenly run down. His taut finger relaxed, his head gradually tilted upward and he leaned back for the first time, and for the first time perfectly oblivious to all the hubbub that ranged around the room beyond them. It seemed to Ned as if the man had never looked at anyone in the face before.

"Thornton." Blue Collar breathed the name slowly, tapping the pen against his palm. The young man in front of him nodded, perplexed. "Just wait there a minute," said the clerk, and with that, he stood up, turned and limped heavily into an adjoining office, closing the door behind him.

As instructed, Ned stood waiting, still clutching his cap in front of him and hoping his borrowed clothes did not betray the plight he was in. Yet all he could think of at the time was how much he longed for a beef sandwich and a bowl of tomato soup.

Several minutes passed. People behind Ned shuffled noisily. The door opened again and Blue Collar emerged behind a taller man. This man wore a fitted dark grey suit of fine worsted, his tie neatly clipped up into the gleaming white tabs of his rounded collar, his moustache carefully trimmed, waxed and upturned at the ends. His hair, deftly parted at the centre, was slicked down to a deep glossy black on either side of his head so that it showed the line of his hat. Blue Collar did not return to his seat but pushed it aside so that his superior could stand behind the desk.

"Your name is Thornton?" It was a British voice, this one. In itself, that might have come as a relief, yet for all that, it was disquieting.

"Sir," affirmed Ned.

"You were a crewman on *Titanic*." Not a question.

"Steward, sir."

The authoritative figure stood perfectly erect, arms at his sides. For a few moments, he looked Ned up and down, much to the young man's discomfort.

"What are we to do with you, Thornton?"

"Sir?"

The tall man was silent for several moments longer. Then he folded his arms and placed two fingers onto his chin, tapping it reflectively.

"Thornton, whilst the *Titanic*..... after *Titanic* had gone down, it was noted by several individuals in the lifeboats that certain..... er....persons - " The word attempted to stick in his mouth but he went on " – escaped the fate of the other poor souls by the ruse of dressing themselves in female garb in order to gain a place in a lifeboat."

"Sir?"

"Have you not heard this?"

47

"Erm..... Yes, ah have heard – well, ah saw that summat were up, in the newspapers. There were some articles ...... like you said. Mebbe some folk got away by wearing women's clothes. So t'papers said, yes."

"So it is said, Thornton. Yes..... So it is said."

Ned felt the tone of the official's voice, saw the accusation in his eyes and his face flushed involuntarily. No words could escape his lips.

The tall official with a gesture deferred to his clerk. "McBride here connected your name to one of those reports. He connected your name, Thornton, because one of those reports referred to a ship's crewman in boat 11 with the name 'Thornton'. The report alleged that you – by name – had escaped the sinking by dressing yourself in female attire to get into a lifeboat."

"What?" Ned was not aware that his mouth gawped like a fish. Nor was he aware that all around them, activity had stopped, the only noises now were in the background. He was only aware that his chest was pounding, a huge tension had gripped his entire body and a pressure was rising into his head, fit to make it burst.

"Sir, I – I ...."

"Is that correct, Thornton?" The tone had now become accusation. "I warn you, Thornton: is the report in the New York Standard correct, or is it not?"

"New York Standard? - No! No, sir! No, sir, it's – it's not correct. It's not! They're mekkin it up, sir, the newspapers. It weren't me! It's lies. Believe me, sir. On my honour, it's not true!"

"Then how do you account for the fact that you, Thornton, are the only person in that whole newspaper report that was named specifically. You – Steward Thornton."

"Sir, I – ah cannot account for it. Ah cannot. Not at this moment. It's the first time ah've heard of it."

"Then I suggest you look at it, Thornton. You will find it in last evening's edition. There is a copy in my office but I have no intention of retrieving it at this moment. And it refers to you by name. No other, just you."

"Oh, Lord! - It's a lie, sir..... It's a lie..... But for the life o' me, ah can't explain it. Ah can't. Ah'm sorry, sir, but it's not true." The words could not rush out fast enough. And yet, as he spoke, it came to Ned that he had been in the lifeboat covered by the coat that Zena had placed over him. At this precise moment, however, there was no way of setting out the circumstances in mitigation of these apparent 'facts' uttered by so distinguished a person as Mr. William Francis Williams, Senior Officer for the White Star Line and Head of Passenger Services.

Williams now chose to sit down. Installed in Blue Collar's chair, he leaned forward toward the young man who was red in the face to the point that he appeared to be on the verge of tears. Looking at Ned in a sideways fashion, with now many faces looking on in near disbelief at what they had overheard, he intoned a statement in a manner that would have befitted any judge in the high court.

"Thornton, your protestation is loud but hollow. I do not think the New York Standard sets itself open to a libel action without due care of all the facts at its disposal. You are at liberty to contest these allegations, and that frankly is not the concern of this company, but I do warn you now that the White Star Line can have no recourse but to terminate your further employment. I suggest you get yourself a good lawyer, and I hope you will consider the integrity of the White Star Line by not seeking employment here again. Other steamship companies may see it differently, but we have our good name and the interests of our customers to consider. I suggest you leave by the exit McBride here will show you, to avoid further commotion in these offices. Good day to you, young man, and may God have mercy on you!"

Utterly stunned, Ned accepted the clutch of his arm by McBride who, despite his own incapacitated limb, hustled him through the ante-room and eventually out into a back street.

"Down there," McBride dismissed him. "And Thornton – there's a lot of bad feeling in this town. For Christ's sake don't let 'em catch you!"

Ned ran.

He ran for fully ten minutes, eager to get himself as far away from Bowling Green as he could. He ran almost under the hoofs of a New York mounted policeman, and finally slumped down in the doorway of a drugstore, set his head on his hands and wanted to shut out the world.

Presently, composed yet still confused, Ned found his way to a streetcar and headed for Zena.

* * * * *

It had been drizzling steadily by the time Ned reached Franklin Avenue. To an extent it was welcome as it subdued excessive fragrance of horse manure to which the city had long since become accustomed. The motor car was beginning to diminish that pungency, only to replace it with another. The rain did mean, on the other hand, that you watched your step rather more than if the streets – and consequently the droppings – were dry. As he mounted the stone steps to enter the building, he was faced with a large cane-wrapped suitcase standing outside the doorway with only a greatcoat to protect it from the rain, and as he entered, Magoolagan was jockeying a second suitcase along the hallway.

"What's up?" asked Ned, wiping the rainwater from his face with a wet sleeve.

"Leavin'" said Magoolagan.

"Who?"

"Shane."

"And Zena?"

"Sure. Her too," puffed Magoolagan, pushing his way past.

"But......" Ned stopped to gather his thoughts.

"It's alright, lad," called Magoolagan. "I said yer can have the room for the week and I meant it."

Magoolagan tipped the case into an upright position and puffed a large breath of relief. "Mother of God," he said, more to himself, "I said he shouldn'a ordered all this stuff off the packet. What in the name o' Bejaysus does them boys need all this stuff fer?"

"Zena's leaving?"

50

"Aye, lad, aye. What else? Did yer think Shane Larkin was goin' to hang around New York forever now?"

"No, I – "

"Look, lad. Yer can have the room fer now, it's alright. Larkin there seen me right and he says you don't owe 'im nuthin'. Yer looked after the girl and that's evens now."

The young man stared back at him with a question in his face.

"But," continued Magoolagan, "after next weekend, then yer's'll have to pay me, right? An' if yer need to work for it, well now, Tom the Butcher'll give yer work peddlin' his meat across the town. Didn' I tell you that already? Then yer'll not have to go down to the five and dime."

"Oh. Aye." Ned was glad of the arrangement. "Although – Woolworths has been good to us."

"Right, lad, true enough, but working for Tom the Butcher can put more in yer pocket than standin' behind Woolworths' counter takin' charity."

Ned only nodded, Magoolagan was right – though he gave credit to Woolworths all the same for allowing *Titanic* survivors to take the profits from sales, for Ned and others would have found things more difficult without it.

Larkin, too, had been generous once Zena had told him, after disembarking *Carpathia* late that Thursday evening, how Ned had comforted and looked after her needs aboard the ship, how he had helped her through the trauma and even found a bunk for her thanks to the kindness of an Italian family. Though to his way of thinking, they had helped each other. She meant only to ask her uncle for the wherewithal to tide Ned over for a few days, but Larkin had seen the young man's predicament and had suggested he take temporary lodging in the tiny room at the top of Magoolagan's apartment building, since anyway the previous young lady occupant had fallen on better times and had vacated a week earlier, much to the relief of Magoolagan and his wife who no longer had to smile vacuously at gentleman callers on the noisy stairway. The mattress had gone with her, at least as far as the tinker's cart.

"That alright with yer then, lad?"

Ned gave him a vague nod of the head but his mind was already elsewhere as Zena appeared on the landing above, looking down at him nervously and adjusting her black straw bonnet. He clattered up the wooden staircase to get to her.

"You're leaving?"

"We're leaving."

He could see she was dressed for it. She had a new full-length coat covering a long straight skirt of brown French serge with several huge buttons dropping in a line down the front. Under her open coat her linen blouse was also new, finished in expensive crochet work at the neck, and on her feet she wore fashionable boots with beige coloured spats. Ned paused at the top step and looked her up and down: all she lacked was a fox fur around her shoulders. She looked older, a very different creature to the young girl he had felt to be his companion aboard *Carpathia*.

"Pittsburgh?"

"Yes," she said, brightly yet with a hint of apology. "My uncle has to get back to his work, and we have things for the families. And..... I have work to do too."

"Ah see. An' you have to go *now*?"

"Yes. Now. Mr. Larkin has arranged the shay for three o'clock........ You'll be alright, Ned. Uncle Shane fixed it with Magoolagan, you can stay here another week."

Ned took a breath and bit his lip.

"Yes.... Maybe. Ah don't know now. Ah think ah'm in trouble."

She put a hand on his arm. "Why? What sort of trouble, Ned?"

He gave her a brief account of his morning.

"Oh, Ned, the papers have been full of nonsense since we arrived. I mean – well, they have, haven't they? All of them trying to outdo the others to get some scurrilous nonsense or other. Look at that report that *Titanic* was still afloat and being towed into harbour in Nova Scotia! They'll print just about anything! Alright, we read reports that suggested some men got off the ship by dressing in women's clothes, so what of it?..... I think it's all lies, myself. They'll cast around for anything or anyone to blame. But, Ned, it wasn't like that with you, was it? You were injured: you didn't even know about the coat I put around you. I think you might have frozen to death otherwise. Heavens, if anyone's to blame for that, it's me! Ned, it'll all blow over, I'm sure it will. Once you get yourself onto another ship – "

"But that's not going to happen, Zena. Not now. They'll put a block on it, ah'll be blacklisted."

"Oh, Ned!"

"And there's another thing. I picked up a newspaper meself. You know they've been printing the lists of survivors? Some of 'em by boat number."

"I didn't see them, Ned."

"Yeh. They have. Well, I looked down the lists. My name isn't there."

"Oh? Maybe they just haven't got all the details yet. Go see somebody about it."

"What d'yer think ah've been tryin' to do? An' if ah'm blacklisted, ah can't get a ship out of here. In any case, ah'm legally bound to attend the board of enquiry next week, they said so. At least *they* know I exist! It's already started, down at the Waldorf. Ah don't know how long they'll be gettin' around to me. So, ah've got to stay in New York and keep me trap shut! Keep meself available, they said. God knows what ah'd do if yer uncle hadn't helped me out. Beggin' around the Church Institute, mebbe."

"But that's not fair! That means if you could sign on with another ship –"

"Ah can't."

"What makes you so certain you can't sign on with another ship?"

"White Star won't talk to me. That newspaper mentioned me by name – *by name*, Zena. Why? Nobody else, just me. Why? – I don't understand it. Who would've given 'em my name? Why would they do that?"

"Well....." An immediate solution escaped Zena, but then her face lit up. "Go talk to the newspaper. Talk to the Standard, find out how they got the information."

Shane Larkin would have overheard their chatter through the open door, but made no sign of it. Appearing from the bedroom with a carpet bag, he effectively terminated their conversation. In double-breasted sack-coat, small Derby hat and bow-tie collar, he looked well out of character. He could have been going to meet royalty. "Come along, young lady. This lad'll have to mind his business."

The carriage was at the door at the appointed time: early, in fact, and Magoolagan and his son loaded the cases aboard before helping Larkin and Zena to step up. Luckily, the rain had stopped, though the hooped canvas over the carriage had not kept it dry.

Frantically, Ned had been trying to think: to suggest he might go to Pittsburgh to see her was a hopeless thought. Even if her uncle were to allow such an association, how on earth could Ned get there with his present means? What was to come of it anyway, himself at sea and her somewhere in the interior of a vast continent?

"Write to me, Zena, will yer? Here. Magoolagan will save letters for us. Ah'll come here every time ah dock in New York, ah promise."

Yet she looked unconvinced, and aware now that their relationship – which to be fair had barely begun – appeared to contain nothing but a lonely lifeboat in a great sea of uncertainties, an injured and confused young man and a frightened young woman.

Larkin lifted her by the waist so that her feet could mount the tail board. Then, before mounting the carriage himself, he abruptly stopped, and with a moment's hesitation turned back to Ned and placed a note in his hand. Ned looked at it, his open mouth biting silently at the air.

"Reckon you can use a sawbuck," said Larkin, patting him on the shoulder. "Good luck, lad." There was an air of finality about that parting remark, whilst Zena could only offer Ned a desolate smile not quite yielding a tear. Sitting upright in the carriage, she blew him a solitary kiss as the driver whipped the reins and the cart with its three occupants and their luggage set off along the avenue. Ned stood watching, a great pit of despair welling in his gut, as the carriage blended with another in the distance and was gone. A motor car rattled noisily past and disrupted his concentration. But Zena had not looked back.

All he could do was take a deep breath as he stood there, aware the lifting of the rain had raised a noxious tincture to the atmosphere. Then a second motor carriage rumbled past him, adding its choking vapours. It was not where he wanted to be. New York held nothing for him now but menace and a prospect of lingering adversity. Its dark tenements closed in on him - the scapegoat to answer its outrage at so great a disaster as *Titanic*. For some moments there in the street, damp and alone, he could only long to be back in England, at a place and time before this nightmare had ever begun.

Yet he missed her already and, back in his room, savoured the faint smell of her perfume on his hands where he had embraced her arms. When he tried to form a picture in his mind of her face, however, he could not.

* * * * *

EIGHT

"Osculation!"

"What?" asked Ned.

"Osculation. I learn new word today, what."

"What?"

"What?"

Ned stopped and looked away to check if he ought to start again.

"Why you say 'what', Ned?"

"Because..... What did yer mean?"

"What?"

"I don't understand you. Why do you say 'what' all the time?"

"I say, 'what'?"

"Otto, what are you talking about?"

"I don't know. But it's alright, what?"

".... You said it again! Why d'yer keep saying 'what'?"

"I am speaking English, English."

"We don't say 'what' all the time!"

"Ja. Ze English say 'what' all ze time!"

"No!... Well..... Maybe some do.... "

"Dat's right. So... Osculation!"

Ned merely looked at him and gawped.

The young German laughed and puckered up his generous lips. "Zis....... zis is what it means. See? Kissing. Zat's what it means."

Ned shook his head. "Ah never heard the word."

"I look it up, what. I look at '*baiser*', you know? – It means to kiss. An' ze book say many words, and zere it is – 'osculation'. So!"

Ned gave him a blank look.

"You don't understand English, English. Look, English, you stay wiz me and I learn you English, okay?" Otto was making fun of him.

"Yeh, alright, Otto, but don't call me 'English'. The name's Ned, but if yer don't like that, just call me 'Tyke' or summat."

"'Tyke'? - Zis is a stupid name! Sounds like a dog. You don't have such a cold nose, ja?" He laughed again and his big belly wobbled.

"Anyhow, where d'you learn such big words? 'Osculation'! Good grief!"

"I read. On ze ship, lots of books, what. And here I go to ze library. Well, some days when I am here in New York. Someone said to me, long time ago, Otto, to understand English you should read a new word every day. So I read. Big books, what. And I am going to be clever, English. You see. I read a lot of books with English words. I learn lot of English, English."

"Ned. For heaven's sake, Otto – just Ned. Alright?"

"Zat's also a stupid name – 'Chust Ned.' Who call you zat?"

"No! Me name is Ned. That's it – finish – Ned. *Verstehen*?"

"I understand. Ned. Okay. But you talk funny, what."

"Ah'm a Yorkshireman, what d'y'expect? Anyway, listen who's talkin'. For a chap who says he's goin' to be clever, ah'd be surprised if yer knew what end to strike a match."

"*Quoi*?"

Otto Bremme was a year younger than Ned, yet looked about five years older. He had large flat feet that rendered his gait more of a swagger, a kind of loping bounce. Aboard ship some called him '*Kipperfuss*', though not to his face. Otto was of a substantial girth, and what's more he sweat quite a lot, an effect not helped by his head of unruly near-red hair. In recent days he had attached himself to Ned whilst the young Englishman delivered meat and bacon to one of the cold stores off 11th Avenue. That whole area around the Chelsea Piers was a haven for purveyors and a magnet for entrepreneurs of all kinds.

"We have somesing in common," Otto had told Ned on first acquaintance. "My ship hit ze ice also."

La Rochelle, the French liner out of Le Havre, had hit ice several days before *Titanic*'s fatal blow, but luckily a heavy mist had forced the vessel to slow right down and the damage, though not insubstantial, was sustainable without difficulty for her present duties. Other than a little water in the hold as a result of a single deformed plate which had required shoring, nothing serious had resulted and *La Rochelle* had docked at New York close to schedule.

"Le coup de grace dans une rive de glace......" Otto thought he would just make up the words and amuse himself. He made a gesture with his hands in the air as if touching a block of ice and pulling them away quickly lest they freeze. Maybe he had heard passengers joke about it. Ned only whistled and then related what he recalled of *Titanic*'s fate.

"So there we are - summat to put in yer diary, Otto."

"Diary? *Agenda?*"

"*Agenda....* Yes. Diary."

"No. I don't have diary."

"Oh."

"You cannot tell a lie to a diary!"

Ned had confided in Otto the newspaper reports, his unequivocal reception at the White Star Line and his deep concern for his present situation.

"Ach!" The German made dismissive gestures. "Zey look for someone to blame, my friend. We take care of you. Don't worry."

Ned scowled and wondered who "we" might be.

"Listen, my friend, I sink you worry much. Is no good to be serious. You should sink about it, life is not a serious thing, Ned – nobody escape, uh? You only escape if you dead! An' zat's it! Poof! *Verstanden?* So don't worry – it only end one way!"

"But ah do worry, Otto. Money, my friend - money! White Star's passed the word around. Ah tried the Holland office, as soon as they heard me name they shut the book and told me to leave. Ah didn't get me Discharge Book - officially ah'm not even signed off! Four years' work down the crapper! So how do ah get to sign on anywhere? What's the Shipping Master goin' ter say? And as for a Health Certificate, well..... Ah can't stay here running around for Tom the Butcher forever. Me room at Magoolagan's is only paid up till the end of the week, he's already given me one extension. What ah'm getting running around for Tom the Butcher won't get me a passage back to England. An' ah shall lose money tomorrer attending this ruddy board of enquiry at the Waldorf."

In the New York of 1912, Tom the Butcher was a remarkable man underneath his quaintly simple pseudonym, rather more remarkable than Ned's first impression after Magoolagan had found him work with Tom's 'emporium'. Far from being an insignificant figure who purveyed meat and other delicacies around Manhattan and Brooklyn from his modest warehouse below 9th Avenue, in fact Tom had influence in a number of areas, not least with the Irish brethren who controlled their share of the black market in the city. Tom was a careful businessman. He didn't go looking for trouble and would steer well clear of kosher or Asian meat markets: there was enough business to go round, so long as everyone stuck to his own stock-in-trade. Not that that would stop him settling a lucrative purchase in molasses or salt or packing materials if one happened to wander his way. New York was a thriving place which opened its arms to industry of all varieties. If occasional help dropped in his lap from someone at City Hall or the district police department, he might well take it with an implicit understanding that such generosity brings its own reward. To most, he was just Tom the Butcher, father of three beautiful girls but also a stocky young son, who discreetly acted as 'muscle' in situations where pressure of a physical kind stood in for wasted words. Tom was a shrewd man. None of his family went short: none of his girls had to wrap cigars as had Katie, his wife, when she had first arrived. None had struggled in the heaving human canyons of New York's East Side, nor had any experienced the Irish workhouse as had Tom as a lad. Tom was content, and life could be good.

Otto put a finger to Ned's mouth. "Ned, *halte fresse*! Be not panic, what. Listen to me. Your friend Magoogle - "

"Magoolagan."

"Ja, him. He did a big thing, he got you work wiz Tom the Butcher, and Tom is good boss. Hey, I don't like his place over there, it stinks of – what's that gasoline stuff that's not gasoline?"

"You mean turpentine?"

"Ja. Turnpintime. All zose places over zere by ze market, all stink of turnpintime – not meat, what. Crazy, uh? But it not make matter. Tom, he knows people. You know what ah'm sayin'? I work with Tom before, many times we work with him, my boss and me. Every time I come to New York we do ze business. Today, what? – Ham hocks. Big backsides of cows! Sheep's er.... what you call it? - livers. Sheep's livers, what. And the balls, ja? And special meats and things. It's lots of business wiz ze ships. Hey, what you think? Tom the Butcher need favours, he gets favours. You know what ah'm sayin', Ned? Tom, he don't deal in ze big stuff, he don't go wiz ze big contracts for – what is dat, Ned – vittels? Vittels?"

"Victualling contracts."

"Ja. Dat's it. Vittels. No, Tom, he does ze trade in smaller stuff - exclusive, ja? Ze 'best cuts' – *c'est le mot, oui*? – ze 'best cuts'? Zey go in ze back door. *Comprenez*, Ned? Okay, you know zis. And for zis - " He painted a strange picture in the air. " - For zis he get little favours. You know? Maybe..... oh, a case of champagne, ze best. Or perfume, ze *Kölnisch Wasser* for ze rich ladies of New York. Best quality. Understand, Ned?"

Ned understood to a point. "So you're saying..... What *are* yer saying, Otto?"

"Oho!" Another grand gesture from the corpulent German. "What am I saying? Hell's bells! I am saying, we make you into a prime rib steak for ze captain, what. Look, I speak to Tom the Butcher. Tom the Butcher, he speak to Monsieur Lagarde and Monsieur Lagarde speak to Monsieur Vuillaume and Monsieur Vuillaume he sign a paper and he pass to Monsieur Genoud wiz lots and lots of papers, and zen ze ship have another chef. And you come wiz me to Le Havre, get you away from zese.... zese nasty men here....."

"Steward," Ned corrected him. "I'm a saloon steward, Otto – ah'm big in the drinks department with a little laundry on the side, not tossin' Caesar salads or prime rib steaks. An' ah don't do cooking unless it's bangers and mash."

"Bangers and - ? Oh." Otto thought for a moment. "Hey, it's not a problem. Chef today, chef of ze drinks tomorrow. Why not? Uh?"

The Englishman was looking troubled. "Yes, but....... What about - y'know - job interviews?"

"Interviews? What? - You are a famous person, Ned?"

"Ah'm ruddy famous in New York! Ah'm in all them ruddy papers!"

"Oh? Ze captain, does he need to speak wiz you because you are so important? Ned, maybe captain saw you already! Uh?... Uh?"

The Englishman shrugged through his face. Maybe Otto had a point.

"Sure! It's not a problem, Ned. Hells bells! Who looks at ze staff on a ship, what? You are a chef here, a steward here, a fireman here....... *Macht nichts* - it's not make matter. You are just anozzer man in ze crew, Ned. Nobody cares, what. You know zis. You have piece of paper – poof! It's done! Vive la France! Uh?"

Ned smiled a tiny smile that hesitated and quivered at the corners of his mouth until it became a bigger smile and eventually he gave in to a quiet chuckle.

"Yes," cried Otto, nodding furiously, "Yes! We get you a piece of paper, Ned. Hell's bells!"

"Will we get away with it?"

"Get away? Oh yes, my small *Nixie* friend, we get away. We get away, Ned. We take you back to France. *Ganz einfach!*"

"But..... but..... Well, heck!"

Otto Bremme just stuck his nose in the air and made a pout of arrogance with his lips.

"Sure. Sure. We do dat. *Quoi qu'il arrive...* Zen you get papers."

"Ah but - like ah told yer - ah didn't get me Discharge Book, they weren't rushin' to give me another."

"Ochh! - Who has papers anyway? You leave it to me. I speak to Tom, you see. And zen, you will have big osculation, Ned."

"What are you talking about?"

"Osculation – you give Tom the Butcher big kiss, say Thank You, what.? Tom, he get a big case of Bollinger next trip. *Special Cuvée! Oui, pourquoi pas?* You see. He will kiss you."

"You're mad, Otto!"

"Mad? *Verrückt?* Oh yes. Hell's bells! Very."

When they had finally stopped laughing, Ned was thoughtful. "You'd do this for me, Otto?"

"For you? Sure. You have ze problems. You have an honest face, Ned. I told you! And I have two sisters who be not married yet.....!'"

Otto let the words hang in the air for a few moments whilst Ned's face told him he really didn't know how he should take that remark. Then Otto burst out laughing again, alternately nodding and shaking his head.

"Ja! Ja! Is true... Anyway," he continued, "I don't like chief steward in charge of vittels on *La Rochelle*: you work two three trips and maybe you be good to push him off, eh?"

"Why don't yer like him?"

"He's Cherman!"

"What?" Ned began laughing again and could not stop giggling into his sandwich whilst Otto was explaining.

"All zat *wurst*, Ned, he eat too much *wurs*t so he fart all the time. Always farting. Very big farter! Very bad for business, what. Chermans eat too much beer and wurst. It's bad."

"But *you*'re German, Otto! Don't you have beer and wurst too?"

"Ja. *Das stimmt.* But I don' like sauerkraut. If you don' eat sauerkraut, you don't fart so much. *Alles klar, nicht?*"

The Englishman looked the young German up and down, trying to hide his smile behind his fingers. Otto was certainly not small himself and very evidently liked his food.

"Don't yer think it's maybe just too much eating that does it?"

"Oh, ja. Eating too much is bad. Makes ze clothes too small, what."

"So eat less."

"Why? - Chust change ze clothes!"

Ned thought he had never met anyone quite so disarming in his life. There was something about Otto Bremme that was quite irrepressible.

"*Jedenfalls*," Otto went on, "Is important to eat, yes? My parents, when I was a little boy zey always say, 'Otto, you talking too much - shut your mouth and eat your food'. And so I say, 'Pappi, what you want me to do? - I shut my mouth or I eat - can't do both!'."

* * * * *

Sometimes, getting through to Otto was a fruitless journey.

"But I keep telling yer, Otto – ah don't speak French!"

"So do I. I'm Cherman. Who needs to speak French? Everyone speaks English."

"Not everyone. It's a French ship."

"Look, I'm Cherman and I can speak enough French, it's easy: I learn you, Ned."

"Teach."

"Teach?"

"Yes, you *teach* me French, and I *learn* French......."

Otto thought for a moment. "Ja. Dat's what I told you, my small *Nixie* friend! You chust have to learn a few things, what."

"Like you learn a new word every week...."

"Ja. Like dat. I learn you."

"No - *teach* – *learn* is different."

"Och! Chust remember - *crème anglaise* is not milk from ze cow in London - it's that stuff Mr. Bird makes, ze yellow powder, what."

"Oh – custard. Obviously."

"Ja. Things like dat.... Ned, why do you say 'obviously'?"

"Um - Because it's obvious, ah suppose."

"Well, I do not understand zis. I know zis word, 'obvious', I heard zis. Obvious means, everybody knows this already - yes?"

"Alright."

"So why do people say, 'obviously', when it is somesing ze ozzer person don't know?"

"Uh?.... Well...."

"*Selbstverständlich*!" said Otto to close the point. "Oh - And you must remember, Ned – ze French invented food."

"Huh?"

"Ja. You never question."

"Never question?"

"No, my small *Nixie* friend, never question! Look - how many tomatoes you have in England?"

"How many sorts, d'you mean?..... Dunno..... Five? Six?"

"Ze French chef, he keep twenty – twenty! And zere are more zan dat. Ja? Okay, he don't keep twenty on ze ship, but he knows all ze names. French is best, ja? If ze steak is too .....erm, too..... uncooked, what you say? – Anyway, ze chef, he is always right."

"Americans like their steaks well done – burned, even."

"I know. Me, I don't serve tables, but I tell zem, zis steak cooked by ze French chef, it is best in ze world, and if you cook too much, it blow up – poof! No good for nossink but stick on your boots or wipe your bottom! Ze best people know French is ze best.. Ze *best*. You are saying *zey* are ze best people and you watch ze chest go up - like zis..... All ze good stuff in ze meat, it goes away if you cook too much. Ze French chef, he know zis, but ze American chef - pah! - what does he know? - He came on banana boat from China!   It's good for you, *madame*, okay? Throw zat one away – stick it on your boots! No, don't wipe your bottom wiz zis!"

"Don't they ever send it back?"

"Send it back? Oho! Ze French chef on *La Rochelle*, he's a big man, Ned...... And he is artist. Ze French, zey invent food and wine, you don't argue with ze French chef. Hell's bells, no."

That seemed to satisfy Otto at least. He sniffed the air and patted his stomach. "All zis talk of food, Ned..... Time for eating, ja? I am ravished."

"You mean 'famished', you idiot!"

"Famished? - Ja, dat's what I said, what. You see, I learn you English."

* * * * *

NINE

Newspaper readers have short attention spans: the rumblings of discontent over the Standard's early allegation of Steward Thornton's escape from *Titanic* under female skirts faded as more and more survivors' stories gained centre stage. Newspapers had been quick to print what they called 'Memorial' issues, which drew attention more to stories of courage and adversity as opposed to protestations of cowardice. So much so that, on Friday the 26th, the Standard printed a column on its third page to remind readers, "Where is the Coward of the Atlantic?" Many readers had moved on, they were more intrigued to anticipate the return of *Titanic*'s dead by the vessels sent out to retrieve them.

Nonetheless, following Ned's unsettling Thursday with the board of enquiry, Tom, with an eye on current events, sent word to Magoolagan that Ned should make himself known to *La Rochelle*'s third officer, using Otto Bremme as his go-between, and suggesting for the lad's own safety he should move aboard *La Rochelle* and wait for fairer weather.

That same Friday, Ned decided he should do something to at least enquire of the New York Standard why it had printed such a maleficent and specific article labelling him a villain, and he plucked up the courage to pedal down to Park Place to see what might be done about it. Whilst dithering at the front desk, however, Ned had been completely floored by the sight of someone emerging from what appeared to be the main office. That person had been Ranulph Knight.

Ned turned his face away until with a furtive look through the office window he could see Knight shake hands with another well-dressed man and enter a waiting motor car. To the surprise of the lady receptionist attending to Ned's enquiry, the young man simply vanished.

Whilst the *Titanic* affair continued to rumble less than quietly along, from across the Atlantic had come the news that, only a week after *Carpathia* had docked with her survivors in New York, the White Star liner *Olympic* -*Titanic*'s sister ship and Ned's previous residence – was once again in trouble.   Firemen, greasers and trimmers had prevented the ship leaving Southampton on her scheduled sailing because it was alleged many of the ship's boats were not seaworthy. Politically-motivated timing aside, the emotive nature of the strike was bound to reverberate in the loudest manner. The matter of lifeboats on ships had of late exploded in the international arena. Virtually the whole of the engineering staff – hundreds of men - had left the ship, giving *Olympic* no option other than to lay up whilst the men's grievances were addressed.

The news had filtered through to Otto from the Marconi Telegraph operator, though when he eventually caught up with Ned on the Friday evening, he found Ned already absorbed in the drift of the event.

"What will they do?" Otto asked, as if an Englishman ought to be better informed than a German on a French ship.

"Ah don't know," admitted Ned. "White Star will fill their places with men from other ships if they get half a chance."

"You sink?"

"Given half a chance," Ned repeated.

Otto folded his arms. "Ned, it is a chance or it is not a chance - how can you have a half?" Ned only smiled.

"But," suggested Otto, "It is *Titanic* again, it's about ze lifeboats. *Nicht?*"

"Ah suppose so."

"More trouble, Ned. I sink zis means more trouble. You should come aboard. Now."

The next morning, Ned took no time at all to leave.

The borrowed clothes, Magoolagan told him he should keep them. Once again, the young man had nothing but gratitude for the hospitality the Irish had shown him for the way he had looked after Zena, even though Ned himself felt he had done but little in the circumstances.

"A young lad in trouble," was all Magoolagan said, placing his hands on Ned's shoulders. Perhaps, having in mind what Clodagh

Magoolagan had told Ned of her husband's troubled youth, it had been a tribute to those turbulent times.

* * * * *

For Otto Bremme, family was all.

Willi Bremme and his wife Marlene had lived in Köln many years before moving to Le Havre. Willi was a skilled steelworker, who had held several positions in the heavy industrial plants of Düsseldorf and Essen. Köln was also the family home, for Willi had two brothers there and Marlene a brother and three sisters.

With the industrial expansion of the era, however, and the establishment of something of a "fortress" character around the burgeoning city, Köln seemed less and less a place where Willi and Marlene wanted to bring up their children, and a chance encounter with a cousin led to a position in the engineering works of the port of Le Havre, where the huge success of the transatlantic liner business was attracting many competent engineers. In 1899 the family moved there, taking a small terrace house in a working class area of the town. Le Havre was a bustling and rather dirty commercial centre, yet the whole family at once took to the more tranquil nature of the countryside in this part of France, and the next years were ones of contentment and hope. Here, the children continued their schooling: Renata, the eldest, Otto, and their younger sister, Brigitte, who was already devoted to her ambition to become a famous actress in the footsteps of France's most celebrated daughter, Sarah Bernhardt, a Mucha image of whom dominated the girls' otherwise sparse bedroom.

It was always expected of Otto that he would pursue a career in *Jura* – the Law, as he had never talked of doing anything else, but in the April of 1910, the young Otto, then 17, suddenly became head of the family when Willi Bremme was the victim of an accident at the Le Havre railhead and died instantly. Otto's responsibilities immediately took on a different tone, and he accepted an offer of work aboard ship, arranged by a friend of his father's, in the knowledge it would provide regular upkeep for the family. To his credit, Otto never once spoke of his disappointment at relinquishing all hopes of a legal career, the prospect of which would have involved years of study at the family's expense.

Renata, the senior of her brother by more than three years, had already been working as a teacher at one of the local junior schools in Le Havre, having had along with her sister the greater success in mastering the French language. Marlene Bremme obtained work in one of the port's warehouses, handling mostly the export of fabrics to North America, whilst Brigitte worked in a grocer's shop, having at this stage little idea what she wanted to pursue other than a dream of copying her idol. Thus, the family managed to maintain the tenure of their modest house, and whenever Otto returned to Le Havre it was understood that there would be a small family party, weather permitting, in their little, not-quite-grassy yard behind the house, and a couple of times a year Frau Bremme would ask her neighbour, Mme. Beaumarchais, to kill one of their chickens for a modest feast. They would never forget that life was but a moment that could be snatched away, and it was necessary to infuse every member of the family with that knowledge that they were deeply loved: Marlene had not kissed Willi and told him she loved him on the morning that he had left forever.

* * * * *

"You know, Ned, when you have shit in your life, you have to deal with it - it don't go away by itself."

Ned grimaced and shrugged his shoulders. "Yer have a way with words, Otto. Be careful how you use that sort of word, ah don't imagine you got that out of the public library."

"What? Shit? It's a good word, ja?"

"For what we're talking about, it's a good word. But be careful – ladies aboard don't like language like that when you're serving up their *bouillabaisse*, so just between friends, alright? Ah wouldn't want to see y'in trouble with M.Vuillaume for learning the wrong kind of English. Besides, they'd blame me!"

Otto decided his point had been brushed aside. "Ladies? Ach, ja, I know what you saying, okay. But shit – Ned, you have to deal with it."

"Or get away from it."

"You sink you can run away? Zis is not going to go away. Zis man, Knight. You tell me about zis man, you sink he is responsible, and you don't know what you can do because zis man is rich and powerful. But do you know what he is going to do next?"

Ned snorted. "Hrrh! If ah get away from here, what's 'e gonna do?"

Otto considered that. "Okay, maybe nothing. Maybe all ze problem will stay here in New York, what. But if he sinks you know things he does not want you to know...... And he is rich and powerful, ja? So he can have.... very long arms. Maybe, uh?" And he made a wide gesture of the hands.

Ned sat down on the edge of his bunk, looked at Otto, looked at the floor, looked at Otto again. "Yes..... As a matter of fact, you may be right. There's the other feller, John Cade."

Otto held out cigarettes. Dieter Pabst in the background had come into the cabin. The two men looked at him silently as Pabst went to his locker close to the door, unlocked it and rummaged for something inside. After a minute he felt their silence watching him and turned around.

"*Was gibt?*" queried Pabst. Otto simply gave him a look and waved a hand, so Pabst re-locked the cabinet and made for the door.

Watching him disappear, Otto made a point of calling after him in English, "And shut ze door - were you born in a field?" He laughed, knowing that he was showing off to Ned and that Pabst would have not understood anyway.

"Ja. You know I don't like him. But he is here. Go on wiz your story, my small *Nixie* friend. Zis man Cade."

"He was here."

Otto was puzzled, so Ned answered the look in his face. "At the gangway. Asking questions. This morning."

"Zis morning? Here?"

69

"Definitely. It was pure chance that ah saw 'im. Ah were in the first class lounge setting up."

"He didn't see you?"

"No. Couldn't have."

Both drew ruminatively on their cigarettes. "I have to go on duty in ten minutes," said Ned, pulling on clean socks.

"Okay. We talk later."

"We could do with sailing tonight."

"*Nicht verstanden.*"

"Tonight. I'd be happy if we sailed tonight."

"No. *Vendredi.* You sink zis man Cade, you sink 'e will try to come aboard?"

Ned had no idea and shook his head. Yet it was clear Cade's appearance was no accident, the fact that he was apparently so close to finding Ned at all pointed to strong influences at work. Who was pulling the strings? Ranulph Knight? Someone at the New York Standard? Ned was weary of feeling hunted, and distinctly uncomfortable about being aboard *La Rochelle* if he might have a better chance of going to ground somewhere else. But where? – All he could do was to get out of New York one way or another. Perhaps after all this French ship could be the best avenue for a young man with no money, no employment and no other means of support, and with hostility waiting around every street corner. How long might it be before the New York Standard were cajoled into another of its witch-hunts? Small comfort that there was more interest in the news from the boats searching for *Titanic's* unfortunates.

"D'yer think ah should have a word with M. Vuillaume, Otto? Try to get my story across to him before some idiot lets Cade aboard?"

"No, Ned, I do not sink. M. Vuillaume knows Tom the Butcher comes with ze best beef – you know zese people just love ze ros' beef. Ja? So zis is how you are aboard, Ned, and when we go you are a part of ze crew, and it's okay. Until zen, we chust keep you small and quiet, like a lil' mouse. And we hope Mr. Cade if he comes again don't have mousetrap!"

"Small and quiet!" laughed Ned. "With Mr. Rosenberg shouting about my Mojitos!"

Otto shrugged his big shrug again that lifted his stomach from the shoulders. "We cross ze legs, my small *Nixie* friend."

"The fingers, Otto, the fingers..... Not the legs. That's summat else."

"Okay, you learn me, then."

"No – I *teach* you! You didn't get that through your head yet. You have dummy kopf!"

"Oh ja? So you speak Cherman so good, Mr. Thornton?"

Ned looked aside and fell quiet. He was still thinking about Cade. "Shit!" said Otto.

"What?" Ned was miles away.

"Shit. New word zis week, what. I like zis word."

It brought a smile back into Ned's face. He said, "Alright, how about my word of the week, my friend – Go shove it up your *Lateinischer Kunst*. Is that right?"

"Ha!" Otto's round face lit up. "You see, English – I *do* learn you somesing!"

* * * * *

The importance of it had not registered earlier, but John Cade had been at the gangway when Ned had left *Carpathia* late that evening of the 18th, following closely in Zena's footsteps. She had left the ship in haste to search for her uncle amongst the crowd at pier 54, but as Ned had filed forward with the crush of people eager to disembark, Cade had been standing at the railing and stepped up as Ned approached.

At first he said nothing, merely looked knowingly at Ned and blew smoke towards him. He held the cigar awkwardly in his left hand, the one with the missing finger.

For a moment Ned acknowledged him, faltered, then moved to the gangway without saying a word yet with an odd sensation of menace.

71

"Take care, mate," called Cade to Ned's back, "and be careful what you say to people, it could land y'in the rattle. Yer might not hide under a girl's frock next time."

Ned did not turn nor look back, and without a coat he was cold again. But he was wondering why Cade had inferred what he did: the tone of it was a long way from any kind of joke. Hiding under a frock?

* * * * *

TEN

There was something 'girly' about wearing a robe that fell virtually to your feet, and in the vestry of St.Paul's church, the boys yanked off their white surplices and purple cassocks with violent enthusiasm. Lads of eight and ten years old would sooner die in mortal combat in a wooden sword fight with the kids on the next street than be seen as 'something girly'. Jibes from other boys about them wearing dresses were just too much for a lad to take. That the new robes were a generous bequest to the church by a deceased high-church parishioner cut no ice with boys like James and Ned. You couldn't have a good fight wearing a cassock, and purple was a girly colour.

Choir practices went on too long anyway, and usually ended when resident prankster 'Nogsy' Normanton played a practical joke on the usual targets, the straight-laced Masters Fleetwood and Etherington, which landed him in trouble with the verger. Nogsy was always playing a joke of some sort. Like dropping farthing coins on the stones of the aisle as the choir processed along it, or dropping a key and then scrambling about the floor to trip everyone up. Or his 'party piece', slipping an inflated sheep's bladder under the cushion of the organist's seat: the fart resounding around the church left not a dry eye in the stalls of the choirboys.

Nor were any of them at all sure about the verger, whom they called "Loofah" for no particular reason except that it seemed farcically inspired. Having the verger hound them for loitering around the graveyard smoking after choir practice would send up the call, "Run - it's Loofah!", a cry the absurdity of which sent a dozen boys home with laughter in their throats. Getting caught by the verger and his bad breath, though, was not a good result.

At nine o'clock they were disrobed and flying out of the vestry in seconds, eager to get to the pie stall and just inhale that wonderful savoury odour that they could not afford until some half-drunken chap would toss them bits of his pie for whatever amusement it gave him. Pie-bating was a popular pastime amongst the lads of the choir. Bolder lads like Nogsy had been known to drop their pants and present an arse-end to easy targets if the result was a chunk of pie, much to the raucous laughter of the other boys. So far as they all knew, it was harmless fun. Though only so far as they knew....

Not that Ned and James were easily led. James was already unsettled about his role as a chorister of any description, scrapping as he was with his father on a regular basis and seeing nothing godly in the act of being packed off to church one evening a week after working all day at the mill, and again on Sundays for Matins and Evensong. Other boys at the mill counted Sundays as their only relief. James had fallen asleep in the choir stalls more than once, something that would never happen in the conker season. If the tiny stipend was the main attraction for a small boy to attend these ecclesiastical communions, the one exception might have been Christmas, when Ned on his own account at least professed to enjoy an evening when the choir - such as it was, seven or eight boys - would go to sing at the local clinic or several of the public houses or even the homes of the poor and elderly. The idea that they might collect money was ostensibly a secondary aim for the choir, and the ad hoc fare they might receive for such singing services was meagre - half an apple, a pasty perhaps, or some sweetmeats, although the effect mirrored in the faces of the old and infirm was supposed to be its own reward, and Ned half-felt that made his weekly church chore just slightly worthwhile. It also brought levity: they spoke often of the time a drunken wealthy gentleman had joined the small crowd assembled on the steps of the White Hart to hear the singing, and loudly bid to buy young Master Fleetwood - "Ah wanna buy 'im!" The poor lad had almost fled, but choirmaster Mr. Kitchen had managed the situation tactfully and no money had changed hands, other than the shilling and tuppence collected from the congregation. Ned and James and Nogsy had almost missed the event, engaged as they were in a competition to catch as many snowflakes as possible in their mouths: there was never a winner to that contest.

Churchgoing was something neither of their parents would ever count on for their own salvation, that was certain. If the boys expressed resentment, their father would teach them "what for" – to which both boys commonly would ask, "What for?" The joke had long since worn away, the crack of their father's belt had seen to that. Eleven-year old James had stood defiant on more than one occasion now, and Alice their mother was increasingly worried for her elder son's safety: she saw that a 'coming together' would only end in one result, as Jubal's threat that he would *"box yer ears for yer, lad"* had acquired less and less effect as time went by. Alice was strongly protective of her boys, naturally, and bore the marks to prove it, for her husband often preferred to use part of a bridle from the stables rather than take his belt off.

Now that he was working, it was time to take James away from the church choir; he stood tall and lanky above the others and gave no impression at all of lighting a pathway to salvation. Before long, anyway, his voice would be broken.

"But why do we have to go to church, mother?"

Alice paused as she folded the sheet and looked at Ned. For a few moments that was all she did. Then she said, quietly, "So you'll find your truth, son."

Whatever those words were, they meant nothing to a boy looking forward to making tinsel chains for Christmas and those small trinkets that hung in big wool stockings by the kitchen range.

"Why church, mum?" the young Ned repeated. "It's boring." It was a dangerous thing to say in those times of stiff moral correctness, but Alice patted him on the head and knelt down to fasten up his waistcoat for him, a completely superfluous act that afforded her the pleasure of love-giving.

"That way, you'll always know to respect your elders and betters," she told him, yet acutely aware that neither she nor her husband ever patronised the church themselves. "Yer father's just too busy wi' the trams," she would offer, but the children knew better.

The young Ned was not sure what respect meant, if not giving in to someone who is bigger and stronger than you are; in other words, the finer part of caution. He grimaced at his mother, deciding he had best put up with the situation until such time as he was old enough to get right away from it. Meanwhile it was easier to just go and sing the psalms and hymns without ever comprehending a word. That was surely a fact.

"Jesus bids us shine with a pure clear light......" Ned often wondered who this chap Jesus Bidsus was and what an amazing lamp he must have had. As to the relevance of the fat bloke in that Christmas carol, he had no idea who Round John Virgin was, let alone his relation to some mother and child.

Other boys in the choir did not understand what James and Ned saw to dislike in getting tuppence for the mere exertion of clutching a prayer book, opening their mouths and singing a lot of words that made no sense. It certainly made no sense at all of anything that they understood in their daily lives at school or – for James anyway – at the mill. Only a few months after he had begun working at the mill, a man had been pulled into a carding machine. It had absolutely nothing to do with going to church and praying. It just meant some of them lost pay for standing around idle whilst the machine was cleared of the mess. James, who went to that floor on an errand, had never seen the insides of human flesh before. He was sick until the foreman told him to 'Buck up and get on wi' yer job!' Amy Garforth smeared soap around his nostrils so that he might put the whole thing out of his mind and not have his pay docked. All his life, James never forgot that day.

Young Ned was in a little world of his own, spelling names backwards. "Yllop Nedgorb ," he said quietly as he worked out the letters of his would-be sweetheart's name.

"What?"

"Nuthin', mum."

"And respect," his mother continued, "for other people. Especially those less fortunate than yourself, young man."

"Like who?" Ned couldn't really imagine anyone less fortunate than himself.

"Well...... You should consider the ladies, for a start."

"'Ow d'yer mean?" Surely his mother had got that wrong - he had never known their father take his belt to punish Grace.

Alice struggled to put any kind of conviction into what she meant. "Well, yer respect ladies, don't yer?"

"Ah suppose so. Like Auntie Ethel?"

".... Women don't always get respect, lad. This is not a nice world for women." Ned stared blankly back at her as she struggled with the means to place her inhibitions in front of the boy, whilst Ned puzzled as to what other world there might be. "You should remember ladies are fragile creatures, not like...... not so strong as you menfolk."

He could at least detect that she was talking as much about herself as anyone else. Neither the boys nor their sister had the least respect for a father who so readily took his hand to his wife and children. The boy nodded back to his mother with what he felt to be total sympathy, whilst all the while struggling to comprehend what had prompted this lecture.

"Be gentle. Always remember, Ned. Gentleness and kindness is the way, not..... not the rough-house-ing and the bad language..... D'yer know what ah'm saying? Bad language is just as much a sin as strong drink, you should remember that. It's not what the bible teaches us."

"Is that why we have to go to church?"

She hesitated, thought for a moment. "Ah want you two lads to get a proper respect for people. Ah don't want yer growin' up like – well, there's plenty around 'ere that'd steal yer last crust an' not think twice on it. Ah've not brought you two up like that."

"No, mum. Ah don't steal crusts." Odd idea, thought Ned – at least steal a whole loaf.

"And you two are bright lads. Ah know yer've not had much of an education at school, but yer father were right, Pretty Fanny Balfour and 'is daft Education Bills aren't fer the likes of us folk, we 'ave to make ends meet first. Still.... Yer can both make summat o' yerselves, ah know yer can."

"Yes, mum."

"That's why we send yer to church. To pray you learn right from wrong."

"Yes, mum. Ah pray every day."

"Do yer?"

"Oh aye. Ah pray our teacher don't find out ah put that stink bomb in 'is inkwell."

"Aah, Ned! Gerron wi' yer!"

And he was thinking, Good job she can't see what goes on with the choirboys of a Friday night! Good job she didn't know of the trade in horse manure young Nogsy had going with regular trips over the wall at the council tram yards. No wonder Ned had got a good hiding from his father for the smelly state of his breeches.

Alice only shook her head slowly. She had run out of ways to show her boys how she adored them. They would grow too fast. As Ned ran off, she stood at the door of the parlour, watching him, and smiled. "Yer'll find yer truth, our Ned.... Ah know yer'll find yer truth.... one day."

For all that, Ned lost his virginity the second time *Orlania* docked in NewYork. The woman had been a whore in her mid-twenties who looked singularly unappetising even when she raised her several grubby skirts, but since Ned and Walter had by that time almost drunk themselves sober, Ned did not obey his first instinct which was to run away. They had in any case already given a wad of pay to a huge man with a tiny bowler hat who sat at the door of the bordello with his braces dangling and his backside squeaking on a frail chair, and Ned wasn't about to ask for it back.

"Five dollars!" Walter had cried out in his broad Glaswegian accent. "You're kidding - We could get a season ticket to the Giants for that!"

"Maybe you could," the huge man had replied, "but who are you gonna get to suck you off, boy – Red Ames?"

When the woman's skirts raised to her garters, there was no turning away.

"Smashin'!" was all Walter had drawled as they left. He was beaming all over his face. Looking down at his pants, he added,

"Ah'm gonna have to get some bigger breeches, Ned. Look, mah cock's grown already. What a bit of exercise does for ye!"

A little further along, he looked down again. "Oh, bugger! Ah'm leakin'! Bloody hell, Ned," shrieked Walter, "what did that bloody woman do?"

"Daft sod," laughed Ned, "What did yer think she was gonna do? This yer first time or summat?"

"Aye," pleaded Walter, reluctantly, "It is. Yours too, I'll bet."

Ned shook a smile into his face. "It is, aye," he said. "Well, put a bloody peg on it and hope it dries up before we get back aboard."

As they plotted a rough course back to their ship, Ned suddenly felt a tiny fear enter his brain.

"'Ere, Walter, what if we picked up some ruddy disease from them women?"

"What? Already? I wouldn't worry about it, mate. Wait for your cock to start swelling and drop off!"

"No. No, really. Ah've heard fellers talk about the pox. They reckon yer start with a burnin' feelin' when yer have a piss."

"Och, away! Listen, I tell you what that is."

"What?"

"You should put your bloody cigarette oot afore ye grab a hold o' yer willy, yer daft bugger!"

If the incident failed to whet his appetite for more extensive female comforts, it was largely down to an episode that followed *Orlania*'s return to Southampton later that month, when Walter took Ned to his father's house in Northam where the boys 'entertained' two local girls for an evening. Walter's widower father being a nightwatchman, the small back-to-back house – by good fortune, above the area that tended to flood every other year - was at their disposal. This time, being entirely sober had been a disadvantage: Ned had almost wished for a negative answer when, deciding that social foreplay was wasted on these girls, etiquette obliged him to ask the one called Miriam if she wanted to share a bed with him, half-hoping that she wouldn't.

"Well," said the girl, feigning modesty, "I wouldn't mind, I'm sure", and so saying drew her petticoats with a practised measure up to the ribbons at her thigh. Ned had reacted to his girl's forward manner after initial fumbling by squirting all down her leg and across his trousers, leaving her quite put out until she showed him how he might pleasure her anyway, saying that the night was young and it was "fun to be a bit naughty". The young man fumbled further and felt awkward but the girl smelled almost good – almost - and had a soft, inviting bosom with even more inviting nipples that she stroked his face with. What's more, she seemed to delight in his innocence, teaching him what someone else's hands could do that cocked a snook at all those Sundays spent mouthing peculiar verses and fingering the Good Book. It was deliciously wrong, he instinctively knew, and yet – if he was going to burn in purgatory for it, it made being on earth in the meantime a hell of a ride. He had never imagined that being inside a woman would be such raw pleasure, yet at the same time it unnerved him that Miriam lay there coolly looking at him panting for breath, with an expression on her face that said, '*Now you know you liked that, and you are mine to command*'. The musky smell of her body, and the sight of all this flesh and frothy linen was just too much for the young man: as Miriam beamed a broad grin of wilful pleasure at him and blew her warm, dubious breath into his face, Ned felt as if he were going into self-destruction.

"Clever boy," she told him. "Now spunk inside me and not every-bloody-where else!"

What seemed like half an hour passed before she asked bluntly, "You finished, then?" She took his hand and drew it to her bushy cleft and with bright eyes flashing at him said, "More, please! Cantcha get it up no more, then?"

After a while even Miriam tired of the mechanical exercise and pushed her skirt down. "I can tell you never played rugby," she opined.

"No," panted Ned, "An' when ah played football, it were all ah could do to blow the ruddy ball up in the first place!"

Yet in that flippant response he somehow said all he wanted to and sat there laughing to himself. He knew that he really couldn't be bothered about this girl, something that definitely went against his mother's teaching but it seemed entirely appropriate. Later, as he and Walter strolled back to the dockyard in the blaze of moonlight, he felt on top of the world. A feeling not that he had reached a state of near-ecstasy but a pride that he had crossed a threshold and not been completely subordinated by the experience.

It was a lesson learned, one that had to stand him in good stead for a long time, since those two early attempts at fornication were not a prelude to regular excess. What Ned learned, however, was that ladies did not necessarily fit the pattern his mother had described years before, and without doubt their language could be the equal of any of Ned's pals. For a long time, the contradiction bothered him just a little, until he began to think that in the world at large, life was very different to the theory, and perhaps his schooling and limited education at the factory had left a good deal to be desired. Those early stolen minutes of fumbling in the wood pile with the girl urging him to "show me yours" now seemed a very simple frolic compared to the adult pastime he had discovered.

He also learned – so he thought – that he was not to be the butt of the standard jokes about men at sea, as he was now confident in the fact he had become a man, and a man that appreciated the comforts female flesh could offer. Somehow, there seemed little wrong in that, but he imagined he could never tell his mother so! As for the habitual greetings of shipmates when a seaman returned from shore, he learned to ride with that too. To the customary jibes of "Did yer get a bit, then?", Ned would always affirm with head and voice, even if it was all a complete load of nonsense. "Got stacks, did yer?" they would ask and he would just nod confidently. Was it any sort of big deal - getting his 'dirty little end away'?

* * * * *

Dieu merci pour les Américains......

81

Mr. Julius Rosenberg, a favoured passenger who had been aboard long before sailing, told the captain, "That boy serves the best Mojitos this side of Manhattan." And he meant it, even if there was something of a confused metaphor in there somewhere. The first officer, too, had been impressed at the new steward's skill with his cocktails, no less than the skill with his mouth. And an impressed first officer was something to shake a cocktail at.

Ned's secret to his sought-after Mojito recipe was, like so many of the best creations, nothing more than a happy accident. Short of bitters on the first evening's duty, Ned had substituted a sliver of grapefruit and a pinch of salt along with the lime, a discreet little slice at that, squeezing and whipping it out neatly from between ice chunks before serving. And all the while presenting his back to the customer – the alchemist protecting his secrets. Yet it was nothing – Ned tasted it himself and thought it sour - didn't work at all. 'No accounting for taste', he thought.

"Mmmm." Mr. Rosenberg licked his lips as part of a self-induced ritual. "It's getting there," he nodded, understanding that he was amongst the most severe of critics and could afford generosity.

Acknowledging genius was the easier part of flattering a passenger, hence Mr. Julius Rosenberg required no convincing that he had found an original. Whether someone had done it before? – Who cares?

"Of course, a classic cane syrup is the thing for a proper Guarapo," said the jeweller's companion, Goldstein.

"D'you think?" countered Rosenberg. "I always felt getting the right Havana was key to a good Mojito."

"*D'accord*," replied Ned coolly, playing with his minimal French for his own amusement whilst knowing full well he had prepared the 'syrup' under the counter with sugar right out of the bag.

"And an ice-cold glass, naturally," Goldstein added in full approval.

Rosenberg wasn't quite ready to give best. "Shouldn't you crush the ice, though?"

With a careful shaking of the head, Ned avoided any direct rebuttal, then said quietly, "Crush the mint leaves, sir..... Never the ice."

"Ah," said both customers together. "The mint leaves."

"Oh yes. From the slopes of Mount Tipitoto."

"Pardon?"

"Peru," said Ned, fighting back his grin. It seemed to satisfy Rosenberg.

"It's in the bitters, you see, sir," was Ned's suggestion. Goldstein nodded knowingly again.

"Did you know," asked Vuillaume in his competent English when they were out of earshot, "that those two think of themselves as connoisseurs of fancy drinks? Even if they absolutely are not."

"He asked me earlier," replied Ned, "if the French Line served Manhattans and Mojitos as well as the American ships do, because he said the British were hopeless. I told him I would serve up something when I came back after my break. I just needed a little time to improvise, and I'll make sure our bitters and syrup are up to scratch for the future."

Vuillaume allowed the vaguest twitch of the moustache to betray a smile.

It seemed Ned had met his new employers' standards of service.

* * * * *

ELEVEN

There were advantages to being one of only three native English speakers amongst the steward staff of *La Rochelle*. Half the world spoke English. *La Rochelle* at cruising speed would take six days and more to cross, ample time for opportunities to exploit - fairly - English-speakers. Ned found himself popular with five or six American travellers and a particular Belgian, a regular traveller whose fluency was sufficiently Anglo-American to gain easy access to their poker games. Confidentially, Ned had to date found poker players the most amenable and reliable of customers. Until they took a heavy loss, then most would just take a bottle and disappear for a couple of days. Unscrupulous play was – whilst carefully on the blind side of the law – pretty much an accepted norm at sea, a player had to be good to make the Atlantic pay and many a sharp player entered New York sporting a quality suit in which he had not boarded at Le Havre. Just as the occasional lady might disembark wearing a quality gentleman that her arm had scooped up *en voyage*. With the prospect of a week at sea, many travellers thought card games a relatively moderate pastime compared with other pursuits. A view which *La Compagnie Genérale Transatlantique* might tacitly commend, so long as there was no trouble – and Ned and his fellow stewards had become adept at steering trouble in the right direction, usually with a complimentary tot of spirits. Then the French line would quietly condone most gaming practices provided passengers actually walked off the ship in a suit of clothes, as opposed to no clothes at all.

The Belgian, he was a characterful man, though at first Ned did wonder if he fell into that classification of gentleman whom gentlemen should not so readily befriend - as it turned out, he could not have been more wrong.

Monsieur Bruno Carelle was a man of imposing manner and charm to match his height of 6ft. 2 inches, so Ned estimated. Outside of his eager poker-playing, he carried himself often in a light-coloured suit with a distinguished sort of air that suggested he might well have been royalty of some sort, notwithstanding the unruly spread of moustache he cultivated. Though he did wax the offending whiskers frequently so as not to frighten the ladies. Carelle decided one evening, whilst using the bar as a kind of vertical bed, to confide to Ned that he was not a native Belgian at all but had been raised near Boma, a former slaving station in the Congo, and by default had inherited the family's business of cocoa beans. Of his background, he said little, except that he was impassioned that Belgians had done so much damage to his home country.

"Thank heaven, the Belgian government eventually woke up," said Carelle, "and curtailed the butchery".

Over time, Ned ascertained that Carelle was now a prominent figure in the cocoa bean and chocolate industry of his adopted country, based in Antwerp, from where his family operated a thriving business importing from West Africa and other places to serve the growing Belgian chocolate market.

"You must visit, Ned. I shall show you beautiful Antwerp. You know, Mercator was Flemish and lived in Antwerp. Our warehouse is not far from Rubens' house." Ned assumed that Monsieur Rubens and Monsieur Mercator must be big in chocolate.

"So, Ned," were his parting words at Le Havre, "I will see you in the Fall when I go again to New York. Mm?" Ned thanked M. Carelle, not least for the substantial tip the big Belgian had placed in his hand, and realised Carelle's invitation had been in earnest - there was in that parting note a covert suggestion that Carelle might have had knowledge of Ned's situation, however scant or intuitive. If he had, he said nothing.

Ned felt little reason now to expect the *Titanic* issue would follow him to Europe, or might still be an issue when he returned to New York. Many nights at sea had persuaded him that was all behind him now, whilst Otto, with less faith in human reliability despite his own convivial nature, maintained he should remain vigilant - a man with the power to malign and impugn the young Ned, this man was to be feared.

* * * * *

La Rochelle berthed at Le Havre in the early afternoon and was quickly set to disembarking her passengers. It was twilight before Otto had discharged all his duties. Ned had finished cleaning up the lounge bar long before and had spent a further hour washing cutlery and *bains marie* to help out.

So the light had long since shrugged itself away from the town as the two men left the *Bassin*, cutting their way through battalions of carts bearing grain sacks and barrels of liquor, mountains of wooden boxes, crates of provisions, spools of cables and all the impedimenta of ocean travel. Clearing Saint François and the dockyards, they set off on foot up the quayside roads as the lamplighter went about his business and whistled his greeting at them as they passed by his ladder.

Yet again Ned asked his friend if he was sure Otto's mother would not mind if he came along uninvited. Otto simply lifted his shoulders in that exaggerated way of his, as if to say, '*You will arrive and that's that. My mother and sisters will be glad to see my friend.*' If a gesture can say all those things, then it was enough.

In reality, what he did say was, "Don't worry, little *Nixie*. Zey will love you. If zey don't, no more schnapps!"

They walked on briskly, for it was not warm, and they were afraid the rain might come. The streets were still busy but at least the aroma was more of fish than the horse dung of New York. Otto carried a linen bag with a few clothes to wash and some meat from cold storage. Ned had a bag containing a clean shirt, a bottle of Black & White whisky, some powdered milk and some chocolate that M. Carelle had recommended from the limited onboard stock. Self-conscious of his appearance, Ned checked that his clothes were clean, though with the privations of ship life, clothing was constantly in a crumpled state. He had shaved, whilst Otto had not: all he wanted to do was get home.

Frau Bremme dropped a pan of water when Otto tripped the latch and burst into the dimly lit room. Luckily, it was not hot water, and she just left the pan to clatter on the stone floor. With one single cry of Otto's name, she ran forward and clasped her arms around her son's big frame. For a minute, that was all, there was a silence as they clung together, and to break that would have been a gross intrusion, so Ned closed the outer door quietly and simply stood there, waiting, with what he would probably have himself called a gormless look on his face. That Otto had been away less than a month was not for him to question, for it was clear there was great love here. What is more, of course, the family would have heard of *Titanic*'s fate, and it was reported in the local papers that *La Rochelle* had hit ice also: that had been a point when his mother's heart had skipped several beats. The age of Marconi transmissions brought a down-side as bad news travelled faster than sentiment allowed, whilst good news failed to comfort an anxious mother.

From a side door a cry announced one of the sisters, who had evidently been alerted in the middle of her toilet for she now made the same exclamation and rushed toward Otto, wearing no more than a camisole over her petticoat and her hair tied up for the night. If she had seen the second figure in the twilight of the room, she did not acknowledge him. She was saying something in both French and German and Ned understood neither. This was Brigitte.

"*Ne, ne, ne!*" called Otto to both women after releasing his mother's embrace. "*Dieser Mann hier - Er spricht kein Deutsch. Wir müssen alle Englisch sprechen. Also....sprecht Englisch, ja?*"

At once Brigitte placed her arms across her chest, before being grasped tightly by her brother. "Gitta........*mein schatz!*" She laughed at him as brother and sister struggled together in a mock-passion.

Ned now realised that, for all his preparation, he was going to have no opportunity to speak German – his supremely limited German – which was in truth both disappointment and relief. They would otherwise be waiting for him to catch up all the time.

Following a general fussing, the first thing Brigitte did was to excuse herself to go and put on her night-dress. The second was to offer her guest a drink. "It's Calva, Ned...... You know, Calvados," she told him. "You like it?"

"Um.... Oh, yes." He had served it at the ship's bar, yet never actually tasted Calvados before. He wondered if it were expensive, since he had brought the whisky to save the family any expense. Then she answered his unspoken question: "It's not a good one. It's more of *eau de vie* than brandy."

She was right. The Calvados was not at first to his taste, but second glasses are generally more palatable.

Whilst Otto and his mother conversed, Brigitte devoted her attention to Ned as befits one who has the status of 'guest'. Brigitte was tall, slim, fair-haired, not quite blonde but very different to the redder hair of both Otto and their mother, though she had their similarly high cheek bones. Her eyes were a bright blue, a very sharp blue which overcame the narrowness of the eye corners to emphasize their almost oriental shape: for all the world, she could have been the product of an Eastern dynasty, a veritable Hun. Now turned 18, she had well-accented breasts which made every effort to draw the eye, a very ample figure and a soft, beguiling smile that belied what at first appeared a forward manner. Ned had not expected these qualities of the sister of his friend, given Otto's somewhat ruddy complexion and considerable proportions. It was entirely clear where Otto had gained his looks, notwithstanding the fact his mother was a slight figure by comparison, but Ned could only assume that Brigitte had inherited most of hers from their father.

Transfixed as he was for some moments, Ned switched back in a blink when someone spoke again. Renata, the ladies apologised, was late, but they assured Otto she would be back soon.

As it turned out, Renata was later than expected. Both tired, Otto and Ned had eaten then washed in the cold water basin and had gone to bed in Renata's room, which at one time had been Otto's anyway. In former times the two girls had shared the second bedroom and spent their nights chattering. Otto's room had always been the smallest and it was still full of his books and a small collection of their father's beer steins that, as a boy, Otto had insisted they should bring from Köln. They were silvery for the most part, garishly ornamental, and precious only to Otto.

And so it was that, around ten o'clock, the door to the room abruptly opened and in walked the tall Renata, preceded by an oil lamp, to find one man in her bed and another on the floor atop a layer of cushions.

"Reina!" called Otto sleepily from beneath a blanket, "*Le Père Noël est arrivé!*"

* * * * *

In New York in the intervening days, Magoolagan penned a letter to Ned's sister, introducing himself as a friend and reporting that Bioscope newsreels were including footage presenting survivors from *Titanic* both as they boarded *Carpathia* and later aboard the ship as she entered port. The fact much of the action was staged for the cameras was entirely missed by the innocent cinema audiences. What was new – reported to Magoolagan by his son's girlfriend – was that the news films now included some seconds of a figure boarding *Carpathia* in essentially female clothing, yet was clearly not female. That this footage differed from the rest by being well defined and somewhat dislocated in its relation to genuine footage was quite lost on the eager audience, who whistled and shouted their protest at the screen. The event was repeated in the second of the week's screenings, with much the same reaction.

"I fear, dear Miss Thornton," wrote Magoolagan, "that young Ned has an enemy strong enough to arrange such false material to have been somehow inserted into the news here. Its purpose is clear and I do not like the tone this business is taking."

Magoolagan inferred a deliberately mounted campaign to discredit the young man, and warned that he should stay away. Assuring her of his best intentions, he concluded, "I pray you, do not be downhearted, for Ned will – God willing – come through this shocking affair the better for it."

Beyond this, he let slip no speculation, he stated only that Ned had "got away" from New York and would no doubt be in touch with the family even now.

Indeed, Ned was. Brigitte posted for him a letter written days before, deliberately not sent by paquebot mail from the ship, in case Cade or anyone else had been able to infiltrate the ship's crew, however unlikely that seemed. "Safe better than sorry," Otto had said.

"Fifteen centimes," said Brigitte, referring to the postage. "It is my gift to you!" Her little joke too.

"Then," replied Ned, "Ah'll find you a gift of fifteen centimes. I think I shall buy you a sunflower!" It was his only image of French flowers.

"No! You can't!" laughed Brigitte.

"Can't? – Why not?"

"It's too soon. Too soon for ze *tournesol*. You are very funny man, Ned."

He was becoming aware just how much he did not know about France.

Those lies of which Magoolagan had spoken had already spread to England, the national papers gave it second page status and the local newspapers were already telling of "Bradford's *Titanic* Disgrace", which might have been the face of cowardice aboard the Great Ship as she went down. Grace replied to Ned via Brigitte, saying the family believed in him. And Otto reminded Ned of the words of Bruno Carelle.

"Monsieur Carelle? Oh, no, Otto, it's too soon for that. Let's wait and see what the British Board of Enquiry has to say, eh?"

"Daft bugger!" Otto exclaimed, in a heavily exaggerated Northern England accent. He looked pleased with himself.

"What?" cried Ned.

Otto beamed. "Is new word. Okay, two words. Is what you told Joubert, no?"

Ned only shook his head.

"New word, Ned. Joubert said, it's good English words for when you are happy. No? It's not?"

"Is he mad? It means things are not good. 'Daft bugger', my foot!"

"Your foot? Your foot is not good? What's wrong wiz your foot?"

"Otto......! Aw, skip it!"

"Skip it? Skip? Is funny way to walk, isn't it? Is that why your foot is not good?"

"Otto..... Just... shut up!"

"Ah, 'shut up' ...... I understand."

"Well shut up, then!"

Otto shook his head slowly from side to side and muttered loudly to himself. "English is not so easy ...... *Himmel, Arsch und Zwirn*..... Not a simple language like German.... *Firmament, Gesäss und Faden*......"

* * * * *

The chicken Otto had wanted served *al fresco* had to wait. It rained. Instead, Frau Bremme made a *ragoût de lapin* largely from lightly-clad rabbit bones and vegetables bought at market that morning, and she had baked fresh baguettes with just a little garlic, the smell of which was pure heaven. Outside it was cold, they could hardly have expected it to be otherwise, yet still there was a warm fire in the downstairs grate as Brigitte had brought in the big logs from the little *abri* for the occasion of her brother's return, not forgetting his friend. Renata came home later than usual, but with a pitcher of red wine that M. Gibault had assured her was the bargain of the week and the best Haut-Medoc that had passed through his hands in months. Renata did not believe him, for she never did, but that did not diminish the fact the wine was good as well as half the price the man in the town would charge.

The men were late too, again thanks to Otto's duties, but nothing was spoiled and only their coats were dampened. Otto produced schnapps whilst Ned took the opportunity to look at two exceptionally attractive young ladies. In so doing, he betrayed his reserve.

"*Prost*! To us!" Otto raised the toast, and speaking in English he said, "To my friend Ned, you are ze welcome one in ze house of my family: always welcome here, Ned. My mother welcomes you, and zese two girls – zey will have somesing good to look at - not me!"

The girls feigned embarrassment, clutching at the brooches at their necks, and Ned did not know what to say, for he was in spite of himself more than a little emotional – excepting his own brother and sister, no friend had ever done so much for him. There was something else too, something sinister and troubling: the last person whom Ned had called a close friend was at the bottom of the sea. It was a kind of taunt that he should not seek true friendship ever again. To do so might mean they were taken from him. There was no rationality in this, nothing that made sense, yet how close a relationship could he allow? One thing you learn from a life at sea – never say 'goodbye'.

* * * * *

TWELVE

By the time *La Rochelle* returned to New York in mid-June – for she had spent time undergoing repairs - Otto was able to report to Ned that all was quiet ashore in terms of ripples in the media regarding the 'Coward of the *Titanic*'.   Ned stayed aboard, nevertheless, keeping himself largely out of sight.

The Board of Enquiry had long since moved to Washington and was completed; attention had since been directed to the return of bodies, with the *Mackay-Bennett* and the *Minia* delivering their gruesome cargo into Nova Scotia at about the time *La Rochelle* had left for France in May. There had been reports from other vessels passing the *Titanic*'s last location. Passengers and crew of the German liner *Bremen* in particular had recounted awful stories of what they had seen: 'fields' of bodies in the most appalling state, sights that reduced women to tears and men to silence.

And there was the macabre. Descriptions of bodies and effects had crept into the papers. They were characterized by the salient details only: gender, estimated age, hair colour, distinguishing marks, clothing and – most despicably of all – a note recommending their social class of passenger. In death, too, the measure of a man was his status in society. To add insult to injury, a shortage of embalming fluid on the rescue boats meant that "prominent" persons would be dignified by their preservation whilst a great many "unimportant" victims' bodies were simply disposed of at sea - no coffin, no ceremony, no pomp, no accolade. The population, it went without saying, had to be protected from contaminants. And neither of Ned's great friends was ever heard of again.

It was July. America had been uneventful apart from the sensation of Mr. Houdini escaping from a box in the East River the day before the ship sailed, possibly the only time that an excited Dieter Pabst had spoken to Ned of his own volition - in German, of course. And there had been a fire in the galley, started by American chef Crazy Colin and quickly put out by Crazy Colin. He was fined and warned for smoking over a range but not dismissed. After that they wanted to call him 'Lucky Colin'. Also, Ned was warned by the first officer for using inappropriate language: sometimes Otto's sense of humour backfired in teaching Ned the more colourful of French language metaphors. Ned was angry but the anger lasted no more than an hour. Otto only shrugged his big shrug – '*Nothing to do with me*'.

La Rochelle returned to Le Havre on a Saturday morning. Otto had seen Brigitte waving from the quayside at the *Entrée du Port*, he had stepped out onto the weather deck and waved back but he fancied she had really wanted to see Ned and not her brother.

"She likes you," he told Ned as the Englishman polished his shoes ready for going ashore.

Ned smiled back and shook his head. "Pass us that Brasso...... She's just glad to see us." He put a wad to the paper-wrapped buttons on his dress tunic before putting it away, then attached his stiff, rounded collar to his neck, fastened his tie, popped the bowler onto his head at a slight angle and turned to Otto for approval.

"Okay," said Otto with no conviction. "But you look ridiculous, what. Grimaldi in ze circus has better style zan you do.... Be good, Ned. An' don't forget ze ham, ja? I see you tomorrow."

Ned had pressed his suit, even had a clean collar this time and a bright pair of studs borrowed from Jean-Louis Dumonceau, yet was still quietly unsure of himself. And as he left the gangplank, he was already wondering how Brigitte would welcome him and what she might be wearing. The scent of those ladies from Chartres in cabin 22B with their silks, their fancy feathered hats and deliberate displays of ankle had given him a kind of appetite.

Clearing the melee of baskets and boxes as he passed along the quay, he looked across to where was berthed *La France*, the new pride and joy of the C.G.T. That ship was breathtaking, he had heard the stories of her interior opulence and speed. Not as big as the huge British liners, though within her smaller frame there was somehow a grace, an insouciance that totally befitted a French craft. For men such as Ned, there was almost a love affair with beautiful ships like this, an intoxication. It had been so with *Titanic,* and *La*

France with her four bright red funnels was as striking. Yet it sent a shudder up his back as those disturbing memories returned. Turning away, he marched up the quay with the evening sunlight lending dark shadows to those nearest houses, the town appearing to shrink back on itself against the expanse of docks. The truth was, on a certain level, Le Havre felt like home now.

These were good days. Otto was content that his friend was comfortable in his new situation and hoped it would stay that way for a long time. Ned learned some French, some German, a little Italian – but only a little. *La Rochelle* continued to pour emigrants into the new continent, with Ellis Island remaining as frantic as ever with the mass influx of European working stock. But this was a cheerful ship. Whereas it amused the bar staff to hear one dear old French lady ask, "What is the American word for Franc?", it was not derogatory laughter.

Wearing his 'practical' hat, Ned was friendly to steerage passengers, mostly Italians and east Europeans, but favoured the rewards of pandering to the British, French and primarily Americans, for whom the French Line held a '*chic*' that the greater formality of Cunard and White Star tended to rebuff. Americans loved the French ships, and if it were a toss-up between Paris and London, most found Paris beckoned with its skirts up where London raised only an umbrella and put you to bed with a hot water bottle. "Going French" was more relaxed, more gay, more sociable even amongst those less sociable classes, all commodities which the C.G.T. was quick to exploit. The French Line had become known and envied for one thing above all – style.

There was Otto too. He was at one and the same time hopeless and completely engaging.

"Lascivious!" cried Otto.

"Okay. So what does it mean?"

"..... I forgot. Someone who gives you a lot of money?.... I don't know, Ned, what does it mean?"

"... I don't know either. Just be careful which passengers you say it to."

Every reason, then, to be in no hurry to return to England or seek employment in British ships.   At this juncture, Ned felt no great desire to return, except for the nagging wound that was the calumny of those false reports and the defamation of his name. For the sake of his family if not for himself.

It was not every night that the pair could get ashore in Le Havre, but from June it had been evident Ned could call on the family by himself, even though he felt at first awkward doing so. The ladies always made him welcome, and he would take something to help meals along and then help with household chores, but if he were without Otto, he did not feel it was yet proper to stay the night. In time he allowed himself to reflect on the qualities of the girls. Their beauty especially: as a young man, friend of the family or not, he was easily capable of arousal.

No, he fancied he was not the gentleman his mother would have wanted him to be. Rather, he preferred to graze – respectfully, mark you, but graze nonetheless - on the beauty of the female sex and become suitably interested, as he felt they might in fact wish. Was that presumptious? Or simply an awareness of desire. It seemed to him that at times Brigitte looked at him in much the same way: on a number of occasions a distinct fire danced in those blue eyes.

Brigitte went for a walk with Ned one afternoon, following mass in the morning when the three ladies dressed in their finest and left early.

On the walk, just a random tour of the town's outer district, Brigitte chatted incessantly the whole time, half in English, half in French, but Ned loved every moment of having to struggle to understand what she meant.   Why, he wondered, had people suggested German was a terribly gutteral language, an ugly language? Words dancing out of Brigitte's mouth were lyrical and delightful. The sound of her voice was like the twittering of birds, though not so high-pitched as Brigitte had a mezzo-soprano voice: it rose and fell, too, in almost a musical fashion. Here in the open air, without the constant drone of ship's engines, it was pure refreshment. Ned smiled at his own lack of invention, evaluating Brigitte's beauty by means of a ship's engine!

"Don't you have boyfriends?" he asked her.

"Oh, yes. Of course!"

"I never see any."

"No. Zey run away."

"Why?"

"I tell zem, my big sea man is 'ere."

He made fun of looking at himself. "Big? Me?" She giggled.

To be sure, Le Havre was not a pretty place, but with these girls to look at and to be with, it took on a particular radiance. Whatever his feelings – and Ned was the last one to know what his real feelings were – he was careful to maintain a propriety that he felt his comradeship with Otto demanded. It was about respect. Moreover, the girls were bright, intelligent as well as attractive, and he had little experience with that combination: all the more reason to tread gently. "*Doucement,*" said Otto at one point, an undisguised reference to his sisters. "*Doucement*".

His mother had heard the remark. Turning away from her washboard where she pounded their underwear, Frau Bremme looked directly into Ned's eyes and winked. "*Doucement,*" she whispered at him. Looking into the tub and observing their shifts and drawers, he smiled back at her, whereupon she butted his side with her elbow and traded her amusement.

Before they left again for America, Otto had a fight with Dieter Pabst. It was over something and nothing – duty rosters. No weapons were involved other than sharp tongues and blunted fists, neither were any passengers aboard at the time, but Otto took a cut to his face from a fall against a galley table. He was a little shaken up and was treated by the ship's doctor. Both men were disciplined by Captain Genoud, and again no harsh punishment was meted out to either, merely a docking of pay and an extension of their duties. Genoud preferred to believe extreme punishment was against the interest of the ship's morale, which lay at the heart of any passenger vessel. Pabst and Otto remained deeper enemies than before, they avoided each other wherever possible and never spoke unless it was on company business. Otto moved his things into another cabin and Crazy Colin took his place under Ned's bunk. Crazy Colin always lost his pay gambling and never went ashore, so Ned spent more of the time talking with Otto in his friend's new billet. Pabst and Ned had little conversation anyway, despite sharing a cabin, and when they spoke, it had to be in German: Ned would try to remember the words so that Otto could later tell him what Pabst had meant. "*Arschgeige*," muttered Otto.

Apart from a severe gale during that crossing, meaning Ned worked furiously to put his customers' belongings back into order in their cabins and mop up water from the bowls, everything went smoothly enough. The Belgian, M. Carelle was not to make another appearance until the Fall.

* * * * *

There was one afternoon that month when Ned and Otto helped out at the school. Ned was not clear on anything much that happened socially - France was still a blank page and would slowly reveal to him its wonders - but he joined in happily with festivities for the little people in Renata's charge who gaily scampered around the small school yard, the little classrooms now released from their educating function and much regaled in festive trimmings and pictures painted by the children.

Knowing little that was going on, Ned stood at Renata's side behind a table festooned with all the goods for sale the children had brought - vegetables, and cheeses that their parents had either made or bartered, spicy *saucisson* and other meatstuffs like the strange white *boudin* that Ned couldn't fancy at all. It was jolly, it was very French, it was perhaps a *'foire au fromage'* or maybe it was a *'salon à bouche'* - at least, words he *thought* they had said. It was mostly baffling for Ned but he did not mind in the least as he enjoyed for the first time Renata's almost undivided accompaniment. So it seemed to him, anyway.

Of the two sisters, Renata always dressed more formally: she was, after all, the schoolmistress and more than four years the senior of her sister and, whether by convention or by dint of her own character, behaved the part. So it was a thrill for Ned to see Renata 'letting her hair down' - whilst not, of course, actually letting down one single ringlet of hair under her wide hat festooned with an excess of flora in the style of the day. Ned did not like ladies' hats. Her smiles, he might have thought, were mainly for him. Indeed, he did think that.

"Ah didn't reckon ah'd enjoy this, Reina," he said to her, "But it's a right good little do, this."

"You like it?" she replied with an air of simple pleasure.

"Ah like bein' here with you," he told her.

She took the money off the older lady, passed her the sausage and put the money into the purse at her waist, but said nothing other than thanking the lady for her purchase.

"It reminds me of fairs we used to 'ave back 'ome," he continued.

"Oh?... Good?"

"Oh aye! We'd get all dressed up an' go out to Barnabas Field in a big haycart, that were a lot of fun.... The lads would all be fightin' to chat up the lasses."

"Chat up?"

"Aye. Chat up the girls, y'know - bit of courtin' and all that. Erm, havin' a good time wi' the girls."

" I see... "

"Oh! No, it were all harmless fun, like. Nobody were serious. Just fun."

Having second thoughts about his loose tongue, he then told her, "Ah didn't mean to be rude - sayin' I liked bein' here with yer."

Her lack of response for a moment told him he may have said too much.

"No harm in it. Just a hayride.... They were good times, an' we didn't get that many good times."

"No?"

"Didn't mean to offend yer," he apologised.

"No, Ned.... it's alright."

Was it alright? She was close, and he would have liked to be closer. One thing to think it, quite another to say it. And the time and the place? No. He would have to take time to get to know these people. Thoughtless. *Impetuous, Ned. Be more careful, you daft sod!* In his head, he heard Frau Bremme's whisper: '*Doucement*'.

By late July, Ned had been made a highly embarrassed guest of honour at dinner at Franklin Avenue. Magoolagan reported that the '*Titanic* business' had fallen out of the pages of the newspapers. Both boards of enquiry were considered no more than a sop to official positions and fell way short of providing answers. Possibly, private accounts of the tragedy were more germane to the real issues, a number of versions were in process of being written. On the face of it, then, no recriminations directed at either White Star or individuals, but neither was there serious debate about cowardly conduct and men escaping the ship in female clothing.

In the Magoolagan household, the only controversy centred on Shane Larkin, whose legs were bad. To answer the questioning face of the young man, Clodagh spoke just a few words of explanation. "The English," she said, and after a few more moments added, "You should've seen his back when they'd finished with 'im...... There now." Her smile was an apology. "Feelings go deep. Not your fault, Ned. Forgive us."

He recalled the stories of their forefathers, how families and friends had suffered in the Gorta Mor and after. The famine, its causes and effects had cut grave wounds into the collective consciousness. Ned placed a hand on Clodagh's arm and was given a look of appreciation.

Prior to sailing at the beginning of August, Ned made an effort to see Tom the Butcher.. The Great Man had little time for pleasantries, merely patted Ned on his cap and said "Good luck, lad," before going into a huddle with his lieutenants, no doubt a crisis in pork bellies or some such.

* * * * *

THIRTEEN

At the end of that month, *La Rochelle* ran back to Le Havre on a short turn-around, all provisioning had to be done over the weekend. But for now..... Catch the moment: eat, drink.

Renata's school principal - and constant suitor - Monsieur Jerome Forget was invited for Saturday's lunch. Frau Bremme was not enamoured of M. Forget, his way of addressing her as "Madame" Bremme was – whilst technically correct – an irritation, when she had previously asked to be called "Frau" out of a respect for her husband.

Introduced for the first time to Ned, M. Forget politely enquired whether Ned found sea life now so normal that he might not feel quite so at home on dry land.

Ned's reply was typically thoughtless: "Well, monsieur, the thing is - when folk see you rocking, they'll not know whether it's the ship's motion or if you're just plain drunk!"

M. Forget looked vacantly at Otto for an answer, for he did not understand the response. Or, if he did, propriety dictated that he should not acknowledge the wit of it in front of the ladies.

Renata frowned. She knew Forget carried the authority of his office too far into social life. All the same, Ned thought M. Forget had a distinguished air about him, though he did tend to wipe his nose a lot above his copious moustache and had a habit of squeezing up his eyes behind his glasses, which he tended to take off rather frequently for no apparent reason, as if to emphasize a point. For Otto, though, the man was an inexcusably archetypal academic.

"He listens to Bach," hissed Otto, as if that explained everything.

They drank white table wine because they had fish, 'borrowed' from the ship's storage, and Otto believed passionately that you drank the wine appropriate to the food. Ned could not care one way or the other: he merely thought it a pity that the smell of the fish masked the fragrance with which the ladies had taken the trouble to anoint themselves.

"I cook fish, so it smell," said Otto. "Always I cook wiz wine.....
Maybe I put some in ze food!"

It pleased Otto to see his friend laugh, even at a very poor joke.
So he added a further thought. "You know, Ned, zere is a magic
with drinking ze wine. You know zis magic?"

"What?"

"It make French men sink zey can sing!" Brigitte smiled. Mostly
at Ned.

The weather had turned much warmer, they were able to sit
outside in the small rear garden of the house where a previous
tenant had set up a wooden lean-to from a high wall, latticed with
small flowering plants. In the evening, they would hang scented
candles from its struts. Further along, bees had invaded the cracked
old wall but seemed to go only about bees' business: they came,
hovered, pried and flew away. It was good as it appeared to keep
the wasps away, but Willi Bremme had some years previous had the
plum tree chopped down to get rid of wasp invasion, now only its
stump remained and most of the rest of the garden was simply
stones or red bricks with grass and weeds climbing around them.
Glorious hollyhocks were disguising the structure perfectly and the
fronds of an overhanging yew from beyond the wall completed a
tiny scene that in the still of the bright afternoon might, if one
closed one's eyes, have been in the countryside. Nature clearly knew
this place, for songbirds would fly in from the meadows not far
outside the town limits.

The rear of this house, though, belied the overall condition of Le
Havre as a place to live. The town's rapid growth had raised
problems, it was one of the unhealthiest places to be in all of
northern France and was said to have the worst T.B. rates of all.
The Bremme house, with its cracked facade and dowdy blue
shutters in need of attention, was at least a little way out of the
lower working-class quarter close to the port area, yet looked down
on by the wealthier merchant class of properties further out, where
now hillside mansions were establishing themselves. Le Havre was

France's second sea port after Marseilles, and bore penalties for its own success.

Whilst their father's death had changed the family's aspirations, Renata, at least, had no desire to move away, having fallen in love with the idea of improving the lives of those children in her charge. The schools of Le Havre were of prime importance in the fight against poverty for so many of the town's families. It was a view respected by some, who also saw Renata as a strong matrimonial candidate for the likes of a bachelor head schoolteacher.

Like her sister, Renata was tall: whilst not so juvenile nor sylph-like in appearance, she had a charm and a kind of wide-eyed serenity that belied her teutonic origins. To French eyes, Renata was very much a French woman, whereas her sister reflected not so much a Germanic look but an appeal more youthful and broadly Euro-modern. She had an equally good figure, Renata, and not too slim, a stature which again commended her as a dependable wife. Moreover she dressed in normal times more soberly than her sister, as befitted her status at the school, and yet in that very maturity there was an essential appeal to Ned's more fanciful desires. Not only Ned's, of course, for if the sisters were out together in the town, the graceful flow of their movements invariably attracted male and female attention alike. "Those Bremme girls," breathed Mme. Beaumarchais to their mother, with a knowing look.

Renata's face, narrower than her sister's, had those high cheek bones, which lent her less of a scholastic air, and Renata's mouth was fuller. That they were sisters was clear, both with hair fair and long, yet it was in the eyes that most distinction could be noted: Renata's eyes brighter, more rounded and alert - those eyes would hold an intense scrutiny as if to judge whether she wanted to know you, whilst Brigitte's faintly oriental, almond eyes flashed a look of hunger at you when she turned on her determined smile. It was possible, Ned fancied, to be reduced to a cinder by basking too long in that smile. One of the crewmen had called Brigitte a 'siren', and such a description may have been unchallengeable. Clearly, however, both the sisters were regarded in local society as distinctive beauties, something Ned had never imagined on his early acquaintance of Otto.

For several weeks Ned had now known and observed the sisters. Known and admired, and secretly desired - such a secret that not one of the Bremme family was unaware of it. It could not be denied, though it was neither polite nor practical as Ned's first loyalty was to his friend. And yet, here was Otto positively encouraging interaction with his sisters, almost as if Otto deemed them his to give away! Yet Ned's desires fought with feelings of his own inadequacy, his poor education and status. He spoke rarely of that, and the family never pried.

Today in their own household Brigitte had left her glorious hair unfettered. Neither had Renata turned up her hair as a respectable woman would but had let it fall, tied at the back with a thin dark blue ribbon that matched her frock. It was something all three men might take note of, though it was merely the way she felt today – something in the weather, no doubt, was pressing the men to divest their waistcoats.

At the table, Ned sat between the girls, and rather daringly tried a little French in an effort to impress that he was not altogether the English bumpkin M. Forget might think he was.

"*Une fleur parmi les fleurs*," he offered, pointing at himself. There was mild amusement, it was the poorest whimsy. *No more rotten comedy*, Ned chastised himself.

* * * * *

"Yes, oh yes," said M. Jerome in the mildest of accented English, "you will find Fécamp very pleasant, monsieur. It is not far along the coast here."

"It gets busy, Fécamp," Otto butted in. "Very popular place this time of the year, what. We were all there last summer."

M. Jerome was not to be put down. "The Fécamp coast is very like your coast of England, Ned. You would like very much, I know. And have you seen Honfleur?"

"No. I've not really seen anywhere around here – "

"Ah, but you must go to Honfleur. It's enchanting! Isn't it enchanting, Renata? In all of France, there is no sweeter place. It's a wonderful old harbour, very much admired by painters. Not painters that I like personally, you understand – today, they are all tapping the paint here and splashing it there, it's not a proper way to paint at all, but they sit all day and paint. Who will buy that foolish nonsense? But you should go, you can take a boat there. Take Brigitte, she will show you."

"Gitta has been already," Otto put in, quickly adding, "We were all there last summer. "

"Yes," remarked Brigitte, more than a little disinterested, "In the rain." Otto frowned. *"Halte Schnauze!"* he said to her quietly.

"I have said – er, *pardon*, I have promised Mlle. Renata that we should go into Rouen next month, *n'est-ce pas*, Renata?" She affirmed, though with little enthusiasm. "I have some business, and there are bookshops there, important bookshops. Rouen has great history, Ned. You should go there. Brigitte would like to go there, I am sure."

Brigitte said nothing and reached for a small piece of gateaux.

"And we were all there last summer!" quipped Otto, his infectious sense of humour turning up the corners of his mouth. Renata flashed a look at him.

"But I do not agree about the painters." Brigitte was not happy to leave it there. "You know, Monsieur Monet was here, in the town, and has had success with his work."

"Impressions!" countered M. Jerome, "That word says everything. It is like he pushed a cloth around the canvas! They are not good paintings, just 'impressions' as they have been called. They made our town look awful."

"But no! I do not think that, monsieur." Under her waves of light hair, Brigitte's narrowed blue eyes tore into the fabric of the afternoon, such that Renata placed a hand on her wrist.

"Chère mademoiselle, they are using that name for the music now – 'impressionist'. Pah! *C'est fou - ridicule!"*

"Rouen is where ze English burned Jeanne d'Arc," Otto put in gleefully, unwilling to have his playful mood diminished.

"Otto!" cried Renata.

"Ja. *Wirklich*! It's true. Ze English burned Jeanne d'Arc at Rouen. Ned doesn't worry, do you, Ned?"

The young Englishman gulped and spluttered at his claret. "Worry? Why should I mind? Hey – I didn't do it, Otto – honestly, it wasn't me!" That gave the two men something to laugh at, even the quiet Frau Bremme had to cover a smile.

"Jeanne d'Arc was foolish!" They were all surprised to hear Renata say that.

"She was foolish, *La Pucelle*. If she had told the court at Rouen that God told her she would be – what is that word? – punished – er, no – that she would be made guilty by ze English and made to death, they would have not burned her. She should have said, 'God told me you are going to kill me.' And then ..... to make the trial - *trial*, Ned, is that right? - to trial her and to kill her would mean she was right, and God had told her truly. That is heresy, ja? Heresy, Ned? – Somesing that is very bad in the bible, yes? – Okay. And the English judges could not kill her if God had told her they were going to kill her – because she would have been right. *Comprenez?* She had received the word of God."

There was a silence. M. Jerome scowled.

"So...." Renata looked down as if studying her hands. "I think she was foolish. Anyway.... That is my... opinion."

"Yes!" It was Ned who broke the silence. "Yes! *Tu as raison*, Reina. I believe you.*"

More silence.

"Yes," said Renata, with a sort of defiant bob of the head. "Thank you, Ned."

For Ned, it was more than that. Standing there in the sunlight, Renata's beauty was something that heretofore he could hardly have dared acknowledge. Aphrodite at her most radiant could scarcely have filled him with greater desire. It was as if a switch had been thrown somewhere in his soul: his mouth had fallen open, and what's more Renata noticed that it had.

Brigitte, however, felt it was time to move the theme along. "Bernhardt played Jeanne d'Arc."

No-one responded. They knew Brigitte's fixation with Sarah Bernhardt: even Ned had been impressed by the Mucha pictures.

"She looked like a boy," Brigitte went on, "I sink she liked to play boys."

"Why not?" mused Otto to humour her.

"She played Hamlet..... Zanetto. She was good as boys. It's wonderful zat her voice was so fragile but so full of.... passion."

"It's funny, ja?" remarked Otto, "In ze plays of your Shakespeare, Ned, all ze girls were boys dressed as girls!" He laughed, until he caught the look from Ned, and suddenly realised the parallel with Ned's recent predicament.

"She has to walk with a stick now." Brigitte rescued the situation without knowing it, but she was really having a conversation with herself. "I saw her get on one of ze ships. Here, in ze harbour. She was going to America too, to make a play about your Queen Elizabeth, Ned."

He knew nothing of this and merely gave a vacant look under an inclined head, embarrassed by his total lack of knowledge of the arts.

"Zey made moving pictures of zis play," Brigitte enthused, but she knew no-one was interested in her girlish obsessions and fell silent.

The talk was now becalmed and Otto looked across at his sisters. Perhaps without realising it, Ned had said the right thing. *Tu as raison, Reina.* Otto sat back in his chair: it was about time Ned became a little more open and he felt comfortable with that.

Yet Otto was not comfortable in his seat for much longer. M.Forget in his opinion was taking up too much of Renata's time, and Renata, fifteen years his junior, could make a better match if she would allow herself to relax her outlook. Frau Bremme had not been one to sit on the fence either: above all else, she considered her daughters' happiness. Renata was afraid that at some point either her mother or her brother were going to embarrass her with M.

Forget or his fellows. She had, after all, to think carefully of her position at the school: if that were to lapse, she would probably have to go much further afield to find work, and for all Otto's bluster, Renata knew the family would find it difficult to cope if she lost her position. Frau Bremme saw all of this too: she was wise enough to maintain her silence.

M. Jerome Forget was not the man of Renata's dreams. No. She had no vision of laying with him nor even undressing in front of him. Yet a woman had to maintain all her options, even those less tasteful ones, and in that sense M. Jerome no doubt had more to offer than most. An excellent position, good connections: he was more likely than most to face a settled, comfortable future. Nor was he entirely repulsive, one had to be grateful for that and one soon learns to ignore a person's annoying little characteristics. As to children, M. Jerome had never touched on the matter, and Renata felt she would be well able to control that situation when it arose. Children would moderate whatever feelings she might or might not have for the man himself, all women knew this. For the present, she kept him content with her attention to his school matters and tended to all the paperwork and the bureaucracy that he preferred to eschew. For his part, M. Jerome enjoyed the companionship of a young lady not only a capable teacher and secretary but regarded by his associates as a most suitable and attractive extension to his arm, one that through her obvious intelligence and grace would fit his social standing.

Of her family origins, few would pass remarks on the capacity of Germans to irritate any Frenchman, but it was, after all, 1912. And to those not familiar with the family, Renata was as French as M. Jerome's family might desire.

As the poor Cognac – for so Frau Bremme described it – passed around the table, debate on cultural and social issues replaced the more mundane talk of the moment, with M. Forget keen to impress on present company his interest in the arts and general social graces. France in his view enjoyed a pivotal role on the world stage: a

Frenchman had shown the world how to fly, a Frenchman had shown the world the magic of film and the cinema, French doctors brought medicine into the 20th century, Paris had outshone the world with *la Tour Eiffel*, in the Arts and sciences France led the world.

"It's true," concluded Forget, "It's why I am a patriot!"

"*Natürlich*," responded Frau Bremme in a quiet voice, and muttered something in German. Otto laughed mischievously.

"What did she say?" asked Ned of Brigitte whilst Forget was distracted by Renata.

"She said, when a country is doing well, everyone is a patriot. When a country is not doing well, all the patriots become politicians and complain how the patriots have ruined everything."

Notwithstanding the fact Forget had no political stomach for that weak southern Republican jack-in-the-box Fallières, it was nevertheless, he stressed, a good time to be French. Besides, Forget was convinced Poincaré would soon be the man in power and then "a few sparks will be flying!"

"Huh, flying!" Otto dismissed the idea. "What would that be good for? Look at that American woman who followed that idiot Blériot and crossed *La Manche* on a flying machine – it killed her!"

"Ah but," continued M. Forget, "France has so many more heroes. Look at our writers and musicians....."

"Bravo!" exclaimed Brigitte, clapping superciliously, "But you yourself listen to Beethoven and Mozart and Haydn and Wagner."

"Yes, I do," came the reply. "They are the masters."

" – And German," Brigitte slipped in quietly.

"But yes," Forget searched for a response, "And look at Herr Strauss and the mess he made of that 'Salome' – that was a complete disgrace. Kissing a cut head – what do you say in English, Ned? – Chopped head? With blood all over! That is how your Germans are behaving now. *Dégoutant!*"

"True," Renata jumped in to mollify the conversation. "You are right, Jerome, it was disgusting. Although personally I like very much what M. Debussy is doing with music."

"Debussy? Him? Ach!......" Forget waved a hand in the air and wiped his nose. "*Mais oui*.... Better Debussy than that idiot fellow Schoenberg. Today it's noise, all bad noise. *Regardez* – that is another German!"

"*Non*," Brigitte responded quietly. "*Autriche*."

Forget waved a hand dismissively again. "Tell me, Otto, what do you think?"

The semi-comatose Otto suddenly became aware that a conversation had been going on. Momentarily, he looked about him, his blinking eyes coming to rest on Ned, who had not uttered a word for five minutes.

"*Je suis d'accord avec Ned*!" said Otto, and belched.

* * * * *

The afternoon had become hot and still, keeping Brigitte busy with the lemonade.

"But what do you mean? - That Ned saved the life of your friend?"

"Friend?" Otto's face puffed out. "*Er ist nicht mein Freund – überhaupt nicht*!....."

"*Aber* –" His mother did not understand Otto's indignation.

"They don't like each other," put in Ned with a gesture of the hands, meaning to infer that it was a stupid and pointless enmity.

"But you saved his life?" asked Brigitte, begging further information.

Ned squirmed a little in his seat. "No, I – "

"Ja!" cried Otto. "Ja, Ned – you did dat. You did. You saved his life, what. Look – he could not swim."

"Yes, but –"

"No! No 'but', my friend, you jumped into ze water and you saved him. Hells's bells! You. You did."

"This is true, Ned?" asked Brigitte.

A long sigh followed a heaving of Ned's shoulders. "Well...."

"Tell zem, Ned! Tell zem!"

"Well – "

110

"He jumped into ze sea and swam to Pabst. And ze ozzer men threw them ze life – er, ze life.....er - "

"Lifebuoys," said Ned. "Look. Pabst went into the water: ah were the first to see it, so ah jumped in and managed to keep 'is 'ead above the water until the lines got to us. It's very simple."

"Simple, Ned? No, no, no, my friend. I tell you – I would not have done zat!"

"Yes, but – you don't like Dieter Pabst, Otto."

Otto scratched his head and wrinkled up his face. "Ja," he agreed, "True."

"*À cause de quoi?*" asked Renata.

Otto gave his big shrug of the upper body.

"It's not important," remarked Ned. "In a way, it saved Pabst from serious discipline. He was drunk, and if you're caught drunk on duty you would normally be dismissed."

"Ja. But you jumped in ze water. You did it!"

"Where was this, please?" asked M. Forget.

"Here. We had just left the roadstead outside the harbour. Luckily it was a calm day – just a couple of weeks ago – "

"Two weeks, Otto!" Brigitte exclaimed, "And you didn't say anything to us?"

"You want me to post a notice in ze *Palais de Justice*? We crossed to New York! I could not shout back from ze ship! I told Mutti yesterday. Zat's all. Ned did not want to say anything."

"Well," continued Ned. "Pabst had some bad news from his brother. We didn't know, of course: Pabst hardly speaks to anyone, does he, Otto? His mother was ill, she wasn't expected to live long. He could've gone home, but ah think he must have been afraid of what he might find - "

"And so," Otto interrupted, "Pabst got drunk ze night before we sail, and still bad in ze morning, he could not serve *Frühstück*. So he would have been dismissed."

"Yes, but.... He didn't jump, did he, Otto? He were drunk and he fell off the ladder an' stumbled into that chap. Ah think the feller threw him away - he went flyin' one way an' Pabst went the other –

111

right over the guard rail. It's easily done." *So easily*, thought Ned, *that I did it myself, in a sense.*

Renata was horrified. "The sea outside Le Havre here? But that is dangerous, Ned."

"Ja," agreed Otto, "Because there are strong – *qu'est-ce-que c'est* - ? – erm, force in ze water?"

"Currents," advised Ned.

"Uh? - Zose little fruits you put in ze – "

"Currents!" snapped the Englishman, "Currents in the water – tides....."

Otto made a sign that he now understood.

"But it were a fine day," continued Ned, "with no wind to speak of. He might've drowned otherwise."

Thoughtful for a moment, Ned may have been holding up a mirror to his own experience.

"*Mon dieu!*" M.Forget had finally become animated. "You saved this man from the sea! He did not swim?"

"No, he didn't swim. You'd be surprised how many blokes at sea can't swim. Nobody thinks about it – you're on a ship."

"But you swim."

"Yes." Embarrassed by the questions, Ned felt a need for levity. "When ah first signed on the *Orlania*, they said, Can yer swim, lad? – An' ah said, Why? – haven't yer got any ships?"

Except for Ned, nobody laughed.

"Pabst went to ze hospital," said Otto. "He broke an arm."

"Fractured," corrected Ned.

"Fractured. Ja. Okay. He could not work. He is very lucky, Ned. He is lucky zat you saw him – "

"Ah heard him shout."

"But because of.... zis matter wiz his mother, Captain Genoud has said he would not execute him."

"Fire him," corrected the Englishman.

"Ned, will you stop making me look foolish, please!"

"Genoud is a good man," said Ned, reflectively. "Matter of fact, it *were* ruddy cold an' all..... But one good thing came out of it – we now know Pabst can speak English!"

"Pabst don't like English," added Otto, licking his lips over some cake. "Because he think English and Americans are all ze same, and Americans make a joke wiz him because they have a beer called Pabst Blue, and so zey call him 'Bluebottle'..... you said in English zat is a *mouche*, Ned - a fly?"

"Yes."

Otto found it funnier than before. "*Stubenfliege*!.... It's a funny language, Ned - English!"

* * * * *

Around 4 in the afternoon, M. Jerome ceremoniously drew out the chain of his watch and flicked open the face. "*Je dois partir; je m'excuse, cherie.*" He wiped his nose, then his forehead.

Renata decided she would take a walk with him, at which Ned felt now would be a good time to leave also: "Duty evening at the ship."

As they walked down toward the town, all the polite conversation was issuing from M. Jerome, until the point that M. Jerome turned, squeezed his eyes up behind his glasses, then kissed Renata three times on the cheeks. After being assured that Renata would be alright walking back, and tipping his hat to Ned, he excused himself.

They stood, Renata and Ned, for half a minute whilst Forget turned a corner by a church and disappeared.

"Well," said Ned, "Come on, ah'll walk you back to the house."

"You..... You will walk me back to the house?"

"Of course."

"We just came down from there."

"Yes."

"But Ned, I shall be alright going back. And you – you have to get back to the ship."

"Yes. Ah do. But not until eight o'clock."

"Eight o'clock? You lied!"

"No, ah didn't. Ah just said ah had an evening duty. Ah didn't say when."

She shuffled a foot from side to side as if imitating a clock. Amused, Ned looked down at the way the hem of her skirt flicked and flounced.   After several moments she lifted her inclined head, smiled and quietly said, "*Tu es fou*, Ned...... Alright. We go back to the house."

So they turned around and began walking back, a little more slowly than they had descended, with Ned listening to the pattern of her tap-tap-tap on the paving stones and savouring every note.

They made small talk. "You missed the Tour de France while you were away," she told him. He knew nothing of any Tour de France.

"It was good. I took some pictures.... you know? Bicycles?"

"Bicycles. Oh. Who won?"

"I don't know – an Italian. It was the last.... what you say? – anyway, the last tour before Paris. They finish in Paris."

"Oh. So who won?"

"I don't know."   Both smiled at the inconsequence of the conversation.

"But you took pictures."

"Yes. I like to take pictures. I have a camera. Little one. I show you, Ned. I have *two* cameras! – Little one and big one. Ze big one belong to ze school. I teach you. You can take pictures. Be very clever."

"I would like that."   And that seemed enough, they fell silent again.

Walking beside her now, and despite one or two other people in the torpid quiet of the street, it became as if they were alone, in a kind of vacuum together. He held his head low, in a desperate thoughtfulness, searching for things to say that would explain himself without giving offence. In his peripheral vision, the kick and sway of her long skirt as she walked was an intoxication in itself, far more than liquor or the heat of the afternoon, and he listened for the short swish of her petticoat under her skirt.

It felt new, though. Ned had begun to feel that something had changed. Something that had been building up in him over many weeks had broken into bud. His action had been a reflex: if he had chosen it, it could only be his desire, nurtured in gentle stages in the hasty interludes that had been afforded him by his ship's periods in the harbour.

114

Enveloped by the quiet street, they said nothing, merely exchanging glances and cautious smiles that sought to probe what the other was thinking, yet failing to prompt more than the most mundane of remarks.

After passing up another street, at the corner, Renata stopped to rest and turned squarely toward him, squeezing her unshaded eyes tighter against the sunlight and pressing her lips together. There were things he felt he should say to her, yet had no idea where to begin.

"Why, Ned?"

"Why what?"

Her head was inclined, the sun glinted off her hair for she had chosen not to wear her hat, and her narrowed eyes were piercing him now from a lower angle, probing his sincerity, questioning his reason.

"Why, Ned?"

"Because..... Don't you know?"

She thought for a few seconds about that. "Ja. I think so...... It's not a good idea."

"I.... Ah thought it were a very good idea." Suddenly, he felt short of breath, the beats in his chest had doubled.

"No. Not a good idea. We do not know – "

" - But... there are lots of things we don't know. Ah'm sorry this is sudden, Reina - it just entered my head. One thing ah've learned in my short time: ah've learned life is something that can be snatched away from yer – just like that!" He extended a hand toward her and closed his fist abruptly. "One minute yer life is so tidy and the next – bang! – it's all turned upside down, and yer've lost it all. So if yer really want something, yer have to say so. Now. Yer have to do it now. That's what ah think. Ah may not say the right words, Reina, but ah know what ah mean."

She thought about that. "Ned.... Gitta likes you very much, you know."

"And I like her. She's lovely, your sister. But ah'm not lookin' at Gitta, she's not up here – in me head. Or here in... well, in my heart. You... are what's in my head. And .... Ah'm with you,

Reina, an' ah feel different.   Ah can't help what ah feel. Ah'm lookin' at you and all ah can see is........ you're the most amazing woman I ever knew...... An' ah have to say what ah feel now because if ah don't ..... well, ah'm back at sea and time's run out." He was babbling furiously in a desperate rush to get it all out of his mouth at once. "An' until this afternoon, ah didn't dare say what ah felt.....
"

Renata was biting a lip. His pain was not lost on her.

"An' now .... Ah can't bear the thought of bein' away from yer. Ah know it's not polite to say these things, but – ah haven't got time to say it otherwise, have ah?   Ah'll be gone again soon.   Can y'understand?"

She nodded. He realised he had been shaking all the way through. Regaining some composure, he imagined he had said all the wrong things it was possible to say.

"Ah've a poor way of showin' it,   Reina, ah know that.   But honestly, it's you that I want.   It's.... well, it's you.   Do yer.... do y'understand? Ah'm sorry ah say it so badly."

For an achingly long few moments, as Ned tried to retrieve his breath, Renata only looked at him nervously; then she looked around her in the cobbled street, deliberating her next words.

"You know, Ned, we like you. Gitta and me - we like you very much.   You are Otto's best friend... And that is good.... But love," said Renata eventually.   "..... You did not say anything about love....."

Ned's face drained. "No," he agreed, and thought desperately. "You're right, ah didn't..... Ah didn't want to sound stupid by saying all sorts o' daft things..... Ah wanted ter sound..... Sensible.... Ah wanted to just say what me heart feels..... Hoping you'd understand..... And ah suppose ah didn't say it very well. Ah'm sorry."

For many moments they stood apart, looking at each other, nothing more, then Renata nodded again. "Yes, Ned. I understand..... And....I don't want you to go back to sea either. But....."

Her remark brought a surprise warmth to him inside, even though he was not quite sure how he should take it. As he drew a long breath, he thought about what had been said for some moments, and Renata thought about it too, and wondered if she could have used better words. Then they walked on, more slowly than ever. His hand wanted to reach out for hers, but could not. There was no invitation.

To an extent, he was pleased that he had expressed his feelings at all, but yet.... her words at best said neither one thing nor the other, and ultimately, Ned felt most dissatisfied with himself.

* * * * *

FOURTEEN

The Grapes looked no different, nor should it have done, and the beer was still too warm for Ned's liking, but it was the right sort of place to go to have a chance of meeting old faces. Seafarers migrated from ship to ship, it was perfectly feasible old shipmates could end up on any of the hulks in port at that time.

Arriving in Southampton on the *Alberta*, which crossed regularly from Le Havre, Ned had spent a night at a poor lodging on the grubbier edge of the town before going again to the docks to observe what ships were berthed there. It was as cold now as it had been wet all through the summer. Le Havre at least had been graced with some warm sunshine in August, though he had wished for a return of 1911's golden days. Were it not for Le Havre and the Bremme girls there, all things considered Ned was ready to write off 1912 altogether, for never had a year seemed so cold and wet and gloomy. With a steady income now, though, he had replenished clothing and other necessities.

This journey had taken on a kind of mystical resonance: at the top of the Cherbourg peninsula, he fancied he had seen the *Nomadic* hugging the shore line, the tender which had delivered so many souls aboard *Titanic* on its maiden voyage. It was no such thing, of course, merely an indication of the damage done to his psyche.

He had done the obvious thing, walking to Oxford Street to make enquiries at the Sailors' Home and the taverns thereabouts.

The Sailors' Home was a sought-after residence. Its ornate edifice that lent an illusion of grand military status to those who held it as their permanent address. The old caretaker knew several of *Titanic*'s crew had lodged there, he knew each one by sight, and knew also that they had not returned. It was, he said, "a cryin' shame - Wish I could 'elp you, son. Try the Alliance, or the Grapes, or the Platform."

Ned went to the old Alliance Hotel on the corner: decorated copiously with shamrocks, it was frequented by Irishmen, but not of the friendly variety he had found in New York. Afraid to push his luck, he went from there to the Grapes, where a barman found one or two of the names familiar and suggested he return in the evening, which he did.

Harry Fenby had been a fireman aboard *Orlania* for over two years. Each barely knew the other but Harry remembered Ned from a card game they had shared, because Harry and his friend had taken all the money from the young Ned and Walter. It was Harry who tapped Ned on the shoulder that evening as he leaned against one of the great pillars that grew out of the bar.

"Wotcha, cock. Tom Ackroyd, innit?"

Fenby weighed up the face and realised his mistake. "Ah...... No. Where do I know you from, mate?"

"*Orlania.*"

"Yeh. S'right. Yer face I remember, can't remember yer name, though."

"Thornton."

"Thornton... Edward Thornton? That snotty kid that went about with Tollivant? Strike me, it is!"

"Ned Thornton. Yes."

"Blimey!" Fenby stood upright, almost falling back. "Well it is, an' no mistake. Blimey!" Fenby was a Londoner and had the appearance of one. He looked around 40 although was probably barely 30 and, quite apart from his clothing pulled up tight into his neckerchief, his face held a kind of ingrained sooty texture that his grand walrus moustache had no chance of concealing.

"You...." Not knowing quite what to say, Fenby stroked his stubbly chin and pushed his moustache up, a habit he repeated constantly. "You're in trouble, Thornton. Aintcha?" Ned did not bother to acknowledge the fact and let Fenby carry on.

"Where you bin anyhow? The word got around the whole of this place. White Star put down some nasty stuff about you – you know that, don't yer?"

"Ah do."

"I..... I'm not sure I should be talkin' to you, mate."

"It's not true, Harry," Ned cut in swiftly. "It's a pack o' lies. They stitched me up. Somebody has it in for me."

Deciding to install himself onto a high stool, Fenby settled against the woodwork and nodded to the sullen barman, who seemed to know what he wanted and delivered a brimming glass, which Fenby attacked with a will before whipping the back of his hand through his frothed-up moustache.

Ned gestured for them both to sit at a table under a window with its fancy cut glass motifs, away from general ear-shot.

"They got it in for yer?" Fenby made no secret of his scepticism. "Do they now?..... Why would that be, then? The word was, you got off a certain sinkin' ship under a woman's skirts. I heard it all. Don't try tellin' me a load o' rowlocks, Thornton."

"It's lies, Harry. It's all lies. Ah was unconscious almost the whole time. Ah don't know nothin' about blokes gettin' away in women's clothes, the newspapers were jumpin' at all sorts of straws and mekkin up a load o' nonsense. Look, an oar hit me on the head. Knocked me stupid. See – see the scar..... A girl put 'er coat over me after they pulled me out the water. Ah bloody well wish she hadn't now..... Ah knew nothing about them lies till after we got into New York."

"Yeh? Straight up?..... You didn't do it, then? That what yer tellin' me?"

"God's truth, man. Someone put the bad word around. Somebody got to White Star and the newspapers. Somebody with money an' muscle. Ah've an idea who, but ah can't prove nothin'."

Fenby drank deeply, discharging half the glass into his moustache, wiped a forearm across his face and sat for a while puffing on his pipe and pushing a charred finger in to try to get it going.

Eventually he rumbled quietly, "Takin' a chance, aren't you, mush?"

"'Appen so. Ah need to talk to White Star."

"And?"

"Ah'm goin' round Canute Chambers tomorrer."

Fenby made a grimace. "I don't fancy yer chances, mate. Look, it ain't none of my business, but folks here say that London board of enquiry was a whitewash - "

"Aye, that's for sure."

"Yair but, the point is, they got the law on their side: if White Star says you're guilty, you're guilty."

"Is that what you say, Harry?"

"Me?...." Harry puffed slowly at his tobacco. "White Star and Cunard put the bread on most o' the tables around 'ere, you know that. Knock on any door from 'ere to Northam, you wouldn't find a soul to back you up. Don't ask a local for an opinion, lad. That business with *Olympic* back in May, that were a one-off, a lot o' them lads suffered for it, they wouldn't try fightin' White Star again, so yer'll find no comfort around 'ere... I wouldn't say you were a villain, no. Yer never struck me as havin' a yeller streak. If you're daft enough to go chasin' 'em, maybe you're telling the truth – a guilty man'd run away and keep runnin'."

"Yes," agreed Ned. "Yes, he would. Ah didn't do nothin', Harry. Just got bad luck."

"Bad luck? – Huh! Bloody good luck, I'd say, if you survived *Titanic* goin' down. Hundreds didn't, poor buggers. Women an' kids too. It's been bad around 'ere, Ned, I can tell yer. Like death itself, most of these streets – yer'll do well to find a house that didn't lose somebody. So don't you tell me about bad luck."

Shaking his head, Fenby went on as if talking to himself. "Kids without parents. Parents without kids. Bad business.... " He scratched his crotch and looked around as he puffed his pipe.

"Truth is, Ned, them blokes what survived *Titanic*, nobody wants 'em. You think that's a queer thing? It ain't just you: folk around the dock reckon they're bad omens. You know what seafaring folk are like. Nobody wants to take ship with a bad omen. So it ain't just you."

Ned bit his lip. "Ah can understand that, Harry. But it's not the same. They've blacklisted me. Ah got no Discharge Book, no conduct record; 'ow can ah sign on another ship? Ah've got to find out why they done it. Ah just want to clear me name so's ah can walk tall again an' work on a British ship. For me family too. You can understand that."

Harry alternately puffed his pipe and sipped his beer, looking about the room as if it would help crystallize his opinion.

"Alright, Ned, I've a feelin' yer tellin' the truth. There's few folk around 'ere that'd grant you that, mind – yer'll need to watch yer back. Chances are, nobody here knows what yer look like, and I ain't gonna say nuthin, but you watch yer back all the same. An' don't go bringin' me into nuthin neither. I don't want it known that I used to play cards with the chap what turned out to be the biggest turd in the pot."

Ned regarded Harry with a frown at first, then his face relaxed as he realised Harry's dilemma.

"So you go sort yerself out, mister, alright?..... Look, I can't help yer meself, and I wouldn't anyway in case my skipper got wind of it, but if yer want to meet me here on Friday night, I'll find out what I can. The wife's sister's hubbie works for the railway – you know the London and South West office down the way? They own my ship an' all, come to that. 'Ere, fancy 'avin' a ship with the same name as the wife, eh? – 'Alma'! Straight up! Anyhow, they're allus talkin' to the lads at White Star 'cos of the ships the railway runs. He's got mates in there. Maybe there's summat to find out, maybe not."

"Friday...... Can that be Saturday, Harry? It only gives me five days. Ah've got stuff to do, like..... "   The other man nodded, jabbed his pipe back in his mouth and pulled his moustache out from underneath.

"Alright, lad. Saturday.   Same time. Not later, though – ship sails on Sunday afternoon – Spain, I hope – borin', eh? "

"Thanks, Harry. Pint?"

"Naah. Gotta be off, lad. Missus wants 'er share o' the old man before I go gaddin' off to get meself some oranges. Serve me right fer 'aving the biggest cock this side o' Nelson's column.   Ey? Anyway, you watch yerself. Grow a 'tache, that might 'elp yer. And some sideburns.   Around 'ere yer stand out like an extra tit. Saturday..... Toodle-ooh!"

* * * * *

It's a generally known feeling that, when you have been wrongly accused of something, you sense that everyone around you regards you as a criminal. Ned could not wait to get away from Southampton. With his kit bag dangling and slapping at his shoulder in a way that might well have had the words 'Titanic Fugitive On The Run' inscribed on it, he hurried to the station to catch an early afternoon train. Every eye seemed to follow him as he passed, and the man at the ticket counter took far too long in issuing the ticket, peering downward as if he had discovered his fly buttons were undone.

The London train was at the platform, Ned found a compartment that was empty and pulled at the leather strop to close the window, hoping no-one else would enter. But a well-dressed man and woman did enter. Politely acknowledging Ned, they conversed intimately at one end of the compartment as Ned stared out of the window at the other. In between times he would look at his Jules Verne novel, but in truth barely read half a page. He was, at least, virtually alone with his thoughts and felt the pressure lifted from his shoulders when the whistle finally blew and the carriages lurched noisily forward to the din of the panting engine.

Apart from a rather smelly individual boarding the train at Basingstoke, it remained that way until Waterloo station, from where Ned crossed to Cockspur Street by tram.

He had been prompted to travel to the White Star offices at Cockspur Street since his enquiry at Canute Chambers that Monday morning had been totally ineffective. There at Canute, in a confusion of small rooms rather like a merchant's counting house, the White Star clerk had merely asked, "What ship?" and nothing else. This man sported a beard at least two sizes too big for him that seemed to want of bowl of milk offered to it.

When Ned had replied, *"Titanic"*, the clerk had looked long at him, then got up, consulted a bank of volumes on the wall shelves, and pulled out a binder overflowing with loose papers. After organising the binder, he then with an insistent bobbing of his beard

123

asked Ned's name, at the mention of which the man simply put the binder down and gazed at the enquirer as though he were something that had crawled out of the Solent to cause a dreadful stench. Ned took off his cap, having forgotten his manners.

"Thornton," the clerk slowly turned over in his mouth, then got up, disappeared into another office to speak to a colleague and returned a minute later only to inform Ned, "Mr. Curry is not here," and if he wished to pursue the matter he should present himself at Oceanic House in Westminster. At which point, Ned realised he should no longer be surprised at anything that happened hereafter.

So here he now was, in the middle of London and somewhat overawed, for the Cockspur Street chambers were a palace - precisely the impression they intended to convey. Here White Star, Canadian Pacific, Cunard and Hamburg-America lines all showboated their grand aspirations to the gentry in gross ostentation. Here the most esteemed of customers could have their servants drop off their luggage and find it again safely awaiting their arrival in their cabin aboard ship at Southampton. Much like the ships themselves, here the chambers mimicked the style of Ritz lounge suites, a style more after Louis XVI than Edwardian England, but the whole calculation behind this facade was to reaffirm the status of wealthy potential customers and the plutocrats who had become the new aristocracy.

To Ned's provincial eyes, the White Star rooms seemed more like the chambers of a law court – experience of which Ned had had just once, for the offence of being an accessory to theft of a cabbage. If ever Ned felt like a complete fish out of water, it was here and now. What was he doing in this place? - He must have been out of his mind!

Using a mirror to straighten himself up, he saw that the round tabs of his collar were soiled yet he had no spare collar with him. He took off his cap, and his brown hair was as it was when he had got out of bed. He put the cap on again, took it off again, and yet again put it on. Dabbing at the ends of his hair with spittle was not something that would impress here.

A well-dressed lady swished her way through to a large oak-panelled ante room, looking over a shoulder as Ned followed. She rustled so loudly that it amused him to wonder whether she had overdone the starch. The ante room was lit with electric light but otherwise was cold and silent and empty save for two walls lined with bookshelves, and around the periphery of the room, a collection of glass cases on stands, each holding a model of a White Star ship.

"Please be seated," she told Ned. He thanked her and did so, placing his small, grubby kit bag on the floor and removing his cap once again. *'At least'*, he thought, *'that's a civil start'*.

All the same, it had already struck Ned from the calm way in which he had been received that they must have had forewarning of his coming. Never had he imagined he could be that important!

The lady took a seat far opposite, under the only window, and both waited silently for almost five minutes before a man in a mid-grey morning suit entered from a different door, finishing off a conversation with someone in the next room as he did so. He placed his cane and top hat on the larger desk and stood in the middle of the room.

Coughing, he began, "You are Thornton, I take it."

"Edward Thornton, yes." He declined to append the word "sir", which was noticed but not commented on. For Ned immediately felt a hostility here and was determined not to be distracted by it.

"Thornton, I am Edward Fox-Fellowes. I am a senior colleague of the White Star Line, have you heard of me?"

"No, I have not, sir," Ned replied in his most polite English. "Ah'm pleased to make your acquaintance." Fellowes coughed again and cleared his throat.

"I take it, Thornton, you know your situation...."

"No. Situation in regard to what?"

"You are – I will get straight to the point – so far as this steamship company is concerned, Thornton, you are *persona non grata*."

"Ey? Is that Latin? Ah'm sorry, ah don't know any Latin except what's in the hymn books."

"It means, Mr. Thornton, you are undesirable employee material."

"Undesirable?"

"Has it not been made abundantly clear to you that you are not welcome as an employee of White Star?"

"And with Cunard, can ah tell yer. Ah were there this mornin' and got a pretty off-handed reception for no good reason. Ah probably couldn't get a job wi' the Isle o' Wight ferry just now. Seems ah'm 'undesirable' to all English lines. Why, ah should like to know."

"You don't know? You obstinate little man, you do know!" Fellowes' well-groomed head shook dismissively as he chastised the young man.

"No. Ah don't. Ah just know as 'ow ah can't get employment, and that ah put down to you lot."

"Don't be impertinent, Thornton!"

"Impertinent? Ah do know the meanin' o' that word. Well, you try signin' on a ship with my name an' see what 'appens. Ah didn't get me Discharge Book neither. An' that's not right."

Fellowes was ill at ease. He had already determined that this conversation should be at an end by now.

"So the question, yer lordship, is why ah'm bein' treated like a plague carrier. Ah were a good employee on board *Titanic*. And *Olympic* before that. So why?"

"Because of your behaviour, Thornton, in saving your own skin during the *Titanic* incident. Surely you know your offence only too well, and now you are being surly and obstinate. Miss Washburn, I trust you are getting this properly minuted."

The lady nodded under her huge bob of hair, peering at him over her spectacles whilst continuing to write in her notebook.

"Aye," added Ned, standing up, "An' I hope she is, an' all. Because so far ah've not heard from you any reason why ah've been blacklisted from White Star and other English lines. Maybe Miss Washburn'd like to know the reason too." Her reaction was microscopic.

126

Fellowes paced the room, hands behind his back clutching white gloves: Ned was holding him up.

"My behaviour, Mr. Fellowes – sir – is simple to tell, just as ah told it to the board of enquiry in New York, and they seemed happy enough. Ah were half-dead in a lifeboat an' a lady put a coat over me. That were some breach of etiquette or whatever yer call it."

"That is not the story our source conveyed to us – "

"Ah! Now we're gettin' somewhere! What 'source' might that be, yer lordship?"

Fellowes stopped pacing, stood menacingly in front of Ned and directed a vivid gaze at the taller young man. "I am not at liberty to say."

"Not at liberty....? Yer put me in the dock and tell me ah'm not to know my accusor? Ah've a right to know what ah've done wrong!" Ned was aware of the pace of his breathing and the heat in his breast.

"That is privileged information. You are being impertinent and should know better. You show a total lack of respect, Thornton."

"Respect? Oh. An' me, ah'm not privileged enough fer yer information? Ah'm just a ruddy skivvy that nobody gives a damn about. Ah'm supposed to doff me cap and run away with me tail between me legs and say, 'Thank you, sir, three bags full, sir'."

"That will do, Thornton!"

"What will do? *'That will do'*, indeed? It most certainly will not do, sir! It's not right and seems to me to be downright bad manners, at the very least."

"Enough! I will not be spoken to in this way!"

"If ah'm not in your employ no more, ah'll speak ter yer as one man to another. An' ah've always respected me betters – nah, then! But in what way do ah need to speak to yer to find out why an innocent man is being persecuted by an unseen person or persons, not to mention the whole of the White Star company? This is the law of the gibbet, yer lordship, not a question of what's right and what's wrong. You're using me as yer scapegoat to draw attention away from yer pride and joy goin' to the bottom o' the ocean, an' you need somebody to take the heat off yer."

127

"Quite enough, Thornton! This interview is at an end!"

"Aye. An' so it is, that's plain enough. But yer wouldn't be sayin' that if ah had me lawyer standin' right here beside me, would yer?"

"You have a lawyer?"

"Yes," Ned lied. "But not 'ere. Ah'll introduce yer to 'im at the proper time. All the same, ah fancy as the injured party in this dispute, ah'm entitled to a copy o' them minutes Miss Washburn's scribblin' out. And a statement from t'White Star Company as to why ah'm not suitable fer employment no more. It could become ..... material evidence, when all this gets to court." He was not sure if that was the right choice of words: he had heard it somewhere, but it seemed good enough.

".... I will have a document sent to your address, Thornton. If you will leave Miss Washburn your address - "

"She knows it. Ah'm a White Star employee, Mr. Fellowes, me name's on yer records right 'ere. Or at Canute Chambers anyway. She can look it up, ah'm sure. Just look at *Titanic*'s crew list – the list *before* she sailed, not the list after because my name doesn't appear after - An' that's somethin' else White Star can explain to my lawyer!"

Fellowes' face went through a contortion, then affected a scornful rebuttal of the sarcasm, yet his facade was visibly dented by it. White Star officials had good reason to feel very prickly about the huge number of dead, the whole affair had become extremely tiresome, company profits had suffered greatly and chairman Ismay had virtually absconded from any kind of public life.

"Very well. You will be at that address, will you?"

"Ah shall."

"Is that where you're currently employed."

Ned chewed at his tongue a moment. "Actually.... Ah'm not at liberty to say. Good afternoon. An' thank you, Miss Washburn, for yer 'elp. At least someone 'ere has some manners."

* * * * *

With London in his nostrils, the flavour of New York came all too vividly flooding back to him: he felt no more comfortable here. This late in the day, the smells of the city and the nearby Thames were rising everywhere - stronger than New York, for as the day progressed, cast-off meat and other foodstuffs tossed into local streams added to the rise of odours most unpleasant to someone not used to the city. By now hungry, Ned took the tram to St. Pancras station where he stopped to purchase food at a pie stall, ate it as he stood there and quaffed a glass of poor porter, of which he drank barely half and that only as a measure against thirst. The grand, tiled public toilet echoed every sound and it, too, seemed to have furtive eyes cast in his direction: was there to be nowhere free from suspicion in this country? Ned had no doubts, he much preferred to be back in Normandy. France was safe, France permitted him to live without accusation. A fortnight's leave, though, was not to be frittered away when there was a chance to see his family.

Remembering the Coal Strike earlier in the year, Ned bought his ticket for Derby in great trepidation. That coal strike had disrupted his travel to Southampton to join *Titanic* in the first place: how odd that he had cursed the miners at the time, when in retrospect they might have prevented his ordeal with that ship. Had the strike been more effective, his recent trials simply would not have been happening.

Slumped in a carriage, Ned longed only to get back to the family home in Bradford, although he might not actually call it 'home' any longer: that dream was somewhere else. For the moment, his destiny lay in the hands of those several railway companies that vied for the rights to operate the length and breadth of England. He was, at least, not short of money, for he had saved most of his pay in previous weeks, and Otto had also given him a generous loan which Ned had had the good sense to convert from Francs at the first opportunity. Wherever he might choose to lay down his head for a night, he was at least able to afford lodging so long as he carefully guarded the moneybelt strapped to his middle, and this he intended to do at Derby, even if the train did deliver him there only shortly before midnight.

The next morning he ate a wholesome breakfast of bread and sausage in the lodge beside the railway yards, and bought his ticket to Sheffield. A journey which he shared with a fellow traveller of notable arrogance: a well-dressed man who spoke interminably of his native Russia in very good English. After half an hour Ned was already convinced he would never wish to set foot in Russia – ever. Russia, it seemed, was greater in every possible context than other European countries this fortunate young businessman had travelled through, and especially England, which he considered dirty and immoral. Ned wondered then why he was travelling second class.

"Be careful, be vigilant," said the Russian, as if he might be addressing the British parliament, "You must watch Germany. Germany is the enemy of my people and your people, do not doubt that. We Russians know this. You are a seaman, you told me. And your British Navy is the best in the world – but only for now."

He may well have a point, thought Ned. "Ah know they've been after the Atlantic trade. There's *Imperator*, the ship they launched not long since: a regular floating palace, I hear. "

The Russian ignored Ned's comment, transfixed with his own theatrical performance. "I have seen things," he went on. "I have travelled far and I know how they think: they want to beat everyone at everything, I have seen them working and I have heard them. Germany is building. They want the Navy that you English have, they want to control the seas. Germany is rising. Do not ignore." And he wagged a finger aggressively as if delivering a lecture.

Departing, the young Russian gave Ned his business card, which was for some address in Petersburg, so he said. It meant nothing to Ned and, once out of sight, Ned threw the card away – it was all in Russian cyrillic script. More than that, the man had insulted Ned's friendship with the Bremme family. On the other hand, thought Ned, there is the likes of Dieter Pabst.....

* * * * *

FIFTEEN

Perverse or not, Tuesday was wash day in this part of Yorkshire: as Ned approached his home, he knew his mother would be up to her neck in it! Seen from the main road this flotilla of gardens was a sea of ships dressed overall, pennants flapping in the light breeze, giving off that faintest aroma of dolly blue mixed with traces of carbolic that Ned would forever associate with childhood.

To save a few farthings of tram fare, and because the walk would keep him warm in this cold weather, he had walked the mile-and-a-half from the gaunt Exchange station with his kit bag slung over a shoulder: he no longer noticed it digging in as his mind became focused on matters of home for the first time in months. It was not that he feared seeing his father on the tram, for Jubal Thornton had for some time been working the Thornbury route, and had complained nightly for long enough over the problems of trying to marry track gauges between rival Bradford and Leeds companies.

Having had all she could take, Alice had one evening snapped at her husband, "Will you shut up about that blasted tramway? Bless me, Jubal, all ah hear is yer blasted narrow gauge!" It had been a watershed. Jubal had kept silence for a minute before stepping outside with his pipe. For once, he did not come home drunk as he often did on a Saturday night, but came to bed in the dark, placed a hand on her shoulder as she lay apparently asleep, and quietly said to her, "Good night, love."

Ned was contemplating with unease his father's reception, the leaden Pennine sky reflecting his misgivings perfectly. Grace had written of Jubal's grim silence in reading the newspapers. There were voices raised at the pub and Jubal said nothing to those either.

Whilst his resolve had actually been strengthened by yesterday's dismissal at Oceanic House, he had grown weary of the preoccupation. Knight, Caldecot, the briefcase, the papers, all these things had weighed on his mind for too long. Reminders were everywhere, even down to billboard posters for soap products.

Only on the train, watching his arrogant fellow-traveller, had it occurred to Ned that the Russian had had a similar attaché case – did not all briefcases look much the same? And he spent a lot of time dipping into his case and shuffling papers, at one point dropping a couple of leaves from his lap and quickly picking them up. Strange how chinks of light shine through this way.

Yet what had he seen of Knight's papers anyway? A big stamp, a crest, a drawing, nothing that meant a thing. Ned had only handled a few before handing them back. Yes, the American senator had appeared curious about Knight's behaviour - but then, he was aware of Knight's identity, and was that not cause enough for curiosity? Knight was, after all, heir apparent to a barony – no doubt the reason why he had chosen his fatuously transparent alias.

In all honesty, Ned had not been ready to return home any earlier. Still struggling with these questions, he left the main road and shortly turned up Southfield Place where he smiled at the sight of all the washing hung out to dry: shirts and underwear and nightwear, for all to see – nobody in this community could be in doubt what their neighbour would wear tomorrow! And if a man coveted his neighbour's wife, the sight of what he might discover in her underpinnings could be so unedifying as to be deflating. Around here, no-one saw irony in the fact the grey of the sky, enhanced by the grey of the atmosphere pouring out of so many mill chimneys, transmuted itself into the grey of the clothes. Clothing had to be washed, no more than that: the outcome was as grey as providence itself.

Alice was in the garden. They called these little frontal plots gardens, though in truth there was hardly a blade of green to be found anywhere amongst the dark stone flags save for a few weeds. Each garden met the street with a low wall, such that the local children played a game of navigating the whole street by racing along the walls without ever putting down a foot on the pavement, other than to cross the end of the cul-de-sac, which they called "barlow", a mystical place of sanctuary whose origin was lost in time, in amongst all the magical regions of a child's unfathomable play mind. There they would play hopscotch and leapfrog, and had their wooden whipping tops, and on the cobbled road they played rounders or football. Between the wall, the road and the pavement, this was the play-world for young children. They might never leave the street.

His mother had not seen him. She disappeared again down the little steps and into the basement parlour through the door that skulked beneath the front steps. Those front steps were for visitors only: Jubal had long since fitted a bootscraper there but it sadly lacked use and was as black as the day he placed it.

Head down and pausing not for a moment, Ned lifted the latch of the rotting wooden gate, fought first with his father's combinations flapping into his face and then the ladies' drawers. He flipped them aside and met his mother about to emerge again with a fresh wicker basket. At the sight of her son standing there above her, Alice gasped and dropped the basket to the floor. With her hand across her mouth she emitted only the tiniest of pitiful cries while her other hand sought her apron pocket.

"Mercy!"

Ned only stood and beamed at her. Slinging his bag to the floor, he descended the steps and clasped the little lady to him, where for many moments they clung together in that embrace which had to span not only nine months but also the whole of the Atlantic Ocean and its dark, dark dread. Alice, her closed eyes squeezing the thrill from her soul, clung to her son so tightly that he felt her finger nails were apt to tear into the skin of his back.

Presently, soundlessly, she took his hand and drew him inside the house and pushed the door to behind her. "Oh, Ned....... Oh, Ned......."

* * * * *

Neither did Jubal see his son come through the door of the Spotted Cow as he sat at a bare oak table chatting with friends. It was one of those friends who saw Ned first, and his silence that was the token for the others to stop and look to their rear.

A cheery fire was in the grate at the left, and the sawdust from three days ago was still on the floor as no-one had actually been sick on it yet and the landlord knew that with such low lighting nobody would comment on it anyhow. Otherwise the large public bar of the Spotted Cow was as dim and spartan as ever Ned remembered it, just a single gas lamp and three candles, with three pictures lifting the gloom of the grey walls. One of those was of Jubal Thornton taking the West Riding belt. The four men at the shove ha'penny board now stopped playing and at the far end of the room the dart board was left idle.

Looking up, Jubal Thornton betrayed not a sign of his surprise. Ned's letter posted in France had not been received.

"Naah then," came a voice from the side somewhere. The atmosphere cooled and the thin babble faded. Faces looked from father to son, from son to father.

"What you doin' 'ere?" barked Jubal. They were the first words he had spoken to his son in over nine months.

Ned had taken off his cap and was thumbing it nervously. "Took some leave, father. To come 'ome."

Placing his glass carefully on the table, Jubal slowly forced his wooden chair around to look at the young man, which he did silently for fully ten seconds. Someone to the side carelessly knocked over an ashtray and nothing was said.

"Leave....?" growled Jubal quietly. "Yer've bin a long time decidin' to come back 'ere, 'aven't yer?"

"Ah couldn't...... Before, ah didn't have the brass, father. Ah had to earn it."

"Earn it? Earn it 'ow? I 'eard as 'ow nobody'd take yer on a British ship."

"Yes."

"'Yes', indeed! That all yer can say? Yer mean to stand there and tell me British ships wouldn't give yer work?"

"That's right."

134

"Aye. Ah dare say. Ah dare say.... From what ah've heard, they'd be right to do so an' all. Bringin' shame on all of us. Did yer think about that, lad, when you were runnin' away from a sinkin' ship like a common scullery rat? Eh? Eh? When ah first 'eard that, ah couldn't believe it. Ah couldn't believe it. But all t'newspapers could talk about were Ned Thornton bringin' shame on all of us 'ere."

"Yer'd be happier, then, if ah'd gone down wi' the ship, would yer?"

"None o' yer cheek, lad!" called his father, "Else ah'll do yer bloody head in me-sen. Nah, then!"

"Ah didn't mean to cheek yer. Ah wouldn't do that and yer know it. Ah've got respect. More than folk in this country 'ave any respect for me, and that's a fact." Shaking, Ned pulled himself upright, determined not to give way to anyone in that room. Not now, not after all he had come through.

"Respect, is it? For what?"

"It weren't true. None of it were true. God's honour! Ah didn't do what they said. An' ah wouldn't shame yer, father. Ah wouldn't do that. Ah wouldn't come back 'ere now if ah'd done that. Yer know that, father – *You*.... know that. You raised me, Mr. Thornton; ah'm yer blood, an' yer know ah wouldn't turn me coat on yer."

Jubal in his chair pulled himself up fully erect as if his body needed to give his brain more space to think. The lad was right. The lad would never dishonour his family and not say so. The lad was right, Jubal Thornton's boys knew respect, he had made sure of that - *by God* he had!

From somewhere in the vacuum of the room, a voice called out, "Scab!" and for a few moments, time itself seemed to freeze, until finally it was Jubal Thornton's face that underwent a metamorphosis as a wry smile crept across his jaw and his head slowly turned in the direction of that voice.

"Scab?.... *Scab*?... Yer stupid, gormless bastard, what the bloody 'ell you on about? This lad's not a *scab* – 'e can't *get* no bloody work, 'ow can 'e be a scab?" The ice in the room melted, there were chuckles and laughs and derisory remarks. It was not to last.

"So," Jubal turned again to Ned. "Yer decided ter come back 'ere. Ah hope tha's not 'oping to find any work 'ereabouts, lad. Yer won't find none. Not fer you. Not fer a lad what let 'is own folk down."

"Ah've not let yer down and ah've not come back to find work."

"Oh, aye. Grace said you were workin' fer t' froggies. A bloody French ship! Bloody froggies, I ask yer, lads!" He looked about him, there were a few who obeyed the call and voiced the same scorn.

"So is that all yer can do now? – Now that yer've disgraced yer family an' yer friends an' yer town? Yer go over to t'other side."

"Ah've disgraced no-one! It's lies. It's all lies. You people here don't know the truth. Ah can tell yer the truth in every detail' Don't pay attention to t'newspapers, they just lie to sell papers, tell folk what they think they want to know."

"Now see thee, lad, don't you try lyin' to me an' all!" Jubal broke into a coughing fit and momentarily crouched in his chair.

Ned was feeling stronger in the face of this resistance. Looking about him, he raised his voice for all to hear. "It's true White Star won't 'ave me no more, yes. An' Cunard neither, an' ah don't know who else. But ah've done nowt wrong. Yer hear me? *Ah've done nowt wrong!* They've told a tale about me an' it's all lies, an' somehow ah'm goin' to prove it."

Turning then and taking two steps closer to Jubal, he continued: "You're me dad, and whatever there might be between us, ah wouldn't lie to yer. You know that, father – *you* know that. On your mother's grave. There's powerful people got it in fer me for no reason that I know about, an' somehow ah've got to find out why. So ah came back 'ere, ter see me family and explain. See if ah can start ter clear me name."

"'E's 'avin' you on, Jubal!" came a shout from across the room.

"Ah'm not!" Ned rebuked the man firmly. "Ah survived *Titanic* goin' down, that's true. Ah were lucky some folk in a lifeboat pulled me aboard when ah were half dead...... Ah'm lucky to be alive, and ah thank God for it, but ah did nowt wrong. That's the truth of it."

"'E's disgraced us all," came another voice.

"Give 'im yer belt, Jubal!"

For the first time, Jubal now stood up, pulled the kerchief from his neck and kicked his chair away from him. The room went deathly quiet as he slowly cast his eye to one side and then the other. Again he coughed, but swallowed it back.

"Enough o' that!.... Listen, you lot. He might be t'last shake o' the bag, but he's still my son. If there's any disgrace 'ere, it's on me. Yer hear? An' ah'll be the one to take it up wi't'lad – not you! Not none o' you."

"'E's let us all down, Jubal! E's let the town down, it were in all t'newspapers. Yon lad's been branded a coward, an' it won't do!"

"An' you, Cyril Greenwood, are you tellin' me my lad's a coward?" He began to cough again, and the room waited for him to settle down.

"Jubal, it were in all't' papers. Yon lad's made a laughin' stock o' this town. We don't want cowards 'ere."

Yet another voice chipped in, "Yer should give 'im a good thrashin'. If 'e were my lad, ah'd take me belt to 'im."

"Don't yer think that's up to me to decide, Sid? Eh?" And he raised his right arm with a fist. Everyone knew what that meant.

"So yer've 'eard 'em, lad, yer've 'eard what these 'ere all think. So do ah take me belt off to yer?"

"You can try, father, if yer must, and it'll be the worse for yer."

Jubal's eyes widened. He lowered his arm and stood straight.

"Same goes for any man 'ere!" called Ned, looking about him. "Yer can take me down if you like, but ah'll kick the balls off a lot of you before ah go under!.... Ah'm an innocent man and ah'll not take a thrashin' from me father nor anyone else.... You all hear me?.... Now don't blame me for what 'appens."

That silence was a cacophony of defiance. Not a muscle moved in the room. Not for several seconds.

"There'll be no thrashin' 'ere. Not 'ere, not nowhere. See? Not till I've 'eard that lad's tale fer meself."

Men breathed again, there were coughs and gasps in the smoke. Jubal himself coughed some more, but then spoke again.

"See here - If any man takes a hand to this lad, 'e's got to answer ter me. D'y'all understand that? *Do yer?* Ah'll deal with this – not you, not none o' you. Ah'm goin' ter listen to what that lad has to say. An' if I hear any o' your kin, Sid, or yours, Cyril, fixin' to bash this lad up, there'll be sparks flyin' an' no mistake. Yer hear me now?" Low murmurs of assent were pronounced. Grudging, but pronounced.

"Well, then. There's an end to it. Tell all yer mates an' all. Make it clear no-one takes it out on this lad, y'understand? If they do, they'll answer ter Jubal Thornton. Ah'm not what ah were, but ah can still flatten any o' you lot and yer know it."

Ned was standing alone in the middle of the room, not quite sure which way he should move now. It was his father who solved the problem for him.

"Go on 'ome, lad. Away! Go 'ome. Ah'll be there in a bit. Tell yer mother. Ah'll not be late, tell 'er. An hour... less, mebbe. Away wi' yer..."

Ned decided he should do as he was bid.

"Ned!" He turned back as he was squaring off his cap.

"Tell Alice to find me best studs. Tell 'er ah need me studs fer t'manager tomorrah. And a collar! Tell 'er."

His son merely inclined his head. Then turned to the door.

"Oh, and Ned!.... Don't take the snicket, lad. Stay on t'road. Yer hear, son?"

Ned took a moment to look into his father's face.

"Yes, father."

He heard. Yes, he heard. It was what he had waited a lifetime to hear.

* * * * *

"German? Ah thought you said French."

"German. Otto is German. Is there owt wrong wi' that?"

"No." James mouthed a shrug. "Nothing. Ah thought you said French, that's all. Either way, they're not our sort, are they?"

138

Ned could have taken offence at his brother but saw it differently. "They're my friends, Jim. The only friends ah've got. Seein' as how everyone in this country thinks ah'm a wrong un."

Their mother sensed a squabble coming on. "Now, now," said Alice. "No scrappin', thank you. Otherwise yer can just go 'ome, James Thornton, an' tek yer leg wi' yer! Yon lad's come a long way, if there's one place he can look on a friendly face it's 'ere with us."

"Aye," protested James, "Ah wasn't sayin' owt that the rest o' yer weren't thinking, mum. I want to see Ned clear 'is reputation - we all do, don't we?"

"Well, fine words butter no parsnips, young James," Alice cautioned. "Now then, show Ned that new crutch what Ernest made for yer."

James reached down the side of the chair and raised the crutch for Ned to inspect, beaming all over his face. "Carved it for us – just look. That's Kentish willow, best quality."

The leg of the crutch was carved in the shape of a cricket bat, albeit a rather slender one.

"Carved his initials down t'side, look," glowed James.

Taking the crutch, Ned viewed it with mixed feelings. He worried there was still a chance James could lose the leg altogether. With a new child on the way, and a poor lodging to maintain along with Christine, James was giving much concern to his parents, who saw the loss of his job at Listers as a catastrophe. James, however, was undeterred.

"Ah've got that job at Salts. Just you see, mum, ah've got it."

"Are yer gonna go temperance, then, James? Yer know what they're like at Salts Mill."

James ignored the remark . "Ben and Maurice both told me. Alright, ah'm not foreman any more, an' scribblin' on paper and punch-cards i'nt right up my street, but it's work. It's work. This leg's gettin' better, yer'll see. Once Christine's had that there bairn, we'll get back on us feet. Yer'll see."

Ned didn't doubt his brother's determination, though part of him wanted to cry. James had risen to foreman quicker and younger than almost anyone else at Listers, and nobody knew their way around silk yarn any better. If anyone needed to tell between strands of Leicester Longwool and Cotswold with their golden fleece, they could call for James Thornton. Mills like Listers or Salts were proud of the threads they derived from different fleeces, particularly the newer Alpaca, which gave a quality not unlike Kashmir at a lower price. James had been one of the principal overseers of the velvets that graced Westminster Abbey for the coronation the year before.

Work in the mills was hard but sought after, with mediocre but consistent pay and good long-term prospects for workers who proved themselves capable of graft without complaint. Hot, dirty, dingy, and with long hours a feature of employment despite the advent of the newer power looms, nevertheless the mill provided a relatively secure living for its workers, not to mention a great many miners in the Yorkshire coalfields not far away, for whom the vast consumption of coal at power mills like these was a shot in the arm. For all their dirt spewing out into the cityscape and countryside, polluting the air for miles around, the mills offered a slightly better place to be than many of the cities' other environments, with open sewers, foul water and rotting rubbish to contend with. Mill girls were less likely to turn to prostitution, and diseases like scarlet fever, typhoid, ricketts and tuberculosis were rife across the populace. If you were fortunate enough to live in a house that had a water closet that was not shared, you padlocked it.

For decades, towns like Bradford had been a magnet for workers of all backgrounds and many nationalities, especially eastern Europeans. Work was there in abundance, as was the wealth amassed by the entrepreneurs, often those from already wealthy families who poured their money carefully into the woollen mills of West Yorkshire or the cotton mills of Lancashire, or any of the many associated trades, making these regions the homes of some of the most fortunate millionaires in the land. '*Where there's muck there's brass*,' went the popular saying: never had it been more true than in the dour townscapes of the North of this twentieth-century England. It was, in so many ways, the workhouse and the gut of the world, with all of its virtues and vices laid as bare as the boney bodies that emerged from tin and *papier mâché* bathtubs late every night.

Accidents with steam-driven power belts were not infrequent. Thankfully not often as fatal as the horrible effects of the carding machines, where some mills would have specifically delegated personnel to clean up so that the main body of workers were not discouraged. That these individuals were given extra pay and time off was small recompense for being what they considered butchers. Children, mostly careless from lack of nutrition and sunlight, would lose fingers in the shredding machines and it raised no more than a shrug amongst most workers. Death was an unwelcome companion and ever constant.

James had just been unlucky, that's all: the girl had been sick on him and it knocked him off balance. Ned cursed himself for not having been around, for the accident occurred shortly before he had left *Olympic* to join *Titanic*, there had been no chance for leave to get home. He had missed his brother's wedding too, last December.

"Yer'll be alright, James," said Ned, clamping a hand on his brother's shoulder and gripping it tightly.

"Aye, kid," said James smartly, "You an' I shall go chumping next week and get t'wood in fer Bonfire Night, eh? Just like we used ter. So long as yer don't throw me crutch onto t'pile an' all."

Ned could not join his brother in his enthusiasm. "Can't, Jim. Ah won't be here. Got to get back to me ship."

"Aah," sighed James. Both brothers saw in each other's face the memory of building those bonfires when they were much younger, of energetically stuffing sacks with rags and straw to make the Guy along with the other boys in the street and sitting there long hours in the perishing cold outside the park gates, cap outstretched for the odd passer-by to toss them a farthing.

"'Ere," urged James, more to cheer himself up, "Remember Wakes Week when you were seven? Couple o'years after t'queen's jubilee. Remember Shipley Fair, goin' all t'way on that traction engine?"

"Aye," said Ned.

"Noisy as ruddy 'ell. My ears were ringin'. An' I told yer to take one o' them toffee apples and yer did!"

"Aye, an' got me ear clipped for it, yer bloomin' idiot!"

"And gettin' under that big Shamrock swing thing and watchin' the lasses' skirts blow up! Eh?"

"It were fun, though. And that gramophone thing - We thought there were a woman behind it, singin' 'er 'ead off. Couldn't believe it!"

"..... And then we got soaked to t'skin on t'way home. Ruddy flamin' June, ey, Ned?"

"Drink yer tea," said Alice calmly.

Their mother had spent much of her life praying her children would all come through the dire ordeal that was childhood and emerge as strong, healthy, capable people. Now this.

Ned pulled his chair closer to his brother, pushed another slice of bread onto his toasting fork and shoved it close to where the coals were glowing brightest. The smell of toasting bread was one of those eternal things that never lost its appeal nor its nostalgia. Alice turned her head into her pinafore and choked back a tear.

"What did yer mean, mother?" Ned asked her in a rare quiet moment when they had the parlour to themselves.

"What, lad?"

"You used to say, 'Find yer truth', mum - remember?"

Alice pushed her frock down over her legs and got up from where she had been warming her feet by the fire, propped up on two chairs.

"Odd time to ask me that."

"Aye, mebbe.... What did yer mean?"

A little surprised, she sought a way to put her thoughts together. "Well...."

At length, she told him, "Stuff yer grandad said sometimes. To us four girls.... He were never much of a talker, yer grandad. So when he did talk, yer listened.... Except Lizzie, she were so empty-headed, she never thought about anything 'cept gettin' wed."

Ned's face urged her to go on.

"It were just.... something he used to say. Ah didn't pay him no mind then, cos I didn't understand. But.... mebbe ah do now."

"It's what yer told me, mum."

"Did ah?"

"Aye. A few times. Yer never thought ah listened."

"No, yer never did, young Ned, that's right."

"Ah!" He wagged a finger at her. "See... Yer were wrong, mother."

Alice smiled. "And so now yer know, do yer?"

Ned took her hand and used it to slap his own cheek.

"Not a ruddy clue, mum!" His mother yelped in his face. "But it allus sounded good!"

The family's support for the moment rested with Jubal at Bradford Tramways and Grace at the newspaper. Ned was holding his own - just. Grace leaned toward the new women's suffrage movement, she had been recently in a brief argument with her boss at the paper, one that she very quickly backed away from. Pay for a man was to support his family whilst pay for a woman was merely for herself - that was her manager's view, a man typical of the era. This and similar outrages convinced Grace women must demand their rights as citizens, even if that meant voting for obnoxious men whose wealth outstripped their propriety and hygiene, not to mention their mental faculties.

"Deeds not words," had said Mrs. Pankhurst, but Grace was not yet ready for deeds – deeds were fine for those whose income made for a soft landing. Valuing her job, Grace for the present held her tongue and kept her ideas largely to herself and her bosom pals. Alice for her part still took in ironing for less than four shillings and sixpence a week, though thinking better of it since it meant keeping a fire going in times when they could otherwise manage without. Ned had given his mother a small amount, as much as he dared, to help out. The trade union, too, had said they would help James, but these new unions gave out much in rhetoric, not so much in cash. Even less in fortitude.

143

Still, James was not giving up where many would and that was good. The doctor had given him a 50:50 chance of a recovery without surgery, and James was an optimist, if not quite the dreamer that Ned had always been. James still had his leg, mangled though it had been, and was unshakeable in his resolve to keep it despite recurrent pain.

Grace rose and crossed the room to Ned. "Little brother," she said, sighing a long breath. "It's so good to have you home." Putting her arms about him, she squeezed very tightly.

"It is that," said Ned. "Unfortunately, not long enough. Ah'm booked to cross back Monday morning, ah want to be back in Southampton Saturday night. Should have some news."

"What kind of news?"

"Don't know yet. Ah've got a bloke keeping an eye out for me. Bit of detective work – sort of."

Grace understood only little from what Ned had said.

"Still don't know why you never got the letter," he worried. She shook her head.

"Never mind, Sis. Ah can tell y'everything face to face. Hey – are you courtin' now? Bet yer leadin' the lads a right dance."

Her smile was coquettish. "Oh, who's got the time?"

"You have! Come on, Sis, y're a good-lookin' lass. All them lads at Salem used ter have their eye on yer. An' y're earnin' good brass now, aren't yer? – For a lass.... Oh, shouldn't ah say that?"

Grace scrunched up her mouth in a gesture that told herself there was nothing to be said that would profit her. Undoing and slipping off her pinafore, she left the room to change into her other dress. *Yes*, she said to herself, *I will go out with William Hardcastle. And if he wants to take me to the theatre, why not? – He can afford it.*

"So....." James eventually wanted to ask: "D'yer speak German now, then? – Sorry - French, is it?... Say summat in French, Ned."

* * * * *

144

SIXTEEN

Ned was early. Though even at thirty minutes past the hour, there was still no sign of Harry Fenby. Not in the mood for more than one pint, he nursed his ale as he sat under the ironwork that dominated the front of the bar. The beer was warm and woody, as it had been the previous week; Ned didn't relish it at all. He much preferred the beer at the Platform.

He had begun to accept the idea Harry was unable to help him when quite suddenly Harry entered the Grapes with a worried look on his face and came straight across to Ned, who stood to greet him, ready to order him a drink.

"Sorry, Ned," said Harry. "I can't stay, mate."

Instead, he picked up Ned's glass and took a single gulp from it, turning the glass around as he placed it back on the bar and then wiping his moustache.

"You was right, Ned. We said you'd got trouble and you surely have. Listen, chum, I've got my missus to think about, and the kid. I wanna help you because I think you're alright but..... if word gets around..... Know what I mean? I have a job."

As he hurriedly said these things, Harry looked about him more than once.

"Listen, I have to go, Ned. Sorry, mate. Look – he'll tell you."

With that, Harry thrust out a finger, pointing to the front door. Then he scurried away through that door, like a frightened badger disappearing down into the earth. In the doorway he ducked past a shadowy figure lingering there. It was John Cade.

"Watcha, me old oppo."

Cade joined an incredulous Ned at the bar, holding the ubiquitous cigarette in his mouth. His dark eyes and growth of beard gave the look of a man who had not slept for days, whilst his blonde hair was more than a little dirty and unkempt, for it burst out from where he had tried to tuck it away under the bowler hat which on him looked oddly old-fashioned.

"'Ow's it going, Ned?"

Cade's thin face gave out different expressions by turns: pleasure, amusement, gravity. Try as he might, his sallow mein failed to convey any sincerity.

".... Cade...." The word came out slowly as Ned regained his composure.

"S'right, my lad. In the flesh. And in the pink, as you can see."

"Ah can see.... Well, well."

"An' the next thing you say is, 'What the bloody 'ell are *you* doing 'ere?' – Ain't that right, china?"

Lost for any other course of action, Ned decided to take that bait. "Alright, what *are* you doin' 'ere?"

"Oh, yes, barman - pint, please! Bitter .... What was that, sunshine? – Oh, yair. Well, I'm a couple of trains behind you, you might say."

The picture in Ned's face was a blank canvas.

"Yes," carried on the older man, "It was raining in Bradford when I left. Does it always rain up there?"

"Bradford?"

"Bit of a dirty dump, innit? Not goin' there again.... They told me you left. Hey, she's a good-lookin' woman, that sister of yours."

"You were there?"

"Don't be so shocked. Soon as they found me, I was away from Tilbury like a shot, but seems I was a day late catchin' you in Yorkshire. So your young lady very kindly told me you was on your way back to France, like. I just had to make a quick stop at Cockspur Street and the word was, you'd be calling back here. We just put two and two together and came up with Thomas Swanscombe."

"Thomas Swanscombe?"

"Harry Fenby's brother-in-law. Canute Chambers told us he'd been asking some odd questions not at all about the usual business."

"Us?" Ned was beginning to wake up and realise it was not all a fantasy. "Who's 'us'?"

Cade leaned back on the stool and blew smoke out slowly as he wagged a finger in front of Ned's face. "Aah....."

"Alright, let me guess.... You and Ranulph Knight?"

Cade clapped his hands in mock salute. "Full marks! You been doin' some thinkin' finally, me old chum. Not stupid, are you?"

Not stupid, but puzzled. "So ah've been doing some thinking. You're going to tell me what about."

"Am I?"

"Well – Isn't that what yer came here for? Yer seem suddenly to have taken on a detective's job. Not workin' fer Scotland Yard, are yer? You solved that headless woman case yet?"

"Don't think too fast, lad, it might not be good for you."

"Meaning?"

Cade took a confident pause, produced a packet of cigarettes and extended one: Ned took it, and the light the Londoner offered. All the time, Cade was looking beyond them both, his eyes and manner appearing to check someone's presence.

"Listen..... You and me, Ned, we go back a bit, don't we? So we don't wanna be fallin' out with each other. Nobody wants trouble, right? All the guvnor wants is that paper. You hand it over and we're all pals again."

"What paper? Ah don't know anythin' about any papers?"

"Hey, whoa, me old mate, slow down to a gallop! Don't tell me you don't know what I'm on about - Bernie saw you - "

" – Saw me what?"

"Pocket them letters."

"Yer said papers a second ago."

".... Papers - yair. Come on now, you're tryin' my patience, lad."

"Just tellin' yer the truth."

Cade stood up. "Look, you bugger, are you tellin' me you didn't pocket them papers?"

"Hey, calm down!"

"You're lyin', mate," Cade accused him. "Bernie said you stuffed them papers down your waistcoat."

"No, ah didn't. Caldecot's lying, then. Are you tellin' me I've got all this trouble because Caldecot said I'd taken some papers? – Ah'm assuming we're talkin' about them that got dropped all over his lordship's stateroom floor."

147

Cade backed off and grinned casually. "Yes, o'course."

"Well, I," repeated Ned with emphasis, " - did - *not* - take them!"

Their exchange had stilled everyone at the bar. Over to one side, a man dropped off his chair and slumped like a half-full hopsack onto the floor, taking with him his beer mug which spilled and shattered. Emerging with a brush and pan, the barman went to the prone figure, crouched and swept up the fragments of glass. That done, he went back behind the bar, leaving the man blissfully motionless under the table.

Fragile moments passed as the two men watched this, then Cade pulled himself upright, leaned forward and quietly said, "I should be careful what you say, me old china. Have you seen the Mail?"

Very obviously Ned had not seen it.

Cade pulled the newspaper out of his inside coat pocket and offered it. "Page two, if you will."

Ned saw the column immediately. The title read, '*Titanic Coward Back in England*'. Beside it was a pencil-portrait that bore a fair resemblance to himself. He lowered the paper silently, needing to read no further.

"There you go," breathed Cade, more at ease and authoritative.

"This is yesterday," Ned noted.

"S'right," Cade blew smoke at him again. "But not to worry, sunshine; I mean, you're not gonna be around long, are yer? Back off over to France, are we? What's it like, that place of yours in Lee Haver?" Cade's comment had the calculated effect, pressing Ned into silence.

Cade knew of Le Havre. He had been to Ned's home in Bradford, he had spoken with Grace. He must know of *La Rochelle*. And more particularly, he must know of the Bremmes and their home. Ned needed to think. There was no sensible reason for sudden reaction or violence, which for fleeting moments had occurred to him. But then, Cade was no small man and probably well able to defend himself. Ned did not take after his father, he had never had need of fighting skills.

So the newspaper poison campaign was on again. Presumably instigated by Knight himself, and all about a couple of sheets of paper. If Caldecot had in fact said those things, he had lied, but why would he?

"Chin, chin, old man." said Cade, raising his glass.

"So yer reckon ah'm off back to France," said Ned at length.

"Stands to reason: where else shall you go? You got to get back to yer ship, aintcha? And with two 'ansome young ladies like that, how could I blame yer?"

Reina and Gitta, he knew of them too. That was unconscionable, that he might do anything to hurt those girls. Or that Knight may somehow exert some pressure there. Unconscionable.

There was no point in beating about the bush any more. Shoot from the hip. "What's in them papers?" demanded Ned. " – If they're so bloody important."

Cade acted surprised. "My, my! How indelicate! You saw 'em, mate."

"Ah didn't – ah picked a few up, but ah didn't look at 'em. It wasn't my business, you know yourself stewards handle all sorts o' stuff and never question what it is. What were they? – Government secrets or something?"

Cade sat upright on the stool, simply looking quizzically at Ned. In a few moments he pointed a finger, laughed a little and let out a quiet, "Ah-ha-ha-ha!" More deliberately, he jabbed that finger into Ned's chest. "Don't you tell me you don't know."

"Whose word 'ave yer got? – Caldecot's? He's conveniently missin'. Suppose 'e was lyin'. If Caldecot took some papers," speculated Ned, "It'd be the easiest thing just to blame the steward."

"Good try, son, but Caldecot swore it were you before 'e died - "

Suddenly aware of what he had said, Cade looked aside, grabbed at his beer and took several gulps. For both men, the words hung in the air like a sword of Damacles, as Ned took a long moment to digest the inference of Cade's remark - that Caldecot had died in a manner other than drowning. Ned's brain crashed to a halt. To say anything at all at that precise point might lead to a place where neither man wanted to be.

It was Cade who broke the silence, muttering into his glass. "Listen, Thornton, if I was you I'd get back across that 'oggin' right sharp and keep yer trap shut. It'll calm down here soon enough, but remember - my employer got long arms. My job to see that he has. Long arms what can reach all the way over to meat houses in New York. You got me, lad? Yorkshire can be a nasty place if people think Ned Thornton's a bad lad. You don't want to see family suffer, do yer? I mean, newspaper owners can be very finicky about who they take on and who they fire." Ned was horrified that Cade was threatening Grace's job.

"If I was you, Thornton, I'd get them papers back... Oceanic House, for attention of Mr. You-know-who."

"Oceanic House wouldn't have anything to do wi' me when ah went there."

"I'm not surprised. Since yer don't exist."

"Don't exist?"

"Not where White Star's concerned. You checked lately to see if you're on the books? - Ain't no mention of a Ned Thornton in the crew list for *Titanic*.... Nor even *Olympic*."

For a few moments Ned was speechless: his name had been omitted from the survivors' lists, he knew that, and now they had doctored the ships' records!

"I should just get back to France.... if I was a clever bloke, like you. Post them papers. They should get through, it's only sometimes that unscrupulous people gets 'old o' the mail and misuses it....."

Cade was revealing all of his hand for a very good reason - intimidation. Whatever the facts, Ned was convinced there was no battle to be won right here, right now. He took in a long breath and after further thought decided to leave, anxious to terminate this odious meeting.

"Alright.... Ah've got me ticket..... You better tell your boss he's won the day."

The other man nodded, a satisfied smirk twisting his face.

"But,"added Ned, "Tell 'im this, an' all. Tell 'im if 'e wants to fight dirty, first 'e'd better be sure about 'is facts before 'e gets 'is hands mucky. Oh - but then, it's you that cleans up all 'is shit for 'im, isn't it? ....Tell 'im ah've got no ruddy papers, so ah shall not be writin' to 'im. An' tell 'im sometimes it's not true that dead men tell no tales."

With that, Ned took a few coins from his pocket and sprinkled them on the bar. Before allowing him to leave, however, Cade clapped a hand over Ned's outstretched wrist. "Twenty-five, Ned."

"What?"

"You heard me. Twenty-five notes... Guineas, in fact. That's a lot of dosh for a kid like you. Set you up nicely with your German sweetheart, wouldn't it?"

Now Ned really did want to punch him between those dark eye sockets. *Thorough*, thought Ned, *I'll give him that.* But the risks were too high, he could not dare put the family in danger.

Wrenching his arm away, Ned pulled his coat about him and headed for the door.

After two paces, though, he hesitated, stopped and turned. He had a last question: "My letter home didn't arrive. Your doing, ah'd guess?"

"Me?" Cade's sincerity was the transparency of crystal. "Ned, boy, what *shall* you take me for? Interfering with His Majesty's mail? – That would be criminal! God love us, 'ow would an honest feller like me manage that?"

Ned rolled his tongue around in his mouth, but he said nothing and grasped the door handle.

"Twenty-five, Ned! Think about it!" Cade raised his bowler to the young man's back but Ned did not turn around, merely stomped his cigarette out on the floor. Once outside, he took a long breath before peering back into the saloon through those ornate glass windows. Cade was already speaking to a large man in dark clothes.

* * * * *

151

SEVENTEEN

Alberta's return passage to Le Havre was a rough one. Ned became for once quite seasick, a malady he never suffered on the much larger ocean liners, which took stronger forces to heave them about, even if they did toss around for longer once they got going. As Walter had observed about the *Olympic* – "The trouble with these bloody big ships is, it takes three days to fire the thing up and six miles to stop the bugger." But sea-sickness anyway happened to those who were doing little, a working steward had no time for it.

It was a relief, therefore, after passing through the dock, that he could return directly aboard *La Rochelle*, which had arrived two days earlier. He would not present an ill face to the girls, and anyway he preferred first to catch up on matters with Otto. No point in frightening everyone, which he felt certain would be the consequence if they knew they had been under surveillance by the mercenary cronies of Ranulph Knight.

"Bremme?" asked Ned. Dieter Pabst shrugged. *"Keine blasse ahnung."* No idea. And he walked away.

Queasy and exhausted, Ned dragged off his shoes and trousers and fell into his bunk. He was in no mood to go searching.

Next morning, Otto shook him awake with a cup of coffee. *"Wilkommen. Wie geht's?"*

It took Ned a minute to come round. They were not alone in the cabin, but the dozing Maurice Louvois understood little English or German.

"Are you alright, my small *Nixie* friend? Did you have fun in England?"

"You could say that," said Ned.

Otto frowned and propped his hands on his hips. "But I *did* say that!"

"No, Otto, I mean – yes, I had some fun in England. The wrong kind of fun."

"Ze wrong kind of fun? What is dat? Is dat fun or not fun?"

Ned smiled and dragged his legs out. "Not. Anyway, how is the family?"

"Oh, ze girls are good. Mutti not so good, but....." He made wavering motions with his hands. "Chust a cold, I sink. *Schnupfen.*"

"Change in the weather, I expect."

"But I don't go home. I don't want *schnupfen*, I got to work, what. Ned, Vuillaume wants to see you. I should tell you when you come back. Are you back? - Okay, I tell you."

"Vuillaume? What for?"

Otto shrugged. "Perhaps he is in love wiz you....."

"You daft bugger!" snorted Ned. "..... Does he really want to see me?"

"Ja. Me too."

"You don't know what about?"

"I sink it's because Pabst saw me take a chicken, but maybe."

"He saw you? That's bad."

"Maybe. But maybe not. He had a girl in ze cabin last trip."

"Ah," said Ned. "Good trip, then? How was New York?"

"No, not a good trip. A woman died. Third class. Polish woman."

"That *is* bad."

"Ja. Doctor Gaucher was serious. But....." Otto gave his big shrug. People died. Others gave birth. Five this month.

"So when does Vuillaume want to see us?"

First Officer Vuillaume was dismissive. He was busy with lists of something or other. "No, it's not me. You need to see the captain. Go on, off you go: speak to Antoine, he will put you in. Now go away, I'm busy."

The captain's steward, Antoine, was casual and surly: he wanted to be ashore but the captain had work for him to do. They found Antoine having a cigarette on the bridge with the duty officer. "Am I a nurse? - Knock on his fucking door, like everyone else does," said the steward, "What? - You think he has an appointments book?"

Captain Genoud was lolling back in an easy chair, reading a thick book.

"Oh yes," he replied to Otto's enquiry, "Yes, I did want to see him. Come in, Thornton, I have seen you before."

"Yes, sir."

Genoud was a small man who did not like his uniform as its emphasis on fitting his corpulence made him look even smaller. In port, he tended to dispense with uniform, wearing only the shoes and trousers and adopting a thick roll-neck jumper rather than a jacket. His hat remained as long as possible on a shelf: it was very flat and very round, and along with his flat feet someone had once commented that he looked like a navy blue milk churn, so Genoud preferred to ignore the whole outfit. Except of course during the transatlantic crossing when it was unavoidable to interact with passengers. He hoped they would react properly to the rings on his jacket sleeves and the gold braid of his hat, and in general passengers did. Genoud may have been small, but he was no fool.

Otto and Ned stood stiffly in front of their captain, who merely lowered his book onto his lap and took his feet off the edge of his bunk.

"You have been on leave, Thornton." Not a question.

"I came back last evening, sir."

"A good leave? You went to England?"

"Yes..... Er, no. I mean, yes, I went to England."

Genoud looked at him carefully, as if answering his own questions.

"You and Bremme are good friends." Again, an observation: both men grunted their agreement, both wondering where this was going. Captain Genoud took his time to close the book altogether and place it on an adjacent table.

"Good. And Thornton, you have learned the French language quite well, have you not?..... I know that your employment aboard this ship was...... Well, let us understand one another, you came to work here in a tentative manner. Would you agree?"

Before responding, Ned glanced sideways at Otto, who returned the dubious look with a raise of his eyebrows. "Yes," admitted Ned, "Yes, sir, that is true. I can explain -"

"- It's alright, Thornton, I am not about to dismiss you. Normally, of course, we take on staff routinely as long as we have some idea they are good at their job. Usually they have worked for the C.G.T. before and so they have papers. You did not have papers. And usually we don't have people join us as a form of political sanctuary..."

Ned had put on full uniform with a collar and bowtie, and now wished he had not, for he felt very warm.

Genoud, though, had a reassuring smile. "As a matter of fact, you have done well aboard *La Rochelle*, you are popular with customers, and we have a lot of English-speaking customers, as you know. Even the German passengers like you because you are – what should I say? – you are more civil to them. As a Frenchman, I concede that a number of our stewards have an attitude problem with German passengers. But you English have much more..... er, much more starch in your collars." Genoud almost laughed as he found the appropriate words. "*Le sang froid*.... Uh? And you can guard your tongue."

Otto laughed fully, and his round body juddered. "Ha-ha, zat's true!"

Genoud ignored the outburst. "So," he went on, "I would say as a matter of fact you have proved an asset to this ship. You too, Bremme: you have your way of making..... making life a little more comfortable for everyone. Although - *crêpes au fromage bleu*?... But yes, you are good workers, both of you."

Ned merely smiled: he would have made a response but was still cautious about being summoned.

"And I shall be sorry to lose you," continued Genoud, then paused to gauge the reaction. "If you wish to take up a better offer."

Two open-mouthed faces reflected their huge curiosity.

"Gentlemen, I shall explain, of course. *La Compagnie* has asked for staff to be transferred to *La France*. Since she came into service in April, *La France* took on a lot of C.G.T. employees on a short contract basis rather than relying on conscript crews signing on for one trip at a time. It was necessary for smooth running and continuity in the ship's initial stages. You are familiar with this. Now, some of the – 'spare wood', shall I say, has been let go, and *La France* needs a further thirty staff to fill the gap. This ship, and *La Touraine* and *La Savoie* have been asked to transfer mainly steward staff to *La France*, to be transferred at once. *La France* will dock here today and she is due to sail again on the 15th – Friday. That doesn't give anybody much time."

The captain paused and looked from one man to the other.

"There are others, but I should like you two to consider transferring, because it will reflect well on *La Rochelle* that she has good staff. Which means of course it reflects well on me!"

Genoud laughed again. "You two are good friends, you will work better together than not together."

"So," Genoud finally got up from his chair and went to the bureau for his pipe. His braces were dangling from underneath the back of his jumper. "Do you need time to think about it? – I should like your answer today. Now, in fact."

"I", Ned began, "I....."

"There is one more thing, Thornton. M. Lagarde has told me the reason why Bremme smuggled you aboard *La Rochelle* in April. Smuggle? Do I mean 'smuggle'?.... Yes, why not!"

Ned quickly turned to Otto who again shrugged his big body shrug.

"Don't worry, Thornton, I judge a man by what I see, not by newspapers trying to work up a story – yes, I know about that too. Some French newspapers also picked up on it and they gave your name - did you know you were so famous? But, unlike Britain and New York, I don't think anyone here cared one way or the other, and they don't trust the British! Actually, French people don't trust Americans either, have you noticed? – Oh, I know, I know – we gave them the Statue of Liberty!" He flung his arms wide in a gesture intended to circumscribe the nonsense of it all.

"It is not my business, what happened to you on *Titanic*, but when one of our regular and most trusted passengers comes to me and says you should have our support, then I have to listen."

"A passenger?" queried Ned.

Genoud had lit his pipe and returned to his chair. He sat there puffing happily as if it were his only pleasure in the whole world. "Monsieur Bruno Carelle has written to me. And M. Carelle is not a man you do not listen to. As a matter of fact, he spoke to me directly about you in September but you will remember we crossed in that gale and there was no time for social chit-chat."

"Ah. It is true, M. Carelle has taken an interest in my affairs." True, indeed. Ned thought back to the late-September crossing, Carelle had re-introduced himself and had proven both proper and forthright. He already appeared to know much of Ned's story, and reassured Ned that he would if necessary find the means to bring some 'balance' into the scenario, though he took no pains to indicate how.

"That is a good thing for you, Thornton, you should be pleased. All the same, it does not alter my question to the two of you – will you join *La France*?..... Your pay will not be any better, not at first, and you may think you are a smaller fish in a big pool, but if you do well, your prospects will be better..... Both of you. And Thornton, you will be a member of her crew – *legitimately*. With papers."

The point was not lost on Ned.

"What's the difference, Ned? We are still here in Le Havre, no? And *La France* is faster than *La Rochelle*, so maybe we are home more often, what."

His captain contradicted that. "Hardly. She makes 23 knots, I make 20, it's half a day at the most. But many more passengers. *La France* is twice as big. And she gets *la crème de la crème*. More money in tips."

"Question, sir," said Otto. "Will Pabst also be transferring?"

"Pabst? I have no idea. I don't believe he is on the list M. Lagarde has given me. Leduc, Merignac, you two..... I forget who else."

"Then I go!"

After that affirmation, Otto looked at Ned as if asking permission.

"Yes," said Ned after a moment's thought. "Sounds good to me. They say *La France* is called the Versailles of the sea."

"That's what they say," said Genoud, nodding. That was that, then, he thought. "Good. Now go and talk to the purser and confirm – he already has the list, there will be nine of you." Then, as an afterthought, he called to their departing backs, "Oh and Bremme..... That's not an excuse to indulge yourself of the ship's meat store before you go. Leave me at least one decent leg of lamb, uh?"

Ned came away from that meeting enormously buoyed up. He had received praise from his captain, he had no need ever to fear recriminations over his departure from New York, and he had confirmation that M. Carelle was, as it were, a friend indeed. Although, at this moment in time, he was not altogether sure how he was going to begin to make use of that friendship, let alone repay him.

He had a new ship! The pride of the French Line, and – it was no exaggeration to say it – the pride of France. Ned felt very good indeed.

"It's okay, Ned?" asked Otto, a little hesitantly. "Isn't it?"

"You knew about this..... You little tinker, you knew about this before, didn't you?"

"Ned, I – "

"It's more than okay, it's bloody marvellous! I'm off at six, let's go tell the girls. Schnapps, Otto, bring the schnapps! It's time for some osculation!"

* * * * *

Before reporting aboard *La France* on the Thursday, Ned wrote three letters. Each was brief, imparting the wonderful news of his new station. This time, he was able himself to take the letters to La Poste. The first, he sent to the address in Antwerp that M. Carelle

158

had given him, and in this letter he mentioned their stilted conversation in September and confirmation that his adversary was indeed that stalwart of the British parliament, as revealed by Cade.

A second letter Ned penned to Magoolagan in New York, before sitting bolt upright in his chair and chastising himself for being a complete fool – He would be delivering the letter himself! He tore it up.

The third letter Ned addressed to his brother James, whose home ought to be entirely safe from any mail-thieves, imagined or otherwise!

He directed them simply to send correspondence care of Mlle. Renata Bremme at the school in Le Havre, marking the envelope "Ned".

Then a further thought occurred to him, the wisdom of which was – frankly – questionable. Obeying an impulse to protest his innocence to his antagonist, Ned wrote a note to Anthony Scott-Chapelle, care of Oceanic House in London, making reference to their short acquaintance aboard *Titanic,* and to the fact that he, Ned Thornton, was now being persecuted for a crime he had not committed and that he – The Honourable Mister Scott-Chapelle – was entirely conversant with the nature of it.

In polite language, he asked the British MP to state that certain accusations voiced by John Cade – apparently on the instructions of Scott-Chapelle – had no substance.

A reckless thing to do? Ned tossed it around inside his head: it seemed he had little to lose since the cards stacked against him had now been played. Perhaps – just perhaps – if Scott-Chapelle were to make reply, some use of it might be made should matters ever result in court action. Those cards would then be on the table.

Over the course of an hour, he wavered this way and that. Then appended his signature in the most official manner he could imagine. "....... I have the honour to be, sir, your obedient servant......."

Ned laughed at himself. A lot.

Yet he did feel on top of the situation for the first time in months, and felt the cards in his own hand were stronger now.

Southampton was a low point, but perhaps a corner had been turned.

He was wrong. In London, a gentleman at Scotland Yard was notified in December that the seaman known as Edward James Thornton, presently employed by the *Compagnie Générale Transatlantique* on French vessels, was alleged whilst aboard *RMS.Titanic* to have stolen certain unspecified possessions, the property of Anthony Scott-Chapelle, and as a result a warrant was now in force for the arrest of the said Edward James Thornton, wherever in Britain he might set foot.

It struck Ned at once that if all trace of his record at White Star had been removed, logically no legal action based on employment on the *Titanic* could be pursued. With the very next thought, however, he decided Knight would find a way around that too.

* * * * *

EIGHTEEN

For a long time, the big, wide world offered nothing that either Ned or Otto knew or cared much about as they got on with their duties on *La France*. Failed assassination of the American president, what was that to them? And all the rumblings going on in the east of Europe, they hardly signalled ill omens to these young men that there was chaos in the Balkans or that the Ottoman empire was beginning to crack open at the seams. The only thing they cared about Turkey was whether the tobacco got any better, and these other things – well, they had never heard of Serbia for a start, let alone a place with such a grand name as Montenegro that sounded like a gambling casino. Where was this new Ottoman state, Albania anyhow? – Somewhere in Africa.

With time barely to get their feet under the table, *La France* sailed for America on the 15th of November with twenty-nine new crewmen and a full complement of passengers. Now in larger cabins, Otto and Ned got down to work without particular difficulty, Otto in the main galley and Ned at first in the second class rooms of D deck. Ned's chief steward was a large and likeable Frenchman by the grand name of Alphonse de Mirabeau, a facially disfigured individual who endeared himself to staff rather better than passengers, who were repelled by his looks. Mirabeau discovered that the Englishman was capable and left him alone to get on with the job, merely reinforcing the way that things were done on the French Line. He soon noticed other stewards went to Ned for help with less-than-sympathetic English-speaking passengers, the Englishman was there to oblige with a mature attitude. If any colleague knew of Ned's experience on the *Titanic*, no-one spoke of it and that was good.

As they had approached the great ship on the afternoon of joining her, Ned had looked up admiringly as he had done that first time months ago.

"Osspissiuss occasion." The words came bravely out of Otto's mouth in a flood of sibilance.

"Is that your word for today?"

"Could be," joked Otto.

"Then give me warning and I'll put on my oilskins!"

"Oilskins? What you saying?"

"You see, it's true – Germans don't have a sense of humour!"

"Och! You British. Always choking, what."

"Even so," mused Ned, looking up at the ship, "Ah get the feeling mebbe we should be dressed up to the nines to present usselves onboard."

"Nines? What is zat?"

"Just another English expression."

"Ja? It's a stupid one. Nines! What sort of clothing is dat? Is dat better zan eights?"

"Well...." The truth was, Ned had no idea where the expression came from.

"Perhaps ten is better, yes? Why not ten? I dress up to ten, Ned – I beat you – hah!"

Yes, you can beat me, thought Ned: he was just happy to admire the ship.

Old feelings had come to him; for *La France*, whilst smaller than *Titanic*, brought back such reminiscences of the British vessel as he had first seen her in Southampton dock. *La France's* four red-painted funnels hinting at her power; her livery a smart white and black; her general bearing as she sat in the water, all seemed to reflect the air of arrogant beauty that *Titanic* had radiated. Of *La France,* though, there was an air of not so much Size or Speed but Swagger and Style. She was impressive enough.

Ned had got used to *La Rochelle,* and *La France* now dwarfed the former flagship *Rochambeau* and her sisters of the C.G.T. Within an extra 50 metres of length, she doubled the passenger capability along with her 24,000 tons weight, and with four screws to *La Rochelle's* two, she cruised 3-4 knots faster than her sisters. For a time, there was a trade-off, as *La France* could suffer intermittent vibrations, but staff would fend off any concerns merely by suggesting she was making up time lost due to adverse weather.

One thing did bother Ned just a little, however: she was equipped with no more lifeboats than *Titanic*. Otto simply screwed up his face in an expression of resignation, as if to say to his friend, 'Lightning does not strike twice'.

Once aboard, it was the elegance of this ship that took the breath away. In a short time, she had already gained that pet name: the *Versailles of the Sea*. A grand title for a bounty of extravagance that showed from even third class cabins: each class of cabin might belong to that of a higher class from a similar British vessel. More than this, there was simply that aura of *chic*: every cabin, every bulkhead even, seemed to exude that almost indefinable flavour imported from the best elements of Paris society. This was the character that defined *La France*, and which in turn became the essence of the French Line. This ship's crewmen and women somehow seemed more relaxed, more convivial, more confident. An appearance of competence was a self-fulfilling observation. Americans would just say that *La France* had Class.

She remained at her dock in New York over Christmas that year. The only parties held aboard were those set up and attended by the crew. In any case, for Christmas Day dinner Ned and Otto had been invited by Magoolagan and the petite Clodagh to join them and their family. It was the first time that Ned had learned Magoolagan's Christian name – Claude. Yes, he allowed them to laugh, and confided that he hated the name. The young German was having difficulty with names: so why not 'Magoogle'? One or two laughed, but no-one objected, least of all the dubiously-named Claude, and the term 'Magoogle' brought a smile - a caring one. Magoolagan would always answer to it.

Shane Larkin came to New York every few months, but little was said of his niece or of what sort of life Zena was leading now, and Ned thought better of pressing any enquiry, only reflecting that the bogus claim of concealment under Zena's coat was recognized for what it was - a lie, a red herring, a distortion manipulated by

Ranulph Knight for his amusement. Amusement for him, serious aggravation for Ned.

But it was Christmastime, and better to not think too much about it. Clodagh told him he would be better to get more into the spirit of the Bunny Hug the young people were attempting at the Dance Palace that New Year, where young American women were recklessly trying to show how they had cast off their Gibson Girl images. Those girls wore rouge and lipstick, and no corset - such scandal! What was far more affecting was on New Year's Day to hear Magoolagan and Clodagh singing in their parlour, 'The Miner's Dream of Home', to the affecting accompaniment of a friend's fiddle.

"…. for the bells were ringing the old year out and the new year in….." It ended in a sweet and lingering kiss, and transported the wistful Ned back to France.

Perversely, however, he was glad – relieved in a sense - that he was away more often now, as he reflected on the embarrassment he had caused the previous summer in his attraction to Renata. A real attraction, a strong attraction that remained. Yet not a wise one. A young French woman hoping for a promising attachment maintained a dignity that had to demonstrate her potential as being sensible and practical. Ned at that time offered only an impetuous response to a situation entirely of his mind's own creation.

"You are wiz zose pixies again, Ned," Frau Bremme had said to him one evening as he washed the dinner pots. She rarely voiced an opinion: someone so astute had no need to.

"Pixies….. Ah, you're right, madame. Of course y'are. I'm away with the fairies……"

"I know where zis head is walking, he is out wiz zat young lady again."

Ned turned the big pot over and plunged the dish mop inside. "Ah don't fool you, do I, madame?"

She smiled and took a pan off the draining board to dry it. "You are family, Ned. You should call me 'Mutti'."

"But I have a mother. In England."

"Zen you call me Marlene. Zey cannot call me zat but you are friend of ze family. You call me Marlene. I wish you do dat."

"Ah will, then," he replied proudly.

"*Aber* – Reina," she immediately changed the subject, "She make up ze mind soon. Maybe. Do not..." She could not find the words. "Ned, when a woman has twenty-four years... many questions. Sometimes ze head is what make matter, not.... not in here." And she patted her chest lightly. "Nossing you can do.... You understand?"

Yes, he understood. By now he understood. And he knew there was a great deal Marlene could have said if she had wished. But .... between a son and a mother, much need not be spoken.

"You see, I am," suggested Ned after a long silence, "I'm just an ignorant man. That's all."

"Ignorant? I do not understand zat. What is zat word - ignorant?"

He had put down the wash cloth. At that instant, an impulse gripped him: he put his arms around the small lady and gently embraced her. It was a very spiritual feeling, water momentarily came to his eyes without reason.

"It means I am a very, very stupid man. But very lucky too."

Otto, on the other hand, had been mindlessly oblivious to anything other than a situation that offered to rid him of a hopeless bore for a future brother-in-law. They spoke of it, Ned and Otto, but not at great length. His friend's only curiosity was that Ned seemed to have been spending more time away from the girls than Otto would have liked. Ned explained that he was standing off more for the sake of Renata's reputation, and in any case, it would give her the time to think. What he did not say was, since the episode in the Grapes with Cade, he had to avoid placing the family in danger.

"Well, my small *Nixie* friend," said Otto, with a logic only he could have summoned up, "You can have Gitta.........!"

Typically Otto! Ned shook his head. "Drink your schnapps," he said.

Otto had not intended the remark spuriously and his light tone quickly changed.

"Ned." He clapped a hold on Ned's arm, "Today she work in ze grocer's shop. Tomorrow..... She is a bright girl, Ned. Maybe she don't wake up yet, but a good wife.... Uh?"

"Otto, Gitta is..... look, she's a lovely girl, ah'm very fond of 'er."

"Fond.... Mm. Vot is 'fond'? Maybe fond is okay. Ned – you are a shy man, I sink – wiz women. Do not be shy, Ned. Ja? You have zat phrase, 'Time waits for nossing'."

" ' – no man,' Otto: 'Time waits for no man'."

"It's ze same! Dat's it. Time don't waits! - Hells bells! It don't wait for Ned if Gitta decides anozzer boy wants her now, not tomorrow. In *März* Gitta will be nineteen, Ned. Nineteen. I sink she begins to sink about herself."

"Ah know, Otto, ah know."

"You know, uh? Most girls are already married years by now. Zese two......." His gesture was one of disdain. But then, he added, "Maybe, because we lose Vati..... I don't know. Maybe it make zem careful - ze husband, he must be ze right one.... Ned?"

"What?"

"I sink you are right. You are ignorant man!"

"Uh?"

"Mutti ask me, What is zis word Ned call himself? - 'Ignorant'. I look up zis word - it says you are not educated. So I tell Mutti Ned think too much wiz a head that don't work very well, what."

"Right," Ned answered, feigning indignation. "I'm going back to my bunk. I'm gonna read Jules Verne and Joseph Conrad for at least a hundred pages so don't bother me till I'm educated!"

Ned had to admit all the arguments to himself, knowing he had to deal with it. Renata had never reproached him nor demanded explanation for his proposal, yet he believed it was Renata he still desired. Marlene understood what was going on in his mind: when he was at the house, she would smile and pay him small kindnesses.

"Your mother," he told Otto, "is a saint."

Puzzled, Otto replied, "No – not yet....."

Life was becoming a series of "If only" moments. If only he were in a better position socially. If only he had more to offer a woman: a sound future, a home, children in due time, and all the security she would demand. Then the spectre of being hauled through a British court of law and outcast by his country.

Yet Reina was always in his mind, whether or not she was on course to marry Jerome Forget. Her stature, tall and slim; her fair hair loose and almost gypsy-like as it was that day last summer, those blue eyes so focused and alert, her voice when he had heard her singing that day of the school concert, her familiarity and popularity with people in the market place. Her skin tanned like the reflection of buttercups; her spoken voice soft, so fluid and enticing. They had not so much as kissed, nor even held hands, barely even touched.

Otto was right, though, about Gitta, insofar as that had relevance for him. With her temperament, he was surprised she had not already had a betrothal, for Frau Bremme had told him Gitta had had more than one young man ask her. Of the two, Otto considered Gitta the more immediately beautiful, and her disposition the more approachable, if at times too mercurial for her own good. Someone in the past had disappointed her, that much Otto hinted, and Ned was not going to ask further. Were there really choices in this? Ned had to draw deep breaths and get to know his place!

* * * * *

Faithful to her promise, though, Renata gave Ned instruction on her camera. He had been looking forward to it enormously: he would have the pleasure of her company, legitimately, so had no need of apologies. They walked, the two of them, to the seaward edge of the town where they could enjoy something of a view that was not simply a fortress of houses. An early suggestion of Spring took them there one Saturday afternoon in February. Not warm, but pleasant enough without the sea breeze, and the sky was bright.

167

She wore mittens, a long coat and complicated hat. Whilst Ned carried the cumbersome tripod and bulky camera with its heavy lens, Renata carried a small box with photographic plates.

There they set up the strange box on its substantial wooden tripod which he had found most annoying, and she pressed down the metal switch with the camera pointed at the harbour entrance below.

"What happens now?" asked Ned.

"We change the plate over."

That puzzled Ned. "Ah thought you said these things had a roll of paper inside that you just wound on. Yer mean to say, this is what that chap had to cart around the Antarctic ter make them pictures o' poor Captain Scott and 'is men? Ruddy 'ell, what a contraption!"

"Not zis one, Ned. That's the little one I have used, not this. There is a new camera I want to get later, a Folding Kodak. Ja - it folds up! But this one here is like the others, it takes these plates. So we have to take these back to the school and develop zem in the dark."

"Oh. Ah see." He didn't.

"So can I take a picture now?"

"When I have changed this plate," said Renata, doing it.

"Alright. Go stand over there."

"Me, Ned?"

"Aye. Why not?"

"But.... I....."

"You're as pretty as a picture. So let's put you in one. Stand over there."

She gave him a sideways look, as if to tell him he was incorrigible, but did as she was told, after showing him the metal arm to press and how to turn the brass lens barrel. He could just see her upturned figure in the glass, one hand pressing onto her voluminous hat.

"Ey!" he called to her, "Yer standin' on yer 'ead!"

As he turned the lens he seemed to be able to see her head clearly, and so he pressed. Nothing appeared to happen, though he assumed it had and was satisfied anyway.

"Champion!"

"What?"

"That picture. It'll be champion."

"Champ - *Champignons*? What? Mushrooms? What are you talking, Ned?"

"No - champion....It's..... er.... it's an expression. It's just a Yorkshire expression."

"*Champignons*...... Mushrooms!"

"No, Reina – 'champion'. That's all."

"Mushrooms!" She laughed. "You are a funny man, Ned."

"Is that good – being a funny man?" He felt as if a door had been opened - just a little.

"It's good..... I sink."

"So yer still like me?"

She was not going to be pushed into that trap, and smiled at him, coyly. "I still like you. Of course. You are my brother's best friend."

Ned paused. That was good enough. Leave it there.

"Oho, we can 'ave fun in 'ere!"

The school second classroom had to act as Renata's darkroom. It had only one big window at the end, and she had been able to make it about as light-tight as it needed to be in the early dark of an evening by stretching two frames of black calico in double-thickness across the top and bottom of it, and tightening the battens against the window frames with turnkeys the concierge had made up for the purpose.

"We are not 'ere to have fun, Ned! You want me to show you ze plates or not?"

"Yes, please, miss," he joked. He knew she would not take him seriously. If he tried too hard, she would walk away. In that respect, he had learned just how much 'fun' he could try with

Renata without offending. Quite the opposite of Brigitte, who was the one who loved to tease yet did not like to be teased in return.

His tomfoolery quickly disappeared, however, once Renata produced the first of the glass plates from the hypo bath and rinsed it. A single candle flickered behind a red glass frame; yet even in that very dim red light, which had taunted his giddy sense of romance, to see the emergence of an image that showed some sort of strange black outline against a lot of other dull outlines, this was something that seized at the imagination. Science? - No, magic! It was a magical creativity the like of which he had not seen before. The cinema with its moving pictures, after all, was what it was, one accepted it and did not look to see what secrets the magician used. This was much better.

"I told you, Ned," was all she said, as he took the edge of the plate with two fingers whilst she held onto the other side. His fascination cut short his amorous foolery as he took the whole plate from her.

"Don't...... drop...... Be careful....." Yes, he was being careful.

"Don't lick ze fingers!" Yes, he was about to lick his wet fingers.

"Poison?" Ned asked.

"*Ja, sicher.*" She shook her head and grinned in the darkness. "..... Like mushrooms."

"Mushrooms? You havin' me on again? Mushrooms aren't poisonous, are they?"

She giggled. "Some."

He peered closer at the plate. "But.... Ah can't...... What are we lookin' at?"

"*Negatif,*" said Renata, "I told you – it makes a *negatif* – er, an opposite. Look closer."

She was right, of course. She had told him before, but he had not been listening.

"So now we..... er..... What do we do now?"

"First, we develop ze ozzer two plates. And then, tomorrow, in ze light, I show you. We put zis *negatif* up close to some special paper. We count. It makes a picture. You have seen photographs, Ned."

"Photographs? Oh aye. Hey! You mean, ah get to see yer standin' on yer 'ead?" There was a mischievous glint in his eye that might have hinted at something else, but she just laughed again. "Of course not!"

"Oh. I get it. You're just standin' by that wall 'oldin' on to yer 'at, ey? Champion!"

"Mushrooms!" She laughed louder. A broad, open laugh, unusual for her. "Yes, Ned."

And that is what it was – "champion". He said it many times, as he viewed the results the next day in late afternoon light. And each time he repeated the exclamation, Renata chuckled and quietly mouthed to herself, "Mushrooms".

She counted out the exposure of the paper, and within a short time Ned was looking at her portrait as she had stood against the wall. The shadowy form of a ship in the background was not so distinct but her own likeness in black and white was there to see and to gaze at. She was quite thrilled that for once he was lost for words.

Eventually, he said, "Can ah keep this?"

Renata smiled. "Of course! I have ze plate. I can make more."

"Amazing! You're a wizard, you know that?"

"Wiz - ? Wiz – what?"

"Beauty and brains in one body!....." He stopped. No. No, it must not go any further, he told himself.

But he grinned as she showed her delight again in another laugh. "Mushrooms!" she giggled.

* * * * *

Then in April, Cade made his move.

La France docked on the 8th. The crossing had been rough, passengers and crew alike were eager to get ashore in Le Havre. For the stewards, there were many vomit-stained blankets to wash!

Particularly keen to disembark was a small brigade of volatile Greek men anxious to return to their homeland following their king's assassination. Ned had heard about that, and did not lack

171

sympathy, yet overall was glad to see the back of them as they had created havoc in his bar. The mess, though, was cleared up quickly and nothing, so Ned was told by M.Mirabeau, compared to the mess that Greece was in.

Once in the harbour, the weather brightened and Brigitte decided she could leave the shop early to go down to the dock, assuming the boys had no more than the usual duties to wind up. She knew Phillipe, the seaman who manned the gangway who was delighted to run an errand for her. A smile and a swish of her skirt was enough to despatch the desperately eager young man, who took less than three minutes to return to her, panting the news that Ned alone would be leaving the ship within twenty minutes. Brigitte waited, pulling her shawl closer about her shoulders in the cool air and tucking her headscarf in behind it, and moving back from the gangway because it was unfair to lead the young seaman on.

The two men were standing by a stack of tea chests. She would have taken no note at all except that they were not moving whilst everyone else was hurrying hither and thither, and when Ned appeared she ran forward, calling his name. He was carrying almost nothing, only a thin sack of clothing, and he wore a coat loosely over his steward's uniform.

She hugged him and he put an arm around her. With a quick turnaround in New York, the ship had been away for less than three weeks, but she hugged him as if it had been three months. In return, he gave her a peck on the cheek like a brother and made to move away from any display of enthusiasm.

Lights were coming on in buildings along the quay. As they came away, leaving the cluttered docklands, Brigitte chatted about her friends and the fact she had made a *lapin* stew for dinner and Renata was away in Rouen and a man had been caught stealing from the shop and -

"*Lapin*? Again?" joked Ned. Brigitte thumped him hard in his side, so that she could hug him again.

Walking out into the edge of the town, Ned felt the unease as a kind of shudder that ran down his back and dragged at his legs. It could not be called a premonition by any means but there was an awareness as he walked that something behind him was not as it should be. His detachment from Brigitte's chattering swiftly erupted into alarm as the first man came forward and grabbed his shoulder. The second, a very large man, delivered a blow into his lower chest that took all the breath out of Ned's body and doubled him over onto the cobbles of the street. Then another blow to the side of his face, and for one tiny instant he could almost have been back in the water with that oar crashing down onto his shoulder. After Brigitte's scream, his ears heard only a kind of deafening whistle, and he was on the stone floor.

"You got 'em!" shouted the first voice, and the man had grabbed Ned by both sides of his collar and was shaking him fiercely. "You gonna hand 'em over, lad, or else!"

" – Run, Gitta! Run!" Was it his own voice? He felt the rough hands of the man, going through his pockets and finding only a handful of loose change, a comb and some bits of paper. The man threw them all away – except for Ned's wallet, which he kept.

"Where you got 'em, eh? - Where you keepin' them papers? You gonna give 'em back, sunshine?"

" – I – I – Ah don't have - "

"Yair, you fuckin' well do, you little bastard! Where you got 'em? At that house?"

Ned tried to speak again but the pain was too much. Then a boot kicked him hard in the side of his face. After that, he could not speak at all, and panted and grunted and knew he was at their mercy.

"You better get wise, lad, or you ain't gonna live much longer. You 'ear me, lad?"

Hear him, yes, he could just about do that. But speak – hardly. All he could manage was to spit blood as they spread him face down on the cobblestones, his left arm up pushed up behind his back.

"You gonna tell us, lad? You gonna take us there?"

Ned felt to be living this nightmare for ever. All he knew was the pain, and he hoped they would not hit him once more for fear that his lungs might burst. With no way of speaking, how could he react to their questions? In which case, the beating would continue.

Then, as suddenly as they had leaped on him, they were on their feet above him as there came a rush of muffled voices. Ned rolled onto his side and saw several other dark figures, and his assailants were turning away. They were running away.... But he could make out little more before the surge of relief overwhelmed him and brought down a muddy red curtain of unconsciousness.

Papa Pascal ran his little establishment La Coquille where the houses of the town met the docks. Part-cafe and patisserie, it was mostly a meeting place for sailors going to and from the docks, where a young woman yelling "*Au Secours!*" at once found the ears of a dozen men who had just left *La France.* That a compatriot was being attacked by two English ruffians was enough to have them dashing to his aid.

At first Brigitte cried out as she held Ned's bloodied face in her hands, but she regained her presence of mind quickly and urged the men to carry Ned back to La Coquille where they laid him out over three tables pushed together. There he was washed and tended to by Brigitte and Papa Pascal's wife, whilst Papa Pascal himself told them how to do it. Fifty minutes later, the motor car arrived and Papa Pascal tendered the fare to the infirmary on the promise of repayment - that, and Brigitte's kiss. As she had already given each man a "thank you" kiss for their help. Despatching one of them to pass a message via Phillipe on the gangway, she stepped into the motor car.

Watching them go, and waving as they left, Papa Pascal lingered in the doorway of La Coquille long enough to notice a figure across the road, close enough to see his face but not to recognize it. Calmly, the man placed a cigarette in his mouth and struck a match. In the fading light, the incandescence illuminated the man distinctly and Papa Pascal noted the man held the cigarette awkwardly in his left hand, from which he was missing a finger.

* * * * *

174

NINETEEN

Bruno Carelle spent ten minutes waxing his moustache before proceeding to the dining room, where he joined with the boring Mr. Andretty and his shrewish wife who smelled excessively of Lily of the Valley, their timid son and the two misses Persimmon, who ran a bakery in Paris and were setting off for their first holiday in seven years – to the Grand Canyon: Carelle was left in no doubt of it since it was half of what they spoke. It was a place which, Carelle was able to assure them, would astound their highest sensibilities since it beggared every traveller's account of it. Dinner was pleasant in the food sense, washed down with a half-decent Beaune, but otherwise tiresome, and he was eager to get away and take his cognac in the saloon bar with the young steward he had instructed to meet him there at precisely 8.45.

Ned was still in uniform - a fresh one - as he approached the table where Carelle had ensconced himself with his Martell, waving his stick in the air for Ned to see him.

"You were right, Ned, this is a busy boat. Even late in the evening, I should not be able to speak with you at any length whilst you were working."

It was rare for the two of them to meet when Ned was not about his normal duties, and he felt more than a little awkward. Strangely perhaps, he was glad that he was not in civilian dress, the uniform lent an entirely proper tone to the occasion, given the chasm of social circumstance separating them.

"It's quite alright, Ned," Carelle leaned forward purposely, "to relax in my company. You are off duty. We can speak man to man, does that meet your approval?"

"Yes, sir."

"Then you must remember you are my equal, Ned. I don't want you genuflecting in front of me."

"Um... Gen-u-what, sir?"

"Paying too much respect. I don't wish that you become my servant."

"Ah," said Ned, inclining his head in affirmation.

"If you wish to call me 'sir', as a customer, I understand, and I will accept 'Monsieur Carelle' but I am not of royal blood nor heir to a title in Perthshire, so once we are better acquainted, my name is Bruno, is that clear?"

"It is, sir."

"I was touched by the letter from your sister. I was particularly touched that she addressed the envelope as 'Monsieur B. Carelle, Chocolatier, Antwerp, Belgium'..... Quite wonderful! And of course it arrived on my desk. Even though I am not in any way a chocolatier. Our postal service is to be congratulated, I shall tell Monsieur Pasquier when I next see him – he will invite me to lunch."

"Ah told her about you when ah were in England, before ah got beaten up – ah don't need to explain, you know the rest. It surely were a big liberty to take –"

"Not at all. Your sister cares for you, that's obvious. Listen, my young friend, I am not a policeman, I am not a detective. I am not the brother of Sherlock Holmes. I sell beans!" Carelle laughed heartily so that the length of his 6ft-plus shook and his watch chain rustled. He calmed and leaned forward again.

"But.... There is money in little beans, and today I have a lot of money. Money is power – well, you know, the sort of power that money makes. When you are in business, you buy people – in a manner of speaking. In my case.... I enjoy, shall we say, a certain influence in parts of the world. In Belgium and of course along the African coast, but I have an office in Switzerland and I share a couple of bean people in New York and Bordeaux. And of course.... oh, contacts in London and Paris and so on. The United States is a big market for chocolate, for instance. It's only money, Ned: it can't make you a good person, but it makes the world go round, as they say. *My* world, for sure.....You asked me yesterday, why would I wish to help you –"

"You're a busy man, ah can't expect yer to take up yer time wi' –"

" – It's alright, Ned. Listen, a person does what he can. Most people are too busy just surviving, but I believe if I have the

176

position where I can help someone like yourself, then I should do that. Let us say, it pleases me to do that. There have been times in my life when I had wished that someone could help me..... But anyway, your sister, Grace. I liked her letter, she impressed me."

" – Ah can't go back to England. Ah'm a wanted man."

"I know, I know. Well, you can go back, but carefully, uh? Nothing is impossible. What we have to be clear about is why this man Cade is following you."

"Cade is just the boot man."

"'Boot man'! What a splendid expression! I can imagine his huge boots walking all over the world... But yes, you mean another man is pulling his strings. I understand..... And Ned, I know this man. At least, I know who he is, even in Belgium we are not out of touch with the – er, the corridors of power in the capitals of Europe... Your Mr. Knight is flying high in the British realm: Mr. Anthony Scott-Chapelle, whose grandfather fought alongside Wellington at Waterloo."

"Did he, sir? - Ah didn't know."

Carelle snorted and laughed. "Huh! I don't know either! Ned, if we believe them, every lord in England is related to Nelson or Wellington, hmm? What nonsense! Anyway, he is a powerful man."

"Very."

"Whose father-in-law, Lord Semper, is presently of ill health and expected to live not long. It's common knowledge. He married money too, you know, our Mr. Scott-Chapelle. Oh yes. Lady Sophie. She is the wealth. It is she whose family brought him the soap business, did you know? The dynasty goes back four hundred years. Impressive, uh? Not that the dynasty in itself is important, the family home came close to bankruptcy during the time of the fourth earl.... Gambling. Yes... Well, it would seem your Mr. Knight will shortly become one - a knight."

Carelle broke off to laugh loudly, attracting other eyes in the saloon.

"When the old man dies, he will become Lord Semper. You could have chosen a less powerful adversary, Ned."

"I – well, ah didn't choose him – *he* chose me."

"A man who can get other men to do anything he wants. No questions asked. And he is noble, is he not? We cannot say nasty things about a British lord, can we?"

Ned for a moment did not know how he should take that remark. Then Carelle laughed again and Ned was beginning to comprehend this man.

The saloon steward responded to Carelle's beckoning cane and was given an order for further cognac and two cigars, the best Havana. Ned immediately said he would prefer a cigarette, which Carelle understood. The steward betrayed a curious glance at his colleague seated there, but turned smartly to his task.

"By the way," carried on Carelle, "You may not have directly recommended it, but this was a good choice of ship, I'm glad I changed my booking when you told me. But in April when I sailed, you were not aboard! – Because of this." Carelle wafted a hand toward Ned's face.

"It costs you more," Ned apologised.

"Och..... A few francs more. For a magnificent vessel like *La France*. Good choice, Ned. I would have chosen her myself eventually but... good choice."

"*La Rochelle* was not half so grand, but ah liked 'er. She got me away from New York in the nick of time."

"In the nick of...... Ah, yes. Only, I had heard that word in another sense - 'nick'. In England a prison is 'the nick' - Is that not so? It was almost a prison for you – New York. But you got away with your friend, the big German chap. You trust him."

"With my life, yes."

"I agree..... You know I spoke to him?"

"Why, no, Otto never said a thing."

Carelle only smiled. "And his sisters, Ned..... Oh, he told me they lead you a pretty dance."

"A *merry* dance, sir. And yes, that they do, ah suppose." Ned was not sure how much he should confide at present. "Gitta looked after me when ah were laid up, wi' this arm. Brigitte, the younger one. She works in the town grocer's shop, like. Reina's a schoolteacher."

"Ah, now that reminds me, Ned – I have some chocolates your ladies may like to try. You know that Belgian chocolates are the finest. And my beans go into the best of them. Naturally!" Again, his hearty laugh.

"I have this little box from one of the master chocolatiers in Antwerp..... They are delicious, your young ladies will love them. And you know, they do say," enthused Carelle, leaning forward a little with a gleam in his eye, "that chocolate is a fine aphrodisiac."

"Aphro-diz....?"

Carelle saw that the word was lost on the young man. He decided not to press the point. "Chocolate was originally a medicine, did you know that?"

"No, ah didn't. Ah don't know anythin' about chocolate, truth to tell. Except the best chocolate's a lot o' brass. Ah couldn't thoil it meself."

"Couldn't........?" Now it was for Carelle to let a strange word go. "But yes, the Maya and the Olmec used to use it as a medicine.... Ned, I am deviating. How long were you – what you said – laid up?"

"More than two months. They looked after me. All me savings went. Ah couldn't let 'em pay for me to eat. They gave me bed and shelter. That's when ah wrote to yer – an' our Grace beat me to it. Mah ribs hurt so much, ah were black an' blue for a while."

"You still are." And Carelle pointed at the side of Ned's face where the blow had torn the skin. It had healed, but the marks were still there.

Ned felt those marks. "Ah couldn't go back to work until ah looked decent. The *Compagnie* wouldn't want a man that looked like the back of a tram smash. Otto kept a good word for me wi' our supplies officer so ah had no problem."

"You are a good steward, Ned, and they know it. You are popular here..... But these men who attacked you, you never saw them before?"

"Neither before nor since. Wasn't Cade, an' ah can't prove it but ah reckon he were behind it."

"And you think – all because Scott-Chapelle believed you had taken papers from him."

"Appen so, aye. Ah've nuthin' else to go on."

"So he gets Cade to... work on you. But why? Why Cade? Just money, you think?"

"Money? Ah suppose so. Why? – You think summat else?"

".... I don't know." Carelle was thinking hard about this. "A man in Scott-Chapelle's position – hey, let's carry on calling him Mr. Knight, it's easier. But this man could buy absolutely anyone. Why Cade? Why a seaman like yourself? Does that make sense?" Ned had no idea what made sense.

"Although, after what you told me about seeing you in Southampton, I imagine you are right, Cade was behind that attack. If Cade knew as much as he evidently did, Knight would not bother to involve anyone else, would he?"

"Suppose not."

"And you told me you worked with him, long ago. But even then he was not friendly."

"Huh! He took a knife to me."

"But....." Sitting completely upright, Carelle was tapping his cane on the wooden deck to inspire his thoughts. "If this is about some private papers, why would all this not have taken place months ago? Why stretch things out? – If you follow me."

That Carelle was prepared to devote thought and energy to his cause encouraged the young man.

"It's them papers. Dunno what they could 'ave been. Some official secret, I thought."

"*Titanic* sank more than a year ago. If you had had papers the nature of which may have been compromising, why would he not take steps to get them back before? Why wait until this April to have those men attack you? Does that make sense? – I don't think so." Ned could add nothing further, and presently Carelle broke out of his pensive envelope.

"Ah – here's our cognac. You know, Ned, there is a saying that men are like these glasses. We say, 'this glass is half full', while another man says, 'this glass is half empty'. It is supposed to indicate a man's attitude to life. All I say is, fill the glass again, there is always room for more cognac! To you, Ned! May you survive all your shipwrecks!"

* * * * *

Almost before *La France* had picked up her tugs to dock in New York on August 21st, M. Carelle was poised ready to leave for a south-bound train.

Carelle summed up his views quite succinctly in idiomatic English: "The scent has gone cold: let sleeping dogs lie."

Carelle would set aside some of his time and influence to dig a little into those quarters of New York and London where information might be gleaned and perhaps in due time, Knight in his own actions might give away some clue. Lord Semper was terminally ill, Knight would become a peer of the British realm, a high profile figure whose many moves would be easily noted by those with weight in the media of the day. Carelle had his own tools of social intercourse, he was a man who knew well how to use the power of his wealth. They were opponents in much the same game, so it was essential to keep cards close to the chest, but for now Carelle was an unknown card in the deck.

It was hardly a plan, yet Carelle himself appeared to relish the chance to take risks, which to Ned seemed the only logical reason for this man of means to want to intercede on Ned's behalf. Perhaps, after his troubled youth, Carelle's ordered, wealthy and cultured life was boring. How much fun could there be in cocoa beans?

The Belgian left the ship that sunny Thursday afternoon, bound immediately for Charleston and later, he planned, for his New York agent, whilst Otto and Ned merely carried on with their duties and the next day went to visit Otto's friend Magoogle.

* * * * *

Carelle's reappearance was more dramatic than his earlier departure. The ship's forward gangway was almost at the point of being swung away when the big Belgian appeared for the sailing of *La France* less than a week after she had docked. It was a particularly busy time for the French liner, with two sailings from Le Havre coming up in September, but Carelle had no wish to wait around longer than necessary before being able to leave. He had, in any case, a ticket for this sailing.

Within the day he had invited Ned to meet him, in Carelle's first class cabin, where Ned found his mentor preoccupied and agitated.

"Damn those bloody daygos!... My apologies, my friend. I have been releasing my energies in a very bad way, forgive me. Drink? No? Well, I have had two already, so please indulge me."

Carelle's steward had left a pot of coffee for him, of which the big man now gestured Ned to avail himself. A plate of small cakes sat on the little table and another plate holding pastry remnants indicated the vols-au-vent had already been consumed.

"One of our agents," Carelle began to explain by way of releasing his anger, "has been poached, you might say. Ach, I should not be surprised, this is a volatile business. South Americans have no ethics at all."

"A cut-throat business," Ned offered, unsure of what was required of him.

"It is, Ned. Any business worth doing today is cut-throat. But in Europe we do not *actually* cut the throat! You understand me? Not in polite society anyway." Ned lent a token twist of the head to the conversation and that was all.

"Ach, I have seen worse. It's annoying but, believe me, I have seen far worse. Here, Ned, have an American cigarette - take the packet." Carelle leaned back in the stout, plush chair. He thought of a cigar, then dismissed it. The cabin was stuffy now: the port was open but Ned saw that the steward had not done a thorough job of preparation. The overhead fan squeaked a little, Ned would get that seen to, and the fresh flowers had been forgotten.

"You would imagine the world of cocoa would be a quiet, genteel sort of business, would you not?"

"Ah couldn't answer that, sir. Ah've seen some rum business carried on around legs of mutton in New York or opium in Limehouse – once, never again – and ah'd never question the goings-on of businesses."

"Wise, Ned ..... When you have seen what I have seen..... Believe me, far, far worse. How are you, by the way?"

"Well, sir, thank you. Busy. Ah like bein' busy."

Inspecting Ned's face, Carelle showed satisfaction. "It's healed almost completely. Good. And the ribs?"

"Creak a bit still. But ah manage..... Ah'll not ask if you had a good visit."

Carelle smiled back at him and, settling into the chair, released a long sigh of frustrations pent up in him over recent days.

"What do you know of Africa, Ned?"

He knew pretty well nothing, and stated the fact.

"My family, Ned, were originally French. A little village in Aquitaine, La Carelle....... my name, you see. Like other families they grew grapes, for the wine. As one does. But one of my forefathers decided there were opportunities in Africa. With land so cheap.... The French government at the time pushing people toward the colonies. As did all the European countries, of course, all building empires. Well, let us be honest, the Europeans stole it from the Africans the same as they did everywhere else....." He paused to reflect.

"So I had family back then in West Africa, they got established along the coast. France had huge colonial possessions there – still does, of course. And labour was cheap too – well, I say '*cheap*'!.....We *owned* people, you don't get much cheaper than that."

"Slaves?" queried Ned, carefully.

"Slaves? Yes, there was slavery, right through the last century in spite of abolition. Arab slavers, they would come through. Congo slaves, millions of them. So many thousands died just in the ships, you know..... Slave ships got sunk, too. But take away the plantation

183

workers and the European owners complain. That's not good for business!"

Finally, he did reach for that cigar.

"My grandfather produced cocoa beans for export. In a nutshell, that's it! I have made that silly joke before, forgive me..... And then, well, families get fragmented and move around; my father and his brother moved south, into the Congo region. Which at that time was..... to call it 'virgin' would be wrong. 'Raw' is a better word."

Ned leaned forward in his chair: to an uneducated Yorkshireman, Carelle was a man who was history itself.

"Boma was not much of a place. It's hardly anything now. Scrappy huts on stilts along the banks of a river that often carried them away. Squalid. Mud banks, long grass, mosquitoes. But – once you've been bitten a few hundred times you lose your flavour for them. We lived in a grand wooden house that cost literally peanuts. Me, my younger brother, our mother and father, servants, a cook...."

Pausing for a further sip of his cognac seemed to allow Carelle to conjure an image in the air at which he stared for some seconds.

"Cocoa beans came across country and down-river along with shipments of rubber – I don't mean together, we had two businesses really. The main cocoa bean business was with Uncle Laurent, he was up north. Well, the European countries were doing whatever they could to rob the wealth of Africa. Flies round the jam pot."

His fixation broke away as he quickly turned to Ned. " – As we Europeans do, ey, Ned? We put a flag in the ground and claim it for our king or queen. Doesn't matter who is already there!" He laughed. "How the proud and mighty show the meek and the innocent what it means to be good Christians! And we are all good Christians, are we not?"

Whilst understanding the irony, the young man did not know how to deal with it. Carelle only grinned with a sardonic air.

"The Congo – a huge river area, Ned – huge, you will never see anything like it. Great trade for Europeans. Ivory, rubber. My family didn't get involved with ivory. But rubber, enormous business in the forested lands in the north. We are talking

184

thousands of kilometres, Ned, you cannot imagine. Dense, horrible country. I had been up into the grasslands as a young man, I hated the forests, couldn't wait to get out of there. But almost inevitably, we became involved with the rubber trade. At the same time – and I was a young man – Belgium became overlord of the Congo. King Leopold, you see, had this grand vision to make the Congo the glorious Belgian colony to match the British and the French – this stinking, wet, choking, festering garden of evil, he wanted to make it his private country. And that's what he did. They called it the *Domaine Privé* – have you heard of this?"

"No."

"No. Even now, nobody wants to talk about it. Because it all went bad. Oh, there was fine talk, fine speeches, fine intentions, but they forgot that people are essentially greedy – especially white Europeans. Instead of protecting the Africans, the reverse happened. Belgian soldiers came in, and mercenaries, and instead of stamping out slavery they increased it. Rubber, you see - exploit the Africans, get them working the rubber plantations while the fat owners got richer and greedier. It's an old story, Ned, and will go on long after you and I are dead."

Carelle stopped to relight his cigar.

"We didn't like that. Apart from the way we are brought up to treat people, the whole economy was .... hopeless for an honest trading company. This is not long ago, Ned, I'm talking 25 years ago, that's all. They took away the rights of the Africans, who had in effect to give up everything they had. They allowed new companies to operate with royal concessions, to do more or less as they liked. Ordinary businesses, like my father's, were taxed to cut them out of the system. Africans were compelled to work for these companies without payment. Slave labour. The worst happened. Carnage! Africans who refused were killed or maimed: they would have hands and legs cut off just for failing to supply their quota of rubber. Have you seen children walking around without arms, Ned?"

The young man found it hard to shake his head, his neck had become so tense.

185

"Sickening! I was sick – the first time I saw such horrors, I was actually sick. I couldn't believe how people could do this to other people. It was not a war, after all, and a war is bad enough. Men, women, even children were murdered without scruples – their value was less than animals. And I don't mean just a few - hundreds of thousands. If the Africans resisted, whole villages were wiped off the map, the people murdered or packed off to company reservations. Soldiers were employed to do the dirty work: they had instructions to bring back chopped-off hands to prove they were doing their job. Much like in North America the English and the French demanded the Indians bring in scalps to prove their claims."

Ned was troubled. "I didn't know that, sir."

"Yes," Carelled breathed out slowly. "Oh yes.... Europeans.... We *'educated'* people. Good church-going Christians. Hundreds of thousands starved or died... And this was my country, Ned. My country."

Transferring his gaze to his glass, Carelle looked and sounded tired now.

"You see, it's easy. Once you have convinced yourself that somehow you are superior to someone else because of culture or education or wealth or religion, it is easy to treat them as if they are cattle, to be herded and slaughtered as you wish. Time and time again it happens. It is the worst side of the human story, and it is our *'advanced'* nations who do it to those we call primitive and savage. Because we can."

Ned wanted him to stop, for he could see that even the refined M. Carelle was suffering high emotional strain.

"I'm so sorry to hear all that, monsieur."

His mentor looked him in the eyes again. "I am not finished....When I was 28, I would come to Europe, to Belgium, we had opened the business there. Few knew what was going on in the Congo. Well – many knew of *something*, but whatever it was, nobody wanted to talk about it. The king's business! Kings and governments know best, isn't that so? The people who were not uncomfortable were the people who made lots of money out of it. That is nothing new, is it? What's a few Africans? – *Oh, they are just*

186

primitive natives! They did what? – Chopped their hands off? – Oh, I don't believe you! And I said to my father, let's get out, join Uncle Laurent up the coast. But my father still had contracts with some men who were reputable traders despite all that was going on. He decided to go there in person and offer them his contacts without strings, provided they helped him wind down the business in the face of pressures from Portuguese traders. So we went upriver that spring. 1892.... Between harvests. I always remember the smell of the sweating. Yes, 1892..."

"The year I was born," said Ned.

Perspiring now, Carelle played with his cigar.

"Myself, my brother Auguste and our father, another Frenchman and three Africans who worked for us - paid. You took your chances with the ferry boats going upriver, sometimes it was just a beaten-up old barge, a native dugout may have been better! We had food and water, and rifles. In Boma we would not need a rifle, but my father was a careful man, he took four rifles and ammunition. So.... And it was a small village - they were all small villages - way, way upriver beyond where they were going to build the railway – I don't even know the name of it." He was in his own private vision now.

"It's the back of beyond, you know? You have that expression – 'back of beyond' – I think that's amusing. It was not a country I ever found attractive. A lot of burnt land: natives would cut down trees and burn them, plant crops in the ashes and hope they would grow. Not fertile. Many natives would burn the grasses or trees just to catch rats or small animals, or even grubs, which they ate."

"We arrived at this place. We were not even there one night. My father went to talk with his business associate, in this tiny shack of a place, with rotting food outside mixed in with human filth, it stank to heaven. And truly, I don't know exactly what happened there because my brother and I were trying to find somewhere to refill our water, but in a small village you quickly hear if there is any trouble and we heard a couple of shots. We ran to where they came from, which was this agent's shack, and there were about a dozen soldiers there outside – a couple European, mostly African. They didn't stop us from bursting in through the door, but when we did, we saw our father and this agent chap both with wounds to their bodies. And even then – *even then* as I stood there, terrified, this African soldier took his machete and sliced it...... into my father's ..... his..... chest..... He never uttered a word, I just saw his eyes looking at me."

Carelle came to a halt as he sat with narrowed, glistening eyes. Then carried on slowly and quietly. "There was more noise and the Africans were shouting something and Auguste and I were running away. Auguste went down in front of me, a bullet right into his head.... Yes... He just collapsed and didn't move again. There was more noise and more gunfire. I ran. I ran, you see.... I ran. Without ever knowing what really had happened there, I just ran. Because I knew both my father and my brother were dead and there was nothing I could do. I just.... ran.... Three of us – myself and two of the natives – we ran along the river bank. Nobody came after us, and I heard more shots. Maybe the Frenchman and the other native, I don't know. But we didn't see them. I had hardly even touched my rifle. I threw it away: I suppose I was ashamed of it. Or maybe it was ashamed of me...."

Seeming utterly spent, Carelle eased his back against the chair and drew a long breath through his mouth. "Auguste was 24. Just 24." Ned decided he should say nothing.

"There you are. That is the worst that has ever happened. Nothing that happens to me now could ever be worse than that. You see. And that is my story. You have the story of Bruno Carelle. There is more, of course, but... another day, perhaps."

His smile was weak, yet one of reassurance, and Ned acknowledged by nodding gently.

"To finish, Ned - indulge me a moment longer. I never did find out the reason for those murders. It was just..... It was the Congo. It was just the Congo.... That's all.... I never went back there, nor anywhere beyond the coast, and my mother and I left the next year and came to Antwerp. We had family in Belgium: an uncle in Antwerp and another in Leuven. But you see, your problems, my young friend, they are slight. Are they not?"

"Yes, " agreed Ned with all his heart, "They are, most certainly. I am sorry for your distress, sir."

"*C'est la vie, n'est-ce pas?* May god grant these things never happen again. Although," he added, with a sigh, "what I see now in South Africa, the way their government is behaving, I see more troubles ahead. After that, who knows where in the world? Of one thing I am sure: history is written by those who profit from deceit, future generations will have no memory of these events, they will be gradually wiped from the collective consciousness as nations constantly believe implicitly in the credibility and honour of their leaders and regimes. And so.... " A sadness had crept into Carelle's normally bright eyes. "These things will continue, because men are men."

Carelle was spent. Smiling at Ned, he waved a hand to suggest it was time he lay down his head, and quietly he took to his bunk and lay face down upon it, taking no trouble to undress. Just as discreetly, Ned took the cane from Carelle's hand before it fell, softly made his way to the cabin door and left.

* * * * *

"I liked your butcher friend."

It pleased Ned to see his new mentor in far more relaxed and affable disposition the next evening.

"You went to see him?" Ned was astounded.

"No. I did not. I have friends that I trust to do some leg work for me. This 'friend' is acquainted with Tom the Butcher and his warehouses. Did you know his real name? – Thomas O'Connell, originally from Donegal. He described the man to me in – shall we say – a frank but warm manner. This 'friend', I rely on for an opinion."

The young man smiled. "Would this 'friend' be someone in the local police department, sir?"

"Astute of you, Ned. I think you mark my card well."

"Then, sir, ah think you have a friend indeed, ah would commend 'im for 'is opinion."

Carelle inclined his head. "How do you know it's a 'him', Ned?"

"Oh.... "

"No, you are right. But for newspaper information, I have another 'friend' who works within the press, and from her I learned that your suspicions regarding Mr. Knight were justified."

From 'her' indeed, thought Ned, intrigued.

"Knight puts money into newspaper advertising: nothing wrong in that, but he pays over the odds to shut out competitors. I had no idea soap was a commodity with power for anything other than cleaning purposes, did you? It seems it has the power to create dirt also!" His laugh was short and only half-amused.

"Anyway, the facts are simple. Knight put one journalist onto creating a column aimed at blackening your character, using that excuse - you know all that, of course. For the purpose, I can only imagine, of a smokescreen. Unless he genuinely thought you did have his papers and he might be able to scare you into giving yourself up. But.... yes, case confirmed. This man and one of the editors, easily bought."

A knock announced the steward with further coffee and macaroons. When he had left, wafting the air as if he were wafting the steward away, Carelle complained, "I asked him for *canelés*, but he brings none."

"Oh," Ned jumped in, "I can arrange that for you. They would have to make them."

"You know about *canelés de Bordeaux*?"

"I do, sir, yes. I will have a word with the pastry chef."

A satisfied smile lifted the older man's moustache. "Tell him, not too heavy on the rum. You tasted them, Ned? *Magnifique*."

"So I believe. Someone ordered them once."

"Good..... Good..... In any case, my friend, I think your Mr. Knight is a man who wears several coats. Or do you say, 'hats'? – Well. I already knew he had 'bought' certain of your politicians, but that is nothing new, is it?... You know, all politicians suffer an unfortunate flaw, Ned."

"What's that, sir?"

"When they make their speeches, they stop from time to time to breathe."

Whether Carelle meant that as a joke, his face did not slip in the smallest detail as he carried on in completely serious vein, "And there was that shooting accident a couple of years ago – did you hear of that? The young man's family are still trying to sue. I am quite sure they will get absolutely nowhere. There had been some mention of a connection with the Fenians. It's hearsay, of course, you cannot openly suggest such things without proof....."

"Fenians? But how would - ?"

"Oh, I doubt it is material, Ned. Merely – should I say – one of the spices this man has in his kitchen."

"So his activities are a bit on the shady side."

"Oh! Come, come, we cannot say that of a British lord, can we?.... Really, Ned, have you learned nothing of discretion? All the same, it doesn't stop us thinking it, does it? So let us say, those in high places are those who walk at the edges of cliffs. You take my meaning?"

"Ah believe ah do."

* * * * *

TWENTY

"He has a girlfriend?"

"Oh yes," said Brigitte, "He did not tell you?"

Ned took off his cap and scratched his head. "No wonder he were sayin' he had extra duties.... The little tinker! He was off ashore with a girl, and muggins here never twigged! Ah shall have a go at 'im!"

"Have a 'go', Ned? – You are annoyed wiz him?"

He chuckled. "With Otto? – 'Ow can anyone get annoyed at Otto?"

"I can! When he was a li'l boy, I would be very annoyed wiz him. He would be – how do you say zis, Ned? – He would .... *battre* .... er, hit my little.... *poupées*."

"Puppy? You had a little dog?"

"No! *Poupées, poupées*..... little people made from cloths."

"Dolls! Aah... Sometimes French is not easy."

"English! English is not easy, Ned – French is easy!"

He smiled to himself. Better let her win that one. She was probably right.

"Look!" she cried, turning away, "We are almost there."

Their ferry boat was steering in now toward that little inlet that imperceptibly led into Honfleur's harbour.

"So what's her name, Gitta?"

She spun her parasol at him. "Sophie."

"Sophie?"

"*D'accord*. Why?"

"Ah.... No reason."

"She is a nice girl, I sink. She and Otto went to ze school at ze same time. Her father is butcher."

"Ah shall 'ave a few words wi' Mr. Otto. Get 'im to sharpen 'is ideas up."

"Sharpen....? Ned, I don't understand." The smoothness of her dark-toned mezzo-soprano voice was like stroking velvet in his imagination.

"It's alright. Yer beautiful, that's all that matters."

That change of tone took her by surprise. Coyly, she returned his look, inhaled to fill out her bosom then looked away and fell to silence, something Brigitte did not often do.

It was a novel situation: he had begun to be thankful for this opportunity. Since she had persuaded him that they should make this trip, and quite apart from the fact M. Forget had suggested it long ago, Brigitte had become fascinating. And really, how could he not find her so? Only the protocol of being a family friend obscured what was in truth there all along. Beauty. More immediately good-looking than her sister, as Otto had opined. Perhaps, through his infatuation with Renata, he had been blind.

Otto's younger sibling, he had become used to thinking of her as that. Yet.... look at her! What a magnificent creature she was. Even if the upturned flan-ring of a hat that she wore today was over-decorated to the point of being a calamity. Still.... it was a balmy September day, and the ladies' costumes reflected that ambience, as indeed they should. Ned felt overdressed - men always were. His one summer suit being quite impermissible at the moment, he couldn't wait to divest himself of his collar and necktie, and come to that, his waistcoat too. Wearing Sunday clothes was a mistake; he only hoped he gave off no body odour that evaded his coaltar soap, and decided that the waistcoat had to go into their carrybag at the first chance. The tie too. After all.... this was France.

Meanwhile, in her bright green dress that shimmered all the way from her lightly-covered cleavage to her feet, Brigitte was drawing admiring glances from men on the ferryboat, much to the annoyance of their spouses who immediately saw through any pretence of unconcern on the part of their menfolk and judged their insouciance coldly. Brigitte just perched carefully if tightly in her seat, spun her parasol and remained of course unaware of any such attentions.

"Look, Ned, look – *les jongleurs*." Away from the quayside, a pair of acrobats were going through their routine to entertain visitors, peddling a strange device evidently cobbled together from several bicycles, a contraption that incorporated little drums and cymbals

193

and horns and other objects that made noises to delight. It seemed to Ned peculiarly French, ingenious and at the same time monumentally stupid, topped off with its even more bizarre operators clad in waistcoats and flying helmets, but if its purpose was to make people laugh, it was an enormous success. Brigitte pointed to the marionettes wielded by another troupe over by the trees.

How could he not have noticed? All those nights of his convalescence, Ned had lain in bed in the knowledge that Gitta was mere feet away from him. Looking at her now, he imagined himself making love to her, imagined somehow she would be different to those girls he had known: they were few enough, yet it seemed incongruous to think of Gitta in the same way at all. He should not chastise himself: he was no more able to disguise his interest than Gitta could mask the language of her own body. For Reina there had been that torch burning somewhere inside, at times he was confused and confounded in equal measure, but Reina was increasingly out of his reach – never having been truly within it. It was time to question those desires and to close old chapters. Reina was a mythical goddess, aloof and arguably outwith his capabilities, whereas Gitta was down-to-earth and here and now and physically the most delightful of objects for his admiration. Was this quest his to make or break?

To cherish her, yes. And then what - beyond mere needs? To love her. To marry her?... To marry Brigitte? Otto would like that. Of course, it was not a question for Otto, but to have Gitta as his wife..... That was a spiritual thing, was it not? And Marlene, what would *she* say? A lowly seaman, with possibly fair prospects, yet what future might that be for the lady's daughter? - To spend her days in the humblest of homes waiting for her man to return from his voyages.

Before he could ever decide, perhaps he needed to distance himself from her intoxication, which was overpowering him now and he knew it.

"Look, Ned. We are here. Isn't it pretty?"

Honfleur appeared at first glance pretty and picturesque, she was quite right.

In a low breath, he murmured, "Almost as pretty as you, Gitta."

But she heard that, and their eyes met in a hesitant awareness.

* * * * *

There was fresh goat's cheese, though Ned was not so sure about that, its flavour was a little ripe for him, and there were delicious freshly baked baguettes, huge tomato segments, sliced potatoes cooked in some sort of salty fat, some green leaves and a kind of terrine that Ned was equally unsure about: being hungry, though, he followed her lead and ate heartily.   And of course, more cheese! Deliberately, they had not brought a picnic, the normal thing to do, because Brigitte had said there was one place of the few that she knew that offered reliable food at a fair price.   The wine was passable, no more than that, yet in the sunshine here at this eating place, it went well with the positive air of everywhere that Brigitte might be.

So they ate, mostly in silence, admiring the quaint buildings of which many required more than a lick of paint, looking at the boats and the fishermen and then back to each other and smiling a lot whilst saying nothing.   Ned had divested his upper body of everything down to his shirt and took every opportunity of his relaxed state to assess Brigitte's looks.

"When I was a little girl," she was intoning the words quietly, almost talking to herself.   "I wanted to be Cendrillon.   Every little girl wants to be Cendrillon, no?   Ze two Grimm brothers, zey are responsible for a lot of children's dreams, aren't zey?   I wanted to go to ze royal ball in a beautiful dress and dance wiz ze prince.   And live happy....." Ned helped her say it: " – Happily ever after."

"Zat's right.   Live in a big *schloss* and probably become very, very bored wiz having everysing a girl always wanted."   She laughed quietly, deriding herself.

"Zen we moved to France.   And one day my papa brought us to Honfleur.   It was a Saturday, like today, a beautiful day, just like zis.

195

And I thought, I do not want to be Cendrillon, I will be happy if I can live here because zis place is pretty and peaceful and everysing seems to be..... just as you would like it if you were God making a new place. Here - away from ze back of zese houses here - zere is a garden behind a small house. It is a beautiful garden full of peace.... you know? Full of ze sort of peacefulness and nice things that every people wants. Everybody wants to live zere. And be - happily ever after. In a garden in Honfleur."

She dropped her eyes. "When Vati was killed, zose dreams disappeared. You have to stop believing in dreams, you have to grow up. Zere is no glass slipper, no castle, no garden in Honfleur. Life is not zat easy."

"At least Honfleur is real, Gitta." She returned his hopeful smile and knew what he was saying to her.

"When ah were a little lad," Ned carried on, "all ah wanted to be were a boxer. Like me dad."

"A what? A box?"

"Boxer. Fighting. Fists. See? Me dad were good. He stood up for us once, flattened a chap that were botherin' me mother in the park. Ah must've been about five, or six. I were right proud of 'im. But....."

"What?"

Ned deliberated.

"He changed. He beat us.... Ah never understood why. Ah still don't understand. Jim allus said he'd beat 'im back some day.... Now Jim has a fight of 'is own. But life – it's like you say, Gitta, it doesn't work out like we thought. Snatches things away from yer."

She said nothing, only nodded slowly. He was speaking of the loss of friends, she knew that.

Momentarily, he realised he was back where he had been with her sister, grasping at an opportunity. He was not going to go that way again. This time he was going to know his own mind and bide his time.

In all honesty, love was a sprite he had never met. The young man might admit he felt passion but had no idea when passion turned into love. He only knew of a desire now for Gitta, and he dared to think she might feel the same; but to have her as his own in every sense.... He had already donned the costume of a fool in that clumsy attempt at courting Reina, he should not insult them further by wielding another loud slapstick that impacted Gitta.

"Can I ask you somesing?" She had been thinking about the question some little while, it seemed.

"Ask," he replied.

"Do you love Reina, Ned?"

He should have expected that at some point, in fact. Yet when it came, with Brigitte's usual frankness, he was at a loss to give the question a well-considered response.

Eventually, he mentally bit his lip and said, "Ah love yer both, yer know that."

"It's not what I ask you."

No, it was not. He knew what she asked. He took a sip of his wine and shuffled uneasily on the wooden chair. "At one time, Gitta.... ah had strong feelings. Ah thought ah had, anyway."

"And you still do, or you don't still do?.... It's not good English!"

"I understand."

"Because I thought you were in love wiz her. And I sink that *she* thought... that... *you* thought... Oh, I cannot say it! Does zat.... do you understand me?"

"Yes."

"Because I sink if you still love her, you may be very upset, Ned. I do not want you to be unhappy."

"Upset because ...." And they both said together, "She is going to marry Monsieur Forget."

"Yes," she said. "I sink so. You know, she talk in her sleep." He raised an eyebrow and she tossed her head back with a little laugh and then explained, "No, no, she doesn't talk in her sleep. I make a joke. But we are sisters, and we are in ze bedroom. We talk."

"Girls talk."

"*Bien sûr*. But.... Reina and me, we are not....mm.... not so close as you sink, Ned. We talk a little... not a lot. She is ze big clever sister. Me? - I am stupid."

197

"No! That you are not! You're not stupid at all, Gitta.... You are intelligent and you are lovely."

"You think?....."

"Yes, absolutely.... You're right, though: she will marry Forget."

"And you are unhappy?"

"No, no. It's best for Reina. He'll be better for her future than...." And before she could cut in again, he added, "But in any case, ah feel different about it all now... It were a daft thing for me to do."

"Daft?"

"Stupid."

"Why stupid? And why do you feel different?"

"Because...." How do you say that you care so much for someone but you are not sure whether you can ever make *them* happy? "Because ah think that maybe you and me...."

He stopped there, and left his gesturing hand wafting in between them.

"You and me, Ned?"

"Yes. If.... if you were to feel the same."

She breathed in deeply, swelling her bosom. "Ah.... You like me?"

He laughed loudly. "Yer know ah do, Gitta. You know it. Don't yer?" Now he relaxed. "You're teasing me! Come on, you're havin' me on...."

She caught his grin and returned it mischievously. "'*Having me on*', Ned? – I don't understand zis."

"Yes, yer do! Teasing. Playing with me because ah'm no good at courtin'."

"Courting? - Ned, is too many words I don't understand."

"Alright, then - making love. You're playin' wi' me."

"Oh, but I don't play! Oh no, I don't play. Love, it is a serious matter, isn't it?"

Was she teasing? Now he didn't know. "Well.... How *do* you feel about me, Gitta? How do yer feel about this fool that's been blind all this time?"

Now she looked warmly at him, knowing she was on safe ground. "*Repose-toi,*" she told him fondly. "Not a fool, Ned. And I like you very much. But you know zat I have always liked you. Since ze first time you came to ze house, and I was dressed for bed, and you looked at me in my chemise – "

"Aye... Ah did, didn't ah?... How could ah forget? My heart jumped – like this – " She chuckled. "And since then...." Now he wondered how much to confess. "Since then, if ah'm honest, ah've often dreamed about seeing you in yer underclothes again."

A tiny breath escaped her. She held her face in a demure girlishness, looked down at her green dress and stroked the side of it for some reason best known to herself. He had no idea what was going on in her mind, but whatever it was, he was certain she wanted him to kiss her. Here, with the busy harbour of Honfleur going about its business metres away from them, that would not have been the thing to do. It was, without doubt, the most ridiculously incongruous place for a man to raise his passion, with the remains of fish from the morning in strongly-scented baskets piled on the quay just over there. Instead, he reached across and took her hand, squeezed it several times then let it go. The thrill of a metaphysical exchange surpassed all those earlier emotions he had felt in a passionate embrace with a woman. Suddenly, the world had changed, his one desire now was to get himself into an embrace with Gitta: it seemed the one place where, right now, he knew he was entirely welcome.

Finally, to his surprise, she said, "Ned, we should make love."

Where did that come from? Oh, yes – this was Gitta. Yes. He might have anticipated her brashness. But he hadn't. More fool, he.

"Gitta, I – " Was there any point in trying to explain himself? Was there really? This was Gitta. In the end, he shook his head with amusement and let go a long release of tightened lungs. "Alright." It sounded like he had agreed to take her to the theatre. He chastised himself for a complete moron before flicking a switch in his head to give his brain a vision of Gitta lying naked on the grass before him. The vision blended with the beckoning, open-mouthed beauty he saw right in front of him. Heavens, she really was a goddess!

"Yes, Gitta....." In a form of spontaneous oath - but in a nice way - he raised his right hand. "Brigitte Bremme, I would love to make love to you.... so help me, God!"

* * * * *

That Saturday was to be a day fulfilled, for which there had been not the least hint at the outset. Honfleur had been a most pleasant distraction on a particularly pleasant day, the best September day of the month - possibly of the decade. Warm, cosseting breeze lifted gently off the land and ushered the little ferry boat back to its quay at Le Havre, whereupon Ned helped her disembark and together they stepped out boldly towards the house. They dared to hold hands for some of the way, but spoke in platitudes and discussed the entertainments of the day.

"*Merci*, Monsieur Forget," said Ned, quite out of the blue.

"What?" asked Brigitte.

"His suggestion. Don't you remember? '*Go to Honfleur, Ned – take Brigitte*'. By god, he were right! What a splendid feller!"

"Splendid? – Monsieur Forget?"

The irony had him chortling. "Yeh – why not?"

At one point, he let her walk a few paces in front just so that he could take in a full view of her, the reason for which Gitta understood and allowed him to soak the image of her into his brain. The fact Ned reflected her radiance made her feel all the more lovely, it brought a thrill to her quite separate from what she was anticipating now. Brigitte had walked out with many of the local boys, and those interludes she would keep to herself, yet for what must have been the first time, this one made her feel like a woman on a pedestal and it felt strange indeed. She had grown up with those boys who pursued her, they offered nothing new, no intrigue. She tingled with expectation, a very odd sensation that she had not felt in quite this way. She wanted to be ravished. But for the moment, she unpinned her hat and let the thing dangle in her hand, swaying with the encumbered sway of her long skirt.

Silence was if anything better than talking, it seemed to foster that smouldering telepathy between the two of them, but as they entered the door of the house in the late rays of the evening sun, Brigitte told Ned that they were alone.

"What, both of them?"

"Yes. Mutti was invited to Monsieur Forget's sister's house – Reina's idea. It was polite. So I do not know what time zey will be back. I hope... late."

That was all. There was nothing of importance to be said, each understood that her candid statement spoke for both of them. The moment had come, they knew it. It could not have been better: for once, the perfect ending to a perfect day. Brigitte pulled herself into his embrace, two pairs of blue eyes met and these two young people were utterly lost.

* * * * *

TWENTY-ONE

"Ned. Ned."

It was Brigitte's mother shaking him. Notwithstanding the early light filtering in through the lace of the bedroom curtain, she held an oil lamp in one hand as she gently rocked Ned's shoulder to wake him without disturbing her daughter. He came round slowly, then suddenly and sharply sat up in bed with the realisation that Frau Bremme had found him in her daughter's bed.

Yet she showed no anger, no disturbance, no intention to upset either of them. "Sshhh!" she said very quietly. Then, "Is alright, Ned. Come."

He carefully took Gitta's outstretched arm from his body and gently replaced it on the pillow. She breathed a heavy breath, did not wake but her breast was implanted against his side: he had to move very carefully. Discreetly, Frau Bremme placed the oil lamp on the little table and withdrew from the room so that Ned could get out of bed and dress his naked body.

Only after he had collected his shoes, his shirt and trousers and gone out onto the landing did he see through the half-open door of Marlene's room that Renata was asleep in their mother's bed. Apparently asleep, facing away from him. For some moments he dared not move, hardly dared breathe. It was a surreal scene, he dreaded the consequences of having to speak to her if she woke and decided to blot the image of her from his brain. Taking one more look at Gitta, whose beautiful body glistened in the flickering light of the poor flame as it strove to compete with the dawn light from the window, Ned dressed at the top of the stairs. It was all he could do to keep saying "Wow!" to himself. She was a magnificent creature: how could he have managed to blind himself for so long?

Downstairs, Frau Bremme had hot coffee waiting for him. Otto, who appeared not to have been in the house long, sat at the kitchen table and looked up at his friend in the poor light of that room, nodding silently to acknowledge him and licking his lips. Frau

202

Bremme passed them both plates with *brötchen* for each and a little citrus jam on the side. She smiled at Ned and said nothing.

Sipping his coffee, Otto said, "Early start, my *Nixie* friend. You forget."

"Yes.... I did forget.... Thanks."

"Okay. I see you later."

"Yes."

"You sleep too well, Ned. Like a baby."

"..... Yes."

Frau Bremme pulled out the chair to sit and Ned looked at her cautiously. Marlene only smiled back through the half-light with her soft, care-worn eyes. Her serene smile told him everything. He could have cried.

"I make you bread and cheese to take, Ned," she said, and patted his hand.

* * * * *

He found Otto filleting some fish in the galley. Otto acknowledged him as Ned stepped over the threshold. All he said was, nodding his head at the fish, "Captain's dinner guest. He don't like steak."

"Uhuh," said Ned. Picking up the chef's meat hatchet from where it sat precariously on the edge of the bench, he hung it back on its hook. "Anything ah can do for yer?"

Pausing from his task to look Ned in the face, Otto said, "It's okay, Ned. We are friends, you know. It's not a problem."

"No.... Ah know. Ah just....."

"You want to talk? It's okay, Ned. You can talk. Mutti, you are worried about her? You don't have to be worried about her."

"She is a saint, your mother, ah've said it before....."

"Ned, Gitta is a woman. Ja? And look, I am not stupid, I see that she is beautiful. Just because she is my sister..... "

"Otto, can ah tell yer something?"

"Ja. So tell."

Ned began to pace up and down slowly in the narrow confines of the galley space. "Would it surprise you if ah said that ah think.... ah think.... ah'm probably in love with Gitta?"

"*Probably*?..... What you mean, '*probably*'? – You don't *know*, you crazy man? Ned, I watch you for weeks, you are like pig with two heads when you don't see her, what."

"Bear!"

"Uh?"

"Bear with two heads. Anyway, go on."

"Ja. Okay. Two heads. And not one of zem straight on your head! Listen, Ned, I see you, Mutti see you. We know you have big.... er, big, er..... big heart for Gitta. Sure. Listen, we see zat before *you* do - *Du dumkopf, du!*"

Ned felt like his brain was in a vice. So much to explain. "We.... we fell asleep. We didn't mean to.... and we didn't mean to offend anyone. Least of all your mother."

Otto stopped filleting his fish and waggled the knife in Ned's direction. "Ned, you talk too much. I tell you zis. Mutti and I, we see Gitta too. And Reina. Mutti, she say to me, Gitta is wanting Ned. An' I say, you sure? An' she say, Yes, sure. It's time. She don't want to play no more. She play because all ze boys in Le Havre want her – yes! *All* ze boys, always, and she play wiz zem. You sink we are blind, Mutti and I? – All ze boys make whistle at Gitta, like zis."

His attempt at a whistle did not achieve a resounding note. Instead, he just waved his hands about. "So, what you sink? – It's easy for Gitta to choose? Reina, she is older, she knows what Mutti thinks, and they know Reina must choose a good man. Oh, okay, okay – Ned, you are a good man too – "

"Otto, ah know what yer tryin' to say."

"No, don't stop me! Reina, she think wiz ze head, not ze heart. Ja? Zat is Reina. But not Gitta. Gitta is..... *Freigeist*..... Gitta wants much out of her life, Ned. Understand? And I want her to have dat. And she wants you. You know why she wants you, Ned?"

"Well, I....."

"Because you don't want her! She think, what. She sees you so much and you have eyes for Reina, and she is a woman, Ned – you don't know how women sink, do you? Hell's bells!"

"But – "

"So Gitta want what she cannot have. And..... listen, my friend, let me tell you zis in case of your head get bigger..... You are little hero to her."

"What?"

"Because - listen to me, Ned! You escape from zis big ship, *Titanic*, ja? It's big, big sing, in all of ze newspapers. Big *catastrophe*. Many men die, but you - you get free. And you get out of New York when you are in trouble. And you jump in ze sea and pull out Dieter Pabst when he is drowning – may God forgive you, you stupid English! And you are zis man of mystery who is being seeked by zese bad men in England. And.... she hears me telling zem how clever you are and popular wiz customers on ze ships. So you are hero.... you see?"

" – Rubbish! Otto, it was you who got me away from New York.. Things just happen to me, that's all."

His friend only laughed, shook that large frame of his and waggled a finger as if to say, '*Yes, well there's no accounting for taste.*'

"Dat's right. You are not bloody hero, you are bloody silly fool! I know zis."

"Hero!" scoffed Ned, dismissing the whole idea.

"Listen, bloody fool! – It don't make matter what *we* sink. It make matter what *she* sink! You sink wiz zat sing in your pants, but a woman, she sink wiz zis...." He patted his head.

"And, Ned, one sing more. Reina will tell us now she is going to marry Monsieur Forget."

"Yes, we thought so too."

"So zat is another reason for Gitta to be.... um.... I don't know ze word."

"Jealous, maybe?"

"Jealous? – No, no. But it put in her mind many thoughts. She is twenty in a few months. Maybe she worry a little bit."

Ned stroked his chin. "Gitta could 'ave any man she wanted. She's one hell of a good-lookin' girl!" That might have been a slip, and he looked anxiously for a second at Otto, but his friend only grinned right back and snorted down his nose.

"Well, you can take zose *mise en bouche* up to ze captain, Ned. An' get out ze best Armagnac, you know zis captain like his Cognac for his guests – not ze stuff he drink ze rest of ze time. I get ze chef now to cook zis fish."

As Ned took the tray and headed out through the door, Otto called after him, "So, Ned – you make two weddings, eh? Reina and Monsieur Jerome and you and Gitta? Huh?"

He stopped and thought about that. "Ah haven't asked her yet."

"You don't ask? Hells bells! Zere is big line of men in ze street at *Chemin des Barques*, have you seen it?"

Ned turned back yet again. "By the way.... You've been hidin' *your* light under a bushel, haven't yer?"

"Bush - Bush? What?"

"Sophie."

"Ah...... Sophie!" Otto tossed his head this way and that for a moment and turned back to his fish. "*Pas grave*," he threw away the remark quietly.

* * * * *

In the event, more than eight weeks came and went before Renata finally entertained Monsieur Forget's proposal and agreed to be his wife. And in the manner in which it all happened, both Otto and Ned were surprised and not a little confounded that M. Forget did not act in the flamboyant, formal manner they supposed he would.

One Wednesday evening, with *La France* on its way back from New York and after the ladies had cleared away the evening meal, he arrived at the house unannounced – for which he apologised - shook his wet cape at the door and allowed Frau Bremme to take his umbrella, then without an ounce of ceremony he spoke to Renata sincerely across the kitchen table and – from the account their mother gave Otto later – quietly and briefly spoke of his love for Renata and said that his dearest wish would be that she consent to be his wife. It was, by all accounts, a more touching – even romantic - affair than Renata herself was ever expecting, and after only the slightest pause for modesty she accepted him with a tear of emotion springing to her eye.

Otto – to no-one's surprise – tried hard to make a joke of it all, yet even in Otto there was a sprinkling of respect for the way that M. Jerome had prostrated himself – in a sense – to ask for Renata's hand. That it eschewed any degree of ceremony or starchiness only spoke all the better for him. Brigitte, too, said that she had been touched, and was delighted for her sister. It seemed, after all, the better part of Forget had come to the surface, and Brigitte noted that Renata retired that night on a higher cloud than she had used as a pillow for some time.

* * * * *

Carelle spoke with Ned once more that year, though the Belgian was travelling with another businessman and had sparse opportunity to impart information. Both gentlemen were concerned with the effects on their businesses of the 'political rumblings' of the day.

"Trouble?..... I think we have volcanoes bubbling under Europe," Mister Abernathy was saying.

Carelle frowned and considered his opinion. "We have powder kegs set up for trouble, that is for sure. In spite of all that euphoria in Petersburg with three centuries of one dynasty, there were a lot of angry voices that we didn't hear much about, I don't see that settling down so easily. Ach, the Tsar needs to wake up. Austria is so asleep it will never wake up, Germany has a petulant empire-builder at the helm and the British still think they own the world and will beat them all at cricket!"

Abernathy was amused at the comment, as an American would be. "And Greece is a tinder box just waiting for someone to put a Lucifer to it. Mark my words, Bruno, the Turks will not take it all lying down, especially with the Arabs kicking up sand in the south, and having the king murdered is only adding fuel to the fire. You know, it's hardly surprising we have these little wars, and suddenly you have the Balkans jumping up and down as well as all these little countries throwing rocks at each other – that whole region is a jack-in-the-box, I think."

Attempting to serve them both as they stood at his bar, Ned was apologetically out of his depth.

"Well, my young friend, when you have all the crowned heads of Europe coming forth from one stem, you are heading for trouble, Ned. Your Queen Victoria is at the very heart of things, even now. Sibling rivalry is an old sickness played at its most sinister by those who have most to lose. We have the greatest players here in Europe - all family members - each determined to get one over on the other. And if it doesn't boil over into something more serious.... well, Bruno Carelle will be the most surprised little bean seller in Belgium."

"Can ah tell you something, sir?"

"By all means."

Ned told the two men about the man he had shared a railway carriage with on the journey to Sheffield last year, and what he had boldly stated about Germany.

"A Russian, you say?"

"Aye. Educated one, an' all. Ah didn't like 'im, but he were very confident in what 'e were saying."

"Your Russian," suggested Abernathy, "is largely right – insofar as you have mentioned the build-up of naval forces and things. Frankly, having in mind Bismarck giving the Danes a very bloody nose not that long ago, there's nothing new about Prussians strutting about like peacocks and the stuffed shirts I've found them to be, nor is there anything new about the arrogance of all the heads of state like Britain and France and Russia, but it's not something to be easily dismissed. Not when everyone else is strutting too. Warships, yes – Big ones!"

"And armaments, Robert," Carelle added. "That Wilhelm seems to have a lot to prove. Maybe he will. Against Cousin Nicholas or Cousin Edward, though? – Who would you choose?"

Ned, who was not really the one being addressed, confessed he had no idea.

"One thing is sure, my friend. Our young German king was born with not just a crippled arm, but with a very large chip on the shoulder."

"Probably true, Bruno, but I can tell you this - Nicholas has completely lost his hold on things in Russia, you know, and that won't end well. Too self-indulgent. Though you can say that of the British too, I suppose. Well, I can tell you the American point of view: they are all Saxe-Coburgs. Your Queen Victoria tied in by marriage. Would that not be enough to swell the head of Cousin Wilhelm? – Maybe he sees himself as the centre of all those sovereign states just as Germany is the geographical centre of western Europe. Maybe he has a right to. Who knows?"

"Otto is worried," Ned told Carelle.

"Yes, I'm sure he would be. But thankfully he is working on a French ship, not German."

"No. Confidentially, he doesn't like Germans all that much!"

"Which is good so long as he tells that to only you, Ned!"

"And now to you, sir."

"Ah, yes! Well, I must blackmail him at once!" The tall man's body shook lightly again. Ned understood the joke this time.

Carelle frowned, however, and his humour was short-lived. Perhaps it was, after all, no laughing matter.

* * * * *

"When should the wedding be?" was the first thing the boys wanted to know when they arrived in the front parlour. It was December 13th, 1913, and all the talk was of whether the Mona Lisa would ever be returned to Paris after being stolen and hidden in Florence for a year and a half. Most thought not.

"Why should I care - " Ned tossed his bag to the floor as Gitta came running down the stairs, " – about any ruddy painting when ah've got me own Mona Lisa right 'ere?" She crossed the room and quickly threw her arms about him whilst her mother coughed as if in shock at the exuberance. Otto simply gave his resigned shrug and said hello to Brigitte's body which was not the least aware that he had even entered the house.

When they had settled and Otto had piled up the fire so that three of them could huddle around it, they finally got the answer to the question.

"Next August? That's a long way off," said Ned.

"*Doch!*" called Frau Bremme, sorting out her pantry, "A betrothal must take time."

"What? – After they've known each other for god-knows-how-long?"

"*Doucement*," said Frau Bremme. "Patient, Ned." She continued wiping the tureen on her apron and lifted it onto a shelf. It occurred to him that she had said the same word a long time ago, in a quite different context. Yet his conscience was no longer troubled, he was sure.

"And you, Ned?" asked the lady, with her head inclined towards Brigitte sitting excitedly beside him. "Mmm?"

"Oh!" Ned put his glass on the floor and looked at Gitta. "Ah don't know. We hadn't -"

"Then maybe *you should*," said Otto, heavily-accenting his words.

Gitta looked into Ned's face. "We should."

"Yes," said Ned thoughtfully. "Life's too short, as they say."

"Too short? You are young!"

"An' hoping to stay that way. But.... yer never know. Like them poor miners just a few week ago."

"Ned...." Brigitte wanted to soothe his brow, "We enjoy while we can."

He stroked his stubbly chin. "Ah didn't propose to yer, Gitta."

"It's alright," she replied.

"Ach!" Her brother jumped up from his easy chair. "Mutti and me, we go clean ze *brouette* in ze garden!" And he made a very obvious performance of leaving the room, whereas his mother gently shook her head at the two sitting there. Winking, she said, "*Nous n'avons pas de brouette!*", and she disappeared also.

"They're right, aren't they? We should make some plans."

Taking hold of his hand, she agreed.

"Ah were worried yer might say No."

"Why?"

"Because... Ah'm just a chap on a ship. Ah don't 'ave much to offer a girl."

"Yes, Ned, you do. I un'erstand you. An' life changes. We all change. Everysing change in time. It get better." She kissed his cheek. And he suddenly felt he was being an imbecile: she was right, things would get better.

"August," said Ned earnestly.

"August?"

"Well, let's you and I get married in August too."

"Ja?"

"Strike while the iron's hot!"

"Iron? You want to hit me wiz somesing?"

" – Nice warm August day, eh? And it'll give me time ter save up some brass an' help get me family down 'ere to meet all of yer."

He hesitated. Had he done it wrong again? Should she not deserve more of a preamble than that? Once again, a fool! She wants what every girl wants – a proposal.

"Ah'm a clumsy man. You sure you want an idiot like me?"

"Ja." It was all she said. So simple, yet so direct, so uncomplicated and honest. It was Gitta, after all. And he loved her for it. She put a warm glow in his heart, all he could do was grin and thank his lucky stars.

"Y'know.... Ah love yer, Gitta.... Will you, Brigitte Bremme, marry this idiot called Ned Thornton?"

There was no eruption or great out-pouring of emotions. Gitta was a girl who had known this moment would come for a long time. All she had to do was recognise it. She held her fond smile for several moments while he drank her in, then leaned forward and kissed him softly on the lips. Very quietly, she said, "Ja." And that was all.

* * * * *

TWENTY-TWO

"*Charmant*, Ned.... *Charmant*."

Carelle almost licked his lips. "Lovely ladies, my friend. You are a very lucky man."

"That I am, sir."

"Well, then. Your health," proposed Carelle, lifting the ubiquitous glass. "And I know you must see to your duties, but first, let me tell you what has been happening."

Carelle sprawled his length across the chaise and looked up at the enormous Rigaud painting of Louis Quatorze above the fireplace. In truth he was looking through it and feeling particularly pleased with himself, having met and entertained the three Bremme ladies here in the Grand Salon of *La France*. Whilst the ship had impressed the ladies, Carelle was himself delighted they were everything Ned had told him they were. They had – naturally – donned their best frocks and hats for the occasion, and whilst their combined perfume approached intoxication, it stopped well short of vulgarity.

Fortuitously, early evening departure had allowed them a visit prior to sailing. As host, with the captain's permission, Carelle had led them around what he considered the salient parts of the vessel, at one point even capturing for a few moments the captain's attention, whilst Ned and Otto simply readied themselves for work.

"Monsieur Caldecot," pronounced Carelle, speaking discreetly as the huge salon was becoming populated, "is a very dead man. There has been not the least mention of him recorded anywhere following the sinking."

"Ah thought not," agreed Ned, glad that he could finally lay one fact to rest.

"There was a memorial service for him in Hackney. June last year. The man's family was there – all two of them."

"Two?"

"His mother and brother. It appears he was not popular. I understand – and I have no confirmation of it – there was a sister at some time... but for years it seems no-one knows about her..... Oh, I must correct myself - I said 'two' but in fact Lady Sophie and Miss Devonshire attended very briefly, by all accounts. *Very* briefly."

"So 'ow did yer find out?"

Carelle tapped the side of his nose with the knob of his cane. "We do what we can, Ned. My associate in London is very useful. Tommy."

"Tommy?"

"His name is Scottish, I cannot get it out of the mouth, but we call him Tommy. He is long in years and long in experience, he knows many people in official circles. And many in less polite circles. Everyone knows someone. You do enough business, you talk to enough people, and you find someone who knows someone who knows someone.... Someone who will sell information."

"Ah see."

"Police, Ned, are good people to know. Because they know bad people. And bad people are the ones you really want to know because always they are the ones with the best information. I am - " He shook his head dismissively. " - not a detective.... not one of Mr. Conan Doyle's creations. I simply move a lot of beans around. This is how I wish to stay. There is another thing, Ned. Mister Caldecot was not a nice man."

"You said he was not popular."

Aware his steward's uniform in the presence of first class passengers did not entitle him to informality in the Grand Salon, Ned stood up, a gesture that Carelle seemed to comprehend for he carried on without the least change of attitude, save for a slightly lower voice so that it might not carry.

"You know he was personal secretary to Mr. Knight. That was only for three years. Go back further, Caldecot had a financial interest in one or two properties in London. Perhaps he still had."

"Is that bad?"

"Prostitution, we might guess, Ned. No blinding proof, but a trail leads to Caldecot through other businesses. He had money, certainly. He kept himself in the clear, but Tommy's friend believes

213

that money changed hands through third parties, and one of those parties was a chemicals manufacturer."

"Chemicals?"

Carelle gave a slow nod. "Mm. Another word for soaps, perhaps? I don't know."

"But.... if Caldecot had money, why would 'e need to be a secretary to Knight?"

Carelle let out a shrugging kind of breath as though he needed to belch. "Who knows?.... Power association, perhaps?"

"Why did you look at Caldecot first?"

"Because he is the only one that is dead." A broad smile twisted Carelle's moustache.

".... And hopefully the others will be around a little longer, so I have more time to find out more."

Looking at his watch, Ned knew he must excuse himself, and arranged to meet Carelle once the initial hiatus of departure had settled.

"Cocktails in the First Class Smoking Room?"

"No. Ah'm actually serving dinner this evening. One of the lads got sick. Ah'll be off a bit earlier. Right here about nine-thirty?"

* * * * *

"By the way, Ned, I must tell you – I am talking to an agent in London about taking a lease on a house there. It's part a matter of policy, and part by way of precaution."

"Yer mean Europe."

"I do. I had been thinking about it for some time, and in the present climate, Britain could be a better connecting point to America. I have been recommended to a property in Barnet. It's possible I could move there soon, maybe before June, in fact. Perhaps not myself personally, but a member of my staff. Though I cannot say I find London pretty, not like Antwerp. But yes, you are right, the European politics becomes more strained with each week that passes."

"And you think it could amount to summat...."

214

"I am a businessman, Ned, I have to be prudent and look at all possibilities. Looking on the dark side, your island has a number of advantages if there is trouble with Austria or Germany."

The big Belgian faltered in his speculation, as if needing to justify his thinking. "Put two eagles in a pit with another eagle, a bulldog and a cockerel and you can guarantee trouble at some point."

Ned saw that the movements of people in the lounge were distracting his friend. "Do you know, Ned, it always seems to me, the fashions of ladies seem to become more extreme when political and economic pressures look like unsettling the normal pace of society. Have you noticed this?"

There was only a blank look from the young man, and Carelle continued in a spirit of amusement. "Don't you think it's curious how ladies' necklines have – erm, relaxed, just in the past year or two? - Not that I object to seeing more of a lady's bosom, of course not! And have you ever seen so much leg on show? Good heavens, you would think these ladies actually had knees! I think it must be all these peculiar new dances, what do you think?"

"Oh, the Tango and things. Disgraceful exhibitions, sir." And at last, Carelle was privileged to catch a glimpse of Ned's sense of humour. "But," continued Ned, "you're not complaining?"

"Complaining? – Oh, good heavens, no! Let's hope this rumoured war holds off for a long time. If it holds off long enough, we may yet see above the knees, eh?"

He chortled mischievously, then switched off his whimsy as suddenly as he had switched it on. "So with a house in London, I shall be in a better position to help you."

"If that is your wish, I welcome it. Ah'll come see you - if ah can get into the country."

"We'll do it properly, Ned - get you a passport. Mm? What would you like to be called?"

Ned was aghast. "A forged identity?"

Another easy gesture from Carelle. "Tommy knows a man…. And I pay him well."

"One thing, though – yer won't be travelling via *La France* – if yer workin' from London."

"Mm, no. We shall see. And you intend to stay in France? With *La Compagnie*, I mean."

"Gitta and I are getting married in August."

"Ah, yes – The 29th?"

"A fortnight after Reina. You *will* come?"

"Of course - you invited me. I have it in my *agenda*. And you – are you ready for marriage, Ned?"

He took a few moments to consider that. "'Appen I am. Ah was 'oping by then ah might've got all the problems behind me. But..... Gitta's looking forward to it, ah know that much."

"A lovely girl... Do you know the Spanish word '*duende*'? – It has a meaning of its own, but in English it is close to saying, 'spirit' or 'essence', but more than that, it has a kind of a magical meaning. A connection with ....er, fairies, you call them, or elves, or perhaps even goblins but perhaps not so much. Sprite! - Is that it? But something else. And in your Brigitte I see *duende*. Well – she has blue eyes, not brown. And her hair..... but..... Have you ever been to Spain? – You should go, Ned, if you can: Cordoba or Seville, go at the festival times, it will open your eyes to life. As I said before, you are lucky. In love, anyway. There is something in that girl. I think you will not find that in any English girl, Ned – a kind of.... a kind of fire. *Duende*. I am not sure what. Cherish her, Ned. These things don't always last."

"Ah'm not sure ah follow you, sir."

On cue, the duty steward arrived with the new bottle. Carelle put something in his hand and the steward touched his forelock, pulled at his bowtie and quickly departed.

"Well," drawled Carelle, reaching forward to pour himself a glass, "Not all things in life work out as we plan, as you know." Ned declined the glass offered to him.

"Cognac." The Belgian was talking more to himself. "I went there once, on my way to Bordeaux. Down in the south-west, you know. Pleasant little town, warm and sleepy. You would never guess that thousands of litres of this stuff is just sitting there, waiting for a suitable age to be put into a bottle. That whole region - the *Grande Champagne* they call it - is just processing the grapes that make

Cognac. I had an idea to stop and view the factory. Right beside the river, most pleasant. Great casks of the stuff, kept below ground – to keep it temperate.... Just as it keeps me - temperate....."

Ned had seen this side of Carelle before: distant, reflective, almost mystical.

"You think Europe's in for trouble, then, sir?" He almost apologised for changing the subject.

"Let us hope not. Your British friends are far too busy going on strike for more money. But... It could be a perfect time for Europe to blow up in its face!"

The young man bowed his head. "Yer know so much more about these things. Ah didn't get much schoolin', an' when ah did it went in one ear and out o't'other. Turks, Greeks, ah know nuthin about all that stuff. Trojan Wars and Wooden Horse, that's about all."

Carelle tapped Ned on the arm as a token of reassurance. "My friend, education tends to be a privilege afforded the more financially able ones among us, but it does not give them wisdom. In fact, the opposite - the greater the wealth, the more impossible it becomes to comprehend what it is like to not have.... That doesn't sound like good English, does it?...You learn life and living, that is all most of us do, so have no shame in your ignorance. Most of us never need to know, it matters little if we do as power tends to be vested in untouchable people far above us. These things are games played by the power elements, the elites of this world of ours, which tends to mean the wealthy and influential. Games, that's all they are. Most of our politicians are just cavaliers having fun. Fun by playing with other people's lives. But, Greece.... Throughout history, Greece was an influence on politics, on thinking, on so many things. The cradle of modern civilisation, but so much more. Your ship, Ned, it was the *Titanic*. And before that, you were on the *Olympic*. Do you know these names come from the Greek?"

Ned clearly knew something – not enough.

"The Titans and the Olympians, they were enemies. They were the rulers, the gods, long, long ago..... And they were giants. Physically – like your ships – giants! They fought a series of wars.

And the Olympians won. That's where Zeus comes from – the leader of the gods. You know that name?"

".... Um.... Monsieur Verne may have mentioned them."

"Yes. And now we speak of 'titanic' battles, don't we?"

"Yes."

"But is it not strange? – The Olympians won, but we speak not of 'olympic' battles but 'titanic'. Curious! You know, Ned, I should like to have been one of those Titans. To be remembered down all the ages. Do you not think so? Would you not like to be remembered that way?" In his smile was a kind of fatherliness Ned had never really known.

"Ah don't know – ah suppose so. Everybody wants to be remembered, don't they? Everybody wants to be somebody's hero."

"Yes... Yes, they do. Remembered as something wonderful. As something more than the simple creatures that we are, with our comical postures and silly wars. Imagine, Ned – imagine: to fight with Titans. Imagine that. Would that not be wonderful?"

His imagination seemed to have exhausted Carelle: he sat back, gazing upward at the vulgar, iconic statues placed ostentatiously about the ship's walls.

At length, he smiled at Ned.

"Cognac is good... I have had a little too much.... Doctor says it's not good to have too much. Yet it helps me sleep when nothing else calms the fire inside me.... Where's the harm, if it only harms my insides? Uh? I never intended to live to an old age. Who does? Oh, don't look so shocked, my friend. There are worse things, no?.... It often gives me a headache, but at least it allows me to sleep. Sleep and forget, eh?"

Ned remained silent, wondering what depths there were to this man. To speak would have been an intrusion. Presently, Carelle regarded Ned quite directly. "Yes.... a beautiful girl. Always tell a woman that she is beautiful, and that she is loved. Never forget that."

* * * * *

218

There was forever idle talk in the crew's quarters. Usually it was smoke-fuelled talk of the football or of their women – or of *any* women! Marcel had become involved with one of the stewardesses aboard: he showed them one of her stockings and laughed. Jean-Louis was worried about his mother, who had diphtheria, and a letter brought only distressing portents of what might come. Ignatio had had a letter threatening foreclosure on his parents' house in Caen. Dutour – who never responded to his first name – had had his trumpet damaged by one of the passengers, and was waiting morosely for the captain's opinion. On the other hand, his wife was about to give birth, and he expected to sign off once the ship had docked. Thornton had expressed a worry that Cunard were tilting for a larger slice of the Atlantic cake by setting their new liner the *Aquitania* off to New York. At almost twice the displacement of *La France*, she was going to carry many more passengers from Liverpool. Coming on top of the news of all those deaths on the *Empress of Ireland*, rammed in the St. Lawrence, it was a disquieting time.

Returning to port one afternoon at the end of June, Ned found a letter from Carelle pressed into his hand by Frau Bremme. Postmarked not London but Antwerp.

'Dear Ned,

I am moving things to the house at Frazier Grove. You may be pleased to hear this. I cannot say that I am – my home is here in Antwerp, and if you were to come here, you would understand why. However, I must think of my company first, and one of my employees will move to London with me quite soon. Belgium will be amongst the first places to be in danger if the present situation in Europe continues. It is a common joke - Belgians think Belgium is always in the wrong place and should be moved! Ha-ha-ha! The news this evening is all about Serbia and Austria, but I feel sure there are enough itchy fingers in the rest of Europe, and we know how much army Germany has been preparing. Your Russian friend,

Ned, remember? Everyone is saying that war is coming, and you know, events have a habit of being driven by the fears of people.

However, I wanted to tell you that on my last visit to London, I made the acquaintance of friends of Mr. and Mrs. Knight. My position makes it possible to move in those social circles, as you know, and I shall gently move toward them - if I can put it that way. I may get the opportunity in the near future to travel to your home and meet your sister, Ned. I am due in New York in August and then back in France for your wedding. God willing. Therefore, Ned, I expect to see you on La France in August and we will talk again. Adieu, mon ami. Bruno.'

"It is good, *cheri*?"

"It's good, Gitta. Ah hope...."

"Ned, why does Monsieur Carelle help you?" He let out a long breath.

From across the room, Otto called out, "He is in love wiz Ned! You know, everyone fall in love with Ned. Not me. Nobody in love wiz me!"

"*Du bist doof!*" shouted Brigitte.

"Er.... Sophie?" Ned reminded him.

"Oh, ja – Sophie, what." Otto chuckled and threw his head into a kind of spin.

Brigitte took Ned's hand. "And I, Ned, I have good news. Ze *corderie* here, I will get a job zere."

"What? Permanent?"

"*Oui*. Good?"

"Oh, that's champion! Ruddy champion!"

From across the table came a hushed response: "Mushrooms!" said Renata.

* * * * *

220

TWENTY-THREE

"*Messdames et Messieurs.......*"

The broadcast system crackled at first, then settled down as the captain's hand took a firmer grasp of the microphone.

"*Messdames et Messieurs......*"

No-one had need of translation of his first words in French, but after delivering his important announcement in one language, Captain Poncelet deferred to his Second Officer to provide the courtesy of the German and English translations, in a considered statement.

La France, steaming in good weather at 22 knots, had never been so quiet. Across the length and breadth and depth of the ship, the gravity of that announcement deserved every respect. Staff stood to attention at whatever service they were working. Passengers halted in their card games, their consumption, their perambulations or their amorous activities. French passengers quickly fell quiet after the captain's announcement had caused a brief collective exhalation, and now paid heed to what it seemed all already knew.

"...... And I regret to announce, therefore, *Messdames et Messieurs*, that there is no doubt of this message: the forces of Imperial Germany have today entered the sovereign territory of Belgium, and Germany has issued a declaration of war on France and Russia..... We have not yet heard of the reactions of Great Britain, which we understand may be expected this evening, but we would suggest it would be foolish to believe that this is not a very grave situation."

"However," the voice went on after a moment's pause, "I must stress that aboard this vessel, there is no question of hostilities. We have already assumed the neutrality of the United States, in whose waters we shall be within the next thirty-six hours. I ask you all, therefore, to continue the voyage in this neutrality to maintain all courtesy to your fellow travellers. Thank you for your attention. *Vive la France.*"

Thirty-six hours was going to feel like a long time, and Ned's first thought was of Otto. Whilst the captain had mentioned courtesy to passengers, and by implication crew also, German travellers on this ship were in an extreme minority, and crew even more so.

Ned went below, taking leave of his duties for a short while, and found Otto attending the meat locker. Seeing Ned, Otto swung the hatchet down into the side of beef and the two men exchanged looks.

"What d'yer think?"

Otto gave a gesture of the arms. "I sink if Lavielle call me *Kipperfuss* anozzer time, I hit him wiz zis!"

"They don't mean it. It's just a nickname."

"Ja, okay." He drove the hatchet down to lodge in the wood of the table. "And zey call me fat. You sink I'm fat, Ned?"

"Fat?..... Course not. You're just..... big enough for everyone to see."

Whilst Otto appreciated the remark, there was a frustration in him, as indeed there was a right to be. A German who worked for a French company and whose family lived in a French town.

"It may pass over quickly," said Ned.

"You sink?"

"Maybe the British will not act."

"Not act, Ned? When Germany and France are at war. And the Russians too. No. *Ausgeschlossen*. It means you and I, Ned....."

" - Will still be friends.... Otto.... We *are* friends."

"Ja."

"We've known for some time this could 'appen."

"*Das stimmt*."

"Since they bombed Belgrade, anyway, and look - when France pulled its troops back, it were obvious even to me what was gonna happen."

"I know, Ned, I know."

Yes, they had talked about it, half-expected it even, but now.... What was real any more?

"I still want to marry your sister."

For several seconds Otto regarded him carefully in silence, then closed the distance between them and spread his large arms around his English friend, something for which Ned's insides heaved a great sigh of relief.

"But what d'yer think – should we postpone the wedding?"

"What? Why?"

He was not saying so to his friend, but Ned's worry was that if anything happened in Le Havre, the girls might have to consider leaving, and it was for their sake a postponement might be a sensible idea.

"Until.... well, till we see how things settle down, like. Ah mean, it might go one way or t'other, there's no way of knowin'. A month.... three months... who can tell?"

"Maybe all finish by *Weihnachten* and everybody go home for dinner, uh?"

"Oh," joked Ned, stroking his chin, "Dunno about that – if it stops before Christmas ah shall 'ave ter buy you a Christmas present!"

"Ach! *Scheisser*! ... Okay, so we make the joke, but zis is serious shit, Ned."

"Serious shit? – Your word of the week, is it?"

Otto only looked at him and shook his head, but in a good way.

"Naah," he said. "Maybe Magoogle find me new word of the week. Magoogle always find me good words – 'bollocks' – I liked dat one!"

It was good to be able to joke. Over past weeks there had been enough tension and speculation. Now that an action had finally broken, in a perverse way it almost seemed like a relief and they could joke about it candidly. There would be a time for worry, a time for contemplation, a time to consider options, but right now they were two friends on a ship in the middle of the Atlantic Ocean and a war had broken out in Europe. It was not good, but it was not something to panic about. They had their jobs to do.

On both their minds, all the same, was the welfare of three ladies in Le Havre. Discussing it later, they decided the family would be in no immediate danger, having lived and worked many years in the town. And.... they were about to marry into local society, even at a modest level. Both men hid their worries. *La France* would not be back in Le Havre for another two weeks.

Two days later, as *La France* closed on the American coast, the telegraph reported that Britain would join the war. On hearing this news, it was apparent the flippancy that it might all be finished by Christmas was not amusing at all.

* * * * *

In the event, it was Brigitte who raised the matter.

"Postpone the wedding, Gitta? ..... Why?"

"Because, Ned, everysing changed. In a few weeks everysing in Europe has been.... I don't know how you say – turned over."

" – Upside down."

"*Oui.* Upside down. Nobody knows what will happen. You need to sink about your family, and perhaps to change your plans, Ned. Zat is why I sink, for now, it's better we –"

"You still want to marry me, Gitta?"

"Yes. Oh yes, I want you. You know zat. Don't you?"

"We said we loved each other."

" – We do! And I want to be wiz you, *cheri – vraiment.* I do not want you to sink you must stay here wiz me, if you want to be wiz your family in England."

"Ah were thinking, maybe you might – y'know, you and your mother and Reina – that you might want to leave. Because maybe you might not feel safe here. An' at the moment, ah don't know if ah could take yer with me back to England. Come to that, love, ah don't know if ah can get back meself. And besides....."

"What?"

"My home is where you are. This - *this* is my home."

"We will be safe here, Ned. We 'ave been here a long time, ze French people know us. And Reina is Madame Forget now."

"Ah wish we could've been at t'wedding...."

"We will be safe here. I'm sure. And, you know, ze English are marching through Le Havre. Oh, it was wonderful! All ze soldiers coming off ze ships and everybody cheering. Last week, hundreds of English soldiers wiz guns and er.... what you say? – *vélos*... And *camions*.... Everybody shouting and very happy."

Her beaming smile slipped, though, as another reality dawned on her. "But Otto, I don't know. He is not like Reina and me. You have seen him, you have talked to him. He is not ze same now, is he?"

Ned let his thoughts pass across his face for several moments.

"No..... He's not the same. He's the best friend I have in the world, but ...... No, he's not the same. He's like a fish out o' water."

"So....." Taking his hand, she squeezed and shook it as though she were trying to transfer her feelings into him. Ned stared at her, drew in her fragrance, looked into her eyes. They were almost pleading with him. It was a curious dichotomy, that she was actually proposing actions that were more or less parallel to the way his own mind had been working, and yet it was a difficult thing to accept, that they should not marry. A postponement until the game in Europe played out and revealed some certainty of events - that was the crux of the matter, was it not? - Yes, it did make sense, even though it went against every desire in his body. He wanted Gitta so much, to make their union official and unbreakable. As any man wants to possess a woman, he wanted that, but also to prove to her that he was worth the faith she put in him.

By and by, Ned clasped her to him, caressed her and murmured to her.

"Aye, love. You're right. Mebbe it's only fer a few months, like everyone said – all that ruddy brave talk! But if it's not.... Well, look at all that's 'appened lately. Everybody's goin' to war with everybody! Yer've got these Zeppelin things droppin' bombs on French and Belgian towns, yer've got these new submarines sinking ships.... Turkey's already tossin' its cap in wi' Germany, it's right the way across Europe. It'll not be easy, an' ah don't think it's goin' to settle down quick like folk said."

But he didn't want to talk politics, he wanted to talk about what really mattered – them. "Ah wanted to come 'ome to *my* wife – to come ashore, settle down to a decent job o' some sort here maybe. Monsieur Verne says, nothing is impossible. Ah'll try anything.

Get our own place and just live – you an' me. You know – Cinderella gets her house in Honfleur...."

"We will. We will. Just – later, *cheri*. Mm?" Then quietly she added, "And I must look after Mutti until everysing become quiet. You understand."

He affirmed that with a nod. "Anyhow, we don't know what's 'appening wi' the ship. There's talk she'll be requisitioned."

"What do you mean?"

"Taken away by the government. For naval service."

"*La France?*"

"Yes."

"*Mais non*! *C'est fou*! *La France?*..... She is everybody's – what you say? – *coup de coeur*."

"Aye, that's right. But we shall 'ave to wait and see."

"What will you do, if you cannot work on *La France?*"

"Find another ship. What else can ah do? Ah can't go back to England. Not sure ah'd want to."

Frau Bremme had been upstairs. Descending into the living room, she brushed against him fondly, lightly squeezing his arm as if to reassure him. "Zere is a letter for you, Ned. From Antwerp. He is here two days."

'Dear Ned,

You English have a saying – the balloon is up! When this reaches you, you will know the worst thing has happened, my country has been invaded. I am rushing this note before all organisation in Belgium falls apart. We knew as soon as we heard the reports in the German press that the French were bombing Nürnberg that diplomacy had failed and it would be only days before the ultimatum turned into invasion. Actually, we knew in the middle of July when Russia and Germany declared war, but we didn't want to believe it. Today there is shooting to the east. Antwerp cannot resist the huge forces we know Germany can send in. I have been preparing for this, of course, as I described to you at our last meeting. I sent my mother to London two weeks ago with a member of my staff. I am following immediately, and from there I shall get in touch with you by some device or other – through Grace perhaps. For the present, our private business must take a back seat. Another English phrase you told me! God willing, we shall meet again in England, and hope all this foolishness comes to a swift end. Though, you know from our earlier chatter I am not optimistic. The very best of luck, Ned, I am so sorry I shall miss your wedding. Adieu. Your friend, Bruno.'

"It is bad news?" asked Gitta. Ned passed her the letter.

* * * * *

For Otto, things could not have been more disturbing. More than any of his family, and probably as he was the sole male, Otto felt the burden of his German citizenship: something he had not sought to revoke even though he had never worn any outward sign of nationality. He had adopted France, but despite whatever doubts he had expressed in the past, his heart was possessed by Germany. Ned tried to reason with him, but he could already tell that Otto believed his destiny lay in returning to the motherland. It was an agonising conflict that could only be decided one way, for despite all the ostentation that might be taken as an ambivalence towards the country of his birth, underneath it all there remained a pride in what he was, where he had come from. He could not go against the conditioning of his birth and childhood.

To his credit, Ned knew it was something for the family and not for him to determine, though Brigitte had agreed with Ned's views. They were not Otto's.

Germany's struggle was that of a nation flanked on opposite sides – opposed, in fact, by those very cousins who had long sought to temper the ambition of a Prussia-dominated Germany with the practicalities of a Europe that wanted to move on from parochial border disputes and militaristic solutions – so long as Britain was still in charge! But, for all his casual manner, Otto believed in a united Germany, a strong, modern Germany that stood alongside the great European nations as it had every right to. And if might was to be right, then that was the means that Germany had to use. For too long, Great Britain had denied the Kaiser his proper place

227

and Germany had so often been pressed into a subordinate role. The tripartite powers of Great Britain, France and Russia had to be shown that they could not simply force Germany to back away as they had long conspired against the position of Austria-Hungary.

From the chest in his room, Otto pulled out the diary from his eighth year: on the cover remained those words, 'Gott mit Uns'.

They had been in port three days when Otto took his mother aside.

Speaking with her hand to her mouth, Marlene found her trembling lips would utter very few words. "*Zurück*?.... Oh, Otto!"

She cried a little, but kissed him and blessed him. Hostilities were in full flow, there would be no way he could enter Germany on any seagoing vessel that bore a British or French flag unless he could devise a route via Sweden, and definitely not a Russian ship. The Italians, after being for some time an ally of Austria-Hungary, did not appear to know what they were doing, which left only the Swiss. Otto's idea was to take the train to Paris and thence to Basel, with an ongoing link to Köln before the Swiss made any decision as to what they might want to do with their army and their borders. He told his mother to be brave, for it might be many weeks before he could get any kind of message to her that he had reached the home of cousin Manfred and his wife, Erika.

"And Sophie?" queried Ned. "Marlene, what will he do about that?"

Wiping her hands on her apron, she crossed to him and put her arms gently on him. "Is for Otto to decide, Ned. I..... we have talk, and he choose. Sophie is..... it is difficult for him, Ned. We have to.... let him go. He wishes to do as his father."

She sobbed a little and Ned embraced her tightly to smother her pain. He could not have loved her more if she had been his own mother, and he did not like to see her so distressed.

"We let him go, Ned. He is German first. He hears ze motherland. He is like his father. Very proud. And I.... am proud because of dat. You understand.... I will not go to ze *bahnhof*, Ned. And ze girls – no. Zey cry. Go wiz him. Please."

It could not have been a more incongruous setting for a farewell. It seemed like pure theatre. The morning sun was breaking through onto a scene of biblical confusion, piercing some of the broken glass in the roof of the station and illuminating patches of people as though they were marionettes in spotlights, each acting out his or her tiny drama. People were rushing everywhere, with the trams disgorging travellers right outside the station building. It was noisy. Too noisy for dignity.

From the house they had walked briskly and talked as amicably as ever, silly little jokes and recollections from their time together.

"And the new word of the week is what, Otto?"

"I don't have a new word, Ned.... Maybe I have a few words.... Zey all say, *Ami.*"

They stopped in the road and looked at each other.

"Ah know that word."

"Ja. Me too."

Otto had walked his flat-footed walk with a confident pace, occasionally turning his head and looking into Ned's face, yet every step now was a league of pain. They wanted it to pass quickly, but there was a long queue for tickets, and distractions everywhere, a mass of people on the move to – heaven knows where. For the most part, Ned stood away, holding onto Otto's bag, not wanting any discussion because nothing they could have said would have been enough.

The ticket bought, all that was necessary was to go to the barrier and look at the trains. "Rouen – Paris". It was there, chalked on the board, with the engine over there hissing to call travellers to embark.

Ned took in a great breath as he handed his friend the bag and knew his heart was pounding with sorrow. There were so many things to say, though nothing seemed appropriate. The German reached out and put his large arms once again around the Englishman and the two stood there in an embrace of love and

229

friendship for several seconds. Over some time neither said a word, for each had a breast that would not release all those torn emotions, all those moments in more than two years that they had spent together and learned to love each other as brothers or better. Then Otto broke the silence.

"You ask for a word and I don't have one. I know zis, Ned: you have my soul, and I have yours, for we are friends. Always."

Then they stood apart, and made eye contact for perhaps the last time. Otto slapped Ned on the shoulder. Smiled. Turned. And carried his bulky frame awkwardly through the barrier and away into the murky steam discharge of an engine.

On the air, Ned felt Otto's final thoughts drift to him as if he had spoken them. 'Goodbye, my small *Nixie* friend.......'

He turned and walked away and cried like he had only cried as a child.

* * * * *

TWENTY-FOUR

His arrival blew the very breath right out of her.

When she had regained her senses, Alice barked, "You're not comin' in 'ere wi' them feet!"

Ned looked down at his boots as he stood dripping rainwater in the doorway and let out a questioning gasp before catching his mother's thrilled smile. With a little shriek, she ran across the room to him and he swept her up into his arms.

"Yer can just get up them stairs to that scraper an' come in t'front door, Ned Thornton."

There had been no firm word, no precise message. Only a persistent murmur in her brain these past days that he was coming.

"Mum," he just kept repeating, trying to convince himself. How long had it been? Two years, and a week.

All the way up the lane as the tram clattered noisily along its wet tracks, he had been saying to himself, *Two years, two years,* unable to believe it.

Once Grace and Jubal were home, their father tired and wheezy, he had to repeat himself all over again, and fight off the embraces of his sister.

Yes, he had come by way of Portsmouth. No, he had no bother getting into the country. No, there were no police. Yes, the trains had been jam-packed in the south, less so as he moved north. No, he was not short of money. Yes, his clothes needed washing. Yes, he would use the tin bath in front of the fire. Yes, he was well looked-after by the French company. No, he was not going back, not until a number of things had been sorted out. Not least, not until the course of hostilities had set itself on the right road.

But..... No, not going back. Should he repeat that to himself? That he was not going back? Why had he come away from that which he held most dear?

Of the fact that he had seen wounded soldiers off the ships at Portsmouth Harbour station, he said nothing. There was no point:

those men had little appetite for conversation, and not having spoken to them, he had no idea how they had come by their wounds.

"You came back to join up?... To join up, Ned?"

"Aye."

"Why?" Grace wanted to know. "Why? Why didn't yer just stay workin' yer French ship? – Yer don't need to join up. Yer were safe there."

It was a question he had asked himself any number of times. Why? But she did not know his heart. And "safe"? - that was a dubious point.

"An' you were gettin' married an' all, weren't yer? What happened?"

So many questions. Ned wished he had wine, but of course there was none and beer was cold and flat and wooden; it offered no cheer in this rainy weather. Alice had made a stew and dumplings using scrag end, it had taken most of her ironing money. They began eating before Jubal as he insisted on washing, and of course it was Grace asking most of the questions.

"Yer love 'er, don't yer?"

"Yes, ah do."

"Pretty, is she?" Alice put in. Ned didn't reply.

"Catholic, I expect," continued Alice.

He breathed a heavy breath. He had to tell it his way. "After Otto left, things weren't the same."

"Fancy 'avin' a German for a mate," said Jubal, emerging from the staircase and tossing his boots into the hearth. His son ignored the remark. "Ah tell yer what, our Ned, yer like givin' folk summat to talk about, don't yer? First yer get yerself in all t'papers wi' that ruddy ship goin' down." That was Jubal again, thought Alice – give the lad a chance.

Ned needed no defending, however. "Now listen.... All o' yer. Ah'm only goin' to say this.... Gitta and I will get wed, but not yet. She wanted to wait – No! No, that's not true – we *both* decided to wait. So we cancelled t'church. She knew ah'd not settle fer long with a war on. *La France* was taken by the government. Ah did the only thing ah could at the time, the C.G.T. offered me a place on *La Savoie* an' ah took it. But... it weren't the same without Otto. An' yes, dad, he's German an' as fine a chap as you'd ever meet, ah'll tell yer that.... an' if it comes to that, Gitta's German too.... So have some consideration, eh? German or not, Otto's my friend, and Gitta's gonna be me wife..... Ah just wish ah could say when."

Alice observed how difficult it was for Jubal to say nothing for once.

"Ah went across to New York, twice. Last time, ah went to see Magoolagan, had dinner with 'im and Clodagh."

"Hah!" Jubal derided him, "Irish! Yer've a fine idea o' friends, Ned, ah'll say that. One's German and the other's Irish!"

"Yer can take that back, dad!"

For once, Alice was shocked. Ned, however, remained calm and went on, "He's a fine bloke, Magoolagan. Did more for me than anyone around 'ere would do, ah'll tell yer that.... Otto calls 'im Magoogle!" Ned broke himself off to laugh quietly. "We talked, any road. He's just as worried about Ireland as we are. It's a bad time all round, no point getting all het up about it. 'Ned,' says he, 'If you're gonna settle down wi' that lass, do it now. Else not at all. Wars do funny things to people,' he says, 'They give us some funny ideas. One of 'em is the duty to our country. An' if yer feel that, then see to it now, otherwise yer'll never settle. An' if yon lass feels as you do in another year, marry the girl an' have some kids.'.... Ah got to thinkin', Magoolagan's right."

"He is an' all," admitted Jubal.

Alice was indignant. "An' what do you know, Jubal Thornton? – When there were that run on the bank back in July you said it'd all be over in a week."

"Aye, well....."

"Storm in a teacup, you said!"

"Aw, come on, woman!....."

"Not that it bothered us none," continued Alice with a diffident air, "When we don't 'ave the cash to pay t'rent man never mind cash in a bank, thank you very much."

Grace couldn't help but catch the look from Ned: *nothing changes!* Both hid their amusement poorly.

".... And what if yon lass don't wait for yer, Ned?" asked Alice, fearful of the answer.

Ned put down his spoon, stood, pushed back his chair and walked across to the fire. "Not sure," he admitted. "But if she don't, that's her business. And for me to deal with, nobody else."

"Naah then," said Jubal, as if that put an end to the matter. "Look, this 'ere trouble with t'Germans, bless me life, it in't for ever, is it? Soon as our lads lock horns with 'em, ah'll bet them Germans back off right smart."

"From what you've told us," said Grace, "Gitta's a nice girl. Intelligent, you said. Well mannered. Pretty."

"Grace....." He laughed, as though hardly believing it himself. "She knocks everybody's eyes out. The lads in the town - "

"Ah know," said Grace with a grin, an admission that she was pushing him, "Bruno Carelle told me.... Beautiful, he said. Both of them. *And* they mind their manners."

"She's straight out of heaven, Grace." Ned faltered, he was not sure this was serving any purpose. "But," he carried on, "Gitta can 'ave any man she wants. Any man. An' the only way ah'm ever goin' to know if it's me that she wants is..... to leave. D'y'understand?"

No, Jubal did not, but only pulled a face. Grace alone understood.

"Yer gonna join up, then, are yer?"

"That were what ah came back for, dad. That an' seein' you lot."

"Yer'll 'ave a pint wi' me first, though?"

"What?" joked Ned, "That cat's pee?"

"'Ere 'ere!" called Alice. "Language, young Ned!"

Jubal coughed several times and Alice looked across at him with a stone expression on her face, keeping her concerns to herself.

"Coughin' well tonight, dad," said Ned. His father looked up. Alice too showed surprise for a second time.

"Gonna have to take better care o' yerself, father. Or ah'll take yer pipe off yer."

None of them had heard Ned speak to his father in that way before. *'Well, well,'* thought Alice.

"Stay home an' put yer feet up, give the Spotted Cow a miss now that nights are wet and cold. Eh? Mollycoddle yerself. Can't be havin' you off work ill, can we? Take some treacle."

"Treacle?"

"Aye, Jubal, treacle," echoed Alice, "An' about time yer took some notice. You listen to't' lad."

Her husband looked around him, seeking support and soon gave up. "Aye, right then." And coughed some more.

"Yer'll be down at Belle Vue tomorrer then, will yer? Sign up? There's a few lads yer'll know that've joined t'Bradford Pals, Ned, yer'll 'appen know most on 'em."

For the moment, Ned wanted to keep his thoughts to himself.

"The buggers killed people in Belgium, yer know," Jubal growled. "Aye.... Women and children too. Just fancy – killin' civilians."

Ned could fancy. He could indeed. Particularly with Bruno Carelle in his mind.

"They'll not stop there, Ned. Mark my words. They'll be over 'ere next. On British soil. Somebody's got to stop 'em, tha knows."

Wars never got any better. This one seemed set to break new ground.

"And ah'll tell yer what, an' all," said Alice, "Yon price o' cheese has gone up again.... and faggots."

La Savoie had been far from his heart's desire. One of the most dependable vessels of the transatlantic fleet, yet after *La France*, nothing had felt quite right. It was not that *La Savoie* was smaller with fewer passengers and altogether less plush. He knew no-one, and it seemed no-one wanted to know him, not of the crew at any rate, and now English passengers were like the proverbial rocking-horse droppings. Life seemed hollow: whilst he had been back to the Bremme house after two out of three crossings, he had not felt comfortable. There was an awkwardness about it now – probably it was himself that was the problem, and then the absence of his friend. It was difficult to know.

Frau Bremme had been as sensitive and warm to him as ever, and of course Renata was now living with Monsieur Forget, so there were two voids to fill. Both he and Brigitte had sensed a change in the air. She too was missing Renata, that was clear. Oh, he would have sworn that he still loved Gitta, but his unsettled manner made her unsure and in turn he was no longer completely confident about her, even though he spent long moments just gazing at her beauty. He loved to watch her turn her blonde hair up onto her head, and then to take it down again and let it flow in tresses that would inspire any poet. Perhaps, he wondered, they should have stuck by that late August wedding and married regardless, as now it was awkward to be going to bed in separate rooms - though neither would have dreamed of offending Frau Bremme's sensibilities by sleeping together.

Oh yes, they smiled and brushed against each other almost as before, and Ned longed to make it right between himself and his beloved, in fact he longed to make love to her again and to be one with her in body and spirit, but in the circumstances that proved less possible than ever. He was not certain anything would make it right at present. Something would have to change.

One morning after signing off *La Savoie*, he kissed Frau Bremme a very fond goodbye and set off for a boat to England. She had cried, and his heart had been in his boots. Brigitte had left early, as she now had to do, working for the rope factory at the end of the town, but Ned had told her the previous evening what he was going to do. There had been no fuss, no drama, and no tears, typical of Gitta: both had accepted the situation in a matter-of-fact way that actually took Ned by surprise. They had kissed, embraced briefly and said goodnight, and in the early morning he was at the door to bid her *au revoir*. As with Otto, it did not play out as he had planned it in his mind, and hardly a word was spoken, it was all accomplished with their eyes and a pained smile that did not linger as he watched her hurry away.

"Yer sure yer've done the right thing, Ned?"

"Yes, Grace.... " Then he looked back at her, straight into her caring face, and heaved a heavy burden of doubt up from his soul. ".... Well.... Ah can't say ah'm sure... No."

"Sometimes," said Alice quietly, "Yer take a leap of faith."

"But, Ned....Yer'll go back to 'er." It was a question.

".... She's me fiancée, Grace. An' ah do want her. When the time comes, ah'll go back. If she'll have me. There's nothin' ah'd rather do." The matter had run its course, Ned wanted to move on.

"Jim?"

His mother and father exchanged looks. It was Grace that relieved the pressure on them. "Not good," she said. "Since she lost the child, they've not been gettin' on that well."

"But he's still workin'?"

"Yes.... But he thinks he got demoted."

"Was he?"

"You have to look at it from their point of view, Ned. He wasn't able to get around the mill as he should."

"No, but he's still at Salts?"

"Yes. Calls himself a clerk now. In a bitter sort of way. It's less money, but at least he's got a job. Could be a lot worse. Course, he can't run to work no more like he did."

Ned drew a hand across his chin. "Mm. Anythin' ah can do?"

His mother placed the replenished pot of tea on the table, passed her husband his tobacco tin and patted Ned's hand. "Not much any of us can do, lad. At least he's still got 'is leg – it don't seem any worse, mind."

"But - " Jubal cut in. "He's not gonna be joinin' up wi' yer. Be careful what yer say to 'im, lad."

Ned agreed that, and promised to give James a little money, as much as he could spare: if he was going to sign on, he would need little for himself.

"Been a big rush 'ere to join up," Jubal continued. "Yer should-a been 'ere at August Bank Holiday, Ned. It were ruddy barmy! Talk about war fever! They took over Lister Park, yer know. Mad, it were. Ruddy brass band an' all. Yer'd think t'ruddy king had come!"

"Well," interrupted Alice, "at least it took everybody's mind off of t'strike at Keighley. That were just as bad."

"Mad as the old hay rides at Barnabas, Ned. Remember?"

Yes, Ned remembered some of the happier memories of childhood. When the local chapel ran a big horse and cart out into the country and everyone climbed aboard. An hour to get there, an hour back, and all the fun in between in the hay fields.

"Any road," muttered Jubal, more disconsolately, "it's been no fun for us.... Bradford Tramways 'as lost a lot o' men. And all the 'orses the ruddy army took."

"What about Little Germany downtown," said Alice. "They've all gone, yer know. Yer go up Church Bank now, it's like a cemetery."

Ned considered that. The sons of German merchants, a strong presence in the town. It took his thoughts to Otto and he no longer wanted to talk about it.

"It were all a bit sad," continued Alice, subdued now. "Not like yer'd think.... Germans or not, they're just more lads goin' off to fight. Even if it is for t' other side.... Strange, really.... Bit sad."

* * * * *

TWENTY-FIVE

The barracks main drill hall at Belle Vue was doing good business. It had eased a lot since the initial high-spirited rush in August, but busy enough. Like most other towns across Britain, Bradford was barely getting itself together after the early shocks. So many men had left that businesses struggled, and horses had been taken into the military effort, threatening the harvest. The price of food was a worry the government's new statutes failed to diminish, however everyone seemed aware it was a time of change, and they would do whatever needed to be done whilst hoping it would all end tomorrow. The common phrase of the time was, 'Don't you know there's a war on?'. It might put a smile on the face, but it put no bread on the table.

"Ruddy hell!... Well, ah'll go to 't..... Hell! It *is* you, in't it? Thornton!"

Ned didn't need this. "'Ow are yer, Jack?" he asked guardedly.

"Hell! Thornton! Ah never thought you'd show yer face around 'ere again." His voice deliberately loud to draw attention.

Jack Openshaw was one of the local bullies when Ned had been growing up. Jack and his 'Carlisle Road gang' would plague James and Ned as they walked home often. Usually it was all mouth and a bit of stone-throwing, though James had once been set on by five of them and badly kicked. Jack Openshaw was not what Ned wanted to see. Not now. Not ever.

"Last time I seen you were at Valley Parade..... Yer still a spineless piece o' shit! 'Ere, where's the sergeant? – This bloke's Ned Thornton!" Turning to him, Jack spat at him, "Yer not joining this regiment, Thornton! Nobody wants a ruddy coward."

It was the last thing Ned wanted, Openshaw alerting everyone in the recruitment line. "Remember *Titanic,* lads? Two year ago? Brought shame on all of us. Remember what all t'papers said?"

Jack left the line and faced up to Ned. "Thornton, fuck off! Ah remember what yer did. Nobody wants your sort. Bugger off!"

In Ned's mind the words formed large and loud – "Oh" and "Bloody" and "Hell"!

He could not - would not - take this now. He had come back to his home and to this regiment to sign on for his country. He was not going to be told he couldn't by a juvenile tyrant. Ned bit his lip and felt the blood pounding behind his eyes.

"Ah'm here to sign up, Jack.... Don't get in me way. We're not behind old man Studd's middin now. Ah don't want trouble, but get out o' me way!"

"Else what?"

As a boy, Ned and his brother had stood any amount of threats from Openshaw and his cronies. They had always avoided trouble, particularly having in mind their background. Ned well remembered the time he ran home, leaving James to fend off five of them. He remembered James' bloody face. But - much as he hated violence - if Ned was going to become a soldier, he may as well start right now.

Other men had broken from the line to watch, many of them muttering the names 'Thornton' and '*Titanic*', though in truth struggling to establish the connection. Jack Openshaw pushed his cap back in a show of defiance. "What you gonna do, then, Thornton? Eh? You allus were a soft bugger, you an' yer brother."

There was one way forward. More than that, Ned was mad now. He wasn't going to waste words or time on this man's sort. Jack's face presented a good target and he had put up no guard, expecting his old bullying tactics would cower the other man. Instead, one swift punch with all of Ned's pent-up anger smashed into Jack's nose and sent him flying off his feet.

That was it. All over in a second. Ned felt his fist - it hurt. Men muttered even more loudly but all stood back as Ned looked around their faces, his heart pounding and his breath snorting. He was up for this now, alien though it was to him, and though they might take him down, by God he would give them something to think about! Two-and-a-half years was enough. It was *enough*!

Then from a corner of the assembly hall, a loud voice bellowed out, "You men! What's going on there?" It was a big man in khaki with heavy boots and large stripes on his arm. His big boots clattered across the floor in a regular military gait. "What's up here?"

"Ah've come to join up," Ned panted.

The sergeant looked about him, saw Openshaw sitting up on the floor, feeling his bloodied nose, saw the other men in a half-circle around them.

"Thornton!" came the muffled cry from Openshaw, pointing a hand at Ned as an indictment. "That's Ned Thornton!"

"What's it all about, then?" barked the sergeant, "You two got some private war? We can take care of that once you've joined up, lads – we like that sort o' thing!"

"It's Thornton, sir!" cried Jack. "The coward from *Titanic*.... 'E disgraced us. We don't want 'im with us."

"*Titanic?*" The sergeant wondered what something from over two years ago might have to do with the here and now. "Yer want to join up, lad? This chap 'ere seems to think yer shouldn't. Why should that be, ey?"

Ned, still panting, said nothing and simply looked into the sergeant's face.

"Come wi' me, lad," ordered the sergeant. Ned followed to one of the desks, where the sergeant brushed aside the first man in the queue. At the desk was a civilian in tiny spectacles and a very tight collar, who appeared terrified of the sergeant.

"This chap 'ere wants to enlist," barked the sergeant. "See that 'e does – 'e seems pretty good wi' his fists already! Name's Thornton - that right, lad?" Ned gave his full name.

"Yes, sergeant," said the harassed clerk.

For a few seconds, that seemed to be that. But then - "Just a moment, sergeant."

The voice came from a police officer in a peaked cap, who had been standing just back from the desk area. This officer stood with a hand across his mouth, regarding Ned thoughtfully. "Your name Edward Thornton?" Again, Ned signalled that it was, now gripped with anxiety. He was well-spoken, this man, and used his voice like a bayonet, jabbing and tugging.

"Thornton?.... Ye-e-es."

"What?" queried Ned in a hushed voice.

"I think this man may be wanted by the police, sergeant. It rings a bell.... I shall have to check. Take him aside, would you?"

"Sir," obeyed the sergeant, he took Ned's arm and led him to one side of the queueing men.

In a softer voice, the sergeant asked him, "Is that true.... what 'e said, son?"

"No."

"Yer don't look like a villain to me, what's 'e talkin' about?"

In a couple of short sentences, Ned explained his circumstances. Perhaps the police officer had seen something from long ago when the fuss about *Titanic* raged. He did not allude to the arrest warrant but referred to the misleading reports in newspapers.

This sergeant was a strong man with a soft heart, it seemed. He listened. That was all Ned could ask. And there was another thing in Ned's favour: the sergeant was already aware that Openshaw was a trouble-maker. He would far sooner have found ways of keeping *him* out of the regiment.

Quietly, the sergeant advised him. "You better 'op it, quick. Ah'll tell that officer of police you buggered off an' ah didn't see which way yer went. Try another regiment, son, not this un. Alright? Go on, quick, jam yer skip on yer 'ead and get out that door over there. Quick's the word, sharp's the motion."

"Thank you," said Ned.

"Oh – and lad!"

"Yes, sergeant?"

"You any relation to Jubal Thornton, the fighter?"

"He's me dad."

The sergeant stood upright and beamed as if he had found a guinea.

"Well, join a boxing club. Yer've a good punch there by the look of it." Ned grinned back and went for the door as he was told. He was still nursing his right hand when he got home.

* * * * *

"Where will yer go, Ned? Ah mean - are yer still goin' to join up?"

"Don't know, mum.... If ah can't join 'ere, mebbe none o' the Yorkshire regiments'll take me..... Somewhere else. What else can ah do?"

"Don't go," said Alice. "After all, lad, yer don't have to, do yer? They'll bundle y'off to Ireland – yer don't want to be mixing wi' them Irish! Nothin' good ever came out of Ireland 'cept a potato. Nah then."

Ned looked into Grace's eyes: she would understand what their parents didn't.

"What about Mr. Carelle?" asked Grace.

"What about 'im?"

"Well.... ah don't suppose 'e carries any weight wi' the military, does he?"

"Still," thought Ned aloud, "It might be a good idea to talk to 'im. See if 'e's got any more news about Knight.... And Cade's been quiet lately."

Ned checked his wallet. He could last about another two weeks at this rate, no more. Not without asking Grace to help him, which he knew she would have done. But he could afford a rail ticket.

Only later did he feel any guilt for the fact they had talked only of him, with barely a mention of Grace and her own happiness. More particularly, her progress with her 'new young man'.

"You're courtin' now, aren't yer?"

It had been touched on much earlier, all Grace would say was, "Stanley? - Oh, he's a big chap!"

Later, alone with his mother, he asked the same question of her and got the response, "What, Stanley Quinn? – Oh, he's a big chap!"

And to his father before he left for work. "Oh, he's a big –"

"Don't!" said Ned. "Ah know – big chap. Got it."

He thought better of enquiring about Stanley Quinn after that.

"You sure she's the one for you, Ned?" Grace, always the practical one. "Because it weren't much more 'n a year ago you 'ad yer sights on the other one – Renata."

"Aye. Ah did."

Grace sighed and shook her head at him as he sat in the warmth of the bath water in front of the fire. There was no other light, for they had turned off the gas light to save the mantle, and only the fire was glowing soothingly, the peace punctuated now and then by a sudden crack from the coal which might send a tiny ember flashing out onto the hearth. It felt warmer in the dark, and mother and father had already gone to bed.

"Ah, Ned," she sighed again. "Sometimes.... Ah never know whether you're just dreamin'. You always were one for dreamin', yer know that."

"Ah were. You're right. Y'always are, Grace. Yer were born with two heads – yours and mine. I got left with a head full o' jam and left-over fireworks. Daft ideas. Ah should've been a Punch and Judy man!"

"Which is why you went off to sea."

"Yeh. Reckon so. Why are you allus right, Grace?"

Convincing Grace of anything had never been easy. "This last couple o' year, ah've grown up a bit – Oh, ah know what yer goin' to say! But working t'Atlantic Railway for a few years, it makes yer grow up."

"Atlantic railway?"

"That's what seamen... That's what the likes of us calls the Atlantic liners."

"Oh."

"An' ah shoulda known at the time it were daft. Ah just got carried away. Ah mean, they're lovely girls.... Aw, yer a woman, Grace, 'ow am ah supposed to explain to you?"

"I'd know soon enough. And Gitta, does she feel the same?"

"Well...."

"Just seems to me it's too easy to get carried away. You make a friend of a German, you meet his family in a French port, you get

244

carried away wi' the idea you can make a wife of one of 'em. All very romantic!"

"Romantic? – Look, Sis, it's been two-and-a-half years. Come on, that's hardly rushin', is it? Workin' ships is a long way from romantic."

Grace had remained seated at the far side of the table. "D'yer want some more hot water in that?" Ned declined, he would be stepping out in a minute.

"So.... You decided not to marry. Because yer'd made up yer mind to join up."

"Otto left. My best friend. Ah know none o' yer can understand that. No good trying to explain to yer, because he's German."

"That's not fair, Ned."

"Weren't intended to be fair. Just tellin' what ah see. None o' yer were thrilled ah'd got in wi' a family of Germans. Even before any trouble started up."

"Ned, that's not true."

"'Tis an' all..... Well, yer might be in a minority of one, Grace. Neither mum and dad nor Jim were taken by the idea of 'avin' Germans fer in-laws."

She did not respond. She knew he had felt this frustration, his accusations were not entirely wild and she would allow him to let off steam. There were, after all, many Germans in the town, Bradford was a well-known outpost for German businessmen, they had brought a certain prosperity and international prestige. Little Germany, that commercial centre of Bradford had been well named. There were, all the same, Englishmen who were happy to see them depart. If nothing else, it would ease the tension as scuffles had broken out in the town which, for a little while, had seemed more like a garrison.

"Ned....." Her voice quieter now. "Why didn't yer marry her?"

"Told yer.... We agreed. She thought .... we *both* thought ..... maybe it'd be better later on. With a war on, anythin' could 'appen."

"You mean you could get yourself killed."

"Yer never were one to mess about wi' words, were yer, Grace?"

"But is that the real reason? Yer weren't just gettin' cold feet?"

"No." He passed the flannel over himself one more time and asked himself the question – was she right? Was that part of it?

"No, Grace. Ah love Gitta. Ah'm not a kid. Look, ah'm twenty-one! You were allus right, ah'm a dreamer, ah know that much. But ah grew up. Mebbe not like you, but ah know me own mind better now."

"And you're not just running away... This thing with joining the army...."

"Listen, Grace. Ah'm gonna tell yer something."

He splashed water over his back again. Grace went to the fire, wrapped her hand in the cloth to pick up the big black kettle and, telling him to pull his legs up, poured freshly heated water into the tub.

"That last trip. Remember ah told yer, ah've been working on the *Savoie*, right? We were off the Normandy coast on us way back from New York, about ten mile into Le Havre, runnin' along with the shoreline. Ah'm in the saloon as usual, an' suddenly the ship's claxon goes. Everybody rushes around, all like 'eadless chickens. Me an' Olivier, we step out on deck ter see what's goin' on.... Over yonder, about a thousand yards, mebbe – there's a German U-boat sittin' on the surface. Large as life, yer wouldn't believe it, Grace. An' we could see that 'e had 'is gun already manned, we could see the gun crew just waitin' there, with the gun pointed at us. It were bloody frightening, ah can tell yer. A lot of passengers were very upset... some women were screamin'. They were signallin' – the U-boat. Something or other, I don't know. Flash – flash – flash, yer know. An' ah suppose we were signallin' back, ah couldn't see. But, yeh, a U-boat.... U-15 or 16, I couldn't make it out clearly. An' yer know, Grace, for a minute all of us were terrified. Then after another minute it were almost like a comedy with all this flashin' goin' on – flash, flash, flash! People dashin' around all over the place. It were like bein' at t'pictures! And we changed course, we tacked further out, and sort of..... sort of went around this U-boat. He just sat there. With 'is gun pointed at us, swingin' it round as we went by. Maybe we got as close as 500 yards, ah'm not sure."

"They didn't fire, though?"

246

"No, they didn't. There weren't any warships around. But ah were not confident they mightn't just take a shot at us anyway. We were flying French colours, after all."

"They wouldn't fire on a merchant ship, would they?"

"Wouldn't they?" he scoffed. "Don't you believe it! If we'd been a supply ship and not a passenger liner, they could've easily put a torpedo in us."

She said nothing, only wiped her hands on her apron, sat down again at the table and contemplated how that story might have ended.

"Y'see.... Ah've been sunk once. No laughin' matter, that. Ah'm not gonna get sunk again, Grace. Never again. Ah didn't decide to leave Gitta because ah wanted to join the army..... An' ah didn't decide to leave because ah didn't love her. Ah left for two reasons – first, because ah'm never gonna get sunk again, and second because ah needed to give them a breathin' space to decide what were best for them. Gitta's as French as anybody, but Reina and her mum, there's a lot of German in 'em. That's no problem for me, but it may be for them. And that's why ah left. Does that sound so daft?"

For some moments she considered that. "No.... As a matter of fact, it sounds pretty reasonable."

"And when Otto left.... well, after a bit it just seemed to me the best thing I could do were to take the king's shillin'. No, ah don't have to. But ah want to. Between you an' me, ah'm not that bothered if ah never go to sea again. So ah had a long talk wi' meself. Ah'm not a villain, but ah still have to prove to me and others that ah'm a free man. Free to come and go, not to skulk offshore for ever more. Y'understand, Grace? If ah stayed in France, married Gitta.... it might be alright for a while. But they've got conscription in France, ah might end up being drafted into a French regiment. An' that makes me about as useful to Gitta as ah would be comin' over 'ere to join the British."

He looked up at her now, as if to say, *Tell me the worst!*

"I'll get y' a towel, our Ned," she said.

247

For the most part, the trouble he took to reach Frazier Grove in Barnet was in vain. An elderly lady allowed him entrance to the house and its dark drawing room upon mention of his name. The lady confirmed herself as Carelle's mother, whilst Carelle himself was away on business for a week, whereupon she gave Ned a note that Carelle had left in an envelope simply marked 'Edward Thornton', anticipating that Ned might at some point come here.

'Dear Ned, If you are reading this, you are seeking me. I hope it does not mean things have gone badly for you – when wars break out, all our lives go into the wash-tub! When the Germans began pressing Franz Josef over Serbia in July, I knew I should leave Belgium for a while. Hopefully, we are safer here, the Germans certainly did not care when they violated the sovereign state of my country, protected by a treaty they all signed 75 years ago! Then our army made a stand at Antwerp. Your Mr. Churchill took his soldiers there in buses, did you hear? Buses, Ned! – against Skoda 305s! And it's a strange kind of war when French taxis go into action to defend Paris! But – we live in a mad world, don't we? Like Johnson fighting Marcussen – absurd!

The Germans took Antwerp two weeks ago. One newspaper says one thing and another says something else. I fear for my friends and for their sons. Our King and Queen have gone to the Channel coast, I am surprised as Queen Elizabeth is German and I hoped would have influence with the oppressors. My first duty, Ned, is to my business, which must continue or several people will starve! Where you are concerned, please excuse me, I have had little time for that. Tommy has further details of Caldecot, and I contrived a future invitation to a soirée with Lady Sophie, but these are things better left for the moment. I write frequently to Grace, but do inform me of your circumstances. Let us hope your postal system is not one of the first casualties of war! Sincerely, Bruno.'

When the lady re-entered the room with a tray carrying tea and biscuits, Ned asked for a paper and pen, whereupon he scribbled a note for Carelle's return, explaining briefly his situation and that he would attempt to enlist with another regiment. At that point, however, he was 'just a ship dragging its anchor'.

Out of courtesy, Ned asked Madame Carelle about their flight from Antwerp. In her limited English, the lady wished to say little and he respected that, but took away a sense that she was pretty much destroyed about it.

Not having seen Carelle was disappointing, but it had always been a gamble. Crossing London again, he made his way to Waterloo and boarded a train to Portsmouth. Perhaps there he would sit and think for a while, evaluating his options.

It was already evening as he sat in that semi-sooty atmosphere with half his consciousness listening to the noises of Waterloo station pattering against the carriage window. He would head for the Lupton, it was a hotel he had used before and if it were full there were other boarding houses in the vicinity.

Rail journeys were seldom a lonely experience: on this one, most passengers seemed more interested in sleep than talk, and at this time the noise of the locomotive might have been a gentle lullaby to his thoughts. The exclusivity of those thoughts was disrupted, however, by a large, cheerfully-voiced soldier who had entered the carriage just prior to departure and insisted on talking as if it was the middle of the morning. His name was Ernie and he talked all the way to Portsmouth. It was clear he was going to go on talking as the two of them headed for Southsea and the soldier's recommended overnight stay.

* * * * *

TWENTY-SIX

"Blanco – blanco – bloody blanco! Boots, boots, boots! Spit and soddin' poxy polish, crease them trousers, brasso them buttons!........ Did I join up for all this, my friends? - My friends, I did not!"

"Pipe down, John!" Bob told him, "Just get on with it! And water it down – you're putting it on too thick. Didn't anyone tell you how to use that brush?"

Happy John jerked the jacket in annoyance, sending the button guard clanging noisily against a bed post.

"I got issued a poxy cape, a Short poxy Lee Enfield, a poxy bayonet, that there poxy button stick, poxy field dressings, a poxy spade and a poxy gas mask," moaned Happy John, "Nobody said anythin' about issuing us wi' poxy brains as well."

Bob Street was the 'elder statesman' of this little group, which had formed from the splinters of a number of training groups. Bob had been in the army before, he was a 'veteran'.

"S'alright for you, Bob," said Happy John, "You done it all, aintcha?"

"Bob's right," said Ned. "We've got it to do. Let's just do it."

"Dead right," agreed young Pugh as he brushed his belt with a sawn-off paint brush. Thomas 'Blind' Pugh was a council worker: his nickname followed him like a loose thread. At school it had been 'Fatty Pugh' - you'd never imagine it now.

"What made you join up?" Bob asked Happy John.

"I was playing three-card brag with Kitchener," said Happy John, "And I lost." Turning to Bob, he asked, "Why did you come back? Missed all the fun?"

The barrack room was quiet on a Sunday afternoon. Lots of men were getting their heads down, some were catching up on 'household' chores. This group had just been served a cup of tea by Ned and were quietly chatting.

There is one thing about the armed forces: they are the greatest leveller on Earth. Bob was a dairy farmer, Blind Pugh a council expert in drains, Ned a seaman, and Happy John was a butcher -

Ned had already traded experiences of his time working for Tom the Butcher in New York, and John wondered how the man managed to corner the market in prime cuts. "I couldn't do that in poxy Faversham," said Happy John.

"He cheats," Ned explained. "In a kind of nice way."

Bob was slow to answer John's question. "Mmm.... We drew straws, me and my brothers. Somebody had to stay behind to look after mum and dad and get the girls milked. Albert got the short straw and stayed home, bless him."

"You didn't answer him," said Pugh. "Not *how* did you join up. *Why* did you join up? I should've thought you'd have had enough of all this."

Bob gave that some thought. "No – somehow, when you've been back in Canterbury long enough, milking cows and sod-all else, the idea of the army wasn't all that bad. Especially when before it was bad for all the wrong reasons, and being raised in India in a military camp was not the worst thing that can happen. Might seem a bit strange to you, Happy. How about you, Ned, what's a northern lad like you doing here?"

"Well," Ned took his time to think, "Ah were at sea, with a girl back in port –"

"Ah!" Happy John jumped in, "You got her up the duff, so you joined up to get away."

Happy John seemed to embrace his nickname in a completely ironic way, and never really questioned the cynicism of it. He shunned his surname, which was Barraclough, though no-one thought to ask why.

"No," replied Ned, a little subdued, "Wasn't like that. We were gonna get wed. Then this ruddy war comes along ..... Yer know, yer get to thinkin', mebbe it's not the right thing to do. Mebbe it's not fair on t'lass."

"You were at sea, ferchrissakes! What's the ruddy difference?"

"Ah were back in Havre every couple of weeks. It weren't that bad."

"Back in where?"

"Le Havre."

251

"Le Aaah?... As in – France?"

"Aye."

"Oh - you were on a French ship?" asked Bob.

"Aye."

"How come?" Happy wanted to know. "English ones not good enough for yer?" He chuckled for his own amusement. Happy John often did that.

"Let him explain," suggested Bob.

Ned gave a sketchy outline of his circumstances, mentioning nothing of *Titanic* nor the matter of his alleged cowardice and especially not the Germanic nature of his adopted family. To his pleasant surprise, no-one connected his name with newspaper reports, bogus or otherwise. French ships, he simply offered, were easier to earn good money.

"Hey," said Happy John, "I'm with you on that – English toffs are as poor as church mice when it comes to handing out tips. I worked in a poxy hotel once. No wonder the buggers are rich - they never give a penny away!"

Bob was thinking. Bob did a lot of that - thinking - and parting his moustache, that was the way Bob was. "Mmm," he would mumble, as if to gather his brain together, then deliver his pearls of wisdom as if he had just had Hermes whisper the words of Zeus in his ear.

"Mmm," murmured Bob, "You're a Yorkshireman, working on a French ship, with a French girlfriend, and you join the Buffs..... Bit strange, Ned."

"Why? Plenty of blokes work on ships that aren't British."

"Mmm.... I think in your shoes I'd have carried right on doing that. I can't imagine I would've been in a hurry to get back to England and join the first regiment I came across...." Bob let his puzzlement hang in the air for a short time, until realising that Ned was not about to elaborate. ".... Well anyway.... Still waters, my friend. Still waters."

The boyish Pugh was looking a little far-away and reflective. "White feather," he eventually said.

"What?"

"White feather."

"Don't be daft – you mean you were given a white feather?"

"Yes."

"Stripe me pink and call me a stick of poxy rock," said Happy John.

Pugh put his tea down on the floor, as if he were about to say something momentous.

"The office I worked in – oh, I worked for Maidstone council, you know - big offices there full of girls."

"Wow!" said Happy John, "What's a shit-faced Londoner like you doing in a posh place like Maidstone council offices? Hey - if you were in Maidstone why didn't you join the West Kents rather than this lot?"

"Free country, innit?" retorted Pugh.

The youngest of the group looked it, in a uniform that made him look as if he had shrunk in the wash. "As a lad we used to come down to Kent on the hopping specials they set on for the hop pickers at harvest. We got paid for it too! In tokens, but you cashed 'em in when you went home. More of a holiday really, you got families galore packed up and off down to Aylesford and places. It were like the whole East End had got in among the vines. When I grew up I just naturally wanted to live in a place like Kent."

"Never mind all that: I meant, lallygaggin' with all them girls in your office? Gettin' your end away."

"I'm married with a kid, Happy.... Yair, anyway...... Blokes went off to sign up – join the Pals, and all that stuff. It was like a ruddy infection, wasn't it? – One joins, everybody joins. I've got a poorly boy. I didn't want to join up. I wanted to see how things went. You know...."

"And here we are, wrong side of Christmas, doubling up and down that poxy hill and crawling through barbed wire and shit. Christ, I've nearly worn out one pair of pants already and they only gave us two! Not to mention bullshittin' boots and bloody webbing. " Happy John brandished the cloth, tossed one gaiter aside and picked up a second. "I'll take a swipe at Black Mack one of these days."

253

"Don't knock it," Bob warned him, "Mack's a good instructor. An army may march on its stomach but you get your feet soaked and you'll soon know about it."

"You be careful," Ned told Happy John, "Black Mack's not divisional boxing champ for nothin', y'know. As drill sergeants go, ah reckon he's doing a good job toughenin' us all up – ah'm tired, yes, but ah've never felt this fit before."

"Shut up, lads," called Bob. "Let Pugh tell his tale."

"Well," said Pugh doubtfully. "... One morning I came into the office, and there was a white feather, stuck up in my ink well."

"Who from?"

"How do you find out who?..... As far as I'm concerned, it was all of them. Soon as I looked up, all the heads went down..... "

None of them spoke for a few moments, then Happy John wrapped it all up by shaking his head and saying, "T'ain't right, is it?"

"True enough," Bob put in. "A chap in the village was boo-ed by the women when he said he wanted to think about it. They all thought it was a big laugh. They can be cruel when they want to be."

"Did he join up?" asked Happy John.

"Don't know. He packed a bag and left the next day. Nobody's heard from him since.... Poor sod."

"I mean," Pugh carried on, "it's alright for them, innit? – Since when were women marched off to fight and get their brains blown out?"

"Mmm," mused Bob, putting tobacco into his pipe, "They want the vote, don't they? Can't see 'em getting it – Americans have just put a block on it, haven't they?......." Perhaps it was a note to leave hanging in the air, but the other three raised no dissent.

"Well," Happy John thought it was time for his little contribution to the subject. "It was just the same for me," he blurted out cheerfully. "I got threats – off you go and fight, or else!"

"You got threats? Who threatened you?"

"The wife - who else?"

Bob joined Ned and Bert Parrock outside, having a quiet smoke in the cold air.

"That wasn't good – that white feather business. Not for a sensitive lad like Pugh. Them girls think it's a lark. They got no idea of a young feller's mind. All this, '*Get the gun, get the girl*' rubbish! A young lad takes it seriously. Y'know, my girl said to me, 'it's terrible but it's thrilling too'...."

"Don't tell me you got a girl, Bob! Thought you were too old for that sort o' thing!"

Bob made a funny face back at Ned.

"They should grow up," agreed Bert. "Pugh's got a sickly son, hasn't he? If anything happens to Pugh....."

"Mmm," mused Bob, thinking through his pipe.

In this group, 'Blind' Pugh was the odd man out. At the outset of war, Pugh had been 18, a boy compared to the others here - Bob Street at 32, much the eldest, Ned who had celebrated his 21st birthday on the very first day of the war, Bert Parrock had been 26, former miner Albert 'Taff' Morgan 27, 'Happy' John Barraclough 23, and Clarence 'Duffers' Duffield 24. Their group had come together by dint of their age relative to most other men in the company, who were generally below 20, and yet Pugh, like an orphaned limpet, had attached himself to the 'old hands'. Pugh was their mascot almost. Even Ned, only three years his senior, felt strangely protective of him. Pugh was just that "little boy lost" sort who did most things awkwardly. It's difficult not to befriend lads like that.

* * * * *

Bob Street was not a talker. Not ordinarily. For all intents and purposes, he was a thinker, the sort of character you would never expect to find in uniform, except perhaps wearing a white collar. His plodding, dour manner came to represent the sort of father figure some in No.2 Platoon had never had. As good as a priest, but without the turned-around collar and Good Book. When Bob spoke, you rather expected those pearls of wisdom: whilst generally this was not the case, he just gave you that feeling that God's right-

255

hand man, if he appeared in human form, would be a Kentish dairy farmer named Bob.

"You know," said Bob, casting an eye around his fellow sufferers, "You fellers need to get wise where women are concerned."

Happy John looked disgruntled. "Sod off, Bob..... Whatcha mean?"

Bob eased himself forwards on the edge of his bunk, as if he were going to break wind, then settled back again noiselessly. "Mmm... How can I put it?... It is the function - nay, the duty – of a lady to intrigue a man to the point where she can refuse him."

If it were possible for this little group to exist in a vacuum, that moment was the essence of it: in their micro-world within the huge barrack room, there was a mystified silence.

"You're right, Bob..... If we could understand what Chinese book you took that out of."

Bob merely inclined his head and clicked his mouth, as if to say, *Well you've had your lesson for today.*

But no, he was not a talker. For weeks, some had pushed Bob to speak of his "first-time-around" experiences in the army. He had joined as a boy soldier, following his wish to see the world – he saw South Africa, at any rate. Getting there and returning much later had cured him of most of that wish, the troopships both ways had gone through rough waters where Bob joined his colleagues hanging over the rail and hoping they were not facing into the wind.

"So yer didn't like South Africa?"

In character, Bob took his time replying, but when he did, Ned and Happy John first paused the cleaning of their kit, then put it down altogether.

"Mmm... It were not bad at first. I started off as a powder monkey – carrying powder to the gun crews. Didn't do much of that, frankly. South Africa gave me a new word to think about," said Bob pensively. "I didn't spend much time at school, and when I did, the teacher - a big ugly chap called 'Simple' Simons – he'd shout at me, *'Concentrate, Street, concentrate!'*...... And like as not, I probably didn't...... But I found a new meaning for that word - concentrate."

Bob fumbled for his tobacco. "The quartermaster, he says to us, 'Any of you lads fancy a spell lookin' after these 'ere Boers?'..... Me and Cecil Humpage, we looks at each other and thinks, 'Has he gone barmy or something?'..... Well, he weren't barmy, and in any case it didn't make no difference whether we wanted to or not, eight of us just got detailed."

None of them had a clue where this monologue was going. Bob drew a long breath and carried on.

"We forgot about fighting Boer cavalry – some of the best fighters you'd come across, by the way... Kruger told 'em, because they were low in numbers, he told 'em to hit and run. And they did. By God, they did! We got sent to a place called Knock Knees – "

"Called what?"

"Knock Knees. I got no idea what the bloody name was because I en't got a word of Afrikaans in me head, see. One of our lads must've thought the Boer words sounded a bit like 'Knees Knock' or something, so that's what it got called." Bob was patting his pockets in a hunt for his pipe. "Got a cig, Happy?"

Bob was given a Woodbine and Pugh lit him up.

"It were a camp. About the size of three or four football pitches, a few huts and lots of tents inside a perimeter fence. Barbed wire. Nasty stuff. No mistake – it was to keep them in and others out."

He took a long pause, staring into the distance, and they waited for him.

"Concentrated. That's what we were told. They called 'em concentration camps, pulled in Boer people from all around. Women and children, mostly. The men were off fighting, see. British forces burned the farms and homesteads, that was our policy. Our army rounded up the families and put 'em in there. Knock Knees. This rat-infested, mosquito-bitten, stinking cesspit of a place where these poor women and kids had to fend as best they could. I felt sorry for 'em, I tell you that straight up. Took me about two hours to feel sorry for 'em after the sergeant filled me head about how devious and vicious these people were. Some of our lads didn't feel anything at all because they were Boers, but I did.... I did. Didn't take me long to feel ashamed neither. Ashamed,

257

Bert. It weren't right. Oh, they got fed – poor slop, half-rations most of the time. I saw one of 'em roasting a rat. I can't imagine what that was supposed to achieve. The wives of known fighters came off the worst. There was a teacher for the kids, they got water, they even got soap - sometimes, and blankets. But.... these were proud people. Proud women who had to cope with lice, bad food, bad sanitation. That's bad for womenfolk – bad enough for men, but worse for womenfolk, they got special sanitation needs and I just couldn't look 'em in the face – they knew they stank and hated it. Not decent, what we made those women do. Some were guarded over as they went to the toilet – what trouble are they gonna get up to there? One or two of our blokes enjoyed all that. They made me sick."

Bob squirmed as he sat, his mind clearly a long way away.

"They struggled on as they reckoned their menfolk would expect 'em to do. We got spat at, food chucked back at us, and worse. Piss and shit. Do I blame 'em?....... Not fit, those camps – there was a lot of 'em, we found out. We heard stories about some of the others. Not nice, lads. We were the British. British!... Not honourable. I looked up at the Union flag flying at the gate....... Don't care whose ruddy idea it was. Politicians in London - I dunno. Tell you what, it put me in mind of the slave camps we used to have in Africa long time ago – British slave trade. Oh yes! Made some families very rich... Of course, they're all 'respectable' now. Tell you somethin' else, too: we had some inspectors come once. Foreign-sounding chaps, I got no idea what. They went round the camp once and back to the C.O.'s hut, and my God! – You should've heard the stink they sent up!"

"But – " Happy John wanted to jump in. "Wasn't the C.O. only doing his duty, holding them prisoner?"

"Duty? Oh, his duty! Oh yes. But his duty didn't include kids dying of disease and bad food and sanitation when the blokes in the officers' mess were served up steaks. His duty didn't allow women getting a beating for not telling what their menfolk were up to. We let too much go on, lads – too much. Prisoners of war? – These were women and children. Like if the Germans locked up your missus, Happy. And your kid, Pugh. Rolling around in filth and nothing to do all day, except worry – worry how your kids were going to survive. To them we were foreign invaders, don't forget."

Ned was trying to reconcile that. "But it was our empire, Bob. They'd revolted against the queen and the empire. Not that I know much..... Ah'm hopeless with things like that."

"Mmm... Revolutionaries. How do you treat your enemies when you catch 'em, Ned? Like shit? Is that how you change people's minds? This was the country they'd been brought up to fight for, right or wrong. I was there four months before I finally picked up the courage to say I didn't want to be there, and another three months before anyone listened. In the end they transferred me out because I had a 'bad attitude' – it's on my service record. In that time, we buried more than eighty kids and several dozen women. I heard other camps were worse. Starving, and sick. Made me ashamed. I'd have far better faced Boer Mausers."

"So....." Ned didn't like the look that had come over Bob's face. "How did you get out?"

"Sabre wound. End of March. I always remember cos Shannon Lass won the Grand National and I got three guineas out of the sweep for it. Three guineas!... Night skirmishers. I was on sentry duty. Boer skirmishers didn't worry about attacking in the dark, in ones and twos. British would have assembled a full brigade. Boers threw the book away, they rushed into any little chance, did their damage and ran off again."

"Devious buggers," quipped Happy John, chuckling.

"Hey! You'd think differently if you'd been there, John. A few thousand Boer farmers against a hundred thousand British soldiers – they gave us a good hiding, man! A bloody nose, that's what they gave us."

"A bloody nose?" questioned Pugh.

"One of 'em gave me a sword wound. Only serious action I'd been in. Not so serious, just in my side. But it got infected, and to cut the story short, I got invalided home, spent a bit of time at the Royal Victoria at Netley. Saw the queen there once: she was on her way back from the island. Never so much as smiled or waved at anybody.... Between you and I, we were vermin really.... Anyhow, I'd been in the Cape eighteen months..... I called a Boer my enemy when I arrived, but I didn't when I left."

"The wound cleared up alright?"

The Canterbury farmer took another draw on his dwindling smoke and looked Ned straight in the eye.

"Right as rain, Ned. But I got a discharge out of Dartford for it. And at the time, I'll tell you no lie, I was ready to go."

"So.... Bad job, then? - South Africa."

"Mmm..... Thomas Paine wouldn't have approved, that I'm sure."

"Thomas who?"

Bob didn't answer. Instead he smiled with a moment of resignation, then shortly said, "Let's just say, Ned, when you treat people like that..... What do you expect in return? Even as a nipper in India, we had respect for the other chap's dignity. Question his reasons, but respect his beliefs."

"You know, Bob...." Happy John wanted to sum up. "You've used up your talking allowance for a whole month." Bob only grinned.

Ned had in mind Carelle and the Congo, and Magoolagan and what he had said about Ireland, and wondered how it was that these three experienced men sounded so similar in their outlook.

"Well," said Happy John brightly, "I've not heard of camps of concentration. It'll never happen here. Maybe we'll never see anything like that again, eh? Still... Wars should be between soldiers."

"Hmmm," murmured Bob, one of his deepest murmurs as he parted his moustache. "Matter of fact, I joined because this time it seemed like a decision to stand up for what I believe in.... My country and my liberty and that of my family. I imagined what might happen if an invader crossed that water and came here to Kent and my farm, and put me and my family into a concentration camp, here on English soil..... I didn't like the idea..... Didn't like it."

"Maybe," suggested Bert, having come late to the conversation, "our commanders will have learned something when they fight the Germans."

"Or the Irish," said Ned, reminding them. "Sounds like we could be heading for Ireland, doesn't it?"

"Does it?" questioned Bob. "I hope not. I fought Orangemen in South Africa, I don't want to face a similar fight here."

Happy John thought about that. "Naaah!" he said. "Poxy Irish! They're just poxy Irish, aren't they? Pah!"

"Who knows where we're going?" suggested Bert. "Everyone's digging their heels in. Look around, there's a lot going on. Them Russian fellers are pushing all over the place, from the Baltic right down to Persia, if you dunces know where that is."

"What's the poxy Baltic?" asked Happy John. "I thought a ball tick was another word for crabs!"

Bob ignored him. "Russians are kicking the Turks' arses good and proper."

"'Ow d'yer know all this?" Ned asked him.

Bob pointed two fingers at his eyes. "I read the papers, my son. Though that can be a caution – you read the papers to get informed, but you can just as easily get misinformed."

That was enough, Bob decided. Getting up, he patted his stomach and moved off toward the latrine. After two strides, he stopped, turned, and in a sheepish manner admitted, "Tell you the truth, when the recruitment drive came to the village, I got bloody drunk like the rest of 'em. If my old mum had appeared on that stage in a German uniform, I'd have run at her with a bayonet!"

* * * * *

Eight weeks after joining the Buffs, Ned bumped into Ernie Waterhouse again. He was surprised he had not seen Ernie before then, since the camp was not so large as to enshroud a big man like Ernie, whose presence was normally announced by a voice as large as his frame, no less than the clatter of his boots.

"Wot'cher, me old sport!" cried Ernie, "'Ow yer gettin' on wiv the Buffs, then?"

"Ah thought ah'd have seen yer before now," said Ned.

Ernie shook his head . "Here, there and every-bloody-where, mate. Had a spot o' compassionate."

"Leave? – You were on leave when we met on the train!"

"An' I enjoyed it! But look, what can yer do? – Old feller snuffs it, I gotta go and see if the old lady's alright, ain' I?"

"Old feller? – Yer dad died?"

"S'right, me old Ned. Too much beer and baccy. Fell straight over – eeeowww! – Bang! Stone dead. The lads said Robey couldn't have done it better – rigid one second, then – eeowww! – Bang! Keeled right over."

"My god!"

"God, nuthin' – booze!"

"So you'd just come back from seein' yer sister in Southsea, and that happens?"

"S'right, Ned. Just like that! Sign the yellow paper, two weeks compassionate, 'op on the bus, china, and off you go, up the Smoke! Poplar's a lovely part of the world - you know it?"

"No."

"Don't want to, neither. I don't go back no more, not now. I signed up at New Cross - fell out the pub, straight into the recruitin' office, and there was I, stark naked, linin' up for the old cough-drop there. So - in the buff - in the Buffs! - If yer follow me. Ey? Ey?"

Ned failed to be more than slightly amused.

"Old lady's gonna move out now, stay wi' me sister in Southsea. She'll be a lot better off there. Clarry will look after 'er.... She liked you, by the way."

Ned had to think what to say, before he said the wrong thing. "She's nice, your Clarice."

"Yair. Noice. That's what I'd say too, me old Ned. Noice..... Not a bad looker, eh?.... Pity 'er feller's a right shit. Still – he ain't there most o' the time. Comfy sofa, ey?"

"Comfy enough."

"You got bacon and eggs in the mornin'! – Noice!"

"Champion."

Ernie smiled but Ned was not going any further with this, Ernie could see that.

"Ere, who's yer instructor? Betcha got Black Mack, aintcha?"

"Yes."

"Aha!" Ernie poked a large finger into Ned's nose. "Knew it! Knew it! You shall get along very nicely wiv Sergeant McAllister, Ned. Lovely man, ain' he?"

A laugh broke out of Ned's face.

"Listen, don't thank me, Ned – I knew you'd get Mack. Guess where 'e's from? Go on, guess – Poplar! Yair, him too! Wiv a name like McAllister, ey? 'E's a rum bugger, that Mack, did yer hear what happened last year – did they tell yer? – Mack and 'is mate got set on by a bunch o' matelots up in Chatham town. Eight of 'em. Mack's mate went to hospital wiv a busted arm, but Mack put five o' them buggers in hospital and the other three ran off. Now aren't yer glad I talked y'into joinin' the Buffs?"

"Well –"

"Course y'are! What did I say to yer all the way down to Pompey on the train? Join the Buffs, I said, don't fuck about with the Hampshires, they're ruddy girlies, I said. Join the real boys. Ain't that what I told yer?"

"Yer did."

"And now look at yer – yer a fuckin' soldier, lad, anyone can see that. Chest out, proud as punch, keep that cock in yer pants if yer can cos all the ladies like the Buffs.... Ey? Ey?"

You didn't argue with Ernie Waterhouse. Ned simply grinned to cover a lack of response and let Ernie grab him by the shoulder.

"Beer, Ned? Friday night. Down the Shakespeare. Know where that is?" Yes, with only two pubs in the village, he knew where it was.

"Good man!" Ernie marched away and began to whistle.

"Good man, Ned!"

* * * * *

263

TWENTY-SEVEN

"My dear Lady Semper."

"Monsieur..... It is 'monsieur', I take it?"

"It is. I am Belgian, madame."

"Ah..... And they told me, French."

"French – Belgian, it is all the same except to the French and Belgians. We are all pastry-chefs and bon-bon makers."

She laughed. "Quite!.... Quite! You are most engaging, monsieur."

"Belgium is a very small country, madame, and we compensate by having very large people – in the sense of personality. We make it a rule never to be less than engaging. To do less would be an affront to King Albert, a national disgrace and would bring down the government."

She laughed again, and her companion joined with her, both fluttering their feathered fans distractedly.

"So tell me, monsieur - er –"

"Carelle, madame."

"Oh, you know, I do so adore the way you continentals speak that word – '*madame*'. So very French, so very elegant, I would say."

"Ah, but it has nothing to do with accent, Lady Semper. Do forgive my vulgar illustration, but does not the word 'madam' have a different meaning altogether here in England.....?"

"Oh! – Oh, monsieur Carelle, you are quite the wag! Quite shocking."

"Oh... shocking. But in a small country we have to make a large statement. *Comprenez?*"

She did. She was quite intrigued. Piqued, in fact, to the point that she accepted Carelle's arm to escort her to the dance floor.

"By the way, Lady Semper, I should like to congratulate you and your husband on your recent title. I am sure I am one of the very last to do so."

"Ah! Yes, you probably are, monsieur! It is almost a year ago that my father died and..... surrendered the title. But it was always a big mouthful, wasn't it? – Scott-Chapelle.... Never tripped lightly off the tongue, did it? And Anthony had worked so hard for it, you know: the soap business doesn't run itself.... Of course he does have managers. So frankly, I am relieved – signing official papers as The Honourable Sophie Scott-Chapelle had become an atrocious bore. Now it's just 'Lady Semper' – so much easier."

Knowing absolutely nothing of heraldic protocol, either in Britain or his own country, Carelle had been briefed - briefly - that a baron was to be called 'Lord' something-or-other, but as to the rest of the whole peerage and lineage business, Tommy thought it better that the less Carelle knew, the better. Ignorance could be an ally, it was something on which nobility tended to smile with maximum condescension.

Tommy's friend Andy – again, forenames only – had arranged Carelle's introduction to a gathering of bankers and associated businessmen, which in turn had led him to this soiree at the manor house of Sir Charles Livesey, a rambling old Georgian retreat that spanned a bend in the Thames. Sir Charles himself had tired of the place and spent much of his time at his Mayfair club until his debtors found his sanctuary.

Carelle never interrogated Tommy on exactly how many 'friends' he possessed, he merely paid over money. Tommy had a word for it – "familyship". It applied to all his acquaintances, all those on whom he could depend for services at the merest mention of money, a commodity which Tommy's patrons – and there were several – could be relied on to haemorrhage, for the right sort of service. Nothing illegal, everything above board, though just slightly edgy, one might suggest. "Familyship" entailed a brand of loyalty, however, and Tommy's friendship could be accompanied by a harsh physical penalty for any in the 'family' who sought to trade outside agreed lines. Tommy may have been getting on in years, but his long fingers retained an ability to extend into the darkest of corners when necessary.

As they danced - a steady waltz was much to Lady Sophie's pace - Carelle was able to explain for the benefit of the Great Man's lady his position in Belgian commerce, the rough extent of his activities in cocoa beans and other commodities - in careful summary, lest he tug at her obvious tendency towards boredom with matters outside her immediate version of reality. He took care to be vague about his associations in this and other countries, making sure Lady Semper gained an impression of this man as a global entrepreneur who operated without flags and – vaguely – an adventurer who would stop short only at the boundaries of recklessness. Such a man, he hoped, might draw the attention of a similarly-minded and free-spirited British peer, one who saw the responsibilities of state or country as no barrier to enterprise. Anthony Scott-Chapelle had been such a man, would Lord Semper be any different?

It was a promising start. Lady Semper in fact turned out to be less of a tiresome assignment than Carelle had imagined her to be. Though approaching her middle-sixties, and older than her auspicious husband by two or three years, Lady Sophie at least possessed the saving grace of good looks and an educated sense of her own history, though little of anyone else's. More than that, she had good taste in perfume and dress, and her gown this evening had an air of subtlety, its silver brocade clinging admirably to her presentable figure without giving away the excess of corsetry to which many society ladies so often succumbed. To this extent, Carelle found her company tolerable, for the moment. She in her turn insisted, tacitly, that he remain in her entourage for the evening.

To a degree, Carelle wondered how different the Baron Semper and his lady might be now from the Mr. and Mrs. Knight of Ned Thornton's acquaintance, as there had been no actual trouble from that direction for a long time. Nonetheless, quite apart from the injustices already perpetrated, an arrest warrant did remain in force in the kingdom and something so prejudicious had to be addressed.

Carelle's master-stroke, or so he considered it, was to refrain from pressing any kind of introduction to Lord Semper himself. Twice he verbally excused himself from an introduction, saying that the peer might have little interest in his mundane business until he had better established himself in England, and long before the climax of the evening Carelle excused himself altogether, complaining that he had an early start for Liverpool the next day and needed a clear head.

Some time after he had left, Lord Semper enquired of his wife, "By the way, who was that odd-looking chap in the pale suit you spent so much time with?"

"You mean Monsieur Carelle."

"Do I? Damned odd-looking, anyway."

"And what d'you mean, 'pale suit'? – It was only slightly light in comparison to the perfectly miserable clothes the rest of you were wearing. I thought he looked quite dapper, actually."

"Dapper?.... Hm. The least hint of a continental accent and you women swoon all over your syllabubs. And what did he drink all evening? – Brandywine, I'm told. Dreadful!"

"No, Anthony, not at all, Monsieur Carelle is a most educated and engaging man. Wouldn't you say so, Olive?"

Miss Devonshire gave Lord Semper a glance before replying. "As you say, dear. Engaging. To a point. And dapper, in a way." Olive Devonshire seldom gave away any resolute opinion.

"Damned odd," muttered Semper.

"Why? Because he didn't look like a funeral director like all these other cronies of yours?"

"But I meant – "

"Well, good for him! That's all I'm going to say."

"What was he doing here anyway?"

"Why ask me? He's a friend of a friend of a friend. Isn't everyone?"

"Oh, really!" he dismissed her sarcasm.

"Well, don't ask me, ask Charles - if you can drag him away from Maxim's. He mentioned Chief Inspector Winstone at one point, I can tell you that."

"Scotland Yard?"

"Hmm? How should I know, Anthony? They're *your* friends, not mine."

* * * * *

'13 March 1915

Dear Grace,

Thank you for your letter. I am pleased James is doing better. Good news, I know that Ned would be happy with the examination. We can understand James' frustration that he cannot join Ned in action – if he ever gets into any! - but he will learn to congratulate his fortune in time. For discretion, as you see I continue to send letters to this address.

Yes, I received word from Ned. Letters are censored, he knows he can say little. It was a surprise to me, too, that he had joined the Royal East Kents, I cannot imagine how that came about, but no matter, it is a regiment with a long and esteemed history. I regret, I have of course no influence with the British army!

You say nothing of yourself, Grace: I do hope you are well, and your parents – I know your father's condition concerns you. I did not condone Ned's decision to join the army, I think you know that. I felt he would be better to remain with the C.G.T. And of course, not marrying Brigitte was a sad thing – a lovely girl, I can tell you. Ned had told me that I was permitted to write to them at Le Havre, but in all honesty, Grace, I do not know where to start in matters of the heart. We must hope this war ends soon, so they can take up where they left off.

I have made the confidence of the lady we spoke of. That must lead to further informations in time. You know of course I have primarily my business to attend to: that has not been going well, although my interests in the pistons and munitions as you can imagine are becoming buoyant now. Where Ned is concerned, I hope to have more to tell once I join with certain events, in particular the "Glorious Twelfth", which is the name you have for shooting a lot of birds in Scotland! Very curious! Apparently I have impressed the lady sufficiently to receive this invitation. That is a long way off, my intention meanwhile would be to come to Bradford to see and talk with you as I also have business to conduct there.

Please write again when you are able. I am here, there and everywhere, more so since I became involved with the CRB, but I promise to receive my post once a week. I hope you do not mind that I use you as a letter box for messages to Ned. It also kills two birds with one stone – you see, I am already an expert in English! I have every reason to hope we shall find him freed from all blame, and I pray he fares well as a soldier for we are hearing stories which – it is pointless to lie – are worrying. Bon courage, dear lady.

Your good friend,
Bruno.'

* * * * *

TWENTY-EIGHT

"Killed anyone? - Blimey, no... Shot rabbits!"

Bob shook his head in dismay.

"You?" asked Pugh.

"Hmmm. Can't say I have, can't say I haven't....."

"What the hell does that mean?" asked Ned, wiping mud off his face.

"Stop that fackin' talkin'!" barked Sergeant McAllister. "Get those rifles up, come on, get 'em up! Get 'em up, you stupid cretin – look, you block the end of that rifle with mud and you know what happens? – Fackin' thing blows up in yer fackin' face! Serve yer fackin' right, too."

"Yes, sergeant."

" – 'Ow the fuck," said Happy John, "can he hear what the hell we're talking about when we're lying down 'ere with all this poxy racket goin' on and 'im facing the other way?"

"Search me," shouted Pugh.

"Didn't you know?" called Bob. "Sergeants keep their ears up their arses – attached to their brains."

"Street!"

"Sergeant?"

"I'll shit in your fackin' cap, lad, and then you'll find out what I got up my arse. Get the rifle fixed on that target, you disgustin' streak of cat's pizzle!"

"Yes, sergeant."

"Jesus!" whispered Ned loudly, "He heard that!"

Bob gestured to him to point his rifle down the range and just get on with it. Besides, it looked like rain, this was a nasty place to get caught in a squall. He wanted to get finished, get back to the hut for a pie and a cuppa, and on the road back to barracks.

It was seven o'clock before all three companies of Royal East Kent soldiers got back to the barracks. Barely in time for a swift evening meal before the canteen closed up.

As they wolfed down the remains of a poorly disguised shepherd's pie – all gravy, no shepherd – Tiny Goff came along with his hands in his pockets, whistling a barely recognisable version of 'Long Way to Tipperary', and approached first his mates in A company before passing along to Bob and Ned.

"Ireland," said Corporal Goff, stretching his white braces in a way that asserted his authority.

"Naah!" dismissed Bob.

"Straight up. Ireland."

"Gerrawaywithyer! You pulling my pisser, Tiny?"

"No! Straight up. Orders came through this afternoon. Next week, Dublin."

"Shit!" said most of the men in unison.

Was it bad news or just *mostly* bad news? At least Ireland was, looked at in a certain way, more or less a "home" posting. They had talked around this subject before. Patrolling Ireland was not like attacking the Boche. It meant less direct action, but it also meant bombs under your bed and that general sense of never knowing quite where the next bullet might be coming from.

A number of men didn't feel the Irish dispute was entirely black and white. Some were not comfortable, in fact, since Home Rule for Ireland had been mooted two years before, and with the Scots introducing their own Home Rule bill the following year, there had been a feeling in the wider populace that the United Kingdom had become very disunited.

Many soldiers felt the cause failed to meet their vision. A majority had joined up to fight the German menace, to meet it head-on in Belgium or France and stop it from creeping across to England. Ned viewed the idea of fighting the Irish with disdain. Mindful of what Magoolagan felt, Ned had no reason to want to face up to insurrectionists that might have a right to their own lands and laws. Bob believed the English should back off Ireland and seek a political solution before the whole thing tumbled into bloodshed. A view Bob kept largely to himself.

An hour later, Tiny Goff was being de-bagged for a bollock-blacking.

Returning to their mess hall, the soldiers were called to attention by the bed-spaces of A company. Captain Randolph Marshall was waiting for them, tapping his riding crop at his side with a measured patience as the men were stiffly grouped together by their drill sergeants. Coughing instantly began as they were silenced, and Marshall then stood on a table. He was a man of average build but assured bearing, very smart and stringently clean-shaven, which matched the manner of his speech.

"Gentlemen....... At ease, men...... I'm sorry to catch you at the end of your day like this. You've mostly been at the rifle range and you're tired. But this is important." Coughing at once broke out again.

"Your training is over. That's official as of this moment. I know you were not expecting that order yet, and I regret to say your passing-out parade will not take place as the battalion's orders have come through and we have to move quickly."

Ned could see Happy John's mouth moving silently as it came to him that he may have no time to see his wife. Pugh might perhaps be able to get a pass on account of his sickly son.

"Strategic necessities come before ceremonials. Anyhow, I believe *all* of you will be glad to know that we embark on Friday for France."

Immediately a rather tired cheer went up. Marshall smiled and let them react.

In the ranks, Tiny Goff drew a twisted smile and bit his lip at the same time. Someone kicked him from behind.

"Now you know why you have been going through trench training at Chattenden. I think it's good news, don't you? We shall be fighting Germans, men. It's what you joined this regiment to do, and I know you will carry out that duty in a manner which brings honour and pride to the Buffs."

A louder cheer went up.

"So you have two days. Enjoy those two days. On Saturday we shall be landing on French soil."

"Where, sir?" came a cry from the back.

"Where? To be honest, I cannot tell you at the moment. I should like to, but I can't. All I will say is that I expect this battalion to be in a front line position within two weeks of today. Believe me, it's something to look forward to – the sooner we go and punch Jerry on the nose, the better we shall all like it, ey?"

An even more convincing cheer went up.

"Carry on, Sergeant Beresford."

"Sah!"

A clatter of boots met the captain's salute, and the C.S.M. dismissed the men, the signal for an enormous howl of voices throughout the hall. Tiny Goff sought to slip out to the rear but did not get far. It took seconds for someone to find the boot polish and Goff's screams could be heard at the far end of the parade ground.

"France, Ned."

"Aye."

"It's what you wanted."

"Aye."

"See your girlfriend, Ned?"

"What?" He looked at Pugh. "Shouldn't think so. From 'ere we'll most likely cross to Boulogne. Wipers is a long way from where I want to be."

"Wipers," mused Bob, as if it were a sanctuary. They all thought that sounded like the obvious place - probably because it was the one place in France everyone had heard of. Even if it *was* in Belgium!

* * * * *

The British army was not renowned for doing the obvious. Troops from Kent, said the logic, would be embarked from a Kent port: Dover, Folkestone, Ramsgate. Heck, there were enough to choose from.

273

But no. The wisdom of it escaped almost everyone. Southampton.

"Well, bloody good too," said Pugh, "Damn sight safer than Dover – Jerry don't drop bombs on Hampshire yet..... I don't think!"

"See yer sister, Ernie," suggested Ned when he next saw Waterhouse at the clothing store.

"Not much chance, young un," said Ernie. "Long way from Portsmouth. Pity. She liked you, Clarry did."

As soon as he heard the news that Thursday evening as their kit was being mustered onto the lorries, Ned spoke to Sergeant Meeker.

"Lee-Hah, lad? Yes, that's right."

"It's where me fiancée lives."

The sergeant was astounded. "Really? You pullin' my pisser, lad? Look, they don't call me Tillie Banks."

Ned assured him there was no deceit, and explained the situation in a few short sentences - could he get a pass to see his fiancée? It might, as he pointed out, be his last chance in a very long time. Or ever.

"Leave during embarkation? Huh! This is the British Army, lad, not a ruddy 'oliday club. What you doin' with a French girlfriend, lad?"

It was pointless to go into depth, but Ned pressed his case, and Meeker agreed to speak to the captain.

Marshall was a busy man, and uncomfortable: his corns were troubling him and he was cursing a new pair of boots. The ship was within sight of the French coast that Friday afternoon before Ned received a summons to the ward room, where he was marched in, ordered to remove his cap and stand at attention as the young captain tried pulling on his boots, and barely looked at Ned at the outset. Another officer fidgeted with an untidy pile of papers on the table which kept fluttering off with the ship's movement. An eight-hour crossing from England had not been smooth and the captain, feeling not a little queasy, was anxious to dispense as quickly as possible with any matters which did not concern his stomach or his feet. So to the soldier's request for a pass, Marshall glibly pointed out the difficulties of disembarking a battalion of men from a ship and re-embarking on a train. Why, then, would he grant leave to a single soldier?

"Thornton? Your name Thornton?"

"Yes, sir."

Captain Marshall for the first time looked him up and down. "You'd better explain."

"Sir, I was marryin' my fiancée here in Le Havre last August, and the war started and we had to put it off. Ah got everything wrong and ah went to England and joined the army. If ah can just have chance to see 'er, sir, ah can try an' sort it out with 'er - explain why ah did that. Try an' make it right. It were my fault, yer see. Might be me last chance. Sir."

"I see." Marshall took another gulp of water.

"French fiancée.... Sounds very colourful... You in love with this girl?"

"Yes.... I am. Sir."

"So.... You would have settled here in France if the war hadn't come along."

"Yes."

"You prefer France?"

"Ah worked on a French ship, and 'appy to do so, that's a fact. But ah'm an Englishman, sir. Ah joined to fight fer me country. Ah want - well, ah'm proud of me country."

Studying him carefully, Marshall nodded slowly to himself.

"Thornton, hmm?"

"Yes, sir."

"Is this man trustworthy, sergeant?"

"Don't know, sah! One of Partington's lads, after Drill Sergeant McAllister. Clean service book, sah!"

"McAllister... Yes... What did you think of your instructor sergeant, Thornton?"

"Very good man, sir. Very good instructor."

275

"Mmm." The captain seemed to relax a little as he took moments to nod in sequence with his thoughts. "She lives in the town, does she?"

"Less than ten minutes from the quay, sir. With her mother."

Marshall took another sip of water, then spent several seconds looking Ned in the face with an inquisitive stare, as if somehow that would tell him what he wanted to know.

"So you know Le Havre. How far to the station once we disembark?"

"Oh, the Gare du Havre? - Ten minutes, sir..... Ah'd say. Depends where we dock. A good ten minutes anyway."

"Look, Thornton. If this show is the usual sort of palaver, we could be at that station till the early hours of the morning for all I know. But I don't know. That's the point. Not with a couple of thousand to embark. I can't have men wandering off all over the show because they know some girl in the town or because they want a quick shag behind the pub. D'you understand?"

"Sir."

"As it happens, nobody else has come forward with requests for leave on any kind of cock and bull pretext except you. Which is quite the point: nobody else is likely to know anyone here, and if they were just after a quick shag, I rather fancy I'd know it."

Silently, Ned was already braced for a refusal.

"As a matter of fact..... For some odd reason, Thornton, I believe you."

"Oh. Thank you, sir."

"My orders are, we train up at twenty-two-hundred hours. Frankly, I doubt it very much but that's the best I can do. You will have -" The captain tugged at the chain and pulled out his pocket watch. "Three hours from our disembarkation time.... No – make that two hours, it's too much of a risk."

"Sir." Ned wanted to burst his tunic buttons with excitement.

"Sergeant, make out a pass for him. And Thornton -"

"Sir?"

"You let me down and I'll take pleasure in personally tying you to the wheel. You understand? Deserters get shot, you know that, don't you? And I have no wish to have to make an example of a man before we have even started."

"Ah won't let yer down, sir."

"I'm sticking my neck out for you and I'm damned if I know why really.... Probably because you may be right, it may well be the last chance you'll get."

"Yes, sir. Thank you very much, sir."

"Two hours - not a second more! Report to the sergeant. Off you go now."

Meeker marched Ned out of the room and then delivered his own caution. "I'm amazed he saw y'in the first place, lad. Now - never mind what that hofficer said - you let that captain of infantry down and I'll personally have your guts for a football bladder. You understand me, lad? Can't imagine why he took such a shine to you. Now bugger off and see me ten minutes before disembarkation."

It was not just the weight of his kit that had Ned puffing and frothing on his way up the Chemin des Barques. The faint drizzle cooled him a little in the dimming light as the evening bore on, but could not still that churning he felt in his belly. He was tired, after so early a rising and the strain of the Channel crossing, but he forgot that he was tired.

Setting down his rifle and bag beside the door of number 48, his heart was pounding at a rate he had surely not felt in all the exertion of his army training, even those frightening hours spent 'under fire' in the training trenches at Chattenden. All he could hear through the rushing in his ears was the sound of his own boots. He did not dare think – thinking gave rise to feelings, and feelings to disappointment. Seconds passed before the door opened in response to his knocking.

" – *Mein Gott!*" Renata clutched at her chest.

* * * * *

TWENTY-NINE

"So how long's she been gone?"

Renata deliberated a moment. "Five.... six weeks. She did not write to tell you." It was not so much a question, only a statement of her knowledge.

Ned had been upstairs to see Frau Bremme, who was in bed, nursing a bout of influenza, which accounted for the presence of Renata this evening and for several evenings now. He had picked up that particular scent of sickness in the air when he had entered. He only wished he had had flowers to give her, though Marlene would not let him touch her nor come close, for fear of contamination. That was a good thing, as Ned realised he must not be sick at this time.

Renata had long since eaten dinner, but she offered Ned a half-stale baguette with butter, a little warmed-over cassoulet and some wine, and he took it.

They spoke for a time in platitudes and about her mother and how long she had been ill – nearly two weeks now. She was recovering, though, for the coughing had eased and her sputum was clearer. Otto? No, there had been no word from Otto for more than two months, and his last letter only indicated that he had joined an artillery brigade, but naturally could say no more than that. Letters must come a very long route, through a string of family and friends, and had to conceal all elements which presented risk. But he was well, she was sure he was well.

"No," he said in the end, chewing at the baguette. "She hasn't written to me. The last letter..... ah think ah got that two month ago. She didn't say nuthin' about joinin' the nursing service. What made her do that, Reina? She 'ad a good job in that rope factory."

"Ned....." She had no answer for him and merely waved her open palms.

"I expect that says what she feels about me," he opined, dolefully.

"No, Ned. Is not true. She loves you. I am sure of zis."

He stared back at her, trying to make up his mind what he really did think, but shook his head lightly, nothing was convincing him.

"So where is she now?"

"Ze last letter was from Beauvais. But she said she would be moving .... And since then.... No more letters."

He took in a great long breath through his nose, letting his body rise and fall.

"Why'd she go?" His voice soft and contemplative and faintly indicative of his own guilt feelings.

Renata shook her head again. "She is not patient, Ned. You know this. With Gitta, everysing must happen now – now! Or she is..... bored. Bored? Ja, dat's the word. Bored."

She made a gesture with her hands wide open in the air. It said everything that Ned already knew of Gitta. He had not overcome his disappointment that she was not here and, whilst so glad to see Renata, still after all this time he felt less than entirely comfortable to be here with Madame Forget.

Gitta was mercurial in many things. She had wanted Ned, but Ned was no longer there. And so there was something else that needed wanting......

Again he sighed a long heavy sigh. Gitta....... He was sure he missed her badly, a sentiment that had to fight with several others.

In the end, a long time had passed, and he was staring into the fireplace, still feeling somewhat misplaced. Untying the strings of her dirty apron, Renata pulled her chair closer to him, reached out and took his hand. She held it for a time and he was glad that she did so, it was a genuine comfort. In response, Ned looked at her in a way that seemed to say, 'I don't know where we go from here', and just continued shaking his head.

"Do you suppose if I had not gone to England.....?"

"But you were not happy on that other ship. Were you? Gitta knew that you were not happy without Otto."

"But did she understand why ah went? It didn't mean ah didn't care for her."

Renata had little left but gestures. What they might be concealing, he had no indication.

"You can still write to her, Ned. Just as you have done. Send the letters to me. It's not different, is it?"

"Don't you think she would have given me word of some sort?"

Renata lowered her head. "Perhaps," she admitted, very softly, "I sink she should have done zat.... But.... Perhaps you also should have spoken more wiz her.... Do you think?"

"Mm." She was right. "Ah think ah'm a lot like Captain Nemo, only not so nice."

"Not so nice.....?" Then she caught his look of irony, of resignation almost.

He wanted to change the subject. "Yes," he agreed quietly, "Suppose you're right... As a matter of fact, you are." Then a fresh resolution crossed his face.

"Yer see...... Ah'm in the war proper now. Next week, any road. So.... well, anything can happen from here on, can't it? Ah'm not expecting a ruddy picnic."

"We are all in ze war, Ned. Here too. We are afraid."

"Here? In Havre? But, you're safe enough 'ere, Reina."

She shook her head slowly. "I don't sink so. You know ze town was attacked."

"No! When?"

"Oh.... The end of January. It was *Unterseeboot*. It attacked ze ships in ze harbour."

"Gosh! Ah didn't know. Anybody hurt?"

"Yes....I sink so."

"Hmm.... But you should be safe enough here, Reina. The fightin's a long way off. And this town's going to be a bridge-head for soldiers coming from England, it'll not be attacked by German troops."

"Oh, but we cannot tell. A few months ago the Germans were walking into Paris, and came into Normandy – we sink zey were coming here! And ze *gouvernement*, zey run off to hide in Bordeaux. Zey are all foolish - ze French *gouvernement*, it runs away, and ze *gouvernmen*t *Belgique*, it comes here, to Havre, to Saint-Adresse. What should that be good for? - Foolish!"

Placing both hands on her shoulders, Ned gave her a pacifying smile. "They'll not come now, Reina. All the fightin's bogged down up north and further east. Don't upset yerself."

He took a swift, forced breath, as if to say there was nothing more to be done about the matter – in truth, the town could be a legitimate target for the *kriegsflotte*, but he was not going to say that.

"It's not 'champion' any more, is it?" His laugh was weak but insistent.

"Mushrooms?" suggested Renata, trying to raise her spirits. Their smiles lasted moments only, before fading away self-consciously.

"'Ow about you, though, Reina? Is everything alright? The school? Yer mum will get well, though, ah know she will."

"Oh, yes. She will. I.... I play doctor wiz her. She must do as she is told, ja? Very strong – er, what you say?"

"Strict." Yes, that was it. He reaacted to her smile again. "After all, yer the schoolteacher – she's got to do as she's told, or else!" She granted his remark with amusement.

"Monsieur Forget?" asked Ned. He had asked cautiously, and she replied cautiously.

"He is well. He is busy."

"Good.... Well, good. Glad to hear it."

Then he looked at her more inquisitively. "Is he looking after you, Reina?"

"Of course."

It should have been a positive assertion, but was not. Some inflection in her voice.... But he chose not to remark on it, that would have been impolite.

"Ah don't have long."

"I understand. And you go to - where?"

"We don't know. No bugger knows! – Oh, excuse me! It's the British army, after all – yer know."

Renata fidgeted with her brooch. "Perhaps you will miss ze Tour de France again." She just wanted to change the tone of their conversation.

"What?"

"Ze bicycles? You remember?"

"Oh yes, the bicycle race. Well, maybe not, you never know. Could all be over by then, eh? And then I can come back an' 'elp yer take pictures of it."

"Yes," she offered a restrained enthusiasm, but then had a further thought. "But with the war, there may not be a race. Or it may not come to Havre again. Somewhere else....."

"Then ah'll take yer somewhere else to take pictures of it."

Stopping himself, he wondered if he should have made a remark that, in other circumstances, would have been an impropriety.

"Ja? You will take me?" The lightness of her reply reassured him. "Ah will that!"

"Oh? - You have a motor car, Ned?"

Was she poking fun at him? - But then, why not? He saw the funny side of it and they laughed gently together. It was good to see her laugh. Like her sister, Renata was lovely when she laughed.

"Well....We shall 'ave to see. Besides, ah'd have to get permission from the boss - yer a married woman."

The light that had been in her face quickly dimmed. At once, he realised he had crossed a line, for some seconds neither knew quite what to say. Time seemed so pressing, those precious minutes ticking away, yet perversely the urgency of it all made it the more difficult to know what to say, and nothing that could be spoken seemed to fill the gap adequately. In the end, it was Renata who broke across their thoughts.

"You must be careful, Ned. It is very dangerous."

"Wars always are, ah suppose."

"Do not make jokes! I have heard the stories. Many French soldiers have died. It is very serious, and we are losing the young men – some villages lose all the young men. Nobody thought it would be so bad, like zis. We hear ze stories about Verdun. Thousands of men killed. Thousands, they say. It is awful."

"Yes.... Well, ah'll try to shoot Germans before they – oh!"

Ned! Cut your blasted tongue out!

"Oh, ah didn't mean – oh! Ah'm sorry. Ah'm so sorry. That just came out..... That was very bad, ah'm so sorry."

She tried to give him a comprehending smile, but it was only half of one. All the same, Renata had already encountered many anti-German remarks in her daily life now. She knew he meant no harm.

Catching that thought, he said, "Ah'm glad at least you belong to a French family, Reina. They won't bother yer...."

"No ... not yet," she answered.

"Ah mean..... after all..... You are Madame Forget......"

A curtain had seemed to descend between them, an awkwardness, a consciousness of a barrier formed by all these events. Gitta. Otto. The war. English, German, French. All these divisive things. Their relationship. Renata did not want any barriers. The war had made living just too critical now, too important. In everything there was an immediacy, and a brittleness which could crack at any moment.

At the point of sensing he was about to leave, Renata ran upstairs and returned with a leather-bound box that she held out to him.

"..... It's your camera."

"Yes. Ze second camera. I use ze one at ze school. Take it, Ned."

"But -"

"No, I want you to have it. Yes. Take it. There is some film too. You have some space for them?"

"Well..... yes. It'll go in me kit bag if ah sort it all out."

"Good."

That took more than a minute, and it was a squeeze. When he was done, they were both standing looking at each other, thinking of things to say. Ned was telling himself that by now she should have been his sister-in-law: a strange, rather alien thought that made him feel less secure in his relationship. In that half-light from the oil lamp, her figure looked more slender and youthful, perhaps too slender and he wondered if she was eating as she should. She had dropped her hair in readiness for sleeping. Her face smooth and pale, she looked a little lost, but also younger. Her lips were parted, trying hard not to express the mood of her eyes.

"Write to me, Ned."

"Ah will."

"Yes.... No..... I want you to...."

"Ah will, Reina. Ah promise. Yer'll tell me about Gitta."

"Yes, of course."

"Oh! An' you'll tell me about..... you'll tell me about *you*, Reina."

Somehow, he had to say that. In the desperation of these times, short-cuts had to be made, there was no time for shilly-shallying. Reina was an island for him. In some ways, the one island that mattered above all others. Despite his awkwardness, there was a bond there now, a bond he felt strongly quite apart from Gitta, a bond that transcended other considerations. She was perhaps his most trusted friend.

"Of course. I will remind you of those walks we had, yes? And ze bicycles...."

"Yes. But, ah mean...." His voice quiet and probing perhaps more than he had a right to. "Not just about you and yer mother and Gitta and Otto ...... Well, yes.... all those things but ...... Tell me about yerself.... Tell me about *you*. Is that alright?"

"Yes."

"D'y'understand?"

"Yes. I sink so."

"Swear on the mushrooms."

He made her laugh. "What?"

"The mushrooms – champion...... Swear..... *Tu jure*."

She laughed again. "*Oui. Champignons! Je jure... Tu es fou*, Ned."

He took a long time looking at her now, though with some self-consciousness. What he saw reflected in her eyes might begin to inspire a confidence that he had lost a short while before.

"Promise?"

"Yes."

"Honest?"

She raised her head a little and they exchanged the trust of their eyes, the only bright things in the gloom now.

"Mushrooms," she said softly.

Two hours had passed in moments, it seemed. Time becomes both friend and enemy in such interludes. How Ned longed to be able to climb the stairs to his former shared bedroom: it felt strange not to do so. Instead, heaving his kit bag onto his shoulder and grasping his rifle, he passed out of the door Renata held open for him. In doing so, he paused so that their eyes met. For a last time, perhaps - who knows? If there was anything to be said, he could not say it: many things had to pass before his mind was clear on anything now, all Ned felt in his heart was a muddle of feelings.

Silently, with a forced grin, he turned and walked away and did not hear Renata's quiet voice say to his departing back, "Ned, *Je suis là. Adieu.*"

* * * * *

"You've been running, lad."

Ned was out of breath, he could not answer.

The sergeant pulled out his pocket watch. "Two minutes to..... Relax, lad. We ain't going nowhere for another hour at least. Usual cock-up."

"Good," panted Ned. "Then we can go for a drink."

"This time o' night?"

"Yer forget, sergeant – I know this town."

"How much?"

"Yer got a couple of francs?"

"No."

"I have. It's just round t'corner. We'll not be missed for a few minutes. It's poor stuff but it'll wet yer whistle."

* * * * *

Frustrating as it had been in some aspects, that evening proved something of a watershed for Ned's state of mind. Not since that night of April 14th, 1912, had he felt any degree of genuine composure, or any sense of being balanced, being complete within himself, of knowing who he was and where he was in the world and that nothing now could really destroy his sense of self. Ned Thornton was that man who had walked a jagged edge for a long, long time, only to reach a realisation that, in essence, he had nothing to fear. The troubles with Knight and Cade, that would pass in good time. Yes, it concerned him Gitta no longer appeared to feel as he would have wished; yes, it concerned him he was still *persona-non-grata* in terms of his identity and those lies still at large about him; and yes, there was every uncertainty about the days ahead and what they would bring that he had never faced before. How would he face up to being a soldier? *Really* face up?

All that notwithstanding, there was a kind of pact within himself now, a kind of agreement that all was struggling forward as perhaps it should. Yes, he was a man who had enemies, but a man whose wealth of friendships were now visible as a broad seam in the fabric of his life. There were places he now felt anchored to, safe-haven ports in the storm of whatever lay ahead. And to his great surprise, he was no longer so deeply troubled that his betrothed had physically become distant. Bothered, but not destroyed. And he - was he distant from her, in fact? She would surely have argued that it was *he* who had deserted *her*. But she was, after all, a free spirit, Ned had always known this, and she might just as easily walk back into his life tomorrow and take up her claim if she had a mind to.

Whether that mattered in the way that it had, was another question. He still loved Gitta... of course he did. He still wanted her. For there was Gitta, and there was Reina, and no matter what other interpretation he tried to put on it, Reina had made it clear his friendship had significance for her. It was good his fiancée's sister was a declared anchorage for them all. Yet there was more. That was it, that was the difference: Reina mattered, and not in his dreams had he made the assumption that he might actually matter to her.

There was some surprise in this, and comfort. A security even, with perhaps one of several futures beyond the veils. This feeling of being valued made an impact for the moment, and perhaps would reveal more of itself in time. Life was uncertain, yet hopeful. All he needed to know was that Otto was alive and well and would return to claim an essential place at the table. As to Gitta - well, Gitta would do as she chose: always had, always would.

* * * * *

"You know you're not allowed cameras, Ned."

"No! – You sure, Bob?"

"King's Regulations. As of this last month, matter of fact. Best thing you can do is keep it tucked down the bottom of your bag. Don't let no-one know about it."

"Yes. Oh – how about kit inspections?"

"Well.... Either blanco it or better still paint it dark green. They might not know what it is but if it looks Army, they'd look stupid asking questions."

"Right."

They exchanged grins but it seemed to settle the problem for the moment.

"Bob.....?"

"Uh?"

"Yer think ah should paint me golliwog dark green?"

"You daft ha'porth!" said Bob, and threw his book at him.

* * * * *

THIRTY

Soon to be advanced to full corporal due to the recent demise of the platoon bearer of that title, Lance-Corporal Parrock felt no ease in the role.

Herbert Parrock of the short legs knew all the usual jibes – "Get off your perch, Parrock", "Stop squawking, Parrock" - all the hugely un-inventive and painfully un-funny phrases each clever idiot thought he had just conjured up. Like Ned, Herbert had joined the army from the merchant navy, and had not enjoyed parting with his 'facial fungus'. Looking in the mirror at his moustache, the sole survivor, he had gawped and exclaimed, "Christ, I look like a fuckin' baby what ate a walrus!"

"You surely do," agreed Happy John with sincerity.

"If I were a painter," mused young Pugh thoughtfully, "I'd paint you for posterity, Bert. Herbert Parrock, the baby's bum with a man's face."

"Go shit yourself!" Parrock dismissed them.

Looking up at cirrus formations overhead and that light breeze coming in, soothsayer Parrock cautioned, "Gonna be some wet stuff coming, lads."

Parrock drew his spoon out of his puttees, stirred the billy can once more then coaxed the scum off it. This time, they had been able to have their Maconachies heated in the pot over the fire, the stew almost tasted good for once. The joke about eating their M & V rations 'hot or cold', as the label stated, had worn thin long ago. The only amusement now was in the way Welshman Taff Morgan pronounced the name - 'Mack-an-*ocky*'. It still brought a chuckle.

"Boys, this is your one sunny day, get your buckets and spades and get to the seaside while you can."

The tea Bert Parrock passed round was already no better than warm. Nobody winced any more at how stewed it tasted: it bore some resemblance to tea, 'wet and warm' was good enough. Thankful for the mug, Ned took it in both hands and sat back on the hard mud shelf someone had created in the side of the trench. That shelf would be slime by tomorrow night. Rain, it had seemed these past weeks, did not stay away for long, the previous few late summer days of relative warmth might last as long as the next man to die for not keeping his head down – for that was how Corporal Riddiough had died, and he should have known better. At least it was an instant death, almost bloodless – just a mass of sticky, matted hair at the back of his head where the shrapnel had gone in. Unhappily, a rear part of his skull had loosened as Happy John had grabbed for the man. Happy John, the butcher from Faversham, had vomited.

They had already seen death, but a close-up death was always indescribably revolting and numbing. One thing to see a comrade in the act of dying, quite another to handle whatever resulted from it. They were, they told themselves, 'getting used to it', whilst in the quiet recesses of their minds they knew they never would. This was what it meant to be a soldier.

Ned still felt shame at his own first reactions of many weeks ago. Back then, the world had shown a new face to them, its darkest face.

"No good crying, lad. It won't bring him back."

"No, sergeant."

"Never pretty, lad, I know that. You'll get used to it. Just control yourself, and make sure next time it's not you. Remember them first rules and keep your ruddy head down when you're out in the trench. The army's not stupid, the army knows yer cap won't keep nasty hobjects off yer head. Get under cover!"

The army did not stop Ned from being sick either. In his mind were the carding machines from the mill. Nor did it stop him from shaking. He shook for hours and could not control that. The sickness, that lasted for days and disrupted his sleep. It was not just the sight of someone's flesh being exposed, like so much meat on a butcher's table, it was also the terror and the spectre of pain to the fragile body, the loss of fingers, hands, arms, legs, or anywhere that was open to the mere touch of a bullet or a shell or metal splinter. And then the smell that might drift in from the fields, that unmistakable odour of rotting body parts. Sickly sweet and truly disgusting, even for men who were used to the festering odours of English cities. "Like my old man's rotten poxy feet," Happy John had suggested, "only fifty times worse." There was no humour in this, only revulsion.

The panic attacks came and then went. One day was never the same as the one before, even though it felt like it. Each day in the front line, Ned told himself he was becoming more attuned to this awful, awful business of waiting around for death or disablement to visit, and yet each day ended with an air of assurance that tomorrow would be better. A man had to believe that - yes, tomorrow would be better.

Only Bob Street and Faversham's butcher were not entirely overcome by it all, yet even Happy John knew that putrifying human flesh, whilst it smelled not dissimilar, was so much more outrageous than that of an animal whose tripes he had left too long in the bin. Whilst maggots in animal flesh would not raise an eyebrow, in the wounds of men even John found it off-putting, to say the least.

For Ned, dying here was so much more immediate than the death that had sought him in the lifeboat. That was more of a mirage to him now, no more than a flavour in the stew of life.

"Cheer up, though, lads – summer's coming!"

"We believe you, sergeant."

Eventually, it did. Not for very long.

Oh, for fair winds every day! To keep at bay the stench of that which the stretcher bearers had not got to. Thankfully, they missed not a great deal, but could not be expected to find everything in this chewed-up land. It was, according to the senior soldiers who had taken pleasure in initiating the young men of C company, just the 'meat grinder'. They had long since become accustomed to their own revulsion and fright, and it was only fair to take it out on the new boys.

Ned and his pals had been told these and other things in the trench training school: it had been a lark then, lots of "Let me at Fritz" talk that was patently ridiculous. Most ridiculous of all was the lack of protection army clothing provided. In the Middle Ages, fighting men had worn armour and helmets; now it seemed wool cloth was deemed fit for the task. There was talk of armoured headgear, but only talk.

Today they had the real thing to deal with, and dealing with it had not been easy for them, not even for Bob Street, who was no stranger to death but completely unused to being under fire. They had been told not to write about it in letters but Ned wrote it anyway, in an effort to expunge the worst of it from his system. He would destroy the paper before it actually went anywhere. Bob thought that a good idea and did the same, perhaps many men did exactly that. Letters and 'whizz-bangs' had to be sanitized to pass censorship: no details, no place names, no fears and no deaths. "Blimey," exclaimed Pugh, "What do I tell 'em? – The Germans were our guests at the May ball?"

Yes, they had listened to all their training had told them of modern warfare: the artillery, the machine guns, the mines. They had listened with belief of a kind, but never convinced. Somehow, the more they had learned, the more 'other-worldly' it became.

"Remember, lads, give it to Jerry before he gives it to you." And up went the cheer, "Aye, Sergeant!" as loud as they could shout their defiance.

"Just imagine Jerry givin' it to *your* wife, private, and yours, and yours."

"Aye, Sergeant!"

"I ain't got a wife," moaned Waterloo Jones. "What do I do?"

"Well imagine Jerry givin' it to yer poxy sister then, " suggested Happy John.

"Ain't got any sisters neither."

"Well.... Yer got any bruvvers?"

"Yeh – one. He's a priest."

"Oh, fuck!" said Happy John. "Reckon you're in trouble, mate."

Yes, sergeant. Oh yes. Do it to him but do it first. Oh yes. Got that. But when that enemy is invisible, when it screams overhead and explodes in a shattering cacophony that jars every nerve and rips any last vestige of courage out of you..... What do you do but climb into the nearest, tiniest, muddiest little hole you can find? Get under! Get under! Stick a sandbag on your back - anything!

The trenches. That training had at least been relevant. All those jokes at Chattenden about being moles sounded hollow now. It was all about the trenches, they came in all shapes and sizes, from gouges carved by a ploughshare to the most elaborate and even decorous affairs that an architect might not be ashamed of. Most had names – Cairo Road, Paradise Alley, The Kitchener Klub. Direction signs pointed - To Ypres. To Calais. To Piccadilly Circus. To French's Fun House. To Aunt Fanny's Place. And occasionally, To Berlin. Officers liked that one.

Do it to him first..... As they charged those dummies and learned how to slice into canvas and straw. To do that for real..... "Ah can't do it," Ned had told Bert Parrock at Plug Street.

"Yes, you will."

"No. Ah can't."

"Yes, you will."

"No - look, will yer bloody listen ter me, Bert? Ah don't think ah can stick it in 'im."

"We all think that.... for a while. Then you think, well, it's bloody Germans, in' it?"

"So?"

"Well - *bloody Germans*!"

How could Ned explain? "Germans or anybody.... Just don't think ah can do it."

"Not soft on Huns, are you?"

How was he to respond to that one? For a moment or two they just looked at each other.

"Just the thought of shovin' it in, that's all. Like a skewer into meat that talks back."

"Look, sunshine, when he comes at you with a stick bomb in one hand and a bayonet in the other, are you gonna stop and ask if you feel alright about it? 'Hold up a second, pal - can we just talk about this?'... Ey?"

There was no answer that he could give other than the proper one. "No, Bert."

"Well, then..... Grow up, lad."

Bert shook his head and stretched a hand out. "Come on, Ned. You do too much thinking for a lad your age. Miss your rum ration, did you?" Then he shook his head more dolefully. "Time we all got bloody pissed, come to that."

Those early days of walking through forest land did not last. Tree stumps were still there, barely slivers of scarred wood, and every scrap of ground had been tossed in the air. On the map, this place was a forest, with clearings where cattle had grazed. Here and there a homestead, a farm, outhouses for pigs and chickens, a sweet little track leading to it, birds singing in the hedges and a little pond over there. On the map. But now..... Look what ten months of war had done.

The battalion so far played no major role, forming only part of a defensive strategy. The barrages were the worst of it, they had earlier decided. They were wrong, for the worst had not yet come. 'Over the top' had not yet come –not a "first wave" over the top. Senior soldiers did not joke with the new boys about that. They knew the worst was not a shell that tore open anything in its path - the worst was a pair of Germans dug in somewhere with a machine gun. Machine guns were the deadliest of all, for they had guided intelligence behind them, not the blind, indiscriminate destructive force that the shells were, but a man-and-machine combination of directed death and injury. Seniors knew when one bullet tore into you, it was instantly followed by another, as the gun spat out its 450 rounds each minute. The seniors had learned its ways – wait for the burst to end, then run, since the machine gun, whether British or German, was a beast that heated rapidly and tired. Its weakness was a reliance on water-cooling. German forces had embraced the machine gun early on, the British and French were playing catch-up, so the match between Spandau and Vickers was at first an uneven one.

"Grow up, lad." Bert was not wrong. Ned constantly questioned his own progress.

New men would find out for themselves. Just as Ned had already found out what it was to see a man's body blasted to kingdom-come by a shell exploding into the ground. The man had been on his way back as Ned observed from the trench wall. German shells had not begun to fall when their sergeant had instructed them to look out for men returning. One or two had periscopes; Ned had none, and there was too much smoke around for a clear view . There was no warning, no thunder, only a noise like a musical ripping of bedsheets before the shock of the field erupting in a whooshing sound, and this man leaving the ground in a mudburst, his body separating as he did so. Ned could neither breathe nor swallow as his eyes bore witness. Absurd. Unreal. Puppet-like, comical, yet indescribably horrible.

He had not looked out again. Whatever Sergeant Partington may have been shouting, Ned felt his body slide down the wall until he was crumpled at the bottom, gasping for breath and trying not to believe what he had seen. Shortly, the sergeant excused him for a break to clean up, as Ned had soiled his pants. That day passed in numbness and a prolonged effort to control his panic, whilst the good sergeant went among his men and quietly watched their every move.

In September of 1915 they were again in action in the field, as the third wave of men to be sent out in the steps of those who were already on their way back, and the action had barely begun. When you are waiting, propped between your rifle and the trench wall, fighting to forget cold and damp and wound up like a spring, it is then that time becomes tortuous and limitless. It became a cold eternity of waiting and uncertainty – *Please, let us not be sent!*

As if waking from sleep, Ned's limbs and muscles had been reluctant to work under the great weight that pressed down his shoulders and neck. All Ned had felt was an overwhelming desire to crawl back into a bunk and hide. But no, they had been 'out there', plodding forward at the insistence of the officer's whistle, plodding as fast as wooden legs would move them, a laboured, dragging pace as the ground had been wet and muddy and spongy, clinging and tugging to hold them back. His kit, too, held him back, and the shovel that slapped him as he tried to run. Barely had they reached the wire than they met men rushing back toward them, some without weapons, bent only on reaching the safety of their own British trenches. Men with terror in their faces, some with tears running down their dirty cheeks, some with injuries, all with the one desire of wanting to live. Some came on so thoughtless of anything but escape that they tore their flesh on the wire without seeming to notice. And so No. 2 Platoon had held themselves there as Lieutenant Donovan made whistle sounds but with arm gestures that told them not to venture further forward, whilst all the time the incredible, deafening noises of thunderous battle threatened to rip the insides out of their ears and shouted at them to go back.

They did go back. As a swarm of men in dishevelled British uniforms came rushing back at them, the field was alive with a horde of huge, dark beetles scrambling out of the smoke, the very ground heaving with their rush for safety, their fight to stay in the realm of the living, whilst ahead all they could hear were the insistent swishy, clanky rattles of the German machine guns spitting and laying into those troops that had gone out before. They had been made to flee, all that came back were men with the badges of blood and fear. One of them fell into Bob's arms as his knees buckled under him, and Bob and Ned picked him up and made to carry him as they sought the directions of the lieutenant, who was still vacillating at the wire, wafting his pistol overhead to usher men this way and that. It was utter confusion, but the men knew the general tone of it, which was to fall back to the trench.

That young man was crying and telling them his arm was hit, but there were streaks of blood from somewhere above his face that he did not seem to know about and his cap was torn. They bore him to the rear, part-dragged this exhausted man, and got him to the edge of the trench where he tried to lunge from them in his haste for sanctuary. Someone else took the weight of him, whilst Ned and Bob scrambled down the wooden ladder to avoid breaking a leg as some did. The man was no longer in their charge, his adrenaline spurring him on faster like a puppet whose operator was yanking the strings too quickly.

Ned let go his rifle against the wood of the trench wall and dropped to his knees, trembling, every nerve in his body jangling and shaking and his ears ringing so loudly that he thought he must surely be deaf. There he crouched for several minutes, watching men return - involuntarily really - a magnetic gaze on what this once-proud troop of soldiers now appeared to be – a routed army, all gasping and coughing and crying and falling around. He recognized few of them. Some were screaming in pain, some were virtually comatose, most were shouting if only in frustration or relief, and everywhere there was a total rabble that none of the commissioned or non-commissioned officers could as yet shout into any kind of order. Quite soon, the injured had been taken to the rear, and the dead left where they lay for the stretcher bearers. Those who remained were the lucky, relatively uninjured ones, who slumped and panted and recovered wherever and however they might. Almost no-one spoke, yet in the volume of thoughts expressed by all those sets of eyes, blinking and looking about them, every man seemed to be asking the same question - *'Why are we doing this insane thing?'*

"Pick up that fuckin' rifle, Thornton!" It was the sergeant. "Might be Jerry comin' in any minute now."

'*Yes, sergeant,*' thought Ned, but did not hear himself say it.

It was not enough. Satan himself must have been waiting for them all to get back into their trenches before signalling the next round. As men strove to pull themselves into some sort of order and thank God for their deliverance, the shells screamed overhead.

"Take covaaaaaaaaaaaaah !"

Suddenly the world was calamity again. Shells fell close to the trenches with the noises of Hell and colossal fountains of earth, of mud and bits of wood and metal being flung up all around them and tearing the heart out of earth and men alike. One shell pounded into the next segment sixty yards away and the cries could be heard above the din. Earth and bits of metal spattered and fell into the trench. Ned shrank himself into the tightest of tiny balls and pulled a board of wood across his back and neck. The shells came again. That fearful tearing noise as they ripped through the sky above them and impacted the earth with terrible, unbelievable, ear-splitting thunder. A lump of shrapnel thumped into the soil close to Ned's feet; it was metallic and black and smoking, about the size of his drinking mug. Wide-eyed, Ned was transfixed by the deathly promise of this inanimate, thoughtless bringer of pain.

He cowered there until Meeker ran by at a crouch, shouting at them all to follow him, and they groped and found the bunker they could not otherwise see as they dared not look.

For more than fifteen minutes the shelling continued. It was the Germans telling the British boys that it was naughty to try to sneak up on their side of the playground. A ticking-off. Then, as abruptly as the guns had started, they stopped and the air sang. The order went out to stand by for a German attack - standard procedure after a shelling. But an attack never came. It was just the guns having their say. *'Don't do it again!'*

Ned looked up at Meeker, stooping at the low bunker entrance and peering out watchfully. Meeker the indomitable sergeant, ever protective of those in his charge. Meeker the reliable, Meeker the strong, the unflappable. Ned bit his lip and choked back a tear, confounded by his own sensibilities.

They were learning. This was what it meant to 'give Jerry a bloody nose'. For they had not, nor anything like it. They had surged out, been made to dance by an invisible Hydra that noisily spat death and pain at them, they had been cut down to size and made to run. It was over. All now left for the stretcher bearers. There were no Germans coming after them in close pursuit, the Germans had had the good sense to remain behind their lines, behind those places where their machine guns made this war easy for them. And yet, these men here had no shame, they felt no disgrace, only a feeling of great ill mixed with relief, a bewilderment of feelings that brought them close to tears through their shredded nerves. They had returned and they were alive: it went against that code which had been instilled into them, like the 'death or dishonour' tattoos that some men bore - meaningless now. They breathed the foul air and were thankful they had not succumbed out there, that they still had their lives and bodies.

And soon the sound of a mouth-organ as all other sounds slowly settled and died away on the fragile stillness. In the next trench, Tommy Tarmey played a slow lament on 'Goodbye Dolly Gray'. The sound began quietly and finally became the only sound in the world, save for the men who were softly singing along. Men had simply stopped, for Tommy may as well have been playing the Last Post.

They were somewhere in an area the sergeant had called "Lows".

The past, the present, the future..... There were no finite limits any more, it was all one monstrous confusion, which had begun to pour into a huge soup of timelessness, this year of 1915.

It was Loos, in Northern France, and it was September, 1915. An awful place and time to be. None of their nightmares had ever conjured up images anything like this. To put a name on a place as being "unimaginable" might have been thought plainly stupid just a few short months ago.

* * * * *

THIRTY-ONE

"Well, I dunno, sarge – where the 'ell do *you* think we are, then?"

When they had first come to this land, those men of C Company thought their disorientation would be only a temporary thing, they thought that events would quickly lead up to one enormous confrontation, one Waterloo, one Agincourt, that would put its stamp on their entire war and would decide matters once and for all. One great charge into battle to surge over the enemy's guns and capture the prize. Whatever the prize might be. That anyway was what they had imagined but, as in so many other matters, they were wrong, and that idea of one massive final burst of energy into an all-or-nothing victory was a vision denied them.

Each reflected on how he had arrived here, in a more pleasant time of early summer - even if a lot of it had been spent shunting in rail carriages and marching endless rough or cobbled roads. At the end of each day, only empty bellies and aching legs and an uncertain prospect of where you got to lay down your head. How they prayed to be back there now.

Heads had been shaking, each man looked at the others. In truth, Sergeant Partington had about as much idea where they were as the rest of them.

"What was that last town where the trucks dumped us? Y'know, after we left Bethune?.... Come on, what were it called?"

"Search me, sarge," said Duffers.

"I'd rather not, son," replied the sergeant, "I've ruddy fleas of my own." He had: it was evident. He had pulled off his shirt in frustration and they had seen how raw was his skin down one side. Wetting the skin gave slight relief, but you could not leave a shirt off for long, whoever you were, and it was not warm. More than that, you could definitely not go without trousers, for the crabs were as bad, despite that oddly-coloured stuff the sick bay gave you to paint over the problem. It would have seemed ridiculous not long ago to yearn for a delousing station, but it was no joke any more. One of the really useful things to bring back from leave was a can of paraffin: trouble was, after applying that, you had to be damn sure not to light up a cigarette. Kerosene, for those mad enough to try it, was worse.

Lice were just one of the joys of life 'at the front', along with rats the size of kittens that someone said they had seen emerge from the canal "over yonder". Ned could see no canal. That was August, perhaps all would be over before another winter, for they had heard about trench-foot and the rheumatics that bedevilled men in the cold mud and rain of winter. Trench-foot was a punishable offence. Commanders seemed to think men contracted it to get out of their duties or to get a Blighty ticket. It was not a bad idea.... Better than shooting your toe off, perhaps.

"Bethune," sighed Clarence Duffield, a Brummie who responded only to his pet name. "That were a right nice place at some time, weren't it? – Bet there were nice bits o' skirt there one time."

"Nice bits o' skirt, my arse!" chided Bert Parrock, "Don't think gettin' a dose o' the pox is going to get you out of this lot! Any road, the best place was that camp back at La Chapelle where your Brummie mates trained us up, Duffers."

"It was, you're right."

"Put a sock in it, Duffers," called Happy John. "You know bloody well the best place was Fuck-Yers."

"Aye, Fuck-Yers!" Nobody had really thought to say it, as if the mention of it might jinx them from ever going back there. Fouquières-lès-Béthune had been a place of rest before being directed to the front. At least, 'Fouquières' had been a name on a signpost, and that was enough to know for they could scarce see any village.

Ned reminded himself. "Good grub, an' a decent kip, even if it were only a barn. Ah'd kill for a bath right now." They all agreed with that.

"It'd just be nice to settle in one place," said Bob, "I'm fed up of being shunted around. In six months, where've we been?"

"Where've we *not* been?" challenged Parrock.

"Poxy Canterbury, poxy Purfleet, poxy Chattenden, poxy Southampton, poxy Hazebrouck, poxy Wipers..... oh, and now a ruddy hole in the world somewhere near a place called Lille. Where's'at, anyhow - Belgium?"

In truth, Ned had largely lost track of where they were: his thoughts were so often back in Le Havre. He had, though, observed their progress by train to Abbeville and thence to Hazebrouck and some other unpronounceable little place whose name now escaped him. He remembered the walk on that long, cobbled road. Cobbled roads had no sympathy for tired marching feet and some of these French roads were straight as a die: they gave the distressing appearance of going on forever. Food was bad on the march, too, and never would they have imagined they did not want to see the sun.

Bob pointed his pipe at John and corrected him. "France...... I think. I'll check with my batman when he gets back with my egg nog, don'tcha know."

"I heard 'em say, *arrondissement*... what's that?"

"It's just a commune, Duffers," Ned told him. "A small place. No importance to anyone but the people livin' there. Search me, though. Ah reckon we've just been goin' round an' round an' -"

"Yeh, we know," cut in Happy John, "finally disappear up yer own poxy Fuck-yers!"

Wherever that place was, it was only memorable as the place before the place where the company first came under fire. June, that was. Not that dates mattered any more: like places, they seemed to blur together. There had been early days when they could recall trees, and birds actually singing in between the exchanges of shells that loosened men's bowels; the luxury of tented camps, and an American reporter who nosed around and asked them about 'Teutons' and how they laughed at that. For a while, all that seemed peculiarly unreal and off-putting, as though at any time a director of the play somewhere off to the side would stride onto the stage and shout, 'Curtain!' It was to be a summer interlude before the war-winter began in earnest.

"Plug Street."
"What, sarge?"

"Plug Street."

"What the bloody hell name is that, then?" asked Parrock, trying to keep in step with his short legs.

"What d'you think I am, lad? – Bloomin' encyclopedia? All I 'eard was, that's where we're going now – Plug Street. That's what that hofficer said."

"Sounds nice," lied Happy John.

Ploegsteert was where the company was headed, what else did they need to know? It was part of what was being called the Ypres Salient, that was all they knew back in that lovely July. On the way there, they passed a field hospital, though not close enough as to attract the attentions of the nurses they glimpsed, despite shouting vigorously. A field hospital was a reassurance in one way, and a shudder of fear in another. Outside, a horse was grazing on almost nothing as it stood in the shafts of a wagon that bore several soldiers who did not move: they only lay there, sleeping perhaps. It was not a good omen.

Plug Street was quieter now, after difficult fighting earlier. The battalion would not be there long.

It was Bert who finally summed it up the best. "Ah feel like Alice in bloody Wonderland." The others gave him puzzled looks. "Ah'm wanderin' around every bloody day just wonderin'...... just wonderin'...... That's all.... "

* * * * *

'4 August 1915

Dearest Ned,

Here is good news – James' leg is a little better, he is walking short paces without the stick, it's wonderful. And Christine told me she is hopeful of another child. That would be the best news, wouldn't it?

But I have more amazing news. Monsieur Carelle came to see us. I received a telegram – bless us, a telegram, Ned! Mother had a fright – well, you know. But she had never seen one before. He had been in Liverpool, he said, and had business that took him this way, a meeting with Hepworth and Grandage, he said it was to do with the new business he has been setting up in England. What a fine man he is, and his manner of dressing, so much smarter than any around here! I don't have to tell you, do I? He arrived on the street in such a fine motor car. A bright red one. Goodness knows where he found that! It caused an absolute shock around the whole neighbourhood, as you can imagine. Drew a crowd. And his driver waiting patiently outside – he probably had to, to stop the children marking his car! Mother and I felt like royalty, and father was livid when he came home to this news, having missed him. He did not go to the pub, he is going there much less now and his coughing is a worry, I have to say.

You can imagine mother whipping up the papers off the parlour floor so that he could come in up the steps! Yet M. Carelle is a man who does not stand on ceremony and is no pumped-up lord. We offered him tea but he politely refused and had his own tin of coffee – He told me how I should make that for him.

He repeated what lovely girls Renata and Brigitte are, believe me when I tell you we would have every wish for your happiness with Brigitte, when that happens. Also believe me when I say their nationality does nothing to offend us, I do understand. He said he would write to you directly as I have given him your present address. It should be easier now, the way they have set up the A.B.P.O. He told me he feels he has the confidence of that lady, and believes in time you will be proven innocent. I'll say no more of that.

I know you can tell us little. You are discreet, only one word was inked over. At least it costs nothing so you can write as often as you like! We pray for your safe return. We cannot get meat, but that is a tiny matter! If you wish to continue in France once the fighting stops, we shall understand, but first we want to see you out of harm's way. By the way, Mr. Holdsworth died very tragically – he was robbed in the street and the thieves even took his stick. Trying to walk and unable to see, he fell over and hit his head on a kerb stone. For a few farthings – I am lost for words. What have we come to, I wonder.

Mother is doing the scarf you asked for, I hope you are right that you will be issued with more darning wool. I don't have a spare darning mushroom, so James gave me half a door knob and I enclose it in this parcel, as you said you lost yours.

I must conclude. Stay safe, Ned.

Your loving sister, Grace.'

* * * * *

'10 August 1915

Dear Ned,

I have been away from Barnet. One of the burdens of managing a business is the need to find another leg to the business when one leg is limping. My venture involves parts for engines, I believe that is the way forward and for the present cocoa beans are not a shining star! Last month the Germans sank one of the American ships that held a cargo of mine. They have set new limits in warfare – none!

My friend, I met your mother and sister. Grace is a very charming girl, and most friendly, I liked her at once. For delicacy I did not – though I thought of it – joke with her that she must have many young men trying to court her, as you have said she does not give out her favours easily. But you will not mind me saying, Ned, a handsome and intelligent woman.

Antwerp has changed from a Belgian fortress into a German one! I get no messages now. We heard stories of what soldiers did across the country, destroying towns and killing thousands of innocent people. Our forces were tiny against a great army, they had no need to do that. I am too old to fight a war, but now I fight in the way that I can, by involving myself with those industries that can produce the weapons to fight back.

Ned, I have seen your Cade. Only for a moment, but I can say I agree with you, I took an instant dislike to him. Surly - I think that is the word. I was not introduced, nor did I wish to be, but he was to our friend Mr. K as is a hound to a piece of shit! – I am a poor foreigner, I can say such things! However, forthcoming events - I am invited to Richmond for the shooting of moorland birds on the

12th - yes, immediately! That is another British custom it seems I must embrace! Not as a guest of her ladyship but one of their political fencing partners, Mr. Ulysses Smith, with whom I recently spent an evening playing billiards - a game at which no Belgian excels! For once, this was not one of Tommy's actions, but my own. Mr. Smith is an acquaintance of Lady S., not so much Mr. K., with whom he argues across the floor of the House. All this could be to our purpose, though I confess that my primary interest is in the acquisition of trade for myself. However, to be honest, I become more intrigued as I become better acquainted with Lady S., and I look forward to the whole meeting - in fact, I leave Durham tomorrow!

Ned, I believe I understand why you wished to join your army, I know it is not simply a matter of duty to king and country. Take care - you have much ahead of you, this I feel sure. Not least a lovely French girl! Bon courage.

Bruno.'

* * * * *

'15 August 1915

Dear Ned,

I hope you are well. I hope you are Champion – yes?

Please excuse my writing is not clear, I am almost in the dark as I am with Mutti again. The doctor has been here, she did not need to go to the hospital, and there is a lot of sick people there, so I come here. I do not complain as I can come from the school and I do not have to cook for five people at my house – Jerome invited his brother to stay with us as he is afraid for Paris. So there are five of us. Henri is a good man, I think. He is a notaire and deals in money, but he and Jerome are always together and Jerome has less interest in the schoolchildren. Madame Forget is a proud woman and does not do cooking and cleaning, I told you before, I think. His sister, Mathilde, is someone I find unpleasant – she does not like that my mother and I are German.

But, Ned, my troubles are small ! We have the summer and people in Havre are good to me. Of course, I teach their children! We had some fêtes in the town and forgot that we may be attacked like before. That may not happen again as your Royal Navy comes, I think it keeps away those Unterseebooten.

Otto, no more news from him since Mars. We think he is still with those big guns somewhere in the west - better than fighting the Russians. We hope he is well. That is all I can say.

I miss my sister. I wish she was here. But I had a letter. She said she was not at Beauvais now. The nurses did examinations or what that was, and she was sent to a hospital for French soldiers near Reims. That may be far from where you are. She said it was very unpleasant to see soldiers that were in battle, but she had to become familiar (?). My English is bad!

So she has not been home. Ned, I am trying to tell you something that I did not want to say and I do not know how to say it. Gitta is going to have a baby. This is so difficult for me but you said she had not written to you, and so I must. She will have a baby in January. Yes. It was a shock to Mutti and me. Gitta did not tell us for a long time - she says it was April and now we have August. She will continue in the nursing, but later this year she will have to finish, and then I do not know - I hope before that, she comes home so that we can look after her.

I know how you feel for Gitta. This news will hurt you. You may understand that I waited some days before writing, but she did not send a letter for you. I am very sorry. I do not know what to say about that. She did ask about you, and I have written to her, saying what I know from your letter of 2 Juin – I keep your letters! She knows she can write to you. I am sorry, Ned, I think that you wanted to hear better news, but I must tell you only the truth. I am sure she still cares much about you.

Mutti and I also care, of course. You are part of our family. Is it alright for me to say that? I know that your letters are permitted to say not many things. But we hope that when you are given some holidays (?) you can come to Havre. Your family in England is more important, we know this.

I have no more words. To be honest, it is lonely here without Gitta and without you boys. Lonely? – is that the right word? *Langweilig*. No – boring! Ned, I should be more honest – it is lonely too. *Einsamkeit*. I tell you this. When there is so much trouble – this war – it is time to open up the heart, isn't it? For everything is so much less sure now. Do you understand me? – I am sorry that I do not speak English quite well, as you know. But we want you boys to come back. You know that. Please write again soon. God look after you.

Reina.'

* * * * *

THIRTY-TWO

'Ned, my friend,

When I reach heaven (!) I must hope God is English! If he is German, I am in great peril. Because I have invested here in machining, I now find myself in a venture which you may not admire - shells and ammunition. But - C'est la guerre, it's necessary.

I have been able to find work for Belgians who fled, as I did, and some injured English soldiers. As well as my involvement in the CRB, there is a new factory at Elizabethville where my business now has a part in the production of munitions. These men were not badly injured but they did not like to be Hospital Blues and wear that silly uniform - you know what I mean, the Blue Boys? I found them work here. These factories are using women - good idea, Ned. I told my men - same work, same pay, and they all agreed.

I hope, my young friend, that you are in good health. I know your letters can say little. For me, friends and informants are more believable than newspapers, I have heard many of the stories and it is alarming. But I must tell you of my activities since, as I told you, I was invited for this curious event, the 'Glorious Twelfth'. Not in Scotland but in Yorkshire........'

"Ah! You must be Monsieur Carelle!"

"I am that poor soul, yes. And you - you are his lordship's private secretary, yes?"

The human beanpole bowed his head ever so curtly. He looked more like a Prussian than an Englishman: his collar starched fit to slice off his head, his moustache waxed and flicked and his hair centrally parted and slicked down so tight against his skull that head lice would have been gasping for air. The only flaw in that persona was the absence of a monocle, for he wore the smallest of wire-frame spectacles.

"Arthur. Your servant, sir."

"Arthur. I see. Arthur, I had no idea we were on first name terms here."

"Oh no, sir! That is my surname - I am Tristram Arthur."

"Ah..... Tristram Arthur."

"Indeed."

"Mmm. Have you ever considered turning that around?"

"Sir?"

"No, your pardon, Arthur, it's unforgiveable of me to be so flippant. Please excuse me. You have stepped into the shoes of someone who - if I am reliably informed - was an astute assistant to his lordship."

"You mean Caldecot.... Yes indeed. Erm..... Sad loss, don't you know." Carelle reflected that he knew quite the opposite, however that was privileged information and Arthur appeared naively under-informed for someone who had been in Lord Semper's employment for two years. Carelle wondered how long he had been in Semper's confidence.

"How do you like England, Monsieur?"

"Like England....? I believe I have no option but to *love* England, as the Germans have loved my country almost out of existence. So I have little choice. Candidly, Arthur, I think your country is full of remarkably resourceful people. What we are doing *here*, though, I am still lacking an education. I thought the Glorious Twelfth was something in Scotland."

"Many people believe that. The idea has a certain *'je ne sais quoi'*, don't you know."

Is this peacock trying to teach me my language, wondered Carelle.

"Monsieur Carelle! Monsieur Carelle!" Lady Sophie's shrill voice carried across the lawn, hit the dry boundary wall and bounced back again.

Whilst Carelle genuflected appropriately, Lady Sophie at once regaled him with all the rigours of their journey, hardly pausing for breath despite protesting that she was desperately out of it.

"And you," she enquired at length as she drew her little party toward the house, like Gulliver pulling a flotilla of Lilliputian boats. "Did you not have a tiresome journey from London?"

"*Au contraire, madame.* I was not in London. I have been in Durham county. *Derram* - isn't that how they say it?"

309

"Do they? I have no idea. There are places one does not go."

"Ah.... It's where my workers make shells for the big guns of war. And no more than two hours from here."

That information struggled to lift even one of her eyebrows. "So what do you think of Coniston Towers? Have you looked around it yet? Has Arthur not shown you? Did you show him, Arthur?"

"Well - "

"Mister Arthur has been most accommodating, Lady Sophie. But I did not yet ask him where is the lake."

"Lake?" queried both her ladyship and private secretary together.

"Coniston."

"Coniston?..... Oh! No, no, that is miles away. You mean Lake Coniston in the Lake District."

"Well - If that is where the English keep the lakes......."

"Oh, but no! Coniston Towers is named after Sir Stratford Coniston, one of Wellington's lot, don't you know."

"I didn't know. I see." Wrinkling up his brow, Carelle wondered just how many more people in this country claimed their pedigree from *'one of Wellington's lot'*.

"Yes. There is everything here: shooting, archery, riding - oh, and you must see the *Avelignese*."

"I must?" queried Carelle, completely ignorant of the word. Observing his nonplussed face, Lady Sophie enunciated the Italian name with greater exaggeration. "Quite delightful horses."

Thus the verbal tour began: the famous Coniston name, the Coniston family history, the Coniston pedigree not forgetting the Coniston English setters, the Coniston riding school, the Coniston art collection and the Coniston contribution to British military history, all of which left Carelle with such a distinct sense of cultural over-indulgence, he doubted he could manage dinner. Until the point where other guests began to arrive, he was beginning to wish he had booked into an hotel at Richmond.

Over dinner - and for once Carelle had resolved to adhere to British standards of evening dress - he had his first glancing encounter with the Great Man himself. Seated well away from Lord

310

Semper - to the relief of Lady Caroline Coniston, Lady Sophie had taken the seating plan upon herself, placing Carelle directly across from her - nevertheless Semper had declared an interest by lobbing haphazard comment at Ulysses Smith whilst standing at his wife's shoulder.

"Are you so short of recruits to your party, Smithy, that you are having to look to continentals now to swell Liberal ranks? Or are you just short of cash?"

"You can ask the man himself, Soapy," called Smith, "He's right here next to your favourite tweeny." Mildred, Oberon Scott-Chapelle's wife of seven years, privately objected to the term 'tweeny', but publicly, for her husband's sake, humoured her father-in-law.

"You are from Belgium, I am reminded," called Semper. Carelle discovered for the first time that Lord Semper had a very slight speech impediment, a tiny difficulty mixing his 'R's with his 'W's. It could almost have been fabricated for noble effect - Carelle wondered if it was. And for his height - Lord Semper was a shoe-insert above 6 feet - the pitch of his voice was unexpectedly high. It was an illogical yet instant irritation.

"I am, Lord Semper. One of his majesty's most loyal Belgian subjects." Carelle gave his moustache a twist.

"I understand the fighting there did not last terribly long."

"Terribly long - perhaps not. Terrible, nonetheless."

"Oh yes, of course, my dear chap. Fierce fighting, I heard this: particularly around Mons, I believe, where our chaps were outnumbered but put up quite a resistance."

When they finally arrived, thought Carelle.

"You are well informed, my lord. A brave action, I was told. Of course, that was almost the last place in Belgium that the Germans came to, but the first place where the British army met them. It would appear the less important towns in Belgium resisted and slowed them down a little, though we were just one soldier to every fifty of them... So I have heard."

"Yes. Yes. Bad show. Your chaps took a hammering from the Germans. We shall sort them out for you, though, have no fear."

Carelle had long since gained control of his hackles in such situations: they strove to rise now, all the same, but his smile overcame them.

"Fear, your lordship? It is not a quality Belgians have been brought up with, when we can look up to our neighbours Britain and France to sustain us."

Semper thought that over for a second, before permitting himself a half-grin.

"Astute, Mister Carelle. I can see it was clever of Smithy to include you as his guest. I must be careful where I point my gun - hah-hah!"

"I too... I'm rather a good shot! But I'm sure we will both shoot well."

Semper nodded slowly. He could not remember when he had last been so contrarily agreed with. At his side, Arthur was not at all certain whether he ought to make a note of that.

So now we are trading blows with Mister Ranulph Knight.... He is all that Ned had suggested... Probably more. In the Drawing Room, Carelle puffed on the finest of cigars, puffing hard to blow away the rancour he had so far managed to contain. *Can it be that he is more clever than his mouth would have me believe?* He would contain that rancour for as long as it took.

Ulysses Smith suffered no such confusion. Tapping Carelle's arm as they passed each other in the entrance to the men's lavatory, Smith curtly nodded and whispered, "Excellent!" and that was that.

"My good feller!"

"Uh - Oh, yes. Mister Judson, is that right?"

"Aye, lad. Ken Judson. 'Ow d'yer like Yorkshire, Mister Carelle?"

Carelle was relieved to hear an honest Yorkshire accent, the like of which he had adjusted to since commencing his business in the North. However, Judson was probably ten years younger than Carelle yet referred to him as "lad": there were things in the language here that Carelle still struggled with.

"God's own country, Mister Carelle..... God's own country. They might come bigger, but not better."

"And certainly not wetter, Mister Judson. I think since I have been in this part of the country it has hardly stopped raining. Except today. Can I help you to this Cognac, Mister Judson? It's God's own drink. Believe me."

He poured a generous measure and they drank.

"Bobbins," said Judson. Carelle wondered if Judson had proposed some sort of toast. "Pardon?"

"Bobbins. It's what ah do. It's what me firm makes."

"Bobbins..... I do not know this."

"Wool. Yer can't make cloth without bobbins, tha knows. An' cloth's what this country turns on, in't that right?"

"Is it?"

"Oh aye. Not soap. Any fool can make soap. All it takes to make soap is a barrel load o' piss an' shit." Carelle could do no better than nod attentively. Where was Judson going with this?

He got his answer: " - An' yon trumped-up scarecrow's full o' that," muttered Judson.

It seemed this Yorkshireman had weighed up Carelle carefully, or possibly Judson supported Ulysses Smith. Semper may have had friends, but he certainly had enemies.

Some time after, Carelle was approached by a man in a poorly-adjusted evening suit.

"Grimshaw."

"Pardon?" asked Carelle. Was this another Yorkshire-ism? *Is 'Grimshaw' a form of local greeting?*

The man bent sideways to ensure the discretion of Carelle's ear. "Arnold Grimshaw. I work for the Tatler journal. I was told to make myself known to you."

Carelle raised his billiard cue and spoke quietly. "May I.... May I continue this game and speak with you a little later."

Grimshaw nodded and backed away. Carelle hoped this man's enthusiasm would not get the better of his wisdom, as Tommy's friend Andy at Scotland Yard had suggested an 'agent of The Tatler

313

journal' would be a useful card to have in the deck. This heavy-handed introduction might jar a little with Tommy's 'familyship' conventions.

Whatever covert conversations they might manage would depend on the level of attention Lady Sophie now expected of Carelle. So far, it was not obvious: the last thing he wanted was to give Semper an impression that Carelle had designs on her ladyship. He was here for business matters, with the business of grouse shooting in the mix; it could be disastrous if his motives should be interpreted as anything else.

To this end, around ten o'clock this first evening, Carelle joined the cache of Semper and friends at the fireplace end of the drawing room, carrying with him his bottle of Cognac as the purveyor of convivial spirits to these four gentlemen. An invitation to a libation of finest Cognac was surely not to be refused.

It was not long before Carelle had revealed his present activities in the munitions industry. Was this a field of national necessity into which these gentlemen might wish to venture? After all, as they all knew, there was a war on.

"Shells and such? Frankly, my dear fellow, a chap can only cover so many wickets in one over. I have two soap factories to run, both of which are working overtime, and my associates at Govan tell me they are pounding ships down the slipways as if they were shelling peas. And you ask me to raid the old piggy bank for spare cash to go into bomb production. I shall have to give that a bit of thought, old stick."

"No, no. I do not make myself clear, your Lordship. I do not seek funding for my own enterprise. I am a simple Belgian who does what he can to help his poor country. I was merely pointing out the opportunities that arise in these troubled times, for patriots like yourself to be able to.... to raise the flag a little higher, should I say, to do the utmost for king and country. I would not dream of suggesting you do not already do that, of course, but .... well, there is no bad thing if this investment means it serves a purpose for one's bank."

"The bank? Ah, now I understand you. Yes, possibilities.... perhaps."

Carelle smiled and nodded his assurance that they were speaking the same language.

"Well, Mister Carelle, if I were able to prevail on the Brantcliffe Bank to invest in munitions, I would simply defer to Oberon here. It is our patriotic duty to ensure we become more familiar with, er.... whatever funding may be necessary. Capital. Oberon and I can talk later about that. Em.... You know my son, The Honourable Oberon Scott-Chapelle?"

So much formality, thought Carelle: *am I really so much in need of being impressed?*

"We have not been introduced, Lord Semper."

The young man casually tossed a smile at Carelle but said nothing.

"Oberon will become Lord Semper after me. The seventh baron.... Won't you, Oberon?... But yet - We'll have words about your suggestion. Needless to say, all of us support England's war interest, eh?"

"And Belgium, my Lord. Do not forget poor Belgium."

"Naturally. Naturally. Respect for an ancient ally, don't you know."

Ancient? questioned Carelle in his mind. *All the way back to the treaty of 1839. Most ancient......*

Carelle's fear of horses was calmed: they were not to ride horses up to the moor. The short dog-carts carried a number of the gentleman shooters whilst Lord Semper had his own phaeton to hand and only Sir Wilfred Coniston rode horse with his two sons. Carelle considered the shooting of defenceless birds an ignoble pastime but for the sake of gaining time with the noble lord and his lady, he would endure it. Fortunately, the weather was surprisingly good, the ride not far and the picnic hampers contained excellent wine as well as a sufficiency of pre-cooked foods of a meat or poultry variety. No lover of salads at any time of the year, Carelle preferred to pick at a scotch egg and a chicken leg or two and wash it down with a decent Beaune.

He had not used a rifle for almost twenty years and staged a frightful shotgun recoil for the amusement of others. Carelle joked and smiled a lot: he was Belgian, after all, and could be excused his awkwardness. It particularly amused Lord Semper's son, who was able to demonstrate how to hold the gun correctly. Oberon was a callow chap who looked his 32 years and more: facially much like his father, lean and pale. He stooped, held himself awkwardly and walked unevenly.

At one point, Arnold Grimshaw caught Carelle on his own as they waded clumsily through bracken.

"I'm sorry, Mister Carelle, sir. I apologise for last night in the drawing room. I was not sure you knew who I was."

Carelle looked around him. "Actually, Mister Grimshaw, I still don't know who you are. If you take my meaning. I imply no offence."

"Ah."

"If you were to be recognised as having anything whatever to do with the police, it would implicate me and undermine my project. We can be acquaintances for the purposes of this shooting thing. You can appreciate that."

"Ah, yes. My boss said - "

"Your boss does not know me. I should like to keep it that way. We have a mutual go-between, have we not? We should keep it that way. You have your business, I have mine. Now, give me your hand."

"Sir?"

"Your hand, your hand! You must take these cartridges - that is why you're speaking to me, you understand?"

"Oh. Of course. I'm obliged to you, Mister Carelle."

"Monsieur."

"Monsieur. Sorry, I forgot. French."

"Belgian!"

Anthony Scott-Chapelle had been for a few years under investigation covertly by the British authorities, this much Carelle had understood from Tommy in confidence. Exactly which authorities, he did not know, nor did he wish to. Too much information could compromise Carelle's own approach as a businessman - precisely what he was, and therefore any investigation by Semper's people into Carelle's background would reveal only that.

As to a police investigation, that might centre on the Semper soap business, but regarding the whys and wherefores of the tale, Carelle knew nothing. Whereas, his own nose had been pointing him towards Brantcliffe Bank as being at the heart of Ned's misfortune. Whatever papers may have been misappropriated, it seemed more logical to associate them with the bank: somehow a soap business did not seem to lend itself to a great deal of intrigue!

Caldecot, long prior to his employment as Knight's personal assistant, had been an employee of Brantcliffe Bank. Could the reason for Caldecot entering Knight's service in the first place reflect issues at the bank?

One thing Carelle did know: Grimshaw was no fool. Whoever was in charge of an investigation into a peer of the realm was aware of the fragile nature of their own position, which might inevitably entail facing up to some of the most powerful figures in the kingdom. Such a person would not employ fools.

"I shall see you at dinner," called Grimshaw loudly, "You must tell me more about the shells business. Any chance to make a few shillings."

* * * * *

"Spinal curvature. Friedreich's condition, would that be the case?"

"Well ! My dear Bruno, you never cease to surprise me. Does he, Miranda?" Lady Sophie turned back to Carelle. "Tell me, Bruno, how did you know?"

"Lady Sophie, I have a head full of silly things. I knew someone before, he had a..... a rounding of the back, as your Oberon does. I believe it is usually caused by some disease contracted in childhood, is it not? Friedreichs."

317

"Oh, you know so much! Yes, this is what the doctors told us. It was very obvious from - oh, ten or eleven years old with Oberon, but - yes, a disease. Diseases are no respecters of nobility, are they?"

Quite the contrary, thought Carelle. And as far as he knew as a layman, such a spinal abnormality was just as likely to have been passed down the family line, regardless of whether or not the family wished to admit it.

"Oberon was never a physical sort. Those ruffians on the rugby field, I didn't want him mixing with those."

Carelle drew his conclusions. It was inevitable that, as Oberon passed out of college, they would toss aside defective statistics and set him into his pre-ordained position with the bank, where he would be comfortable behind a desk. A young man of social standing needed a position through which to demonstrate the entitlements of his lineage; particularly the grandson of Lady Sophie's father, Clement Val de Chapelle, the fifth baron. Someone had to make people aware of that. As Lady Sophie did all the time.

"Ah! So - if I have it correctly, he was the Fifth Baron."

"Exactly."

"And so it is your side of the family - oh, forgive my impertinence, Lady Sophie."

"No, no, monsieur, you are correct. Anthony gained the title by marriage, and of course on the death of my father - it was my father who was Lord Semper." As Carelle already knew.

"Of course. So you and Lord Semper......"

"Anthony."

"Yes.... He was not Lord Semper before...."

"Before he was my husband, no. Before that, you could say he was *nothing* - ha, ha!" She laughed gleefully. "Just a distant relative in charge of a soap factory."

"Ah.... You make it crystal clear, *madame*... And as Lord - er, your husband - has been a member of the House for some time, he would not simply drop it all, as it were, and jump into the other House as if he were playing chair music."

She carried out a mental calculation and then laughed. "Aha! Musical chairs.... Yes. Oh, Bruno, you are amusing! I shall be glad when it all falls properly into place. Heavens, it's not as though we need the headaches of all these people - you know, those at Westminster. Let them find somebody else. We have quite enough to do, thank you."

Carelle reflected on the dynasty as she carried on. Tommy had stumbled upon the rumour that there had been a daughter, Carelle would have dearly loved to uncover more of that. A daughter prior to the Scott-Chapelle marriage, when plain Anthony Scott married Sophie Val de Chapelle. Intriguing, but hardly meat for conversation here.

"And the name 'Semper', that comes from - "

"Latin!" interrupted Carelle.

Lady Sophie slapped a knee through the brocade of her gown and turned to her companion. "Goodness, Olive, how much he knows!... "

"But I don't know, dear lady. Do tell me."

"The family crest, have you seen it?"

Carelle admitted that he had not.

"Semper Excelsius. It means -"

"Always higher."

" - Why, yes! 'Ever Higher', we would say. Why, Bruno, you are well-informed."

He gave a light shrug as if to say it was no magic trick. "You see, there is a place in my country, it is called Leuven. You English would say, Louvain."

The brow furrowed across her forehead.

"There is a religious college there, very old." She sat back, frowning. What was this to do with them?

"I think you would say, a university. Over the door and again in the main hall, the motto inscribed there is 'Semper Excelsius'."

"Really?" She was almost imperceptibly interested. "How extraordinary..."

"A crest.... er, you would say 'coat of arms', I believe.... Almost a year ago, the German army came to Leuven. They burned the town, they murdered hundreds of men, women and children. They set fire to many wonderful old buildings, including the catholic unversity. Even the priests were killed."

"Oh my! How awful," conceded Lady Sophie.

"Oh dear," remarked Fairbrother, who hardly uttered a word in Lady Sophie's entourage, "I say, that's a bad show."

"Oh, aye!" exclaimed Judson. "Louvain. Ah remember readin' about that. It were in t'papers."

"Yes.... It was for a little while. I learned later of people who had suffered... Friends of mine."

Lady Sophie was more concerned that the atmosphere had turned a little chilly. "Olive, dear, where is my wrap?"

Carelle snapped his gaze away from where it had been transfixed. "Would you please excuse me, your ladyship?" He stood, smiled, placed his playing cards back on the table, gave a curt bow of the head and walked away, tapping his cane on the floor as he went.

"Extraordinary!" remarked Lady Sophie quietly.

"Remarkable man," suggested Judson to the Belgian's disappearing frame.

"An unusual man," offered Olive Devonshire cautiously.

"Hmmm," Lady Sophie deliberated. "He can certainly be odd at times." She turned away to watch the drinking game the younger men had started.

Delicately, Smith knocked on the door of Carelle's room.

"You alright, old man? Here - I brought you a whisky."

"Thank you. I prefer Cognac. But very kind."

"Louvain?"

Smith could see that a nerve had been touched. He had no wish to intrude on the man's privacy, only to acknowledge that some people cared.

"He was my uncle," said Carelle at length. "His son and his adopted son. I do not know the full story. They were taken out and shot. He was a professor of philosophy... A great danger to an invading army, don't you think?"

Smith allowed the gravity of his face to speak for him.

"Your country, Ulysses.... It has not been invaded. Not for a thousand years. People here.... Well, I should not expect them to know, should I?.... Where are you from, Ulysses?"

"What? - Originally? Liphook. Why?"

"Imagine if Liphook were seized and destroyed, people taken and murdered in hundreds. The town burned and looted. For five days that was Leuven. Think of it as Liphook.... It was as if Germany had to teach Belgium a lesson just for being there. Hundreds died. Ordinary people. My uncle and his boys. Each one of those people had their own story to tell. Now we shall never know, shall we?"

Smith decided to down the whisky himself. "So sorry to hear that, old man. It's every war's story."

"You know, Ulysses, your country's fighting men are brave, I'm sure they are. I only wish.... sometimes I feel that the further up the tree, the view becomes more and more distant from reality..... These noble people here.... it's no more than a game. Others fighting and dying, it is getting in the way of their pleasure. A bayonet in the stomach, a gun at the forehead..... You know, Ulysses.... I think that - what shall I call it? - that culture of looking at war as if it was a game of chess or something, I think these people have no understanding of invasion by a foreign army... That is not my idea of what people of position and power and wealth should be demonstrating. They are only concerned that what happens to others is an inconvenience. 'Bad show', they say.... 'Bad show'.... What does that mean, Ulysses?"

Smith looked at the floor and drew a long breath. "I think it means we take time to learn the lessons of history, Bruno."

"Lessons of history?... You think?... I do not think that. I think many do not want to know the lessons of history. It is not 'convenient', and always someone else's fault, so why should they care about history?"

"You're probably right, Bruno.... But I think it is going to be a long, terrible war, and I'm glad you are working for this country, my friend."

"Mm. But what will history tell of it? The bravery? The courage? Or the foolishness of pride and arrogance?"

"There will always be proud and arrogant men. I expect this war is no different."

"Until that foreign army invades your country. Kills your family. Rapes your wife, Ulysses. Destroys all you have. *Then* you will open your eyes."

"And then what?"

"Then you say - there should have been another way. Because we have learned nothing from history."

Before retiring to bed, Carelle felt the need of a stroll to clear his head. Descending the rear staircase and slipping through a back door, he was careful to be seen by one of the servants in case this man might be ready to lock up the house. The garden was warm, fragrant, still, and bathed in the most beautiful moonlight. Standing there taking in deep breaths was a tonic to the system after the stuffiness of the drawing room.

"Mister Carelle."

He turned, startled to have his lonely vigil observed. ".... Miss Miranda!"

"Such a lovely evening, is it not?... Do forgive me, I actually thought you were my uncle. Silly - because my uncle isn't here! .... By the way, may I ask you - well, we were talking at dinner, and someone asked the question as to whether you were married."

For the merest of moments, a vision of Lucie came into his brain: he dismissed it at once. "Married, dear lady? No. Not that I am aware of."

"Ah. It was just that - "

"A talking point at dinner. We are curious creatures, are we not? After all, there is only male and female in our species, so to other animals we must appear identical, and yet the single most vital thing we humans find to discuss is the nature of our differences. Oh, I mean no offence, young lady, but I always find it fascinating that so many are absorbed in the most mundane of things.... But, forgive me, it must seem rude of me. I was almost married..... once. I have no wife, put it that way. Does that answer your question, *mademoiselle?*"

"Oh, yes, monsieur. I shall inform my mother, she was very interested - Um, no, no - I mean she was curious."

"Ah! I believe that the curiosity of a woman rises in accord with her social position, does it not?... No disrespect."

"It was only...." She hesitated, indicating a reluctance to show more of her hand perhaps.

"Yes?"

"You see, you have no servants, monsieur.... It just struck us as unusual, that's all. A man of your position with no wife and no servants."

"Oh. You think that is important?"

"Important?.... Unusual, surely."

"You think I need servants?"

"Of course."

"Why? - Because I am overburdened by my wealth?"

"But, I mean - Your social position - "

" - Is not really relevant to my needs, is it?"

"But.... How do you manage without servants?"

"Oh.... I have two hands and two legs and a head that works provided it is oiled regularly with Cognac."

"Sir, you're mocking me!"

"Oh, my dear!..... I would never mock beauty, *mademoiselle.* But as to servants - you have a number, no doubt."

"They come and go. Only last week daddy fired his head butler."

"Why was that?"

"He was clumsy. He spilled a glass of sherry."

"He was fired.... for spilling a glass of sherry?"

"Of course."

"Ah... And will this person find other employment?"

She gave a light laugh. "I shouldn't think so. Rowlands was at least forty-five. Who's going to want him?"

Carelle found his mouth had opened but the words would not come out immediately. At length he asked, "And this man - Rowlands - how is he now to take care of himself?"

"Take care of himself? - Well, how should I know? It's not our concern, is it? He should learn to be less clumsy."

A little crestfallen, Carelle found the conversation lacked appeal.

"But surely, monsieur, in your own position.... I mean, you are such an erudite and sophisticated man."

".... Kind of you to say so. But, do not let appearances deceive you, my dear - erudition is not the exclusive property of those most socially and financially fortunate. At the risk of upsetting you, Miss Miranda, I must tell you I am from the most lowly of beginnings, and yet profoundly proud of that condition."

"You are outspoken, Monsieur. I like that."

"*Mademoiselle*, I am - "

"Would you be offended if I were to have myself seated beside you at dinner tomorrow? - Frankly, all the other men here are great bores. Even my brother. Well - especially my brother!"

Carelle paused, deciding not to rise to the bait. "Oh, I think you have the exaggeration of youth. I am sure they are not all bores as you say. But.... Of course. It would be my pleasure to remove you from the tedium of others... And bore you with mine."

"Tedium? Oh, no! You know, I am just so tired of being patronised as a woman that people think should simply wear fine dresses and appear at country balls on somebody's arm. I'm sure it would be much more fun doing reckless things."

"Reckless?... Spilling a glass of sherry, perhaps."

"Monsieur Carelle - now you are mocking me!"

"*Pas du tout*, dear lady. But do you mean reckless as - for example, going out into the world *without* wealth and privilege?"

"Um.... I wasn't thinking of that exactly."

"No.... Of course..... That would be foolish in the extreme, would it not? And as they say in my country as well as yours - *noblesse oblige*. Is that not so?"

* * * * *

324

THIRTY-THREE

For Carelle, the paper-chase was not a good idea.

It is one of those curious facts that whoever states, "I don't like to be the bearer of bad news", invariably is quite delighted to be the bearer of bad news. Oberon Scott-Chapelle was a good actor, at least: he never let his baby face slip whilst announcing at dinner there was to be a paper-chase and all the guests were *expected* to participate. This of course did not - as Lady Sophie was swift to point out - include the ladies. Ladies simply did not do that sort of thing.

Lacking the appropriate wardrobe, Carelle had to borrow a jumper and a pair of shorts. Fortunately, his steamer trunk included a pair of light boots that would suffice. It was an immense source of amusement to Oberon in particular to view the "troops" that morning - which luckily was clear with an absence of wind. At least Miranda - a year younger than her brother but a generation apart in terms of outlook - had entered into the spirit of the affair, she had decided that being a pretty lady should not disbar her and was determined to show the men a thing or two. Judging by the approving male glances, she did.

Of fifteen 'chasers', Carelle imagined he must be the eldest. He would - he made it plain - be taking the event "at a very slow canter", by which he meant a walk. Whilst minimal clothing drew attention to Oberon's physical condition, that did not in any way hamper his abilities as he set out with his wife Mildred at his side to uphold family honour. She trotted the first hundred yards before pulling aside, whilst his mother and father applauded from the sidelines as the chasers left the local village inn to follow the 'hare' laying down his paper trail ten minutes ahead.

The opportunity having been provided for discreet conversation, Grimshaw held back with Carelle so that they might exchange facts, citing their lack of the proper clothing as an excuse for a poor pace.

325

"Oh yes, no doubt of it. We thought he might be acting in a duplicitous fashion as much as five years ago," confided Grimshaw.

"Five years?" queried Carelle, surprised. "Why so long?"

"Tricky, these things. You give someone the freedom, or should I say, permission, to act as a spy, and you have to some extent to allow them to weave the web of their choice."

"I don't understand."

"MI5 approached him several years ago. He was not a baron then, but it was clear the old man was on his way out and Anthony had more or less assumed the title long before the last rites. Apart from that, it's not uncommon for people in diplomatic circles to have their political leanings exploited one way or the other."

"And what were Lord Semper's political leanings?"

"In mundane parlance? - Extreme..... And someone so far right is bound to give off the right kind of - should I say - signals to foreign powers."

"Germany, you mean."

"No.... though Germany might be a start."

"So what did he do?" Carelle was impatient to get to the point.

"My boss told me that you are a 'trusted' party, so I will tell you what I can. But I don't know everything."

"Then what did he do? Did he steal some papers? That is where my concerns are pointing."

"Papers?..... He had access to highly confidential matters. Foreign Office stuff. He was not involved directly with the military, if that's what you mean. "

Grimshaw indicated they should start running again, though it was not so easy to converse as they jogged.

"He was prominent in an affair between the Germans and the French. We - MI5 - thought he would be using his position to gain information for our people, but...... later, it was evident his activity was duplicitous."

"I do not understand - 'duplicitous'?"

"Trading information back the other way."

"With whom?"

"The French, the Russians, perhaps."

"The French?" The idea quite shocked Carelle. The French were allies! Though they say all is fair in love and war, and countries being diplomatically allied was no different to being 'in love' - it was usually a lottery over who cheats first.

"You must remember, sir, in any country there are factions who stand to gain from a war situation."

"Yes, I would agree."

"We have every reason to believe that Semper - himself, perhaps, but certainly the people he associated with - had something to gain by setting up Serbs against Austria. Viscount Grey had suspicions."

"You are puzzling me again, Mister Grimshaw. What is a viscount?"

"Sir Edward, then. He had his reservations about Anthony some time before he became Lord Semper."

"Really?..... But you mention the Serbs. You're not suggesting there was any involvement in the Serbian affair which sparked off this whole war? Surely not?"

"I'm not suggesting anything."

"But you are!"

"If there is no proof, Mister Carelle, a chap can suggest whatever he likes. There is no proof Semper had a connection to the Black Hand Serbs who assassinated the archduke, but it's an appealing idea."

"So you *are* suggesting it!"

"Simply stating the view you'd get from anyone at MI5 that international disputes begin because people ensure there's something to be gained. For those who are able to make war a profitable proposition....."

"'Profitable' in a material sense?"

"Material, yes, or political expediency."

"Like myself, for example. I deal in *material* things, after all - to my advantage, you could say."

"I did not include you, sir. We have a full knowledge of your situation."

Somewhat taken aback, Carelle reacted to that. "Do you?...... Do you?.... Indeed, perhaps you do."

"And so..... Lord Semper having a reputation as far-right, that would have an appeal for right-wing factions in other countries. MI5 thought - originally - that he could be useful in gathering information for Britain. As it turns out, he seems to have found it more profitable the other way around. Is that clearer?"

"Yes."

"Not all politicians and businessmen are patriotic to their own country, are they? If their interests lie elsewhere, they don't consider themselves unpatriotic - quite the reverse, in fact, they may consider themselves brave to fly in the face of opinion. Mister Carelle, we are men of the world. Do you consider that the leaders and crowned heads of Europe each put the needs of *their* country first? We don't believe that, do we?

Carelle did not demur for a moment. "We would have to be very naive, would we not? .... Though I am not sure if it helps me particularly. You think he was trading information with *all* of them?"

"Who knows? Certainly with France, we know that for a fact."

"How do you know that?"

"Because, sir, we employ more than one spy!"

"But France is an ally, surely!"

"Very much so. But how many shades of grey do you see in the French Tricolor? Just as with this country. Go to the visitors' gallery at the House and look down, do you see black and white or do you see shades of grey? Do you see altruistic patriots or those with self-serving interests?"

Carelle gave Grimshaw a searching look. He was certain Grimshaw would not have made *that* comment to his superiors.

"I take your point.... And you knew this about Semper for a long time?"

"A considerable time."

"But you didn't do anything. You didn't arrest him."

"We couldn't. We didn't have proof of the right sort. And the Americans wanted to catch their own traitors, and saw Semper as a useful pointer to *their* nest of spies, so they were keen for us to extend his leash. It takes time first of all to suspect that something is wrong, and more time to gather the information you need to substantiate your fears, and by that time, Europe was already locked into a war."

"So do you have enough proof now?"

"Not yet."

"Excuse me a moment, I am changing my socks!"

"Those foreign diplomats would merely deny the accusations and point to the fact Semper was the responsibility of the British government. You know the sort of thing - if you can't control your own wild cards, don't expect us to help you.... And lastly, Mister Carelle, there is the biggest stumbling block of all - the power of influential friends. People like Semper spend their time cultivating friends in very high places, I'm sure you know what I'm saying."

Carelle presented a grave nod of agreement. "Most of the worst scoundrels in history have had the ear of some king or other. But from information at MI5, you are saying it's possible Semper had a hand in events in Serbia - you are really suggesting that."

Grimshaw paused a moment, looked away and then looked back at him. "I trust you not to repeat this. I'm not 'suggesting' it - I believe it to be an unproven fact. But that is Arnold Grimshaw talking, not MI5. Semper had a relationship with two gentlemen of the Austrian court whom we know were instrumental in fostering a hard line against Serbia for the shootings there."

"..... 'Relationship'? Are you now telling me this was something more than diplomacy?"

"I'm not suggesting any deviant behaviour, only that these gentlemen acted to pressure Franz Joseph into the hard line he took over his nephew's assassination."

Carelle for a time digested these notions. "But what did he say to them? - 'It's alright, chaps, if you go ahead and take over Serbia, Britain will not stop you'?"

"..... In effect, yes."

"Good heavens! I thought I was making a joke! You mean, he would actually undermine the Foreign Secretary like that?"

"Of course not. The power of suggestion is often more effective than words on a paper. No, we can't prove any of that. We have no documents, no informers who will turn state's evidence - nothing."

"And this was Semper alone?"

"Who knows? He has other, erm... sympathisers. Some more extreme than him, I fancy."

"*More* extreme? You are joking! You mean, people in high places who might just say to the Kaiser, 'Come on, we won't stop you'.....?"

Grimshaw gave a kind of laugh down his nose. "Since you put it that way - quite possibly."

"Coniston, for instance?"

"Coniston? Oh no, not him, no. Look, if you were Semper, you would hardly surround yourself with men of like mind, would you?"

"Wouldn't I? ... No, I suppose not."

"Together, they would stick out like a sore thumb."

"..... And his family, what of them?"

"Not Lady Sophie. Miranda has her own agenda and Oberon's ambition would hardly outpace his wit."

"He has a strong position at the bank."

" - Which Semper makes use of. Yes, we know."

Further along, they passed underneath an arch of the viaduct and fell to rest on a rock which gave a splendid view of the arches as a train approached and dumped a cloud of bad-smelling vapour on them. They no longer spoke at a hushed level as they were quite alone in the moorland. Each took his water bottle and drank.

"You know, for a man who works for a society magazine, Mister Grimshaw, you know a great deal about politics. But what of Caldecot?"

"Caldecot? You probably know as much as we do. We left that to the Americans. We think Semper killed him, but there's never going to be any proof."

"Yes." Carelle's head dropped. "That is what my young friend believed. Now you say as much. But.... Is Semper the sort who would kill someone? On the face of it, I would not have said so."

"Nor I. Toffs don't usually do that sort of thing, do they? They get someone else to do it."

Carelle's head came back up. "Say that again!"

"What?.... Toffs don't do that sort of thing?"

"You said, they get someone else to do it." The frown turned into a wide-eyed smile from Carelle, who shouted, "*Imbecile!*" Upon which, he immediately turned to Grimshaw to apologise. "Not you, my friend, not you! I was addressing heaven. But of course! You are right. Of course!"

"What, sir?"

"All along, I have been thinking in straight lines. I did not connect the lines together. I should have seen..... John Cade."

"John Cade? - What of him?"

"You know this man?"

"Cade, yes. We know he's worked for Semper on and off. He's a shifty character that hangs around and makes trouble. Has a police record. There is a story - "

"A story?"

"I'm not sure I can tell you."

"Why not?"

"It was not thought important."

"What was not important?"

"All we know of Cade is that he's been in the background with Semper for a few years now. More or less since Semper's trip on the *Titanic*."

"Yes, yes."

"The idea was, Cade's mother was a servant in Semper's household - oh, a long time ago when he was plain Anthony Scott, with a couple of businesses in the Midlands."

"Go on."

"It's so long ago, not material to our investigations. Don't forget, it's only since Scott married Lady Chapelle and then his rise to parliament, etcetera.... It was only once he was a VIP active in diplomatic areas that he caught the attention of MI5."

Carelle became reflective. "It occurs to me, if the mother of John Cade was once employed by Semper, it's possible she may have been involved with him."

"It's possible, I suppose... If she were in that household."

331

"You have never investigated?"

"Why would we?"

"Cade is about - mmm, 30 years old, would you say?"

"Probably."

"So.... 1885..... Nine months earlier .... 1884."

"Nine months. Mister Carelle, that's a pretty explosive conclusion to make!"

"Where was Semper around 1884?"

"Scott..... I would have to find out. Don't know about the woman, though."

"Can you do that?"

"Yes. Shouldn't be difficult. But even if you're right, I can't see the connection would suggest Semper murdered Caldecot. "

"He didn't," Carelle told him, suddenly developing a broad grin. "Though he may as well have done."

"I fail to see a connection: what would that have to do with Cade suddenly coming on the scene after Semper went to New York on the *Titanic*?"

"Because Cade was on the *Titanic*."

"Cade was on the *Titanic*? Really? I didn't know that. Good grief!... I knew he'd been a seaman. I thought Cade came into the picture after *Titanic*."

"I imagine a lot of people didn't know that. Why would they, after all? He was not important. You said yourself - 'VIP'. Who cares about someone who is not a VIP?... Uh?...Who, apart from the shipping company, would have been looking for Cade's name on the crew list? Who would even bother to think of a connection? Ned Thornton told me Semper had got White Star to remove all trace of his name from the crew lists. What if they were instructed to remove Cade's name as well? Uh? It's only just occurred to me. Caldecot died in the sinking - who is going to investigate ideas that nobody even thought of?"

Grimshaw's countenance went through a number of contortions.

"I have only been with the department two years. But Mister Carelle, if what you're suggesting were true - You're saying Semper is

Cade's father. That's a strong assertion to make. And besides - father and son - so what? Where is the motive to kill someone?"

"I don't know. But blood is thicker than water..... It's only a possibility, Mister Grimshaw. "

"And also a possibility that we might be able get evidence out of Cade that implicated Semper."

"Can you check on Cade's mother?"

"Yes, when I return to London. Don't forget I also have an article to write for The Tatler."

"Do you know her name?"

"Not off-hand, no. An Irish name... Can't just remember."

"Please find out. It may not be important, but it may be. Perhaps not to you, but perhaps to my friend. Come, we must chase some papers!"

"It's all I ever do, Mister Carelle - chase papers!"

"Isn't that better than chasing aristocrats for a society journal like Tatler? I think you are going to become one of Mister Conan-Doyle's favourites, Mister Grimshaw."

Carelle was tired when they finally reached the end of the chase, directed by Coniston's ostler to another inn in another village. Tired but happy. The chase had been a success. Sir Wilfred Coniston attended to show his hand at downing the traditional stirrup cup, even though the eponymous cup with its fox's head ought to have been served before the event rather than after. Miranda Scott-Chapelle and Andrew Coniston had already been declared the victors, and their lordships applauded with suitable restraint.

* * * * *

THIRTY-FOUR

More rain had come in overnight. Who needed this? Along the entire front the ground was a series of swamps that sucked at boots and made disgusting noises. In the trenches, men stood in water a foot deep in places, those who could not climb onto something. From October a wet winter had started. As bad as this country had looked before, it now looked worse.

To describe the men as 'marching' was laughable. C company coped, that was about it. Coping was all a man could do, whilst still carrying the impedimenta a soldier had to carry. From the weight of his overcoat and the rucksack on his back, extra clothing and personal stuff, water in a canteen along with food rations, gas mask and cape in a bag, a rifle and bayonet and a hundred rounds of bullets in his webbing, down to the shovel many of them had to carry. This prodigious load tired a man after fifty yards, never mind the expectation of plodding several hundred yards to reach an enemy position, over horrible ground and under gunfire. To be first in the line of attack was a double imposition: those men not only faced the enemy first and were more likely to suffer for it, but they carried the full weight of kit so that the men behind did not need to carry so much – the generals had reasoned they could collect what they needed from the bodies of men who fell before them.

Sound military thinking of the time. Bob Street thought otherwise. "Why not," argued Bob, "have the men that go first stripped of food and kit, just guns and ammunition, give them a better chance to reach the Germans, a better chance to fight and to take attention off the lads coming up behind, who could carry more kit to give them once they'd taken the German trench?"

The four of them looked at each other.

"Ah'm gonna call you Professor," said Ned, who carried on stirring the dixie.

"Yer can't do that, professor!" said Parrock. "Them generals needs us to carry all that stuff over so's we can 'ave their spatchcock dinner cooked and ready for 'em when their chauffeurs bring 'em up."

"What the fuck we need poxy mules for anyway?" cried Happy John. "We're all just flippin' pack-'orses, aren't we?"

"Shit in it!" shouted Corporal Parrock. "Tell you what – when you fall over we'll send you to the horse hospital. 'Ow d'you fancy the knacker's yard?"

As if to shut him up, another shot rang out.

They passed mules stuck in mud, their handlers scratching their heads as the animals braced their front legs to heave their rears, the men straining to guard the machine guns or ammunition or whatever they bore. These were exhausted animals, it was frequently no use. In the end the men would uncouple the mule from its load and put a gun to the unfortunate animal's head. Ned pressed his eyelids down for a few moments as if that would obliterate the sound of those poor beasts being relieved of their burden. Someone else would come along and break up the mules' flesh for meat. The men passed by.

It was if anything slightly less upsetting than those poor devils of horses who had suffered caltrops into their hooves. First used centuries ago by the Chinese against Mongols, the spikes drove deep into raw flesh. Those cries were not something to be heard, men covered their ears and the agony was – again – only relieved by the mercy of the pistol. It was bad enough that they were dumb animals, and not men who could speak their agony. You did not look into the eyes of a horse about to be shot. They had heard the tale of the handler who had first shot the horse in his charge and then turned the gun on himself.

"Takes skill to handle horses." Taff was good at stating the obvious. "Our chaps worked with pit ponies down the mines in Wales. Some stayed with ponies when they got taken. I wouldn't wanna be a handler."

"Oh, I don't know," offered Wally, "You can ride 'em when you get tired. And if you sleep with 'em, they keep you warm provided you don't care how you stink."

"We all stink anyway," laughed Happy John.

"Maybe," countered Bob, "But you try pulling an ambulance or a big gun in this lot. It's murder."

"Let's give these buggers a hand," suggested Wally.

"No, don't!" cautioned Bob, "That's not a good idea if you don't know how to handle mules."

"But.... long as you keep out the way of those back legs?"

"You're wrong, Wally. Horses maybe, but mules will kick you in any direction. Just keep away."

"Chapter seven," said Ned.

"What?"

"It's chapter seven in yer Field Service Book, Bob – how to kill a horse. Yer never seen that?"

"Lovely," said Bob and strode on.

It was no more terrible than so much else that happened, and the worst of it was, they were becoming accustomed to it. Ever so slowly, the war was taking over their minds. The terror never diminished, yet it dulled with every new shelling, each new attack. There were few of those – attacks, but they filled every waking hour with dread of what might be.

"Give us a tune, Ned," said Duffers, but Ned could raise no enthusiasm for song. Not this time. He watched another officer lift a horse's forelock, place his pistol close to the skin and fire. *Five,* thought Ned, *that's five; and three yesterday.*

"'Ere," chirped up Happy John, "Talkin' about horses - Did you hear the one about the chap what came up big on the gee-gees?"

"Shit 'n'it!" said Parrock. Happy John carried on anyway.

"He goes to Rolls-Royce and says, 'Ere, I wanna buy a fuckin' motor car'. The lah-de-dah salesman says, 'Sir, we don't use that kind of language here', and the bloke says, 'I don't give a flyin' fuck what language yer use, I wanna buy a fuckin' car, mate'. So the salesman tells him again, 'Sir, if you insist on using language like that, I shall have to fetch my manager.' And the geezer says, 'Fetch the bugger, what the fuck do I care?' So the posh manager comes over and the bloke repeats that he wants to buy a Rolls-Royce. The manager looks down his nose at this scruffy individual, so the bloke says, 'Look, I just won ten thousand nicker on the gee-gees an' I wanna buy one of your cars to sit outside my mansion in Chelsea. Is that too hard to understand?'. The manager pauses a few seconds then points to the salesman and says to the geezer, 'Sir, is that fucking prick bothering you?'"

Happy John had his uses.

* * * * *

Pugh had been the first.

Poor, innocent Loos had been taking lives: they should not blame Loos, though that was how they felt at the time. Battle began there on a grand scale at the end of September and raged on in various stages. Two weeks in, the 12th were sent to the front quite late on and were engaged in attacking the quarries. Heavy bombardment from the British artillery had failed to weaken enemy positions as anticipated - those lofty expectations, they had heard it all before.

Ned had not been there with Pugh, he had his own problems. Breasting the wire, something silently took a bite out of his coat. He paid no attention at first, for he was terrified at the thought they might be heading toward gas, and the shovel at his back was a nuisance; he could crouch but found it trickier to maintain pace. As the man ahead of him slumped forward, face down into the sodden earth, Ned had to question why he quickly felt a searing sensation in his side, like a hot coal had lodged itself into him. It was, he decided later, Private Beckwith who had saved him, by taking the sniper's bullet straight through Beckwith's flesh and into Ned's side. It could have been the hot toasting fork from the fire at home: it stung, and then stung more. Putting his hand there, he felt fresh blood, then a sensation as if he had a "stitch", but in the wrong place. Ned extricated the shovel from his back and dropped onto all fours – *à quatre pattes*, how extraordinary that at this minute he should remember how Brigitte had teased him as they rolled about the grass that time! Then he felt suddenly weak and faint, as the masking adrenaline of the attack gave way to a realisation of pain.

337

It had been too clear a day, that was the trouble. Wet, but a clear sky apart from smoke plumes drifting across. Soldiers would blame anything. *Anything* was unlucky, if it tied in with going into battle.

Once he had been able to fall over, he had felt a rush of blood to the head, and a fearful mixing-up of all his senses. No gas came, thank heaven, for he began to feel a kind of paralysis that would hamper the fitting of a gas mask, and he gave up attempts to pull the field dressing from that awkward little pocket at the bottom of his jacket. Men coming back heard him groan and he was dragged by the arms until two men were able to lift him from the coal-spattered ground and return him to the trench, where he lay in a contorted heap for a while until being stretchered off to the Triage.

The field hospital was as much chaos as the battlefield. Many had been injured in the failed attack, efforts to prioritise their wounds by risk of mortality were arbitrary at best. Ned waited there just inside a tent flap for three hours; he watched the afternoon wear on into a dreary evening and felt cold before a male orderly found him an extra blanket, taking it off a corpse. They were into lamplight by the time his own wound was properly looked at. Not severe, he was told, just as before, he would be happy to know he should be out of action for perhaps two weeks. Ned was happy he was alive, at least. Then he gave in to the morphine and fell asleep on the stretcher.

Bert Parrock found him on a rickety bed in a tent, reached out and placed one of Ned's own cigarettes in his mouth.

"What's the time, Bert?"

"Seven. Butler brought your porridge and toast yet?"

Ned had slept well and the nurse had told him he was "doing fine", the pains would return as the morphine wore off but would ease later. He had no reason to disbelieve her, he only knew that it damn well hurt anyway and was bloody awkward to move with the skin pulling beneath the dressing.

"Thank the sarge," Parrock told him, "Meeker pulled you back." Ned merely opened his mouth, he would remember to thank the sergeant.

"What you got there, Bert?"

In his hands Parrock held a little rag bundle. "It's a doll," he said, looking down at it as he settled onto a wooden box. "Found it out there... lying in the dirt."

"Looks pretty hard done-by," offered Ned.

Bert smiled at the doll. "Some poor kid probably still crying about losing it..... Funny, really, just finding it there. What place has a kid's doll got here?"

"What place 'ave any of us 'ere?" suggested Ned, thoughtfully. Still, they were perhaps of similar minds. Children. It seemed absurd that there could ever have been children in this landscape. What place did any idea of family or children have here?

"You 'eard about Pugh?" said Parrock – it was hardly a question since he knew perfectly well Ned could not have known.

"Yes," said Parrock, lowering his eyes. He placed the doll almost reverently on the floor at his feet.

"Oh." Ned could only think how Pugh hardly ever stopped talking about his little boy, Jack. Now Pugh's wife would have to cope with the lad on her own. It was an awful thing to contemplate, and best not to.

"Beckwith?" queried Ned, having remembered most of what had happened.

Parrock gave a violent snort up his nose as if his moustache were irritating him and looked away.

"You don't want to know," he said.

Tired of the squashed-up cigarette, Bert took out his gold Princess Mary tobacco tin and proceeded to stuff his pipe and light up. In this war, one thanked heaven for just a couple of things, and tobacco was first on the list. A hot bath was really the ultimate, but one never came across one of those. Bert was looking down at his boots, which he then unlaced and changed over – in his haste to waken up, he had put them on the wrong feet before wrapping his puttees. Ned watched him struggling and grinned.

"Ain't got no Foxes any more and I just get confused," Bert explained.

As he watched, Ned began to laugh cautiously. Foxes puttees had indicators for left and right, but that did not excuse the mistake with his boots.

"Only got two minutes, Ned. You gonna be alright?"

"What happened?" asked Ned. Bert scratched at his crotch and pulled from a pocket a set of pliers that he had jammed into the wrong place.

"Dunno really. Walked a straight line, I expect," he said.

"Poor Pugh... Machine gun?" It was more supposition than question.

Bert blew a cloud of thick pipe smoke into the disinfectant air. "Didn't stand a chance. Here – and here." He pointed to his face and neck. You did not want to describe those injuries. Ned respected that and asked no more.

"Marshall's got a job on," said Bert reflectively.

"Oh?"

"Thirty-eight, Ned. Thirty-fuckin'-eight."

"What?" An admission of horror, it took time to sink in. "Who else?"

Bert mentally counted, puffing steadily. "Cartwright.... Henderson..... Macey..... Mostly A company.... That twat Hamilton.... He won't bore us all no more..... Poor bastard."

"Thirty-eight......" Ned recalled how Hamilton had always boasted what a marksman he was....

"Anything you want, Ned?"

Coming back to earth, Ned gave that a thought. "Missed me rum ration, Bert. No chance, is there?"

Bert shook his head. "How long they keeping yer?" He had already looked at the diagnosis sheet dangling from the bedhead and understood nothing.

"Dunno. It's not a Blighty wound, is it?"

"Don't knock it, mate: being here with a light wound might be a lot better than some of the poor sods we've seen going back with a Blighty wound."

He was right, of course.

"So.... They're not sending you to base, then?"

"For this? Not unless one o' these buggers coughin' 'is guts up 'ere gets me an infection."

"Speaking of infections," said Bert, "Next time your nurse comes round, tell her to change your water bowl."

"She did, didn't she?"

"Not unless this frog's jumped in since then." He lifted the bowl up, grabbed the slippery frog in his hand and tossed the water onto the floor, then shrugged. "I mean, honestly - what the fuck are these nurses here for? Ey? Bet they don't even give a bloke a decent gander at their tits - most of the blokes in 'ere don't want medicine, they just want a good pullin' off and an eyeful of what they keep under their skirts!... Really, Ned, *what is* the world coming to?!!"

Ned only grinned, more to himself. His friend was not usually one for irony.

"I tell yer, mate," concluded Bert, "there's no charity left in the world... Anything else yer want?" The frog hopped away under the bed.

"Ah could do with a good piss."

"Yair.... I can do that for yer. I can reach that bucket from here."

These men!

When Bert had left, Ned found himself choking back a number of emotions. More than anything, the men kept you alive, they kept you from going insane. He loved these men, they were closer to him now than anyone in the world. Almost.

But 'Blind' Pugh was gone. Their young mascot was gone. Left alone to his thoughts, Ned remembered how Pugh had been the 'ugly duckling' who had never found his swan feathers. Life was not fair. Pugh was the most harmless of men who had simply wanted to belong. As with all these men, they had known each other mere months, yet this was family.

Being alone with one's thoughts for long was a bad thing. Only the nurse noticed the melancholy in his face as he sat so still: she simply forced a smile, dabbed his face with the hem of her apron and carried on to the next bed.

* * * * *

They did send Ned further back, though. Motor-driven ambulances came to the Triage, though such grand transport was denied Ned. Instead, he was led to a stretcher inexpertly lashed to four bicycles, one of which had a strange two-stroke motor attached to a rear wheel with a cylindrical fuel tank above it that looked more perilous than any bomb. Dubious, Ned questioned the orderlies as he was clumsily placed aboard and tied down.

"Be thankful, lad," said the first rider, "An ambulance is a big target."

As the rickety contraption *phut-phut-phut*ted Ned precariously along behind, the ambulance bounced perhaps ten of them along the track to a near village, whose name nobody knew any more as there was really nothing left of the village except for a few chimney stacks and a silage pit that stank. Along with a few houses now occupied by the military, there were tin huts there that cowered in the shelter of several large Red Cross flags. The huts formed a V.A.D. hospital, with proper beds and nurses who looked like they had only recently arrived, still with their starched aprons and collars and white bucket caps that almost covered their eyes – perhaps deliberately. From the next bed, the soldier told Ned of a man with a head injury who, the day before, caught one of these nurses off-guard, reached out from his bed and lifted her skirt. She reacted by dropping her medicines tray and slapping him across the face. The man had slumped back against his pillow and begun to cry. He cried not from the pain.

Might Gitta be here? – What a wild, stupid thought! He soon dismissed it. Why on earth might she be here, scores of miles from where she most probably was? Yet the flavour of the idea hung around in his head. It was so long since he had seen her face, he struggled now to construct a mental vision. The remarkable thing was that it did not bother him quite enough, and he lay thinking about that. Just what did he want any more? Months without any word at all only prompted the obvious - she no longer cared. And pregnant. If she had still cared...... The question he put to himself was also the obvious one - how much did *he* care?

There was a day when the sun shone brightly. Able to move freely around the encampment, Ned put a hand against his side as he walked stiffly to the perimeter where flattened earth simply gave way to grassland, where clumps of trees intruded and fluttered their last depleted leaves in a gentle breeze. For the time of year, winter did not feel to be in full control, though he was well wrapped up against any cold. The flowers had gone, of course: perhaps they had been like the little blue and purple and white flowers in the grasses that encroached on the outskirts of Le Havre where he had walked and sat with Brigitte, and they had run in the damp grass of an early summer, ignorant of the calamity about to engulf Europe. In a hollow and against a willow tree, its huge shock of branches hiding them from view, they had kissed and fondled and made love and knew of nothing else but each other. He could relive that overwhelming sense of vitality as he pushed into her and knew nothing but her brittle voice urging him on - "*Oui,* Ned, *gib mir*!" That exciting confusion of raw language which had heightened his passion.

There had been long grasses of pale purple, so many plants whose names were unknown to a boy brought up in a northern England industrial town and made to marvel at the beauty of the Normandy countryside and those coastal buttresses so reminiscent of the South of England.

Now, here in some field in the Nord-Pas-de-Calais, as he edged slowly beyond the boundaries, he brought it all to mind, Brigitte and the countryside of Normandy: as fresh as yesterday, even to the scented air, that scent of land and stillness and warmth, and the butterflies and dragonflies – large, beautiful ones with bright blue bodies - dipping and probing around them and alighting with amazing deftness on the tips of the tallest grass stalks. It had been as if he had noticed nature for only the very first time. There too was a memory of that July Sunday in 1914 when they had ignored the storms of meteorological and political climates to enjoy a music recital, provided free in the town, when Ned and Otto had accompanied the two girls and Monsieur Forget, to sit in the untypical sunshine listening to musicians warming hearts with a variety of classical and contemporary compositions. Brigitte and Renata, he remembered, had applauded that solo pianist for giving them the Liszt *Liebeslied* and Monsieur Debussy's *Arabesque* and other diversions. Otto had been bored. M. Forget fell asleep. Ned had to hold the girls' parasols whilst they got to their feet to clap. How lovely they had looked that day.

Would he ever make love again? He turned his mind outward, not wishing to contemplate such matters as were now far too distant beyond the sound of guns and the smell of war. Brigitte and Renata - they were both out of reach, both too far away. It might almost have been that they never existed.

He only barely heard the woman call out. Part of his daydream, perhaps. No, she called again, not loud but sufficient to catch his attention. What had she said? – He had missed it.

"*Quoi?*" Ned called back.

"You are French?" the woman asked.

No, Ned told her in French, but he could speak the language.

"Ah! But you speak very well, sir. I am surprised. So many of your comrades......" She shook her head and gave a dismissive grimace to match the movement of her hands.

The woman was probably in her late-twenties, Ned considered. Without any doubt a prostitute: not that it bothered him in the least. But her manner of dress, whilst desaturated in comparison with the Armentières ladies that he had encountered, informed such a view. And those ladies had an off-putting reputation – "inky, pinky, parlez-vous...." Yes, all the British soldiers knew what happened when *'the German officers crossed the line'*. The verse struck entirely the wrong chords in him.

She was standing in the shade of an oak tree, simply standing there, as if calmly waiting to serve at a table. Behind her she had placed a thick rug on the ground – *heaven knows how far she has carried that thing!* Unless of course she had obtained a lift from one of the military transports.

It took him some moments to gather himself: she had, in a sense, interrupted his morning, broken into the channel of his thoughts.

"You are a long way from the town, mam'selle," he suggested.

"Well." She threw away a word that said absolutely nothing and absolutely everything.

"At least it's a nice day," he offered.

She only shrugged. "How did you learn to speak French?"

"I worked on French ships. And I have a French girlfriend."

"Ah! A girlfriend. She's pretty?"

"Aren't all French girls pretty?"

"You are a diplomat! You should take the place of Poincaré – it could not be worse for the Third Republic."

She laughed, and he laughed too, to be polite. She had a tooth missing in the upper centre.

"Oh, I would not want to be in his shoes," he said.

"You want some business?"

Prostitutes were nothing if not matter-of-fact. It was purely business, after all, she might have been selling cheese – you sniff it, you take it, you leave it. The woman was not unpleasant to look at, but meaningless fornication was not a companion to his mood at this time. *How desperate must she be*, he wondered, *to come out to the hospital?* And on a morning.

He made an excuse – his wounds. She nodded but was clearly unconvinced.

"No?.... Your girlfriend, she must be good." With a gesture, she pointed to his trousers. "Jig-jig. I can do better. But perhaps you are in love."

He thought about that. "Perhaps I am."

"You don't know? *Zut!* You men are stupid!"

"Yes. I think we are."

"What is she called, this girlfriend?"

The woman was close to him now, her perfume was pungent and cheap.

"Renata."

"Renata? It's a German name!"

"A German name.... yes. Well... German - French, it's no matter."

"No, it doesn't matter. I do not mind Germans. They killed many people but nobody I know. They make good business for me. Bring all you nice young men here. If you object to me not minding Germans, you can go to hell, I don't care."

Ned gave that a thought but further comment was redundant.

He appeared to her to be losing any interest he might at first have had. "You did not ask me how much?" she said, as if it were a demand. "And look, I am clean. Wash every day." She flounced the linen of her dress as if to prove it.

Declining this sort of business transaction with dignity was not so easy. "I tell you what," said Ned, "I have no money on me. I will go back, and I will bring you two francs."

"You want fuck?"

"No.... But I will give you two francs. It's all I have here."

"Two francs?" The woman spat on the floor. "For what?"

"No, no – I will *give* you that. Just give it to you."

"Englishman... Are you a little boy? For two francs you might just lick my tits! I pull cock really good for twenty. But two francs – listen, I'm a great fuck! Come have a look."

"I.... No, I can't. My wounds.... Thank you."

What the hell are you thanking her for, Ned? The absurdity of his etiquette brought a smile to his face, which the woman did not understand. Now she looked sideways at him distrustfully, perhaps he had insulted her. There was no honour in this - a trade is a trade, why should she bother?

He decided he should move on, and with a shake of the head, he did so. Off to one side, he glimpsed one of the male orderlies waving at him from the perimeter, so he picked his way back through the damp, dying grasses to hear what the orderly had to say.

"Weren't you warned about them?" asked the orderly, giving out a broad grin from behind his spectacles.

"No."

"There's two of 'em. Come out here regular. See that old hut over there?" Ned could see it now, hidden in the trees more than a hundred yards away. "There's a mattress in there. They take turns. And while you're shagging the one, the other sneaks in and takes everything you've got of value. Know what I mean?"

Yes, he could understand that now.

"Lean pickings, ey? From a bunch of wounded blokes. Wouldn't never fancy it myself," said the orderly. "Imagine that mattress, eh? Probably crawlin' with nasties. Chuck up some too with all that piss and bejizzle! Ey?"

"Expect so."

"A bloke'd have to be really, really hard up to fancy some o' that cunt, wouldn't he? ......Might be better off with that rug, ey, lad? I think that's just for quick gobbles and short time. Maybe if some of these lads 'ere ain't got long to live..... know what I mean? Just imagine, coughing yer last guts up and this hag here frantically suckin' you off as you croak!" He laughed loudly. "Cor, the stink o' that mattress, eh?..... 'Ere, I'm laughin' now, but I'll tell you no lie, that's a fact - a bloke died out there a couple of months ago. Yeh. Straight up. Another chap found 'is body. Them women had given him a good time and he must have croaked on it. Too weak, see. They just dumped his body by the path. Shell wound in his chest. Poor bastard. Left it. No names, no pack drill."

"Really?"

"Oh yeah. He had no pants on. His dick was covered in spunk and muck, know what I'm saying? And that hag there was lining up the next bloke! What a business, eh!"

The orderly had conjured up his own mental imagery and gave in to the complete absurdity of it, laughing convulsively and slapping his thigh.

Ned decided the orderly was in a reality of his own, he found it all rather surreal. Perhaps, though, it was in fact one of the least absurd things about this war, that men could laugh at the most horrific and bizarre situations, imaginary or otherwise. He thought about that rug, it was almost threadbare. Maybe business had been good.

347

"Still..... You 'ave to admire 'em, aintcha? Enterprising ladies. Ha! There's always someone profits from a war, ey? And why not, I say....."

Enterprising. Ned's thoughts passed to Carelle, what he had said about getting into the machinery business. But Carelle was not in it for money, he intended his wealth for causes he believed in: if this war had to be fought, it had to be fought with the best equipment and hopefully the best intentions. And a hope you were on the winning side – God's side... 'Gott mit Uns.'

Leaving the orderly, Ned was pondering his reply to that woman. How, instinctively, he had given her Renata's name. It had been a surprise, just declaring it like that. Was it time he told himself where his heart was? Was Gitta, then, a one-time thing? An affair he had passed through? Gitta's light had shone brilliantly, he had been consumed by it, whereas now – in this colder light – what had been his first reaction? - To give Reina's name. So what did he feel about Gitta - truly? And Reina, how did she feel about him?

He could find out only one way. It was time, wasn't it? It was time for him to place his feet firmly in the earth and end this nonsense of delusion with which he had dallied far too long. From so long ago those words came to him: *find your truth, Ned.*

Yet, when it came to it, his letters failed to deliver that commitment. Too much still hung in the air. He had not heard from Gitta, and might only know what he really felt once he saw her again. And Otto - never could he let Otto down. He wished to insult no-one, and anyway, Renata was a wife, how could he ignore that? Was Reina his heart's desire? Choice was not his prerogative, after all. Frustrated in his vacillating to the bitter end, Ned could not write the letter.

It was – after all was said and done – perhaps not that time. The war came first. *Let the war have its way, and then we shall see.*

* * * * *

THIRTY-FIVE

"We've been lucky so far," Bob had said, which raised quite a few eyebrows.

Lucky..... *Yes*, thought Ned, *Perhaps we have been lucky, seen from a certain perspective.*

They had been lucky at Ypres, the action had been largely over by the time the 12th arrived, fresh and green back then at the end of April, 1915. Crack Canadian troops had countered German attacks and ground was re-taken, though no-one really knew whether counter-offensive tactics were working, and there was soon talk their general would be replaced. Billeted well to the rear, C company had been stood down whilst the main force regrouped and waited for General Smith to formulate his counter-attack.

They had heard of gas attacks even before Ypres, the Germans had just launched a chlorine gas attack on French positions there. That news had been, if anything could be, more frightening than the thunder of the guns. The big guns - terrible weapons that they were - were not new. Tear gas was not new, the French had used it early in the war. Chlorine - no-one had heard of that before. What could that do? Choke you to death? Was that a fair alternative to being shelled?

But C company got the shelling. In a bombardment, you crouched in the deepest hole, or prayed non-stop, or you might play cards, or talked as much as you could, or simply sat there clinging to your rifle, letting your thoughts drive you insane. Or wet yourself. Conversation was difficult, but without it a man might go mad. But they had been lucky so far here at Loos.

By the end of October, they had been in 'the khazi' for some days. It was an apt term for a shelter, because it stank worse than most dugouts, and the word 'Khazi' soon replaced the words on the makeshift signboard at the entrance, which had been "Members Wives Only", until some humourless officer had had the wording removed.

While a barrage was on, there was nowhere to go to relieve yourself unless you soiled a billy can. A hole at one corner was the best they could do. The chamber was about 12ft by 10, and men stooped the whole time. Constructed around an upright railway sleeper with numerous bits of wood bashed into the sides and ceiling, it was shored up to resist shelling other than a direct hit, being submerged and accessed by a shaft of six rough steps. It had been dug into the muddy earth of a field and not in amongst the slag deposits of the area, so its structural integrity seemed promising.

There would have been thousands of 'khazis' all along the front. At various times, as many as twenty men crowded in and clung to the hope they would be safe. The air was acrid, full of noxious odours that you got used to, and if the makeshift bellows pumping air were put out of action they would struggle to breathe. Pumping would stop anyway at the first cry of "Gas! Gas!", when candles and Davy lamps would be snuffed to save air, and they would have no light once the flap was closed. In a sense, it was safe, but in another sense, it was a death chamber. Below ground, gas was a major risk, but in this war everything was a risk.

"Poxy mole, that's all I am," moaned Happy John.

"Shit in it!" said Corporal Parrock. He was thinking about that cup of hot tea he hadn't had for nearly three days, and trying to forget his itchy clothes.

"Pray for sunshine," said Parrock.

"Why, Corp? We're not going on parade, are we?"

"Because Jesus wants me for a fuckin' sunbeam," mocked Parrock. "You seen that board covering the entrance? When rain really comes, what protection is that? One surge down the trench, the mud gives way, the board goes, and we start doing duck impressions."

Marching past a dressing station, they had seen and heard the terrible effects of gas. A line of men waited mostly in silence, heads and eyes bandaged and each holding on to the man in front as they could not see. To lose one's sight was an awful thing to contemplate.   It was quite enough to make every man vow always to have his gas mask in the peak of readiness.

Only after persistence did they find out what the gas did to its victims. Chlorine brought on congestion in the lungs that, in a short while, "drowned" the sufferer.

Happy John remained quiet.   This was no honourable battle-charge of a war. There was nothing funny in any of this.

1915 had been a mess and little of it made sense, but they were learning, they told themselves.

It had taken Ned a long time to recover from that first sight months ago of the soldier being blasted into the air before him.

"He blew up, Sarge....... He blew up!"

Partington had dealt with it the best way he knew, by slapping Ned and forcing him to crouch down into a ball as the shells came in overhead. He probably saved Ned's life.

All that pre-war fervour had never envisaged this.   The moving-picture houses had shown just how easy it was to kill someone without the least drop of blood or mangled flesh in sight.   Not unpleasant at all. Death was easy - it happened to the "bad guys".

Instead, they had to get used to this frightening world of bombs and howitzers and machine guns and obvious, alarming mortality. Strange new privations, washing and shaving with almost no clean water, the most basic equipment for eating, sleeping, defecating and keeping dry, clothes that stank and crawly things they would not tolerate in their parlours.   Above all, a lack of those essential freedoms taken for granted: to walk away, to be free to move as they wished, and to be comforted by wives and mothers and sweethearts.

At least they were free to sing, they cherished that.   From the front-most trenches came the loudest songs, all the popular music hall ditties of the day and going back twenty years. Even Bob Street sang along with "Goodbye My Blue Bell" as he had learned it so well during the Boer War.   How strange, though, to hear at times the Germans singing in their own trenches, how bizarre was that? Even more bizarre was the familiarity of some of those songs.

"Did they pinch them songs from us?" mused Bert, stroking his fresh beard,. "Thieving bastards!"

"And we pinched 'em back again," suggested Bob.

"Aw, Bob Street! You an' yer ruddy education - you just love to spoil everything, don't yer?"

An Englishman could not think of Germans as human: to give credence to that thought could be one's own destruction. Do as the CSM tells you - screw those Ten Commandments! - he's not your brother, he's the Hun! Hate him, kill him - wipe them off the face of the Earth! It was all the reason a British soldier might need. Last Christmas Day when British and German soldiers met together, that was a serious error: the generals would ensure that never happened again.

As a boy, Ned had read of wars, or the French Revolution, when Madame Guillotine parted heads from bodies. To a boy, an abstract thing. Was death instant or for how long did it hurt? To the young Ned, it was far away and once upon a time, that was all. Facing the reality was another matter. Men were not to be considered with the detachment of Legallois as an experiment in the conscious nature of the severed head. Dignity and compassion, where were they? It was for every soldier to deal with, each in his way.

Ned would settle for a Viking's end - dying with weapon in hand, challenging his enemy. In hand-to-hand combat with a young German, perhaps, with a bayonet or the blast of a rifle. But up to that point, he had not had proper sight of a single German soldier, no more than faint bobbing pointy helmets glimpsed from afar. Nor did he wish to if – as he imagined – it might by some wild chance be Otto coming at him with fiercely flashing eyes and a bayonet in hand. Time and again, he tried to wipe any vision of Otto from his brain. It proved impossible.

* * * * *

Gas.

At Loos in late September, the gas came. They had been relieved, returned to the rear for two days, with decent food and a chance to sleep, but brought up again after one day to a forward trench that faced an elevated German position some four hundred yards away. The coming of gas was akin to one of the seven plagues of Egypt: stealthy, silent and almost unseen.

There had been artillery shells falling somewhere. Then a whistle, and a cry went up - "Gas! Gas!"

The word froze all the senses. More whistles set soldiers scrambling for gas packs. There was at once a temptation to break and run, but where to? Running along trenches not only risked being shot by an officer as deserting a post, but would create a jam with other soldiers doing the same, and you might just be running directly into the gas anyway. Bunkers were out of bounds as gas would settle there.

First to react was Sergeant Partington: ever-reliable Partington, the consummate soldier. In seconds, he had fitted his mask and was shouting through it to the others to do the same. Quickly, quickly!

Like most of them, Ned was all thumbs, despite the training. The mask itself was a cumbrous affair of khaki-coloured heavy linen, a hood which required the wearer first to unbutton his collar to tuck the thing in. Jamming it over the head, the soldier breathed in through a filter and out through a mouthpiece which garbled speech. Once on, goggles had to be aligned, though it was impossible to see anyway! Their training had prompted jokes - they were visitors from the Moon - but they made no joke that day. Ned got his mask on, tugging it so that it tore at his hair and felt as tight as possible. Not comfortable but if it was painfully fitted one imagined it was secure.

They stood there, trying to look at other Moon creatures, almost choking anyway at the thought of what might be heading for them. The impregnated fabric was bad enough, an unforgettable flannel smell, and the act of breathing was laboured, but the notion of gas beyond the thin shell was truly terrifying.

"Stand up! Up! On your fuckin' toes! Up!"

Peering about him, Ned felt like that Moon creature. He could see little - a blur of strangely-clad statues, comical but unreal. In a lunatic thought, he wanted his camera to hand. They all knew he had the camera and no-one would say anything. So far he had taken two photos only: Renata would not have been impressed. Some men carried cameras that would fit into a pocket: his box Kodak was much too big for discretion.

From above the trench wall, yellow-green wisps of vapour began to waft and dip into the trench. Men stood, rivetted in position as thin, sinister mists approached them — they saw little but knew it had to be there. Sergeant Partington passed out boards to three or four men; as instructed they wafted the boards in an awkward action to usher the gas back up the wall, to the front or to the rear, anywhere to lift the gas out of there. Men used unintelligible words and hand signals. Other sounds came, men who perhaps had not fitted the mask in time or not fitted them properly. Soon the voices were screams. Wounded men sat up, crying out to be lifted up. To hear men screaming like children was an awful thing.... An awful thing.

Ned did his best to contract every single piece of clothing he had about him. "Gas! Gas!" It paralysed him, seized every muscle, every nerve tensed to breaking point. He was back in the lifeboat, staring through a dazed vision of *Titanic* and completely frozen in time. He wished only to be somehow sealed within his clothing and mask, fearing that even an opening in his collar would suffice to allow poison to attack him. Would it invade the ears, or stick to flesh or hair? He stood on his toes for as long as he could and counted to himself - to one hundred, slowly. Then again. Close the eyes and count. The only sound in all the world - the sound of one's own thought. And the worst of it all — the imagination.

They longed to trade this position for an enemy they could see, each wanting that harbinger of death to have human form, a German soldier to retaliate against. Not .... this horror against which they knew no means to fight. The troop remained rooted to the spot, sightless, hardly daring to breathe, the glass lenses of the

354

masks fogged and useless.   If German troops should storm their position now......

By and by - a seemingly endless passage of time - they heard the all-clear, heard whistles and the positive shouts of those who dared open their throats. It was a full minute before Ned dared take off his mask, and only then at a slap on the arm and a 'thumbs-up' from Duffers.   Gingerly removing the mask, he took a breath. He had returned to this planet!

Despite barely moving, they were exhausted. They had survived a gas attack. Screams and coughs and retching sounds from not far away told them some would not, and some men were just sick anyway.   Ned saw Bob retching and worried, but it was just the stress. Yes, Bob too. Yet they would learn from this. They would learn in particular that their linen masks - a product of intelligent military thinking - were no more effective than a handkerchief soaked in urine. The only problem with that idea was, as Happy John pointed out, when you heard that gas was coming, the last thing you could muster was a good stream of piss into a handkerchief! "What stupid wanker came up with that idea?"

"Stand by!"   Lieutenant Donovan alerted them.   "Stand by for enemy attack!"

They stood by. An attack never came. The battlefield in fact was strangely quiet and still, as cold as the dirt they stood in. It was as if the gas had tranquillised everything and neutralised all the weapons.

"Stand down!" came after fifteen minutes.

The men of C company looked at each other with the kind of relief that needed no words to qualify it; each nodded reassurance to his comrades. Ned moved, then stopped. His pants were cold: they were cold because they were wet. If anyone noticed, they made no remark, and Ned did not feel ashamed, only annoyed it was not the first time and disappointed that he was not yet a soldier.

Shortly, Parrock passed him and noted, "It's good for the crabs, Ned – drown the little bastards!"

Ned called back, "Can ah put a chit in for a new pair o' bollocks?" He would put lotion on that when they returned to camp, whenever that might be.

"You know," mused Taff Morgan, "I never knew what really useful stuff piss is. Just think what we've learned, gents: we piss on our boots to make 'em easier to wear, we piss on a machine gun to cool it down when it jams, we piss in our pants to kill the ruddy crabs, and now we know we can piss on a hanky to use as a gas mask! About the only thing we've not been told to do yet is drink the bloody stuff. An' after Happy John's excuse for tea, I'm not sure I wouldn't prefer my own widdle. Tell you what, I've got a proper respect for piss. Think I'll bottle it and sell it. Or we can just squirt the stuff on the Germans - piss *them* off!"

For a Welshman who talked rubbish, Taff Morgan made sense at times!

They had come through their first gas attack. It would not be their last.

They were worn out, having been stood to arms at 0700. More than anything, it was the tension of waiting that exhausted soldiers. Waiting, feeding off their fears. Shivering in a trench with the cold, the mud, and mostly cold food. Above all, the wet. No soldier could maintain his spirits with wet feet, this was the hardest fight. Dry socks inside dry boots, that was the prayer. Soldiers dreamed of that more than they dreamed of sliding into bed beside a warm woman. Duffers had lost a coat to the barbed wire. He would go to the field hospital and get another a dying man no longer needed.

The mark of the soldier was how he stood up against the misery, tedium and fear. It was not what they had signed up for. Yet, sign up, they had, and they saw it as their duty to make a good fist of it. It ran counter to all instincts, yet each would say that it was their duty, above all. Duty - a word stronger than any chains.

Thank heaven for Happy John Barraclough! However low they might all be feeling, Happy John was invariably the first to lift his spirits - and the first to complain at the least little thing. "There's always a bright side, fellers."

The men only looked at him and waited.

"Think of it this way. You get caught in a barrage, you get yer poxy leg blasted off. All of a sudden, you got a pair of boots you can sell for ten bob!"

Later that evening, they boiled up tea and opened their rations. They had regained something of their appetites, albeit the biscuits were now too soggy after soaking most of the day. If they had remembered their spare socks, they rubbed down and changed them. At least it was not raining.

Led by a muzzled torch, Sergeant Meeker came along the trench and spoke to Sergeant Partington. Ned saw Partington's face change. Meeker only clapped him on the shoulder and went on his way down the trench.

Ducking his head inside the funk hole where they boiled up the kettle, Partington lit a cigarette, covering the flame carefully. He sat for some little time on the broken end of a wooden wall before standing up and beckoning those that were at hand to listen to him - Ned, Duffers, Happy John, Wally Myers, Frank Philips, Tommy Tarmey and Albert Morgan.

"That gas attack," sighed Partington slowly. "It was ours."

He gave them time to take that in. "Somebody cocked up. Got the wind direction wrong. Yair."

It was a sort of statement that questioned if he should say more. He did anyway. "They were our gas canisters. Fuckin' idiots just aren't used to using the stuff ..... Tough break, lads...... for them that got caught."

"Many, sarge?"

"Five or six, Sergeant Meeker told me."

"Fuck!" said Happy John quietly.

"Yup!" was all Partington could say through taut lips. He breathed a harsh breath and went away to check the sentries. They knew his sigh was to cover his real feelings. Inside, Fred Partington was livid.

* * * * *

Becoming a soldier would not come easy. Clearly, Ned was not what he had thought he was. Very probably, each man there was thinking much the same.

Whatever else, a soldier in battle was there to blindly obey the orders of senior officers who in turn blindly obeyed what orders they were given by more senior officers. None of whom, in actuality, knew the effect of what they were doing. It was simply, "The Plan". The generals had devised The Plan, a blueprint for the actions of perhaps a hundred thousand men, but as to the informed and sensible nature of that plan...... You may as well have tossed dice! Plans needed continual intelligence to guide the operator to alter The Plan to reflect fresh information which would influence the outcome. Rigid adherence to a Plan that had been nullified by new circumstances was utter stupidity and, by any other name, a death warrant. In practice, however, once committed, The Plan was not adjusted: it was to be seen through, verbatim, and that was no more than the blind leading the blind. It became clear to see that the military strategy of the entire Western Front came down to nothing more than the vagaries of the brain of one man.

Inevitable, then, that soldiers under siege "went mad", developed "the shakes", tried to desert or became so taciturn as to wish only to die. None of these conditions was understood, none was accepted as any kind of excuse, and none was likely to gain the unfortunate individual any recognition except that of cowardice, subject to court martial and summary execution at the will of the commander-in-chief.

Men had volunteered to fight for their country: ordinary men, good men, yet their country would punish and even execute them rather than accept any notion that its leaders got things wrong or failed to understand the nature of the war they were fighting. Or that they pushed men beyond all reasonable limits. High-ranked commanders did not understand because they could not: like noblemen born to riches, doomed never to know the debility that is poverty, the burden of not facing death robbed the generals of any such comprehension. They had faced it themselves in a bygone time, some different world..... So they knew it all..... What they had endured, others could endure.....

Life at The Front had to continue.

Attacks were infrequent and few Germans ever advanced much more than half-way toward them either, but the mark of a man was whether he could force his legs up that ladder and over the top of the trench, for the officer was there as much to shoot anyone who did not as he was to encourage them forward once out there.

Mostly you kept your head down and listened for tell-tale sounds from the other side. Shelling was blatant and mortars gave themselves away. "Whizz-bangs" arrived swiftly, exploding in the air: their name was a stroke of onomatopoeic genius for that was precisely what they did. Later came the "minnies" - heavy mortars. Men got used to those too, they learned to dive for cover the second a distant thump from the German side raised the signal.

Luck.... So far, it had been with them, Bob was right.

There was luck, and there was care. If you took care, you might sidestep the luck, until it ran out. A man might play his luck like a pack of cards. But once an offensive started, and you ran out across that well-termed 'no-man's-land', you could throw the deck of cards away, for the machine gun was waiting.

Behind the front line, there was relief. They could wash and partake of decent food, perhaps even meat though more likely a stew with vegetables. A pudding to follow, stodgy suet though it may have been. It was still a feast compared with the stagnant, tasteless diet of tinned beef they got in the trenches and the interminable supply of cardboard biscuits that nearly broke the teeth until they had been softened. A chance to rest, to read letters, 'La Vie Parisienne', even descend on the local town and get drunk. After that folly of the gas, the men of 12 battalion needed to get drunk more than anything else.

And in this fashion they trudged a path toward 1916.

* * * * *

THIRTY-SIX

'Dear Ned,

Ven. 17 Decembre 1915

I read "between the lines" of the letters you send. There is much you cannot say, I know this.

We found Ellen McKitteredge, the mother of John Cade. A pleasant cottage outside Tunbridge Wells. When I arrived at the door there was no-one at home. I went to the local post office - I have always found that ladies who staff post offices anywhere are pleased to have their tongues made a little loose! No money changes hands, it is wonderful! This lady wanted to know who I was, I mentioned a few names. It is like turning a key in a lock. She said cheques arrive. An envelope had once been opened by accident, inside was a cheque for thirty pounds. Ned, the cheques are from Brantcliffe Bank. I laughed out loud! Always the same size and shape of envelope, several times a year. She was sure each contained a cheque, and nothing more.

I went back to the house. There was a man in the garden, though I do not think he was the gardener. He said she would not want to talk to me - perhaps I made the mistake of mentioning Anthony Scott. And of course, I am a foreigner! I knocked on the door anyway - well, I had come a long way. There was no answer, but as I left I saw a little movement of the net curtain in the window above.

There you are. Grimshaw has discovered Ellen McKitteredge was a scullery maid at the Scott house in Burton from 1881 to 84. She would have been 19 when she left. He found she was living in Kentish Town more than two years later and appears to have continued there for a long time. So, we may be no nearer to understanding the root of your problem, but at least we are tracing a path. Actually, Ned, I was excited - I wish I had more time away from my business. There was a problem at Elizabethville, a man was killed and four women injured. When I heard, I was in Liverpool, and I went up there right away. My car misbehaved on

360

the way back, we spent the night at a crofter's house somewhere in the north of Yorkshire. I am getting to like your Yorkshire!

There is another soirée by friends of Mrs. Knight. I believe I shall be ill and tender my apologies - you have a saying, "playing hard to get". These evenings can be boring, and I don't want them thinking I am keen for their acquaintance.

I hope to spend Christmas in Barnet, with friends. Take care, Ned. Good fortune.

Your friend, Bruno.'

* * * * *

Christmas 1915 was little fun at their encampment near Givenchy where there had been heavy fighting months before. By now, no authority could screen fighting men from the fact British efforts were not advancing. Hundreds of thousands killed - how could they not hear? Regardless of whether you believed the newspapers or what the military was saying - and the military were saying no more than they were obliged to. Few soldiers were blind to this madness of placing two enormous lines of opposing men for hundreds of miles, it represented no kind of solution to a problem instigated by heads of state. All the protagonists followed the same principles and practices: how was it possible anything could be achieved this way?

Soldiers were willing but not stupid. They saw comrades shot to bloody pieces, blown away like rag dolls in a hailstorm of shells or petrified by near-invisible clouds that tore out men's insides. These were friends, colleagues they had gone to school with, worked alongside in the factory and prayed beside at chapel. Now so many were dead, blinded, or maimed, and they all had names, they were real people that you stood next to and smelled their fear and cheered their spirits as they cheered yours.

This war had become an enormous thing. So big, it seemed no-one could possibly have a way of sorting it out. Frustration and lack of hope gnawed away at everyone. Perhaps the generals were right, perhaps the only way they could succeed was by smashing their way across the other side. Yet to do that needed ever bigger armies and more weapons until everything - men, machines, supplies and money - was exhausted. The military command could not disguise the fact their tactics had led only to a massive stalemate. You may as well, said Bob Street, have two boys playing conkers in the school yard, winner take all. Field service stations had to fend off men reporting sick in their droves. The sickness may have taken many forms but had just one name - fear. Fear without hope.

Conscription , introduced in January 1916, was essential now, the war's bad press had seen the volunteer army vanish. Men dying in unprecedented numbers was a sensitive issue not just along the front line. In England, as soldiers knew, women were taking over men's jobs, thanks to government intervention to put more women into the workplace. The working age for girls was reduced to twelve to provide for this, allowing boys to be conscripted into the army. Soldiers worried their jobs would not be there when they returned home - whenever that might be.

Winter brought its own misery. No soldier escaped the cold and the wet. Trench foot - a punishable offence - was becoming as common as a sneeze. Men were alert to the smells of their fellows, for gangrene was not a million miles away from athlete's foot. All of them knew they stank, but there was a good way of stinking and a bad way. The poverty in England's cities could not smell like this. Food rations were unappetising and hardly nourishing, dry clothing was in ever short supply, heating non-existent, shelter just a lottery. The only thing the men had in abundance - if you excluded the lice - was time: days were long, dismal, tedious and yet still fearful. For amusement, men might bait mice and rats, which had come in to feed on corpses, or they burned lice in tin lids over candles just to hear them pop. Only shelling got rid of the rats - for a time. Going to the toilet was an event in itself: latrines, such as they were, were disgusting places and lime could be choking. Infections were easy to catch. And all the while it was horribly cold and the news from the world outside brought nothing of tangible hope - so many

362

thousands killed at Ypres, at Festubert, at Loos.   French soldiers fared no better.   Shipping sunk and Zeppelins raiding English towns; more marching women, and interminable rumours of new offensives on the horizon. There was a lack of football fixtures to follow, no horses to bet on other than moonlight events. Even Jack Johnson winning the heavyweight title failed to relieve the gloom. The only relief of winter was that it brought fewer barrages and very few offensive activities. The rum ration went up at one point but dropped down again.

C Company spent Christmas Day out of the trenches in exchange for New Year, they enjoyed a meal of beef stew, carrots and dumplings with apple turnover to follow, though the beef was hardly more tasty than the apples, which had almost no taste at all and were more "squelched-in" than "turned-over". At dinner they sang songs and warmed their hands over candles dressed with peculiar waxed leaves.   They managed to get their own team together in the grey afternoon light and put on a game of football with a company from a service battalion of Royal Fusiliers.   On ground that was firm though not quite frozen, the 'visitors' won, 7-3. The score didn't matter, it kept them warm for a while, and in the evening, two platoons of C Company were granted leave to the local village.   There was no festive bunting, no fancy candle lights, no Christmas tree. A line of French flags had been hurriedly stretched across from the church to one house, and here two French men of late middle-age and their unattractive wives sold them cheap beer and a little sausage that had hung around too long, though there was some hot fat to toss it into. Other than the wives, there were no females, no glamour of a presentable skirt in sight, but here at least there was a fire in the grate and a chorus of ready voices to lighten their spirits. Even the French joined in with English verses and the two ladies received thankful hugs from every soldier, thankful simply that a female was here to care about them. One of the voices was that of Taff Morgan, who proved the value of Welsh male voice choirs.

"What - the river?" queried Taff to somebody's question as to why all Welshmen were called 'Taffy'.

"How the bloody 'ell should I know, boy? - I'm from Acocks Green via Cardiff docks!"

To the accompaniment of a squeeze-box, Taff brought the house down with a gentle solo rendering of "Wait till the sun shines, Nellie". Nobody had heard it sung that way, so respectfully, so plaintively, and the air of almost tearful nostalgia that descended on all of them delayed the applause by several moments.

After the fourth jug of beer, the cold seemed to abate somewhat. "God, that beer's fuckin' terrible..... Give us another jug, pops! *Plus de bière, plus de bière, Papa!*" Then one of the elderly men produced a bottle of *eau de vie* from local fruit of some long time past. It was too rough to have been called *Calvados*, yet too precious to be taken for use in munitions as much *Calvados* had been. One bottle and one little glass passed around seventeen men before the old man relented and brought forth a second bottle. It was all he had. After the cheering, each soldier took his turn to kiss the man. They were kisses of genuine gratitude.

Not one had had the presence of mind to bring a lantern. And it was cold - very cold. They would have to find their way back to camp in near-total darkness, through a frost-laden canopy of still, damp air.

Goodness knows what time it was: nobody had bothered to check earlier, and in the dark even the best Rotherhams could not tell you the time. After the candle-light of the house, everyone was blind for a while.

They decided to hold hands, form a chain, and Bob led the seven of them off in what they fancied might be the direction of camp. Over an hour later, they did turn up there once they glimpsed the flickering, shrouded lights across open country where once the trees had been. One of their number, however, arrived separately from the other six.

Taff Morgan, at the back of the chain, had dislodged himself to take a pee and carried on purely on voice contact - they were making a fair bit of noise anyway, mixing up music hall songs with Christmas carols.

Then at one point they heard Taff's voice calling, "'Ere, lads, what's this hill doin' y'ere?"

"What poxy hill, Taff?"

"I'm on a bit of a hill, like. Can't see you - can you see me?..... I seem to 'ave....... climbed onto somethin'...... Feels a bit funny underfoot."

"We can't see you. Funny how, Taff?"

"I dunno .... Smells 'orrible too!"

"What smell, Taff?"

"Well - Aaaaaaaaaaaaaaaahh!"

"Taff! You alright?" They were all shouting at him.

"Shut up, lads, shut up!" yelled Bert, "Let's hear him."

"Awwwwwwwwwwwwww...... Shit! Shit!"

"Taff, you alright?"

"I suppose so. Get over y'ere, will you?"

Cautiously, still holding on to one another, they shuffled towards Taff's voice. There was a low wicker fence in the way, which they carefully stepped over. It was Wally who saw him first, three yards away. In the near-total dark, the outline of Taff seemed to disappear from well above his knees into the "hill".

"What's that ruddy pong?" Everyone smelled it. The most appalling smell of animal dung.

"Bloody hell, Taff - did you do this?"

"What you gone and done now, Taff?" Ned moaned.

It was a dung heap. As high as a cow and twice as smelly. It was more than a dozen feet across in either direction. A frozen dung heap, its surface had been frozen solid, but the surface crust may have been only an inch deep, underneath that the dung was still - relatively - warm and soft.

"Holy shit, Taff! Holy shit!"

"Bloody right," called Taff, "Aw, fellers, get me out, ferchrissakes, will you?"

"Taff! You mucky bastard! Did you shit this lot? "

"What the hell's this muck pile doing here?" Wally asked. "I've not seen any cattle around, have you?"

"Who cares?" Ned answered him. "Maybe God's had a crap!"

"Come on, fellers, don't bugger about - get me out!"

"How we gonna get you out, Taff? - We can only just see you!"

"Well - I dunno - I can't move my bloody legs, man - grab a branch of a tree or somethin'..... Get some boards on top and climb over."

"You what? - Not bloody likely, mate! Get yourself out!"

"Bob! Ned! Come on, fellers!.... Please!.... For God's sake. I'm gonna freeze my ruddy balls off y'ere, man! I don't want my tombstone to say 'Died in service to a pile of shit'! Get me out! "

They did. It took them quite a time, but they got him out. Casting around in the dark, and careful not to come across a second pile of slurry, one of them found a broken limber from a gun carriage, and after tying a coat to one end of it, they improvised a pole and got the coat end to Taff so that he was able to hang onto that whilst they hauled him out.

"Down-wind!" shouted Ned. "Get down-wind of us!"

Even in the dark, Taff Morgan looked utterly wretched. "But.... there isn't any wind."

"We'll keep whistling and you follow us."

"Aw, lads..... Look at me...... Just look at me!"

"We don't mind lookin' at yer - just don't want to catch the poxy stink of yer."

"Well, I like that," cried Taff in disgust. "That's the last Christmas fuckin' carol you're gonna get from me!"

"We can live with that," Duffers told him.

* * * * *

The church in Hackney had not been easy to locate. It seemed to be in the wrong place, sitting as it did between buildings that looked more like warehouses. Once through to the far end of the narrow church, Carelle was surprised to find a large stretch of open garden with a number of trees, most of it given over to gravestones, stretching back a hundred yards or more. An absence of large tombs told him this was not a resting place for the wealthy, but a pleasant and peaceful place all the same.

In tapping his way along the stone floor, through from the street to the rear, Carelle's presence had attracted the attention of the vicar, not least because of the discord of Carelle's opulent and stylish appearance.

"May I be of any help, sir?"

"Ah.... Yes, I have no doubt you can."

"You were looking for something?"

The vicar was an elvish, pernickety sort of man, thin and wasted, whose enormous sideburns seemed to be striving to accomplish what his lack of cranial hair failed to do.

"I am looking for a particular grave. You know most of these graves?"

"I am the Reverend Christopher Vanstone, sir. I have been the vicar here nine years and thirty. I think I can say I know most things that go on here."

"Nine years and thirty?.... Ah. Do excuse me, Reverend. I am Belgian. I did not mean to be impertinent."

"Oh, no offence taken, sir, none whatever. Belgian, you say - my, my! I have not seen a Belgian since..... erm, well, what were you looking for?"

"I was looking for the grave of a Mr. Caldecot. Mr. Bernard Caldecot, he was buried here three or four years ago."

"A grave, you say? Oh, you won't find it."

"I won't find it?"

"No. There's no grave."

"Oh."

"There is a memorial stone. Mr. Caldecot was lost at sea, I recall. Yes, one of our maritime deaths. God rest his soul. So there is only a memorial stone. No grave..... No grave if you don't have a body."

"Ah.... Yes, I see."

"Most unfortunate, not having a body. Still, there we are.... Would you like to see the memorial stone? I can show you. Do come this way. I will take you to our 'lost at sea' department."

Carelle was momentarily nonplussed. The Reverend Vanstone turned stiffly and smiled. "That is my little turn of whimsy, sir, do forgive me. You are Belgian... I'm so sorry." Then by way of further apology almost, he added, "We don't actually have a 'lost at sea' department..... Perhaps we should make one.... Although we don't get many people drown in Hackney.... There's no sea, you see...."

The reverend was half-chuckling, half-muttering, and Carelle found his attention wandering.

As they walked through the garden, the vicar paused at several different monuments to give Carelle the benefit of his knowledge.

".... And this - this one here, this is Minnie Goodenough. Yes, I know, it's an odd name, isn't it? - Still it was good enough for her, d'you see?....."

And a little further: "This here, this one - this is Sidney Merrydown. Yes, really. We have some wonderful names here, you know. Yes. Sidney was mayor of Lambeth. At least, he thought he was. The rest of the parish seemed to think differently. Poor man. Died of a nail...."

"A nail?"

"Yes..... He was very poor, because he had no job and lived in somebody's back yard. He was starving. So he tried to eat one of his boots. And a nail lodged in his throat.... Killed him. Poor soul - ah, poor soul ! - 'Sole', d'you see? Boots!... "

Carelle wondered whether to laugh, but decided he could not. The situation was too bizarre. A joke-making priest at a cemetery! Too bizarre.

"Oh," apologised the Reverend. "Oh, no, you're Belgian. Do excuse my little whimsies."

Carelle was beginning to see why the Reverend Vanstone had remained vicar of this parish for thirty-nine years.

"Here... Yes, here we are. This is the one, this is it."

368

Vanstone stopped in front of a small grey stone plinth that had a vessel on top for flowers: there were no flowers in sight. The Reverend bent down and plucked one or two blades of grass from around the edge and fed them into the holes of the flower holder. "There, now. There, now," he chanted.

The whole thing was small - smaller than Carelle had expected, and very plain. The inscription was also simple, it read: "Bernard Caldecot, 2 July 1870 to 15 April 1912. Much missed."

"It's wrong," commented the Reverend. Carelle turned to query the remark.

"Should have been the third of July. Somebody couldn't read straight... But it was not worth changing it. I think he is probably looking down on us now, from heaven, d'you see - saying, 'When are you going to change that blasted date?' Do you not think so, Mr. - erm?"

"I see."

Pausing for a short interval to pay a semblance of respect for the departed, Carelle then asked, "Did you know the gentleman, Reverend? - Mr. Caldecot?"

Vanstone for a second raised his eyes, as if consulting heavenly guidance.

"Know him? Why, yes. To a degree. As I know all my flock. Though he was not a staunch parishioner, you know, not a regular attender, none of them were. And once the boys had grown up, well......"

"So you could not say what manner of man he was?"

"Couldn't I? - Well, he was known to be ambitious. Yes, I do remember that about him. He sought position, and money, I believe. Ambition doesn't get you very far in the eyes of the Lord, you know. 'Do not store up for yourselves treasures on earth, but in heaven'. Matthew 6 verse 21. "

"Oh."

"I fear so. I have no personal experience of trying to get a camel through the eye of a needle.... You know, I always considered that one of the least effective metaphors in the Testament, wouldn't you agree? - How many people in Hackney have seen a camel, do you suppose?"

Carelle shrugged at the absurdity of it all.

"'For where you have envy and selfish ambition, there you find disorder and every evil practice.' - James 3, you know, from the Testament."

Carelle thought it best not to comment on that. He had no great familiarity with the Bible. And yet he wondered if 'every evil practice' might have some relevance here.

"Did you do the ceremony, Reverend? - I understand only two people attended - is that right?"

"Is it? - Oh, oh yes, I think that's right, yes. I do remember. I have a very good memory, you know. His brother and their mother. Oh yes, I remember it very well. It was windy and my cassock was getting blown about, I did hurry things up, I must confess. *Mea culpa, mea culpa*..... She was very, very unhappy, Mrs. Devonshire, very distressed."

For a moment, Carelle went quickly through his mental processes. Yes, he had been told Lady Sophie and Olive Devonshire had attended very briefly - *'very briefly'*, he remembered those words exactly. He could well imagine that Lady Sophie would not want to waste time excessively with such matters.

"You mean - " Carelle put it to the vicar, "You mean - *Miss* Devonshire."

The Reverend straightened up, turned, and for the first time looked strangely normal. "Do I? - No. No. Oh no - *Mrs.* Devonshire - definitely. *Mrs.* Devonshire."

"Oh, but.... Miss Devonshire is not married, to the best of my knowledge."

"Not married? Why, that would be extraordinary! No - oh no - their mother - Mrs. Devonshire. Definitely married."

"Their mother?"

"Yes. Quite so. Their mother. Are you a friend of the family?"

"But.... I am so sorry, Reverend, do forgive me. I have to get this straight in my head - their mother was *Mrs.* Devonshire?"

"Well.... yes. Yes, she was. Of course she was. Would she be anyone else? She was the mother of the two boys - er, the two young men. Why do you ask?"

"And the brother - "

"Norman."

"Yes. Was he Caldecot also?"

"Caldecot? Norman? Oh, no. Norman Devonshire."

"I am now a little confused, sir, I must beg your pardon."

"That's quite alright... It's not often we have Belgians here. I remember at Christmas once - "

"No. No. The name. Devonshire. Are you saying that was the family name?"

"Family name. Yes, of course."

"But this man was Bernard Caldecot."

"Certainly. Yes. I knew their mother for quite some time. I have been here forty years, you know. So many families come and gone. And that Boer war, we lost a lot of young men from around here...."

"Mrs. Devonshire - can you tell me about Mrs. Devonshire? Where does the name Caldecot come from?"

"Well... She remarried."

"Aah!" The sound roared out of Carelle's throat as if a lightning bolt had just entered his brain and instantly he wondered how he could have been so stupid.

"Oh yes. Twice married, she was... Her first husband was Frank Caldecot, and he died, and so the second husband would be..... um, yes, that was George Devonshire. The man's name was Devonshire, he was a pawnbroker, I believe. Or was it a stockbroker? Something to do with handling money anyway - "

"So Caldecot came first. And so - Bernard was the elder, was he? So Bernard would have had that name. But Norman didn't."

"Of course, yes. He was the younger of the brothers, and adopted the stepfather's name; Bernard didn't wish to. Though we might have wished he had - Odd sort of name, Caldecot. Almost foreign-sounding. Caldecot - sounds like some African tribe or something. Hottentot. Something like that."

371

"Ah!" The bramble hedge opposite may as well have been a burning bush as Carelle stared through it. "Now I see. Thank you. Thank you so much."

"Thank me? But whatever for?"

"Oh - but tell me, vicar, the brother, Norman - can I get in touch with him?"

"Norman?... Well, he's here."

"Here?.... I'm sorry?"

"Yes, his grave - in the far lane, I can show you."

"He died?"

"He died, yes..... Drank himself to death. Sad, you know, very sad. Only a year ago actually."

"And Miss Devonshire, Mr. Vanstone, what of her?"

"*Miss* Devonshire?"

"Yes, Miss Devonshire."

"Was she? Who?"

"Miss Devonshire. She was there."

"Where?"

"Here."

"Here? What? - Here? I never saw her. Never knew her. Knew *Mrs.* Devonshire - not Miss."

"But.... But.... No, she was here, with Lady Sophie."

"Sophie? Who's that?"

"Lady Sophie. Lady Semper. You don't know her, then?"

"Semper? No. No, I don't know a Sophie. Sounds French. Or was she *Belgian*? - Oh, is that why you're looking for her?"

"No. No, I'm not looking for her."

"Mmm. Good thing, perhaps. I don't trust the French. Do you? Would you like to see some similar memorials? There is a lovely one just over here...."

Carelle stopped for a second and thought. This inquiry had gone about as far as it might go. Making an excuse that he had kept his driver waiting in the street, Carelle shook the vicar's hands vigorously and took his leave.

As he was driven back to Barnet, Carelle mulled over this development. The man had quite legally been 'Caldecot' after his father. How accurately did anyone check these things in any case? Above all, no-one would have seen any need to check the details to form a correlation with 'Devonshire'. The man that went down with *Titanic* was Caldecot: why should there be a case to do anything other than rubber-stamp the formalities?

However, Carelle had tripped over something he did not know before, and suspected the people at MI5 would not know either. Whilst chastising himself for not having looked at this matter earlier, Carelle was pleased with his morning's work. What an idiot not to see it before - Olive Devonshire was Caldecot's sister!

* * * * *

THIRTY-SEVEN

From Givenchy, where the 12th battalion had shared activities with the 6th, the men were moved in February to a billet near Busnes, where they undertook further battle training and Captain Marshall handed over his authority to Captain Parminter whilst he went on two weeks leave. Randolph Marshall had earned that. "A good officer," his men would say, and few said that of their officers. Parminter was a different kettle of fish: he was 'old school' and they resented his attitude, which was more 'do as I say, not as I do'. He had some sort of medal on his chest, so they imagined he must have been useful for something. "Services to brown-nosing," was Happy John's suggestion.

Luckily, they were involved in no action: somehow, going into action with Parminter in charge seemed like a bad idea. But it was no 'rest' period either. Training was intended to "gird up the men's loins", according to the chaplain: pep-talk and bullshit, to everyone else. Whether they learned anything was another matter, the NCOs appeared to be marking time. No.2 Platoon felt if they had to fight, in a perverse way they would rather just get on with it. They got their wish, even if it was a choice of evils: by the end of February they were back at the front line in the Loos sector, in unfamiliar trenches that were in need of repair, which it was their first task to address.

For more than a week it was quiet. There was a scandal when a soldier from B Company was accused of stealing and eating a messenger pigeon. The men laughed. Wally Myers looked at Happy John and accused him, "'Didn't you do that?"

"Me? - I only eat rats and lice, mate. You tryin' to spoil my diet?"

"What message d'you reckon that pigeon was carryin' when he scoffed it?" wondered Wally.

Happy John had an answer. "It said, 'Send No.2 Platoon a dozen poxy whores to stop Wally Myers wankin' himself stupid!'"

"Shit 'n' it!" called Bert Parrock.

At the end of the month, an assault, with a familiar lead-up. A bombardment of German ground for two hours, and then the command, "Fix bayonets!" The legs stiffened. The gut seized up. The throat had been dry for ages. Every muscle already ached, and the feet were frozen. It would be like stepping up out of an ice cave. Each man now had his own steel helmet, all those hopeless cloth caps had been consigned to history. But he still had 70 lbs of kit on his back.

Bert Parrock came round with the bucket. "In the bucket, lads - all your stuff, come on. Church roofing fund."

"Y'know, Bert, I reckon while we're out there spitting blood for king and country, you're back here doin' a nice little business with the local pawnshop with all this stuff of ours. Bet you jump on yer posh new motorcycle, straight down the town for a spot of how's-yer-father with the girls."

"Shit 'n'it, Myers! Get to your post!"

At the whistle, they once again did the most unimaginably stupid thing it was possible for a human being to do - they climbed the sandbags of the trench wall, stepped out onto crisp mud and moved forward to the wire. The whys and wherefores meant nothing now, you either did it or you didn't do it - passage to the afterlife was a step away in either direction. A man's life, his body, his mind, his soul, his very being, were all outside his control. His motivation was a prayer he would come through it, and the officer at the rear who would shoot him if he turned back.

Ned was as terrified as ever. His legs were a combination of frozen immobility and a twitching organism that needed to be pressed into some sort of action else he would remain stationary, a prime target.

Sergeant Partington was ahead, and Ned was determined to follow Partington. The good soldier Partington was always the man ahead, always leading, always urging, never fearing and never faltering. Fred Partington was a model soldier.

Yet there was another ahead. It was Meeker, and the boys of A Company. And Meeker was on his knees, scrambling about the soil. He had been hit by a sniper, and they were perhaps a hundred yards out from their own trench and more than two hundred from the enemy. Suddenly, the sound of machine gun fire. A single German machine gun. Everyone fell to earth. Each knew how difficult it would now be to make any progress whatsoever. The shouts of charging had started somewhere to their left, but not here, not where this group was being pinned down by a Maxim. The machine gun was too far away to hit them with accuracy, yet its short sweep this way and that meant it was suicidal to pursue a charge from here. Lieutenant Donovan was over to the left, they could hear his whistle, but could not respond to it.

Partington ran forward, and Ned followed him, straight to Meeker, now on the ground, clutching his stomach. His face was a picture of agony, though he emitted only gurgling sounds that could scarcely be heard over the noise of the battleground.

"Get him up!" shouted Partington. "Pick him up. Come on, Ned, help me pick him up!"

"Go on!" gasped Meeker, with as much vocal sound as he could muster whilst groping about his torso, "Go forward! Leave me!"

"Ned, get Duffield. You and Duffield get the sergeant back. Understand?"

"Sergeant."

It was not a command Partington made lightly. It was specifically against orders. Just as a man could be shot for turning back, it was equally forbidden to help the wounded, they were instructed to leave them and let the stretcher bearers see to them later - by which time, how many wounded men would still be alive?

Meeker was a good man. Fred Partington was not prepared to have a good man wasted in that way. He knew the penalties.

Partington waved to the men behind him. Warily they came on, crawling or stooping low, coats dragging in the dirt, each holding on grimly to his rifle with one hand and his webbing straps with the other. More bullets! The men all fell to the earth, some diving into shell craters. They were like crabs washed up on a beach, seeking out furrows in the sand.

Ned struggled to pick Meeker up. He grasped at Meeker's back to pull him, Meeker only yelled and gripped his middle. "Get your hands behind him," shouted Duffers. "Make a chair. Sling your rifle. Get our arms behind him. Like this."

Meeker screamed with the pain of being handled. Ned pulled Meeker's field dressing out from his jacket, tore it open and pulled at the linen, but on opening the coat further, he could see the great red patch on his jacket now. No simple bandage was going to stop that sort of bleeding and none of their first aid training was going to be of any use at all. In any case, the greater danger was that they were exposed to further injury if they tried to treat the wound right there. It was a magnetic thing to look at, but Ned had to ignore it and put the pain out of his mind, just concentrate on moving him. It seemed a supremely idiotic thing to be doing, all three men so burdened with their clothing and kit, and in all of this, a single small bullet that had reduced three men to this pantomime performance!

Between the two of them, they lifted Meeker off the ground and began to move to the rear. Another man from A Company joined them, he had lost his helmet somehow, but grabbed hold of Meeker's legs. Like a drunken crab, each pushing a little on the man they were carrying, the three of them progressed with their burden toward the British trench. It was slow and clumsy. They heard the chatter of the Maxim, but in a fatalistic way, they knew it would be more dangerous to stop and take cover and then begin again, and all the time Meeker would be losing blood and compounding his injury through their rough handling.

Reaching the wire, they crossed it where a dead soldier lay spreadeagled over it, weighing it down. All the same, the erratic wire cut into their clothing and flesh. Time had slowed down, and their limbs with it. As he breasted the wire, Duffield raised his back to help the others over, and that is when it happened. The shock jerked Duffield bolt upright, and for a second he hung there in the air, like a statue, before dropping his hold on Meeker and falling like a post into the earth.

"Duffers! Duffers!" Ned shrieked, but Duffield did not move. Dropping Meeker down, the other two jumped over to Duffield's body, his face down into the earth. The back of his head showed a quite small hole with little blood, and as Ned pushed himself into a position to attend his pal, he realised to his abject horror that Duffield's face was almost gone. There was instead a mass of bloody, wet, slippery flesh and the outline of a cheek, and then a whole lot of tissue that represented what were his nose and mouth. Ned turned away as quickly as he had looked. No training had ever prepared him for this.

Yet the adrenaline still surged, and the other soldier had grabbed Ned's arm and shouted at him, "He's dead! Leave him, leave him! Come on, get Meeker, get Meeker. Grab hold."

Yes, yes. That was the thing to do. Grab Meeker, get him back, get him back.

They hauled the sergeant by the shoulders of his coat, dragged him along the ground on his back, got him to the edge of the trench. All the time, the sergeant moaned loudly, as if he were about to vomit. Responding to their shouts, three sets of willing hands came to the trench wall and took him, slid him clumsily down the wall. Ned fell over the edge, down into the partly-frozen water, tore his coat on a plank of wood and hurt his leg. The soldier from A Company was in the trench now too. "Are you alright?" He slapped Ned on the shoulder and decided Ned was as 'alright' as he was going to be, and that was enough for him, he went back to helping Lionel Meeker, to try to stop his moans turning to screams.

Ned clutched his ears, they were used to the sounds of the battlefield, but could not take the screaming of one who was so close, one of the family.

Meeker was hurried off and the sporadic screaming went with him, only to be replaced by others. It was utter confusion anyway, men were rushing this way and that, it was complete madness. Shortly, as Ned sat there attempting to recover his breath and check his leg, more men came back. Ned only felt drained. All he could do was sit there, seeing Duffers' face. With shaking hands, he fumbled in his pocket. Another soldier came by, quickly assessed the situation and shoved his own cigarette in Ned's mouth before passing along to somebody else. Discovering he was sat on his rifle, Ned pulled it out awkwardly from under him. He had not fired a single shot.

"You alright, Ned?"

"No. You?"

"No....."

Bob Street was coated in filth. An exploding shell had showered him with muddy earth. As muddy as they all were, Bob was muddier.

"I'm not. I feel sick, if I'm honest."

"Aye.... Aye...."

"Meeker? - Did you get him back?"

"Aye."

"Is he gonna be alright?"

Ned made a hand gesture - this way, that way. Had Ned voiced an opinion, he would have said No.

"Where's Duffers?" asked Bert Parrock. "He came back with you, didn't he?"

They each stared at one another through dark, tired eyes.

By noon, stragglers had either returned or been given up for dead. Stretcher bearers were out there, hoping their red cross flag would be honoured, as it usually was. No-one envied them their job. What sort of a game was this where one side pitched itself at the other until the men were forced back, the damaged bodies then collected in preparation for the other side to cast the dice and throw their own men into the game? There had never been such a game. It could have been better played on a gigantic chess board. Your turn - my turn - your turn, my turn....... Throw the dice: a four or higher kills one, throw a six and you can kill two. We have plenty of those... Men. Throw it......

Moans faded from the battlefield. Someone brought warm tea and it had begun to drizzle - living only for the moment, these were the things of which Ned was aware. Little else. In the light raindrops was a taste of smoke and cordite. Ned stared at his .303 rifle and spat on the ground.

Around 1pm Lieutenant Donovan came along the trench. He looked dreadful. Not hurt, but just looked dreadful. "You're C Company, aren't you?"

"Sir."

"Sergeant Partington - have you seen him?"

Every face was a blank stare.

"No?"

"Not here, sir. Further over?"

"I've covered pretty much everywhere. I'll take roll call a bit later - everything's in such a bloody mess at the moment."

The lieutenant looked around him, shook his head and made a tutting noise with his tongue. "Hell..... Fucking mess...." Then he strode away down the trench. The five of them looked from one to the other. Nobody had ever heard Lieutenant Donovan talk like that before.

But the good Sergeant Partington would not return. They would not see Fred Partington again.

Boots off, Happy John rummaged for dry socks. He knew his feet stank, but the cold air was like God breathing freshness across his toes.

"Five men..... Five, Bob."

"Mmm. I know, John, I know."

Ned joined them, placed his rifle against the boards and sat down on someone's unclaimed field pack.

"And how many injured?" continued Happy John, not really a question. "Twenty? Thirty?"

"I don't know, John, I don't know."

"Forty-two off to V.A.D.," said Ned. "One of the ambulances broke down, Galloway told me. Dozen blokes carried off by hand. They should still be usin' the mules, never mind these blasted motor cars."

"What poxy difference does it make?.... Uh?"

Bob raised his eyes to take a considered look at Happy John. "Careful, John," he said eventually.

"Ah know what he means, Bob."

"So do I know what he means. You be careful too, Ned. Watch what you say and who you say it to. Come on, think where you are."

The other two did think about it.

"It's just that - "

"What?"

".... Aw, shit, I don't poxy know!"

"Ah think what you mean," Ned ventured, "is - what are we proving?"

Bob Street sipped at his pipe. "Proving?... You think we should be proving something?"

"Don't you? After all, Bob, you served in South Africa. You know what yer saw. You know what yer did. Would yer do that again?"

"Can't say I would."

"And looking back on this ten years from now, would we ask the same question?"

"What? - Would I do it again?"

"Aye."

Happy John laughed a sarcastic laugh. "Tell you what, Bob - if you go out there and get your poxy legs blown off, don't come runnin' to me!"

Bob smiled. Perhaps the question should not be answered.

"Does it bother yer, though, Bob?" Ned persisted.

The older man looked at him. "Bother me, Ned? - What, in a religious sense, you mean? Will I go to heaven and all that? That's a strange question to ask a soldier. A soldier has God at his side..... So they tell me."

"Mebbe. But if yer die tomorrer, what's the point? What will any of us have proved? Who will it mean anything to?"

Bob only shook his head slowly and sighed. " My brothers, my mother... Aggie, perhaps - "

"Aggie?"

"Aggie. Agnes. My girlfriend."

"My god, Bob Street - how long've we known you and that's the first time yer've actually mentioned yer girlfriend's name."

"No it's not...... Is it? Is it really?"

"Er.... No, it's not! - But that just shows yer - 'ow many times've you ever said owt? An' yer've known the woman ten year."

"Thirteen!"

"Thir - ! Thirteen? Just a girlfriend? You never thought of gettin' wed? Even after thirteen years?"

"Never found the time, Ned. Does it matter?"

That stopped the conversation. Ned had to ask himself, did it matter? He supposed not.

"So anyway, lads.... Who else would it matter to, if I died tomorrow?"

"When yer get right down to it, Bob, that's about the size of it. There's only a few as would grieve over us."

"Grieve over us? - Oh, I thought you meant, who would be depending on us for income. I hope there'd be a lot more would miss us, lad, in that sense. Every man affects so many other men: I mean, if you weren't here my life would certainly be different."

"Yeh?... Ah'd have to say the same, Bob."

Listening to all this, Happy John shook his head in amazement. "Jeeesus!...So when are you two gonna get married, eh?"

They ignored John's remark. "Maybe," continued Bob, "that's the only good thing to come out of all this... Doesn't that prove something?"

"Does it?.... I don't know."

"Be careful, lad, that's all I would say. You're not going to achieve anything by asking the army what we might be proving."

"None of us is ready for a court martial, Bob. But yer know this isn't what we joined the army for."

"Maybe I do at that. But here we are, my lad, and we have two choices: we can stay or we can leave. One way we'll get shot next week, and the other we'll get shot once Mr. Haig has signed the papers. Are you telling me you're ready to desert?"

Ned inhaled. "No." He settled back and reached into his pocket for a piece of biscuit to nibble at. "You know me better than that."

"Yes, son.... Thank heaven, I do. And John as well. You're good lads."

Bob reached out and clipped Ned across the back of his head with a light pat.

Well, thought Ned, *we have proven this much at least: friends are what we're fighting for. As to the rest, though.....*

And at that instant, Ned thought about Otto Bremme.

* * * * *

"Ah-ten-shun!" Corporal Parrock brought the men to attention the instant he spotted Captain Marshall at the tent entrance.

As Marshall tossed aside the tent flap, the whole squad jumped to their feet: Bob, Happy John, Ned, Tommy Tarmey, Wally Myers, Taff Morgan and 'Chunky' Philips. Ernie 'Stench' Waterhouse had just popped out to relieve himself.

"At ease, men," said Captain Marshall in a very ordinary voice. Taking off his cape, he shook it to shed most of the rain, and took off his cap, which he gave Ned to hold.

None of them had the slightest idea why the captain had come. It must have been a serious matter, the adjutant never came to an individual tent. In any case, it was a surprise to see him, he must have only just returned from leave. What that meant for the disliked Captain Parminter, they were not going to guess.

Marshall dispensed quickly with the pleasantries. Yes, they had eaten - the usual tasteless fare. Yes, they were comfortable - as comfortable as understatement permitted. Yes, they had fresh blankets issued the other day; yes, their ammunition locker had been replenished; no, the requisitioned puttees had not arrived; yes, their mail had come through. Superficial but normal protocol. No-one aimed to be the first to breach that protocol, perhaps with a question about future movements, or leave, or even the end of hostilities. It was not done. And anyway, the captain must have had something on his mind.

"It's not been going too well, chaps, has it?" The good captain knew better than to try the open bullshit that the top brass so readily trotted out with not the least conviction on either side.

Marshall looked from face to face. He knew full well the losses in the battalion. "I can only say how sorry I am for the families. And that somehow we make it up to them.... But I can't pretend I have brighter news at present: we just have to keep pushing Jerry until he cracks - which he will... I'm sure of it."

The men again looked across at one another.

"I'm here because I want to share something with you. Private Duffield was a good chap.... Every single man in my command is a good chap - I'm thoroughly proud of all of you.... I have been going through Duffield's things." That in itself was unusual, it was an NCO's job to check the belongings of dead soldiers, not the commander's. "Did any of you know that Duffield wrote things? - I mean, not letters home - he wrote poetry, or prose anyway. Did you know?"

Only Bert Parrock eventually confirmed, "Yes, sir. I did. He didn't pass it around. He was a quiet young man."

"Yes. I don't imagine he meant any of this for publication... I want to read something to you. Oh, be seated, by the way, sit on your bunks. Carry on smoking."

Marshall took the paper from his inside jacket pocket. It was a little crumpled and he straightened it out. He seemed to study the paper for several moments, then began quietly.

"There is no title, and he left it undated and unsigned, it is simply headed - 'Poem 3':-

'Peace tonight, lad,

Dream of home,

Take your yearnings to your cot.

Taste the thoughts of love unfulfilled,

Taste the bitter brew of leaving that which life had promised,

Here in this lunar landscape, this savage country.

Sleep tonight, lad,

Savour the taste of a last kiss,

That tremble in her voice as you left her in the throes of uncertainty,

Refusing that life of bliss.

Shall it ever be so sweet again?

384

Or shall the hell of this foreign garden pull you in and
Shall you ever be consumed?
A soldier's duty, a young man's dreams, the conflict never ceases,
To do the right - to fight the fight, the anguish never eases.
We stand here at our nation's bidding,
Reluctant gladiators in a Hades of some other vision,
Obedient to their will, no matter what the cost,
Yet at the end, is not every cause but lost?
No tears tonight, lad, no more fears,
Dream of home,
Dream of fragrant fields of peace,
We shall rest there by and by.'"

A long silence followed his words. Marshall appeared to be
paying respect, it showed against the judgement in his face. The
men no longer looked at each other, they wanted to hide their faces.

At length, Marshall spoke again. "I was moved, I will not deny.
It brings a clarity to the life of someone we had perhaps taken for
granted. We all do that, don't we?" He broke off, looked at the
ground and clenched his cane in both hands.

"But I have to tell you, much as I admire Duffield's spirit - and
giving his life as he did - there is a danger here. We cannot allow
ourselves to be diverted by the sentimentality of sweethearts at
home or the lives we had before. The only way we can win this war
is to focus all our attention on the task ahead. We all become
sentimental in our letters home. But we are soldiers, we have a job
to do. My job is to make sure we do it, and bring us home to the
better world we know exists beyond this place. I don't speak of the
parade-ground honour of the Buffs, I know you men respond to a
higher call. But let us not allow sentiment to get in our way."

His speech delivered, Marshall took another long breath and
looked around the tent from man to man. "Now.... Do any of you
know if Duffield had other material like this?"

Seeing only blank stares, he continued. "Duffield wrote a number
of things, apparently. I am placing his things in the hands of the
C.S.M. They will in due time be passed back to his family."

The captain looked around once more. Duffield's comrades had been enlightened. Hopefully emboldened. He had done his job.

"Thank you, corporal."

"Sah!"

Captain Marshall threw his cape about him and, turning to take his cap from Ned, recognised him.

"Thornton.... Still with us, Thornton."

"Yes, sir."

"Ah - the girlfriend in Le Havre, wasn't it?"

"Yes, sir."

"And is she still your girlfriend?"

"Yes, sir. She is."

Marshall looked into Ned's face a moment longer, as if he were trying to read the future. Then his concentration broke.

"Good man. Good man.... Carry on."

On leaving the tent, he passed by the large figure of Ernie Waterhouse, who had been standing in the rain, not daring to enter.

When the captain had gone, Ned turned to Bob. "He put that paper back in his pocket.... D'yer think he'll keep it, Bob? Why would he?"

"Same reason you would, I expect."

"What?"

"That it meant something."

Ernie came in and clapped large, wet hands at them. "Crikey, lads - I didn't know the gaffer was back. 'Ere, why is it every time I go for a piss something happens? ... You're never gonna believe this gorgeous blonde I just bumped into."

* * * * *

THIRTY-EIGHT

Jubal was sitting bolt upright in the chair by his bedside when Grace entered the ward with Ned following behind. Wards smelled strongly of carbolic, this one held a slight sweetness in the atmosphere, intended to combat the odour of urine and faeces. All beds were occupied by older men: most were quiet, subdued, within themselves. One man with a crutch was spending all his time hobbling up and down. Tap. Tap. Tap. Green tiled walls amplified every sound in this building which felt more like a public toilet.

A long winter should soon be over, with April so close. Ned struggled to think how long before the woods hereabouts would again regale themselves with carpets of bluebells as they always had – far, far away from anywhere a war might stop them.

Her father was staring right at Grace as she approached, his eyes wide in their sunken sockets, his cheeks drawn as if sucking in air. His lips dry and cracking nevertheless formed a strained smile as if his flesh were reluctant to permit it. Jubal wore only a thin dressing gown that appeared to have been pre-owned by several people, their cumulative stains little moved by numerous bleachings. In one hand he clutched a rag that had dried blood patches on it, as he recognised the daughter who brightened every day for him now.

"Someone to see you, father," she told him.

Jubal's stare moved to the figure behind her. His eyes widened and his lips parted. "Jim !"

"It's our Ned, father," corrected Grace with a resigned, even tone.

"Ned....... it's Ned....... Ned," rasped Jubal, almost wrenching tears of joy out of himself.

His son approached him and bent on one knee to take him by the hand that was not holding the rag. The hand was old, blotched with black, and gave only bony resistance under a skin that moved and creased like the skin of a part-cooked chicken.

"It's Ned...... Grace, look, it's our Ned."

Jubal moved as if starting to raise himself from his chair, then stared long at his son and allowed his hand to savour the exchange of trust. He looked and looked. And smiled. A big smile. "Our Ned..... Oh, mercy me! ...'Ow are yer, lad?"

"Good – good, father. An' how are you?"

"Ah can't piss proper no more," Jubal spat out, as if it were something to blame on someone else. Grace perched on the edge of the bed, smoothed down her skirts and played absently with her decorated purse.

They spoke for a while in platitudes. Some things his father said made perfect sense, at other times his mind seemed to be somewhere else.

"Ah knocked 'im flat !" exclaimed Jubal.

"Who?" asked Ned.

His father looked vacant. "Who?" he said, after a few moments. Ned shook his head.

"But you know, Jim, you mustn't let 'em send you to war. Tell 'em, they mustn't send you to war. Them lads are gettin' killed over there, hundreds on 'em......."

"I *am* over there," Ned tried to get his father to understand, and patted his chest to indicate the army uniform he was wearing. "I *am* in the war..... But don't worry, ah'm alright."

Jubal's eyes lowered and saw Ned kneeling in front of him. He took a long, long heaving breath, and then seemed to calm himself.

"Ned," he said. "You alright, son?" That met with a nod too, as Ned realised that his father was in the same world again.

"Ned..... You've had a rough time, lad. Those bastards have really buggered up your life, haven't they?..... But I knew....." He stiffened, and Ned felt his hand tighten on his own. "Ah knew my lad were a good un. Ah knew no son o' mine 'd act the coward. It were all lies. Don't you worry, son, I knew. An' ah'll give 'em what for, just you see if ah don't. You watch: the White Rose'll flatten the lot of 'em."

He had been coughing intermittently and now gave himself up to a convulsion of coughing and spluttering, reaching for a metal spitoon as he did so. In alarm, Ned turned to look at Grace but she retained a vague smile of resignation and simply gestured with a flat hand to calm himself. She had seen this many times. In a little while, their father's convulsion passed. Jubal sat gasping for a minute before composing himself and speaking again to Ned.

"They're all the same," he began, coughing a little in between times, "Ned, it's like that musical box. D'yer remember, lad, yer Grandma Hensby had that musical box.... She were a nice lady - died too young. She had a musical box, you wound it up and it played a tune over and over – ah can't remember what tune it were. She used to play it, and then after she died ah think it just got lost somewhere....... There were these figures on top: a lad an' a lass, fitted together, like. An' as the music played – plinky-plonky-plinky-plonky - they danced, up and down and round and round, bobbin' around on the top o' this 'ere box......"

Jubal's words were softer now, his coughing abated, he was staring straight ahead, looking at the memory in his mind's eye, almost a child again, fascinated by the twinkling of a bauble on a Christmas tree. For some moments it lit up his face.

"We're all like that musical box," he continued, setting his eyes once again on his son. "They wind it up and we bob around and dance to their tune. *They* do it - bosses and politicians, them as has all the brass and control all our lives. We just dance, like ruddy marionettes. After yer were on that ruddy ship, Ned, an' they blackened yer name wi' them there lies, they wound up the box so you had to dance. 'Gerroff my bloody ship!' they tell yer, and yer've got to dance. Off you go to war and they say, Dance! Them generals play the tune an' you lads go waltzin' off and get yerselves killed. Yer can't stop dancin' cos yer fixed to t'box. An' when they've finished wi' yer, they'll wind it up again and get some other poor buggers to dance.... An' they do it because they can. Nobody to stop 'em. 'Cept poor sods like me and ah'm fer t'boneyard now, lad."

He exploded into a coughing fit again and both Ned and Grace went to him and held him as if, somehow, merely holding him would make him better. A nurse passed by, only cast a glance and carried on.

Ned looked at Grace with a question in his face: '*Is there nothing we can do?*'

"But you, lad, yer've been fightin' more than a war, haven't yer? Yer've been fightin' these years, fightin' for yer name they took from yer. It were a ruddy great big musical box, Ned, it weren't fair. Ah knew you were a good un all along. Ah know you'll show 'em. Ah know yer will."

Jubal slumped back in his chair. They moved to shift him onto the bed, but he pushed them away. "No, leave me be. If ah'm dyin', let me be where ah can see t'world proper, not lookin' up at a ceiling."

"You're not dying, father......" Grace touched Ned's arm and silently shook her head: the question was not one to answer. Presently, Jubal composed himself.

"You're a good lad, Jim. Ah'm right proud o' yer. Yer know, lad, I was always right fond o' yer mother. She's a good lass, Alice."

"Yes, father."

"Never fall in love, lad. Don't do it. Messes up yer mind. Ah never wanted to fall in love. But she's a good lass, Alice. She never wanted me in t'ring, though. She could never understand what fightin' were about. It weren't the prize money. It were..... it were just me..... it were just me showing that old bugger..... what I were worth...... Ah showed 'im...... Ah showed 'im...... He beat me black and blue, yer know..... But ah showed 'im...... He used to take me behind t'middin an' beat me black and blue...... That bastard!"

Placing a hand on her father's shoulder, Grace bent towards him. "Calm down now. Just calm down. That were all long, long ago. You work yourself up so."

Jubal began coughing again and Grace beckoned Ned to leave the ward; she would follow.

"We'll come again, father."

* * * * *

Outside it was still raining a little. The air was chilly and full of a scent of manure wafting across from the park land adjacent where

390

someone at least was preparing hopefully for another season's roses. Negative of Ned, then, to light up a cigarette, but he felt his nerves on edge. The smell of the hospital ward lingered in his nostrils, he needed to blow that from his senses and manure was not enough. Quickly he puffed at the cigarette between his lips whilst his fingers buttoned up his tunic.

Before he knew it, Grace had joined him and for a little time neither said anything.

"That fever is recent," Grace reflected.

"The emphysema, though," Ned suggested, "it's been gettin' bad for a long time."

"Yes.... It has. But he may last months, you know." She might have been trying to convince herself. "You never know..... T.B. – it can take them in weeks, or years..... But then, if it's not one thing, it's another. Dad's not been the same since Sid died last November. Dropsy, they said. Do people die of that? – I don't know. That took the heart out of him."

There seemed to be much left unsaid. So she went on, "I told you, didn't I? – There was no luck with the sanatorium thing."

"Yer told me. Didn't expect the money from Tramways would run far. And ah suppose......"

"You suppose mum and I are at risk too from T.B." They stopped walking and he looked at her, as if weighing up whether to pursue that matter.

"He's fifty-four, Grace. Fifty-four. And looking like all the life has been sucked out of 'im. T'in't fair, is it?" He blew out a long, weary breath of smoke and lifted his face to a grimacing sky.

"Well" said Grace, with a philosophic air, "But then, anything can happen - it's wartime.... Can't it?"

She kicked at a stone with her shoe and ambled on. He followed, squaring off his army cap and folding his arms across his chest as if it would ward off the rain and shield his cigarette.

"Y'know... Ah used to think ah could hate 'im...... But..... Yer can't, can yer?"

Grace adjusted her linen bonnet against the drizzle, and at length she said a simple, "No."

"Ah wanted to...... But ah've enough fighting in my life. He were right about that. Fighting Germans, newspapers, aristocrats... Ah'm fighting things ah never understood......Too much fightin'."

"I know, Ned."

"Ah have to stop somewhere..... Ah don't know if ah shall ever...... find a time when someone's not tryin' to get at me. Maybe he's right, maybe they'll just keep windin' up that musical box. Ah never will get away from.... an act of kindness a young woman bestowed on a half-dead young man in a shipwreck. Will ah?"

She stopped and faced him.

"Aye, Ned, you will. This war's already changed a lot. There'll be a way ..... Bruno sees an end to it, he said so. I was having a word with Harry, he's deputy editor on the paper. Maybe when the war's over...."

Ned laughed a laugh of ridicule. "Over? Tell you what, Sis, in the trenches we don't even whisper the words 'War' and 'Over' in the same sentence. You start talking that way and yer get caught by a terrible disease – it's called Hope. Yer get a dose of Hope when you're waitin' out a barrage and you forget yourself. Next thing you know - Ping ! – That's the bullet with your name on it. Or the shell, the one yer never hear."

He realised she had stopped and was looking hurt.

"I don't believe that, Ned. You must have hope. What about your lady in France?"

"Reina? Ah'm not sure how she is."

"Reina?" Grace shook her head. "Reina, Ned? You were going to marry Gitta! What more is there you've got to tell me?"

How could he blame her? He had not explained himself for months in his letters as he had no clear idea what might happen. He had withheld the news Brigitte was pregnant, as well as his feelings about Renata.

Time to set things straight. And, in as few words as he could get away with, he did.

"So.... Fine fiancé you turned out to be, Ned Thornton! You're a right giddy kipper, aren't you, lad? .... Alright, then.... Reina.... A married woman! Did you think about that? And where's Gitta now? Has she had the baby?"

"January. In Paris. Regine, she's called. Reina says they're both well - she went there to see her. She's livin' at a friend's house just outside Paris."

"And the father?"

He shrugged. Doctor Ardant, that was all Renata had said. Except that Dr. Ardant was not living there.

Drawing in a long breath, Grace seemed to breathe the whole picture carefully into her brain. "Well," she said, giving herself time to think.

"Listen, Grace. You're right, yer know me better than ah know meself. You allus did. Ah've been as blind as a bat – it were Reina all along. It were always Reina. Ah just didn't know it."

"Oh, fine!.... And the fact she's a married woman?.... What about that, Ned Thornton - have yer thought about that?"

"Ah think of Reina every minute of every day ...... I almost wanted to give up the idea of ever seeing her again, Sis. She's German. And what the heck am I doin'? – Trying to kill Germans. My best friend and the woman ah love, they're Germans. And I'm fightin' Germans. It's ruddy madness!"

"Don't you think Reina understands what you're doing and why you're doing it? Don't you think she wants you to come through? Just as we all do."

Ned flicked away the cigarette butt, stopped and looked straight into her eyes. "I imagine she does. But ..... y'know, letters, there's often no way of knowing what the other person's really thinking. An' ah've already messed up enough for one lifetime....." He breathed a long sigh and she squeezed his arm.

"Thanks, Grace. 'Appen yer don't believe me, ah wouldn't blame yer. Ah didn't know for a long time that ah loved Reina, but ah do now – an' ah think she wants me."

"Ah should ruddy well hope so!" But she gave him a long look, the sort that tells somebody they forgive everything. Though in a cautious afterthought, she reminded him, "She's still married, don't forget."

"Forget!" cried Ned, "Ha! Funny! 'Ow could ah forget?..... With a name like that. Madame Forget.... But he doesn't love 'er, Grace."

"And you do...."

He made no reply.

"Well, if she's the sort of girl you've told me she is, I'd say she'll cope with all that and sort it all out for you." She said that in a way that closed the matter. It was time to move on.

"Tell you what, though, Sis - ah've got me back-pay: ah shall get some tickets for the three of us to the Theatre Royal or the De Luxe before Thursday when ah have to get back. We could do with lettin' our hair down, eh? Our mum an' all."

She beamed at him and squeezed his arm again. "Good idea, Ned. What's on?"

"Harry Champion, Florrie Ford, Little Titch – Who the hell knows? – Ruddy Caruso himself for all I know! Who cares, any road? Bugger it, let's enjoy ourselves fer once - tomorrer can take care of itself."

Perhaps he *was* a changed man. Her smile lingered and faded, however, into a series of question marks that all seemed to throw up the same conundrum: where was Ned going? The lack of hope he had voiced, the frustrations he felt, the constant pressure of trying to break out of what life had forced him to become. To where? There was no single answer: so much was down to him, and if he had lost sight of all those goals that a young man started out with, what would be his future focus? What would lift him back into the cheerful optimist he once was?

Probably the only answer lay in Le Havre.

* * * * *

THIRTY-NINE

There was a heavy frost that morning of early April. Drifting into the port through light Channel fog at Le Havre was no pleasure, the way it used to be, everything felt cold and bitter and repelling. The entire harbour wore not just its winter cloak but a shroud of war-weariness. It had been tricky enough getting his travel warrant arranged around a stopover at Le Havre, yet his adopted 'home town' no longer spoke its welcome to him. No longer were the quays lined with bright, eager, well-dressed passengers, patiently waiting in a spirit of bonhomie to get aboard their transatlantic ship that would take them to new lives. No longer festooned with bright wooden chests and piles of luggage and sacks of foodstuffs and drinks intended for an ocean voyage. Now the port heaved with a different tone, a swell of grey and light blue and khaki as military personnel of many denominations came and went or simply sat around waiting. Strands of wounded men on crutches or in bandages or lying on stretchers with very little cover to sustain them. Metal and rope barriers made quadrangles of everything. The whole port of Le Havre was like many mounds of beetles, seething this way and that, everyone fighting to stay warm and to stay alive. As Ned passed down the gangway, his heart was at once heavy and light. Heavy at the sight of all the human carnage here, yet lightened by the knowledge he was about to see his love and his other family again. In whatever state they now were. Oh, how he had looked forward to that!

His other mother was at the door. Marlene was standing there, all in black, her head covered by her shawl, standing at the door as Ned stomped up the cobbles of the street, kit bag on his shoulder. She knew. Somehow she knew he was coming. And yet shocked in equal measure to see him.

Ned stopped thirty yards from her, amazed that she was standing outside as though waiting for him, and set his kit bag down in the street. Panting from the walk up from the harbour, he straightened and gazed at her, his mouth open and speech-resistant.

"Ned! Oh, Ned!" she called, and ran as best she could into his embrace. She looked well, which was more than he had expected.

As ever, they conversed in a mixture of poor German and poor English, with a little French thrown in when all else failed: it was a routine he had become used to being without and he relished it now.

"Otto is alive, yes." She breathed an excited breath that swelled her chest with huge relief, but her emotions came out in little spurts. "He is – *verwundet*....... *blessé*......."

"Wounded," Ned confirmed.

"Ja. Dat's it. Wounded. In ze... in ze.... here," and she rubbed her hip. "Oh, I sink..... two months. Ve got ze letter.... from Manfred, he is wiz Manfred."

"Thank God! You can still get letters?"

"Ja. Still. Ze letters go from Manfred to Wiesbaden to a friend, to his aunt in Schweiz – ja? And zen from Schweiz to Lyon, anozzer friend. And zis woman post to me. Is good. Is very good."

"He is alive."

"Ja. He is." She broke down in little convulsions and clutched at her shawl, so Ned took her head in his hands and cradled her to him, stroking the back of her head.

"That's wonderful, Marlene," was all he wanted to say. "Very good."

Otto had been under a collapsed wall some way behind the front line. A bomb from an aircraft had toppled the village *mairie*, in which he was billeted, and the wall fell on him. The hip wound was bad, but his other injuries were minor, a lacerated jaw and a broken tooth. He had spent three days in the field hospital before being transferred to the rear and thence to another hospital near Aachen after a further week. They had saved his leg, and now he was – as of six weeks ago – in safety in Köln.

"He won't look so beautiful to Sophie now," Ned joked, a poor effort to lighten the tone. The letter had not said where this took place, or how long his injury might keep him away from the war. Perhaps for good. How Ned hoped it would be for good!

"You must talk to Reina, Ned. Go talk to her."

He lowered the spoon from his mouth and slowly scooped up another portion. The broth was offal and onion, but tasted good, with all the French flavour he had admired of Frau Bremme's cooking.

He had asked her about Brigitte, all she would do was shake her head. "Talk to Reina."

"But -"

"He is not zere. He is in Rouen. He is always in Rouen.... I do not know." She lifted her arms in an expression of exasperation. "Monsieur Forget do as he wish."

In the late morning a breeze blew scant snowflakes against his face as he strode briskly down the Chemin des Barques and along the lane towards the school.

He heard the children singing as he entered the school yard, and when his face appeared at the half-glass partition between the classrooms, a number of distracted children hesitated and turned their heads to him. As he put a finger to his mouth, to tell them to ignore him, one or two of them laughed. This drew Renata's attention, for she had her back to him and was singing heartily to encourage them all. Now she turned, wide-mouthed, and froze almost completely for some moments.

His smile radiated from his very soul. A huge, huge smile, a smile that helped him fight back the water that was weeping into his eyes. Renata recovered and beamed back at him. She did not halt the class, but she conducted them to a crescendo of rather beautiful - if not quite total - harmony, and then quickly set them a task before turning to the door.

Task or no task, the children's attention was all on Ned. They reached and peered back through the glass as he backed away, whilst Renata came through the door and stood there, three yards from his grasp.

"Ned!"

"Ah didn't mean to give y'a fright, Reina. Sorry."

397

"No. No, it's alright..... it's alright. I am.... I am ..... I am delighted to see you, Ned."

"Should ah come back? Ah mean, when yer've finished yer class, like?"

"Yes – er, no! No, no, stay."

"I.... I just have 24 hours."

"Ja."

"Ah'm on me way back from leave. Ah were in Bradford, seein' me dad. He's very sick. Ah got leave..... Compassionate. Ah was due some leave anyway."

"I understand."

"Ah have to report back day after tomorrow. So -"

"You don't have much time."

"No."

"Ned....."

And they both said together, "Gitta." He with a question in his voice, she with a reluctance in hers.

"Yes, Gitta," he affirmed. "How is she? Where is she?"

Renata moved a couple of steps closer. "Still in Paris."

"She's with that doctor?"

"Ned – " Her voice had an abrupt note of urgency that stopped him. "She is well. But – little Regine.... she will have a problem with her legs."

"Her legs?"

"Ja. It's okay, it's okay - she is not in danger. But she has zis problem. Ze doctor thinks she will not walk. Maybe a little, maybe not. Ze birth - it was not easy."

"Ah." Ned knew better than to try to make intelligent guesses where women and childbirth were concerned. Let Renata tell it. She had held it from her letters all this time. Regine had suffered in the birth, there was some suggestion of damage to the hips.

"But she will be alright?"

"Yes, I sink so. But.... it will take a lot of time if she can be made right. And ... a lot of money. We don't have zat."

"No.... No. Ah see. You mean, there are things they can do, but it needs money."

"Yes," said Renata after a moment's consideration, "Exactly zat."

He pulled out one of the small chairs that had been tucked under tables and sat down awkwardly to let the news sink in. In other circumstances, he would have looked comical, as indeed he now appeared to the children, whose sniggers they could hear but ignored.

Renata moved across to him. She first stooped, and then knelt in front of him, catching one shoe in her thick black skirt: she pulled it free and after exchanging glances took hold of his hand.

"Gitta is alright, Ned."

Some other chattering children came through the classroom, and hurried outside after noting that serious words were being exchanged here.

"But..... Ah mean, is she bein' looked after?"

"She is staying with friends..... A friend from the nursing. But not – not with him."

"Ah see.... Ah see.... "

Her posture became more upright. "She told me she is not needing money. She has good friends."

"Well, then. Ah suppose there's nowt much ah can do. So long as she's not struggling."

She pressed his hand tight. He was not entirely sure what signals were coming over but cast a hopeful look into her eyes.

"And you, Ned. Are you... alright?"

Was he? As he looked at her, he asked himself the question. Gitta had been far distant from him for a long time. And he knew only too well how he had been withholding his other feelings for Reina, feelings that even now he scarcely dared reveal. Doubt can be a cancer that eats away truth. As far as Gitta was concerned, however, what may at one time have hurt him now gave more of a note of conscience and little more than that, if he was honest.

There was such an earnest expression in her eyes. This was a different Renata from the woman he had known months before. Pursuing a line of thought and concern for Brigitte was one thing, but feeling the closeness of Renata was not altogether on his agenda. Not because he did not want it, but because he was not ready for it.

But then... what *was* his agenda now? One body blow, the fact Brigitte's child had a deformity, was quite enough for the day.

In every perception, Reina was the closest she had ever been, certainly closer now than the night the battalion had arrived in France. Physically closer, and emotionally too, there was no doubt of it. It did not render any easier the fact he had to return to the war.

"...Yes," he finally intoned a little unsurely. "Ah'm.fine. As fine as..... well, yer know. Fightin' at the front ...."

"No."

He let out a heavy breath, a breath laden with visions of men fighting and men dying and men being blown to bits.

"No fun, Reina... And me dad.... he'll die soon."

She was looking into his eyes, not sure that they were staring back at her, or whether they were far away, and for what reason. On a sudden impulse, she leaned forward and put her arms around his neck and pressed her face tight into his. Immediately there was a wash of little voices from behind the partition.

He said nothing, nor did she. He only raised a tentative arm and placed it on her back and gently drew her to him. There they remained for many, many long seconds, not exchanging words or kisses but faces pressed into the most tender of embraces, drawing recognition and strength from each other. He told himself this was the caring hug of a sister and might be no more than that, yet his nostrils took in the fragrance of her as if it were an ether that would overwhelm his senses and forbid him to release her. And - oh - the touch of her flesh!

They were parted only by the rising sound of giggling voices from behind the partition wall. Rather than show any embarrassment, Renata simply drew back and smiled at him, an acknowledgement that they had nothing to feel embarrassed about. In times of strife, a great many things may be overlooked, and in moments like these there was no space for the normal proprieties of life. Sometimes life was to be seized upon and taken whilst it was still on offer.

"Ah!" He suddenly remembered, a need to end the moment in spite of himself. "I changed yer camera, Reina - Ah hope yer don't mind. Only, that box was just too big.... and ah didn't know at first, but cameras aren't allowed." She registered mild surprise.

"So ah changed it while I were in England. It's not much smaller, but it folds and fits in one o' me pockets so if ah'm careful nobody really knows.... Ah heard a feller talkin' about it and ah thought it were a good idea. It's a bit like that Kodak VPK, but this one's German.... ah thought yer might approve, like."

"Was it a lot of money?"

"Yes - well.... Ah traded yer Kodak. And ah've got a few photos.... Still on film rolls, though. If ah leave the film with yer, maybe yer can get it developed for me - yer'll see me mum and our Grace..... Oh, and Bob and Happy John. Ah can only take a picture when t'officers aren't looking.... Ah hope ah didn't do wrong, swoppin' it." She simply gave her approval with a smile.

"You will come later for me, Ned? I must stay wiz ze children now."

"Yes."

"Mutti will have a good food for you, I know. I will come there."

"Good. Good, Reina. Tell me what time – I will meet you here, we'll walk up the hill."

* * * * *

Many times that night Ned cursed his brain for not shutting up!

Was there any point in reasoning? Transcending the veiled curtains in his mind, Otto's two sisters wandered through those deep canyons of his imagination and frustrated his sleep.

Brigitte had been the overt beauty that delighted the eye, whilst Renata had a beauty of subtlety, of greater depth and mystery. Brigitte was fire, Renata was peace. Gitta was the raw creature that had infatuated him, it was at once her attraction and her flaw. She shone out like the brightest of stars, a light that would dazzle and fade. She had blinded him, once he had woken up to the notion he could ever be thought attractive. But Reina, he had dreamed of Reina constantly, though in a measure of being way beyond his reach: from the beginning, it had been that way, his stumbling approach had only made the wall a higher climb. As to Gitta, reason said that it was not a matter for guilt - Gitta was what she was, always had been, always would be - a free spirit, a firefly. If there was any justice in all of this, it eased his mind that Gitta had done as she had wished. More than that, though - Ned was now crystal clear it was Reina he wanted.

It had been Reina keeping him from sleeping. Until finally, in a muddled dream of revealing his passion to her, he had let go his consciousness.

A cold morning brought vague light, he knew little else but that he did not wish to leave. Despite poor sleep, he rose quite early, but Renata had been up earlier still and the *brötchen* she made were fresh, warm and fragrant. He ate them gratefully with some *confiture de lait* and a thin mixture of *fraises* which Marlene kept for special occasions. Coffee stimulated his awareness.

Her mother had called for Renata more than once in the night but the coughing had not lasted long. Marlene's intermittent illness was puzzling, but a convenient excuse to offer the Forget ladies - once again Jerome was away on some political pretext that was more and more the norm now and, having made his mother a broth, Renata had excused herself to see to her own mother's needs. That was *her* norm now.

After that light breakfast, she had spent time making her mother comfortable, it was good to hear them talking and laughing, their voices echoing down the staircase with the light that was spilling from the oil lamp up there. Always they conversed in that way of mostly German with French words spattered here and there in the mix, and always it intrigued Ned as he listened, understanding much but not all of it.

"She is feeling better, Ned. Thank you for that *mélasse* you brought her - for ze *toux* - ze cough: er... ze *sirop*. She says it tastes nice."

"Will she be well?"

Renata could only smile her uncertainty. "Who knows? She goes up, she goes down. Ze doctor says she is mostly alright. She is missing our father.... And her family back in Germany."

He gave a quizzical shake of the head. "Yer not thinking of going back there?"

"Me? No." She had been tidying towels and stopped to look at him, seeing the suggestion was not one he wanted to contemplate. "No," she reassured him.

He sat up in his seat and his lips let out a little noise that showed his relief for her to see. It was also in his mind that he had not been alone with Renata for a long time before last evening, when they had talked many platitudes. Too many.

"Whatever happens, Ned, I would not go to Germany."

"Of course - Ah mean, you're married to a Frenchman, right here."

"Married - yes..... A piece of paper."

Ned was unsure what to say about that, and decided to say nothing. Whatever she might consider about her marriage was her business.

"Ah wouldn't want yer to leave, Reina. Ah hope .... well.... ah rather hoped that, once this war's ended....."

"Yes?"

"Um..... Ah don't know.... After the war, a lot of things will be different."

"A lot of things are already different."

"Yes..... And mebbe - "

"Ned."

"Yes?"

"I think.... Ned, I think you love me."

It came like a blow to his chest, that knocked the wind right out of him. Speechless for some seconds, his face underwent a variety of contortions.

"Is zat.... Is zat true, Ned? - You love me? Little bit.... Yes?"

His open mouth bit the air.

"Reina..... Ah said long ago, ah'm an ignorant man..... Ah've been a foolish man. For a very long time. Sometimes ah don't know whether ah'm doin' right or doin' wrong."

"You don't answer my question."

".... You're an intelligent woman - Ah know yer can see right through me.... You're right, Reina... ah do love you. Yes.... Ah think I always have, right from the start.... Ah just didn't know what was really, really important in my life."

"You are important in my life, Ned."

"Am ah?"

One of the candles had burned down, leaving just two candles to illuminate the walls and make the shadows dance, for the curtains were still drawn against the arriving light. He stood as she moved closer to him, and now her face in the dim light was the brightest radiance in the room, and her eyes the centrepiece of that radiance - a magnet, drawing him to her. Extending his arms, he took her. They did not kiss at once but remained for long moments looking at each other, reaching out to blend their senses in a confluence of emotions. In his mind was a whirlwind of thought and fear and hope and desire. One desire overcame all else as he met her lips with his and was gripped with that overwhelming surge of passion to hold and possess her.

"Reina..... Oh, Reina..... I'm sorry."

"Sorry? Why, Ned?"

"Ah was so wrong about everything. So stupid. Thoughtless. Ah couldn't see what was staring me in the face all along - you."

"But, it is not only you, Ned. I was wrong also. *Je méjuge.* I judge you..."

"Misjudge."

"Yes. I mean dat. I misjudge. And now - "

"Now you like me?"

"Now I like you..... Yes..... Now I like you." Her face lit up. "Now I am in love wiz you, Ned."

The glow that had been embers in his chest burst out in flame, overwhelmed him and took his breath again.

"Tell me that again - please!"

404

"I am in love wiz you. Yes."

All he could do was clench her body ever more tightly in his arms and repeat her name - "Reina.... Reina.... Reina....." Her name meant everything.

Ned donned his coat over his uniform and buttoned his collar. The train would not wait.

For some reason, as he readied himself, all he could think to say to her was, "Otto will be fine, ah'm sure. He'll come back. Someday soon."

Renata signalled her agreement. It was not what was on her mind at that moment.

"You come back," she told him in a faltering voice, and her impulse was to put her arms around him and pull him tightly to her again. It was what he most desired, and yet he had to leave.

"You come back, Ned...... You come back, my love." He responded, wrapping his arms about her shoulders and feeling her bosom pressing firmly into him.

She kissed his bristly cheek and drew back fractionally so that he could be sure to see her eyes. Those large clear blue eyes held tears – tears fit to melt his desperate heart. Her breath now so warm, so real to him as never before. This was Reina - finally! Reina, his desire, his love. The one thing he craved for more than anything else in the world, yet he had to leave her. Every instinct was telling him to tighten his hold on her, to ravish her, to love her.

"You come back soon."

"Ah will."

"Promise me."

"Aye, Reina.... Ah promise you."

"Mushrooms?"

"Aye.... Champion.... Mushrooms."

It was the hardest thing, to walk away and leave her.

* * * * *

"Wait, Ned. Why are you only telling us now?"

"Why? - Because you asked me, that's why, yer stupid blighter."

"Don't get mad! What did we say to upset you?"

"Yer talk about it as though she's just another whore. Come on, you're me friends. If ah didn't think yer'd understand, ah'd never have told yer."

"'Just another whore'? - We didn't say that."

"As good as.... What did you say, Bert? - D'yer remember what yer said? 'Do you mean to say you didn't shag her?'...... Isn't that what you said?"

"... I just meant - well, there's a war on, Ned. Come on, it's the first thing you're gonna get asked when you get back from seeing a girl. Nobody means anything by it. We're all glad yer had a good time."

"Ah were on leave to see me father.... He's dyin', for Christ's sake. Hardly a 'good time'! Came back by way of Le Havre, that's all. A few hours, that's all."

Bob tried to mediate. "Ned. Ned, we didn't mean any harm. We just think - look, you've always seemed a naive sort of lad. Y'know. You're one that never talks about getting his end away..... Not like the rest of this bunch of clowns."

Ned looked from one to the other with impatience.

"Aye, that ah may well be. Doesn't mean ah can't fall in love wi' a girl an' treat 'er right."

"No.... It doesn't, lad, it doesn't.... Listen, we've had some drinks tonight, you caught us with our mouths open."

"Obviously.... My fault for feelin' sorry fer meself, ah suppose. Thought you blokes 'd cheer me up."

"Look, lad", Ernie wanted to contribute, "it's a right bloody let-down coming back 'ere at any time. We're not in the best of spirits either. Cyril Wilson got it yesterday."

"Cyril?"

"Took his arm clean off. Took him five minutes to die, poor sod."

A few deep breaths calmed Ned somewhat. "Right sorry to hear that. Cyril were good on that banjo."

"He was. Beats me how he managed to carry that banjo around. Old beat-up thing. Often cheered us up. Specially when he did his Chaplin impressions."

"And with Tommy on his mouth-organ," Wally put in.

"Well....." Ned began to feel less prickly.

"Ned, look. Bert meant no harm."

"I didn't mean no harm, Ned. Honest. I'm right sorry. An' I apologise to yer girlfriend. Honest, I do."

"If you love the girl," Bob carried on, "then naturally you're going to respect her. You know, we all took it for granted - with you knowing her for so long.... and .... well, you never talk that much about them."

"Why don't you just marry the girl, Ned?"

"Ah would, Bert..... Ah surely would. She's already married."

There was puzzlement, and Bert passed his hip flask around again. "Thought you said you were engaged before the war?... And now she's married?"

Yes, thought Ned, *it's not an easy one, is it?* And how he wished he could confide that the family was German. But that part he had withheld all this time, and he was not going to reveal it now. In any case, they had not cheered him up, far from it. On the other hand, he should not hold their ribaldry against them. It was, after all, only stupid banter - soldiers' banter.

"Ah should know better, fellers... Ah'm sorry."

"Forget it, lad. By the way, we've got a new sergeant."

"Oh?"

"Name's Longbottom.... Great name for a sergeant."

"Yair," whined Wally, "Better not drag it along the ground.... Likely get it shot off!"

'7 April 1916. Dear Monsieur Carelle,

I am so grateful for all you have done for me, and especially because you didn't have to. But I want to ask you very humbly for a great favour, and I do so not for myself, but for my friends, who are very dear to me.

407

When I wrote to you in October I said that Gitta was having a baby and that it was all over between us but I wish her well. I want you to know that - as stupid as I am - I know now that Reina is the love of my life and I shall do everything I can to make her happy once this war is over. I know that is shocking, but it is the truth - I have been very stupid.

That's one thing. This is something else. Little Regine was born on the 4th of January and there is a problem with her hips. The doctor says she will have difficulty walking, but there are things they can do to help. Only - these things cost money. I know that you will not be offended when I say, I have no-one else to turn to. I would gladly give all the money I possess but it is not enough. I have never begged for anything in my life, sir, but I ask you now if you would help us. And you know it is also true when I say I have no idea how I could repay you, though I promise I shall.

I cannot say more at the moment. I am not a good writer as you know and my letters are always short compared to yours! All the same, there is nothing more important to Reina and me than the health of little Regine, for she will be our future.

I send you my thanks and very best wishes as always and hope you are well.

My greatest respects.

Your friend, Ned.'

* * * * *

FORTY

"In police custody, Mr. Grimshaw, how so?"

Carelle tapped the telephone a couple of times to clear the indistinct line. Grimshaw repeated himself and then went on, "It seems his lordship may have jumped before he was pushed."

"Can you explain that to a poor foreigner, please?"

"Hang him before he hangs you. "

"Hang him? - You are joking, aren't you?"

"In a manner of speaking. I don't mean literally, hang him. Semper has alleged that Cade was blackmailing him. Whereas Cade has told the police Semper was shopping *him* to cover up the fact *he* was being blackmailed by Semper. All very confused, but in effect, you set one blackmail against another."

"Ah! And who are the police going to believe? - That is what you mean."

"Quite so. Can you hear me alright now?"

"It's not so bad. Carry on, please."

At the other end of the line, Grimshaw evidently paused for a drink of something.

"Cade doesn't have a leg to stand on. A man like that against a prominent member of the House - not a chance."

"Cade's bad luck, I suppose. Nothing good was ever going to come out of that relationship, was it?... So you followed up what I found out about Miss McKitteredge."

"It wasn't difficult. Never is when you know what you're looking for. It's *Mrs*, by the way."

"Mrs? Oh."

"No, she didn't marry. Women of her age don't like to be thought unmarried."

"I thought perhaps - that man in the garden."

"Don't know who that might be. Anyway, young Cade spent a lot of time in trouble with the police one way or another. Then later joined the Royal Navy, but after getting as far as Leading Seaman he somehow blotted his copybook and they threw him out."

"Which is when he joined the Atlantic liners, I presume."

"Something like that. As I said, nobody had any need to check on all this until you made the connection. You don't call the fire brigade till you see there's a fire."

"Where is John Cade right now?"

"Awaiting his majesty's pleasure. With his former record, he'll go to prison again."

"I see. So.... There may be every chance we can talk to him, then?"

"Mm. Doubtful at present. I can't say too much, but the MI5 operation with Semper isn't ready to be compromised just yet. This is a new twist: their little pow-wow with Semper focuses on other matters, don't forget."

"I must speak to him on Ned Thornton's behalf to find out what happened between him and Semper aboard *Titanic*. And the connection with Caldecot and his sister. So you think I cannot speak to Cade?"

"You should understand that convicted felons can now sign up with the army as a way of mitigating their sentence. You know how badly the army needs men. It doesn't take long for the deed to be done. God help the army, is all I can say."

"Oh, but that could be a *catastrophe*! We could lose him completely."

It was almost as if Grimshaw gave a shrug down the telephone. "Possibly," was all he said.

"Should I speak to Mordecai Winstone, do you think? Would that help?"

"You could try, sir, though I don't think Scotland Yard will help you much. I shall not give you any hindrance, so long as you keep the name of this department out of it. "

"Then how did you get this information, if not from the police?"

"We find it's best not to get directly involved with the bobbies, Mr. Carelle, they can be useful but they can complicate things. They have to stick things down on paper and keep to the rules. The department likes to keep things simple. No names, no pack drill. There's no service manual for MI5, Mr. Carelle."

"Then I will see if Tommy can get me into the prison before Cade gets his sentence."

"He's to come to trial yet."

"Do you imagine they won't find him guilty?"

"Mm. Fair point, sir. Anyway, good luck with that. Remember, I've not heard of anybody called Tommy."

"One thing, Mr. Grimshaw. Apart from thanking you, of course, for your help. But in regard to Lord Semper being blackmailed: do you know what Cade was using against him?"

"Frankly, little that Semper couldn't get around easily. Whilst Cade refuses to actually name Semper as his father, nobody really gives him a chance. His case is based largely on Semper's political activities in peddling information to foreigners."

"What about his associations with the Fenians?"

"Well, the term isn't strictly relevant now, but with reference to the Irish Brotherhood, yes, there is that too. This Easter's flare-up in Dublin, it's likely his fingers have touched the money behind that."

"I see. You'll pardon my observation, Mr. Grimshaw, but these executions of Irish men by the British are not helping, do you not think? Blasting to kingdom-come a post office, of all things!"

"Thinking in that sense is a luxury such as yourself can afford, Mr. Carelle. As a public servant, I cannot. I have to be content to catch our right honourable friend with his fingers in the till - with actual evidence of the secrets he traded."

"Which is what we were discussing before. That flame gun thing."

"The S.A.P., or KA5 flame projector contraption - whatever they call it. And other stuff. You should not mention that, by the way - you know that, of course."

" I do. And can you prove that yet?"

"Forgive me stressing the point - if it were to come out that a foreigner - yourself - had knowledge of these matters, I should be on a very sticky wicket.... Prove it? - *We* can't yet - no. But we have a very good idea the Americans can."

"You *will* get him?"

"We shall, though it won't be easy with someone in his position."

"Why not? If he has committed treason, why not?"

"Mr. Carelle, surely a man like you must appreciate what it is to have pals in places where they can pull strings. He has powerful friends, we have said this before. Neither will it be in time to alter anything that happens to Cade."

"No. So Cade's blackmail is not about his own birth?"

"There are still things that have to come out, Mr. Carelle. I will take you further into my confidence when I know more about the foreign connections."

"As you pointed out, Mr. Grimshaw, I am a foreigner too.... I wonder that you do not investigate *me*."

"My dear sir, with the best possible intentions, we know more about you than your own barber does."

Grimshaw may have heard Carelle wince at the end of the line.

That late April evening, Carelle spent time in his kitchen preparing a rhubarb and chocolate cake before writing a letter to Ned and one to Grace, saying he would be in Bradford within the week and hoped she would join him for dinner. He made no mention of the fact the dinner would be hosted by two associates from the local company and another gentleman who was involved in Carelle's work for the Commission for Relief in Belgium.

A week later, he arrived to collect her from the house at Southfield Place and caused the usual sensation in doing so. He also presented her with a large package, containing the dress she should wear for dinner, and hoped she would not be offended. It was an admirable fit in a purple fabric - a restrained purple, but nonetheless very much a Carelle hallmark. Grace told her mother she needed a cup of tea to get over the shock - instead, Carelle offered her a brandy from his flask, and she took it.

Alice let go her stick and flopped back in her rocking chair. "Sal volatile!" was all the speech she could muster.

* * * * *

In May, 1916, the 12th was again relocated. C and D companies found themselves uprooted from their base by the Lys river and ordered to a camp well to the rear. Training for what, they had no way of knowing, other than the routine assault courses, but a change of venue was no hardship when it took the men away from the front line. For a time, they even had running water in the billet - sometimes it was actually warm: they could wash and shave!

Brigades of New Zealanders and their support groups had come into the Armentières sector. Shipped over from Egypt, they had been active in the Dardanelles. These were not stumbling raw recruits, they were men with fighting experience. Rubbing shoulders - if only a little - with New Zealanders was a novelty for Englishmen, who delighted in provoking conversation if only to hear the strange accents of cousins. The arrival of colonials in some numbers to join the affray was a great source of optimism: to recognize allies from the Empire other than simply British and Canadians was an immensely satisfying stimulus, and in no time at all these men were talking to each other as old comrades.

It lifted the men's spirits after the news from Ireland and the reactions in press and public alike to the recent executions of revolutionaries following the uprising there. Bob Street lit his pipe and slowly shook his head from side to side. For the men fighting in France, it almost felt like a 'back-door' action, that British soldiers in similar circumstances to themselves should be slamming down the iron fist against a people that could in so many ways be compared with their own British folk. Opinions, naturally, were wildly divided. It was fortuitous, then, that the arrival of antipodean troops imparted a feeling of solidarity of empire.

So far as ordinary soldiers like Ned and Bob were concerned, however, all of the movements taking place were none of their business, it was a general rearrangement to enable the French to move their Tenth Army into the Verdun sector, widely known to have been the most senior battle zone of all. At least - according to Sergeant Barcombe. Sergeants always knew what was going on.

For the men, though, relocation meant packing up and putting down again somewhere, rain or shine, with a whole lot of pain and aggravation in the doing of it: tired legs and an empty stomach until it was all accomplished according to the dictates of the sergeant-major.

"I'll tell you what I poxy think of it," rattled off Happy John in a music-hall duologue with himself as he dug yet another latrine, "Oh yes, and what do you poxy think of it? - Well, I'll tell you what I think of it - I think it's a downright poxy liberty, that's what I think - Oh, you think it's a downright poxy liberty, do you? - Damn right I do. All this 'Pack that poxy wagon - unpack that poxy wagon', without so much as a 'by your poxy leave'......."

"John!" interrupted Wally to no avail. "John...... John..... Will you just shut your stupid gob and get it done, you pathetic Kentish sheep-shagger!"

Happy John threw down his shovel and pointed to the large hole. "Second time this poxy month! Second poxy time! I ask you, my friends, do I look like a shit-shoveller? - My friends, I do not!"

"Yes, you bloody-well do!" chorused Wally and Ned together.

"John, you are king of the scavengers," Bob added. "I trust my night soil waste with you as if it were my life savings."

Happy John spat in the hole and carried on digging and complaining at the same time. "Bet you the Boche soldiers don't have to put up with this shit! Bet you they got special shit-shovellers to do it for 'em. Fatigues, they said! Fatigues! D'you know, I used to think a fatigues party was where we all laid down for a kip and then got pissed out of our skulls."

"Alright," said Bert Parrock eventually. "John, I'll have a word with that nice Mr. Haig and get him to award you the 'Excused-Shit-Shovelling' medal for fellers what are full of it."

It took a wandering C.S.M. Beresford, inspecting the site with a practised casual thoroughness, to shut him up. To his eventually departing back, Happy John muttered, "All this for a poxy shilling a day! - British Army's got to be the most canny employer ever!"

"7962 Barraclough - shit'n'it!" called Bert.

* * * * *

414

FORTY-ONE

Within a brief period, Ned's insides were twice challenged. He had diarrhoea for a time - the chloride and lime added to water might well have killed germs, but it also gave men 'the trots'. No sooner had he worked this through his system than something else came along that achieved in him a very similar response.

"It's coming down," said Wally.

"It can't come down," scoffed Taff Morgan, "There's no landing field over there."

"What's it doing, then?"

All four of them watched the aeroplane circle lower. They had just eaten breakfast and were returning to the tent to get kitted up.

"It is...... Look, he's definitely landing. Come on!"

"Why? What's it got to do with us?"

"Maybe needs some assistance. What? - Yer prefer bayonet practice, do yer?"

What had been a low hedge was now an even lower hedge, they could see the biplane dropping to a patch of relatively even earth three hundred yards away. As they ran, the pilot nosed the aircraft down onto the earthy field and brought it to a halt. He was already out of the plane when they approached, but had not switched off the engine, so his first gesture was to warn them about the propellor to the rear of the main body.

"Fuck!" was the first thing they heard him say as they arrived. "Help me get him out. Poor bastard." He was evidently a Canadian, this pilot.

The aircraft was a twin-winged creature that looked like the front of a gondola had been hacked off and grafted onto a pair of wings with a tailplane hung off the body by slender tubes. The idea seemed oddly simple - stick half a rowing boat onto the front of an aircraft body, with the propellor at the back. Simple, but it looked truly ridiculous.

These men had never seen such an apparatus close-up before and were first impressed by how open it was - no protection whatsoever. Most had only ever seen an aircraft in the sky.

"Get him out, come on!"

"Is he alright?" called Bert.

"No, he's fucking dead," the pilot yelled back. "Help me get him out, now!" By the man's accent, they confirmed him Canadian, though he bore the insignia of the British Flying Corps.

Bert, Ned, Wally and Taff helped get the dead observer out of the front binnacle. A large wound across the chest, they could see that right away through the man's thick flying coat.

"Bastard!" shouted the pilot, checking the body. It seemed planes carried rifles, the observer had taken rifle fire from another plane. Reconnaissance aircraft didn't look for combat. This one was of a type the officer referred to as a "pusher". On the ground it looked smaller than these craft did in the air.

After crouching for a few moments to examine his comrade, the pilot wasted no time in jumping to his feet and, through shouting and gestures, made his purpose known.

"I'm not going back without pictures," he told them. "Sixty bloody miles - best part of a bloody hour! No way I'm going back without pictures!" He was angry, amongst other things, that was plain to see. Very angry and perhaps not rational. But the soldiers looked at each other as if debating how this could have anything to do with them. They knew little of what aeroplanes did.

"You guys know anything about cameras?"

"Ned does," volunteered Bert at once. Ned looked at Bert as if he had just suggested a stroll in front of a firing squad.

"You use a camera?" the pilot questioned him.

"What?"

The Canadian shouted louder. "The semi-auto camera, that big thing in there. It uses plates. Forget that. Look, Harry always had a backup, in case the ALC got smashed up. He's got a small film camera taped up inside. Before these automated efforts came along, we used a regular camera anyway. Not brilliant but okay. You know about cameras?"

416

"Well, I - "

"It's a folding camera. German, I think. Might be a Kodak, I dunno. All I know is, it takes about eight pictures on a roll."

"Maybe an Ica," called Ned. "I have one similar."

"Great! Listen, son, you ever been up in a kite?"

Ned was horrified. He had jumped sixty feet into a freezing sea, but it was hardly time to bring that up.

"No, never!"

"Nothin' to it. We strap you in tight - don't worry, you're not gonna drop out, son, I wouldn't do that to yer! You take that camera and when I give you this signal - " He made a jabbing, vertical movement with his flat hand as if chopping wood. " - you take as many pictures as you can of what's directly below us. Got that? Count twelve seconds between each. You got that? Look, it might sound fucking crazy but I've gotta have pictures! You don't need to stand up or do any acrobatics, just hold the camera out - make sure it's not going to snap the side of the plane. You understand?"

"But I've never been in an aeroplane before."

"Hell, son, I never had my observer shot before. In times like these - look, I'm making this up as I go on, but I need to get pictures this morning. I can't fly this fuckin' thing and take pictures at the same time. In any case, our guys are lucky if they get a few hours training in the air, so what's the difference? Twelve second intervals, you got that?"

"Twelve seconds. But - "

"That's right. One-little-second. Two-little-seconds. And so on. As steady as you can. I'll keep the plane still while you do it. I'll just have to fly a little lower than normal. Real steady - honest injun! And listen, son, you just ignore that Lewis gun up there - you don't know how to fire it and I'm not asking you to. Yeah? Damn thing shouldn't be there anyway - I told that fuckin' mechanic..... aw heck, what does it matter? Anyhow, you'd wreck the bloody plane if you tried firing it! I just want you to steady yourself, point the camera down - we lash the camera to a strap round your wrist - and go click

417

- click - click, and get me some pictures. Yer can do that, son, I know yer can!"

"Ah can take pictures but - ah don't think ah can manage the flyin' bit. "

"Sure yer can! Sure yer can, son! Just trust me - I do the flying. I'm the best there is, you've nothin' to worry about. You just sit up there in front and you've got a whole sky open to you, nothin' to get in the way. Just enjoy the view."

"But - "

"Look, these guys will tell your C.O. that I requisitioned you to do a job with the Flying Corps. We'll get yer back here in one piece. Once we're back at base, I'll give you all the bits of paper you want."

The pilot rounded on Bert Parrock. "You there - you tell your C.O. that Second Lieutenant Sam Pickett stole his soldier and I'll send him back when we've got pictures. You got that?"

Bert knew this was piracy, the C.O. would never permit it. But what was he to do?

"I've got that," yelled Bert. "Oh - what unit, sir?"

"Hell, soldier, who gives a shit? You think I'm a Jerry stealing British soldiers one by one? Look, Fritz, I found a new way to win the war! ... Pickett, Second Lieutenant, attached to 5 squadron. You just tell him I'll get your man back. Oh, and get Harry's body back to St. Omer for me."

"Good luck!" shouted Bert, directing his remark at Ned.

In that instant, Ned felt as though he was about to learn to swim all over again whilst having a tooth pulled. He didn't like surprises like this, his legs were already beginning to crumble.

"The - the camera," stuttered Ned. "D'yer know if it's a 6.8 or a 4.5?"

"What? Hell, kid, it's a fuckin' camera, how the fuck should I know? Why?"

"It's a difference in the shutter. Faster is better."

"Can you work the fuckin' thing is all?"

"Ah can, yes. Long as you don't fly upside down!" It was meant as a joke, but after further thought, he was no longer sure.

They took the helmet and coat - wet blood and all - from the dead observer and the pilot saw that Ned was properly dressed before ushering him to the aeroplane, its engine still cackling noisily.

It was like climbing into a boat on the local park lake back home - just up instead of down. Far too open, too unprotected, and nowhere to slide down and make yourself small. The seat was bare metal and the retaining harnesses looked none too reassuring. Ignoring the proper camera equipment - he would have found it impossible to master even if it was semi-automatic as Pickett had said - he discovered the small camera in a bag taped onto the seat bracket as the pilot pointed it out. Nervously, he cut the tapes and bag, extended and locked the bellows to make sure it worked, and hoped no other little bits needed twiddling that he didn't know about. A quick wipe of the finder - well, it seemed useable. He only prayed there actually was film in there!

"Put them gloves on, son, you'll need 'em - it gets cold up there. But take 'em off just before you start taking pictures. Don't drop 'em - make sure the cords are round your wrists. Oh, and be careful with your feet - don't want any holes in the side of the plane, got enough ventilation as it is. Keep an eye on me, I'll give you the nod when to get ready. Get me eight good pictures, son," the pilot shouted, "and I'll buy you the best shag in St.Omer." At that moment, all Ned really wanted was to crawl back into his camp bed.

"If I bang on the crate and wave my hand like this - " Pickett used the flat of the hand in a horizontal sweep. " - then cut, and we'll go home. Okay? Fill the camera, that's all I ask. A poor picture's better than nuthin' at all, that's why I need yer. But keep it still as possible. You savvy, cowboy?"

"Yes, but - what do you want me to photograph?"

"You let me worry about that. Just point it down. Hun positions, son. Especially their artillery. You'll know what I mean when we get over there. Oh, and son, one more thing: whatever you do, don't let anything get loose and fly away, understand? That's fucking A1 important!"

Ned only stared back at him. With a few sharp jabs pointing at the rear-mounted engine and propellor, the pilot yelled, "If something gets loose and hits that - you and I are buggered. Get it?"

Ned's colleagues were backing away from the 'plane but looking warily at him. He almost expected them to go down on their knees and say a prayer. *Heavenly Father, don't give this idiot his wings yet........*

After a few more quick explanations of what he was intending to do, Pickett jumped aside and was ready to mount his aircraft. Then a sudden thought occurred to him and he extended an arm to the young man.

"How old are you, son?"

"Nearly twenty-four."

"Hell - you're older than me! Name's Sam, by the way, what's yours?.... Okay, Ned. And if you're gonna throw up - and *you will* - throw it down into the pod, got it? - Not up and out and all over me! Oh, and keep your mouth closed when we take off and land - so's you don't chop your tongue off."

Instruction over, Pickett directed the three soldiers to pick up the tail of the aircraft and swing the whole plane around to face the other way.

Was the bumping, bouncing run along the field the worst part? Ned thought so, then instantly changed his mind as their chariot suddenly leaped into the air and left his stomach behind in a rush of wind and a complete lack of equilibrium. The ground dropped away beneath them, leaving him battered, winded, and gripping the edges of the gondola. Sam Pickett could read the young man's terror through the back of his head: as Ned strained to turn round, Pickett reached forward a hand and made a shaking 'ok' sign with his thumb and forefinger. Ned was not okay. He might have been inside a great bag, tossed and bumped by an invisible giant. His heart was in his mouth and his stomach was about to join it. At any second, he would die in a way he had never reckoned on doing! Desperately he looked about him - anywhere that would take his mind off what they were actually doing. Up in the air! - It was about the most perilous thing he could imagine doing..... then he remembered stepping out of the trenches into no-man's land. Which madness was more survivable?

The dizziness and surging stomach would have their way. And what made low clouds so solid that it felt like the plane was crashing into them? Pickett was right - Ned threw up after dropping his head forward as far as he could. What he had eaten for breakfast and more besides all cascaded down his leg and boots. The vomiting over, for long moments he felt his head light and his face as cold as winter, but the buffeting of the air now speeding by quickly freshened face and mind, and after another minute, he was able to turn and stick up a tentative thumb. Pickett shouted something that Ned could not hear for the wind buffeting his helmet. His gut still aching, he clung to his seat, not daring nor wanting to move any further forward to peer into the abyss beyond the nose of this contraption, that felt not the tiniest bit secure nor rigid. Only once had he been at the top of a ferris wheel: this was not dissimilar, except that the ferris wheel had not been bouncing and dipping and moving at a frightening speed.

In less than two minutes, the biplane was flying a level course and Ned, nervously inching forward to peer over the prow of the craft, could see the grand vista of the Western Front spreading out before him. Totally unprepared for a sight of such vast proportions, Ned found his terror almost completely distracted by the enormous network of man-made earthworks that stretched as far as the eye could see - simultaneously, a breathtaking spectacle of human endeavour and a lunacy of a magnitude greater than any words could possibly describe. It was a folly of incomparable stupidity, that only here at this height might the brain take it all in. From here, the two rivers of trenches looked like a gigantic pot of stew had been poured liberally across the land with a mesh of chains in two streams running parallel with each other, stretching out to infinity. Each stream of chains led into smaller rivulets that spread out in a myriad fingers.

What on earth were the armies doing? Scores of miles of the most utterly ludicrous mind games ever devised to test the capabilities of one nest of ants against another. Once seen like this, how could it ever be seen as anything else? How were airmen able to return to this spectacle day after day and not be utterly overwhelmed by the nonsense of it all?

Peering over the sides of his gondola, which was moving into whiskers of thicker cloud, Ned saw nothing apparently happening below, no sounds fought with the noise of wind and engine to give anything away. He had no idea at what height they might be flying and did not wish to know, his stomach was beginning to teeter at the neck of his throat again. *Up in the clouds! - Unimaginable!* And yet *- Would not M. Verne have loved this!*

To suggest he might be enjoying the experience of flight would have been folly, but Ned began to see what made men want to fly machines like this: Nature's overwhelming power revealed in all its splendour as Ned now saw green fields far in the distance, clear multi-coloured patches where neighbour met neighbour, little hamlets and ponds and a town way over there, all sheltering below a canopy of dirty white that from here he could touch if it were not so forbiddingly cold. And then to contrast that with the incredible other-worldliness of what lay immediately below: a grand folly, a monument in earth and wood and stone and metal, an agglomeration of all the best things on earth but in all the worst manifestations.

Here was one colossal contradiction, this illusion of a life made necessary by the defence of a realm, and that realm the exclusive property of each nation, the illusion that no other way but theirs was just. All those grand illusions - what an absurdity! It was no more than earth and fields; grass, dirt and water, and all those dwellings and buildings that man in his struggle to establish himself had set on the land in a vain effort to make himself recognisable in the landscape. Earth was a timeless thing, man a mere transition.

A metallic tapping from behind him - Pickett was banging on the fuselage to attract his attention. As Ned turned, Pickett was already giving the signal. He nodded back and prepared his hands with the camera, fighting the wind as it threatened to tear the device from his grasp, as well as straining to see clearly through his goggles.

Concentrating on the view ahead had been taking Ned's mind off his upset stomach and that disgusting taste in his mouth, not to mention soggy trousers. As they headed southbound along the line, he readied the camera, similar enough in its actions to his own, and found he could get into position if he leaned and stretched his two arms out to the left, allowing for the curve of the gondola. Ned had anxiously scanned the horizon for other aircraft and had seen none, whilst below, within the frenzied zig-zag lines of the trenches and their tributaries, he could just make out groups of soldiers. What lay between British and German lines made no sense at all, most features were nothing but a grey-brown murk, a dirty sea of bizarre shipwrecked debris and everywhere puddly craters flickered like tiny starshells as they reflected sunlight. As Pickett dropped the noisy plane lower, Ned saw that they were drifting over the German line. He felt sure soldiers must be firing at the aeroplane from below but he had no way of telling and sought no proof of it. He looked around at Pickett, who put up his hand and showed five fingers twice. Ten seconds! Ned had set the shutter and wrapped the cable release between his fingers, now he held out the camera as far as his arms would allow and tried to make sense of the finder but that was no help at all, and the light reflecting on the metal rendered it useless: he would take the pictures by dead reckoning, relying on his own sense of balance, which up to this point had been far from its best.

Pickett banged on the aeroplane body again and, when Ned looked, was chopping his hand in the proscribed manner. Ned ripped his goggles down around his neck, to rid himself of that air of unreality they gave to everything. Immediately fighting the cold wind in his eyes, he aimed the camera down, pressed the cable to trip the shutter, then reset it, pulled his arms back, and counted twelve seconds. Another shot. Twelve long seconds. Then another. Each time, resetting the shutter meant a two-handed operation and his hands were cold and his eyes wet from the force of the wind, but he counted out the seconds, repositioned the camera, and tripped again. At shot five, the camera slipped from his grasp, taken by the strength of the wind, and banged against the side of the pod as it danced on the end of the tether. He recovered it, checked it was alright then looked back at Pickett who only nodded emphatically to continue.

Another minute and he was done. Turning once more to his pilot, Ned jabbed out an arm and gave a firm thumbs-up, whereupon Pickett at once put the stick over and banked steeply toward the South and then West. He was heading home. Job done.

There was good reason for that hurried departure. As Ned congratulated himself in completing the task, his eyes roaming the horizon now spotted the other aircraft. He could not tell if it was heading their way, but it may have been only a thousand yards away. Pickett would know if it was British or German. Either way, the aircraft bounced and shuddered as Pickett dived to gain speed. Again, Ned's heart was in his mouth as he saw the ground and sparse trees coming up to meet them, but he could not be sick again.

The rushing landscape changed. Passing over the sights of civilisation once more - villages and fields all set out like a giant green patchwork quilt - Ned looked back and saw no sign of the other plane following. One in the far distance was on the same course as their own, no doubt a 'friendly'. His hands were cold, he had not replaced the gloves as he put his goggles back on, and did so at once. The camera secured, it seemed all he could do was to watch the scenery, and hope for no further incidents. Hope also - God, hope against hope! - that the images he had taken were safely captured on film. Surely they had not risked their lives in vain. Later, Pickett would tell him that they had been shot at from the ground and there were new holes in one wing, something of which Ned had not a clue. He had flown above six thousand feet at more than sixty miles an hour - the statistics were almost too monstrous to be comprehended! What amazing excitement! Though only afterwards did he acknowledge that.

Landing was by far the easy part, Ned closed his eyes and mouth as the ground came up to meet them. There was nowhere else to go, so what could go wrong? A barrage of bumps almost convinced him otherwise. They had arrived at Pickett's base field near Montreuil, a satellite of the RFC units at St. Omer. It was little more than a single hut and a rag-tag bunch of tents with a marked absence of any military identity other than the number of planes parked there bearing British RFC roundels. Ned was amazed that Pickett could navigate his way there at all - from the air, so much on the ground looked the same. After Pickett had cut the engine and in this oh-so-peaceful field, Ned's ears thought they had entered paradise.

"Cup of tea, sir?" said the aircraft mechanic who rushed up to help Ned out of the gondola, then recoiled in puzzlement that a wrong man had arrived in the right clothes. When Pickett asked Ned if he was feeling alright, Ned was surprised that most of him was, though still dizzy. His gut ached, but the adrenaline rush had squeezed the queasiness out of him.

"By the way, sir," asked Ned, "if anything had gone wrong, how would we have got down?"

Pickett smiled and used arm and hand in a diving motion to suggest that the words 'plummet' and 'crash' would be appropriate. Then he added, "We can always jump. Look for a lake and pray that you only lose both legs and not the bits in between!" In those early years of the RFC, injuries were either light or fatal, there was nothing else. You had to be either very good or very lucky to last three months as a reconnaissance flyer.

"Were we in danger?" Ned asked him.

Pickett laughed. "Always, son. Did you see that Hun plane up there?"

"I wasn't sure it was a Jerry."

"Those black crosses - dead give-away. That was the guy whose wing man shot my buddy."

"No!"

"Oh yes. We got out of there just in time. He could have followed us, but thought better of it. Maybe he was low on fuel. But those Fokkers are faster than my kite."

"Those what?"

"Fokkers! ..... No - you're probably right, Ned. Come on, I'll introduce you to Hattie."

"Who's Hattie?"

"The guy who'll develop that film."

"Oh.... a bloke called Hattie?"

"Thinks he's a girl really. Listen, I don't care. There's gotta be a use for all sorts in this war. I mean, we don't have to shag 'em all, do we?"

The creature called Hattie was their genius of the photography department and more civilian than fighting man: he would himself suggest he was an amateur serviceman and a professional civilian. In forty minutes, he developed the film and printed pictures. Someone else telephoned St. Omer and a despatch rider took the enlargements to headquarters as part of the morning's batch of photographs.

"They were okay, then?"

"You did alright, Ned. There were four he managed to get workable prints from. For a small camera, not that bad. Wouldn't want to frame 'em, but good enough. I can't give you copies for souvenirs."

Ned was looking at the blood stains on his jacket.

"Not sure you'll get those out," said Pickett dubiously. "Tell them to requisition you a new jacket and charge it to the RFC. As to your shitty trousers, though.... Listen, just keep the ones I gave you."

"What now, sir?"

"Call me Sam, Ned - we shared a flight together, you're as good as adopted. Well..... We get you back to your unit, that's what we do. You ride pillion?"

"No.... That'll be two things in one day that ah never did before."

"When you get back, ask yourself which you preferred - your balls will tell you which. Stomach alright now?" Ned made a sign, just so-so.

Pickett slapped him on the shoulder and gave him a picture of an aircraft. "This is an FE2. You were privileged, son, they haven't been in service long. And that feller there would be you, sat in the crow's nest."

"Is that what they call it?"

"Hell, who knows? - I just made that up. Take the picture, show it to your C.O. Give me ten minutes, I'm going to write a report for him. Don't hand it to anyone else."

"But ah'll have to pass it through the company sergeant major."

"Well.... If that's how you guys do things. But make sure your C.O. gets it - I want to be sure he writes you up in his dispatches and sends a reply to me. You got that? My report will corroborate his. If he doesn't, I'll come and kick his balls in - you tell him that!"

"First thing ah'll do, Sam," Ned assured him.

* * * * *

'18 June 1916. Dearest brother,

I hate it that letters take so long. It's so cold, to have to tell you things I know you cannot hear. Thanks for yours of the 10th. What amazing times! We were all utterly flummoxed you went up in an aeroplane - how incredible! And a mention in dispatches - what does that mean, Ned - do you get any more pay for it? Just so long as you are safe.

I am glad you were busy and did not have time to reflect long on my last news. Father's passing was expected, still a shock to the system. We were glad his pain was over. The funeral was a gentle affair at St. Pauls, well attended. He was popular at Tramways and many remember his time as a fighter, he was more respected than perhaps we imagined. So tiny in that coffin. James seemed at peace - I'm glad. He threw the first handful of earth and I heard him say a few words. No malice, Ned. I hope you would say the same. What is done is done. I leave the big words to the vicar but if there is a hereafter I feel sure he will be a happier soul there now that his torment is over.

Robert Illingworth and Frank Halstead were killed. You all used to play together and go to chapel, I don't need to remind you. Sometimes I think it was a bad idea for all those lads to go marching off to war together. We pray you fare better. Mother says, when you come home she will steal us a side of bacon to celebrate even if she goes to prison for it!

I try not to be negative, but working for the paper opens our eyes. We are censored in what we can print, like the strikes. A meeting of conchies in Leeds was broken up by police, we couldn't print it. I am not sure I agree with the conchies but the police beat them. Police stopped a Labour party demonstration too. Using bobbies like this isn't right. Harold tells me all this! Bruno told me the Durham factory has more contracts for shells, they have to tender to the Ministry. One of their shell case suppliers is letting them down, so I think - reading between the lines - Bruno is something of a trouble-shooter for various firms now! He's probably very good!

I must tell you this. After the evening Bruno took me to dinner at the Midland with his colleagues from Hepworths, I had an invitation for interview from a manager, this man said he needed some "intelligence" in his offices. I shall go and find out, at least. I know it's down to Bruno, he's so good to us.

I must conclude. Look after yourself, Ned, we think of you.

With love, Grace.'

* * * * *

'5 July 1916. Oh, Ned! I have cried all morning. Both of us. Isn't it awful? We just could not believe the news on Monday, it was so horrid. Forgive me, I think I am writing to you as a prayer you come through all this. I know you are with a different regiment and not at the Somme where all the Pals have died, but all the same, it's frightening, mother and I are very anxious. It is in all the newspapers so I cannot imagine you do not know the events of Saturday. I went in late and there were glum faces all around. I was so upset, I cried all the way up the lane. Everyone knows someone who has lost a son.

Mother and I went round to Laburnum where we knew Mavis Greenwood had lost her boy. She was inconsolable. She held his school book in her hand the whole time and couldn't put it down, even to wipe her eyes. Norman was eighteen in March.

Harold said it was a place called Serre. We never heard of it. What must there be there that so many young men had to lose their

428

lives? The Telegraph said at first nine hundred, which was bad enough, but later it was almost eighteen hundred - out of two thousand men. I am still crying, just talking about it. None of us here can understand. I am sorry, Ned, we are all so upset, I suppose I am trying to get it out of my system.

On every street there are glum faces, people cannot believe the Bradford Pals could just be destroyed like that. In one day. First day of the campaign, they said: it beggars belief. Frank Middleton at the paper told me that our West Yorkshire soldiers have suffered the biggest losses of any regiment. All those poor widows and families - it seems only a short time ago we were all celebrating the town winning the FA Cup.

We are going to see Mr. Hayley at the greengrocers, his wife took ill after hearing Robert had been killed, we want to help if we can. We pray you can come home soon, Ned, take good care of yourself. I am so sorry to send such a miserable letter, but I wanted to tell you we all have you in our thoughts. I have not seen James, I know he will say the same.

With deepest love from mother and I,
Grace.'

* * * * *

429

FORTY-TWO

Lady Sophie was most impressed with Carelle's new motor car - a large white one, she took pains to comment, with exquisite red leather seats and trim. She was not sure she was quite so impressed by Carelle driving it, rather than letting his 'man' do it. She was not very sure about his 'man' either. Motor cars gave Lady Sophie the vapours, and his grim face showed that Carelle's driver was equally unhappy about being relegated to the passenger seat.

It was by intent that Carelle's poor sense of timing should determine that they arrived around lunch time at the rowing club where Carelle knew Semper was going to be that day, having a meeting with his confidants. When it came to information, Lady Sophie was an open book. Charming in a certain perspective, and completely without guile. Arthur spotted them arriving immediately and passed word to his lordship that Lady Sophie had chosen this moment to visit. "Damn!" was all that Semper let slip.

They exchanged pleasantries, naturally, and whilst Lady Sophie took Miss Devonshire aside to show her the men of the club going about their 'training' on the river, each man keen to demonstrate his physical condition before tucking into beer and sandwiches, Carelle stood a round of drinks for the parliamentarians. It was the least he could do for having disturbed their conference.

"Valentine, Snelson, you have not met our Belgian friend, have you? Carelle, this is Lord Chadlock." Carelle as usual employed his Belgian-ness to best effect by being suitably convivial, although after reading earlier of the casualties at the Front, he lacked committal until Cognac had restored his spirit.

"His lordship is chair of the 1908 Committee. And of course, a very good friend."

"I should be," commented Lord Chadlock cheerfully, "his factory sits on my land."

"Ah," Carelle came back, "What better associate to have than one whose arse you have to kiss every day of the week, my lord."

The two peers looked at each other, not quite believing what they had heard. Then Chadlock saw the funny side and laughed: at first a little cheeky chortle, then a loud guffaw. The other three men followed his example once they had the mood of their senior in their faces.

"You're a bit of a card, Mister Carelle," said Chadlock. "You would do well in the music halls. You've the balls for it."

"Balls, my lord? Do you mean, as a *jongleur*? Juggling comes naturally to me. As I constantly point out - I am Belgian: we have to have more balls than other people if we are not to be ignored."

"Ignored? Come, come, sir, I see no danger of that. Bit of a wag, Tony - you've been hiding this chap from us, haven't you?"

Semper was not comfortable with raucous laughter on a Wednesday lunchtime, he tugged at his gloves whilst returning Carelle a considered grin. "Mister Carelle is in the chocolate business, Stephen, and is used to serenading us with his sweet tongue. But do not judge him lightly, I have found his cane bears a sharp point. He has made some shrewd investments since making this country his home. Is that not so, Carelle?"

"I do prefer *bon-bons* to piston rings and primers, your lordship, it's true. But your factories are a refuge for many of my countrymen and women, and so I say, may their efforts bring a swift conclusion to this war."

"You see, gentlemen: the man is flawed, after all. Who would put sentiment before business?" Semper delivered these clever words to his gloves, but their tone was not wasted on the others.

"Well...." It was easy to let Semper take them to a place Carelle did not wish to go. "I am no philanthropist, my dear sirs," he commented, "only a simple businessman - "

"Munitions," reported Semper, "Mister Carelle sets his future in armaments, gentlemen. Noble intentions, I have no doubt, but prompted by golden ambitions, I'll wager."

Chadlock was quick to interrupt. "Why, Tony! It's not long since you were telling me of Brantcliffe's proposal to put a foothold in munitions. Come clean, old chap, you can't say one thing one minute and disagree with yourself the next."

431

Delivering a withering stare to match the naivety of his colleague, Semper attempted to paper over cracks. "You forget, Stephen, it was I who put a veto on that motion when Cranleigh raised the issue with the board. Had you forgotten?"

"Had I? - Oh, I may have. Well, it's all grist to the mill anyway!"

It was an expression Carelle did not understand. "Gentlemen, I was merely saying I am a businessman who wishes to help his country, however I may."

"And harvest a tidy profit, I dare say. Come, come, Carelle, no need for reticence."

"Capital!" laughed Snelson, trying to slip in his own pun.

"Sir, you have me at a disadvantage. In present times one may not have one without the other. And yet .... appearances sometimes deceive."

"Meaning what?"

"I have a love of chocolates, your lordship - not war. To survive this war, my business must pursue activities which may not be popular in times of peace."

"But we are not at peace, Mister Carelle," interrupted Chadlock, "and frankly I find it commendable you put your resources into the best interests of this country - which at the moment is dedicated to winning a war with Germany by whatever means. Survival of the fittest, isn't that so?"

"I agree, Stephen. But where will Carelle take his money once this war is won? I wonder... And won by whom?"

"We are not competitors, my lord, are we?" countered Carelle, "I thought we had interests in the same boat - if you take my meaning."

"Ah!" called Chadlock. "Boats! Got you there, Tony!"

"I merely wished to point out," drawled Semper, " - I'm sure Carelle will not mind my saying - that he is Belgian, and Belgium is a country occupied by the Germans. I don't doubt Mister Carelle's short-term sympathies but what of the longer term? Of course I have no desire to impugn you, Carelle, but the less-informed might be bound to wonder, some would say."

Carelle showed no sign of being hurt, and only grinned a little awkwardly whilst he sought a response. Was Semper playing double-bluff? - Accuse the other man of treachery whilst keeping your own powder dry? For Semper to counter the intentions of Brantcliffe Bank to finance munitions could equally suggest a ploy to allay suspicion that he was out to profit from the war over and above his already lucrative activities.

"How should I put it?" offered Carelle. "When I left my country, I brought little clothing. A businessman may wear many suits, but a patriot is a person who wears the same suit whether for work or for Sunday best - is that the expression, 'Sunday best'? Whilst I work in this country, I wear just one suit, for Sundays and all the other days."

"Come, come, Mister Carelle," interrupted Valentine, "Tony didn't infer any stain upon your character, sir - or on your suit, if you wish!" They laughed, and Carelle laughed politely with them. Inside, he was prickly, but a long history of dealing with all manner of business had taught him the politics of deceit and how they can be assumed to disguise the angered breast.

What this day was teaching him - as he already suspected - was that Semper did not like him. It was, at one and the same time, an inconvenient turn of plan and a badge of self-approval.

Their conversation became more casual as Valentine remonstrated with Snelson and Chadlock about a recent vote in the House, and on another matter both of them disagreed with Semper as to who - if anyone - had won the battle of the fleets at Jutland.

"Where the Dickens is Jutland anyway?" Lord Chadlock wanted to know, "And what the blazes is wrong with the Navy these days?"

Carelle knew little of their party politics and wanted it to remain that way. Chadlock appeared a traditional noble steed of the Right, and the other two mere light cavalry. He would underestimate none of them. Arthur meanwhile stood to the side, evidently admiring his manicure.

Presently, Lady Sophie and her companion re-appeared and the tone of the proceedings lightened beyond measure, and almost beyond tolerance. Until, that is, the subject of artillery crept into the conversation, and Lady Sophie, supremely comfortable in her boredom with such matters, carelessly responded, "Tony, not that flame gun nonsense again, surely? I thought we'd had enough of that."

Semper for a few moments looked like an actor caught in the limelight without a line. "My dear, we were not talking about - ?"

"Oh, it's boring, it's boring! Flame gun, this, flame gun that! You and Bernard in little huddles in the corner. Daddy thought you'd gone and bought some new contraption you were sinking everybody's money into. Bet it never worked, did it? Crackpot ideas like that never do."

Lord Chadlock was nervous. "Sophie, we're not talking about guns, my dear."

"Oh, this was a horrible thing you put petrol into - wasn't it, Tony? Horribly beastly anyway! I don't like all that talk. I wish, Tony, you would be done with this whole war nonsense. Why don't we just go over to America until this silly war's over? What about Biarritz, are they still open for business?"

Carelle saw his moment. "But, Lady Sophie, I have been for weeks trying to get your husband interested in exactly those beastly things. As an investment. But I fear he remains unconvinced."

"Shipbuilding," Semper countered, "is an equally noble activity at this present time of national emergency. I have put considerable investment into that. Let Winston and the Welshman shout at other people to get what they want, I've enough on my plate."

"Well, good!" cried Lady Sophie. "I'm glad to hear it. No flame things at least."

"Flame gun, your lordship?" Carelle wanted to turn the screw. "I heard the Americans had some mad scheme with a big gun that squirts flame. I didn't know the British were working on such a thing, too." His inflection made a question of it, and Semper seemed a little subdued. "No. Not at all," he offered.

"Ah. Another rumour, then. After all, had such a resourceful man as yourself been behind the project, we should all be talking about flame guns by now. Perhaps it didn't work, so many of these ideas don't...."

"Oh," Chadlock waded in, "There's always some new wonder machine, isn't there? We've all heard about this land-ship idea, I see that's busting out any time."

The others looked at him. "Well, come on, we all know it is! 'Tanks', isn't that what they're calling them now? You can't keep secrets for - "

And the look from Semper at that precise second made Carelle wish he had brought a camera.

Chadlock only stared at each of them in turn, then gave a shrug and called the waiter over.

Carelle returned to his motor car mid-afternoon, leaving the ladies in the hands of his lordship's party. Carelle's driver was pleased to have his boredom terminated, and eagerly drove them away.

"Thought you'd care to know, Mister Carelle, whilst you was having your lunch with the toffs, that Mister Arthur came and had a few words with me."

"Really? What about?"

The driver paused before replying, almost as if he had felt offended. "He offered me money, Mister Carelle. Twenty pounds, to be precise."

"Twenty pounds? For what?"

"Information. He asked me in a round-about sort of way if I'd be willing to keep him informed of your movements, Mister Carelle."

"Ah! And what did you say?"

"I told 'im the truth: I said I was not a reliable person and temptation would only lead me to make similar questionable requests of my employer - meaning yourself, Mister Carelle."

"And how did he react to that?"

"Like I'd just farted in his face... I thought you'd approve, Mister Carelle."

"You think correctly, Tommy. I do approve."

"It's a good job, Mister Carelle, that I don't make a habit of doin' this sort of thing."

"I'm sure it is, Tommy. Think only that you allowed Sam to have a day off."

* * * * *

"Really, Mister Grimshaw, this is a bit too much like a 'penny dreadful', isn't it? Scribbled notes delivered by hand and meetings in the park? Aren't we getting a little melodramatic?"

"Perhaps so, Mister Carelle, and I apologise. I have to be aware that, even a young organisation like MI5 is not immune to spying activities, especially now there's a war on. It's not every day we catch somebody like Lody - getting him was quite a feather in our cap, but the question arises - how many more are there like him? Sometimes, using the telephone is not the best idea. Here in the open no-one can eavesdrop on us."

The agent's appearance amused Carelle to the extent that he almost laughed. "You know, Mister Grimshaw, if Conan-Doyle wanted a model for his detective stories, he has only to look at you. You seem to lack only the big pipe."

"I don't possess a calabash, sir," muttered Grimshaw, choosing to ignore the exaggeration. Even if his coat *was* too big.

"The point is, the Americans have arrested James Martin."

"Martin?"

"Yes. The Washington correspondent Semper was in touch with - I dare say Carl Lody was too. Martin's the chap he was going to see when *Titanic* went down."

"I read about Lody. A very amateur spy, by all accounts. What does this mean for Lord Semper?"

"For the present, perhaps little. Martin was known to be a contact for a number of foreign agencies. Evidently the Americans used a double-agent to flush him out. He'll go to trial, but the devil knows how long that may take - America isn't at war as we are, and if certain folk have their way, wild horses won't drag 'em in."

"That would suit Semper. Now they've got Martin, he will do his utmost to cover his tracks, won't he?"

"He surely shall, Mister Carelle. If he knows we suspect him - "

"How would he know?"

436

"Well, stands to reason. For one thing, he knows you don't like him because you told me so. For all he knows, you might be one of our people."

"Yes," agreed Carelle ruefully, "That was a mistake. I did not plan to get on the bad side of him."

"Carl Lody's trial eighteen months ago implicated a whole lot of people the Americans have been watching, and now Martin, so that's another thing. Lastly, our other agent has been finding out a thing or two."

Carelle was surprised. "What other agent?"

"Mister Carelle, you know I have to be careful what I tell you. Don't blame me, sir, I have a job to do like everyone else."

"Alright - but tell me anyway!"

"Since last year we've had another party working within Semper's organisation. She - "

"She?"

"Yes. She works in the offices at Brantcliffe."

"Alongside Oberon?"

"Not him, no. Semper's man there is Bernard Pettifer."

"Another Bernard!" Carelle laughed.

"She's been under cover for us for nearly a year."

"And found out what?"

"I can't tell you. You know I can't tell you. What I can say is, we have certain information. We know for instance Semper had paid Fenians through the bank - you as much as knew that yourself. The Serbs - she got some information on that too, though I don't have the details. And after we mentioned Ellen McKitteredge, she confirmed that too. Thanks to you, of course."

Carelle licked his thumb and drew it down his chest. "Anything else?"

"The case is still building up. I tell you what, Mister Carelle, we're going to get this bugger. But getting him and keeping him may be two different things. Oh - and the other thing was, John Cade has been taken into the army."

"Damn! I should have got onto that sooner. Damn all this red tape!"

437

"In a way, it could make it easier to keep track of the blighter On the other hand, if he does the smart thing and takes off - "

"The *smart* thing?"

A wry smile came over Grimshaw's normally gaunt face. "Smart from his point of view. He could easily desert. If he does, it could be weeks before he's caught again."

"Won't the army take measures to see he doesn't get away?"

"I don't know what they do, to be honest, Mister Carelle. Look at it this way: you're in the middle of a battle and a soldier nips back and steals a motorbike or something. Not difficult in my opinion with all the chaos going on. You can't send a bloke into battle with chains on his ankles, can you?"

Carelle made no reply.

"And anyway, who's to say where he'll be posted. He might easily get sent over to Ireland or Palestine or somewhere. He'd probably love that!"

It was not what Carelle wanted to hear. Rightly or wrongly, Carelle had always felt the best plan to gain exoneration for Ned Thornton was to get authenticated statements out of John Cade and, if possible, even Lord Semper. Prison could have made that task easier, but as it was...... Somebody, he had to hope, might make a mistake.

"I could always write to General Haig, I suppose," mused Carelle.

"Hmm..... If you think it would do any good."

"Mr. Grimshaw, I meant that as a British joke, not a Belgian one."

* * * * *

FORTY-THREE

'Cheri, 28 July 1916

I want to say this - I love you. I want to say it because I want to read it and if I read it, I will believe it. I know - I am a mad woman! Do not ask me to explain this. We are in a simple situation. It is simple because there are only two things that make matter to us - You make matter to me, and I make matter to you. I want to tell you something. I wrote to Gitta last month. She is still working in that hospital militaire at Vincennes. She thinks about coming back to Havre, but not yet. And Regine is well. Doctor Neveux is looking at the first examinations. I cannot tell you how we feel that M. Carelle has insisted he pays for special treatments. He is wonderful. I have written to him.

For a long time I thought to say to Gitta what I am feeling, but I think anyway I do not have to tell her. Although, we have not spoken as sisters for a long time - you understand this. That man Ardant, I do not know what to think.

I said to her, Gitta, forgive me - I love Ned. And this morning I got a letter from her. She said, Reina, I know that you do and that is wonderful. Yes, darling, she said that. She said I am lucky to wake up my heart and find what was there for a long time that I didn't see. She is right. And she sends her best wishes. She is not angry. I was worried because - well, I told you.

Ned, I sat at my table at the school and I cried. The children came to ask me what was wrong. I said, Nothing is wrong, it is good news. Why do I love you, Ned? - I do not know. Because inside my heart I did not feel any different for a long time. I am a little girl. Is that what you want? A foolish little girl? But - Mutti said to me some weeks ago, Reina, it is time for you to be foolish - you love him, so tell him. So - !!!! If I say nothing, what should that be good for? And I have seen that you love me.

I have thought. I shall go to Amiens. Yvonne has an uncle there. And I thought this - please ask for some leave. You said it will be your turn soon, but I do not know how soon. Tell your officer that your girl friend must marry you! He does not know that I can't marry you, does he? Maybe he wants to see the marriage papers. Then you come to Amiens. It's a foolish plan? I want to see you so much. We can be together, it's possible? Write to me, Ned. Quickly, chéri.

I think about this. And because it is difficult to wait for letters, listen to me - Yvonne's uncle is Roland Morineau, he works at the Relais, Rue Victor Hugo in Amiens. If you only have time to write, "I am coming!" go there, and I will come. If it is not possible for you, I understand. I must wait. But I cannot be patient! There are too many times we should be together.

Nothing has changed in Havre, Jerome spends much time away, and I do not like his mother and his sister. No. I must leave that. I do not care what they say. I think one day with you is better than a life with them. Please do this.

Reina. xxx'

* * * * *

"Getting to be a habit, Thornton."

"Sir."

"At ease. Smoke if you want to. And you can take that worried look off your face - I can't kick you with this gammy leg, can I?"

Marshall's pained grin was settling enough. The captain hobbled round from the wash basin on the oak dresser and negotiated a wary collapse into his padded chair. There was little else left in the farmhouse that had not been taken for use as shoring timber in the trenches. Marshall had gained the wound several weeks ago, it was taking its time to heal. Whatever happened, Ned considered Marshall the best officer in the battalion, and that was important.

"Yesssss," hissed Marshall, steeling himself against his pain as he wrestled his behind into the seat. "Now. You may have wondered why I sent for you."

How true! Ned had been worried to have been summoned by his captain: any routine matters would have seen him appear before Donovan first.

440

"And you'd be partly right. Lieutenant Donovan has already considered your request - I'll come to that in a moment. There's something else first, and as a matter of fact, one thing leads onto the other, rather."

Ned was now not only anxious but highly curious as the captain rummaged in a drawer of his bureau.

"I see you've got your new helmets at least," said Marshall without looking up. "Damn good thing too and not before time."

"Yes, sir. "

"Those first efforts weren't much use in the trench stores, were they?"

"No, sir. One of the lads said now we've got summat to shave in."

"Ye-e-es. Well.... Don't let me catch any of you chaps using them to shave or anything else for that matter. I dread to think."

"No, sir."

"At ease," Marshall repeated. "D'you want to smoke?"

"No, sir. Thank you, sir."

"Well, we've had an odd request. That is - I - I have had an odd request. This paper is from the clerk of courts martial in St. Omer. He writes me a rigmarole about the difficulty he had in locating me - well, the battalion.... well, in fact, you, to be exact, Thornton."

The blood in Ned's veins momentarily froze. Taking his time, Marshall looked up at Ned and smiled.

"Don't worry. It's alright. You are not in any trouble, Thornton.... Are you sure you don't want a cigarette?"

"Yes, sir - erm, yes, thank you, ah will have one."

As Ned fumbled a cigarette into his mouth and lit it, Marshall appeared to be studying him, though not in an unkindly way.

"Of all the men in this battalion, Thornton, you appear the most innocent and yet you seem to attract the most attention. Do you know that I had a police warrant presented to me last year?"

Ned felt his face turn bright scarlet. "No, sir. Ah didn't."

"You know what for, though...."

For the briefest of instants, Ned deliberated a reply, yet thought any elaboration would only exacerbate his position.

"They said I'd stolen some papers, sir."

The captain smiled. He admired a man who faced him instantly with the truth. "That's right. That's right."

"Yer didn't have me arrested, sir."

"No.... No, Thornton, I didn't. For one thing, the warrant was quite old and the army needs every man, and I wasn't going to let you go and then have to fill in a great pile of paperwork just because of an old arrest warrant for some cock-and-bull story back in England that nobody really cares about any more. The police don't tell the army what to do. And anyway.... To be absolutely candid, you've given me the impression of being a decent chap and I must have thought so back then. I like to trust my own instincts."

Trying to choke back a metaphorical tear, Ned resisted an urge to grin.

"Of course, it's not every day I get presented with a police warrant, you can't just ignore these things, not when it's come down through Brigade. I did enquire further into it, and to be honest from what little I could find out it just didn't ring true.... Not that I'm any judge of police matters. But you know, the army is pretty capable of handling people of all types..... So - now we have this."

He slapped the paper against his other hand. "It's a letter that requests your presence. Not for a trial - that has already taken its course: the defendant, this letter tells me, has been found guilty by court martial. He may well be shot. However, it asks that I release you to go there and speak with the guilty man, who evidently has asked for you by name. I can only assume it's by way of a last request or something like that. Sounds like the sort of thing you read in detective stories."

Ned's astonishment was genuine. "Sir - who would that be, please?"

"Um.... A private in the Royal Engineers. A private John Michael Cade."

Ned wanted to sit down at once. His jaw dropped and his frame hung as if suspended on wires. It was a body blow of stupendous proportions.

"John Cade...."

"You obviously know the man or you wouldn't react that way. Yes, John Cade. Whoever he is. Here, are you alright, Thornton? Do you want to sit down?"

"Er - no, sir.... I mean, yes, sir, I'm alright."

"Are you going to tell me who he is?"

"Ah'm not sure ah can..... Not in a few words. John Cade were a seaman like me. A friend told me he'd been drafted into the army but ah hadn't a clue what happened to him... What's he done? Ah mean, why the court martial?"

".... It says here, 'for striking an officer'. Doesn't elaborate. In any case, he's been sentenced, it's only awaiting authorisation by General Haig. But from what this adjutant says, he'll most likely be shot. Cade means something to you?"

"In a strange sort of way. Not a nice way. It's a long story, sir."

"Does it have anything to do with the police warrant I was shown last year?"

"It does.... But it's not easy to explain. Ah'm not tryin' to be awkward. It's a long story."

"I don't have time for long stories. Not even from you. That ruddy bloke Pickett bent my ear quite enough about you,."

"He did, sir?"

"He did! And as you know, I dealt with that."

"Yes."

"Much against my better judgement, but there we are...."

"Ah'm sorry about that, sir."

"You meant well, Thornton, I do believe that. You were put on the spot. So I didn't press charges."

"Sir."

"And...." Marshall sat back and looked Ned straight in the eyes. "To be absolutely candid with you, private, d'you know... I envied you....."

A brief moment of recognition passed between the two, as if for that moment they were not officer and soldier but comrades who shared aspirations. Brief, however, was all it could be.

The captain's batman appeared at that point with a mug of tea. Marshall quickly took up the mug, sipped, put it down again and

443

then gestured at it for Ned. "You want one?" Whether he did or not, Ned declined, not wanting to push his luck. Marshall squirmed in his chair and rubbed his leg.

"Alright, well look here. I'm going to release you to go to St. Omer. The paper from the clerk is a request, not an order, but a man being executed is not something I take lightly. So tomorrow - ah wait, Brigade Commander's inspection - No, the day after tomorrow. The execution of that man is set for Wednesday, the 16th, if it's confirmed, so you'll just have time. I'll give you three days. Ah! Now, then. That brings me on to this other matter: your request for leave - you and your girl friend who wants to get married... Donovan mentioned that to me with his tongue right in his cheek."

"Sir."

"You're telling me, she *has* to get married, is that it? - It usually is."

For a few moments Ned looked at his captain and chewed at his lips before giving a reply.

"No, sir.... No, it's not. Ah'd be lyin' to yer, sir, if ah said it was. And.... well, quite honestly, Captain Marshall, ah don't want to lie to my captain, sir. Even for summat really important like this."

Marshall slurped his tea, all the while looking intently at the young soldier.

"I see," he said, with a note of understanding.

He kept looking until Ned felt thoroughly uncomfortable, then he said, rather quietly, "Thornton, of you I don't believe I would have expected anything else. I have dealt with a lot of different soldiers in my time - some are slackers, most are good men - and I can honestly say not one sticks in my mind as much as you do. As a matter of fact, lying would not have been the easy way out for you, would it?"

Almost choking on his relief, Ned thanked his lucky stars that of all the officers in the British army, their company adjutant was one of the most human. Ned had never even seen Colonel Williams, the battalion's commander, at close quarters, but would be happy to shine Captain Marshall's boots any time.

"So....." Marshall shook his head slowly from side to side. "Ordinarily, I would not have grounds to give you extraordinary leave - you know that, don't you? Not just because you want to get married. Or simply because you have a lovesick girlfriend." His ironic smile could only have been seen by someone below the desk.

"However, as I'm releasing you to go to St. Omer on this other matter.... and I did check that you are well up the leave roster, so Donovan tells me.... it seems, Thornton, I am going to accede to your request. Why? - " He chuckled to himself. " - As before, I'm really not sure. It was the same when you asked for leave in Le Havre, wasn't it?... Same girl, is it? - You're a lucky blighter, Thornton. Most don't stay with our chaps once they see how things are... You really should marry this one, shouldn't you?"

The matter dwelt in Marshall's eyes for several lingering moments, as though he were reflecting on his own life. Then just as suddenly it was as if he were ordering a cavalry charge.

"Very well, I'll give you a pass for five days. You can go to St. Omer and see this pal of yours, for as long as that takes, and then you can go and meet your girlfriend. As to getting married - well...... Amiens, was it?"

"Yes, sir. Amiens."

"That's a deuce of a way from here. You'll need travel warrants for both places, though I'm damned if I know how much use you'll be able to make of them. Ruddy rail system in this country is right up the chute. Make sure Beresford gets that organised for you. Tell him to make you an advance of pay. I'm writing this chit - give it to him. And Thornton - "

"Sir?"

"..... No, never mind. If you're going to get married, have a good wedding and be back here on Sunday. No, no, wait a minute, you'll never be able to get a train anywhere on a Sunday - be back Saturday midnight. Here, let me alter that note. Give her my best wishes. I have a feeling that she's worth it."

Ned stiffened and, once again, felt like kissing Captain Marshall. It was clear the captain liked him and he could not fathom why.

445

"Thank you, sir. She *is* worth it. I.... I wish you could see her, sir.... Thank you very much. Oh, sir - one more thing."

"What is it?"

"Can ah send a telegram, sir?"

The captain looked long at the soldier, stroked his leg and silently mouthed the word 'telegram', then grinned and wafted Ned away with his free hand.

* * * * *

FORTY-FOUR

It was late afternoon by the time Ned found the office of the Clerk of the Court in St.Omer. He was not hungry as the lift he obtained from a supply truck - the third he had managed to get that day - was laden with foodstuffs that had been directed to the wrong unit, and rather than face disciplinary action for allowing rations to be distributed to a non-approved source, the lance-corporal driver had turned around and taken the whole lot back. No chit - no rations. "More than my job's worth, mate! What you think I am? - Ruddy delivery man for Selfridges?"

The military policeman who staffed the clerk's office instructed Ned to report to the Duty Officer at the chateau. Headquarters - the chateau - was no different from anywhere else in the western theatre of war - chaos. There, Sub-Lieutenant Bryan had diarrhoea and welcomed no-one below the rank of Major.

"Who?"

"A soldier from the Royal East Kents, sah!"

"What does he want?"

"He's got a letter from Captain Willoughby who has - hang on, sir - What's he authorised, lad?"

The difficulty of conducting a conversation through the closed door of a toilet was bad enough, and they had already waited some considerable time. Ned realised the sergeant did not read well, if at all, and took it into his own hands to speak up in his best English so that the lieutenant might hear.

"Authorisation to see the prisoner Cade, sir, following his court martial. Captain Willoughby wrote to my C.O. asking that I should be released to come here as the prisoner had requested."

There was a groan from within the chamber. "Really? Does it have to be today?"

Ned looked for permission to speak again, to which the sergeant assented.

"Ah'm afraid so, sir - he's to be shot tomorrow morning, ah heard. Ah'm very sorry, sir."

447

Another groan emitted from the chamber. "Oh, very well. If you must, you must, I suppose. Wait out there in the office."

The two soldiers made a tactful retreat and after about ten minutes the lieutenant appeared. He was younger than Ned, blonde haired, boyish and red of face. By the state of him, he had tucked his shirt into his tunic a dozen times already. Under his breath, he appeared to be cursing his luck for having eaten something French.

"Sergeant, change that water bottle for me, would you?"

"Sah!"

Sub-Lt. Bryan placed himself gingerly into the chair at a desk, pulled at the wad of papers he had already looked at many times today and put down again, sighed heavily and looked up at Ned as if the soldier was there to give him an enema.

"Cade?"

"Yes, sir. He - "

"Yes, yes, I know the case. Very tiresome. We've got him downstairs in the boiler room.... This place isn't a prison, private, it's one of the few secure buildings in the town..... And why am I explaining to you? Let me see that paper from your C.O."

Ned placed the letter of authority in front of him and the lieutenant took his time to read it.

"It says here Cade requested you under convicted man's privilege. You do know his sentence has been confirmed, don't you?"

"Yes, sir. The sergeant told me. Ah'm sorry to hear it, sir."

"I'm not. You don't go round bashing an officer in the British army and expect to get away with it. He's been sentenced, he'll be shot at seven tomorrow morning. The firing squad have already been detailed. If you're a friend of his, you may as well know I am a hundred per cent behind the sentence. We don't allow this sort of thing to go unpunished."

"No, sir.... Ah'm not a friend."

"Then why did the blighter send for you?"

Ned realised an explanation would be futile. Gulping back his feelings on the matter, he simply said, "He's got nobody else, sir. Ah'm a sort of old enemy, if yer like; maybe ah'm the closest thing 'e's got just now...."

The lieutenant for a few moments stopped thinking about the toilet, leaned back in his chair and stared at the soldier.

"Curious," he eventually said. "... Still, I suppose you have your reasons. Anyway, you have a signed authority, and as a matter of fact here - " He reached out and plucked a paper from the pile. " - here is the memo from Captain Willoughby. It confirms you have permission - if you arrived, and you obviously have!"

The sergeant at that point returned, carrying a large jug of water. "Sergeant, has Cade had his dinner yet?"

"Not yet, sir. About six o'clock. Chef's not started it yet. Got a nice bottle o' wine, though."

"Then it's a good time. Take this man down, he is allowed to see the prisoner. Let's see, how long shall we give him?....." As if it meant anything at all, the lieutenant scrutinised his pocket watch. "Give him forty minutes, sergeant. May as well be generous, it's the last meeting he'll have except for the chaplain."

"Sah!"

Sentence confirmed. Ned had truly been hoping otherwise. He knew only as much as the next man, but in general it was thought less than a quarter of all men given the death sentence by court martial were actually executed. The dealings of courts martial were not made public knowledge, nor were the reasons for sentencing a man to death, but it was a widely held view that numbers of executions rose prior to a major offensive, for self-evident reasons.

The offence of desertion was high on the list, yet even here there might be mitigating elements. Striking an officer, however, presented less of a moral dilemma: it violated the basic Army code, in no circumstances could it be tolerated. Cade, it had been stated, had been disliked within his unit by most, not least his sergeant-major, whose testimony had been unequivocal: "This man is not of good conduct nor character and is undisciplined. He joined the Service from prison and should have remained there. The charge is proved since there were witnesses to the attack, and the accused is unrepentant."

449

In the old chateau the boiler room was one place that was still lockable, and window bars made sure there was no exit other than the door or the various pipes that rose out of it to heat the rooms above. During summer months it was not in use, the boiler itself stood open and cold. It was a large room mostly given over to machinery, though seemingly none of it sharp or dangerous enough to present an obvious alternative exit for the incumbent. In a corner beneath a small window, a bunk had been arranged with a generous amount of straw and a pair of thin mattresses to cushion the rope base of the wooden frame. Beside it were a table, a tall-backed wooden chair and a bucket, and that was all, other than the well-thumbed book that Cade had to read - 'Tom Sawyer'.

Shaking as he entered, Ned looked around the room and saw Cade scratching something on the wall with a small piece of iron.

"Thornton!" Cade almost did not get the word out. It was as if an apparition had arrived that he had never expected.

Still in full uniform, Cade had his jacket buttoned up to the top. The air down here had not quite caught up with the season, and despite several blankets on the bunk he spent most of the time wrapping his arms about him to huddle from the cool of the room in which he had languished with little exercise.

"Cade.... I..... I......"

"Cat got yer tongue?... Don't be frightened, I ain't gonna eat'cha. Though if I did there ain't nothin' they can do about it, they can only shoot me once."

A grin spread across his face. Ned was not sure what that grin said, but approached and stood by the seat Cade had gestured him to. Ned wondered whether to extend his hand as a common courtesy, though he did not wish to and so far everything felt awkward.

"'Ow yer been, me old china? Giving Jerry a pastin', are yer?"

"No."

"Ooh! I sense a slight tone of disillusion there, Master Thornton. They gettin' to yer, ey? - Them officers?"

"No. Not really."

Cade took that on the chin and stood for a moment, trying to size him up.

"Well.... Young Thornton. Been a long time, Ned."

"Not that long. The Grapes."

"I know, my son, I surely do. Gave y'a bit of a fright, didn't I?"

"You did."

"Hah! Well, there we go, ey?.... Still... Different kettle of fish now, innit? You fighting off the Boche and me about to get me Discharge Book. Might get Saint Peter to stamp it! 'Ere, d'you think they'll give me my finger back when I get up there? Ey?"

Ned felt in no mood for weak jokes. "Ah were sorry to hear - "

"Aah, fiddlesticks! Don't be sorry, Ned. Not your fault. Just 'ow the dice falls sometimes, luck o' the game. Fair do's - I clobbered an officer. I did. Fuckin' enjoyed it, too. Right little prick, he was. I busted 'is ruddy nose an' I shall do worse if I ever see him again. Did they tell yer?"

"No."

".... Ain't sorry at all, Ned. Bastard deserved it. Even the court martial as much as said he was pushin' his luck. So I give 'im one!"

"And now - "

"Now they're gonna put me up against the wall and blow me brains out. Well, good riddance! I ain't that fond o' this life, I'll tell yer that fer nothing. Bastards, most people! - Bastards! Look, I'm as bad at scrimshanking as any of 'em, but I just 'ad enough."

For a second Ned faltered, but then ventured, "Ah heard as how you were related to Lord Whatsisname."

"You're not wrong... Another bastard! Well - both of us are, put it that way." Cade laughed. Ned was startled: at this time, Cade laughed.

"Listen, Ned, that bloke is a right honourable shit, that's the only word for it. He ain't fit to shine my boots, and I'm just a bag o' washin' so what does that make him?"

"But..... What I don't understand is - "

"Sit down, Ned! Lord's sake, sit down, relax. It's me they're gonna shoot. And listen, Ned, do me a favour."

"What?"

451

"Call me John. Will yer? You and I have known each other a long time. Thick and thin, and all that."

Ned thought about that. Calling this man by his first name would not come easily. He said nothing.

"No hard feelings?" Cade held out a hand. Ned took it. This time it seemed half-right, despite their differences. Hard feelings? - Yes, many. Though he sensed his view could change after he left this place. As the sergeant watched from the doorway, they shook hands - full of tension on Ned's part, but they actually shook hands.

"When I asked the captain," Cade began, "if he could get word to you about this court martial, all I knew was that you was somewhere in France with the Buffs. That's all I knew. He said he'd make some enquiries. By god! - he did, didn't he? That might be the first time I've ever got to thank a pig for anything.... Anyhow, the word come through - sentence to be carried out. Thanks, Mr. Haig for keeping me waitin' a month... I was..... I had my fingers crossed it wouldn't happen."

So saying, Cade lifted his left hand and showed the missing finger. He smiled: it was a last bitter joke, as if he knew that his failure to cross fingers spelled his dreadful fate. For Ned there was no humour in this.

"Signed by Mr. Big. My claim to fame, ey? Well.... yer've come all this way, lad, we can't let yer down now, can we? By the way, how far did yer come?"

"We're camped by the Lys river, near Armentières."

"Oh yair? Mademoiselle from Armentières! I 'eard there's lots of French fanny up that way. You're doin' alright for yourself then, Ned."

"Still alive anyway."

"I'm just amazed you're here - truly fuckin' amazed!"

"Ah've got a decent C.O., he let me come."

"Amen..... So what don't you understand, Ned? I had a feelin' yer'd be wanting some answers."

"You know I didn't have any papers of Knight's."

"I know that."

"So why did you try to kill me?"

"Didn't try to kill yer. Honest. But fair do's. Look, you was in the wrong place at the wrong time. I know you didn't have the stuff that Lord Tony wanted - cos I had it! Yair! Oh, yair, there were some papers about secret stuff - that flame projector thing was one. Tony and Bernard had a fight about that because something wasn't right - I don't know what it was exactly, but it don't matter. Lord Tony was trading plans for that flame thrower with this chap in New York - "

"Martin."

"Oh! You know about him? Yair, Martin. But the really touchy papers that went missing weren't to do with that, they were private papers about Oberon."

"Oberon?"

"Yair, that useless streak of bejizzle. Private stuff, nasty. Powerful stuff if it got out. Oberon gettin' his leg over one of his pals.... Oh, listen, me old china, I'd invite yer to cocktails but me butler's not turned up yet - yer don't mind, do yer?"

Ned almost managed a grin. "So why did you make all that trouble for me with White Star and the newspapers? Why did yer give me such a hard time? Ah couldn't get a job."

"I know, Ned, I know. Sorry, mate. Like I said - wrong place, wrong time. Not my idea. Lord Tony wanted a smoke screen. To him you were just a nobody - well, like me an' all, we're *all* bloody nobodies to these toffs, aren't we? We don't matter to aristos like him. He jumped on the rumour some blokes got off the ship in women's clothes, and you had that girl's coat on yer, didn't yer? And you were there when them papers fell out of the briefcase. You was a ready-made villain, Ned. Who are they gonna believe? - A star of the British realm, or a cheap steward runnin' away from murderin' a bloke. Eh? We were keeping our eyes open, see.... Any port in a storm."

"Easy to say. So what was that all about - that twenty guineas you offered me in Southampton?"

"Twenty-five."

"Was it?... Anyway, why? - When you knew ah didn't have any ruddy papers."

"Pocock."

"What?"

"Charlie Pocock, off to one side, watching us. One of Tony's employees. Bloke as beat you up that time. He were watching me watching you. I made it look good."

Cade's hands seemed to offer an explanation for him and leave it there.

"Knowing the Americans were getting wise, Tony thought it would be smart to create a diversion, which was you.... It nearly worked, the Americans thought it was you they should be lookin' at. Anyway, you can blame me - I told him you'd pocketed some stuff."

"Which ah didn't."

"..... I know, me old china, I know. My fault - can't deny that. An' I'm sorry. But remember, at that time, we didn't know *Titanic* was going down. When we got rid of Bernard, for all we knew the evidence could've been found if the ship stayed afloat."

" - 'Got rid of him'?...You killed him?... You're admitting that."

Cade paused for a few moments, looked at Ned as if weighing up the odds, then shrugged. "*We* killed him. Yair. Not me - *we* did it. Listen, I'm not proud of meself..... There we are. Tell you the truth, up to him getting aboard *Titanic*, I'd not seen him for ages. He were always a curse on my luck, I tried to get away from the bugger. I never knew he was comin' aboard. But *he* knew I was aboard, he'd got Bernard keeping an eye on me for a long time - he didn't trust me and how right he was!" Cade laughed again. Ned considered this: Semper's power game must have been at work for many years.

"You could've floored me when I got summoned to his cabin and there he was, grinning at me like some ruddy Cheshire cat. Course, that was before she struck the iceberg. Anyway, what was I saying?"

"You killed him."

"More 'im than me! Tony grabbed hold of Bernard and I hit him over the head with a brass lamp to knock him out..... Just knock him out, right? He went down, and lay still. Tony said to me, 'Is he dead?' and I suppose I said, 'Can't tell'. At which point he took the lamp off me and bashed him again twice as he lay there, bashed his head in. Surprised me, honestly - I didn't reckon he could do that:

454

thought he was all mouth and trousers. Anyway, the water was creepin' up further down, we just left 'im. But Tony thought Bernard had got you to pocket them letters about Oberon. I just didn't tell him otherwise."

"..... So you're as much a villain as yer father is." The reference to Semper as his father seemed to sting Cade, then he ignored it. Looking Ned in the eyes, he sought no compassion and asked no quarter. He was a broken man, only the verbal spirit remained.

"I done bad things. I know it."

There was no way Ned was about to sympathize. For some seconds he stared at his adversary, with many thoughts passing through the clouds of his memory.

"My god!" exclaimed Ned quietly in the end. "The trouble you went to..... All that stuff in New York.... The newspapers.... Those newsreels that Magoolagan told me had been falsified.... Beating me up in Le Havre." Cade was hanging his head and nodding.

"Was it worth it?... For.... For what? - A bunch of state secrets? Not even that .... And you murdered a man!"

Cade had no responses and Ned's brain was moving along. "Not that it matters, but why is your name Cade when your mother and father both have different names?"

He smiled. "My landlord, see. When I joined the Andrew I gave his name, seemed like a way of leaving everything behind, like.... What's the Navy care?"

Up to now, Ned had been standing. He took the chair and flipped it round to straddle the seat and lean against the backrest.

"Are you going to tell the priest these things?"

"What for? The good of my soul? Listen, I'll be judged if and when I get up there, and take me chances. I've done wrong, I own that. A lot of stuff I shouldn'a done, but there we are. We make our bed, we gotta lie on it."

"What about your mother? Does she know where you are? Does she know about.... tomorrow?"

Cade breathed a big sigh. "Dunno... I ain't heard a word from 'er. Can't say I blame 'er. Can you?"

Ned had to think about that. "Let me get this straight, ah'm a bit confused. You were planning to extort money from his lordship, based on some letters from Oberon to his fancy man - if ah've got that right."

"So far."

"So.... what effect did that have? Where did you go from there?"

"Nowhere. Stalemate. The bastard threatened to cut off my ma without a penny. He'd got her fixed up at a house in Kent."

"I know that."

"Just the same as he fixed up his other kid, Irene, when she was born the wrong side of the sheets.... Well - they had one helluva quick wedding, put it that way."

"Ah didn't know that."

"Bernard did. He found out about Irene Scott when he worked for Brantcliffe. Tony was paying for 'is daughter to live in a house in Uxbridge, so long as she kept her trap shut and kept away from the family. See, Bernard was a clever sod, he found out Tony raped my ma - way back when she was in service at the Burton house. Raped 'er, Ned... My ma... Nine months later - me! He did the same with her ladyship, and Irene was born just after Tony and Lady Sophie rushed to get hitched. Caused a bit of scandal at the time, but people have short memories - shorter if you pay 'em!"

"So Irene Scott was legitimate."

"They shoved her out of the way in any case. It were a mistake, Irene weren't wanted - Sophie disowned her at birth. Tony as good as raped her as well. Bit tough on Sophie, eh? - Not that I have much sympathy. I mean, if she gets herself involved with the first cousin she knows so's she can hang onto the old man's title and give 'erself a cushy life, why should we have any sympathy? Imagine the to-do if Irene shot 'er mouth off in them big society circles. Most people only know that their lordships' children are Oberon and Miranda. The 'honourables'! - Nuthin' honourable about Tony. Nor anybody in them high society circles from what I can see. I'd sooner deal with crooks and honest beggars... So you see why I hate the bastard."

"You worked for him, just the same."

"I did. I did. I made a plan to get him, and I would have too, if I hadn't been stupid - "

"Yer got caught half-killin' some poor bugger and ended up in the army."

"S'right, me old china. I said you were a bright lad. Me - I'm not so bright. But they'll get him eventually. They'll get him for 'is politicals and misuse of bank money."

"Well, I did hear about that. He used the bank to finance his extremes."

"And White Star."

"White Star?"

"Sure. How'd you think he got White Star to put down the poison on you so fast? Surprising what yer can do with the power of soap in your hands, innit?"

Ned rubbed at his chin. "But you said stalemate. You threatened to blackmail him, and he threatened to cut your mother off. Instead, you worked for 'im. How was that supposed to work out?"

"If you can't beat 'em, join 'em! Where's the best place to be to know what the bugger's up to? And I had to fix it so's ma wouldn't get her income stopped even if something nasty happened to his lordship.... "

"You were fixing it through Brantcliffe?"

"Bernard Pettifer. There's another one that don't keep all his eggs in one basket. Ways and means, Ned, ways and means. Business is business."

Ned felt a long intake of breath was needed. He could muster little sympathy for Cade even now, yet he began to see how corruption grows in a man for what may seem legitimate reasons but ends up eating him away.

"There you are. His nibs won't get off scot free, they're onto 'im. Nobody likes a traitor in the ranks."

"Carelle said they had more or less got the evidence they want - "

"Carelle? What - that Belgian chap?"

"Yes."

457

"Carelle..... Yair..... Belgian feller. Suckin' up to 'er ladyship. I thought 'e were after her money. Certainly couldn't have wanted a shag!" The idea amused Cade.

"Carelle has plenty money. He just wants to see fair play."

"You surprise me. This Carelle's a friend o' yours?"

"Yes."

"Well, well! Good luck to yer, then. Ah thought we'd put you off the scent."

"You mean your bully boys beating me up in Havre."

"Not mine - Tony's." Cade smiled ruefully.

"But hang on! When you had me beaten up, you already knew ah didn't have anything yer wanted."

"Lord Tony didn't know that. He thought yer did. Those boys were employed by Tony, not me. I just paid lip-service to keep it rolling along for me. I know, I know! - My fault. I wouldn't have let 'em kill yer, though, honest. I kept an eye on 'em."

"What? - You were there?"

"I saw that pretty girl, too. An' I thought, Good on yer, Thornton: she'll look after yer. You're a lucky man."

"So some people have told me. But - When you caught up with me at the Grapes that night you made out I'd taken stuff. You knew damn well I hadn't, so why the ruddy pantomime?"

"Like I told you - Charlie Pocock. His lordship's eyes and ears. Smokescreen. Tony didn't trust me - very wise, really. Same bloke that beat you up, like I said. I sort of played to the gallery, yer might say. I had to make sure he was convinced I was playing it straight."

"Alright...then what did happen to the papers?"

"Olive."

"Olive Devonshire?"

"Her and Bernard. Before it even got to the ship sinking that night, Bernard had taken the letters from the briefcase and given them to Olive. Don't ask me how he did it - he did it! Letters the Honourable Oberon had written to his honourable bum-boy. I don't reckon Tony had planned it, I reckon he'd done some rush deal with Whitbridge as he left London. Fuckin' idiot, Oberon! - Fancy billin' and cooin' in a load of ruddy letters like that! Who did he think he was - Oscar Wilde? Idiot should've known they were dynamite."

"What bum boy? Who?"

"I dunno - some senior clerk called Thomas Whitbridge. D' you want me to draw you a picture?   I don't like that sort o' carry-on, turns me right off. One thing havin' call-girls but bummin' other blokes - naah! - Not for me. Didn't go down well with the Baron and his lady, I can tell yer.   Tony got certain letters back from Whitbridge on a threat him and Oberon would both go down together - if you'll pardon the joke! So Bernard and his girlfriend hid them letters away."

"How?"

"Remember her stuffed cat?"

"Ah do, aye. And her jar of toothpaste."

"Shoved the papers up its arse. That's how. Simple."

"Heck!   So I imagine Caldecot and his sister were going to blackmail Semper with Oberon's letters?"

"Sister? What sister?"

"Caldecot's. His sister was Olive Devonshire."

"What? ... You're pullin' my pisser, Ned! I thought he fancied 'er."

"No - brother and sister.   Carelle found it out. I've known about that and your mother for some time."

"Well, bloody hell ! There's something I never knew. *Well, bloody hell!* Bernard Caldecot were a brighter spark than ever I thought. After all, in a world where yer can't trust nobody, who better than yer own kin?"

Ned doubted that. *Not in the case of you and your father.* "Perhaps Caldecot got the last laugh on you all."

"And here's me thinkin' all the time what a clever geezer I was for knowing she had the evidence."

"So she's got the letters!"

"No. I got them off her."

"You stole them?"

"Well ...... I asked her nicely. Then I persuaded 'er! And she gave them to me - for a share of the profits."

"Once you'd blackmailed Semper."

"Smart, Ned - smart."

"No. Carelle found out most of it."

"Yer Belgian pal. Tony thought he was police."

"Did he say that?"

"That pet monkey of his, Arthur, he's always puttin' his foot in it."

To the sergeant, still leaning at the doorway, Cade called, "Time for tea and scones yet, sarge?" The stoic sergeant remained in his place, smiling implacably and saying nothing.

"I thought not. Tweeny's afternoon off, is it?" No response.

Cade sat back on his bunk and only shook his head slowly from side to side.

"'Ow's your bit o' stuff, by the way? Yer French piece."

"Ah'm gonna marry her. When this lot's over."

Cade let out an envious whistle. "Y'know, at one time I took you for a right dummy.   But you done alright.   Became a mensch, didn't yer? Kept yerself in one piece, got respect ....."

His words fostered a pregnant pause.

"That's important to you, John. Respect."

Cade seemed to react to his name being spoken. The bravado had gone, he began to look like a man in search of friendship, a man with weakness, a man who had not yet understood how he should face up to his last hours.

"When I were a nipper, Ned, I got stuck up the top of a ladder. Don't ask how, it don't matter. The thing was, I looked down and it looked like I was on top of a mountain, so far down to fall. And these other lads, they were all laughin' and shoutin' at me to make me fall off, and shakin' the ladder.   I were only a kid, I started cryin', and that just made 'em all worse. In the end, this bobby came along, and the kids scattered, and it was, 'What you doin' up there, lad? - Up to no good, I'll be bound'. He climbed up this ladder, got a hold of me by my pants and talked me down. An' when I got down, he give me a good tickin' off and a clout round me ear and sent me on my way."

All the while, Cade was visiting sour memory.

"You know something? - After that, it weren't the lads I hated, it were the bobby. For treating me like a dumb, useless prick up to no good. I wanted somebody to help, and that's what I got. And ever since, I never let any o' these high and mighty types do me down. I wasn't ever gonna get pushed around and put in my place. I was a frightened kid, but I grew up fast after that."

And, thought Ned as he watched Cade wrestling with his demons, *maybe all you ever had was the law of the gutter and people doing everything they can to kick you down.*

After a silence, Ned asked him, "How did you lose the finger?"

"What, this?.... Card game. Not one o' them rough card games like the gin palaces down Whitechapel, oh no. One of Tony's clubs, long time ago when I was lackeying for the bastard and wet behind the ears. I wasn't playing - Tony was. This particular night, he lost - oh, I don't know how much, he lost a lot. Went out to the 'ansom, him pissed and in a bad temper. He slammed the cab door as I was trying to help 'im in. Right on my hand. He laughed, sort of half-apologised and carried on laughing.... Three fingers bandaged up for ages. Finally one of 'em got infected, the clinic took it off.... now I pick me nose with me right hand."

"I wonder why in that case you worked so long for him."

"Greed, really. The longer I stayed, pokin' this stupid head into his business, the more I figured I could get on him. A bigger pot for blackmail. Greed, see. And I let him think I was doin' his dirty work but all the time I was stackin' up information..... Like them poncy letters and other stuff from Paris and Petersburg. Some military stuff he bought off his mates at the ministry. Never gonna get to use it now, am I?"

"You won't have to. The police have quite a dossier on him."

"They should have. He were never that careful covering 'is tracks. He's rich and powerful, what's he got to be afraid of? Money to his mates, you know. The City, Irish Americans, Austrians, big-wigs in high places, secret stuff he tried to sell off."

"There'll be quite a stink when it all comes out."

"You reckon? Seriously - you reckon?... How did he get hold of all that classified stuff in the first place? Uh? He's got toffs in his

461

back pocket from 'ere to Christmas. 'When it all comes out,' you say - hah! It's not gonna *come* out! Get real, Ned, this is the British aristocracy you're talkin' about! They'll never let all that stuff get public and lay 'em all open to question, drag 'em all down together. Birds of a feather, my friend...."

"So....."

"Two ways he comes out - dead, or he disappears. End of story."

Ned had to admit either suggestion was plausible.

"Listen.... It don't come easy to say some things. Being the stupid prick that I am. But.... I had a lot o' time to think. I wanted to say something. I wanted to say I'm sorry. Honestly."

It was not a simple thing to accept, and looking into Cade's face still did not give Ned any feeling of forgiveness. All he could do for the moment was look back into Cade's eyes and finally see the essence of the man there. Cade was leaving this life, and wanted to account for it. John Michael Cade had - perhaps - finally become a human being.

"Yer can hit me if yer want.... Might make yer feel better."

No. No, it would not, Ned decided. Not now.

Cade became more subdued. "What's it like, Ned - facing death? What's it like when you're starin' up the barrel of some German's rifle?"

After thinking for a moment, Ned decided he had no idea and said so.

"In the trenches, though, you're facing death all the time, aintcha?"

"Mm. 'Appen so. But ah can't tell yer, cos ah never yet faced a German man to man. If ah do, ah'll probably shit meself."

Whatever he thought, and however that might apply to his own situation, Cade merely nodded calmly and lay the idea aside. "Have y'ever thought, Ned - in another time, another place, you and me might've been friends?"

That took Ned aback. That was saying something more than he had ever bargained for, and in truth, his answer would have been No - no, he could never be friends with this man who had cheated and murdered. The failure to answer hung around Ned's face for several seconds, before Cade saw the futility of his question.

"Can you do something for me?"

"If ah can."

"I've a letter I want to write tonight. I don't trust them buggers to post it for me, and I don't trust no chaplain neither."

"Alright."

"It's for my wife."

"... I had no idea you had a wife." Cade affirmed silently. Taking the empty envelope from his pocket, he held it up. It was addressed to Mrs. C. Cade at an address in Bermondsey. He would write the letter that evening and hand it to Ned in the morning.

"She'll appreciate that. She's a good woman, Catherine. God knows what she saw in me. I gave her a bad time. I never deserved her, and that's the truth."

Ned turned away. Truth. It was here somewhere. "Find your truth," he said quietly to the floor.

"Ey?" puzzled Cade, "What's 'at?"

"Oh, I was only thinking.... Maybe she saw a little of what I've seen these past few minutes."

Cade's reflex was to smile. That smile had no understanding, but held only regret and nostalgia.

"Yes, of course," Ned assured him, "Ah'll do that.... And would you do something fer me?"

"What?"

"Take this piece of notepaper. Write what I ask yer?"

Cade' s natural suspicions got the better of him for a moment. But only for a moment. He already sensed what was expected of him.

Sleeping in the guardhouse, Ned passed a fitful night's sleep, waking twice and having difficulty nodding off again. The bunk was uncomfortable and the smell of straw irritating. He could only imagine what sort of a night John Cade might be having.

It had not originally been his intention to attend the execution, but Cade had asked him to do so, and Ned was not about to deny him now.

At 6am the guard woke him with a cup of tea. He washed in the cold water of a basin with water fresh from the well and spent time pulling bits of straw off his uniform, which had been clean when he had set out from camp. All the time, he felt the stillness of the morning, his senses becoming awake to every tiny nuance of the growing day, as if he had never known a morning before, as if time had curiously stopped.

It was a strangely difficult thing to do. To see comrades die in battle was one thing, and very awful. To be present as an adversary was ceremonially executed was entirely another. There was no comfort in this.

He was not allowed to approach Cade as the prisoner was led, bound only at the wrists, from his 'cell', but Cade paused regardless of the four-man escort and bid one of them hand to Ned the envelope.

That was his last act in this world, and as the eyes of the two men met, Ned found himself facing a man he no longer knew, who had become another man whom he knew intimately.

Involuntarily almost, he found words leaving his mouth that he had never imagined he would say to another man's face.

"God take you, John".

Cade dwelt a moment and smiled weakly at him, and then walked sadly on.

They were in the large rectangular courtyard of the chateau where there were small trees and flowers, and the wall at shoulder-height gave a view beyond of a meadow, green and vibrant and peaceful, with only a handful of buildings to obstruct the view out across the countryside and into the distance. The August air, even so early in the day, was light and warm, white butterflies were already descending on the flora, and the sounds were only those of birds and of the clinking of military hardware.

There was no post to be bound to, Cade stood where he was placed, erect and looking sternly at the men who were lined up to shoot him.

Captain Willoughby read out the charge and the sentence and asked the prisoner if he had any statement to give. There came none. The proceedings was brief and formal.

Across the far side from Ned, the medical officer coughed and pulled his jacket to his neck.

Offered the hood, Cade silently refused. He did not wish, he had told Ned last evening, to depart this life in darkness, he wanted to raise his eyes and have them filled with sky and as much of the earthly environment as they could see.

One thing that dwelt in Ned's mind particularly: in all their conversation the night before, Cade had never once referred to his father by that title. Was that not the greatest sadness?

There being no military chaplain immediately available, a French priest had been co-opted. This man read out in French the Lord's Prayer from his book while Cade looked around him, breathing in the air of a last morning as he stood there, unfettered save for his bound wrists. He had not shaved for a couple of days, his skin looked more sallow than ever and his shock of fair hair was open to the breeze, for he was given no cap to wear though he was allowed his service jacket. His blue eyes looked more steely-blue than ever, and his jowls held a grim sort of resolve. He had not breakfasted, nor drunk anything other than water. In a perverse kind of way, he felt as pure as he was ever going to feel as he filled his lungs with the drying air. It was as though he approved of the morning.

The sergeant of the firing squad approached in a military course of straights and ninety-degree turns, offered the blindfold one last time and Cade again refused, whereupon the sergeant pinned the white square to his chest, backed off a couple of paces, nodded to Cade as his salute to the condemned man, then made an about-face and returned to his position. Without delay, he raised his right arm.

"Ready!"

Preparing himself for the shots, Cade lowered those wide eyes and looked across at Ned Thornton with an open mouth. Despite all the odds, there was something called comradeship passing between them.

"Aim!"

As the officer waited for the six men to steady their rifles, Ned chose to murmur in a low breath, "Goodbye, John Cade."

"Fire!"

* * * * *

FORTY-FIVE

Trains at these times were not exactly rapid, nor exactly comfortable - there were, for one thing, more than enough people needing to travel for comfort to be excluded to pretty much everyone. With so many troops in transit, travel for the public was less easily acquired. At least, once aboard, and provided the carriage was not full of wounded men, there was a certain amount of peace to be had, insomuch as one was not travelling by road. As viewed from the train many roads were seen to be a nightmare of confusion and congestion. With upwards of three thousand Allied casualties every single day along the Western front, it was not surprising that ambulances large and small were everywhere, fighting for the space with military vehicles.

Ned stood for a while until a young girl gave up her wooden bench seat for him. She found room to sit on the floor under a window at her grandparents' feet. The two grandparents smiled through their absorbed misery and Ned offered them brandy from his hip flask, which the old man accepted with great thanks. Ned mustered in return as warm a smile as his spirit could allow: it had been a distressing morning at St. Omer. He still shook, and he prayed the day would end differently.

Troop movements were via 'regulating stations' at Abbeville and other places, where men and commodities alike were reorganised for different areas, which imposed restricted services on ordinary civilian passengers. Through first Boulogne and then Abbeville, three separate trains took Ned a distance of around a hundred miles in more than six hours, and arriving in Amiens was not the uplifting experience that he had hoped for as he found no vehicle to take him the last leg of his journey. Yet, it was a matter of a few blocks' walk only. He had been allowed leave without his full kit and carried his essentials in a light knapsack. Amiens at this time was not a friendly-looking place, just as so many French towns and villages still cowered in the shadows of what had been and what might yet be to come. Like Bradford, Amiens had been a textile city, a famous one, but until this war, Amiens had despite the industrial revolution at least preserved a character its English rival may have envied, with distinctive architecture and a most wonderful cathedral.

Destruction, however, had not escaped this place. War had come to Amiens in August 1914, leaving many buildings scarred if not destroyed and roads still lightly scattered with debris, but the German army had been beaten back by the French and the town astride the river was now in a relatively secure situation some miles back from front line activities. It remained, nevertheless, a bustling town with a fortress mentality so long as hostilities dictated every discretion.

Ned was tired now and the walk was not welcome, asking his way as he went, but it was still light when he finally reached the Relais that Renata had described. Monsieur Morineau was not there, a girl told him that Madame Thornton had arrived the day before, though she was not there either, and he would probably find her within the cathedral or at the river bank.

Having in mind his own weariness and hunger, he felt at first a disappointment, but reasoned that Renata could not have known when he might arrive, if at all - with the briefest of messages to go on, nothing at all could be assured. *At least*, he contented himself with a great release of inner tension, *at least she is here. My god - she is here! She is here!*

Gathering his remaining strength to consult his senses, Ned asked the girl if there was food he might take quickly, as in any case the latest of shops closed by 8pm. She immediately went to the kitchen and he was provided a brioche, a piece of cheese and a jug of wine. He would have preferred water, but perhaps wine was safer. He found the cheese to his liking but had no idea what it was: it looked like a piece of melon, and the girl called it mimolette. After eating a portion of that, though, he sought out his tooth powder: the last thing he wished to present to his love was an odorous mouth, even if he had not yet washed from his body the trials of the day.

Following along Rue Victor Hugo, Ned traced the girl's directions first to the cathedral. If he did not find her there, he would continue to the river. It was not far and he could still have seen the cathedral anyway in the fading light. In Amiens it was difficult to *not* see the cathedral.

At ground level, the approach along an ordinary street still offered a surprise. Old houses ranged either side, with here the occasional gap where the war had reduced a building to rubble, and suddenly, as though you stepped off the cobbles of the street straight into it, there it was - the cathedral, two great pillars rising up to flank that very French huge circular panel of windows. Ned had no great awareness of religious buildings, yet even he was strongly impressed by the immense size of this building and its intricate Gothic architecture. Apparently undamaged by the city's recent war scars, Amiens cathedral towered into the evening sky like a colossal church organ, its enormous decorated edifice and spires a noble testament to the endeavours of men. Sandbags piled around the front of its finely hewn stones could not mask the quality of its sculptures: not merely piled around but piled up, thousands upon thousands of them, a protective wall against bombardment.

Once inside the huge doors, more sandbags, walls of them to bolster the internal structure, with parts of the area fenced off. For all that, the staggering height and length of the vaulted chamber still took away the breath. No splendour, however, could distract Ned from his purpose: she was here, he would find her.

Happily, no service was in progress that he might otherwise disturb, although the cathedral had drawn inside it many of the faithful and the dejected, the discouraged and the hopeful. A sole English soldier had no wish to announce his presence with clumsiness. Stepping as quietly as he could, with as little show of his urgency as he might betray, Ned wandered down the nave, taking in the smell of incense and looking all about him. She was here - somewhere. She *had to* be here. Older ladies clad only in black regarded him with suspicion as he passed their pews, along the chequerboard floor and across the 'labyrinth' at the building's heart. Anxiety set in as he could see no sign of Renata. Up into the choir stalls and the sacristy, around to the small chapel. Where might she be?

At length, as he returned along the North side, his searching eyes were drawn to the flickering of candles and there, peering further into the half-light, he observed two figures, both women, both with shawls across their heads. One of them was Renata. Immediately his pulse thumped.

She had lit three candles and was standing back to allow the other woman access. Ned stood transfixed for seconds. Yes, it was clearly she - his heart leapt, his pulse raced even faster, and at that moment he felt he could barely move. It was as if some secret force were holding him back, and here he was, little more than twenty feet away from his most precious love, mute and immovable, his mouth wide and soundless!

Renata stopped attending the candles. She straightened, and slowly her head turned, her body following, aware of a presence in that vast chamber.

She saw him, and her eyes and mouth both widened before breaking into that silent expression of purest joy, the recognition that her love was here.

Ned gulped and could hardly swallow, nor even speak. They were facing each other now, he in his dirty uniform, right down to his puttees and boots, and she in a long, slim dark brown dress, her head and neck covered in a beautifully crocheted shawl of deepest violet. For these long, long moments, Renata and Ned stood facing each other whilst the tears welled up in her wide blue eyes and he panted his thanks to whatever god he had brought with him on this journey.

Then they were in an embrace, an embrace of pure silence and passion and love, a long, long embrace, clinging and grasping and pulling and holding tightly - ever tighter - oh, so tight! Her light perfume in his nostrils, her warm, fragrant breath in his face. The feel of her face in his hands. For Renata, the strength of his solid frame within her arms. And not a word for ages. Not a word in this vast chamber of unspoken dreams.

Presently, the older lady turned, saw them together and smiled a huge smile, a smile of gappy teeth but warm and sincere. Renata had no idea who she was, she was simply there, in that moment, almost like a friend, almost to betoken the approval of the world.

Renata however had eyes only for this lean, smiling man with the unruly dark hair and questioning blue eyes; his skin never had caught the sun and the smell of his body was pungent after the trials of the day. Ned, she knew, would never shatter the world with his learning or his prowess at being anything other than a normal human being, but for his honesty and his steadfastness, she adored him. Just as significantly, she knew beyond any doubt now that he loved her, even if he himself might hardly believe it.

It was Renata who finally spoke in hushed tones, respectful of their surroundings.

"Oh, Ned! I was not sure you would come."

"Nothing was goin' to keep me from yer."

"I was afraid...."

"Me too. Anything could have happened to stop me getting 'ere but.... well, it didn't. Thank heaven."

"I was so worried. You know, there is a saying here in France, *le pire n'est jamais sûr*: it means - oh, what does it mean? - It means, the worst things are always possible, but - "

"- But we hope for the best - English saying.... Ah made up me mind, Reina, after this mornin', nothing were gonna stop me from seein' yer. There had to be a better world than what ah saw this morning. So nothin' was gonna stop me. Not any more. Ah've got to be with you - always. Ah love you, Reina."

"I know, Ned. I know, my darling..... Oh, I am so pleased to see you.... Oh, Ned!"

"Ah'm lost fer what ter say....... Ah just.... Ah want the world to stop right now. Just leave you an' me like this. Just like this."

She laughed. "Yes. Yes. We will stay like this. Forever. Like in the Bible - two pillars of salt."

"Yes...." Then he let out a little laugh too. "Are we mad?"

"Oh yes. Yes. We are mad. And Ned - we are in love! We love each other! After how many years? - *That* is the madness, Ned."

"Ah told yer, didn't ah? - Ah told yer, ah were just a stupid man."

"No - you said an '*ignorant*' man, Ned. I remember what you said. It's not ze same. No?"

"Might as well be. Either way, ah've woken up. Ah want you, Reina. Ah want you like ah've wanted nothin' else in all me life. Nothin'. If all ah can have is you, then ah'm a happy man."

"Ja..... I know. I am ze same."

"Oh, god, let life just stop right here! Like this. You and me together."

"Be careful, Ned, when you call to God - zis is His house. He may hear you! Zen poof! - He stop your life if you ask for it!"

"Ah don't care. Ah don't care. Ah don't need gods when ah've got the whole world in me arms."

Her broad, flashing smile made his soul complete. Gods and men, what did they matter? - All he wanted in the world was this woman. To share his life. And now - after far, far too long - they were together. The tiredness had gone from his body, the execution and the cares of the war settled into some back quarter of his brain. Reina was the 'here and now' and that was all that mattered. She was his love, and nothing now would ever change that.

"Ah like the shawl. It sets off yer eyes."

"Zere is somesing wrong wiz my eyes?"

"No, no. Y'know, brings out the beauty in yer eyes. A shawl makes yer look kind of.... Spanish. Mysterious. Darkly beautiful."

"Dark? I am not dark, Ned."

"You're the dark, you're the light, you're everything beautiful."

"I am not beautiful."

" - And you've cut yer hair! Gosh! It makes a difference."

"I didn't cut much. You like it?"

"Um..... No, it's awful!"

"Ned!" she protested, but realised his joke as he smothered her face in kisses.

"Yes. It's just different, makes yer look younger. Yes. Honestly. And you *are* beautiful.... All women are beautiful. But you - you are the most beautiful woman ah've ever known because ah look into your heart and see everything good about you..... "

"Ned."

"What?"

"Ssssh!"

"Ah'm sorry. Ah'm too excited!"

"Yes."

Ned looked around the street, in the evening light a few couples were strolling toward the river. One or two pairs of eyes observed them, but none acted like they took offence.

"Ah'm sorry. But ah do like the shawl, when you have yer hair like that underneath. Ah'm not fond of women in hats. Don't like hats, all decked out with feathers and lace and stuff: they cover up one of a woman's best features. Yer've got lovely hair, Reina, ah like to see it like this."

"Well.... You will see it. You will see much more of me now. Much more, Ned. I will show you much more."

"Ooh - that's brazen talk, my love. Yer gonna get me all excited again."

"But I want to get you excited! At ze right time. Yes. Ned, Ned, listen. We do not have much time togezzer. I want to live in every second, you understand? I do not want to wait. I do not care what people say or think, I want us to love each other. As much as we can when we have zis time. To love each other - because we throw away so much of our life before."

"You're right. You're always right. To hell with it, all that matters now is you an' me."

"Dat's right! We say to the world, 'mushrooms'!" And she laughed.

"What?"

"Ja - mushrooms, Ned! Is champ- er..... what you say?"

"Champion."

"Ja - *champignons*. Mushrooms! Dat's right, Ned."

"My god! - Have yer gone a bit potty?"

"Potty? - What is potty?"

"Mad. Are yer mad, Reina?" Now he was catching her spirit.

"Ja! Ja! Mad! I am free, Ned - and very mad!"

"Free?.... Yes. You are..... As free as you want to be, my love."

473

"Free. In here - in my head. And dat is what make matter. You and me. Dat's all. Mushrooms!"

She was laughing now, openly laughing, with a joy he had rarely seen in her before, but he understood what it meant to her, and he was glad. Bathing in that joy was easy. As he did so, it came back to him again - *Find your truth, Ned.* Had he found it?

"What is it?" she asked him, having caught the detached nuance in his eyes.

"Oh.... It's just that I think I found something today..... Maybe more than once."

She shook her head, not comprehending, and he spoke no more of it.

"And ah will make love to you, Reina. Ah may be that clumsy fool still but ah'll do me best, ah want to make yer happy and ah want yer to love me."

"But I do! Already. And I will try - though we cannot marry - I will try to be a wife to you, Ned. I will be your woman, and you are my man."

"And when the war's over - "

"*Before* it is over! - I leave him and come to you. Wherever you are. It don't make matter. I waste my life wiz zis.... zis man who does not love me."

"Never?"

"Mm. No. I sink no. I am - what do you say? - I am part of.... *les meubles.* Ze sings in ze house."

"Furniture. Property."

"Ja. Because he does not make me feel.... what you make me feel. Wiz you, I feel... I want to be loved and you want me, and I know zis. I want you to put your hands on me and make me feel wonderful - you can do zis, Ned, but him - no."

"You are his wife, but he does not own your body and mind."

"Ja. He has piece of paper. Well...... Look, Ned, ze lights along ze river. It's pretty."

They had strolled down to the bank of the river through the old quarter, an area that was populated by many old wooden and brick buildings, many tall ones lent the place a claustrophobia. It was not strewn with romantic cafés as they might have hoped from its setting, it was largely drab and cluttered, but here and there were lights that reflected romantically into the water from houses and occasional streetlamps which gave the river, especially on a summer night like this, a tranquil, friendly feel that seemed so far away from war. The night smelled good.

"We can go for a swim," she joked. "Ja? Why not? We get soaping wet, ja?"

He laughed loudly. "Soaping wet? - You mean, *soaking* wet!"

"Ja. Oh, ja. Soaking. Dat's it."

"Yes. Well. We could just go for a soaping, ah suppose...."

She knew she was being teased. It was good to be loved so much that nothing mattered.

"Aah," sighed Ned. "This is a beautiful river, isn't it? We should live here, Reina, on a river like this. People should just live beside rivers like this.... What's this un called? It's beautiful here.... "

"Zis river? It's ze Somme, Ned."

His face had changed as he turned to her. "The Somme?...."

She knew. Of course she knew. Not even in Le Havre could news of such monstrous events be contained. Everyone knew the events early last month and the way the battles there had reverberated ever since. Only Ned's ignorance of the local geography had failed to make the connection for him.

"Aah...." He breathed out a very long sigh that said so many things without words.

All along the Front, names like Bazentin, Pozières and Delville Wood had come into the language. The Somme had already come to mean not a river but a whole essence of infamy, its name standing for a notoriety that might supplant its rural identity forever. The men of the 12th battalion, along with every other, feared the Somme battlefield.

It broke the spell. Momentarily, Renata knew her man was back on the field of battle. She knew also it was not something either of them could brush aside. Significantly, she knew that the lines were drawn up little more than twenty miles east of where they were standing. By what fortune they had not so far heard the guns here at Amiens, she could not guess. As of that moment, however, they were standing on a narrow stone foreland and could see a wide sweep of the river, much of it reflecting light.

She gripped him ever more tightly as she allowed his mind the space to consider his thoughts and feelings. At length, he looked at the ground and shook his head slowly, then turned to her.

"Were you serious, Reina?.... No, don't answer. Of course you were serious. Ah should know you better."

"But what are you talking about?"

"Us making love. No, wait a minute - that's sounds like I'm a complete idiot. Of course I want to make love with you. But - what I meant was.... Are you completely happy with that?"

"Of course. You love me?"

"Yes."

"And you have respect for me, monsieur?" That sudden amused coquetry, the feigned propriety of her impish question, sparked his own return to light-headedness.

"Yes - as a gentleman, I give you my word I respect you."

"Well?"

"Ah didn't say what word it was, mind!" Instantly he was the teaser again, and she fell for it gladly. She slapped him and shared his laughter. It was good. She had not lost him to inevitable fears that must not soil their opportunity for happiness. Not now. In all the world there was nothing better than being together right there, right then. And so they walked and talked and held onto each other as it grew late.

He had spoken little of the execution of John Cade. Renata sensed he would speak of it in time and left the matter alone once she had registered her shock. Nor did she press him on matters of life at the front line or the fighting, although at one point he did let go a long sigh as he wrestled with the feeling that this war was making him feel older than his years.

With great presence of mind, she countered, "It's alright, Ned - you can catch up wiz me." He simply melted in her smile and wanted the moment to last forever.

476

A little further along, he grew mellow and Renata sensed a moment of unease.

"It's just...." he began awkwardly, "Ah'm fighting Germans...."

She understood the doubts and the conflict within him, that he was at war with her own people. Those German soldiers: she knew, they too believed - *Gott mit uns.*

She gripped his hand and said quietly, "They are not the enemy."

Françoise, Morineau's daughter, was preparing herself for bed after locking the doors, but she had made coffee afresh for them, with another portion of that brioche. They sat for a short while in the little parlour and did nothing but look at each other. The guest from Nantes was already in his room.

"*Choisissez,*" Françoise said to them, pointing to bottles in the wall cabinet. "*L'armoire là. Je vous en prie.*" There were just three bottles of spirits, nothing extravagant, and they left them there.

Already they suspected from the looks she returned that Françoise did not believe they were married, but it was of no consequence: neither Françoise nor Yvonne's uncle would be reporting back to Le Havre society. Françoise anyway was taken by the charm of this handsome and friendly couple, and would say as much to her father.   Love was important, and lovers very important, more important than ever as so many young men were dying. It was a practical consideration, if nothing else, and France was a practical nation: once this war was finished, the cost would surely be the loss of manpower to the nation which needed to be replaced as soon as possible. Everywhere one saw whores plying their trade amongst the eager young men, many of whom would not survive the fighting: all the greater reason for congratulation that some young men and women were still able to fall in love in whatever circumstances and, hopefully sooner rather than later, to procreate. Monsieur and Madame Thornton, then, were as welcome as if the mayor of Paris had chosen to stay at the relais. It was clear to anyone that they were very deeply in love.

The bed squeaked and the floorboards squeaked and creaked as they went to and fro. At first disconcerted, they decided to make it a source of amusement. What did it matter if they could be heard? Let everyone know they were here to make up for lost time!

And Ned was clean! The bathroom along the landing held a large, ornate bath: the water was not very hot, it had been boiled and taken to the bath in buckets, but there was soap and a temptation to relax and just luxuriate for ages in the soothing water, a temptation he found easy to forego when he had his lady waiting for him. To dress again or not? - There was a corridor to be negotiated. Pants, then - damn it, this was 1916!

In all those years of tense or tender moments in each other's company, they had hardly ever been alone, and even in those rare instances, never entirely removed from family or an inquisitive environment. For the very first time, they were free to be as they wished.

When Renata and Ned closed the door of their room that night and undressed, it was as if they had met only that evening, so intense was their pleasure in watching each other's every move. Renata thrilled as she saw Ned carefully studying her taking off her dress, she wanted to be naked before him and to drink in his gaze as an elixir of pleasure. At no time did their eyes not communicate: his eyes held a pride that she trusted him so, and her eyes held the promise that she would always be his and no other's. There was no spurious modesty, no embarrassment, no notion of propriety that had to be addressed. He was embracing her even before she had removed her underwear, a passion he knew he could unleash only ever with her.

In gentle silence, he drew up her chemise and caressed the luxury of her breasts, she followed by slipping her palms within his pants, pressing them into his tight buttocks and around to his manhood. There was no false awareness of self, only a desire of the one to pleasure the other. Trust was implicit. Reina was the love of his life: with every kiss and caress he meant to show that to her, in whatever way she desired. She returned his advances with all the lack of the guilt her years with Jerome Forget had built in her.

478

Against Forget's approach, she had steeled her body and tried to comfort herself mentally as he tore at her clothing, entered her and thrashed and writhed in a clown's pastiche of copulation that left her tired, bruised, ill-used and utterly frustrated physically and mentally. Now as she gave way to Ned's body she welcomed the warmth and the firm yet tender, playful yet caring responses he gave her, subtle nuances of his hands playing along her face, her skin and into her sex.

They kissed and murmured and cooed to each other, entwined their bodies and thrilled to each other's touch until, at exactly the right time, she led him into her and they enjoyed the most wonderful of earthly ecstasies in each other's arms, rising and flowing and pulsing and imparting all the loving pleasures both had so long craved. Many times they repeated verbal manifestations of their love, and after Reina and Ned had both achieved physical climax, their bodies finally settled alongside one another, supremely contented, and they lay for a long time open to the warm air, simply looking into each other's face to gain every last grain of recognition of what they had.

Her face radiated to him its loveliness, her clear azure eyes looking into his, searching, flashing, daring, coaxing, trusting, and finally calming. He could conceive of nothing more exquisite in all the world than Reina's superbly crafted face, all he wanted was to continue sucking and pecking at those lips until he had drained every last vestige of love out of her.

In the late hour, they washed again in the cool water of the bowl, dried and cuddled up together in that sumptuous bed, the marriage bed of their imaginings. Quietly they talked a little of slight matters and shortly succumbed to sleep. A day which had begun in stark, unremitting despair had ended with the happiness Ned had wished for. A new beginning.

* * * * *

FORTY-SIX

The sights of Amiens seemed, at least for this pair of star-crossed lovers, a redundancy. Yet the day was bright and warm, as had been many of the days of this summer, such that one might entirely forget bloody hostilities raging only miles to the east, and once they had pulled themselves from their room for a late breakfast - Morineau and his daughter both tolerant of the nature of their guests - they decided to enjoy whatever there might be to enjoy in a city that, for the present anyway, was not far removed from a state of siege. The importance of Amiens as a rail hub had grown and a military presence was all-pervading in much of the city, such that another British uniform would have gone largely unnoticed if not for the highly attractive lady who clung to the soldier's arm.

The dress Renata wore, a pale yellow dress trimmed with blue - whilst of dubious propriety for the mood of 1916 Amiens - was entirely appropriate to the summer weather of any other time, and certainly appropriate to the summertime Renata possessed in her head. For Ned she pulled her hair up into a cluster at the back, tied off with a slim blue ribbon. No hat, by request. What did it matter if observers considered her a little gauche? Renata felt free. For once - free.

As Ned complimented her on her beauty, she responded, "It's Gitta's dress. I hope you are not offended. I have never worn such a dress. And," she added to make it appear a sensible choice, "it was easy to go in ze *valise*." For this day alone, she was determined all their missed summer days should be rolled into one. And of course he was in no way offended. Quite the opposite, for it was a huge statement for Renata to make. She was now 27 as of June whilst Ned had turned 24 just six weeks after her, but she had no trouble feeling 19 again, radiating a vigour and a youthfulness that belied those years. She was, for the first time since Ned had known her, truly enjoying life - whether it was wrong to feel so at a time of such tragedy for so many people, nothing could drive from her heart this feeling of being wanted. It was her day of fulfilment, something she intended to savour. Moreover, she could now tell Ned that Brigitte would be returning to Le Havre, something that would please and unite the family.

"You too? - Pleased?" she asked him carefully and he paused only for a second to make a choice of positives. "She's yer sister. Ah can love her as your sister, can't ah?"

Her eyes questioned that statement for a moment. "You sink?.... It's not difficult for you?"

"No more than it is for her. An' you too, come to that. She's gone through a lot, Reina, ah know that."

"Yes."

"And I'd say ah was at least partly to blame for that, wouldn't you?"

"Yes."

"More than partly," he conceded. "Anyway, it's good she's coming home. I imagine she's a different girl now. "

Renata smiled. "You sink? You don't know Gitta so well."

"Do you know where we are, Ned?"

It seemed an odd question to ask of a complete stranger to this place. Mildly bemused, he looked about him: a pleasant enough street, apparently undamaged, with trees across the way. She grinned a broad grin. "Boulevard Longueville?" she prompted.

No. That rang no bells for him.

"Monsieur Verne?" she prompted.

He looked at her with a questioning frown. "What? - Here?"

"Yes! Right here. Number 44. He lived here. And I sink, he died here. Yes."

"In Amiens? I didn't know that."

"Zey give ze street his name. But you didn't know because you didn't look. I looked for you. I am your eyes, Ned." She was his brain, too, that much was evident.

The building, though, was modest in itself. A house. A very French house, pleasant enough. But... that Jules Verne had lived here! Yes - thoughtful to bring him here. It made a kind of bridge.

"I read Verne," she added. "A little. *Cinq semaines en ballon.* The older children, they like those stories from long time ago. Ned, you said you are like Captain Nemo? - I do not sink so."

He turned to her with a warm grin. As usual she was right. For all his genius, Nemo could never see that humanity's better face was love and compassion.

"You are not impressed, Ned?"

He was looking wistfully at the unremarkable building, turning over in his mind the impressions Verne had given him over the years. "*.... Not for less would I make a tour around the world.*"

"What?"

"*.... To make him the happiest of men.*"

"Who?"

"Me.... Mr. Fogg went around the world and came back with nothing but the love of a charming woman."

"Ah."

"That's what I did. More or less - ah've sailed as far as goin' round the world, ah'm sure. And what do ah have to show for it? - Nothing but the love of a charming woman..... Ah finally found my way to you, Reina.... An' heck, ah do love yer."

Her eyes reflected the contentment of his. For these moments, she had waited a long, long time.

That was another sort of landmark for him. Renata was not only intelligent - far more than he - but she was mindful of little things like this, discovering the Verne house. Although, the 'little weeping angel' in the cathedral had no significance for him, and he declined that suggestion. It was a symbol, she said, of the tragedy of war, but it was far from his mood this day, and he preferred instead to walk to the river again. Sensing that he might have offended her, he quickly added, "But if yer want to go to church, Reina....."

"No. No, no. It's not necessary, Ned. *Je suis contente.* I have made the prayers, last night. It is enough."

A strange thing, that he had not previously given more than passing thought to the fact Renata and her family were Catholic; a point which Grace had alluded to and he had instantly dismissed it. Brought up in an Anglican environment, Ned no longer felt the relevance of religion: with the war raging literally just along the road, only the chaplain in the trenches might be any reminder at all that God had any part to play.

Clutching his arm tighter as they walked, her own essence radiated through his body. He knew she understood.

"Ah don't need gods, love. No offence. Ah've lived through things nobody should 'ave to see. The world bein' looked after by some kind of all-seeing, sweet-natured old man in the sky.... It's not for me. Ah'm not bright like you. Ah never had much schoolin'. Ah see what ah see. Goin' to pray is alright for some - if it makes yer feel better. But me.... Fairy stories now."

"But I understand how you feel, *cheri.* It is alright. Someday we will talk... Not now."

He pressed on a little faster. The war had entered his head again and he did not want that. Not today. Not if there were some way of avoiding it. And Verne too was bothering him, somewhere in the vault of his brain. It came to him that a man like Verne could see the possibilities for mankind, if war and greed and corruption were first banished. Yet this world of 1916, it appeared to have learned very little of that. In fact, it appeared to have learned nothing at all. He wondered if the world of men ever would.

They found they had strolled down to a bridge over a canal and a thinly grassy area. Here Ned made use of his camera, packed discreetly into his haversack as he left camp. Knowing he now had only two exposures left in the camera, he set Renata by a colourfully decorated barrow that might normally be festooned with flowers or vegetables, but held neither. After posing for him, Renata insisted she take one of him, but noticing an older gentleman close by - well-dressed and slow of pace - she called to him and asked if he would be so kind as to photograph them both.

" *Enchanté,"* said the old man, placing his stick carefully against the barrow, "*Avec plaisir! Vous êtes les jeunes mariés, n'est-ce pas?*"

"*Oui, monsieur, c'est vrai. Nous nous sommes mariés ce matin.*"

"*Ce matin? Oh, la-la! Mais - c'est merveilleux, mes enfants, formidable! Malgré la guerre, uh? - Bravo, bravo!*"

That she was clearly French and he clearly English bothered the old man not at all: in age there is wisdom to transcend all notions of class or country.

Handing the man the camera, Renata instructed him how to take the picture whilst at the same time vaguely touching on their wedding that morning and the circumstances of why they were now alone, instead of being surrounded by well-wishing guests.

Carefully, without his stick as a support, the man framed the couple and took the snap. *If it is no good*, thought Ned, *it cannot be repeated.*

Elated, the old man waved his farewell and hobbled cheerfully away. Ned beamed at her and said, "You enchantress! Yer could charm the birds out of the trees! Yer told that pack o' lies with the honesty of a virgin."

"Virgin?.... No, no, not me," she laughed. "I am your wife..... He said it. So it must be true."

Their broad grins slowly faded into a serenity of recognition. "That you are," agreed Ned with a stilled passion in his voice. So saying, he pulled her into his arms and kissed her luxuriously.

Further along, the old man turned his head back to the couple and grinned with satisfaction. He wished he could have given them a wedding gift that matched his admiration for her untruths.

* * * * *

Making plans. Making love. Getting to know each other as they had never before been allowed to. That was the order of the day. Their day. Their one day together completely without ties or responsibilities. It would swiftly pass, they knew, and to an extent the portents coloured their time, although they tried hard to set such thoughts to the back of the mind. Renata did not press him as to his time as a soldier: she knew there were horrible things he had no wish to describe. He would tell her what he wished her to know, and what he suffered she knew with very few words.

Life went on in Amiens, they were not in a vacuum, they wandered its traumatised streets for a time, moved aside for the occasional brightly coloured tramcar navigating fine tree-lined avenues and for a few francs each ate a splendid meal at a small restaurant they came across in the town, a leisurely lunch in company with others trying desperately to ignore the clouds of war jostling in on the once-pleasant halls of Amiens. A veiled sun shone out its cosseting ambience and all the time Ned had to keep looking hard at Renata to assure himself she was here - his dream, in the flesh. It could have been the perfect day, except for that canker in the back of the mind that their clock was ticking. From the East, rumbles of man-made thunder crossed the sky.

That Friday evening they went to bed early, both a little more subdued than the previous night, and said little that could be of any consequence as - still living their dream - they watched each other undress and closed their naked bodies together. She stroked the broad scar on his side and kissed the more recent shrapnel tear to his upper arm as though it might heal further, and all her hopes and fears for him she kept to herself. Tired but still resolutely happy, they talked quietly late into the evening, made love with a tender ferocity, and again fell into slumber in supreme - if not total - contentment.

Mercifully, they did not stir to the muffled sound of the guns in the far, far distance, a dawn thunderstorm.

* * * * *

"You wanted to apologise?.... But why?"
Renata gritted her teeth.
"Because, Ned, I.... I had bad thoughts. When I was coming here..... I wanted you so much.... and I dreamed that somehow we could .... go away. You and I, just go. And live our own lives.... somewhere.... anywhere. Somewhere we can just love."
She gripped his hands.
"It's not possible. I know it's not possible. Because I should know you better. You will go back.... because you have to. Because you are you. And.... zat is one sing I love. You say you are just a simple man, and zat is true. But you are an honest man and a brave

man, you have ze courage to do what you don't want to do... and what I do not want you to do. You go to fight because you believe your people need you to fight. I am just a selfish girl. I want you alone. But I cannot have you, because it would not be you any more.... You understand? Well - it's no matter - me, I understand. You know it's difficult to say in English what I want to say."

"Your English is wonderful.... An' ah think ah know what you're tryin' to say."

"Yes," Renata signalled in a low breath, "Yes, Ned, I believe you do know.... Oh, my love, I am afraid....." Impetuously, she put her arms about him and gripped him tightly to her. "Forgive me, *cheri*.... I am afraid."

Ned knew that fear. He had smelled it on himself many times. It was the fear of fear itself. The fear of a future they could not know. Inwardly, he nodded to acknowledge it, then carefully extended her to his arms' length.

"Ah know, Reina.... Ah know... The only fear I have now is.... being without you."

He put a finger to the underside of her chin and lifted her face to look into his soothing smile.

"But we will get through, ah know we will.... Just remember - it's champion. It'll be champion. It will."

Her face lit brighter for some moments. "*Oui, cheri....* Ze mushrooms..... Always."

A breeze blew strongly across the platform. He was only grateful that her train was to come first: it would have felt wrong somehow if it had been him leaving her alone at the station. Alone and yet surrounded by all these soldiers, here at Abbeville. It was far from ideal: there was noise, there was hustle and bustle, there were the pungent odours of unwashed bodies, there was clutter everywhere, it was not the stuff of romantic fiction. Yet their clock ticked ever faster, their time drawing inexorably to a moment of closure. This they had known as they had travelled slowly up from Amiens that Saturday morning. How to avoid those moments of dread? It was impossible. All lovers know those moments.

So their morning had been pensive, caring but overshadowed by the parting that was to come. Renata wanted to shout out, "Stay with me!" yet she could not, it would only make worse the nature of what Ned had to do. Similarly, he ached to be able to carry her with him for as long as time endured, yet he too knew there would have to be another time, and they would have to wait. How does anyone in love part from that which they most desire? It is the shocking wound whose scars are unseen. Lovers know the despair of being parted, perhaps never to see each other again: in time of war, the poignancy was almost too much to bear, and yet millions had to bear it just the same.

They held hands and were silent for much of the time, knowing the complete inadequacy of words. On the train from Amiens, they had sat as closely together as was humanly possible, cursing those powers that would tear them apart and uncaring as to what anyone might think of them - those eyes which saw this young man and woman in love would forgive all indelicacies. Yesterday was now a million miles away. Renata, in brown once again, wiped away the occasional tear before he could see it, yet he knew they were feeling the same.

"Will you tell Otto about us?"

"Yes."

He nodded. Clearly, it was right she should.

"When you write to 'im, tell 'im 'e remains my dearest friend. Tell 'im ah shall want to see 'im once this ruddy war is finished. Tell 'im ah miss his ruddy awful cooking. But ah'm so pleased he's still in Köln with your cousin." He did not mention that the nightmares had stopped, that he no longer dreamed of charging a German trench and facing Otto with a bayonet.

"And Gitta.... Please tell her ah hope everything goes well for her. Ah wish her well, Reina - truly. Regine will be alright - she's bound to be, with you three women to see to 'er."

"Yes. I will write to Monsieur Carelle and tell him everysing we have done. And thank him, because he is so generous."

"What about Monsieur Ardant?"

"No.... We do not know what he will do. He is still working at that hospital. Gitta said maybe he goes back to Chartres. We do not know. I wanted to write to his family, but Gitta said no.... You know, when I saw zat money from Monsieur Carelle, I could not believe it."

"He is a good man. The best."

Small talk, no more. These were things that mattered, but at the same time felt of slight consequence beside the anguish they were feeling.

"Ned... You can dance?"

A strange question. He scowled in spite of himself.

"Not really. Why?"

"Every year there is a big *jour de fête* at Rouen. Everyone is very happy. People drink a lot and be very happy and there is dancing. Since I was much younger I had always wanted.... to dance with the man I love at the *jour de fête*. I never did that yet. I.... I never had a man that I loved."

"When this fightin's all over, ah'll come an' ah'll take yer to the *jour de fête,* or anywhere yer like. You teach me, sweetheart, an' ah'll dance. Ah promise."

"On ze mushrooms?" She smiled the meaning of the word.

"Aye, love" he said softly, "Aye."

Abbeville was no place for lovers. That station was hateful now. Every stone gave out vapours of despair at their parting. Every step was a leap into an abyss of hopelessness.

And with the train approaching, so that sense of desperation overtook them, inexorable and insurmountable. Each clung to the other with sufficient space only to look into the other's face, and words did not come easily. Their two bodies were about to be ripped apart.

"Perhaps," ventured Ned, "it was our misfortune to be born into the wrong time and place."

Renata only cherished him with her eyes. It was her turn for courage. "But we were not," she said.

"No... ah mean.... Ah wanted us to live.... To live."

She kissed his cheek.

488

"Ned.... I have lived."

As the train for Dieppe drew in and noisily disgorged so many bustling bodies, another melée of bodies rushed to get aboard. Ned took her by the hand to a carriage that was no more than full, entrusted her small case to the custody of a large woman seated there and, once two or three more people had embarked, stood at the door, clinging to her hand through the open window. Other passengers looked but made way for them, understanding and compassionate. They had already made their final embrace, which had lasted a brief eternity whilst a doleful psalm played out inside Ned's head.

"For all of my life", he finally told her, "in whatever world there is for us, I love you, Reina,". Renata began to cry. Whistles blew, the train lurched ahead with a great roar, the carriage shook and parted their hands through the open window. Summoning all her remaining inner strength, she smiled through her pain and slowly mouthed the words, "*Je t'aime*, Ned."

As long as they could, they watched each other, waving more slowly, until it dawned on his consciousness that the train was gone, she was no longer there. It was over. He could no longer hold her. From deep within his soul, a gigantic howl sought to burst out of his breast: *Reina! Reina!* Around him, soldiers and civilians alike continued to bustle, yet in that repressed morass of pain, he was utterly alone in a universe of despair.

A little over an hour later, he was seated in that awful place as the train rattled and crashed its way forward along his return journey to Hazebrouck. Anywhere would have been awful. He was without her. All he had left to feel was the sensation of her body at his fingertips, the taste of her lips, the all-healing power of her smile, the softness of her voice saying those things no-one else could say to him, the memory of all those moments with her.

Would it have been so difficult not to go back? 'Stay with me, Ned. Love me.' Words like that should not be spoken. What difference does one soldier make? One more among hundreds of thousands. One more to make no difference to anything but a list of names. A man's duty? To whom? To a king who would never even know nor care of his existence? To a country that had not wanted him? That musical box.... it goes on playing. The dancers go on dancing. And oh! - the hurt of wanting her!

What did I ever know of loving?

Love. An ecstasy. A torture. Exquisite, and diabolical. It tears you apart then puts you back together only to tear you apart again. Sweet and brutal. Strange. Why do we do it? - It's a lucky bloke that knows.

But unless we have that essence of someone inside us, we're not complete, are we? Well... Maybe I'm not that ignorant child any more.

I love her, it's all I know. She is everything. Those days with her.... They'll be our 'forever'. For as long as I last, anyhow. They'll be a torment, and a joy, and every moment now is a step towards the next time with her: that's the only way I can look at it otherwise I destroy myself.

She's the music in my head: like a sweet, soaring violin and then a deep, melancholy cello and finally a heavenly choir. Yes, that's her, that's my Reina.

My Reina... Hell, I can't lose her now, I couldn't bear it. She has my soul.

So the pain begins.

Oh, Reina..........

＊ ＊ ＊ ＊ ＊

FORTY-SEVEN

"How was the leave, Bob?" asked Happy John. "Bring us back any paraffin?"

Bob eased himself onto the camp bed and took his time stretching out and pretending it was luxury. He needed to relax, it had been a tiresome journey, all the worse for knowing what awaited him when he got back.

"Lost five cows," muttered Bob. "Five! Poor old girls get sick. There isn't the same feed for them any more, we just have to make do with what's left to us."

"Sounds a bit desperate."

"Mmm. Desperate is the word. Sad to see them cows sold for meat. I reckon I'm gonna have to start sending rations home soon."

"That bad?" queried Wally. "I thought in England it was all chin-chin and cocktails at dawn, old sport."

Bob only shook his head morosely. He didn't want to talk about it in a jocular way. "How's it been here?"

"Oh, the usual thing, y'know. Jerry invited us to dinner but the soup was cold and the caviar was definitely off. We said No thanks, we'll stick to our M. & V rations.... Did you hear about those tanks we sprung on the Jerries down the road at Flers? *We* could do with some o' them."

"Why do they call them 'tanks'?" Taff wanted to know.

"Because they look like bloody tanks, idiot!"

"Good for putting a crease in your trousers, Taff," called Ernie.

"Maybe we can get a ride to the Jerry trench.... keep the rain off. Oh, I got a card from Wilf, by the way."

"Really? How is he?"

"Living.... Well, that's something, innit?"

"Depends," Ernie put in. "Without a right arm, what's 'e gonna do?"

Happy John carried on. "Leaving hospital, he says they're sending him to a cushy place, Summerdown Camp in Eastbourne. He's gonna be havin' a holiday. Splashing about in the poxy sea, I shouldn't wonder. One o' them boys in blue, he is now."

"Don't joke about it," said Ernie. "Who wrote that card for 'im? Ey? Think about that. What's a train engineer do with no arm?"

Nobody wanted to take him up on that. They all felt the chances of surviving this war were getting slimmer.

"Mmm. We were right anyway. Said we'd not see Wilf again.... How's Ned doing?"

"Out of the infirmary. Bert reckons he'll be back with us shortly."

"He's a jammy bastard, that Ned," said Wally. "If it'd been me, you can bet they'd never have found me under all that earth. Next time a shell lands on my dugout, I want to have Ned on top of me. And you can take that any way you like, I don't care."

Ernie chastised him. "You want to trade places with Ned? - He looks like a rat nibbled his face."

"All the same, he's a jammy bastard. Ned spends more time away from this company than any three blokes I know."

"Change places with him then," suggested Bob. "He's missed his long leave, hasn't he? It was his turn. 'T' still follows 'S', I believe. So don't talk about lucky."

"Brought you some sausage, Ned. Straight from the butchers on the high street. Cooked it myself yesterday in some fat we got off that farmer. Horrible stuff but they taste alright. Better that than have it go off. How's the er..... the, er......?"

Ned felt the side of his face. "Bit better every day, Bob," he rasped. "Still a bit deaf, though..... M.O. says it'll get back to normal.... But ah can still fight once the bandages are off - ah'm thrilled about that, as yer can imagine!"

"You were lucky only to lose a bit of your ear. Harry Pearson's in a bad way and - well, you know about that new lad."

"Poor sod. Few weeks at the Front and that's it. What happened to Smithy?"

"Three fingers. How many times do we tell 'em? - Don't put your hands on your head to hold your helmet down! - What's the chinstrap for?..... If it don't take your ruddy head off! But... the way they're rushing these conscripts through now...."

"We were green not that long ago, Bob. Needed our bums wiping."

"You still do!"

"'Ave we learned anything, d'yer reckon? Maybe Smithy learned that losin' three fingers is a trip home. Right hand, ah suppose?"

"Yes... They panic, don't they? They're not getting anything like the training we got. Conscription's shovin' 'em all through like a bloody sausage machine."

"Aye, well.... I still panic. Ah don't know anybody that doesn't from time to time."

"Mmm. Me neither."

Bob waved his hip flask under the other man's nose, his eyebrows signalling an invitation. Ned declined and adjusted his head bandage so that he could hear better, though he winced as the wound still smarted where it pulled his hair.

"You know what I think, Ned? They've heard so much about the Somme and they're so relieved to come here instead, they're just not prepared for it to be as bad. They're terrified when they hear names like Pozières that they've read in the papers and they don't think it's as bad here. You get killed just as easily here as on the Somme. Bloody newspapers have got a lot to answer for. *'British casualties were light'*.... Oh yair, light means less than a thousand.... *'And our forces inflicted heavy losses on the Germans'*..... We're having an easy life, Ned! We're overpaid!" Ned was recalling what Grace had said about censorship.

"That's a fair old outburst fer you, mate."

"Yes, well..... Trouble is, back home they believe the papers. They don't want to hear it from a chap like me. In the pub last week, I heard them silly old sods talking - like it was all far worse back in the day..... I got narked, I can tell you. Nice lies is better than rotten truths. But you know about the newspapers, Ned - I don't need tell you, do I?"

"You kept all that to yerself, Bob?"

493

"Course I have. That was private, what you told me. Oh - here - brought your letters. Four of 'em. Three from Le Havre. That woman is just too good to you."

Ned grinned as best he could. "She is. Ah'd like yer to meet 'er sometime, Bob. Ah tell 'er about you."

"Do you?.... Well.... This much I do know, lad - Bremme isn't a French name. Or am I much mistook?"

She had endorsed the back of the envelope as usual. Ned always destroyed envelopes before they saw them.

"No. You're not mistaken. Her 'usband's French, ah have to write to 'er mother's house - Bremme, see. That's why she writes the name and address on t'back, so's he don't find out."

"Bremme.... German? If your humble servant is not mistaken again."

Bob had given him a sidelong look of inquisition, so Ned returned the query with a condescending grin.

"You are not mistaken, Sherlock."

".... Married a Frenchman...."

"Family's German, Bob. So now yer know. The woman ah love is German. An' ah'll tell yer this, Bob Street - they're family to me. There's not one of 'em ah don't love like me own kin."

"Uhuh. No wonder you never say much. And nobody else here knows this?"

"Ah wouldn't own up to anyone else."

"Mmm. Privileged information. I'm in your debt, young sir."

"Ach, don't talk wet! Ah would never lie to you, yer know that."

"So.... What happens? Weeks ago you said you were going to marry her."

"Soon as we can. She'll leave 'er husband."

"Sure about that?"

"Dead sure. She loves me, Bob."

"Hmmm. I shall surely hope so, lad. Because you're not going to have an easy ride, whatever happens. You know that, don't you?"

"Aye... But it won't make a scrap o' difference if the whole of the British Empire's against us."

"Alright, Ned. I got the point. Just worried for you."

"Don't. If *Titanic* sinkin' didn't stop me and Lord Muck tryin' to get me locked up didn't stop me, ah can tell yer now the British Empire don't stand a chance of keepin' me from Reina."

"A bullet might."

"... A bullet. Ah'm not an easy man to kill, Bob."

"And what's that about *Titanic*? You never said anything about *Titanic* before. You telling me after all this time that you were on *Titanic*?"

Ned chewed at his teeth. Bob deserved his confidence.

"Well, bugger me! - Just how long have we known each other, Ned Thornton? All this time and you didn't tell me - God, you're a dark horse and no mistake! I ought to start calling you 'The Cat' - you've got as many lives, apparently. And what lord, did you say?.... Is that the chap you told me caused you bother in the newspapers? 'Bout time you told me the rest, isn't it?"

It surely was. Bob was the closest thing in the world Ned had to a father, it could do no good to keep secrets from him. It was just something he had got used to. Friends like Bob, though - they don't grow on trees.

"Anyway, it's all very well, Bob Street, to lecture me on stuff ah've not told yer. What about you? Took wild 'orses to drag it out of yer that yer'd got a girlfriend. Thirteen years! Did yer see her on leave?"

That changed Bob's attitude completely. He had not been the brightest of souls since returning.

"It's over," Bob told him.

"Over? What? - Thirteen years and suddenly it's over?"

"Mmm.... I hit her, Ned."

"You what?"

"I hit her."

That took a little time to sink in. Ned only looked at him, in a way that indicated Bob would tell him when he was ready. Bob hitting a woman? - Absurd!

"I found out she'd been seeing this other bloke. Oh, I don't know - some character in the town, reserved occupation or something, I neither know nor care. She said she couldn't hang around waiting for me forever..... I just..... " He sighed with frustration and shook his head. "I hit her...."

"That's not like you, Bob."

"No.... It's not." Seeing his friend struggling with the episode, Ned regretted having raised the matter.

"Stupid thing to do. Sorry I done it now. Course I am."

"Did you hurt her bad?"

"Bloodied her lip..... Slapped her across the face..... Hadn't meant to..... Anyway, it's over."

"Naah! Listen, feller, don't write it off so easily. It's not a new tale, is it? They get bored waitin' for us. Mebbe they shouldn't, I dunno. Women don't know how it is for us here, do they? They don't know we're desperate to get back to 'em. Do they? They've got no idea what this lot's like. How could they? For a lot of 'em, they just want a quick fling and they'll settle down again. Leave it a while, Bob. Bet you she writes to you."

"Mmm. Doubt it. Anyway.... " He had made up his mind to put it out of his head for now. "What's the news from your French lady?" Bob nodded in the direction of the photograph that Ned pulled from one of the envelopes. "That her?"

Ned's face was transformed, he was a hundred miles away. "Oh, wow! It's the snap I took at Amiens... Oh, wow!"

"Let me see.... Gosh!.... " Bob broke off a biscuit to nibble at. " I can see why you're smitten... A very lovely lady. Very lovely. She loves you, that's plain to see."

"Is it?"

"Plain as day. Look at them eyes. And I've never even seen her before. Oh - nearly forgot - here, there's this other letter from your friend in London. Postmarked the 25th: they're improving."

* * * * *

'Barnet, 24 September 1916
'Dear Ned,
Illum habemus! - We have him!

496

Great news! - Scotland Yard is to issue a warrant for Semper's arrest! At last, my friend, we shall shout your story from the rooftops! Forgive me, I am elated. I had to write straight away, I do not know when the newspapers reach you - they have not yet been given a story to print and today is Sunday anyway, but Scotland Yard will act tomorrow. It will be in Tuesday's editions unless there is a block on the information - which, frankly, would not surprise me. Grimshaw swore me to secrecy - I promised not to say a word to anyone within these shores!

Since I saw Olive Devonshire, she has given a statement to the police, which implicates herself but particularly Semper. By coming forward she will gain leniency. The case now will focus on documents Semper took in contravention of the Official Secrets Act of 1911. Regarding those personal letters, I don't know, it is not a criminal matter for Semper. The paper you got Cade to sign will carry some weight - often the testimony of a criminal is discounted, but they cannot ignore the statement of a man about to be executed and witnessed by a priest and a British army officer. Again - well done, Ned.

Olive Devonshire has confessed to her part, as 'accessory'. Her testimony means the police can act. They already had the information about Martin from the Americans. Arnold Grimshaw is almost sorry it is coming to an end! Perhaps he will get a promotion.

So that you have some satisfaction in this, I called at Highgrove Place this evening where for the moment he is under house arrest. They are trying to keep it quiet but I cannot imagine the newspapers will not sniff something out before long. I was permitted entry but Arthur told me Lady Sophie was not at home. Our conversation was short, because this man has even less wit than character, if that is possible. However - this you will like, Ned - Sophie had been listening, she appeared at the top of the staircase and called down to me. I forget the words, she called me Bruno and she said she was disappointed to hear what I had said. So I said, "Lady Sophie, your husband is a traitor not only to England but also to you, and he has caused a great deal of trouble to a young man called Edward

Thornton, whom he will remember as the steward from Titanic. Please tell him that name - Edward Thornton."

That is what I told them, Ned, and I left. I can tell you, it gave me so much pleasure!

Amat victoria curam. Our diligence finally won the day!

Now, I must go north. Tonight, if I can catch a late train. But I wanted to write this news to you. I shall make my way to see Grace on my route, I believe they will be happy to see me.

With the very best of wishes, Ned, for your good health and safe return.

Your friend,

Bruno

p.s. My Latin is bad - I think my school-teacher would be kicking my Latin 'Ars'!'

Ned's smile widened as he put the letter down. Otto came into his mind: it was Otto with his obsession for vocabulary that had taught him - *Lateinischer Kunst* - Arse. Maybe a dead language still had a point to make.

* * * * *

Every day came the threat that they were to move forward. So often it didn't happen until the day when suddenly it does. Suddenly they were not in reserve any more, they were up to the Front again. This time the very front, no more supporting roles. Yet how long had they been away from the trenches? Less than two weeks? It was all the moving around that confused matters. And anyway, in the grand scheme of things, one trench was as good as another. Or as bad.

"Wish people would make up their poxy minds."

"Ah," said Ernie, "Happy John's happy again. Got something to moan about."

"You can shut your poxy face, Stench, or we'll send you back to A company."

"Goin' south again, by the sound of it. You get a better class of trench further south, don't yer? And - don't forget - it's nearer the equator. Take your parasols and bathing suits, girls."

"Nearer the what?"

"Shit n'it!" shouted Corporal Parrock.

"Nearer the bloody grub tent would do me fine," said Tommy under his breath.

"D'you think Ned will be joining us, Bert?"

"Soon, Wally. They'll not keep him there long. They'll push some new straw in his chest, give him a new clockwork spring, a carrot for his nose and wipe some fresh paint across his face and send him off good as new. You'll see."

"I mean, Ned's never here, is he? - Always off for one thing or another."

"You would be too if you got buried alive and got yer ear shot off, Myers."

"Yes, Corp. Sorry, Corp. Three bags full, Corp."

"Myers, put yourself on a bloody charge!"

"Yes, Corp. Could I have my cocoa and afternoon nap first?"

* * * * *

FORTY-EIGHT

From the Belgian coast the line ran all the way to Switzerland: at times they felt they had walked that far. Walking was just something troops did, something troops simply had to do: according to Happy John it was written into army law - 'Thou shalt walk till thy boots learn to walk off on their own'. In Ernie's case, he was warned never to take them off as the smell drove others to drink.

A few more miles made little difference, so long as there was food at the end of it. For most, the end of it meant rolling up sleeves and getting the camp set up: supplies, ammunition and equipment all stowed away before there was any chance of food. Things had to be done the army way: as if the men would rather feed their bellies and lie around idly passing the night away before giving thought to tents and security. As if! The army relied on its men, yet did not trust them.

Somewhere along the way, they marched past a group of prisoners at the roadside resting, with an armed British escort every few yards. It was an uncommon site, the only curiosity was the variety of expression on the faces of those men. Mostly tired, gaunt, careworn faces: strangely un-foreign faces even beneath their large helmets and cloth caps. They had been given permission to smoke, and someone was passing around a water can. As Ned's eyes examined them, he saw that the nature of those soldiers ranged from the utterly defeated through to the nervous and anxious, right along to the arrogant and defiant. From within the marching Britishers, someone shouted out, "Bastards! One of you killed our Pugh!"

A response came swiftly from Sergeant Barcombe: "Private Barraclough - be silent, lad! Eyes front!"

The sight of captive men caused Ned to reflect that one day one of them might be a friend of Otto's. He had to fight Germans and to hate Germans - because they were Germans, nothing more. Watching them, Ned affirmed to himself that he could not hate - the response was not in him. To kill a man who is ready to kill you, that may well be one thing, but to hate? He thought of Renata, and how much he adored her.

This morning they were on the road to La Bassée, itself in German hands, not far from the village of Neuve Chapelle, an area that had seen major action eighteen months before as part of an Anglo-French offensive when the tug of war resulted in consolation for neither side for the loss of thousands. A large proportion of British losses had been Indian. Whilst India as a nation was beginning to explore a path away from empire, its sons gave their lives in this war so far from their homes and families, and in truth scarcely loved by those whom they served so well. No-one knew what losses the Germans had incurred since, if figures were published, no-one believed them anyway as Germans were known to be lying and deceitful and evil whereas British newspapers and politicians could be relied on for the truth. Naturally.

As with so many major actions, the lack of any ostensibly positive outcome for the Allies called into question the strategies of those on whom the fighting men depended for their very lives. Veteran soldiers of late 1916 were cynical of the dogged attitudes of the General Staff in obstinately pursuing their strategies. Many believed the stalemate could not be broken by generals or senior staff negotiating positions with their opposite numbers and politicians over months and years, whilst thousands on either side were allowed to perish as if their lives were just the value of the last piece of paper tossed into the waste bin. No-one, though, took bets on the notion that things could be done differently, and such talk could be treason.

The tall Lieutenant John Donovan called his soldiers to a halt just as dusk was getting the upper hand. For some, there was to be a farmhouse for the night, derelict and shell-worn, whilst three platoons of C company were relegated to tents as usual and they put them up in semi-darkness before getting permission to light fires and cook. It was colder now, this October of 1916, they had seen little sunshine of late and some said worse was on the way. 'Worse' arrived the next morning, C company set to paddling and setting up

501

the tents more securely. Bert Parrock found a wall to serve as a wind-break, they anchored the tent beside that.

A former bloody theatre like Neuve Chapelle still had to be managed. Trenches here were as active as anywhere else, they just had fewer concentrations of troops now that the Somme had become the primary focus of Anglo-French offensives. The men of 12 battalion were here to relieve the present garrison and, whilst British and Allied forces gathered further south along the Somme salient, it was to be hoped the Germans might not be doing a similar thing here in the Vimy-Neuve Chapelle sector.

For Ned Thornton, after rejoining his company the evening before the march, it was reasonable to debate that success or failure with the present tactics came down simply to one side having more men than the other. Even the new tanks, the super-weapon, had failed to have major significance on an early showing. As it was generally accepted that one man in defence was worth at least two in attack, the arithmetic worked well for the German defenders. This much Ned was contemplating as he stood trying to see from the high walkway that characterised this deep trench, so deep he wondered why it had been so constructed.

"You never seen a firestep before, feller?"

Ned looked back at the man. Yes, he had seen firesteps: not this deep, though.

"Jerry built this trench. This is a Jerry trench."

"Yer kiddin'?"

"No. Where're yer from, lad? Up my way, by the sound of it."

"Bradford."

"Gerraway! Ah'm Tommy Tucker, from Colne."

Ned's mouth must have dropped open.

".... I know, I know," said Tucker, "Look, d'yer think I make it up?" He showed a resigned face and shook his head. "We were with t'Bradford Pals a bit back."

Giving his own name, Ned extended his hand. "Where was that?" Tucker's mouth turned downward.

"Yer should be right glad you weren't there, lad. That West Riding Regiment - it were criminal. Ah tell yer no lie."

"Aye, ah got all that news. Wish ah hadn't."

"Horrible, Ned. Three quarters of your lads gone that day. Two battalions nearly. Pure murder."

"You were there?"

Tucker only nodded and clicked his teeth. He changed the subject and asked Ned about the side of his face. Could he still hear alright behind that mess?

"As well as the next man."

"Doctors done you up, then," said Tucker.

"Half past nine!" shouted Ned.

Early the second morning, a bombardment began. The rain had stopped, perhaps the German gunners felt the need to dry out with some target practice. As usual, British defenders sought the deepest of holes to keep out of the way. It began at first light and continued more than two hours, a sure sign this was no impromptu caprice, a follow-up was coming.

Those British soldiers used to being under fire settled down as best they could to the usual games of hiding away and ignoring everything, whilst every sinew in the body was taut as a spring. Perhaps settled down to card games with that old dog-eared deck with the missing five of spades where someone had substituted a piece of biscuit packing. One way or the other, the shelling would be over in due time, and there was nothing you could do about it - the trick was to consider yourself half-way to heaven already, sitting there in God's waiting room. You either got called through, or you didn't. The younger replacements were, as ever, hard to control. Ned and each of his comrades knew exactly how they felt and did their best to calm them. Regardless of all else, it did not come happily to Ned that he was once again hiding in a deep shelter when he had recently been buried in one. Like his friends, he was now unofficially an 'old hand'. In the army barely two years, he never ever felt like a 'real soldier' or a real anything before. The war made old men out of young men very, very quickly.

At around 7.30, the guns ceased. To the newer soldiers, the relief might show in their trousers as well as the looks on their haggard, ever-startled faces. Older soldiers disguised their fear better, hung back and waited. Ned looked from Bert to Ernie, across to Wally and Bob, Tommy Tarmey and 'Postie' Jackson. Something in the air that morning tied all their thoughts into one channel. Only the younger conscripts spoke, excitedly expressing relief, while the older men exchanged their thoughts until eventually Bert Parrock broke their silence - "It's on."

No sooner had he said it than they heard the whistle blowing. Someone blowing furiously. It could have been for the entire Canterbury police constabulary.

"Outside!" came the cry. "Outside! Get out! Get out! Man your posts!"

Bert calmly pulled his helmet strap up. "Right, lads. Let the cowboys see the indians."

"It's about time," croaked Wally in a dry voice. Like the others, Wally was almost shuddering with fear, yet at the same time relieved that unpredictable and indiscriminate death from shelling was being replaced by a human enemy they might actually fight.

Curiously, there was haste but no panic. Training, after all, counted for something. Bob slapped Ned on the rump and helped him up onto the firestep: in this trench it was like an upper gallery with the duckboards running along the length several inches out of the muddy trench bottom below. With the parados of the original German trench lowered, the parapet that now faced forward was high compared to most British trenches. A man falling into it would probably break his neck.

German forces early on in the war had had the advantage of where and how to build their trenches. After being driven back by the French from their initial gains, they had chosen the best places for defence, often on high ground, and many of their defences were formidable. So much so that their dugouts could often be thirty feet below ground, deep enough to withstand bombardment whilst usually avoiding descent to the water table which was a hazard their Allied opponents, with less choice in the matter, often faced. C company felt secure in that former German trench.

504

Using his periscope, Sergeant Longbottom was peering keenly over the top of the timbers whilst his free hand waved a series of signals to the others.

"Anything?" asked Donovan.

"A minute, sir..... Nothing..... Smoke.... Wait.... Jerry coming, sir!"

The Lieutenant stretched his neck and shouted to the trench, "Company will fix bayonets..... Fix!" Then the command for every soldier to man that wall instantly. There was no thinking about anything now. From here, it would all work on instinct. All those questions from training sessions, they didn't enter the mind now, it would be reflex or nothing.

"Steady, lads," shouted Percy Longbottom. "Don't shoot till you've got a clear target now, d'you hear? If you can't see him for the smoke, he can't see you, remember. Wait till you've got clear sight. You may not have enough time to reload."

At Ned's left, the young soldier was a distraction, clearly in a blind panic and unable to get his rifle to stop shaking. The poor boy was unaware he was dribbling down his tunic, and possibly worse.

"Steady, lad, calm down. Pretend you're shootin' them metal flags at the funfair. It's just target practice, lad, just target practice, that's all it is, right? Settle down, just squeeze yer trigger when yer've got a bloke in yer sight. Don't snatch, don't let the rifle kick yer shoulder back, keep it tight in like yer training taught yer. Aim for 'is body, not 'is legs or 'is head - 'is body's a lot bigger target. Keep yer ruddy head down, wait till yer see 'em properly without stretching up."

The young soldier's face turned to him and grinned a gaunt grin of wide-eyed terror. He could not have been older than seventeen. Ned felt sorry for the lad but knew there was nothing more he could do for him now. More to the point, Ned himself was shivering - that, he told himself, was just the cold.

The grey of greatcoats danced in the smoke. German soldiers were at the wire. Foolish, brave men! But they had to be monsters! They had to be evil! They had to be shot!

Off somewhere to the left, amidst lots of other noise, there had already been the sound of a British machine gun, but in this sector a relative quiet.

Ned levelled the first man in his sight and was ready to squeeze the trigger but the man fell, knocked sideways. From off to his right, he heard Happy John shout, "Bloody apples in a barrel!" until the sergeant told him to shut up.

It was not apples in a barrel, though. From being one soldier, it became three or four, and then through the smoke came a dozen more, and suddenly their eyes were filled with German ogres at the wire, coming through the wire, dancing in a storm of bullets, more and more of them in their large helmets like some mediaeval teutonic knights, darkly threatening. On they came, these fearsome, oversize helmets, relentless: several dozen now, all shouting and screaming and holding their bayonets out to the front as best they could whilst they leaped over rough and slippery ground.

"Shoot! Shoot! Shoot!" John Donovan was beside his sergeant, waving his pistol in the air as if to signal a cavalry charge. With his well-trimmed moustache and uniform tailored to his slim body, he could have been the hero of any American motion picture.

Beside him, from the corner of his eye, Ned glimpsed his young companion fall away. He did not look down to see why or what or where. Two Germans were rushing directly at his position: he might only get one of them with a bullet. The shot went true and struck the first German soldier at the base of the neck: this man instantly fell forward, whilst the second German came on with incredible speed despite the awful ground under foot, shouting at the top of his voice, his eyes so wide they were almost leaping out of their sockets.

It was too late, the German was there and steadying his rifle to fire down into the trench, only needing to stay his forward momentum and bring the rifle to bear on the nearest occupant, but together the bayonets of Ned and Wally Myers thrust savagely upwards and together they caught the German's lower legs. This man screamed as he pitched forward over the top of the pair of them, crashing onto the duckboards seven or eight feet below. He lay still, but Ned had no time to check whether he might be alive, more soldiers were coming at them. As the sound of a machine gun close by now opened up, a blow from a boot caught Ned on the side of his helmet, yanking the strap hard into his already-damaged face and he tumbled from the parapet walkway as this second German soldier more or less slid into the trench and tumbled over and over.

In moments both men had regained their senses and, more importantly, their weapons. But the German, with more mud on his boots, failed to get himself upright and, crucially, had to raise a hand to adjust his spectacles which had jolted out of position. Ned, acting entirely on reflex and with a swift action born purely out of mechanical practice, thrust forward his bayonet into the man's coat in a position that would have pierced his upper chest. That action took all of Ned's focus, nothing else in the world existed at that precise moment as the steel point entered the man with a surprising amount of resistance, despite the weight of the rifle behind it. Nor could Ned easily pull out the bayonet, the whole feeling of it was bizarre and unreal and very frightening, it was only the movement of the man in doubling over that helped pull it clear.

In that instant, as the soldier's hands moved to the point of impact, Ned felt a reaction of horror that he had taken a tool to smash a man's chest, to destroy a man's body. Ned saw the soldier's wide eyes, and with the crystal vision of men in battle, flooded with adrenaline, he saw they were the brightest of bright blues that shone out right through his spectacles. There was a kind of surprise, a kind of disbelief, a kind of question, a kind of apology, a look of disappointment and despair. Their two pairs of eyes were locked for as long as it took for the man slowly to fall backward, gasping a long, loud gasp as he fell with blood appearing at his lips. Then Ned flopped back onto his bottom, legs straddling the duckboards, in an exhaustion of the mind. Notwithstanding other combat around him, he sat there, numbed, a statue for long seconds, gazing at this man whose death was on his hands. This tall, curiously familiar-looking man who was dying in front of him.

There were more scuffles around and about, much shouting, much swearing and panting and grunting, a great deal of noise. However long that went on, Ned was not in the least aware.

Unguarded against attack by another soldier, he sat and stared. He could gauge nothing in these moments. He had killed a man....

"A soldier kills without thinking," their training instructors had told them. "You're like them Roman gladiators. If you stop to think for the tiniest part of a second, it's too late, and you will have his steel in your belly. If that happens, Thornton, and you are dead, do not say I did not tell you so!"

War seen from the air, war seen through the thunderous shell-shower of a bombardment, war at the receiving end of a spitting machine gun, that was one thing. This - this was killing. This was taking a life.

The face of that German person, underneath his comically-large helmet, was stained across Ned's whole mental vision. A young man with glasses. A decently good-looking young man, he would have attracted many young ladies in his town. A tall, quite fit young man, perhaps just twenty years old and perhaps he ran two miles before breakfast in the hills behind his home or perhaps he ran to work at the steel mill or the office. A book-keeper perhaps, or an accountant, a medical student, a steelworker or a tramcar conductor. He would have a name: Friedrich or Albrecht or Gunther or Klaus. He would take off his glasses and polish them before going into battle, and he would worry that they became dirty and he could not see. He would check his gas mask, terrified of being caught in the open in a gas attack.

And he would struggle to cross that muddy, awkward open ground with his boots slipping and his greatcoat and backpack weighing him down, and wishing he had not had breakfast that morning and wishing also he had taken a pee before lining up at the trench wall. Trying to keep his rifle at the ready and wondering what it was going to be like meeting his enemy face to face. He would be shaking, Klaus, and he would be feeling sick, he would be hoping the British machine gunners were slow and not alert and he would be feeling that he only wanted to be home with his wife. Perhaps his wife and children. Perhaps his mother and father. He did not want to be here, facing British rifles and British gun batteries and suffering all the privations of the trenches. He wanted to be at

508

home, just doing his job, just spending his life trying to make it that bit better for himself and everyone. He would have feared a meeting with Ned, and all the other Neds on that battlefield, and he would have wondered what manner of man it was that he was about to kill. He may have not wanted to kill, he may have not seen good reason for it but he would remember the words of his drill sergeant telling them how they had to kill the enemy before the enemy killed them. Remembering also - 'Gott mit Uns'. And having killed, Klaus would have been sick to his stomach and sought to go no further with this war. Klaus would have wanted another way.

So Ned sat there, looking at the face of Klaus underneath his spectacles, his sightless eyes telling Ned his story. Frozen in time.

Only now did it come to Ned what the first German had been shouting - the man who fell into the trench and broke his neck. In his headlong rush, he had been shouting out, "Ilse! Ilse!" Ned could only imagine this had been the name of the man's wife or sweetheart. It sickened him, deep in his gut. And yet, it was perhaps the reason he died - in battle, you cannot allow yourself the luxury of thoughts of loved ones. And for a moment, Ned pondered, when it was his turn to make a charge like that, would he be yelling out "Reina! Reina!"? Klaus had a woman who loved him, just as Ned had a woman who loved him. Ned had just created a widow. It was a terrible, mind-destroying thing to have done. Now only one person, not two. A kind of robbery.

Shortly after, Bob found Ned, still sitting there, with a single tear cleaning a line down his grubby face. Bob helped him find his feet. They looked at each other and knew there was nothing to say. This was victory. This was glory.

* * * * *

FORTY-NINE

"Ernie?....."

They could not believe it.

"Not Ernie?...."

The big man was dead. Their big friend from Poplar, the man with the biggest grin in Kent was dead. Nobody had felt like eating much anyhow. Ernie Waterhouse had taken a bullet straight into his skull and had died instantly.

After a time, Ned said thoughtfully, "Ah shall 'ave to write to 'is sister, Clarice...."

"You don't have to do that, Ned. Not your job."

"No..... Ah want to. Ernie were the man that got me started in the Buffs. Ah spent a night at his sister's house in Southsea.... Seems the right thing to do, like. Ah want to anyway."

They had not wished to know all the details but somebody told them. Twenty-eight British men had died in that attack. So far as they could see, seventeen German soldiers had died there, with so many more out in front of the trench. Now the officers wanted to know how the German soldiers managed to get through to the British trenches and why no nearby British machine gun had opened up. As if it mattered now. Twenty-eight British lads had died, that was what mattered now. To Ned. To Bob. To Wally. To Happy John. The tactics were not important. Colleagues had died, that was what was important. Ernie, a bullet in the head. 'Postie' Jackson, bayonetted. The young conscript, also a bullet through his head. Eating was not what seemed appropriate right now, but they ate anyway in the gloom and Bert Parrock brought the tea round as he so often did. Taff Morgan had gone off to the Triage with a shoulder wound. Percy Longbottom with a torn leg. But Ernie 'Stench' Waterhouse was not sitting with them.

With a kind of detached emptiness, they had been watching as the burial detail took away the cadavers, British and German. Already those bodies were getting stiffer and set into grotesque positions: the absurd, obscene sight of it all made Ned feel utterly cold and alone. He wanted to think of a place less than two hundred miles away, but dared not.

Bob was looking at the personal effects of three German soldiers as they lay in the earth where they had been collected.

"*Lebensmit - Lebensmittelhändler*," Bob tripped over the word. "What's that, Ned?"

"He's a grocer," replied Ned, a little dreamily.

"Was," corrected Wally. Ned gave a curt acknowledgement with his head.

"His wife and kids, I imagine," said Bob, holding up a photograph. Nobody spoke. They simply lifted their heads and looked at Bob. Wife and kids. "Lovely woman," said Bob with no intonation. These German soldiers have wives and kids. Well.... of course they do.

"This man," said Happy John as he slowly went through another man's belongings, "was called... Karlheinz.... is that right, Ned? - Karlheinz Neckermann. Heck, these Germans have long names."

Drained, Ned added nothing to his consternation.

"Took this belt," said Happy John at length, "as a souvenir. Thought I'd get something I could carry... Not sure I want it."

None of them seemed enamoured with the idea of souvenirs.

"Says here," muttered John, examining the belt, "Says here, 'Gott Mit Uns'."

Ned looked up, straight into John's wide eyes.

"I understand that," said John. "Funny, that, innit?.... *Gott Mit Uns...*"

"'Stench' was always such a big, strong feller," said Bert, his mind far away. "Seemed like nothing was ever going to knock him over.... you know?.... Never the sort you think of as a hero, but he was.... in a way..... wouldn't you say?"

"About as much as any of us is a poxy hero. D'you think of yourself as a hero, Wally? - I don't."

"What's a hero?" asked Bob of no-one in particular. "A hero to whom? That's the thing."

511

"A state of mind," murmured Ned into his Jules Verne book. Then, raising his head, "Isn't that about the size of it? ... Really? ...We do what we react to at the time. We do what we've been told and we fight because we have to. What other people think about it.... that's up to them. You're right, Bob. It's about who thinks of yer as a hero. Not us... Certainly not us."

The fruits of such a question were left to rot. After roll-call, they fell largely silent and each in due time curled up with the approaching night and placed the day into memory. It was already colder. There could be no more miserable place on earth.

* * * * *

Morning came as before: by daybreak, German guns sent the British to their holes. The pounding of shells into the earth made cowards of the men who had bravely defended the trench less than 24 hours before. C company once again took to the shelter of German-built chambers which faced the wrong way - not that it mattered which side of the line the defences faced, the shells still did their frightful work. Men squatted, praying that no shells would directly impact above them. Ned in particular was more nervous than usual. Happy John threw dice on the floor and picked them up again time after time. Henry Calder, novice cleric, counted his beads and prayed. Frank Philips recited poetry to himself from a very small book. A young conscript called Mackintosh screamed and clawed at his ears, yelling at the top of his voice. Sergeant Barcombe took hold of him and cradled him for a time like a mother . "There, lad. Hush now, lad. There, lad.... Be over soon. You'll see."

Along the line, shells fell, earth and timbers flew in all directions and dugouts crumbled. Screams were heard but generally it was the noise of thunder that drowned out all other sounds and drove away every sensation but fear. At one point, a rat ran across and hit Ned's boot. It froze as Ned looked at it, the rat seemingly looking back at him in curiosity. It sniffed the air around his boot and shortly scuttled away to safety, vanishing into a tiny crevice. In his

512

contorted mind, Ned for once saw the humour in it and his face twisted into a grin as a mad tirade from the rat walked through his brain. *'Too much noise! - Can't a rat get any sleep? - You people, are you out of your minds? - When are you going to get civilised?'*

Luckily no-one noticed, for they could have thought him as mad as any of these young soldiers. Two-and-a-half hours to the minute, the cacophony over and around them abated, though the noises did not stop. In another minute, Bob said, "They're pounding the reserve trenches." Many of them knew what that meant. Cautiously, they climbed out of their hiding places. No whistles were blowing, no orders being shouted yet.

A light frost had descended that morning and the explosions pitching earth up into the air also threw up little clouds of frozen vapour that came to Ned's nostrils and immediately brought back to him the smell of ice he had not sensed since *Titanic*.

"Where are they?" asked Bob, almost as if he were afraid of the answer.

"Dunno. Havin' a barn dance."

Clomping along the duckboards came Lieutenant Donovan.

"Bayonets, lads! Bayonets! Get up there, keep an eye out!"

"Blimey!" called Happy John, "Do we have to take our poxy eyes out as well?" John made no apology for the poor joke, only straightened his balaclava, secured his helmet and slapped his gas mask for good luck. He was suffering more than usual from itches this morning. He wanted to throw out another joke but could not think of one that Chaplin hadn't already done better.

"Anything, sergeant?" After several moments scanning the horizon through the periscope, Reg Barcombe gave a negative response. Then they heard the sound of a machine gun. Pash-pash-pash-pash-pash! It was a British gun from a forward position. Moments later, a second Vickers joined in.

The men at the parapet strove to peer into the distance. It was not smoky, but mists were rising and falling in patches.

"Jerry's coming, sir."

"Company will fix bayonets!"

"Holy shit!" Wally exclaimed. "They must be crackers!"

513

Each man lining the parapet strove to see into the haze. Sure enough, out there were German soldiers advancing. This time, however, a machine gun had opened up close by and they were dancing long before they reached the wire. Along the line, no more than a handful of grey coats could be seen getting close to the trenches. One threw a stick bomb, it exploded in the trench perhaps thirty yards to Ned's left. Someone shrieked. Ned felt something bounce off his helmet.

There came a second wave, or so it appeared, this time a denser mass of bodies hurling themselves forward in a furious attempt to reach the British line, firing rifles as best they could. Again, only a handful reached the trenches, and the section of No.2 Platoon easily overcame the three that got to their trench. Almost as quickly as it had started, the assault dissipated. Only the chatter of the Vickers guns continued for a short time after that.

Half an hour later, Donovan stood his men down.

"Tea and muffins before tennis?" asked Happy John of everyone.

Having secured his position, Lieutenant Donovan handed the trench over to Sergeants Barcombe and Harrison whilst he went to report. It was not long afterward that a commotion at the wall drew men back onto the parapet. A single shot had been fired from somewhere, but then, silence.

Bert Parrock drew attention to a German soldier who was lying alone many yards away, just this side of the wire; he was groaning and yelping and struggling hopelessly to sit himself up. Motioning to Sergeant Harrison, Parrock then pointed to Wally and Ned to accompany him, and the three of them set out carefully to go to the man.

The mists were clearing. Along the distant stretches of the field, German stretcher-bearers were out collecting their men.

"*Wie heissen Sie?*" Ned asked the fallen man.

"*Danke,*" gasped the soldier, "*Manfred Mayer.*"

Ned almost grinned at the name. "That's like John Smith in English," he said to the others.

"*Aus welcher Stadt?*"

514

"Stu - Stuttgart."

"Stuttgart," repeated Ned to calm him. *"Sehr hübsch, nicht?"* Ned had never been anywhere near Stuttgart in his life. Mayer struggled to answer but the pain gripped him.

"Haben Sie keine Angst, Herr Mayer," Ned continued, *"Sie sind hier sicher."*

"Ja," groaned the soldier plaintively. *"Ja. Vielen Dank..... vielen Dank...... vielen Dank....."*

"Sie haben noch einen langen Rückweg vor sich, nicht?"

"Ja," smiled the man with difficulty. *"Ja. Dreihundert Meter... Wirklich langer Weg."*

Bert stared at Ned with a wondering look but Ned made no attempt to translate, and nobody was asking where the Yorkshireman had learned his German.

They carried the man back to the lip of the British trench where several hands took him down, helped lay him on sandbags and someone gave him a cigarette, which he took in his lips as his hands were shaking impossibly. Mayer had difficulty moving his lower body: whether his back was broken or whether he had problems with his legs, they could not tell, there was only a bullet wound in his lower side, to which Bert applied a dressing from his own pocket as best he could. Shortly, British stretcher-bearers arrived to take Manfred Mayer away. As Ned rose to allow them to attend the man, Mayer shot his arm out and grabbed Ned by the wrist. Looking him directly in the face, and stifling his obvious pain, the German spoke. *"Ich werde nie vergessen..... Niemals.... Niemals. "*

They manoeuvred him onto the stretcher then and, grimacing through his pain, the German gasped at them, *"Danke, Kamerad..... Danke...... Danke, Kamerad......"*

Several men helped get the stretcher away. Watching him go, Ned lit himself a Woodbine, left the others and went into the shelter alone. When Bert followed, he found Ned sitting in a corner. He didn't wish to talk and Bert could imagine why.

* * * * *

FIFTY

'Barnet, 17 October 1916

Ned, my friend,

I hope this note finds you well. This must be short as there is a little drama in the north - there are always 'little dramas' in the north! It is not a good time, I had some upsetting news from Belgium. However, that is another matter.

In case the newspapers did not catch up with you - Semper has gone. Frankly I know little more than the newspapers do, but Arnold rang me and confirmed what Tommy had already said, Semper was freed from custody and at once has disappeared. Tommy had said this would happen - he suggested Semper's friends have him on a boat out of England, he is probably right. Ned, this in no way affects your own situation, we have all the evidence we need to ensure you will be exonerated in a court of law - if it should need to go that far. That old arrest warrant will be withdrawn, and so on. Of course, you may choose to stay in France - with a lady like Renata, to be honest I would do the same!

These events work in your favour, but I shall discuss the matter with my lawyer once I have returned. The law, my friend, is not perfect: whilst no man is above the law, some either by privilege or purchase find the means to jump from its grasp. It is wrong, but it is the world we live in.

For myself, I am angry he has been helped to escape, and I have my own suspicions as to who is responsible. It disappoints me but does not surprise me.

If my fears are correct, I believe all the evidence against him will also melt away with him.

I shall write again soon. My very best wishes.

Bruno.'

* * * * *

'My darling, darling, darling,

516

31 October 1916

We write letters almost every day, I often wonder what I will say tomorrow that will be important, but tomorrow comes and I say the same things! I thought I was a sensible woman but I am not!

Amiens is a long time. You will come when you can, but you said you were late for leave because of your injury. I know you cannot always tell me the truth, but you left the hospital so I must think you are better. Will you get leave soon? I am not strong like you.

Otto is well, Ned. His leg is damaged for always, but he says he will be alright, he continues with Manfred and Erika and will get work. Their conditions are bad, but he says they are bad everywhere. Horses and animals are killed for the fat and meat. Germany's condition is as bad as France, I think. He is still a soldier, but if they make him fight again, what would that be good for? He is starting to work for friends of Manfred, he is making some money, I think.

Gitta hopes to go back into the rope factory. She takes Regine with her to the shop, she is a good girl. There is 6 weeks before she sees the doctor again. Mutti has made little clothes and Charles Vaugeois made a cradle (?) for her. It's pretty, I painted little flowers - she will like it! Charles makes attention to Gitta, he is a nice man, they were amoureuses a long time ago as you know, but I think she tries to turn him away. He walks with a stick, and cannot have children. This is what Verdun does for the men. Gitta does not love him, but we never know what Gitta wants! She said she will go back to nursing, but not yet.

She wants to be demoiselle d'honneur for me when you come! It is our joke. We laugh because it's not possible! We have become friends again. You asked about M. Ardant - I know nothing more. Jerome's mother is worse, but I show her I am not affected. She throws away my food, and I see that look in her eyes. I am French first and German second, but she does not let me be French.

Do not let your anger spoil your life, cheri, that was a bad man and if he has run away, he cannot hurt you again. His punishment is in God's hands.

Ned, I want you so much. Mutti and Gitta understand, so it is good, isn't it? I want you here so that I can hold you and make love with you. Yes - I am a bad woman! I don't care. We will look for a little house - somewhere in the Valmont, perhaps. When you come, I will leave Jerome. He knows that I don't want to be with him. Of course he does not know I love you, I tell him nothing, though he is not a fool. But I will leave him and we will be together.

Be careful, my love.

Reina.'

* * * * *

"For Christ's sake, where now?"

"Orders is orders, John. Just another big push."

"Not the Somme. Say it's not the Somme!" Happy John frequently behaved like a child seeking attention in class.

"I dunno, John. Look, don't have a go at me - even us corporals got mothers, y'know."

"It will be. It will be. Ah heard 'em sayin' the poxy French 6th army's on the push, yer can be bloody sure Tommy's got to wade in as well, just so them poxy generals can keep their noses up at the chateau ball."

"Nah then, nah then! Careful, John. Talk like that's trouble. You know that."

Yes. They all knew that. They had spent all that time and energy getting these trenches up to scratch, with rain virtually every day through to the end of October which had seen the solidity of the trench compromised. Even the guns, quieter now on both sides, signalled that change was in the air. In a week, C company had lost only one man, and five injured. As cold and dismal as the rain was, at least the severity of it was saving lives: neither man nor beast could move far in these conditions - advancing an army was an impossibility, and that was true for both sides. Rain and mud made progress by foot exhausting and anything other than foot hopeless. Yet every cloud has a silver lining - how were they supposed to fight a war in this?.

518

"Well," reasoned Bob, "you had your glorious summer. Now you got your winter of discontent."

Happy John gave him a hurt look. "Poxy Shakespeare, innit? - You think us clowns don't know these things, Bob Street?"

"Oops!" said Bob, "Sorry to hurt your feelings, ladies."

"Anyhow," added Wally, missing the point. "Summer wasn't glorious, was it?"

Happy John sang his thoughts: "God save our gracious weather. Let's hope it pours forever. Long may it rain......"

"Shit 'n'it, John!"

* * * * *

The Somme. Yes, it was.

They did not know where, but the march was long enough, with only a short pleasure trip tossed about on wagons, and along the way they saw the signs. Signs were unreliable, but it was Somme country alright. Despite the weather, it was plain for all to see that there was - as Tommy Tarmey put it - a "right old rumpus" going on.

"Send off your whizz-bangs now, boys," said Happy John, "You'll not be writin' home much for a while, is my guess. Here we go again...... 'Somewhere in France, November 1916: Dear Lizzie, Remember when we went to church as kids and we were told, There's always someone watching over us?.... Turns out, it's the company sergeant major.'"

Other battalions of the Buffs were in the vicinity, they would be joining them. Somehow, whilst plainly illogical, there felt to be safety in numbers, and they had heard of the deeds of the Buffs at Flers and Thiepval because their commanders had boasted of them.

During the autumn of 1916 it was clear to anyone along a 50-mile arc of the Western Front that major operations were under way. 12 battalion took position as one of many units of what was known at that time as the Reserve Army, under the command of General Gough. With its operational zone in the northern sector of the

Somme salient, the Reserve Army had been committed to a northerly offensive from the area of Thiepval village, the town of Bapaume being the eventual target to the east. By the end of October, Gough's Reserve Army had been renamed the Fifth Army to legitimise its situation alongside Rawlinson's Fourth and Fayolle's Sixth Armies. Further to the north stood Allenby's Third Army and to the south Micheler's Tenth Army. All in all, to the hundreds of thousands of soldiers on the Somme and the Ancre, this was the place where the screw was to be turned. To the likes of Ned and the others, it made no difference whether it was one river or the other, for as Happy John pointed out, "I forgot my poxy swimming costume anyhow".

By late October, succeeding against the mud had become a task of Herculean proportions. The effort for men was bad enough, for horses and mules it became a nightmare, moving even a single ammunition cart or gun carriage on its wheels would put to task a dozen animals. Roads blocked up, schedules all but collapsed in the encroaching wintery weather. Whilst in the heat of the summer the men of No.2 platoon had described themselves as 'sleeping on the march', the new reality was stark. Fortuitously, they found a popular farmhouse with its roof mostly intact, lit a fire, stripped to the buff and stood around drying their clothes whilst dancing to avoid spitting brands of the wrong kind of wet wood. Tommy Tarmey even gave them an accompaniment on his mouth-organ.

Men also fell ill; statistically, many more than those casualties of battle. Frank Philips was taken away with what became pneumonia. Assaults went ahead in a general confusion of who had gained or lost what, whilst peculiar names emerged to describe standout features - 'Stuff Redoubt', 'Schwaben Redoubt' and other manufactured landmarks.

In this sector of roughly four miles, Allied troops were just about gaining an advantage, though the daily to and fro for many weeks had never made the picture more than tentative. Success was measured in yards, and every yard meant hundreds of men dead or wounded. The battle for the River Ancre was yet another synonym for the great battles of attrition being fought. If there was indeed a plan at work here, it was a crude one: use a lever to force open the door, and when that doesn't work, a bigger lever.

'Just up the road' was Serre, where the boys of the West Riding Regiment had been cut to pieces on the 1st of July, and 'round the corner' were Courcelette and Pozières and Thiepval where battalions of their own Buffs had fought fierce actions only weeks before, acquitting themselves with distinction as the company commander again reminded them. The Australians, who gave up huge numbers of men in those actions, would speak those names differently.

It was in these conditions of "muck and murk" that C company men in the second week of November found themselves in the arterial lanes that fed the forward trenches. Their own division was now in support of one Canadian and three other British divisions: in this Ancre sector alone around sixty thousand fighting men, including neither transport nor medical units nor artillery. Across the whole of the Somme salient, some estimates said that approaching a quarter of a million Allied soldiers were waiting to oppose German defenders of possibly similar numbers. Put that way, such power was not only unfathomable, but suggested an invulnerability the men could hardly refute. Ned, however, reminded himself that *Titanic* had been deemed unsinkable. Only a fool could really take heart from numbers that might, in Napoleonic times, have held an advantage. This war had taught everyone very differently.

Individual days blurred. 12 battalion settled into trench routine once more. Two days and nights in the forward trench, then a day and night in reserve, as heavy barrages continued on both sides. There was nothing new, it was the same pattern of attrition, the war of nerves and the pressure felt in every sinew. The Somme offered no revelations despite all the hyperbole coming down from high places. One newer recruit called Leach ran from their dugout screaming and was sent to the rear. Within 24 hours he had been returned, endorsed as 'fit' by the medical staff: he spent his time cowering at the rear of the dugout and would not move even to eat. His face was sickly, he stared into space, transfixed by terror. He had, according to Wally, the smell of death about him. Soldiers found it difficult to cope with other soldiers like that - they might try for a time, then give up, for they had their own concerns to deal with. Leach would die soon. Then there would probably be someone else. It was hard to adopt such inhumanity, yet each knew the only law that counted was that of survival. Ned wondered how long it might be before they heard that wooden gas rattle again, something they had been spared in recent months.

* * * * *

FIFTY-ONE

On the morning of the third day, they gathered to launch an attack. Their objective was given no clarification, only that they must move forward and take the opposite German positions. The ground here was undulating, gently rolling chalk land, but apart from that bore a strong similarity to all the other ground they had fought over, in that its features had been largely wiped away by some colossal sweep of giant hands, leaving only the surface pock marks, craters filled and filled again with the debris of life.

It was cold, wet and exceedingly murky. As a heavy barrage fought for possession of the darkness around them, men shivered miserably in their greatcoats in the early morning long before daybreak, facing the dichotomy that they needed to move, yet to move increased the chance of death. German shells were already raining down on the rear trenches when C company along with all the other assailants mounted the parapets and moved out across the muddy ground. All the discomforts of hell were once again forgotten as the only point of focus through shrouds of patchy damp, chilling fog was the evil wire in front of the German trench, so far away in the early gloom that it seemed impossible to overcome if the machine guns opened up before they reached it. In the event, smoke from the barrage combined with the fog and poor light to make life difficult for attackers and defenders alike, though for a time it was a screen under which to hide.

As that cloak of deception thinned, German machine gunners observed their targets. Three orderly waves in which the British had left the trench soon dissolved into a horde of clusters, men flinging themselves this way and that in the general direction of forward. Men fell, men screamed, leaped in the air, crumpled, and cried out. Was it the ninth or the tenth time that Ned had made this wild excursion into lunacy? This time was broadly no different from that very first time, except that he now had in his brain the pattern of movement to adopt . More than that, speed - an ability to overcome the natural inertia, that impulse to freeze in the face of gunfire. Survival was a matter of how long they could maintain presence of mind. Through all the British wire, in and out of craters, through the muddy, freezing water, over obstacles that had been flesh and bone, past dwarf stumps of trees, the speed and that practised measure of caution allowed Ned to surge forward towards the enemy wire without mishap. Until the cloak of invisibility failed altogether and he could move no further, pinned down by a machine gun which raked the tops of those dunes formed by the craters. He waited before lifting himself but it was impossible, the machine gun swept again, spattering the muddy earth. Phat - phat - phat - phat - phat! Ned wished for German stick bombs, which could be tossed twice the distance that a British bomb could.

"You alright, Ned?" Wally was beside him.

"Smashin'!" called Ned in a flat voice. "You?"

"Never better!"

The nonsense language of crazy men. You might as well be crazy. Ned felt his foot give under something. A man had dropped into the crater, his leg had come to rest on Ned's foot. Shaking free of the leg, he recognised Mervyn Clutterworth, a corporal of A company. Clutterworth's eyes were open, gazing up at the sky, sightless. At one time that would have been a magnetic image, but the Thornton of nineteen months' soldiering took his gaze away and pillaged the dead man's pack for food and ammunition: there was no telling how long it would be before they might move away. The machine gun might be overcome, or it might not. The day's terror would go on, and the day had hardly begun: it was shortly before 7 o'clock.

With no means to communicate other than stupidly peering over the lip of the crater, there was no way to learn their situation, for shouting only added to the general confusion. In time, and by interpreting the sounds, it became clear no British attacker had reached the German trench. It was a game in which you had no clue what to do, a game when you chanced all and took the consequences. The logic of the insane.

Stealing a glimpse ahead of them, Ned saw only a line of bodies stretched out in a series of humps in front of the German wire.

They looked like a family of seals that had swum in and decided to stay for a while.

Clinging to the ground and flinging themselves from one crater to another, Wally and Ned made their way from around 8am back towards the British line through the moonscape. This was not even close to the marshlands by the river, yet their path was a series of muddy ponds and thickets of tangled wire and wooden fencing. Remaining out here for the rest of the day was not to be countenanced.

"You up for this, Wally?"

"I'm not staying here, pal. We'll be frozen solid by evening."

The third man agreed, a soldier of A company. Holding their rifles across their chests, they moved off by making their elbows work along the ground like paddles. With the level of battle easing over the whole area, they swam and crawled for half an hour, taking risks wherever one crater raised up before forming another, waiting generous intervals to allow German spotters to forget where they were. They passed bodies, some they recognised and had to ignore. They came upon more C company men behaving like crocodiles as they were doing, and Bert Parrock was one of them. He had blood on his face, but there was no telling whose it was.

"You alright, Bert?"

"If I could unfreeze my bollocks, I would be! You?"

"Oh, aye," said Wally, "but I had to leave my deck chair back there."

By nine o'clock the sky was clear. Within ten yards of the British trench, the sniper's bullet hit almost silently, betrayed only by a distant crack, and Wally slumped as he poised ready to move. Sliding to him, Ned found Wally spreadeagled on the ground with his chin in the mud and his eyes wide open, staring forward. He looked like one of those wild tigers that had been shot and made into a rug for a Victorian parlour, the head always there to trip up anyone with careless feet. No blood was visible above the mud in Wally's face, the bullet had smashed his neck and his collar was a mass of red. Had he been an animal, the white hunter would have claimed a 'clean kill'. His expression gave nothing away, neither peace nor care nor pain, simply an emptiness, as though he were some sort of vessel that had never known human vitality. It was fearful to behold - once a comrade, a laughing, friendly man, now a spiritless shell. There was no antidote in the whole world that prepared a man for seeing his brother like this. The person that had been Wally Myers looked like a museum exhibit. No goodbyes. No sentiments. No reason. Instant cruelty.

Ned lay there in the mud, staring into Wally's empty eyes and trying to comprehend that his good friend was dead. Ned was soaking wet, cold, hungry, exhausted, very numb, very upset. Another awful place, this. He never wanted to learn its name.

* * * * *

Before that assault had ever begun, Tommy Tarmey had been carted off with a shell wound to his upper body. Recently returned from hospital, Taff Morgan was missing. No. 2 platoon was losing its older hands. Late in the day, they heard Reg Barcombe had not returned. In all, it seemed the battalion had lost something like 78 men, a disastrous day.

Retired to the rear, the platoon 'elders' had taken as much punishment as was endurable in one day. They cleaned up as best they could and ate unappetising food in a manner that served only the function of their bodies, for their spirits were elsewhere. Ned had felt that wretched cold which he had thought never to feel again after *Titanic*. He and Bert lit a fire and the water was getting hot: that and their pipes or cigarettes were the only objects of cheer, even the arrival of the mail was met with a lack of vigour.

"Bet she's pregnant again," said Happy John, but there was no humour to be extracted from his remark and he read the three pages from his wife with scant emotion. At one point he was heard to mutter something about "fucking landlords", then at the end of it, he put the letter down and turned to the others. "Thank fuck for the SSFA, that's all I can say."

"All well, then, John?"

526

"Pregnant again! That's the fourth poxy time this year. Beats me," he said, shaking his head innocently, "I dunno how she does it!"

Bless you, John, thought Bob, *you always try to cheer us up.*

"You gonna open that?" Bob asked Ned, nodding at the letter from 48 Chemin des Barques. Bob had read his letter from his brother and one from Agnes, and that made his evening faintly brighter.

"Later," said Ned quietly.

Bert Parrock smoothed his moustache. "Says here," he drawled, straightening the newspaper, "the French have been fighting the Germans at Verdun for two hundred and eighty days...."

"Mmm," observed Bob thoughtfully.

"Two hundred and eighty days....That seems impossible, don't it? They reckon half the entire French army is fighting at Verdun." The others seemed little interested. "This paper reckons with three major fronts to fight in France, the Germans won't have enough men left for the Russians before long."

"Three?"

"Verdun... Ypres....and here."

"Well, yer've taken a load off my poxy mind there, Bert."

"Corporal Bert, if you don't mind, soldier."

"Sorry - Corporal poxy Bert."

"That's better, poxy private."

"Anyhow.... got poxy Christmas to look forward to, haven't we? It'll all be over by Christmas, yer know. Did nobody ever tell yer that?"

"Shit 'n'it, John!"

Where does it all go from here? Each man in his way reflected on that question. They tried not to leave space for silence as they knew every one of them had an awful lot of desolate silence in him now.

"Getting fewer, Bob...."

"Mmm."

"Us old fellers."

527

"Mmm. I know what you mean. 'Old' is the word. Next time I'll think twice before joining up at 32."

"Wait till you're 48 at least," Bert told him. They chuckled, but it quickly died away. Each man knew of his longing not to be there, yet each man knew also he could never speak of it.

"How is she, Ned?" Bob called out.

Ned's sigh told neither one thing nor the other. "Alright, ah suppose," he owned up in the end. "Plus ça change, plus c'est la m ême chose.... You know?"

They didn't, but they said they did.

"She still loves you, though?"

"Aye....."

"So come on - when you getting married, Ned?" asked Bert. "You gonna wait till you've shot every ruddy German?"

That jolted Ned's head up. He looked troubled. More than that, Bob's face had taken on an alert. Bert wondered what he had said. "What?...."

Happy John put down his tea mug. "Am I missing something?"

"It's alright," Bob told them. Turning to Ned, Bob said, "You know he didn't mean that."

"Mean what?" queried Bert, sensing the atmosphere.

"Tell 'em, Bob," said Ned, biting hard on nothing.

"No - no, let it go. He didn't mean - "

"Tell 'em!"

"What?" pleaded Bert.

"Ned's girlfriend..... She's German."

A heavy breath escaped both Bert and John as their mouths framed a very long, 'Oh!'.

"But she's French, essentially. Isn't that right, Ned?"

"German," Ned corrected him. "She married a Frenchman. She's German, my Reina. So's her mum, so's her sister, so's her brother - the best friend I ever had... He's in their army - over there somewhere." And Ned tossed his head to one side, indicating the front trenches. "So.... Now yer have it all."

Bert put his fist to his mouth. He and Happy John looked at each other and settled back onto their haunches.

528

"Makes no difference, Ned," Bob told him, then said the same again to the other two. "Just one o' them things. War makes enemies of friends just as it makes friends out of enemies, but it's not gonna happen here. We're too intelligent for that. Aren't we, Bert?"

Their corporal at first didn't know quite what to say. Then he agreed. "... Sure, Bob, of course.... It's alright, Ned. We're not going to say anything."

"Ned don't mind so much what you might be saying, Bert. It's more what you might be feeling."

"Tell you what I'm feeling," put in Happy John after a short lull. "I'm tired of bein' without my missus and reckon Ned's feeling the same. Expect we all are. For what it's worth, Ned mate, if we upset you any time, I'm right sorry. Hope it works out with your girl. Doesn't bother me if she's German or Chinese!"

Bert wanted to express his own thoughts but didn't find it easy. "He's right, lad. We just had no idea.... You know me and my big mouth. I reckon.... that lady must be something special.... Guess that's all I can say. It's gonna be rough for you though. Expect you know that." Bert's response tailed off into embarrassment.

How could Ned could get angry? What would have been the point? Giving them a half-smile, and tapping Bert on the head, he got up and went to relieve himself up against the wall before finding a place in the light of the next tent to read Renata's short letter again.

'....... Regine is growing well, they put her again into that wooden thing that I told you about so that her legs can grow as they should. They have said once she is perhaps eight or ten years, she should be able to walk more like normal people. Bruno replied to my letter and he is very pleased. He is a good man, Ned. We are so lucky.

I miss you so much and I count the days and weeks. I know I say this in every letter. But you did not say when you can come.

There is cholera in the town. Only a few people but we keep away from the harbour. Everybody seems to be careful but we are afraid. Perhaps it is people from a ship, we do not know. Gitta

529

knows, she has seen cholera before, she said it is a horrible sickness as you lose all the water (?) and death is painful. So we will be very careful, darling, believe me. Madame Forget said it was Russian sailors because she does not like them, but nobody knows. I must not annoy you with our little problems. We have enough to eat and we can stay warm in the house, so it is enough. I pray for your return, Ned, and I say it every day, but sometimes I feel so helpless. I will write again because I do not know what is wrong with me at the moment. I love you, that is all I can say.

Your Reina.'

'17 November 1916
My darling Reina,
I too find words difficult. I did not write yesterday as my hands were cold. The last days have been tiring so please forgive me. We lost a friend. We are all looking forward to some leave, but there is no chance of that at the moment as we recently relieved this position here. You know I cannot say where, but there is a lot going on. I should like clean clothes but that will not happen yet and the old wound on my side is annoying me. We are going to be busy tomorrow. Fingers crossed. At least we got a good dinner tonight. These are the wettest autumn days I can remember. There is so much mud, sometimes we cannot tell if we are being fed vegetable soup or hot mud. The men were saying French soldiers at Verdun have been fighting for nearly three hundred days - I hope we shall not be saying the same in another year! You will understand when I say - Mushrooms, it is not!

We joke, but this land has suffered so much. You could not believe that once there were fields and forests here, wars are a terrible thing for everyone. I long to be back with you, dearest, to tell you how much I love you and want you. Then we can start living, and look for that house at Etretat or somewhere. And I need to say this - I had never really known who or what I was before. Thanks to you, I know now who Ned Thornton is and what he wants and stands for. You know I was never good with words, but my life means something to me now, and my life belongs to you.

This war will not be forever. It is a longer night than my night in the lifeboat, but it must end soon. I do not have your religion, but I do pray that it does. Then we will dance at the jour de fête, I promise.

You are my thoughts and my life, Reina. Always.

Ned.'

* * * * *

FIFTY-TWO

"Sergeant?"

"Don't say it loud! - I'm never gonna live it down."

"But Bert - it's high time. If anyone should be made up to sergeant, it's you."

"Acting sergeant, Ned - *acting*. Let's not go mad. And let's hope I'm a better actor than I am a cook."

"Reg Barcombe would approve... if he were here."

"Yair. Funnily enough, that's what Donovan said."

"Well," said Bob, "So what's your first order - *Acting* Sergeant Parrock?"

"Alright - you, you and you - get yer ruddy hair cut!"

"Fat chance!" laughed Happy John.

"Well there y'are. Now that's it - I ain't gonna give you fellers any more orders. Right?"

"Sergeant!"

"Yes, Lieutenant, sir!"

"Form those men up. Sharply now. This is not a girls' hockey team outing."

"Sah!"

Parrock turned back to his platoon with a grimace and wiped the snowflakes from his nose. "Alright, you rotten lot - get fell in, like the hofficer said."

Monday's previous attack had begun in darkness and fog. Saturday's assault was going to commence in snow. With any luck, this attack would replicate the success of the British yesterday at the other Ancre river battle at Serre, which was being reported along the line, news which Ned heard with mixed feelings.

Augmented by further Canadian troops, the Ancre offensive was cranking up a gear: calamitous weather was not going to call things off now, the generals had decided - it was the same for the enemy, they pointed out. Small comfort. With the biting cold, it was no surprise to anyone that the rain in the night had come in as snow, although as dawn approached it was already turning to sleet. With a driving wind, it might prove more of a problem for the German defenders little more than three hundred yards away, for they would have snow in their faces. The British, though, might make full use of those shovels on their backs. As Happy John put it, "We'll build ourselves a poxy igloo, fellers, and throw snowballs at the Jerries!"

"You know what?" said Ned.

"What?"

"John's got a point. If they issued us with white sheets to cover our uniforms instead of this ruddy khaki, we'd be invisible to Jerry, wouldn't we?"

Bob looked directly at Bert. "Now why didn't *you* think of that? - *Sergeant.*"

* * * * *

The two company sharpshooters had spent the morning on the improvised practice range once the shelling had calmed down. Harold Hancock and Sidney Holloway were rivals for the role of battalion marksman, and although they didn't go so far as to have notches on their rifles, they were good at it. If pressed, Sidney would admit Harold was the better, and Harold would too. Not, they conceded, as good as the Germans, who had turned the role of sniper into an art form, but good enough. Harold's expertise was the distance shots, where a marksman had to take greater account of light and wind velocity and direction, even the dampness of the air. Both reckoned they had the best job in the entire unit. All the same, it was cold and miserable in this pre-seasonal winter and difficult to get excited about anything once you had stood peering through a loophole for an hour. Telescopes were a luxury but, given all but the worst weather, the typical Jerry soldier was as distinctive to spot as was the British 'Tommy'.

Two days before, they had been up to their knees in mud trying to get carts with ammunition lockers brought up, so it was a light relief to be back at the sap head keeping an eye open for people on the battlefield that wore the wrong clothing. Devoted to his art, Harold felt British tactics did not keep their snipers in location long enough to accustom them to the nuances of each individual trench sector, since they would be moved along every few weeks. Sidney, on the other hand, could not care less so long as he had his tea and 'baccy', balaclava and extra socks. Both agreed, all the same, that their most important function - the real challenge of the job - was to spot and hit a German sniper before he could be as deadly to British troops as Harold hoped he was to the Hun. Concealment was every bit as important as accuracy. Theirs was no 'cushy number': German snipers were on the lookout for *them*, and German snipers were good: their Mausers may not have matched British Enfields in rapid action, but they were superbly accurate. What's more, a German sniper could be anywhere, they tucked themselves away in the oddest places. *Devious little devils*, thought Harold, *but effective.*

Sidney had learned his craft in Africa, taking money for tutoring rich Europeans in the courageous art of shooting defenceless animals. He was as practised and as cool a killer as any sniper in the British army, whereas Harold had developed his skill at the funfairs, shooting clay pipes and little tin flags to impress the ladies, something at which he was so good that he was banned from Kent country fairs as soon as any stallholder spotted him.

Their score for the month so far had been in Harold's favour, so Sidney promised his Mark 3 Enfield a good work-out today.

* * * * *

For the attackers, the going in the event was rougher than before, if that were possible. What had been mud was now half-ice. Noise underfoot betrayed any attempt at stealth - not that subtle noise was an issue in battle, but later it could be. Progress in the semi-blizzard was poor, it slowed the infantry's pace and took away any advantage, so on balance the weather tipped the scales in favour of the German defenders. Tanks, had there been any, would have been unusable at any time in current offensives, their promised killer blow for the Allied forces was yet to become evident.

As with Monday, by mid-morning the result of the attack was predictable, it had descended into confusion as the snow and sleet gave way to light rain. Moreover, this sector seemed to lack the leadership of an officer - where was Donovan? German machine gunners were taking full advantage of men approaching their wire on a broad front with little or no apparent central thrust. A few Allied soldiers penetrated German defences, but not for long. As before, this field of the Ancre was liberally strewn with British and Canadian fatalities. It was to be the last major offensive of 1916.

Happy John had been with Ned all the way forward to within thirty yards of the German wire. Those coils of serrated steel looked more angry and vicious than British wire and there were no gaps, the Germans had closed them in previous days. Their machine gunners were enjoying a game of forcing attackers first this way then that. John and Ned flung themselves from one crater to the next until John hurt his arm on a piece of machine gun abandoned there. Separated by a crater, and slightly hurt himself, Ned was unaware John was not with him until he heard the thundercrack and a cascade of mud and chalky debris fell on him. Above all other sounds of battle, this was absolutely close and distinct - a German stick bomb. Scrambling through icy water, Ned saw at once that John had taken the impact and, crying out his name, Ned threw himself across the crater, terrified at what he might find.

John was conscious, fearful, lying almost in a sitting position against the slope of the crater, holding his belly, his lips chattering uncontrollably as he looked down. His head was bloody and dirty, and as he saw Ned approach, a panic rose into his eyes.

"Ned! Ned!" He was able to speak, though indistinctly and in short bursts.

"John!" shouted Ned, utterly shocked. "You alright, John?" Clearly, he was not.

"Stu - stu - stomach!....... Ned! - Oh, Ned!.... This time they done for me..... poxy ..... oh, God! Not like this!... Not like this!"

"Where? Where? Wait a minute. Let me get a dressing."

John's wide eyes were the only white parts of his face. The rest was mud and blood and the perspiration of panic. "Oh God! Oh God! They done for me!"

"Wait! Wait, John! Give me a second. Let me get yer coat open so's ah can see."

As Ned dragged off his own pack, hauled aside John's webbing, unbuttoned and then pulled up the coat, John's blooded shirt partly tore away with it. There was almost nothing to see that he could recognise, the whole area of John's stomach was a mass of blood covering tissue peppered with little bleeding points. Some of that tissue was where it should not have been. John was alive, but his stomach was a mess of torn skin, ruptured vessels, flowing blood and the suggestion of grey organs about to slip out from within. Beyond that, it was impossible to make more than a guess at his chances of survival. Out here on the battlefield - slim. Ned's fingers hovered around John's belt, uncertain as to whether to investigate further whilst John heaved and jolted. When the dark brown sac of something moved above his belt, Ned's heart sank, he knew he could do nothing here.

This was his friend. His brother, John. This was awful, truly awful. Ned was already in despair beyond his shock.

"Ned! Ned! It's bad, Ned! It's bad! I know it's bad!.... Tell me, Ned! Tell me, Ned!" With a feeling of sickness welling up into his throat, Ned's pallid face hovered above John's eyes. He could not speak for fear he would vomit, for his tongue was numb, he was close to gagging.

"It's bad, Ned!... Tell me! I know..... I know..... It's bad. Oh, God! Help me!... Help me!"

Drawing himself more upright against his own shattered reflexes, Ned slowly shook his head at his friend. Above the continuing noises of battle, Ned shouted, "Ah can't, John..... Ah can't. Yer need doctors. Ah can't move yer. It's a .... it's a nasty wound. Ah'm sorry, John.... Ah'll get Red Cross to yer."

John's breath came in short, panicking staccato gasps and grunts as his upper body heaved and shook with a series of shudders, his pain so severe.

"I'm gonna ....die, Ned.... aren't I?..... I'm gonna ..... I'm not.... I'm not ready.... "

There was nothing Ned could say. He hung there, open-mouthed. John had his hands on his stomach: he knew he was losing all feeling in those hands, but he also knew what he felt.

"Lord, Ned!..... What 'll they say.... in Faversham... when they hear... their butcher.... died with his... tripes hangin' out?" His tortured grin bore the irony of futility. "Mother! Oh, mother!... Not like this..... Not like this..... It hurts, Ned..."

As he watched John crying, Ned could barely stop his own eyes from filling up. "Ah know, John. Ah'm sorry." In his entire life, nothing before had ever brought to Ned the meaning of utter desperation. All he could do was to sit there shaking his head and choking back the sobs.

John grabbed Ned's wrist. His hand shook, there was little power left in it, but he grasped as hard as he was able.

"Shoot me, Ned! ... Shoot me!"

His friend recoiled in horror. He could not pull free of John's hand but - shoot him?

"Please!.... Please, Ned!..... While there's ... still time.... I don't wanna..... I don't wanna.... Like this..... Me guts fallin' out..... Please, Ned! Please... It hurts... I'm frightened!... Mum, I'm frightened!"

Terror gripped Ned as it had gripped John. Killing an enemy was one thing. Killing his friend.....

"Please, Ned!..... Do it!... I'm frightened....." John's eyes would open wide and close again, squeezing mud and blood out of the way. The pain was seared into his gaze and his words gargled in his throat.

From his jarred, hazy awareness, Ned's brain brought him a picture of himself as a little boy holding the hand of his elder brother. "Please, James..... Please..... I'm frightened..... Don't let him hit us.... I'm frightened....."

"Please, Ned ....." It was his friend, John.

There was little rationality in anything. You did things or you did not do them. Regret was not an option. You were a soldier. You did a soldier's job.

Ned wiped his eyes and hurried. John was in pain. His brother was dying in pain. He could not let the pain go on.

"John..... Listen... You are my friend, John. Always will be..... "

John had pressed his eyes together with the pain.

"I love you, brother," rasped Ned hoarsely, water blurring his wide eyes.

He placed the tip of his rifle at John's chest and told himself he must not think. Do. Don't think. Do.

The bullet blasted into John's heart and he shook upward just for one moment, then his body sagged, a gurgle came from his throat, his tightly closed eyes stilled and his head lolled to one side.

"There, now....."

The soldier let the tears come and spill from his face onto the other soldier's face. With one hand he caressed the dead soldier's cheek and stroked it tenderly.

"There, now....."

Ned put the rifle down, rocked back on his knees, put his hands to his face and sat there crying for a long time... A long time, oblivious to the battle raging on around him. His despair was the only human cry that anyone could hear at that moment, and no other soldier interrupted his grief.

$$* \quad * \quad * \quad * \quad *$$

For an age he felt only numbness. No longer knowing quite where he was and feeling the cold most severely, Ned realised he must move and crept away from that dreadful crater, resorting to all fours to keep below the sweep of the machine guns. At no time did he look back at John Barraclough's mutilated body. It was all he could do to steel himself from looking. But in another crater, encountering another corpse in the filthy water, he stayed quite some time before trying to move away.

It was quieter now, the field was clearing and from the sound of things, the German defenders had beaten back their attackers once again. The rain was more drizzly and all the snow that had fallen earlier was now melted into pools within the craters. Visibility remained poor, nor was there any sign of a sun in that gaunt, pressing sky that might give him a bearing. Ned imagined he must still be little more than 30 yards from the German wire and moved carefully in crab fashion, dragging his rifle along the ground and steering a course around bodies and equipment strewn all about. He covered perhaps sixty yards and met not another living soul, yet as he looked around him he could judge he was no nearer the Allied trenches.

The guns had stopped, that was a mercy at least, the sounds were the usual ones of men crying in pain, men crying out for help. Whilst the firing had stopped, though, he now knew he must beware of snipers. Off to one side, a German song came wafting on the faint, frozen breeze. It was not a song of pleasure, it was a song of defiance. That was the direction he must not go in. So he kept moving, he knew he must.

Suddenly, the earth at his fingertips crumbled away, and with a slushy collapsing sound a whole lot of earth disappeared into a hole that as he watched grew larger. Peering into it, he saw it was a tunnel, perhaps a tunnel formerly used by Germans as an escape route when their earlier trenches had been overcome. The idea it was a British tunnel did not appeal, it appeared older and very well made - as well made as tunnels might be. Far too carefully made to be one dug by British mine-layers hurriedly burrowing under the German line.

There were floorboards and there had been electric light here. It did not matter to Ned what it had been, here was a refuge from the searching guns of snipers. Head-first, he slid into it, slewing his body sideways to land on his knees. He winced at the pain in his side: could his old wound have opened again? - He had no time for that. The very first thing that he saw was the body of a British soldier. Quite dead, evidently for some time. From here it was possible to deduce that it had indeed been a tunnel, not far below the surface, and that surface had been dropped with successive bombardments until the 'ceiling' was barely three or four feet below ground. Moreover, it was well built with wooden timbers shoring up the sides, not the wicker-work that characterised many German trenches. Nor was it deep enough to be able to stand up, but it was at least a yard wide, and it moved off in only one direction, for the other way was clearly blocked by subsidence some yards along. What is more, Ned now saw the signs of two more bodies in the rubble of that blockage, and a foul, repulsive odour intimated what had become of them.

Following this tunnel slowly and stealthily, Ned drew his bayonet to lead him. The water in the tunnel varied from nothing to several inches, and there were holes in the ceiling that let in the light as the earth above had been exposed, but at least it was not generally open to the elements. On the other hand, there could be great dangers here: for one thing, the ceiling might give in, and he had no idea which way it was going, though the compass in his brain told him he was probably heading the wrong way.

Shortly - he had gone possibly thirty yards - he stopped as he heard voices. The voices then stopped too. Pausing to check that his rifle had 'one up the spout', Ned moved cautiously forward, and the tunnel then took a step downward, and another step, so that the chamber he was now in was both deeper and wider. Some sort of 'halfway house' perhaps. He was still bent over, and as he moved a wooden plank to one side, suddenly a sharp voice came at him.

"*Wer ist da?*"

Instantly recognising his situation, Ned called back, "*Schiess nicht! Ich werde nicht schiessen!*"

"*Sind Sie Deutscher?*"

"No," said Ned in German, "But I will not shoot you. I swear. Put down your weapon. I am not going to shoot you."

"Who are you?" The voice was brittle but strong. This was not a badly injured man. It would be wise to keep his rifle steadied in his hand.

"I am English. But I am not going to shoot you. I will not hurt you. If you have a gun, do not shoot, or you will force me to do the same."

Ned saw them now. Dim light was scattering around the chamber through a hole at the top of one side wall where water was trickling through and splashing. There were two of them that he could make out.... No, three..... No, there were two men who were semi-upright, and two others who were lying down. This chamber was perhaps eight feet wide and around twenty-five feet long. With eyes gradually adjusting to the gloom, he could discern no exit at the far end, for he was afraid there might be others further along.

"English?"

"Yes."

"Alone?"

"Yes."

"You are not going to shoot?"

"No.... I am not going to shoot. I do not want to shoot. Please put down your weapons."

The soldier seemed to shrug in his big grey coat, and he tossed something out to the front. It was his dagger. "I don't have a gun," he said, "And if you shoot us, you are a murderer, Englishman."

"I am not going to shoot you.... See - I put my rifle down.... See? I put it down." Ned felt for the ground to lay his rifle safely. It was almost dry there, no running water. He held onto his bayonet.

For some moments, there was no response. Then the larger of the two shapes moved forward just a little and Ned could see in the very dim light that he had the insignia of an officer. Neither man had headgear. The second man was a private soldier.

"Who are you?" the officer asked.

"I am a soldier in the Kent regiment."

"Ah! The East Kent or the West Kent?"

Momentarily, Ned was stunned to silence. "Er.... The East Kents."

"Ah! Then I believe you. Yes. We have fought them. They are strong men."

"Strong - ?"

"Mister Kent - do you have any food?"

"I..... I have a little. Are you hungry?"

"These men have been here two days and I have been here one day and two nights. We are very hungry."

"And the other two?"

541

"One is dead. Ziegler is nearly dead. Pabst and I are alive, but he is only just alive."

"Pabst?" Ned was thunderstruck. "Pabst? ... Is he - ? It's not Dieter Pabst!"

"No. Who is Dieter Pabst?"

Suddenly woken, the private soldier's head came forward from where he was sitting in a self-aware stupor, his knees bent up. Like the officer, his head was quite shorn of hair and his gaunt cheeks held several days' growth. He was like a badger who had come up to sniff the air. He looked at Ned with a wide-open mouth, then spoke. "Dieter? You know Dieter?"

"I know of a Dieter Pabst I used to work with. But that can't possibly - "

"Dieter? - Where did you work with him?" The man coughed and then controlled it.

"Where?... Erm... Aboard ship. Aboard a French ship. *La Rochelle.*"

"*La Rochelle!* - My God!"

"You know it?"

"Yes! - No.... I mean, yes. Dieter was on *La Rochelle*. Yes. Yes, he was. And you knew him?"

"Yes. Not well, but.... yes, I knew him. But... That's incredible."

"Yes," said the man, slumping back into his previous position, seemingly exhausted. "Yes."

"Food!" the officer interrupted them. "Do you have food?"

Ned shuffled his pack from his back and went into it, pulling out first some biscuits and then a tin of M & V. The German officer came forward and grabbed the biscuits off him. Eating one ferociously despite its relative hardness, the officer passed another to the soldier.

"If you help me get this tin open, there is some meat in this tin you can both have."

The officer needed no second invitation. Ned held onto his bayonet just in case, but the officer produced a can opener - along with a huge, wide smile - and quickly removed the can top, taking a portion himself and passing the can to his fellow. Standing back watching him, Ned would not have been in the least surprised if the officer had produced a bottle of beer and two glasses.

"Kaltenbach." It was not easy to stand on ceremony in their semi-crouching positions, but the officer managed to extend a hand to the Englishman and his face held at least the promise of sincerity. "Helmut Kaltenbach. Oberleutnant. Third company, 94th regiment. What is your name, Englishman?"

Ned took the hand. "Thornton. Ned Thornton. Private. 12 battalion."

"Thornton?" It was the soldier Pabst again, his voice loud and shocked. "Thornton? *You* are Thornton? Really? I cannot believe it! ... Dieter spoke of you."

"He spoke of me....? Who are you - his brother?"

"Yes! Yes! Dieter was.... Dieter was my brother.... He was my older brother..." The man's voice dropped and his grin faded quickly. "Dieter is dead, Thornton. He is dead now. I have lost him."

"How? Where?"

"We joined together. We joined the army... with all the men from the village. It was.... like a party.... like a beer party. We played skittles! We joined the infantry because Uncle Gerd said we should become soldiers... as he had been. It seemed.... it seemed like a big joke....Dieter was not married and I was not married. We thought.... we thought we should fight... for the motherland, Oberleutnant - you know."

"Pabst, who is this man? You know him?"

"No, sir... No, sir. It was my brother. You did not know my brother, sir. In the First company. We joined together. Dieter was killed at Serre.... He was killed, sir."

"And this Englishman was his friend? This man here?"

"Yes - No.... Not friends. But they had known each other. Isn't that right, Thornton? ... Dieter told me. Dieter told me... he was in the sea, he almost drowned... but this man Thornton saved him from the sea.... Yes. He told me." Turning to Ned, Pabst continued, "He did not like you, he told me... He did not like you at first, you had a friend, a German, and he did not like him."

543

"Otto Bremme."

"Bremme. Yes. That was the name - Otto Bremme.... And he did not like you. But then, he said... you saved him... from the sea. He told me. Yes.... And now ... you are here, Mister Thornton."

"Yes... " Ned shook his head. He could scarcely believe it. "I am.... well...." Ned raised a smile at his hopeless lack of speech.

"So that is where you learned to speak German?" Kaltenbach suggested.

"Uh?.... Oh..... I was friends with the family. A German family."

Three men. In a hole in the ground. With injuries. With almost no food. Stuck between the lines. It was bizarre, Ned thought. Yet here it was. How glad he was that he had not fired. Without doubt, he could have killed them both, but.... For what? Because they were Germans? That no longer was a reason, if it ever had been. There had to be something else.

"You are wounded, Leutnant?"

Kaltenbach peeled his coat to one side and there by his shoulder board Ned could see the patch of blood now mostly dried into his jacket. "It is alright," said Kaltenbach, wincing a little. "I will be alright. Except that I cannot carry anything. I think it is broken. But him - I am not sure. What do you think?"

Ned asked Werner Pabst about his injury. A bomb blast to his side and upper leg. With difficulty, he showed them: the whole area was dark and bloody and dirty and impossible in this light to gain any indication of severity. He could no longer walk, and Ned was not sure the bleeding had completely stopped, or if it had, whether it would start again if he moved.

"I am no doctor, Oberleutnant. I cannot do anything for him, except perhaps apply the dressing I have here, and I doubt that will help."

"I must get him back," said the lieutenant. "He must have treatment or he will die here. Like - like these." A gesture of the arm now showed them both that the third German was virtually dead. Lacerations across his neck and face, exposing muscle tissue, and an obvious loss of blood. There was nothing to be done.

"Do you have matches, Thornton?"

Ned fumbled. "Somewhere here."

"Are they dry? There is wood. Over there. It is fairly dry. We kept it dry. We had a fire, but when it went out we had no more matches."

Together Kaltenbach and Ned gathered the few sticks and brands and tried to set them alight. After three matches, they had failed.

"We shall have to move. We cannot stay. They died last night. We cannot stay another night, we may all die. And we must have food and decent water."

Looking around, Ned thought of a splint to help them get Pabst moving. Kaltenbach agreed, but explained that he could not manage to move the man himself because of his shoulder wound.

"We can try, Leutnant. If we use some of these timbers and that lighting cable there, we can make a sort of sledge to drag along."

"We?... What are you suggesting, Englishman?... You mean you will help us go back to our lines?"

It was not something Ned had given any thought to. Not something he should need to give thought to. After all, why should it be any different? Three wounded men.

"You would do the same for me, wouldn't you? Men wounded in battle."

The lieutenant gave him a long look.

"I am not sure that I would, but I thank you for the suggestion. You are either very foolish or very brave, Thornton."

"I'm not brave. It's just that - well, right now I can't think of any other way of keeping him alive, can you?" The lieutenant had no answer.

"If you are not brave, then you are mad. Around here, it is probably the same thing.... But between you and I, it will be dangerous for you, Englishman, there is a risk you could be shot by my soldiers." All he got in response was a shrug. "Are you sure? ....Very well. In the circumstances, I will say 'Thank you' before we go.... Thank you... Whatever happens. Let us hope we both live through it so I can thank you again."

He looked at his pocket watch. "We have about four hours before it gets dark. After that the sentries will most likely shoot us anyway because they won't see that we're German soldiers. We must move now. What about your injury?"

"It's only a twisted ankle."

"No, it is not. You have fresh blood on your coat. Look - here."

"Oh, that. I think it's an old wound that I tore again back there. I'll be alright. I'll make it to your trench and rest up there for a time."

The idea that he might 'rest up' rather took the lieutenant by surprise - it intrigued and amused him. Was this man truly mad? Soldiers didn't just come to visit! "But.... We could make you a prisoner."

"Mm. You could."

"It would be better for you. Safer. You would go to hospital and be treated. Then for you the war would be over, and you just sit in our prison until it is all finished, then you go home."

"Or you could just patch me up and let me go back to my wife. Oh, and give me something to eat before I go. Some schnapps if you have any."

"Schnapps? - Oh yes, we have barrels of it, don't we? Ha-ha!..... But.... Our soldiers might think you are a spy." He was only semi-serious and Ned knew it.

"Yes, well - obviously. Look, I've got my notebook and pencil right here. If you will just tell me how many men you have and in what positions....."

Helmut Kaltenbach was almost laughing. Who was this man that they could make jokes? This was the most unusual enemy he had ever encountered. Two opposing soldiers finding humour in their adversity!

"You would do this, Thornton? Truly?" He had become serious again.

There was little to think about. "Oberleutnant, I just lost a very dear friend. I watched him die out there. I have lost friends and so have you, I'm sure of that. I don't know about you, but I can't go on watching us all kill ourselves for no good reason."

"No good reason? - But we fight for our way of life, Thornton. We fight for our country and our families and our beliefs."

546

"As do we, Leutnant... In the end, you and I are no different... are we?.... But we are all fooling ourselves. Do you not think? If you and I - here, now - if we can talk and not shoot each other and tear each other apart like mad dogs, why cannot the next two men, and then the next?"

Kaltenbach only let go the suggestion of a doubt.

"I've been fighting too long, Leutnant. I know you won't understand but I've been fighting since 1912. I just want it all to stop. Let me help you do this, and then let me return to my people."

"If that is what you wish.... Then I tell you this, Thornton," said Kaltenbach. "If we get through this, I make you a promise - I will make sure my father hears about you."

"Your father?"

"He is a big man in Württemburg. Our little kingdom, you know. That's where I am from. He is a big man in the system. He will be interested to hear about you, I know he will."

"As you wish," replied Ned.

"I do wish. Truth should be told. After all, there are plenty who will say it was not true."

The Englishman reflected on that. Truth. Had he found his truth? To be true to yourself, that is all, and there was no valour in that, merely the mark of humanity. Ned considered these things, then set about in the gloom finding pieces of wood.

"What were you doing here in the first place?" asked Ned.

The lieutenant explained that the others were a scouting party of four sent out three nights before to reconnoitre the British line. A flare had caught them in the open and small arms fire had pinned them down. One German had signalled, but he had been cut down, and the lieutenant and another had left the trench to reach them, help them back and more importantly discover their information. Caught again by British fire, they had taken this shelter once they had discovered it. By the next morning, it was too late and, severely weakened by their wounds, they stayed another day and a night and into the Saturday when the British assault began.

* * * * *

In the early afternoon Kaltenbach declared Ziegler the third German dead even if he was not certain rigor had set in.

Together, he and Ned managed with great difficulty to get Werner Pabst out through the large hole they had made by enlarging other holes, then onto the raft that was formed of several uneven timbers lashed together by electric cable. They would drag it by means of a bar that Ned had secured at the leading edge, and several strands of cable made into a loop to get hold of. Pabst would be held down by a coat taken from one of the dead men and then in effect 'lashed' to the raft by wire.

Not sighted by the German line due to the rising terrain, they were still visible to the British at some considerable distance, so this 'caravan' would need a good helping of luck to get through to the German trench. With darkness approaching, and the fading mortality of Pabst, they had no option to wait.

It had stopped raining, though the skies were full of the portents of more and the light was already becoming dimmer than previous afternoons. They worried more snow might be coming in but for now the wet, stubborn earth was the main hindrance.

"Wait!" called Kaltenbach, "Wait a minute! You can't leave in that coat. Look, if our men spot you before they see me, they'll shoot first and ask questions afterwards. Wait."

He slid back down into the tunnel whilst Ned did his best to keep very low and shuffled Werner into a position on the raft where he might feel least pain, tightening the sleeves of the coat around him. Ned was almost exhausted, and the trouble in his own side was more annoying now.

"I hope your lot have got the tea on," he rasped at Werner Pabst.

"Coffee!" corrected Pabst in a croaky voice. In his dissociated state, he was still in considerable pain and doing his utmost to hide it, whilst under his already sunken, stubbly cheeks he was pale and very cold. Ned believed they had only hours before he would be beyond saving.

A minute later, Kaltenbach reappeared with the greatcoat of the other of his dead soldiers. "Here, Thornton, put this on."

The coat had the smell of a dead man about it, a smell of urine at the edge and a large blood stain down the back, but he tugged it on. It was damp and colder than the one he had just discarded.

Ahead of them, as they peered above the lip of another crater, the German trench lay about fifty yards across much the same terrain, and through the German wire. Heaving the sled down into a crater was not such a problem, but taking it over the other side needed every ounce of strength. Together, Kaltenbach and Ned dragged and yanked that sled forward as far as the wire whilst Pabst moaned several times and was told to be quiet.

The German wire was evil: coils of serrated steel that took pleasure in ripping chunks out of the body.

So far, they had managed to avoid attention, but at the wire, they had no choice.

"Help! Help! We are German. Patrol returning! Patrol returning! We are coming in. Don't shoot! Don't shoot!"

Immediately, a rifle bullet sent up dirt in front of Ned's face.

"No! No! We are German. Don't shoot! It is Kaltenbach. Kaltenbach. Do you hear? Kaltenbach. We are coming in. Don't shoot!"

"Kaltenbach?" The voice sounded distant, but at least the soldier didn't fire again.

"Oberleutnant Kaltenbach. Do you hear me?"

"Yes, Oberleutnant. What company?"

"Third, from the 94th. I need cutters. Do you hear? I need wire cutters. Quickly. We are all injured."

A few moments later, there was another voice from the trench.

"Oberleutnant Kaltenbach?"

"Yes."

"It is Sergeant Engels, Oberleutnant. You want cutters?"

"There is no gap in the wire here. Cutters! Quickly, quickly. We have a man dying here."

"At once, Oberleutnant."

He was a brave man, the soldier who scrambled out of the trench with cutters. The British snipers would be watching the trench, and they had a few good sharpshooters over there.

Harold Hancock and Sidney Holloway had come on duty at 1400 hours, having missed all of the morning's actions and glad of it. Visibility was better now, for a while at least. It even felt just a touch milder.

As usual, they had tossed a coin to see who would take the first turn as observer. It fell in Sidney's favour, but they would change over every half-hour or so as eyes tired. Rivals perhaps, but above all they worked as a team, wherein lay their success.

The Red Cross were still active in some parts of the field: they were always very careful of them. And unless Jerry sent out patrols, often there was precious little to get interested in, except to play the game of spotting the other side's snipers.

So when Sidney's eye caught sight of something moving over to section B of the German trench, the decent thing to do was to tap Harold on the shoulder and draw his attention to it. If there was something that needed to be hit at that distance, Harold was the man. Sometimes, being stuck out here in the most forward part of the sap trench felt a bit close for comfort, but it had its rewards and, unless they were careless, generally their job was safer than many others. Not that shells were selective, however.

"Where?"

"There. See the double-post on the right. Come back in five degrees. Just below. See it?"

"Ah.... See it. What you reckon, Sidney? - Three-fifty?"

"About."

"Right. Let's 'ave 'em, then!"

Harold's first shot was on the mark. The target jolted and slumped further down. A second man was on his knees at the German wire.

"That's one," confirmed Sidney, blinking through his binoculars.

"Right. Don't put me off! They've got something they're pulling. Could be an ammo box. If I can hit that, maybe it'll all go up........ Nope, wasn't an ammo box. Can you see the third?"

"Wait..... Damn! - Naah, they've gone to earth."

"'Ere, let me see.... Yair, you're right - "

At that instant, a bullet struck the loophole, taking a shard of wood past Harold's ear. Hancock and Holloway dropped away from the edge of the trench.

"Blimey! - That were bloody close, Sid!"

A second and a third German soldier scrambled out to help them. Between them, they managed to drag the sled up to and over the lip of the parapet and into the arms of several waiting soldiers. Kaltenbach with his one good arm pulled at Ned's collar to help him slide through the gap in the wire and another soldier came out to manhandle both of them along and down into the German trench.

"Thornton! Thornton! Are you alright, Thornton?"

".... Tell you what, Leutnant..... Those British have... some good shooters over there!"

Kaltenbach had immediately got his men rushing for medical supplies.

"Pabst?" Ned gasped loudly.

"Pabst is dead. They got him too."

Ned groaned. "Yes.... I think ...they did a good job.... Don't you?"

"Thornton, wait - we have a stretcher coming. Just keep calm. We will get a dressing on you and get you to the hospital."

"I have to.... tell you, Leutnant.... I didn't bring my passport."

For several seconds, Kaltenbach stared into the face of this man who grinned at him and made a joke through his obvious pain. Then he saw Ned black out.

It could only have been seconds that Ned was unconscious: now the pain was really biting, making him feel dizzy and giving him a cold sweat. Kaltenbach was barking orders at his men, but Ned did not really hear much of it.

Turning back to Ned, the lieutenant's urgent voice told him, "You will be alright, we will see to you. We will get you to hospital, Thornton."

"I..... What did you say your name was, Leutnant?"

"Helmut."

"Ah.... Sorry to disagree with you, Helmut.... I think we both know.... that's a bit too far now..... It's just.... you know, I have bad.... I just have bad luck..... with other people's coats."

Ned was bleeding badly from his back, he had begun coughing and his speech was rasping now. His lung had been breached, his panting breath lifted his shoulders at each gasp and the pain was severe. As Kaltenbach pulled away the hand that had been supporting him, it was clear there was great loss of blood. He knew better than to make foolish promises now.

"Your family, Thornton ... "

"Jacket pocket..... " Ned coughed. "... pocket.... There's a letter....."

Kaltenbach pulled out the letter as Ned indicated. Looking at it, and seeing the name, he paused to get the meaning of it, before looking back into Ned's fading eyes with a question in his. It was the name Ned had spoken earlier, in conversation with Werner Pabst. Otto Bremme, Ned had said.

"Yes, Oberleutnant.... that's right..... Renata Bremme.... A German lady, my wife...... A lovely... German lady.... My wife."

Reina......
Reina.....
My letters, did they find you......?
I wish.....
I just......
I never wanted anything so much. Just to look at you again. Just to feel you again. To smell your face against mine. Feel your soft skin. Stare into your lovely eyes. Simply hold your body to me. Just once. Not like the fool I was before, not that foolish boy who saw without seeing and spoke without thinking.

Just once more. It's been so long without you. So many empty days and nights. I ache for you, Reina. Nothing else. There is nothing else I want.

552

It's all passed me by. Inside, I'm still that same boy, though. Somewhere. That same fool. I will try to be better. And I wanted to return to you one more time before...... Before the next time!

It hurts, though, to think of it. All these things hurt. I cannot bear the memories, it is the pain of all the things I cannot have again.

I cannot remember if I told you I love you. I cannot remember if you said you loved me. I can't think of reasons why you should.

No matter - It is enough that I can say it now.

Reina.....?..... Reina.....?

Kaltenbach waited for the eyes to be still, then he and Sergeant Engels released their hold on the body and set Ned Thornton in repose where he lay at the wall of the trench. Engels placed a cigarette in Kaltenbach's mouth, lit it and said nothing. The lieutenant sat there, unmindful of his exhaustion, his stare dwelling on Ned Thornton's still feet for a long time before he was aware he was cold.

* * * * *

FIFTY-THREE

"They've done what?"

"Given him a medal."

"What?"

"Given him a medal, sir."

"Given who a medal, sir?" Lord Asquith was not in the mood for parlour games.

"Thornton, sir."

"Thornton? – Oh, the soldier you were talking about."

"Yes, sir.   Thornton.... As I was saying, sir - mentioned in despatches. Loos and the Somme."

"Are you out of your mind, Millbank? The Germans have given one of our chaps a medal?"

"It's here, your lordship, in this communiqué.   We had it translated from the German and ...." Millbank's voice diminished markedly, as if in shame, ".... well, it says that the *Eisernes Kreuz Erste Klasse* – that's the Iron Cross, First Class – is awarded to the private soldier Edward Thornton during an action at the field of the Ancre River on 18th November, 1916."

Lord Asquith scowled and growled. "Given a British soldier a German medal?...Good God!"

"Yes, sir." The secretary sounded almost apologetic.

Asquith flopped back into his chair and repeated, "Good God!"

"Yes, sir," agreed Millbank again quietly.

Asquith's brow tightened and he looked incredulously at Colonel Blashford for some sort of answer.

"Can they do that?" Both men returned blank stares. "What on earth are they playing at, Airey?"

"I don't know, sir, first I've heard of it. It's a ploy of some sort: you can't trust the Hun, can you?"

For many moments all three men were suspended in the silence of the large room before Blashford disrupted the stillness.

"Well, the blazes with it! Who the devil do they think they are? Heavens, I'm not having it!"

"Not having what, Airey?"

"Why – why – why, I'm just not having it ! This is the bloody British army, for God's sake. We can't have the Huns telling us what to do!"

"Calm down, Airey, calm down. They're not telling you what to do. They've given a British soldier an award for bravery. That's what they've done...... Devil take 'em!"

"They can't do it!"

"Well no, of course they can't – except that they *have*! Just because you don't like it, it doesn't stop them giving a man an award for bravery. Even if it is from the other side...... If it were the French, you might credit it...." And Asquith shook his head, as though he did not believe his own words.

"Sir, I move we disallow this award."

"What the Dickens are you talking about, Millbank? Disallow? You can't 'disallow' it unless you get the blasted Huns to withdraw it. Are you going to do that?"

"Um..... Perhaps not. Sorry, sir."

Lord Asquith let out a deep, deep sigh of apparent remorse.

"Aah! ..... What sort of a war are we fighting, gentlemen? What sort of a war are we fighting when we're giving medals to the other side? I don't know..... Not done, is it? Just not done.... What do they think this is? – a game of cricket?"

"It isn't cricket, sir," Millbank found a tentative amusement in the remark, "I'm sorry, sir - I just coined an old phrase there, if... if I may ....."

Asquith was not to be cajoled with witty remarks, his withering stare sealed the lips of his secretary, who hung his head and cowered to the rear of the room.

"No," said Blashford, "No, my Lord, you're quite right. It really isn't done. In fact, we can't reject the award, the offence would register with the German High Command and the next thing you know, His Majesty will be getting nasty letters from Cousin Willi in Berlin, raising matters of protocol. It would bounce around all the crowned heads of Europe and land everyone in a ghastly mess. What do you think, sir? I mean, having a war with Germany is one thing but getting His Majesty into a state of anxiety - well... I hate to think what Parliament would have to say about that. Especially with the sabre-rattling we're getting from a certain Welsh gentleman who flexes his muscles at any opportunity."

"Does the Welshman know?"

"I should be surprised if he didn't, sir. He's only been PM five minutes but he pokes his nose into everything!"

"I should have thought," offered Millbank, almost apologetically, "that the crowned heads of Europe were already in deepest animosity..... for the last few years anyway."

Lord Asquith ignored the remark completely and sighed again. From the vacant expression in his eyes, he could have been reflecting on the tens of thousands of souls whose lives had ended at the Somme battlefield, but Millbank knew his superior was more likely turning over in his mind the embarrassment of having to contend with Mr. Lloyd George in the House.

"Damn man.... He'll lay it at my door, just you see."

"But why? It's March. If this thing happened back in November....."

"Yes, but just you see, he'll seize every chance to say it happened on *my* watch."

"Ye-e-s," Millbank cast around for another possibility, "but after all, he was Secretary of State for War then. Wasn't he?"

"Well," breathed Asquith eventually. "Well......"

Millbank and Blashford moved forward, awaiting a pronouncement from the Great Man.

"Well, then!" It came out of Asquith's mouth like the muted crack of a muffled cannon. "Dammit, he shall have a medal from His Majesty also!"

"He shall?"

"By God, yes! And the Welshman will like it, damn him! I'll make sure he does. We'll just present him with a *fait accompli*. Millbank, get onto – get onto – who the devil is that chap at the War Office who handles citations and such?"

"Major Walters, you mean?"

"Major Walters! Get onto Walters, tell him there's to be a medal for this young man – erm, what was his name?"

"Thornton, sir."

"Thornton, sir!"

"Are you sure, sir? - After all, he *was* mentioned in despatches. Doesn't that cover the matter?"

"Of course it doesn't! Imagine what the press would say - the other side's giving out better awards than we do! Look, tell Walters I want a top drawer medal for this chap – um, what do we do, Airey? - What about a V.C., is that a bit much?"

"Can't do that, sir. Officers only."

"The devil ! Alright, then, the D.S.O."

"Officers only, sir."

"The deuce it is! – Don't we have any blasted medals for ordinary soldiers?..... Alright, then, Airey, what are we going to give him? The Germans are giving him a what? – An Iron Cross, d'you say? Iron? Iron? Can't they do better than that?"

Blashford coughed against his fist. "One of their better medals actually, sir."

"Is it?...... Is it?..... Iron doesn't sound very grand, does it? Not very grand at all. Strike me!"

"What, sir?"

"You don't suppose they're trying to insult us, do you? I mean – iron. Sounds more like they're giving him a bathtub! You'd think an award should be gold or silver. Or have some fancy clusters on it, I don't know."

"First Class, sir," remarked Blashford, advisedly.

"*First* class? *Firs*t class? Don't they know this man's not an officer?"

"I expect they do, sir. From what I know of it, First Class means they give him Second and First Class at the same time. Sort of - "

"Do they do that sort of thing in Germany, then? – Give First Class honours to other ranks? ... And what about their trains?"

Blashford and Millbank betrayed completely baffled faces to each other.

"I...... I think we would have to accept that they have a different protocol, sir. After all – well, they're German."

"Mmm. I see your point, Millbank. Very well, what are we going to give him, Airey, eh? - A blasted knocker for his front door? Come along, think of something, we can't have the Welshman stealing this one."

Millbank had for some moments had an itch that he couldn't scratch, and wanted to add a point. "There's one more thing, sir."

"Is there, Millbank? Does it get any worse? What sort of 'one more thing' might that be?"

"Well, my Lord, do you remember the case of Lord Semper?"

"Semper? The soap king? Heavens, who can forget? Yes, of course I know it, Millbank. Went to prison, didn't he?"

"Erm – my Lord, you're forgetting.... He – um – he ran away. Didn't he? Um – if your lordship remembers."

Asquith appeared to consult his brain. "Ah!.... I credit you that, Millbank, I credit you that – he did, he did. He left the country."

"To America," added Blashford.

"Yes. Something like that."

"Somebody made a boo-boo," suggested Blashford in a tentative voice.

Lord Asquith pretended to have not heard the remark and sniffed at the window as if he could smell rain coming in.

"Blasted Americans," persisted Millbank, "Giving safe harbour to a chap like that."

"The deuce!... Yes, confound it, Millbank, get to the point, will you?"

"Sir, there was in that affair the case of the young steward aboard the *Titanic* who was dishonoured in that awful disaster. Is your lordship aware of that young man?"

"Am I?.... "

"It came out at the trial, your lordship."

"Oh, yes! I am, Millbank, now that you mention it. It did, it did come up at the trial, did it not? I remember the column in the Times. What was it? - Refresh my memory."

"The young man was the victim of a campaign of discredit by Semper."

"Oh, yes, yes, I remember. Damn the man! – Never try selling state secrets to the French, Millbank. Mark my words, no good will ever come of that. Well, anyway, what of it?"

"Sir, that young steward from the *Titanic*, it transpires, was Edward Thornton."

"Oh?"

"The same Edward Thornton."

"The same Edward Thornton?... What? – *This* Edward Thornton?"

"Indeed."

"Are you sure?"

"Yes, sir."

"The deuce! But - that's extraordinary!... He was the man who left the ship in women's apparel, wasn't he?"

"Yes, sir. It's the same man, anyway."

"Are you sure?... Escaped the ship in a dress! Wasn't that it? Well, how on earth did he manage that? - A coward one minute and a hero the next?.... That can't be right, can it? .... *Can* it?...Beggars belief.... And does Mr. Lloyd George know this?... Heavens, but that's certainly extraordinary!.... How remarkable of you, Millbank. Are you about to offer me some sort of explanation?"

"No, sir, I am not. I'm only suggesting there is a possible controversy at foot. I am raising the matter as it would seem we are about to honour - as you yourself point out - a hero in the one circumstance who was branded a coward and a villain in another circumstance. A fact that may strike a particular chord with the British press, I fancy ..... I felt you might like to be aware of the dichotomy, my Lord."

Asquith sagged back in his chair and looked around the room for the cat.

"I see.... Astute, Millbank, astute.... Well.... We must give the matter some consideration... as to the ramifications in the public media, must we not?"

559

"Should we not consult the Prime Minister on the matter, sir? Out of courtesy, if nothing else."

Lord Asquith appeared to chew on something that was stuck in his teeth.

"You know, Airey, if this chap was a coward......"

"Sir?"

"..... I was wondering if perhaps the Prime Minister might not in fact be the best person to announce the medal...... Something to ponder, eh?..... Yes... Yes, it would perhaps be better coming from him... But before we do that, let's sort out the medal business so His Majesty won't catch any flak from the Germans."

"Let me look into that, sir," offered Blashford. "I think I would be correct in recommending the Distinguished Conduct Medal."

"Is that good?"

The corners of Blashford's mouth twisted upward in a faintly apologetic sort of attitude.

"I would say, good enough, my Lord. It's the highest honour we can give a serving soldier who is not an officer or an N.C.O."

"Well, do that, Airey. Speak to your friend Walters, arrange it. And for heaven's sake, Millbank – for heaven's sake, make sure that Iron Cross nonsense is not leaked to the press until we have promulgated our award here, is that clearly understood? – Not leaked! No mention of an Iron Cross from anyone, or I'll have the Intelligence section of the War Office shot for collaboration with the enemy."

"Understood, my Lord."

"Oh - and for heaven's sake make sure you notify the Prime Minister's secretary, otherwise there'll be hell to pay."

"Yes."

"We must be sure the press and the man's family are notified of this D.S.O. –"

"D.C.M., sir."

"Yes, capital ! Do that. Does the man in fact have family, do we know? Where are they?"

"I believe....." mumbled Millbank, conjuring with his notebook, "I believe he had family in Yorkshire, sir."

"Yorkshire? ..... Oh, dear.... Well, make sure the announcement of our medal is issued at least a week before anybody goes to press with this blasted iron medal thingumajig, are we clear on that?"

"Clear, sir."

"And above all, my dear fellows, make sure you keep yourselves one step ahead of that bloody Welshman! No telling what he'll do to snatch a few points on the floor, never mind the hustings. Oh, and Churchill too, don't let him get wind of it yet or we'll have him charging up Whitehall in his blasted buses again, wanting heads on the end of his sabre!"

Suitably commanded, Blashford bowed curtly and left the office, leaving the redoubtable Millbank to administer whatever opiate their leader might need to settle him as he peered purposefully out of the window in search of inspiration.

"Bloody Germans! Who the devil do they think they are? And how the devil are they going to present the chap with this iron medal, eh?"

"Present the chap's family, sir. He's dead, after all."

"Eh? Well.... Is the Kaiser going to sail up the Thames in the 'Rheinland' with the whole Imperial Navy coming up behind?! Heavens, Airey, what next? - Giving medals to cowards now. It makes one wonder just what one is fighting this war for, doesn't it? .... Airey? .... Airey?"

Asquith swung his chair back around. "Wonder what this chap Thornton did, actually.... "

* * * * *

FIFTY-FOUR

"And if you ask me, Mr. Welch...."

Atkinson drew closer to the tall man, looking around him furtively as he did so, as if he half-expected a plain-clothes detective to be thrusting a well-trained ear toward them from somewhere in the churchyard. "... If you ask me, I think it has something to do with that other business. You know – that business about the soap millionaire chap and the state secrets he was peddlin' to the Russkis – or was it the French?"

"Both," Maurice Welch answered him.

"I dunno," continued Atkinson with barely a pause for breath, "That whole story got very confused. From the start I reckon there was something shifty about that young lad and these medals: as a newspaperman I got my doubts about that whole palaver. Seems like both of 'em got their come-uppance now, dunnit? Yer know what ah'm talkin' about....."

A warmer breeze stirred by a burgeoning sun swept a thin branch across Welch's shoulder and sent a shiver of leaves onto the back of his neck. Taking a thought-inducing draw on his cigarette, he stared through Atkinson to a point some distance beyond.

"Aah," he breathed to clear his throat. "Well, Mr. – erm..... If you're referring to Lord Semper, he got clean away, didn't he? As to young Thornton, whatever he did or didn't do, he paid a high price. You may be right - no smoke without fire, they say... Getting their come-uppance, though," cooed Welch, "I'm really not convinced that's all there is to it, you know. Still, it's very interesting," His mind seemed clearly reinforced about something. "It's certainly worth burning a bit of the old midnight."

He was silent for some moments further, then asked Atkinson, "Tell me - Have you heard of a chap called John Cade?"

"John Cade?.... John Cade? Don't think so. Why?"

"Mmm. I expect the name never filtered through this far... Thought you might have, though, because his name came up at the trial. Probably not important. Still, you have to follow up these things. My paper got a letter from a Mrs. Christine Cade three or four weeks ago. She'd heard all the fuss about the medal and wrote in to say all that stuff about Thornton being a coward was nonsense, said her husband reckoned Thornton was the finest bloke he'd ever known. Only a short note. Strange."

Atkinson was dismissive. "Well, you know what some people are like. Comin' out of the woodwork to get a share in the glory."

"Oh, no," corrected Welch, "No, not at all. The fellow never showed his face. Why? – Because he was shot in front of a firing squad in France last year. In fact, the note was delivered by hand to my office, the chap's wife must have been in London. But no address, she just left an explanatory note addressed to my editor. We were hoping people here could shed some light on it but – well, mostly drawn a blank so far, especially since I could get nothing out of Thornton's sister, though when I mentioned the name Cade there was a reaction. That's all, though, she didn't want to talk."

"Not surprised. You wouldn't want a coward for a brother, would yer?"

"Ah, that's the point, isn't it? - The barrister at the trial was clear that all the evidence against Thornton was lies. And the judge agreed. After all, had there been a case to answer, we would have been hearing about another trial, one imagines. As it was, any case against young Thornton never materialised."

"Aah! You don't wanna go fallin' for that! You often get these clowns come out of the woodwork - you know, ' I was 'is best mate, guvnor, give us a guinea and I'll tell you all about it'. This Cade chap – his wife's probably one of those. Bet you she's using your money to buy 'erself gin."

Welch's face refuted that. "Quite wrong, I'm afraid. She didn't get any money from the paper. We don't know where she is. You know that she wouldn't be getting any kind of a pension from the army. Wife of a disgraced soldier shot at dawn and all that. Personally, I don't imagine I'd begrudge her the money if it were me, poor wretch. And it strikes me...."

"What?"

"Mmm. Maybe nothing at all. The trouble is, you know, newspapers often *are* the law, aren't they? - Take that trial of Semper's, there was quite a bit about the way he had used young Thornton as a scapegoat, in fact quite a lot of protestation about Thornton being a victim, and yet how many of the papers actually printed any of that?"

"..... You askin' me? - I couldn't tell yer."

"Exactly.... None, as a matter of fact. Not one. There are times, you know, when I feel our scales of justice tilt too much one way.... And I'd not exclude my newspaper from among the guilty parties, even though they pay my salary."

"Well, anyway," Atkinson carried on in a surly tone, having entirely missed Welch's point, "if you want my opinion – and you can print it if you don't mention any names – I reckon this whole thing's a smokescreen by the army. You know how they like to drum up a hero or two when things aren't going so well. I mean, the Somme's looking like another big cock-up, in't it? So they go dream up another hero to boost morale an' cover their arses...... Pardon my French! If you ask me, it's all my eye and Peggy Martin! Now me, I'd sooner trust what I read in my paper than what the army tells us, what d'yer reckon? This young lad had been found out a long time back; no smoke without fire, just as you said. Look, he was a kid that used to get thrashed by his dad – did you know who his dad was?"

"A tram worker, so I heard."

" – A fighter. That's what 'e was. A prize fighter. Going back a good few years. They used to call 'im the White Rose. Good with his fists, was Jubal Thornton, one of the best. But the best times never last, do they? And his family suffered for that. Died only a couple o' year back, 'e did. T.B. That lad there, him and his brother used to get beaten regular by a chap that didn't know when he was in the ring from when 'e was out of it."

"Oh? And the point you're making?" questioned Welch, becoming impatient.

"Well..... The point is, the lad got beaten enough to cow any young man, 'e probably learned to cower away and that's what 'e become, like – a ruddy dyed-in-the-wool coward. So, gettin' off *Titanic* in some woman's clothes, then gettin' involved with that ruddy lord so-and-so and 'is dirty work, it all fits, dunnit? Does to me! A proper picture of a wrong un through and through. For my money, any road. "

Welch shook his head gently, thoroughly unconvinced, as Atkinson pressed on. "It were a big thing around this town a few year ago, all t'papers ran it and there were a lot of bad feelings. Ah mean, his sister's been workin' for the Argus for a little while now so yer can imagine why they back-pedalled on it, eh? But at the time, well, there were quite a to-do, ah can tell yer. Quite a to-do. No smoke without fire, Mr. Welch, as you said before."

This run-of-the-mill grass roots opinion was quite disappointing, Maurice Welch felt. No imagination. A provincial newspaper, of course.

Welch appeared to be using his cigarette to give him answers to the questions in his head, waving it around erratically. He was already formulating in his mind the story the Standard would publish the following evening. Here were the makings of something to run with. Perhaps Horace had been right all along.

"Oh, by the way," Atkinson voiced a thought that had been intriguing him. "Who was that big chap in there with his sister, Grace?"

"What, the big chap with the ornamental cane? Don't you know?"

"Search me. I thought 'e were a rich uncle or summat. Looked like it, the way he took 'old of her arm."

Welch simply smiled. "Just so," he said condescendingly, "..... Rich uncle 'or summat', as you say, Mr. Er..... Actually, I know that man. He's a Belgian businessman of some standing. He's played quite a role in the war effort. Munitions, you know."

"Ah!" scoffed Atkinson. "Yer mean, there's always some bugger does well out of a war."

"Did I mean that? No, I don't think I meant that. And did you notice too the lady and young child that gentleman had with him?"

"Matter o' fact, ah did, yes. Foreign-looking lady, the way she were dressed. 'Andsome, too. Are they related, d'yer think?"

Welch did not bother to answer. His thoughts were already elsewhere.

And then just as abruptly, Welch said, "Well, then! Perhaps you're right, Mr. - Erm...... Still, it's interesting. Perhaps we shall see in due time if you're right, shan't we?"

It was a brisk signal to bring everything to a closure just as the big Belgian gentleman was passing their position, carrying the lady's little girl on one of his large arms. She could not have been much more than eighteen months and was entertaining herself with the Belgian's moustache.

The tall, fair-haired lady who walked with him was totally in black with a dark veil, yet elegant and even through the gauze, clearly a beautiful woman. Struck by this beauty, even more than the sheer presence of the Belgian, Welch sensed an air of resolution about her, an air of defiance to her grief. If anything lent total credence to the story that had built up around Ned Thornton, surely this lady was the key to it.

Ignoring the Yorkshire newshound, the man from Fleet Street patiently watched her passing by, captivated by her graceful movement and admiring her apparent resilience to her sorrow.

Welch drew himself erect again, looked around and sniffed pleasanter air. His smile was for the church and these people rather than for his fellow journalist.

Yes.... The more Welch entertained the idea, the more sure he became of it.

"We shall see... *'Died on the Titanic'*.... that has a nice sort of ring to it, doesn't it? Yes, I like that.... Well, I have a train to catch."

END

EPILOGUE

Anthony Scott-Chapelle - Lord Semper - was accused of treason in September 1916 when Scotland Yard produced evidence that Semper's American contact, James Martin, had attempted in 1912 to broker a deal with both French and Russian military representatives based on highly secret British ordnance plans for a large, ground-based flame projector. Martin gave a full confession to the American secret service and was gaoled in 1916 for crimes over the period 1909 to 1914. The flame projector never went into full production.

The FBI attempted to consolidate the case with testimony from John Cade presented by Bruno Carelle's lawyers regarding the disappearance of Bernard Caldecot on the *Titanic*, leaving Lord Semper also facing a suspected murder charge - which under the terms of *Habeas Corpus* would remain unproven. Semper's career and reputation were nevertheless destroyed, and as a peer of the realm he faced the charge of High Treason. The case caused a sensation for a short time - in 1917, the crime of High Treason against the sovereign carried the death penalty. Additionally, the scandal of Oberon Scott-Chapelle's relationship with a male employee, whilst not a punishable affair for Lord Semper, broke into the media with an impact on the public consciousness not seen since the trial of Oscar Wilde twenty years earlier.

Lord Semper, despite being refused bail, was 'allowed' to leave his prison and immediately fled the country with - it is strongly inferred - help from 'friends in high places'. Documents signed by a 'senior authority' were cited that enabled Semper to walk from the Tower of London and disappear: those documents have never been seen again and their existence denied. Semper took ship to Charleston and thence to Venezuela where, in 1919, he was reported to have a large plantation and a white concubine. Lady Sophie refused to speak to the Press on the matter for the rest of her days and in 1919 retired to family estates in Normandy. Oberon Scott-Chapelle died two years later from influenza. His sister Miranda entered a nunnery and gave family money to the order, though she left five months later and married a Chicago businessman whilst on a round-the-world tour. Olive Devonshire rose in the civil service, never married and lived to be 86. Irene Scott developed an haute-couture business in Chelsea, having married a banker in 1924.

Thomas Whitbridge ended up in the river Thames in 1916. No evidence of foul-play was ever presented.

Helmut Kaltenbach survived the Great War and went into production of oil filters in Solingen with his elder brother who, following in their father's footsteps, became an official in the Weimar Republic . In 1934 Helmut joined the Nazi party and in 1936, against his brother's wishes, merged the business into the developing armaments industries of the Ruhr. Helmut was killed in a plane crash in 1942 on a flight with the Nazi Minister of Armaments, Fritz Todt. Helmut's wife and two daughters were all killed in a single Allied air raid on Essen in 1944.

Bob Street also survived the war, albeit less one eye from a wound he suffered in August 1918. He returned to his Kent farm to work with his brother and married his childhood sweetheart, Agnes, in 1921 at the age of 39. They had a son, William, who became a reporter for a Kent newspaper. Bob was an active member of the Labour Party and attended a mass rally in East London on 4th October, 1936, where a huge march by anti-Fascists against a smaller procession of 'Blackshirts' - the British Union of Fascists - led to serious confrontation. In what became known as the 'Battle of Cable Street', Bob was assaulted by police sent to control the marchers, he suffered a heart attack and died in the arms of his young son and two friends. He was 54. Shortly after, the passing of the Public Order Act severely curtailed the activities of pro-Nazi Fascists operating in Britain.

Otto Bremme was invalided from the German army in 1917, and remained in Köln where he became a book-keeper in family businesses. He married Katrin in 1924 and they had two sons, but he became increasingly distanced from political movements in Germany in the early 1930s and moved back to Rouen, sharing a house for a time with Brigitte. Otto died of an infected ulcer in 1940. His elder son was killed near Limoges in 1944 whilst working for the Maquis du Limousin, the French resistance, after imprisonment and torture by the German SS. Their younger son became a chef at a Normandy resort.

Brigitte Bremme eventually returned to nursing, first in Le Havre, then Rouen, where she raised her daughter. Married to a local man in 1922, she lived there till her death in 1949. She has five grandchildren, all living in France. Her eldest daughter, Regine Ardant, became a reporter in France and later with the BBC World Service. Every other year Regine travelled to see her Uncle Bruno's grave in Antwerp, remembering the man who had helped her to health as a child and who accompanied her aunt Reina to "that sad town in England", carrying Regine on his shoulder at Ned Thornton's memorial service in 1917. Regine died in 1988 following a long history of malaria.

Grace Thornton married one of her newspaper's sub-editors in 1920. She remained in Yorkshire and had four children, all of whom survived the Second World War and became successful in the newspaper and cloth industries. She became a great-grandmother for the first time in 1970 and died ten years later, aged 90. In between, she had written a respected book on the military conflicts of 1913 to 1918 and their socio-political aftermath. The medals awarded to Ned Thornton remain within her family to this day.

Bruno Carelle sold out his assets in Britain after the Great War and returned to Antwerp, where he died of pneumonia in the summer of 1929 at age 66. He was the recipient of his country's Civic Decoration for acts of devotion and humanity, which included services to the Commission for Relief in Belgium. He never married, and whilst he had no children of his own, he was called "Uncle Bruno" by hundreds of his employees and their children both in Belgium, in London, and in Durham. Before his death, he commissioned the building of a clinic in Brussels for war victims: it was finished in 1932 but destroyed in 1944 during an American bombing raid. Bruno maintained a correspondence with Grace Thornton right up until the week he died, when he wrote to her that, after the death of his young fiancée Lucie in a boating accident in 1896, he had never looked at any woman other than Grace.

Renata Bremme continued as Madame Forget for a time and worked at the school in Le Havre until 1920 when her mother passed away. She had left her estranged husband some time before. Renata moved to Southern France where she established a photographic studio at Collioure and developed a reputation for portraits of celebrated people. She had no children and never remarried, but was beloved of her family, whose children visited her at her small house among the fig trees. She died of cancer in 1952 at the age of 63.

Many asked about the photograph, framed and placed in isolation on the wall of the studio: it was the photograph of Ned Thornton and herself that the old man had taken at Amiens in 1916. Taped to its underside she kept Ned's final letter, relayed to her from Germany by the British Defence Services.

Renata had the name of the studio placed prominently above the entrance, and whilst many enquired as to the origin of the curious title, to very few did she ever tell why it was named 'Mushrooms'.

She never wished to visit the war graves of northern France and returned only once, during the summer of 1929, after visiting Antwerp, to the cemetery near Bradford to stand at Ned's memorial stone, and she did it alone.

*

END NOTES

The Author

John Hopkinson is a Yorkshire-born photographer and writer who has lived in various parts of England and France and currently resides in Sussex. Now retired, he began his working life at sea and has worked in a variety of "jobs good and bad". He has written a number of articles and stories, his first publication in Kindle was the novel, 'Assassinating King Bill', an anarchic satire "far removed from any sane enterprise". He began writing this novel, 'Mushrooms' in 2008 as a short story based on rumours: it was on the back-burner for several years until the centenary of the Great War encouraged a re-appraisal of its themes.

If you wish to learn more, you would be welcome to write to him at the address below.

Author's Note

Thank you for reading this novel. I am proud to have completed it. It was, as you may have gathered, a work of passion on my part, touching on elements of justice, of human strengths and weaknesses. There is a Ned Thornton in many of us, such that none of us should ever be taken at face value.

Remember that 'fiction' is seldom fact-less, and 'fact' is what is left when a myriad of fictions are stripped away.

If you have enjoyed this book, please leave a positive subjective review, as reviews are highly respected by writers and help put wine on the table. In any case, I should be pleased to receive any comment and will do my best to answer.

bartonkeyescouk@gmail.com

JH

By the same author:

"Assassinating King Bill" 2017

"Hybroid" 2020

Printed in Great Britain
by Amazon